Book 1

Confessions
Of A
Church Stalker®

Apryl Butler-Bennings

Prayer and Confessions
Change Things

Confessions Of A Church Stalker®
Copyright © 2010 Apryl Butler-Bennings
Atlanta, GA

Library of Congress Control Number: 2014922568
Imagery Publishing, Atlanta, GA
ISBN-13: 978-1-940681-00-9
ISBN-10:1940681006

Printed in the United States of America

"Confessions are good for the Soul
But
Can be harmful for your Reputation."

Be careful of whom you confess to and what
you confess.

Dr. Luke S. Hall
Lukeism

DEDICATION

First, I would like to thank God for giving me the inspiration for this written work. He has been the One I was looking for who was with me all along: God has also sent angels into my life to protect and guide me, for which I am very thankful. This book is indeed dedicated to all the angels in my life.

To my Mother: Thank you for forcing me to read and express my feelings on paper.

To Christi: Sissie, thank you for always remaining levelheaded and calm when I temporarily lost the ability to be. You are always there when I need you. You are the greatest!

To Whittney: My Shadow, thanks for being both my mentee and my mentor. Your encouragement and love will never be forgotten. Thank you for tagging along, shadowing me, researching with me, and being the first one to experience *The Confessions Series*® many years ago.

To Lori: You pushed me beyond my limits. Your inquisitiveness prompted me to provide more than simple answers to the challenges of writing—and life. Thank you for holding me accountable.

To Pastor Andre´ Landers: My Spiritual Father, thank you for the mission and teaching the Word. Thank you for SHAPEing me into a Disciple. I appreciate the hand you have had in this shaping process. You have equipped me with many of the tools I need to live up to my potential. You are an incredible man of God and I appreciate you more than you will ever know.

To Dr. Luke S. Hall: My Spiritual Godfather and extended church family, I am grateful for you. You have helped me to know and to understand my purpose. You have taught me to endure the changes and transformation required to live up to the potential, power and position my purpose brings. Because of you, my labor has not been in vain. I now, fully understand that it has been all GOOD! Family, you have blessed me tremendously and I am so incredibly grateful for the Vision.

To Raquel: I cannot explain it. We are two separate beings living off one mind. Our thoughts are intertwined. It is no coincidence we met. We were in the right place at the right time for this purpose. I value you, your work, and your opinion beyond measure. Iron sharpens iron. You jumped right in and ran with it. After months of me pestering you, you saw my vision immediately. I could never repay you for all you have done. You have been faithful with little and our Heavenly Father will reward you with much!

To my husband Scott: Thank you for your patience. You have been my backbone throughout this process and have given me the time, space, technological assistance and the resources I needed. You understood my solitude as I worked diligently to bring *The Confessions Series*® to life. You are my chief advocate and supreme helpmate. You are the greatest. I love you!

PREFACE

    We have all loved and lost. There are times when love will knock you down; we need to be knocked down to learn what we do not need, and how to get what we do need. These experiences are often painful and unavoidable. But one thing is for sure-- we survive being knocked down by love. *Confessions of a Church Stalker*® is the story of getting back up after being seemingly defeated by love. It is a reminder to keep the faith, to remain strong and focused on the goal of true personal fulfillment. Before you know it, you will be a contender in the challenging and rewarding life-battle that is love.

PROLOGUE

    There are millions of people that the church, the pastor and intercessors will never reach because these people will not be found in a church building, with the exception for a wedding, funeral, or baptism. I believe the only way to overcome the obstacles of life is by the Word of God. Therefore, we have to take the Word of God outside of the four walls of the church and take it directly to the people. The Confessions Series®, discusses love, life, family, divorce, sex, fornication, blended families, success, finance, pain, hurt and disappointment; all with the goal of directing people to God through His Word, without "beating you up" with the Word. My hope is that this series will encourage people to study more of the Word for themselves, to dig deep into it and become *HOOKED* on the Word.

REFERENCES

The Holy Bible – King James Version, The Message Version
Pastor Andre´ Landers – Higher Living Christian Church
Dr. Luke S. Hall – New Vision Christian Church

Special Thanks to The Confessions Team

Chris Quarles Branding & Design
Cool Pink/King Pen Writing Services
Irvin Productions
Juva Alexander/J. Z. Alex Editing
Lori Hanes
Maleka Watson
Raquel Pam Singleton
Scott Bennings
Sheneita Astin
Syreeta ShaNee
Weather Proof Designz
Willie M. Smith II

TABLE OF CONTENTS

INTRODUCTION

All Danielle's life she had a connection to a church home. Her mother, Mama Rose, made sure Danielle, or Dani as she was affectionately called, was in church every Sunday and any other time the doors of the church were open, even if Mama Rose was not present herself. It all began when Danielle was three years old. Her first day of day care was at the church. From that moment on, she was always in the house of the Lord. At the age of five, she started a Christian elementary school where she began to find her voice and participate in both academic and spiritual activities.

Dani was an intelligent student. She received high marks in both schoolwork and conduct while serving as the devotion leader the majority of her primary years. She was not shy to stand in front of the school and pray, recite scriptures, poems, or sing. Little did she know that this devotion leader position was laying the groundwork for the life she would later lead. Over the years, she learned thousands of scriptures.

When Danielle was not in school, Mama Rose had her at revival, Sunday school, children's church and every other function or event that her church, the church across the street, the church around the corner, and any other church in the neighborhood hosted.

As Dani grew older and went to high school and college, church was still a major part of her life. However, she began to have more of a say concerning when and where she wanted to attend church. The more she socialized the less important church became. She was a young girl and friends, parties, dates, shopping and "worldly things" became much more important. It seemed as Danielle matured in age, the more she digressed in her spiritual walk. However, she made it a practice to always attend church. Sometimes this included a wedding, funeral, or baptism. It was still considered church in her increasingly secular mind.

While in college, Danielle participated in all the college "activities." She partied, hung out, traveled, drank and cursed. And, yes, of course, fornicated. But some way, somehow, she always found herself back at church, sometimes with the alcohol still on her breath from the night before. Dani attended church with her friends, long-term boyfriend, and her family. She always remained a part of the church she grew up in, but it was beginning to feel entirely too large. She felt like a number in the midst of thousands. She could remember when the church began in the Reverend's living room and now it was a mega church. It was almost as if Rev had no idea who she was anymore.

Danielle's long-term boyfriend was a member of the same small church he had been in his whole life. After giving it some thought, Dani decided she was going to join his church. She wanted a church home that gave her that small, intimate family feeling again.

***

Years have passed. High school and college have come and gone. Danielle tries to remain balanced, focused and in tune with God and His Word. She undoubtedly veers off the path of righteousness numerous times but is always willing to keep trying. Dani and her boyfriend are in an extremely rocky relationship at this point. They are more like enemies but hide this from the rest of the church and continue to worship together weekly.

Danielle does not hold a title, position or office in the church she began attending because of her boyfriend, but serves where needed. She cleans the church, prepares, or purchases food when the congregation hosts dinner, tutors the children, types, and prints the Sunday programs, coaches the cheerleaders, heads the dance ministry, and a multitude of other duties. Originally, she thought she was "being about her Father's business." Then suddenly, she began to feel like the church members were taking advantage of her willingness to be helpful, therefore, she slowly removed herself. The sad part was that no one ever asked her why. It was just as if no one at the church even noticed she was gone. That was Danielle's confirmation that it was time to move on. She and her boyfriend were on a hiatus and to lose him and her church all at the same time was a bit difficult, but it was what she knew she had to do.

By now, Danielle is in her mid-twenties. Life has taken all kinds of twists, turns and even led her to a few dead ends but she is still doing her best to stand on the faith her mother instilled in her years ago.

For over a year Danielle worshipped at home via television sermons while she worked. Over the next few years, she dedicated her life to her career. Then she realized this indirect form of church attendance was not really acceptable. Danielle popped in and out of church for a year or two until she finally made the decision to get back into the church one hundred percent. After making this determination, she wrote out a list of between sixty five to one hundred churches. The list was comprised of churches people invited her to, churches in her neighborhood or churches she had heard of but never visited. The list of churches should have been enough to keep her busy for the year. As Danielle began to search for a new place to worship she got sidetracked from the list after she had gone to about half of the churches when one of her girlfriends told her she joined a church on the first visit and her life changed. Dani was shocked because her friend, up until this point, was a CEM (Christmas, Easter & Mother's Day) worshipper.

■■■

Therefore, Dani asked, "What happened during the church service that prompted you to give your life to Christ?"

Her friend replied, "The pastor said we did not have to tithe."

"Wait a minute. Back up. Rewind. What pastor would ever say that?" Dani asked.

Danielle's friend stated the pastor's name and the name of the church. It was a well-known, respected church on the rise and not far from Dani's house. However, it was further down on her list. Being the naturally organized person she is, Danielle is already feeling slightly guilty for not keeping up with her list the way she should and she does not want to continue distracting herself from attending all the churches on the list she created. But as the conversation between Danielle and her friend continues to unfold, she decides she may have to attend this church to get clarity on the "no tithing" issue for herself. Danielle also hopes to purchase a CD of the pastor's sermon from the previous week so she can listen to the message and engage in a more informed discussion with her girlfriend after she has evaluated all the facts.

FIRST VISIT

Sunday arrived and Danielle was prepared to check out the new church her friend raved so much about. Whether these church congregations were aware of it or not, Dani was taking them through an interview process, and before she made a decision on which church to attend she wanted to check out all of the possibilities. Unless The Spirit of the Lord moved profoundly and immediately let her know the church she was sitting in on any given Sunday was "home," she was not planning to make a hasty choice about something so important. This was serious business to Danielle. It was like searching for a daycare for a newborn baby. She would not leave her baby at just any daycare facility, so why on God's green earth would she lay her life down at the wrong altar?

As Danielle exited the highway, she realized she changed handbags earlier and her directions were not with her. This was turning out to be a fiasco. "Get thee behind me, Satan," she breathed to herself.

She was already fuming. *Oh God! I cannot believe this! I actually took a chance and listened to the crazy friend of mine when I should have just stuck to my original plans. This cannot be the start of anything good.* She circled the block a few times. She went up and down all the side streets but she could not find the church. Dani called her friend, but of course, it was too early for her to be awake. *I should have never listened to her,* Danielle thinks as she feels herself becoming more irritated. *Now I am searching for a church that she is not even on her way to. This is turning into a disaster.* There was one church she could clearly identify in the distance, but there were no people in the parking lot. She sat for a moment and wondered out loud, "What should I do?"

Danielle continued thinking to herself: *I am all dressed up and cannot find a church to attend. Satan is always busy. What next?* While she was in the empty parking lot, she saw quite a few cars with people dressed for church driving in the same direction. *That is my cue-I will follow them,* Danielle thought. As she followed the crowd, she noticed the parking situation. This made her angry all over again. *One thing is for sure,* she resolved, *I am not parking in that tall grass. I have no idea how deep it is or where the utilities are, and my toes will be dirty by the time I get to the sanctuary not to mention I will have wasted a car wash. I KNEW I SHOULD HAVE STUCK TO THE PLAN!* Danielle was fuming.

"Excuse me sir," Dani tried to speak as pleasantly as possible to the parking attendant.

"Good Morning," the man responded.

"Do you have anywhere else to park?" Dani asked.

The attendant quickly replied, "No, parking is full."

Danielle became irritated again. "Why do you not have additional parking when you have this many members?"

The parking attendant was matter-of-fact but apologetic. "Ma'am we are working on extending the parking lot. Can you pull to the right?"

"No, I am not parking in that tall grass," Danielle quipped. "Why is it not cut?"

"I'm sorry Ma'am we don't own the property," the man explained. "We rent the space and the landlord will not allow us to pave space for an additional parking lot or cut the grass."

"Who is your pastor because this is unacceptable?" Danielle was furious.

"Is this your first time here?" the man asked.

"Actually, it is and I am not even sure where I am," Danielle answered. "I could not locate the church I was looking for, so I followed the cars in front of me, but maybe I've made a mistake. In addition, you did not give me your pastor's name. I'd like to send him an email and possibly speak to him about your parking situation and how unappealing this is." she spoke with disgust, but was also thinking with the mind of an engineer as she conveyed her disappointment. She saw a problem and was ready to resolve it. "And can you please direct me out?" she asked the parking attendant. "I will not be staying."

The man answered, "I'm sorry to hear that. Our pastor is Pastor Hunter."

"This is Victory Hope Greater Faith Church?" Danielle asked.

"Yes it is," the man replied

"WOW!" Danielle nearly shouted.

The parking attendant looked confused. "I'm sorry is there a problem?"

Dani softened a little as she responded. "Well, sort of. This is actually the church I was looking for. Is there a sign out there?"

"Currently, the name is on the office park marquee with all the other tenants' names," he explained.

Danielle thought to herself, *she did not tell me the church was in an office park building. No wonder I was not sure where I was! This is getting more and more interesting. This is a little scary for me but I am going to give it a try. Now what am I going to do about this grass?*

The parking attendant interrupted Dani's thoughts. "Ma'am, I would hate for you not to worship with us all on account of a parking spot." He speaks into his radio and says, "Deacon W, I have one coming up. Allow her to park next to Pastor, please." He waited for a response.

"Give me two minutes and send her my way," the voice replied.

The man smiled warmly at Danielle. "Enjoy service Ma'am."

As Danielle pulls up, a nice looking man in a suit walks towards the car with a radio so she is under the assumption the man was called to direct her. *The parking attendant probably told this guy about the way I behaved earlier,* she assumed, as she tried not to appear too embarrassed. This prompted another change of heart in Danielle. She began to calm herself with a pep talk. *Dani, I think you may have been a bit rude,* she thought to herself. *Why didn't you just follow the rules? I'm sure the parking attendants have walked the terrain of the parking space and know where all the dangers are. Maybe you're just frustrated from getting lost. Get ahold of your emotions. Don't let the devil dominate your attitude.*

The gentleman is now standing next to Danielle's car waiting for her to roll her window down. Danielle is impressed. He is dressed immaculately and is extremely attractive. *If I were not in such an uproar, he would be very appealing to me,* Dani thought. *Surely, if this was a few hours ago and we were at a club I would have definitely made the first move.* Dani internally motivated herself one more time. *Get thee behind me, Satan,* she repeated to herself.

The attractive gentleman brought her thoughts to a halt with his pleasant greeting. "Good morning Ma'am. Could you pull up next to the white car?"

"Sure. Thank you." Danielle responded.

Then she actually took a look at the car she was asked to park next to. She gasped and whispered in a tone only she could hear, *white car? Yeah right. You meant White drop-top Bentley Coupe on eye-catching rims that is spotlessly clean! I hope this pastor is single, because I'll definitely be calling him-forget the email. Think, Dani. You read his biography online. Is he married? I think he is but I can't remember for sure. I only remember his name is Hunter—Trevor Hunter.* Danielle is so wrapped up in her thoughts she doesn't realize the gentleman is waiting for her to get out of the car. Dani laughs to herself. *I'm sure this day can't get any worse.* Danielle clicks the lock on her car as the man extends his hand to her.

Why did I have to buy this tiny sports car? Dani scolds herself. *It's so difficult to get out of this vehicle like a lady. I hope I'm not showing him "the goods" as I get out of the car. Then again, maybe I should. He is pretty fine.* The gentleman speaks to her again.

"Good morning beautiful, I'm Deacon Randall Washington. I'm sorry you had an unpleasant experience this morning in the parking lot."

Danielle responded in the sweetest voice she could muster. "Good morning, I'm so sorry to be in such a bad mood, but this morning has gone completely downhill for me. Please explain this to the parking attendant and give him my deepest apologies."

The man extends a million-watt smile to her. "I certainly will. I'm sure a beautiful woman like you would never be rude intentionally. As you probably know, Satan is always busy—especially when we're about Kingdom business."

Danielle agreed. "Yes, he is. I was lost looking for the church this morning, since a friend recommended it to me. I discovered I left my directions at home, so when I saw all these people coming in this direction, I decided I would follow them. Then I was instructed to park in a field of grass instead of a decent parking space and all my frustration just tumbled out. But I guess the good part is that I ended up at the place I was trying to go even though I had a few hiccups along the way."

The deacon responded in such an understanding way. "God will get you where you need to be every time even if he does send you through the wilderness. It's not by accident you arrived here this morning. Do you have a church home?"

Danielle playfully looked at the deacon's nametag, pretending she forgot his name. "Well go right in for the kill, why don't you, Deacon Randall Washington," she joked. "No, I don't have a church home right now. It's a long story, but I'm looking for the right place to worship."

The deacon smiled. "I hope you make Victory your new home. We'd love to have you."

Dani returned the sentiment. "Thank you so much. I appreciate you being so accommodating and offering me a more ideal parking space. That was very generous of you."

Deacon Washington replied, "No problem at all. It's all in a day's work. Let's go in so I can give you a quick tour of your new church home."

Danielle thought, *Deacon Washington definitely takes that "speak things that are not as though they were" Bible verse literally.* She smiled to herself. *This experience has turned out not to be so bad after all. However, I still need to check and see if this guy is married. If not, I'll take this as a sign from God that I'm at the right place at the right time.* Nevertheless, all that came out of her mouth directed toward the deacon was a witty, "Modest, aren't we?"

He replied with, "I'm sorry—I didn't get your name."

Danielle quickly answered, "I apologize. I am so discombobulated this morning! I promise I usually have more manners than this and I am much more likeable." She hoped her hint got across effectively. She extended her hand. "Rose—it's Danielle Rose."

"Mrs. Rose," the deacon repeats. He ignores Danielle's outstretched hand and reaches for a hug. She counteracts this gesture by giving him a firm, almost professional handshake. *I see where he was going with that,* Dani muses without showing any outward excitement. "No, it's Ms.," she corrects him. "And you can call me Danielle."

The deacon corrects himself. "Ms. Danielle, it looks like I have a bit of bad news."

Danielle was about to worry again. *What now?* She thought. *Things were just starting to go well!*

Deacon Washington continued, "It looks like the sanctuary is full and you will be directed to the overflow section."

"Oh." Danielle responded with minimal enthusiasm.

"The congregation has doubled pretty quickly and we're not as prepared as we should be," the deacon explained. "But we consider it a blessing. We hope the landlord will allow us to pave the field into a parking lot for our members." He could sense her disappointment and irritation surfacing again. "Here," Deacon Washington quickly interjected. "Let me get you one of Pastor's cards. The service times are listed. Will you be visiting again?"

Danielle couldn't help but respond favorably to the deacon's charm. "I hope so and again I am sorry to be a bother this morning. Thank you dearly for your kindness."

He opens the door to the overflow room and gets Dani an offering envelope and visitor's card before escorting her to a single seat along the wall. Randall (Dani hoped to be calling him by his first name soon) whispers, "I hope to see you before you leave. I would worship with you but I am on duty in the main sanctuary. I will catch you next time."

Danielle sat down, thinking, *what a spectacle you have made this morning. I think I need to sneak out before the doors of the church are open and come back when it falls on my calendar to visit this church again. I hope no one will remember me by then.*

Danielle looks at the monitor to watch the pastor speak and is surprised to see the leader of the church is a friend from college! She is shocked. *There's no way he should even be allowed to be in the pulpit of a church!* She thought silently. *Then again,* she reasoned, *I'm not even sure if I should be here. So, either: a) the church is full of heathens or b) I really do need to be here, because if he can change, anyone can.* She takes another intent look at the monitor. *I can't believe that's him! I need to go home and make a few calls, take a look at the church website again and pull out some old photos to make sure that's actually him.* The pastor preached a wonderful message. Danielle almost forgot the main reason she had come that day—to get a CD of the message from last week. However, the pastor did mention something in his sermon that answered Danielle's question.

The pastor made his position on tithing clear. "If you are tithing because you think a check will appear in your mailbox today when you get home, Newsflash! The mailman does not run today and that is not how it works. So spare yourself the trouble and don't even tithe."

How did she confuse that? Danielle wondered about her friend who insisted that the pastor did not want his members to tithe. *She's new to the Word and the church—that's how,* Dani concluded. Now that Danielle's question was answered, she put her focus back on her escape plan. *Okay, you got what you needed,* she said to herself. *Now all you have to do is sneak out and not come back for a few months.* The perfect opportunity came for

Dani to excuse herself. Since she has grown up in church, she knew the proper protocol for leaving. It was improper to move during the benediction, so if she didn't move now, she'd have to stay until the end of service. Danielle politely dropped her head, held up her index finger to indicate she needed to be excused, and headed toward the door. On her way out, Danielle put together a mental checklist of the things she needed to accomplish. *I've got to check my calendar to see the exact date I'm scheduled to come to this church again*, she thought. *Then I need to clarify to my friend the actual statement the pastor made concerning tithing. I also have to find the old pictures of my college-friend-turned-pastor for verification.* Danielle was consumed in her thoughts and was startled when the parking attendant pulled the door as she was pushing it to exit. Dani wasn't expecting anyone to be at the door at the time of her escape—especially not him— the person she was trying to avoid.

He smiled, "Leaving so soon?"

"Yes," she responded matter-of-factly.

He asked, "Are you planning on coming back?"

Again, Danielle's answer was abrupt but honest. "Yes, I am."

He seemed satisfied with her response. "Good I'll see you next week. If you're here before a quarter till I'll make sure you can park on the pavement."

Danielle had to think fast without appearing flustered. "I'll be traveling next week so I won't make it, and the week after I have another church to attend."

The man was determined. "So, I'll see you in three weeks-great! I'll be looking out for you then."

The parking attendant continued walking with Danielle as she attempted to get to her car as soon as possible. "We're about to pass the video stand," he said. "Let me buy you a CD from last week to cover you for the next two weeks."

Danielle began to panic a little *God, what are you doing.* She wondered. *The person I was so rude to is blessing me and buying me the very item I came here for.* She felt a little ashamed and immensely surprised but tried not to show it.

Dani apologized to the parking attendant for her behavior. The two formally introduced themselves to one another and exchanged kind words and a quick hug before departing. *Now I have to keep my word and come back in three weeks*, Danielle concluded. *Otherwise, I'll feel terrible if I don't*, she confessed.

The next two weeks went just as Danielle had planned. She went out of town one weekend and attended another church the following Sunday. The third Sunday was quickly approaching. *I really need to stick to my original schedule but I also don't want anyone to feel as if I lied to them*, Danielle mulled her decision over. However, she knew she was leaning toward going back to the church where she had behaved so rudely, especially after she was treated so warmly. *What's a girl to do?* She asked herself. Suddenly she came up with a solution she felt was feasible. *Remember, you acted so ugly in the parking lot. Give them time to forget you before you return. Okay, that's my plan. I am back on schedule. It's not like I'm never going back--just not this week. And really, how many people does he shake hands with anyway? He won't remember I said I would be back. As long as I eventually show up, everything should be fine.*

WEEK 3

Saturday night I laid out all my clothes. The church I was going to visit started at eleven the next morning. *That time may be a problem*, I begin to think. *I already sense that church will run into extended service. It will be well after one o'clock before I even make it back to the parking lot.*

The more I thought about it, the more I talked myself out of going to church. I like to go to church early and have the rest of the day to work, chill, rest or do whatever I want.

I am sure this will not be my church home because of the service schedule, I concluded. Then I immediately tried to soften my stance. *Danielle, stop tripping*, I told myself. *You are talking yourself out of a church home before you even get there. Keep an open mind. Maybe they have other service times that were not listed on the website. You know how easy it is for you to let the devil come in and take over.*

As I prepared for bed, I decided I would still go check the church out. *One thing is for sure*, I reasoned. *I will be able to sleep late at least one day out of the week. This may be a plus after all.* As usual, my eyes popped open at a quarter to four. I clicked the remote and checked to see if I had any text messages. Nothing. I searched for email notifications on my phone then rolled over to my laptop. *Goodness, I am connected to so many gadgets!* I took the realization as both an ironic reality and a subtle warning to myself that it was time for a change. My favorite gadget of them all was hard to determine. It was a toss-up between my old faithful television set and my iPhone, since I could text when I did not feel like talking.

I am so glad times have changed and the TV does not go off any more. I no longer have to wake up to the star spangle banner or a fuzzy screen. That immediately brings back fond memories for me. *How many TV sets have Mama Rose and I burnt out over the years? I am so glad the price of televisions has become more affordable. I remember the times we would have to take the television to the repairman every time it started acting up.* I glanced at the TV and couldn't help but smile. The show on the screen definitely brought back vivid childhood memories for me. *I used to love the Flip Wilson Show. I couldn't wait to get to the TV to watch shows like Green Acres, Happy Days, Inspector Gadget and That's My Mama. Zoning out in front of the TV was the life. Now, I have no idea what life is supposed to be. Oh well, nothing wrong with reliving my childhood just a little and entertaining myself with a little TV Land for a few hours.*

The television advertised that one of my other favorite shows, *Sonny and Cher*, was having a marathon. I have to admit, the commercial made me a little excited. Too bad I don't eat much junk food, otherwise I could curl up on the couch with a bag of Doritos, a bag of cookies and a pint of ice cream,—all of which would make this TV marathon much more enjoyable. *I'm actually glad church doesn't start until 11AM*, I decided. *I can catch a few hours of The Flip Wilson Show and take a quick nap before I head out.*

I am dying laughing at Flip as Geraldine. What I am amazed about is how the attire that was fashionable then has come right back around. I hate to say it but I am getting some fashion ideas and putting some outfits together in my head. I bet Flip never thought this comedic concept would be so popular. There are plenty of male comedians who are borrowing that act in one way or another these days. As I was chuckling at Flip Wilson's musings, a thought crossed my mind. *Why not go to both churches? That way, I won't feel like I haven't kept my word, and a little extra time in church never hurt anyone. That's what I'll do.* I feel so much better with this decision. I remember the parking lot attendant said if I arrived by a quarter til he would make sure I could park on the pavement. I'll make sure I'm not late.

***

I'm sure you can guess what happened next. I didn't turn the TV off. I actually watched television until it was time for me to get ready for church. I put on the clothes I laid out the day before, checked the mirror (and checked it one more time), and headed to the car.

I usually like to play the latest music while I'm driving. But there's something about heading to church that makes you turn the volume down on your music and put yourself in a more solemn mood. Kind of like when you drive past a cemetery or a funeral procession—you automatically adjust the volume on your music. So I turned on Yolanda Adams—her music always seems to help me get my head together before church. I've learned over the years that you have to have already engaged in your own praise and worship before you enter church in order for the service to be effective for you. One of the best ways for me to do that is to listen to spiritually uplifting music. I dropped the top to the convertible I was driving and allowed myself to get (responsibly) lost in the music. Before I knew it, I was turning into the church parking lot and turning the music down to just above a whisper. And whom do I see as I enter the lot? None other than the parking attendant I had been so rude to during my first visit to the church. *Maybe I can drive past without him noticing,* I hoped. I was in a different car than the first time I had come, so there was a chance he wouldn't know it was me.

No such luck. The parking lot traffic slowed down and I ended up having to pull up right next to him. And, of course, he remembered my name. "Good morning, Ms. Rose," he said pleasantly.

I tried to match his pleasant tone without showing how embarrassed I was. "Good morning. How are you?" I responded.

He smiled. "I'm well, and you?"

I returned the courtesy. "Same here—thanks for asking."

Just when I thought the small talk was over and he was about to direct me to a parking space, he said. "I'm glad you made it back. I didn't think you would—I must admit I'm a little shocked. You'd be surprised how many people say they'll come back and never do."

I suddenly felt very proud of myself for making the decision to come back to this church today. Integrity is very important to me and I pride myself on being reliable. Even though the parking attendant doesn't know me, I want him to believe in me—I told him I would return and am glad I made good on my word. But I answered him with an emphatic yet gentle, "I told you I would."

"You sure did," he agreed. "Enjoy service. Take that spot up ahead on the left."

"Thanks and I'm glad I'm on the pavement this time." I was in such an uproar the last time I was here that the parking lot looks foreign to me. *Where do I go in?* I wondered. *I'll just sit here and watch what the other church members do and follow them.* Once I saw the direction everyone was going in I got out of the car. I was so focused on figuring out what to do until I didn't even notice the deacon I talked to last time I was here was opening the car door for me.

There was definite excitement in his voice. "Mrs. Rose, welcome back!"

He remembered my name. It's officially time for me to inspect this man's ring finger. He's definitely striking me as a viable prospect. But of course, I had to give him a bit of a hard time. "It's Danielle—don't you remember?"

He formed his hands into a praying pose to convey mock repentance. "I'm so sorry. Please forgive me—and welcome back Mrs. Danielle."

I used the opportunity to continue our playful and flirty banter. "Thank you but I am sure I told you the last time it is Miss. I am not going to come back if you can't remember that." I smiled to indicate the real message I wanted my words to deliver.

He laughed. "Oh now you are clowning me. I'm only human. Please pardon me. Let's start over. Ms. Danielle it is so nice to see you again."

I responded with a deliberately flirtatious "same here." I'm not sure how appropriate that was at church. But after all, he did start the flirting first. I continued speaking. "It's nice to see you again Deacon Washington."

I could tell he was impressed I remembered his name even though I hadn't been to the church in a few weeks. He said, "Maybe I failed to mention this, but please call me Randall."

"No Deacon Randall, you didn't mention that," I answered, hoping the flirting would continue.

"You're not paying attention," he quipped playfully. "I didn't say anything about calling me a deacon."

I said mischievously, "Well, that is your title, correct?"

He laughed. "Yes, you are correct."

I offered him a challenge. "Once you drop the 'Ms.' from my name, I'll drop the 'Deacon' from yours."

He grinned. "I'm sure that won't be hard to do, Danielle."

"I'm glad to hear that Deac...I mean, Randall."

His flirting became a little more intense. "Sounds like you're going to have trouble with this, Danielle. We may have to practice it."

I couldn't help but laugh. "Now you're clowning me," I told him.

Randall smirked. "I would never do that."

He opens the doors to the sanctuary and walks down the aisle behind me. I can barely contain my excitement.

This guy is fabulous, I think to myself. *He's sexy, he seems intelligent, and from what I can tell, he's a God-fearing man.* I breathe a quick prayer as I head down the aisle to find a seat. *Okay, God, I'm leaving this up to you—but you have a willing participant in me.*

Randall escorts me to a seat and leans in close to ask me "Is this seat okay?"

A combination of intrigue and arousal grips my body. *Help me Lord! This is the last time I can come to this church. This man has caused parts of my body to tingle that should not be active right now! Not in church and not due to the whisper of a complete stranger.* I then realize his seat is next to mine. *Oh Lord, this is going to be a long service. I can smell his cologne every time he moves.* I could feel myself becoming more and more drawn to him. However, from where we were sitting, I still couldn't see his ring finger. The entire time we were talking, Randall kept his hand in his pocket. A move I like to call the "Playboy stance." Remembering this sobered me up a little. Now I could think more objectively, despite my attraction to him.

Danielle, get a grip. This is the church flirt. Don't get tied up and tangled up in the nonsense he'd be sure to bring to your life. You are looking for a church home--not a date. Don't forget the reason for your search. You are looking for a church home because you and your long-term, serious boyfriend broke up and you don't want to worship where he is. Don't make the same mistake again. And don't forget Mr. James.

I almost burst out laughing in the sanctuary at the thought of Mr. James. I can see from the corner of my eye Randall is looking at me because I accidentally made a noise that started as a laugh—I tried to cover it by turning the sound into a "cough." Mr. James was definitely the pimp of my home church. From the way he dressed in those gaudy suits that were color-coordinated, snakeskin, gators, Stacy Adams Boots, his blinged out pinky ring to his dripping wet Jheri curl, his entire image projected the notion that he probably "managed" a group of girls who had been hired to "do his bidding." And then there was his highly adorned Cadillac with a diamond in the back and the sunroof top. Apparently he was appealing to women for some reason, since they flocked to him, seemingly without any concern that Mr. James entertained several of them at one time. Maybe he was balling. The more I think about it, the more I begin to wonder what all the hype was about with Mr. James. And the more suspicious I became of Randall. Maybe I had gotten too excited too soon.

That's right Dani, I said to myself. *You need to get a grip. You're in the house of the Lord. Maybe God brought you here for a substantial reason, so pay attention.* But it was hard for me to stay focused. *Randall is sitting much to close for me to be completely enthralled in the church service. I haven't felt this giddy about a guy since high school.* I try hard to pull myself together and listen to the pastor.

I struggle to remember the last phrase that came out of the pastor's mouth, and then have to admit that I simply don't know. I resolve to get to church earlier next week in hopes that this tactic will make it easier to actually devote my attention to the service. I sit up straight so my body will indicate that I'm concentrating on what is happening in front of me. Then the pastor says, "Everyone stand to your feet and grab hands with the person beside you for prayer."

Oh no! I'm officially in panic mode. *Randall and I have to touch.* I don't look up to face him. I can feel he's wearing a ring.

A wave of disappointment washes over me. I try to get a look at the ring, but Randall has positioned his hand in a way that makes the ring invisible.

Give it up Danielle. I force myself to come back to reality. *The man is married.* But a part of me still wants to rationalize the presence of a ring on his finger. *He seems younger than me, I reason. Maybe it's a class ring or a championship ring he earned from playing sports.* Randall is holding my hand both firmly and gently, and I begin to melt. *Please end this prayer Pastor.* I think to myself. After we say "amen" Randall holds my hand noticeably longer than the person on my other side. I'm pretty sure I didn't hear a complete sentence of the sermon. I decide I'll buy the CD of the service after the benediction. *As long as the pastor doesn't ask us to hug our neighbors, I'll be fine.*

Then it came. The pastor said "Hug your neighbor to the left and right of you. Go in peace and have a blessed week. I'll see you all Wednesday at seven o'clock."

I hugged the person on the other side of me first, hoping Randall would be gone by the time I turned around. *I'm not sure I can handle any more physical contact from him.* I fumble with my purse to buy myself some more time and turn around slowly. I have to pass by Randall in order to leave the sanctuary. He's looking at me with an expression that says he's not going to let me get away without a hug.

I look up and smile, trying not to appear too flustered and uncomfortable. He reaches for a hug and I give him the "church embrace" to make it clear I'm trying to keep our interaction as appropriate as possible. I made as little contact with his body as possible.

I'm so nervous that I drop my car keys. Randall and I both bend down to pick them up at the same time. Our eyes meet and neither one of us looks away. I can feel his breath on my face. I can see every part of his face. I'm pretty sure he sneaked a glance at my cleavage.

The interaction seemed like it took forever. All Randall said was "nice toes."

Did he just compliment my toes? I ask myself. *Yeah, he definitely just said that. And that is considered flirting. Stay cool, Danielle. Stay cool.*

"Thanks," I said nonchalantly. "And thanks for grabbing the keys."

His response matched my casual tone. "No problem. Have a great week."

I cordially responded, "Thank you; same to you."

This encounter would not have been this perfect if I were anywhere else. If I were in the grocery store, mall, or the club this is not how things would have unfolded. However, there are two main reasons why I absolutely cannot come on to this man: 1) we go to church together, and 2) I don't know if he is married.

I'm definitely stuck between a rock and a hard place. At this point, I just want to purchase the CD of the church service and get out of here as soon as I can. Now, where was the place where members can purchase CDs, again? I ask myself. I try to remember as I walk out of the sanctuary and intentionally go in the opposite direction of Randall. I don't see a place to buy CDs, so I turn around, only to find Randall walking in my direction. My heart starts racing. "Ms. Danielle you look lost," Randall says playfully.

"I am looking for the bookstore to buy a CD, Mr. Randall," I answered, barely able to look him in the eye.

"It's Randall. Follow me," he graciously responded.

"It will be Mr. Randall until you call me Danielle. So, Deacon Randall, if you could point me in the right direction I can handle it from there." He ignores me and walks me right up to the purchasing counter. "Do you want a CD or tape?"

I give him an awful look of disbelief and irritation. A look so bad the lady behind the counter laughs.

"I'll take that to mean you want a CD. Danielle, some people still listen to tapes." He laughs and I find myself enjoying the sound of his laugh.

I couldn't believe Randall not only walked me all the way to the purchasing center but proceeded to speak for me throughout the entire transaction.

Randall spoke to the woman at the counter. "Beautiful and funny," he grins, as he nods in my direction. *That was a pickup line if I ever heard one.*

The lady looks up with a look of both enchantment and suspicion. I could tell the woman was attracted to him but was likely much older than him.

The woman smiled and said, "That will be eight dollars deacon."

I reach into my handbag and before I can grab my wallet, Randall pulls out a money clip and hands the woman a $20 bill.

This can't be happening, I gasp. *God knows I love a man with a money clip. More importantly, I love a man who has a nice stack of bills in his money clip. And yes, the collection of bills in Randall's money clip was impressive. I would guess about $4,000. The clip could hold no more. This leads me to believe that if he carries this much money to church, he definitely had more money on him on a regular basis.*

I politely told him, "No, I got it. But thank you."

Randall quickly countered with, "No, it's on me."

I was insistent. "That's so nice, but you've done more than enough."

He displayed a slightly shocked expression. "Oh? What have I done?"

At this point, we have the full attention of the woman at the counter.

"You pointed me in the right direction. I can handle it from here."

Randall smiles at me. "Beautiful, funny--and independent I must add."

The woman looks up and raises her eyebrows. Almost as if to say, "Never mind the fifty people in line behind you. You two stand here and keep entertaining me with your flirtatious acts of kindness."

"Can you please give him back his twenty and swipe my card?" I ask the woman as I hand her my credit card. Randall grabs the card and the CD and gently pulls my hand. "Thanks," he says to the woman. "I will be back before you close to get my CD and Pastor's."

Randall mockingly scolds me. "Don't diminish a man's ego. When a man is paying let him pay. Didn't your mother teach you that?"

I quickly retort *what my mother actually taught me was to look for a man who is six feet, 200 pounds, black, handsome, exclusively interested in me, wealthy and willing to spend money on me.* But I didn't speak it out loud. Randall may have fit this description precisely. He may have been a little under the weight I preferred, but I could easily handle that with one or two sweet potato pies using Mama Rose's recipe.

Randall tosses my credit card in my handbag and hands me the CD. "Enjoy," he instructs. "Please don't insult me by offering to pay again. I hope you wouldn't hurt my feelings like that if I gave you a gift."

Did he say "gift"? I was gushing a little. *He is definitely flirting.*

"I wasn't trying to insult you," I said. "And you can buy me as many gifts as you want. However, just be aware that I can buy my own."

"I'm aware," the deacon answered. "You don't have to reiterate it. Anybody that meets you can tell you know how to handle your business."

"Oh, really?" I ask. "And what makes you say that?"

"It's the way you carry yourself," he responded. "Which way did you park?"

We begin to walk towards my car.

"By the way, how do you like this car?" he asks me.

"I love this car!" I say excitedly.

He smirks. "I wasn't expecting such a strong reaction. So, what do you love the most?" he inquired.

"I like the that you can drive the car in either the standard or automatic setting. I also like the speed of the vehicle," I responded.

"A girl after my own heart," he says smoothly. "So, you like speed, huh? How fast have you pushed it?"

I answered, "Pushed it? I would not say pushed. The car provides an easy smooth acceleration."

He asked again, "So how fast?"

I gave him a sly smile. "I'll say this--the speedometer reads one eighty."

"So I take it you are running it at one eighty?" He joked surprised at her comment.

"You might be the police. I plead the fifth," I quipped.

He laughed. "I am nowhere near a police officer. When are you taking me for a spin?"

I return his flirtation by answering, "You name the time."

"I'll have to take you up on that soon," Randall responds.

"It's a date," I tell him. *Date—did I just say "date?"* Maybe that wasn't the right choice of words. Well actually, that term is pretty accurate. Technically, we're outside of church, since we're in the parking lot.

Randall opens my car door and leans in to take a look. "Nice," he says.

"Thanks," I respond.

"This car suits you," he tells me.

"What do you mean?" I ask.

"You ride real clean," he responds.

I smile warmly and say "I appreciate that. And I'm holding you to that date." I wanted to emphasize the "date" concept once again to make sure we are on the same page. I'm admittedly flirting at this point.

"You got it," he answers. He makes an effort to give his voice an even more alluring quality.

Randall waits until I'm comfortably in the car, hands me my seatbelt and bends down, with one knee on the ground so that we're face to face. "Drive safely," he says.

"Yes sir," I respond.

"Let me correct myself—drive safely and at the speed limit," he jokes.

"Okay," I say shamelessly giggling.

"I'm serious," Randall has genuine concern in his voice.

"So am I," I tell him.

He becomes serious. "No racing. No breaking records. No speeding."

I playfully poke back at him. "You didn't say no drifting."

He quickly adds while shaking his head, "No drifting!"

"Gotcha," I give him a wink.

"And lastly," he says.

"Yes, State Patrol?" I interrupt, completely comfortable with flirting with him at this point.

"Will I see you next week, Danielle?" Randall asked without hesitation.

I pause. I literally feel like we're on a date at this point. "Umm, maybe," I say.

"Maybe?" he asked miffed.

Before I can answer Randall, the radio host announces the time. Once he hears the time, he tells me, "I've got to run. I am sure they are looking for me to count the money. It will really make me happy to see you next week."

I smiled. I was so glad Randall couldn't see my heart was melting. I was also glad he couldn't tell that my heart wasn't the only part of my body that was feeling something.

"So let's make that happen. I hate to run. We could stand here and talk all day but I have to go. Make sure you grab something healthy for breakfast. Enjoy your day and I really hope to see you next week."

"Have a good one." My response is sincere.

He closes the door and stands there to watch me pull off like it hurts him to see me go. I really would like for him to walk away so I can gather my composure together before I pull off. *I swear I have not felt like this since ninth grade—and I remember the feeling clearly. Sade was just a little girl and we had been to a football game and the captain of the football team kissed me. I waited until we got home to completely "lose it" i.e. scream, run around my room and jump up and down. With Sade in arms, I slid all the way to the floor in utter bliss. I never forgot the boy—or the kiss. Any time I felt attraction or love in a romantic sense I thought about the captain of my high school football team when I was in ninth grade. Right now, I feel the same way I did as a teenage girl. To be honest, I maintained a crush on the football team captain until the day he was tragically killed.*

Ironically, thinking of that ninth grade kiss took my mind off of Deacon Randall temporarily. Before I know it I'm pulling up to my house. *I guess that's what I'll have to do from now on when I need to be distracted from thoughts of Randall,* I think to myself. This also made it painfully obvious that I had to think about a painful memory and a love from years ago just to stop thinking about Randall for a few minutes. The deacon's impact was more powerful than I ever thought it would be.

WEEK 4

The week goes by quickly. Before I know it, it's Friday again and I am looking forward to Sunday morning. I must admit, I have thought about Randall an awful lot this week. I've been dreaming about him as well. The dreams haven't been extremely inappropriate, but they have definitely been racy enough to get my attention. I feel a little guilty thinking about a man of God in this way, but then again, I really don't know that much about him.

Just calm down, I remind myself. There may not be anything wrong with dreaming about him in a romantic way if he isn't married. Wouldn't it be great if God led me to this church to find Randall? The Lord does work in mysterious ways, and stranger things have happened to me. And if I can't find a decent man at church, then where in the world will I find one?

I know I shouldn't think like this but I feel that I need to get more prepared for church. I need to make sure I look my best. My hair, nails and outfit all need to be very attractive yet tastefully sexy. Of course, I want to be just as prepared mentally and spiritually. This is clearly something I can't discuss with my girls. I'm almost embarrassed to admit I've given this much thought into getting ready for church. I'll only mention this whole Randall situation to them if things start to progress. My friends already think I'm 'holier than thou' and I'm tired of defending myself, which I will definitely have to do if my friends find out I'm interested in a deacon! Not to mention the fact that my crew will suddenly start showing up at church to check Randall out, which could be very embarrassing. I need to work through this situation on my own.

I go through the process of choosing an outfit for church and finally narrow it down to two choices. I'll decide which outfit is the winner when I wake up Sunday morning. Both looks are flattering. Now I have to figure out if I can wear Spanx, and if the foundation garment can be felt through my clothing. I don't want Randall to feel it when he hugs me, but I really need to wear them. They give my waist definition and make my stomach appear flatter than it actually is. Don't get me wrong, I spend my fair share of time in the gym to try to stay in decent shape, but God knows I hate it. But in order to truly to be ready for church Sunday, I've got to get a good workout in, eat a balanced meal, and get a good night's rest.

Part of my mental preparation for church will also entail turning my phone off at 6:00 PM Saturday evening. Otherwise, my phone will ring all night with random texts, online notifications, and voicemails filled with gossip I don't want to hear. I've decided to call it an early night Saturday. After my workout, I'm going to eat a healthy meal like a grilled salmon salad and catch up my Tivo'd shows until I doze off. I'm sure my body will thank me for the extra care I'm taking of it—and I'm hoping Deacon Randall will be appreciative as well.

■■■

On Saturday night, I'm in bed by 10:00 PM, which is completely unheard of for me. I also did two things I never do, to make sure I'm on time for church the next day—I set my alarm and turn the television off before going to sleep. *Wow, this deacon really has a hold on me;* I have to admit to myself. I haven't even spent any time with Randall outside of church and already he is influencing my daily habits. But that may not be a bad thing. Change is good—especially if the change is for the better. Right before I get in bed, I kneel to say my evening prayers. As I'm trying to concentrate on praying, I unintentionally start practicing what I'm going to say to Randall. Once I'm

satisfied with the imaginary conversation, my mind brings me back to reality—
kneeling by my bed.

I'm half-praying; half-encouraging myself when I think, *Danielle, just relax.*
Whatever is going to happen will happen. Just enjoy the ride. Don't be too pushy or try to rush
things. The man is supposed to pursue you. I laugh to myself. *He sure is fine. Maybe that's why I*
am putting so much thought into this. Randall better not let me catch him off of church property, or
he's going to see another side of me. I smile slyly to myself, crawl into bed, and doze off.

My eyes pop open at 4:49 AM. Much too early. I said I wanted to be fresh and
ready to start the day, but not quite this fresh. I'm starting to regret going to bed so
early. I lay in bed until my alarm goes off. Time to get ready! I jump up and get
dressed. I feel at ease since I have plenty of time. I carefully apply my makeup and
make sure every strand of hair is in place. Then I debate on the outfit I want to wear-
- pink and gray or black and white? I opt for the pink and gray—a pale pink jacket
with a charcoal gray skirt. It's soft and classy. The skirt is short enough to show I've
been spending time in the gym, and the jacket gently hugs my hips and highlights my
waist. Randall looks fit, so I need to look like I work out, too.

I take my time driving to church as well. I turn up VaShawn Mitchell on my
stereo and enjoy the ride. The parking attendant stops me as I arrive at church.

"Good morning," the attendant says.

"Good morning!" I sing.

"Glad to see you back again," he responds.

"Thank you. It's good to see you, too," I tell him.

"You are in time to get a spot on the pavement." The attendant informs me.

Of course, this is great news to me. "Now today is my lucky day."

He motions toward the nearest parking space. "If you think you can get into
that spot there it's yours."

"It sounds like you are challenging my driving skills," I respond playfully.

He smiles. "I am not sure if you can get in there or not."

I answer him with a bit of nervousness in my voice. "Oh Lord! Now, if I get
into this spot then it's mine every Sunday."

"Yep, and after the fourth visit you have to join," he teases.

I laugh. "Y'all are a group of characters over here. Where did Pastor get you all
from?" I easily back into the spot. I must admit it was a little tight, but nothing I
couldn't handle.

The parking attendant is shocked. "Ms. Rose you are all right with me. I really
did not expect you to be able to park in this spot."

"Remember you promised me this spot every Sunday." I respond confidently.

"Show up every Sunday and it is yours," the attendant tells me.

Thinking about Randall when I respond, I simply say, "will do."

I check the mirror one last time and open the door. I try to relax and wipe my
hands on my skirt because they are already sweating. I approach the door and to my
surprise it is pushed at the same time I pull. I look down to see a pair of gray men's
dress shoes in front of me. Well, if it isn't Randall! I feel myself losing composure
right away and I try hard to hide the fact that I really want to melt. I love a fine man
in a suit. More specifically, a pinstriped suit, which is exactly what Randall was
wearing. It was like he was waiting for me to arrive. *Just keep remembering Psalm 121,* I
tell myself. *My help comes from the Lord. Keep repeating this in your head and you'll stay focused.*

I feel completely weak in Randall's presence. He has no idea what his suit is doing to me. "Ms. Danielle, such a pleasure to see you this morning," he says.

"Thank you. My pleasure as well." I'm surprised I got the words out without stuttering.

He reaches out for a hug but this time I give him a true, almost passionate hug. It was so intense I swear I moaned when his face touched my neck.

"Wow, you look beautiful and smell wonderful," he tells me, confirming that I chose the right outfit. "And I love that fragrance."

All the stuff I rehearsed to say before coming to church has slipped my mind and all I can do is smile. The things I want to say right now would be totally inappropriate in church.

"You're always so nice. And although I do enjoy your compliments, my grandma always told me to never trust a man that is always flattering you, because he only wants one thing." I make the most skeptical face I can, even though I'm elated.

Randall laughs so hard that I look around to make sure no one else notices, but of course now we have an audience.

"Do you compliment all the ladies?" I ask him.

He's still laughing. "No I don't. You are so funny Ms. Danielle. I love it. I need to be around you more often so you can make my days brighter."

I'm not sure if he's coming on to me or simply being friendly. If we were in another setting, I would have questioned his comment. But since we're at church, I'll continue to exercise decorum.

I respond, "We can make that happen any time. But don't just use me for my comedic skills. Nobody likes a user."

"Oh no, Ms. Danielle I would never use you. There are many other things I would rather do instead."

Oh no he didn't! How am I supposed to respond to that in church?! "Would you care to elaborate, Deacon Washington?" I ask.

"I would love to later. But right now it's time for service."

By this time, we are at the threshold of the sanctuary. We walk in side by side and nearly hand in hand. Our feet are on the same step. Our arms are swinging on the same beat. I am hoping his thoughts are on the same track as mine. We approach the same seats from last week. He ushers me to mine and jumps right across the aisle to his.

This time I was very coherent. Service was especially thought provoking. The praise team effectively ministered to me and sounded wonderful. I was fanning myself before the second song was over. I gently wiped the perspiration from my brow. Before I can lower my arm, Deacon is passing me a Kleenex, and I'm back in my thoughts. *I was doing so well. I was focused on the church service and not thinking about Randall. His simple act of handing me a tissue tells me two things. One, I have to make sure I don't perspire next week. Two, he's paying attention. Can't pretend I don't like that.* The doors of the church opened. My heart pumped. I was hoping no one could tell my chest was heaving. *God, let me come a few more weeks before I make a decision. Right, now I would be making a drastic and emotional decision because I want to be close to Randall every week. I really would prefer not to make the choice to join the church while he is so close to me.*

Then here it came again. Pastor Hunter instructed everyone to "hug your neighbor." This week, I can't get out of hugging Randall during this part of the service—no matter how hard I try. As I am hugging my neighbor, Randall speaks softly, clearly and extremely close to my ear. He is so close that his lips touch my ear. "I need to go to the back. Meet me in the vestibule at the same place you were this morning. Do not leave until you see me. Are we clear?"

My entire body is motionless. All I can do is nod. *Damn! He did it again! Father I stretch my hands to thee-- no other help I know.* As soon as I am able, I look around to see Randall practically running out of a paneled wall. He must have unbuttoned his jacket because it was swinging behind him. Then I become more observant of my surroundings. Which other panels are doors? Why are there hidden doors in the sanctuary? Where are the cameras and security staff? I scan the room really well. Now, I am a little perturbed with myself. I'm usually much more aware of my surroundings but I've let Randall distract me. And why did he have to run off so quickly? My inquisitive nature is starting to kick back in, since Randall isn't here to blind me with his fineness. I take a seat in the pew and take in the scene. There was nothing extremely unusual. Then something catches my eye. Who is that? There is a man looking like James Bond in basic training. Is he at the Palace? I watch him for a few minutes, and he does not move or crack a smile. *Security Man # 1,* I think to myself. The man's stance and the way he is dressed makes me think of Men in Black or Bad Boys. And it's impossible to even think about Bad Boys without singing the theme song, which I immediately start hearing in my head.

In the midst of laughing at myself, I see another man who looks like the first. I try not to think too much of it but the only thing that comes to my head is Deacon James. Deacon Washington maybe a new version of Mr. James after all. I think of Mr. James and laugh to myself. *Next Sunday I'll be all eyes and ears so I can pay more attention to my surroundings.*

As I walk down the aisle to leave, I make eye contact with everyone I pass. I wonder if any of the women are Randall's girlfriend or wife, or if the men are part of the pastor's security team.

I have no idea how much time has passed once I'm in the vestibule. Have I made Randall wait on me, or am I waiting on him? I don't see him yet. I take a moment to look around so that I can make more observations before Randall takes up all of my focus. I'm looking for men who look like they're part of the security team. Now I'm curious about the rest of the church. I decide to wonder off. Where is the ladies' room? The water fountain? Medical station? What about the book store? Does the church have a nursery? Even though I don't have any children, asking about the nursery was valid, since people always push children on me for some reason. I turn my attention to the announcement board in the foyer. It is nice to see what services the church offers.

A hand gently grabs my waist and pulls me back. I know who it is. *You may not want to do that, Deacon. It's been a long time since a man has touched me.*

"There you are. I have been all around the building looking for you. I was about to give up," Randall says, slightly seductively.

I tried to answer in the most nonchalant voice I could. "I went to our original meeting spot but you weren't there. So I decided to walk around."

Randall was playful but spoke in a slightly formal tone. "I'll let you slide this time but this is not where I told you to meet me. Beautiful, smart, funny, and hardheaded. You are an interesting combination of traits."

I was still very much attracted to him, but slightly annoyed. "Speaking of traits, you know, I've noticed that you're a tad bit demanding."

"You think so?" He asked.

I couldn't believe he had the audacity to be surprised. "Think so? No. I know so."

Randall inquired, "Is that a problem?"

"For some it may be," I answered.

"What about for Danielle?" he probed.

"Oh, now, I get called Danielle?" I observe.

"I guess now you do."

"I am not sure if I have moved up in ranks or down." I make the observation jokingly, but still want to know what he's thinking.

"You could never move down only up."

"That is nice to know."

"But you eluded the question."

"No, I didn't."

"Okay and your answer would be?"

"In all honesty, I kind of like it. However..."

"However what?"

"Are you willing to receive or are you only the giver?"

His laugh was deliberate and strong. "I like how you said that."

"Well?" I pressed him for an answer.

"I'm not sure."

"Why not? If you're demanding with me, are you going to be cooperative when I am demanding toward you?"

"I guess I really am not around people that demand much from me."

"Well I have news for you."

"And what would that news be?"

"There is a new sheriff in town."

He laughs really loud again. "I'll take that."

"And in my city what is good for the goose is always good for the gander."

"I got you."

"I hope so." I smirked.

"Basically, you are saying the only way you will adhere to my demands is if I adhere to yours?"

"Yes. And let's change the word from "demands" to "requests." "Demands" sounds so submissive. And, by the way, that is the way you communicate your requests to me—as if you want me to submit to you."

"You sound like you have a problem with the word submissive," Randall observes.

"No, I don't."

"Are you sure?"

"I'm positive. I have no one to be submissive to."

"Maybe you do but you don't know it yet."

"Maybe. But if I'm correct the Word said wives be submissive to your husbands. Husbands love your wives."

"That is what the Word says. What is your point?"

"I have no husband."

"So you say. He has met you and knows who you are if you will be patient he will present himself."

"If he knows who he is the right thing for him to do is inform me of this, don't you think?"

"You know him and you will know he is the one for you when the time is right and not a moment sooner."

"That does me no good."

"It will be for your good in the end. Be patient and wait on the Lord." He said positively.

"I guess that means I have no control."

"I guess you are right," Randall agreed.

"Huh?"

"Am I too hard or harsh?" he asked in an abrasive tone.

"Not really."

"Well what is it?"

"Humph." I was deep in thought by that point. "Nothing," I muttered.

"Oh, it's something," Randall prodded.

"No it's nothing."

"Don't be like that."

"Like what?" I asked confused.

"Don't hold back on me."

"I'm not holding back."

"What would you call it?" He asked, sincerely looking me in my eyes.

"Keeping quiet."

"Why?"

"I don't think this is neither the time nor the place."

"Where is the time and place?" he asked suspiciously.

"Anywhere outside of here."

"Anything you can say outside here; if it is within the will of God, you can say it in here."

"Who said it was in the will of God?" I was beginning to regret my choice to be celibate. There were definitely some ways I wanted to get to know Randall now. But I was too far on my abstinence journey to turn back now.

"I know you want to do things under His will," Randall said assuredly.

"I like to do things in decency and order. If we get back to the submission conversation, we will be out of His order."

Some random woman walks by and Randall speaks to her. "Good morning."

"Good morning. You and your wife look beautiful. You've coordinated your outfits perfectly," the woman responds.

We both stare at the woman with confused expressions.

"The gray and pink looks nice on both of you," she explains.

We both look down at each other's outfits and then at ourselves. We are actually dressed similarly. I paid attention to the stripes on his suit but nothing else. He is wearing a gray pinstriped suit with a pink shirt and a pink and gray paisley tie.

He looks me up and down and said, "See they already think we are married. Let's just do it and submission will no longer be a conversation."

"I think there are some other factors involved."

"Like what?"

"You may be crazy?"

"What if I am not?" he asked sounding hurt.

"Then congratulations."

"Thank you Mrs. Danielle Washington."

"I wish it were that easy."

"It is."

"Really?" I asked totally shocked he assumed it was that simple and easy.
"Yep."

"Now that we have that established, I have a question." I said.

"Yes, I will marry you."

I laughed. "That wasn't my question."

"Go ahead with your question." he frowned.

"Where did you go?"

"When?"

"When you went behind the paneled wall."

"To assist in opening the safe."

"How did the wall open?"

"I really can't answer that question."

"Why?"

"It would be a security breach."

"Oh. Okay. Are you a Deacon or Security?"

"I thought I was just Mr. Danielle Washington."

"Not if you can't answer my questions."

"Actually, I am sort of responsible for both."

"Really?"

He nods.

"Seriously?"

He nods and raises his eyebrows.

"How or why do you get to do both?" I ask persistently.

"I guess because I can fight." He lifts his sleeve and shows me his communicator. I get a glimpse of his cuff links and his monogrammed shirt. Now I am confused. Either he is gay, or a really well put together man, or worst of all—married.

"Are we under surveillance now?"

"Actually, the church is always monitored. We have been recorded at some point during this conversation."

"Is our conversation heard now?"

"No. Not until I depress this communicator will my volume be activated. However, my earpiece is always live. Meaning I can hear every noise made on my locator at all times. My locators change randomly during shifts. But I will not bore you with details."

"You are not boring me. I really need to know."

"You need to know or want to know?"

"Kind of both."

"Curiosity killed the cat."

"Don't you know the rest of the cliché?"

"No I don't." he replied.

"Satisfaction brought her back."

"That is the least of my concerns. You will always come back."

"Don't be so cocky and arrogant. You leave me no room to compliment you if you're always tooting your own horn."

He laughs. "I'm kidding."

"Oh my! You two coordinated nicely. You and your wife look beautiful this morning, Deacon." Another church member comments while passing by.

"I told you that you need to marry me." He whispered in my ear, which made me tingle inside.

"I don't think that is the way you ask for someone's hand in marriage."

"You are correct. But don't give up on me yet. I will do better." We exchange smiles and continue walking. I enjoy and savor the moment. It feels so right. I find myself wishing for more. Randall walks me to the sidewalk. He places his hand on my back and at the same time, he puts his wrist up to his cheek and says "10-4" into his device. I gave him a questioning look.

"I'm sorry. I gotta run," Randall says abruptly. "I will see you Sunday. Have an excellent week, beautiful. Be safe and be blessed. Hey, and stay out of trouble."

I was caught off guard. I was really hoping I could get him away from the building so I could ask some more specific questions. Clearly, a monkey wrench was thrown into the plan. But at least I knew he was expecting to see me next Sunday. Then he called me beautiful.

What are the chances that we would wear the same color? That is so strange. I'm intrigued by the coincidence, but I try not to read too much into it.

Dani, get a grip. It is going to be a long week. I take a deep breath, crank up the car, and begin to pull off. As soon as I put the car in drive and release my foot from the brakes Randall runs off. I am not sure what I am getting myself into to, but this is getting stranger by the minute.

The rest of my Sunday is pretty ordinary. I work out and do a few chores, but the day is pretty uneventful. Before I know it, it's time to go to bed. I kneel to pray. *Dear God, I claim and thank you for another prosperous day. Thank you for your endless grace and mercy. Thank you for keeping your hedge of protection around me, my family and my friends and their friends and families. Father, I humbly come to say thank you for the use of my limbs, organs, mind, and sanity. Father, I thank you for all that you have done thus far. I thank you in advance for all you plan to do and even for the things you did not do because they were not in your will. I thank you for strengthening me to make the right moves in my life, and to move on when necessary. I bless your holy and righteous name. I ask that you continue to lead me and guide me along the path you have set. In your son Jesus' Name, Amen.*

I rested at the foot of the bed after ending my prayer. I have no clue how long I was there before I move and get into the bed. I lay there flat on my back looking at the ceiling. All sort of thoughts went through my head. I felt a sting in my heart, which prompted me to start thinking. *How did I get here? Truly, where am I? How did I go from a long-term relationship to being by myself? After four years, I still feel like this place is foreign to me.* During the break up, my life changed completely. I lost the majority of my friends. They were our mutual friends. It was easier to let him keep them. I moved to a new place. This is my first time living alone. I am not sure if I made the best decision buying a house instead of renting an apartment. Not to mention, I am worshipping in a church I'm not familiar with at all. Don't get me wrong. I am being spiritually fed at my new place of worship. I think about whether I can honestly make that assessment since I had been so sidetracked by Deacon Randall. Then I remembered I've been listening to the sermons on CD, so I actually could say what I was learning at church was beneficial. But there was no denying that Randall is a distraction. I felt the need to pray about the issue further. *God please speak to me. Am I doing the right thing? Am I going to the best place for me to worship? I need to truly and consistently be fed spiritually in order to grow and become a disciple in your kingdom. Please reveal your plan to me Lord. Why have you placed what seems like an obstacle in my path? What does all of this mean? Help me Lord. Lead me and guide me. I can't make the right decisions without you. Give me wisdom and direct my steps.*

Those were my last waking thoughts that night. The next thing I knew it was morning and time to think about these things all over again.

WEEK 5

The week was pretty normal. Nothing particularly good happened, but nothing bad took place, either. I worked, went to the gym, and did it all over again the next day. *I really need to get a life,* I concluded.

It's 3:16 AM on Thursday morning. I'm wide-awake. *Well, if you want to talk to me Lord, I'm listening,* I say in my mind. Almost immediately, I hear God respond to the statement I've just made in my heart. God instructs me to go to service at a different time this Sunday. I knew this was confirmation that I was, indeed, going to the right church. I had asked God for clarity on whether I had found my church home, and He responded to me. Perhaps I'd be able to avoid the temptation named Randall Washington if I worshipped at a different time. *Well, now that I'm awake I may as well make good use of my time,* I reasoned. I prayed, read my daily scriptures, and exercised my abs by emulating the workout routine on my exercise DVD. Then I get dressed and head out for the day.

Saturday came so fast. *I had better figure out Sunday's attire. I haven't worn a hat to this church yet; maybe I'll do that this week.* Then again, I don't recall any of the women wearing hats. The hat may be a little too overwhelming for the general fashion sense of the congregation. I stand in my closet looking at my hats, shoes, and suits. I am not sure what I want to wear. Nothing is jumping out at me yet. I decide to pick the shoes first.

What about the light blue shoes with the ribbon that ties around the ankle? I have many outfit options with those shoes. And they're so attention getting that I should make sure the rest of my outfit is pretty low-key. I think I'll go with my navy blue suit with baby blue pin stripes, a baby blue camisole, a light blue hat, and a soft blue flower to accent my lapel.

I need to try this skirt on. It's a little short. I want to make sure it's not inappropriate. But I can take a lap scarf if need be. Oh, I completely forgot this skirt has splits on both sides. I was trying to make sure my outfit was especially modest, but the skirt is bound to draw enough attention on its own. I should pick out an alternate outfit just in case. I checked the church website Friday to get the service times. I am planning to attend the later service in order to avoid distraction, since I definitely received the Lord's response.

Sunday comes. I go through my normal routine to get ready for church and leave the house. I arrive at the church parking lot. The parking lot attendant stops me and motions for me to roll down my window. *Uh oh, what have I done?* I wonder. For some reason I begin to feel uneasy.

"You are late." The parking attendant is stern and not as friendly as he was last week.

I try to make the best of the situation by playfully saying, "Better late than never-- and who says I'm late? I actually think I'm early for this service."

The attendant softened his tone. "You have a point. I was expecting you earlier."

I immediately respond to keep him from asking any questions. "I like to switch things up. Never let the right hand know what the left hand is doing. It keeps me on my toes." I figured referencing scripture would help me to avoid any further interrogation.

The attendant sounded a little disappointed on my behalf. "We'll see how you feel about that in a few hours. I have a feeling you won't like this service. It is much more crowded, lasts longer and the line to enter and exit is like rush hour traffic on a Friday. You will have to be here early to get your parking spot. Or else, you'll be on your toes walking from the field to the building. And God knows you don't want that."

This doesn't sound good. "We'll see," I tell the attendant. "But I think I'll take your word for it."

I pull up to my spot, jump out of the car, put my hat on, and proceed to the front door of the church, ready to worship. In the distance, I notice a line of men standing a few feet from the door. The closer I get, I notice one of the men steps out of formation. *Oh gee. It's Deacon Randall.*

Before I even get close enough he has his arms out for a hug. "Ms. Rose," he greets me.

He insists on calling me Ms. Rose. Two can play that game. With all the resolve I can muster, I extend my hand to shake his and say, "Good morning. Deacons."

I was still holding his hand and shaking it as deliberately as I could. When I let it go he said, "Oh you are clowning me."

"Enjoy service." I respond.

One of the deacons comments, "That's a beautiful hat."

I throw my hand up politely as a gesture to say, "Thank you." I hear Randall's feet hitting the pavement just behind me. He grabs my waist. I am slightly out of his grasp, because I barely feel his touch. Before I can completely turn around, Randall spins me toward him and steals a hug. "You look as beautiful as ever," he says. "Why are you late?"

"Why does everyone keep saying that?" I ask. "I'm not late. I'm actually early."

"I was expecting you earlier," Randall says. "This is not your hour."

I ask skeptically. "Oh, is this the hour your wife or girlfriend comes to church?"

"You don't even have to worry about that," Randall assures me.

Oh my goodness. I was not expecting Randall to be here. And I didn't think he'd respond to that comment so quickly.

"And, once again, you look like my wife. We're dressed alike this week, too," Randall observes. I look at him and then down at my outfit. He was wearing a navy suit and light blue shirt. He wasn't wearing a tie today; his jacket was open and his cufflinks were beautiful. And his shoes were particularly stylish. He looked so handsome.

He teased. "Why don't you just call me next week and let me know what you're wearing so I can stop going crazy trying to figure out what to wear."

I'm effortlessly flirting again. "I can do you one better," I say.

"I'm sure you can," Randall responds. "What did you have in mind?" He looks around to see if people are eavesdropping on our conversation. Then I realize that someone may be speaking into his earpiece. *Great, not only am I possibly competing with a wife or girlfriend, but I have to be in competition with this earpiece, too.*

"Too many ears around here," Randall says, a little annoyed and very serious. "We have to go." The tone of his voice is very urgent.

We walk into the sanctuary like a couple. He leads me to my normal seat. Randall places his Bible down to save his seat and walks to the side of the altar.

During praise and worship, he walks over to my side instead of going to his seat. This immediately makes me uncomfortable.

He stands there for what seems like hours then grabs my hand and leans into my ear. His lips touch my ear each time they move. "I will not be in the sanctuary for this service." Randall says. He becomes demanding again. "Do not leave without seeing me. You look extremely beautiful. I was afraid you were going to stand me up. But it was surely worth the wait. Are you okay?"

I nod slowly. I am not sure if he's asking me if I'm okay because he's leaving, because he can sense how tense I am, or because he can feel the heat escaping from my body.

I was going to miss his presence in the sanctuary, but that may not be a bad thing. I really need to concentrate on the service. I was able to enjoy praise and worship and Pastor Hunter preached a very timely word. I am convinced the man is anointed to preach. When he began to compare baptism to the process of pickling, I was completely enthralled in the message. I was glad Deacon Washington wasn't nearby. This was a message I needed to hear. I could definitely relate to it. I had been "pickled" numerous times but I still don't feel my dill is right. Just as a Christian may not feel like his/her walk with the Lord is right, even though he/she has been baptized. Pastor Hunter gave the appeal for salvation or rededication and opened the doors of the church. I wanted to move. I needed to move. But I still was not one hundred percent sure. *I don't know what I am waiting for or on. Am I ignoring God? Am I being disobedient?* Then I hear Pastor Hunter speak.

"Last call," the pastor repeats. "We will wait for you. There's someone else who needs to come down to the front of the church. Your hands are sweating and your heart is beating. My daughter, my son, don't miss this opportunity. Saints, pray that the right person makes the right decision today." As I looked down to pick my purse up, I hear the congregation clapping. A woman is making her way down the aisle. *Maybe I wasn't the person Pastor was referring to.* The benediction was given and my favorite part of the service came. The pastor said, "Hug your neighbor on the left and on the right of you." I only had one "neighbor" today. Randall's Bible was still in the chair where he left it. I hug the church member next to me and sit back down. Then I look around me to see if there are any cameras or hidden exit routes I didn't observe last time. I don't see anything out of the ordinary after surveying the ceiling, every light fixture and monitor in the sanctuary. I get up and proceed to the door, still looking around me. Randall, surprisingly, was far from my mind. That was the first time he wasn't at the forefront of my thoughts since we met two months ago. I was relieved. As I approach the double doors, I could see a foot and a hand outside the door and as soon as I got close enough, he turned around.

"Hey babe." Randall said.

I almost looked back to see who he was talking to. "Hey there," I said, with less enthusiasm than I would usually speak to him.

"Everything all good?" he asked.

"Most definitely." I say.

He grabbed my bag and we begin to walk. He jingled the change in his pocket as we walked along the sidewalk to my car. I feel at ease. It gave me the indication that I made him as nervous as he made me. This was so unusual. A guy had not made me nervous in years. But now I know he feels the same way.

Two elderly women approached us. "You all look so beautiful."

The women turn to each other and one says, "Hazel do you remember when we could wear those stilettos?"

One of the women faces me and says, "We got to leave them to you now Deaconess. Keep our legacy up."

They both address Randall. "Deacon keep up the good work-- you two look so happy."

He says, "Thank you" and grabs my hand.

As soon as they are out of sight, we look at each other and laugh.

"Why does everyone think we are married?" I said through my laugh.

"Because we should be," Randall says pleasantly, but with serious tone.

"I don't know if I should agree or disagree." I tell him.

"Why would you disagree?" he asks.

"Because we don't know each other outside of here."

"That is a minor technicality. I can tell you anything about me you want or need to know." Randall seems so sure we should be a couple.

"More like a major technicality," I tell him.

"Change your thoughts. We will enjoy each other better getting to know each other as Mr. and Mrs. Washington. There is no need for dating. Dating is not sound doctrine, anyway."

We are at my car. He opens the door. I reach for my bag and throw it on the passenger seat. As I begin to step into the car, he grabs me so intensely that it almost startled me. *For him to be as thin as he is he surely is strong.*

He leans in to talk to me, and again his lips and breath touch my ear. "Six more days until I see you again. Take care my love."

I reply, "That is by your choice. The six days you're waiting to see me again, that is."

He replies. "Yes, it is. For the things you see are temporal but the things you don't see are eternal."

What? Did he scripturize me as he holds me in the church parking lot? We release our embrace, but I still have my hand around his waist. He is much thinner than he looks in these suits but his body feels solid. Our arms stretch until we are hand in hand.

I sit in the car and roll the window down. He taps the roof and says, "Drive safely until we meet again."

I am completely perplexed.

WEEK 6

Saturday

The week goes as usual. I see a change in me. The kind of change a woman has when she is either in love or "gets some" in the morning before going to work. And of course, there are other reasons—especially if you know me. I could be in just as great of a mood after finishing a session of shoe therapy or buying the newest and hottest handbag on the market. Very few things make me feel better than getting a little blue bag from a certain fine jewelry store or getting diamonds as a gift. Even my colleagues and crew are concerned. All hell broke out this week at work, but I have remained calm. Every project that needed to be completed this week has been off-schedule, and I haven't worried about it one bit. Virtually every person in the office has scolded me for some reason or another, and it hasn't affected me. Why? Because it is less than twenty-four hours before "we" meet again.

Saturday morning's routine has changed. Instead of jumping up hitting the gym by five and the salon immediately afterwards, now I need to plan for Sunday before I leave the house in case there is anything I need to pick up while I'm out. I also need to think carefully about the hairstyle I get. So now, I am hitting the gym around seven and the salon by ten. This is not my preference, I have to admit. I do not like spending my Saturday in the salon with a bunch of cackling hens. But my mind is so preoccupied I don't even hear the gossiping antics from the women in the salon.

Before going to get my hair done, I decide on a three-piece cream and black suit with wedge cream and black strappy heeled sandals. *I may need to pick up accessories. A nice chunky neckpiece would top this outfit off. I think big, full hair would be nice.* The suit includes a black pair of pants and a black skirt. I think I am going with the pants. I am really not fond of wearing pants to church but I know it's chic these days. My old-school tendencies kick in and I'm leaning more toward wearing the skirt. I'll decide in the morning.

■■

Workout done. Hair done. Nails touched up. I need to make a stop at the cleaner's and then to Arthur's to check out the necklaces. *That is all I am looking at and I'm not making any other stops.* Then I realize I'm hungry. Sushi sounds good, but Spondivitis sounds even better.

Danielle no can do, I say to myself. *Be disciplined.* I hop out of the car to race in Arthur's and don't even get into the store before I'm interrogated.

"Danielle, where have you been the last four weeks?" One of the employees asks.

"Dang has it been four weeks? I'm behind schedule. I will be back on track." I run into the store.

"Danielle, you're late." Another employee playfully chastises.

I am usually here every Saturday at ten. This has been my routine for over ten years.

"I know," I respond. "Work-out and hair appointment times changed." Men can change every aspect of your life. And to think I did not even know Randall well and I was already changing.

"And you seem to not be rushed like you usually are," the employee observed.

Everyone that knows me knows I live on a timed schedule. I am always going from point A to point B. Tell me where I am supposed to show up and what to wear and I am there. It's kind of a sad life and frankly, I'm really sick of it. Sometimes I want to do what I truly want to do and not go by an agenda to fulfill everyone's expectations. Then I remind myself of the Bible verse that says, "Don't grow weary in well doing." *But who was I trying to do so well for?*

The sale associate interrupted my thoughts, "What are you looking for today?"

"An ivory and black chunky neck piece," I respond.

Instantly three choices are on the counter for me to inspect. I pick one and say "I'll be right back."

The ladies in the shop jokingly say, "There she goes."

I like to be very coordinated and in order to do that I have to actually put my pieces together before making a purchase. I run to the trunk and grab my suit from Sharp Suits and my shoes.

"Do you live out of that car?" The sale associates ask me.

"Basically, I pay for a place to shower every now and then." I tell them.

"Where is your hat for this outfit?" The woman at the counter inquires.

"I'm not wearing one," I tell her.

"That cream and black hat you have goes nicely with this," she reminds me.

"Yeah it does--but not for tomorrow," I tell her.

"Why?" she scolds.

"I started going to a new church and I am not sure if they are ready for the hats yet," I say casually.

"WHAT?!" They all say in unison.

The look on my face confirms their surprise. "So where are you going to church?" The ladies ask.

"Victory Hope Greater Faith Church."

"My neighbor is a minister there," one of the women tells me. "My son attends every week with his son."

"Oh yeah? I like it there a lot." I tell her. "What's your neighbor's name?"

"Minister Stephens," the lady answers.

"I know exactly who he and his wife are. That is a praying man. You should come to church sometime," I say encouragingly.

"I can't," she answers. "I am here on Sunday and Wednesday."

"Check it out live on the website." I offer her a practical solution.

"I will," she tells me then turns her attention back to the jewelry. "You were right. The one you picked works the best."

I pay for the necklace. "Thank you. I will see you Saturday."

The ladies continue to taunt me as I leave the store. "And she is off and running, beating her own weekly time. Six point three minutes."

Sunday

Morning comes. I opt for the skirt. I knew that I would. I get dressed and leave the house. I take my time driving. No need to rush. I'm doing well on time. Besides, I'm trying to convince myself that I'm not always rushing—even though it certainly seems that way. I arrive at church and as I walk in the door, I see that Randall is not in his usual place. I check my watch and realize I'm a bit early. Then I see him moving at the speed of light. He seems to be very quick on his feet, like a cat. I watch his feet as he moves closer and it is as if they don't touch the ground--like a runner or a ballerina. This is ridiculous. *He has me so mesmerized that I can't see his feet hit the carpet.*

Randall greets me. "Good Morning Beautiful."

"Good morning." I sang.

"Where is your hat?"

"Huh?"

"Your hat? I liked you in the hat."

"Umm, at home."

"It needs to be with you from now on."

I can feel my eyebrows touch. There he goes with the assertive talk again.

"It was a long week?" he asks.

"It always is for me," I tell him.

"The past six days were torture." he sneaks in.

"I'm sorry to hear that. Again, that is by your choice." I remind him.

"I know-- just be patient with me. It will be well worth the wait."

"What am I being patient for and waiting on?" I probe.

"Time will tell." he answers coolly.

"You are not making sense to me." I say, slightly irritated.

"I promise it will be worthwhile. That's all you need to know."

▪▪▪

As praise and worship goes on my leg begins to cramp. *Oh crap. I overdid it.* The door is a long way from where I'm sitting. I really need to walk this cramp out. I begin to shake my leg and stomp without being too obvious. I rub my leg. I pray. Nothing is helping. I kneel down and massage my cramped muscle. Suddenly I see another set of feet next to mine.

"Everything okay?" Randall sounds concerned.

Panting, I answered. "Yeah."

"What's wrong?"

"I have a cramp."

"A Charlie horse?"

"Probably due to two hundred pound leg extensions and two hundred squats," I tell him.

"Impressive. Can you walk to the door?" he asks.

I look to the door and say "No." The sweat is popping out on my forehead.

"I can see the knot-- sit down," he instructs me.

I sit, but my leg remains stretched. Randall touches my leg. My eyes close instantly. I am not sure what he did but in one second, the cramp is gone. I flex and bend my leg to make sure the cramp is no longer there. It's really gone. I thrust my arms around his neck and laid my head on his shoulder.

"How did you do that?" I ask, thoroughly impressed.

"Years of practice."

"You are a life saver."

"You're welcome. I want to be in your life permanently. Lay off the leg extensions."

"Why?"

"Two hundred pounds is too much for you," he said without looking at me.

"I can handle it." I was not questioning the work out advice. I was questioning the "permanent in my life" comment.

"I know you can. But your legs can't. Get more potassium in your diet." Randall stood up and went to his seat.

I could see from the corner of my eye that Randall watched me the entire service. When I did look at him, we made direct contact and I moved my lips to mouth the words "Thank you."

He nodded. I winked. He smiled. Service was coming to a close. He stood shoulder to shoulder to me and when the timing was right he said, "Are you able to walk?"

"Yes."

"If not, stay here."

"I can walk."

"I will meet you in the vestibule," he replied quickly as he started to walk behind the pulpit through a marked door.

Sure enough, he was standing there with his hands behind his back when I got to the vestibule. "Hey." he grinned.

"I have something for you," he said.

"Roses or diamonds?" I joke. Both being my favorites.

He laughed. "Neither. Something to show my love and something you really want and need right now." He pulled his left hand forward first and it was a banana.

"Thanks. That is so thoughtful. Where in God's name did you get a banana so quickly?"

"I keep them with me at all times."

"Okay little monkey," I tease him.

Then he pulled the right hand forward and it was a bottle of water.

"What are you trying to do to me?"

"Take care of you."

My heart begins to beat so fast I hope he can't hear it. "You didn't tell me you were a doctor, too."

"Why are you working out so hard?" he inquires.

"It helps me to relieve my stress and it keeps me in shape."

"Why are you stressed?"

"Just the daily dilemmas of life. The norm."

"We need to do something about that. What can I do to relive your stress? There is a healthy level of stress but something tells me you are at the level where stress is not normal. Let's erase that thought now."

Take me home and make love to me until I tell you to stop, I thought. That would be entirely inappropriate to say here at church. I decide not to. Instead, I responded by saying, "You don't have to do anything."

"Yes I do." he assures me. "Life should not and will not stress you."

"God said we will have trials and tribulations," I counter.

"But where did he say that you should be stressed? Give your stresses to me and to Him and we will handle it."

"Watch what you ask for, Deacon," I warn him.

"I am capable. Where do you work out?"

"Mainly at the gym and at the track."

"Gold's or LA Fitness?"

"Neither. I go to a neighborhood gym—I've been working out there before either of those commercial gyms became popular. All types of people work out there—the retired body builder, coaches, the ex NFL player, the boxer, etc. We are all family. The owner runs the facility like the YMCA. He keeps the kids in the hood out of trouble. He has a boxing ring and he lets the boys with anger issues and fighting habits get in and work it out. I love it."

"What? So you know about the ring?"

"I get in every now and then to let them know that just because I'm a girl doesn't mean they can or will walk over me."

"Anyone get in the ring with you?"

"No one there would fight me if I paid them to."

"I would hate to come up there and shut it down."

"Would you, now?"

"I sure would. The neighborhood would not be the same."

"There goes the neighborhood."

"I will." He said seriously.

"We shall see. I know who to call now if I have any issues."

"So you like boxing?"

"I sure do?"

"Don't lie!"

It caught me off guard. I do not like or use the word lie. And he said it harshly. It wasn't that serious. "What reason do I have to lie to you?"

"You don't. Who do you like best?"

"Past or present?"

"Either."

"Of course I have to go with the home team always and say Evander. But I was a Tyson fan in his day. Currently I love Mayweather--hands down. There are some other guys out there I feel a lot. I think they have strong potential and talent. There's a lot of talent out there."

"Good choices. I won't challenge you."

"That is mighty nice of you but feel free to do so."

"No I won't. Where do you walk the track?"

"Howell High School."

"Really?"

"Yep."

"How often do you work out?"

"Tuesday, Thursday, and Saturday at the gym. Monday, Wednesday, Friday, and Sunday at the track."

"Why so much?"

"I don't know."

"Are you training for anything in particular?"

"Yeah a wedding dress someday."

"Looks like you are on the way. Any prospects in mind?"

"Not at all. Does LL Cool J or T.I. count?"

He laughed. "You never know. What times are you there?"

"At the track from six until sun down. At the gym from six until I burn out. The gym closes at midnight."

"You are doing too much. You need to take a day or two off," he tells me.

"Naw, I'll be okay."

"Yeah, if you have someone to massage your legs daily."

"Is that a question or an offer?"

"I would like an answer," I can tell he's looking for confirmation that I like him as much as he likes me.

Just then, the two older ladies from the previous weeks walk up. "Deacon, you, and your wife look nice in your black and ivory," they say pleasantly.

I never paid much attention to his attire. He was wearing black slacks and an ivory shirt outside his pants that had black stitching and black buttons—he was also wearing cuff links.

"Thank you," he said and we walked off.

"We have done it again," I quip.

"I guess we have. God is speaking to us. I don't know about you but he is answering my prayers. I need to comply and be responsive and obedient to him," Randall says.

"I would hope that you do," I said, staring at him. He is really fit. I have never seen him without a jacket. He is thin (the way I like) but fit. I would love to see what is really under that shirt.

"Drink your water." He opens the bottle and puts the top in his pocket. "As soon as you get in the car eat that banana and have some protein for dinner."

"Yes, Daddy." I respond sarcastically.

He laughs nervously. As if calling him "daddy" triggered something. I sense he liked it.

"I will. My dinner is cooked. All I have to do is make cornbread."

"Girl, you can't cook!" He said loud and in shock.

"Shh." I put my hand over his mouth. "WHAT! Yes I can!"

"You heard me girl you can't cook."

"You see a girl, slap a girl. I didn't get this thick eating bananas, Monkey Man."

"Who said you are thick?"

"I did."

"You are just fine."

"From your view."

"I love the view. Take the compliment and lay off so much working out."

"I will." I said, referring to the compliment.

"I'll be watching you."

"Ooo. I may like it." I said and put some swagger in my step.

"I'd hope that you would." We hugged and his hand touched mine and he said, "Six more days until we meet again. Be blessed and be safe love."

"You too, Deacon."

I pulled off. He realized I never answered his question.

WEEK 7

Monday was a drag. Tuesday at the office was even worse. By Wednesday, I was ready to walk down the hall speaking in a "known" tongue everyone could understand. Instead, I slammed my office door, kicked my heels across the room, pumped up my Toni Braxton, and shut the cell phones down. All three of them. I cupped my hands over my face. *Why, Lord? Why does everything go wrong at the same time? This job, my life--what next? Get thee behind me, Satan.* Then God spoke--clear as a bell. "It's not that serious, Danielle." I gathered my composure together and searched my desk for change. I was going to get junk food from the vending machine. I needed instant comfort. I may even go out for a few minutes to get a milk shake. I was really going against my norm. *Okay, scratch that.* I came to my senses and called Paige.

Her line rang once and with the chirpiest voice ever, she answered, "Paige Rose."

"Hey," I said like a zombie.

"Hey girlie. What's up?" Paige responded.

"UGH, SISSIE!" I was both yelling and whining at this point.

"What happened?" She said in her sisterly and mother tone. I could hear her closing her office door.

I did not come to my sister with a lot of drama, but when I did, she was always there and knew what to say, when to say it, and how to say it. That's what big sisters were for. At that moment, I hoped I was as great of a little sister and friend to her as she is to me.

"I don't know," I started. "It's everything and nothing. I am having the day from hell. Every project is off track. Every bid is too high. Every submittal is denied. I am never going to make partner like this. Why did I jump gung-ho in this men's arena? I feel like they're kicking my ass and laughing about it. I bust my ass harder than anyone in this building. I am here before the rooster crows. My office at home looks as if I work from there full-time. I can't work out or have a social life unless it involves my Crackberry, iPhone, and earpiece. I don't know which is going to be worse--my carpal tunnel syndrome or my vision from looking at these damn memos and plans all f'ing day. I'm sick of it. I should have gone to beauty school and right now, I would be enjoying gossip over a wash-and-set with a cup of Chai tea. Bump that. I should have been a baby mama—with a balling baby daddy. But no, y'all had high hopes and expectations for me. Look at me now—I'm a damn basket case! Work, work, work-that's ALL I do!"

Paige listened patiently and responded calmly. "Oh Baby Sissie, it is just one of those days. Tomorrow will be much brighter. Don't take it so seriously. Take a few deep breaths. Inhale. Exhale. Don't stress yourself over a damn job and especially not over a man. The last time I looked, that building said Sanders, Carmichael, Morrison, and Shwatz. I don't recall seeing Rose anywhere in there. Besides, you don't want your beautiful name up there with some old-ass fuddie duddies anyway. You want your own name on a building, in elegant cursive script. Rose, Rose, and Rose."

I enjoyed her encouragement but I had to interject. "Sissie."

"Yes, Pookie?"

"Why are there three Roses in my supposed business name and only one of me?"

"For me and Sade of course."

"I have a feeling your names will be on the marquee but I will be doing all the work," I partially joked.

"And your point...?" Paige countered, clearly teasing me.

I gave her my best Ike Turner impression. "Anna Mae, you see that sign? That's my name on the marquee. This is my show. You understand Anna Mae?"

"Okay fine," Paige relented.

"Eat the cake Anna Mae," I respond.

We laugh until my stomach hurts.

I can hear Paige's smile through the phone. "I knew I would make you laugh. So what's the plan?"

"I think I'm going to put on a halter top and booty shorts and paint the town with some twenty-one-year-old ripped basketball player in top physical condition, and drink body shots off of him—all of him. Then I'll give him the keys to my brand new Phantom that I plan on buying this afternoon and go out drinking until the bar is empty and hit the nearest soul food joint to get smothered pork chops with cream potatoes and gravy, fried tomatoes, mac and cheese, sweet tea and a whole sweet potato pie."

"Hell yeah! What time we start?" Paige laughed at my plan, but I knew she was in full support.

"Now," I told her.

And of course, Paige had a more logical, yet equally satisfying suggestion. "How about some sushi and a bottle of Vino, and maybe a quick shopping spree? Or we can do massages and a haircut. I feel a trip to our good friend Louis in the making."

It only took me seconds to agree. "Yeah we can do that. But I may go to church tonight to recharge. Can we do it tomorrow or over the weekend?"

"Yep."

"Set it up."

"Okay fine."

"We can make it an all-girls day. We haven't had one this week."

"We are so bad." She said slyly.

I laughed. "I know. I'm calling in sick tomorrow. They won't keep busting my ass."

Paige didn't believe me at all. "Yeah right. You have never called in a day in your life. Wake me up at the normal time. Have a good night at church."

"Thanks Sissie."

"Girl please, you're welcome. Don't get mushy on me."

■■

I pull up the church's website to check service times. There's a seven o'clock service tonight. I will be in the house with bells on. I am scanning the website to see what else the church offers when there is a light tap on the door.

"YEAH!?" I am a southern belle. I never use the word "yeah" as a response to someone wanting my attention. That is so abrasive and rude. Southern belles always say "yes." My answer let my assistant, Leigh know I was highly irritated.

"It's Sade on the phone," Leigh said.

"And?" My aggravation was growing.

"She said she's calling and texting and you won't respond."

Oh crap. She texted me a few hours ago before I went on my tirade. "Send her through," I tell Leigh.

Leigh talks to Sade before transferring her. "Sade, I want to warn you she is in a bitch of a mood. I think they have stepped on her last nerve around here."

"I know," Sade answers unsurprised. "Mommy called me and told me to call."

Leigh sounds relieved. "Okay, you've been warned. Please make it right because I can't imagine dealing with the devil wearing Prada for the rest of the week. I don't even know why she let these old farts piss her off so much."

"Me either. She takes that job to damn seriously," Sade reassured Leigh.

"She needs a man," Leigh said with conviction.

Sade laughed. "Don't you dare tell her that or you will be in the unemployment line and you can kiss your nice gifts and bonuses goodbye."

"You're right," Leigh responded. "I'm keeping my mouth closed. We do get to go to some great events, compliments of the absence of Danielle's non-existent love life."

"Don't you mess it up. Neither of us will come up," Sade jokingly warned.

"Gotcha girl," Leigh answered, with a wink in her voice, as she finally transfers the call to my office.

"Hey Pookie," I said as I picked up the line.

"What's up, Auntie?"

"My blood pressure that's what's up." I tried to sound like I wasn't completely stressed out.

"Why? What have they done to you?" Sade said soothingly.

"Got on my freaking nerves," I answer.

"Jerks." Sade is immediately on my side.

"You got that right," I tell her.

"So what you doing now?"

"Kind of two things. I am looking at a church website and checking to see what is new at Louis."

"Auntie, BACK AWAY FROM THE INTERNET! Do not do it!" Sade warns me.

I'm immediately distracted again. "Pookie, there is this hot new bag on the website from the summer collection. It is a banger. I think I am going to "get some air.""

"Auntie, I know what that means." Sade laughs.

"I'm not going to take my wallet," I tell her. "Just five dollars so I can get a milkshake."

"Auntie, a shredder smoothie with five extra shots cost more than five dollars and is not considered a milkshake. Besides, I am sure they have your card on file and I know you know the number by heart. Who are you fooling?"

I was busted.

"What's up for tonight?" Sade inquires.

"Church," I tell her.

"Don't lie! You're going to the mall."

"When you have a job you can go anywhere you want, any time you want and buy whatever you want."

"Auntie please don't start with that. I am looking." Sade whines.

"Whatever! What do you want?" I know she is up to something.

"What time are you going to be home? No stops. No track. No gym."

"Five thirty after the mall. You did not say no retail therapy," I tell her.

"Don't do it, Auntie!"

"Okay--would you rather me go to a therapist, a bar or have hot steamy XXX sex with a nineteen-year-old thug?"

"Stop it I say! I am a child with virgin ears." Sade laughs.

"I thought so. I am going to church--you coming?"

"Yep, I got to keep my eye on you. Come straight home," my niece instructs.

"Don't you mean go straight home?"

"No, I'm chilling on your couch. See you soon." She clicks the line.

I yell out to my executive assistant, "Leigh?"

"Yes Ma'am."

"Get Sade back on the phone and tell her I'm kicking her you-know-what when I get there and to get her hind parts off my couch and do something. I know she is not going to answer if I call."

"Will do."

I knew when I said it Leigh was going to call Sade and talk about everything except what I told her to say. They worked together to keep me in line or to bamboozle me. It was all good. Well, it was mostly for good.

■■■

We talk smack all the way to the church. I have never been on a Wednesday so we kind of show up a little early to make sure I get a spot on the lot.

"Ms. Danielle. How are you?" The parking lot attendant is there.

"Good and you?"

"I'm great thanks for asking. What brings you out on a Wednesday?"

"Rough day. I thought I better come out before you all have to come to see me behind bars."

"We do not want that to happen. Who do we have here?"

"My partner in crime."

"Okay partner you two behave yourselves. I'll be checking on you."

We both giggle before I pull off. Sade is my niece but we are like best friends. Our relationship is very different from me and her mother's but the same. We hang out and have so much fun. It's like I am more like her big sister than her Aunt. We are so silly and please don't get all three of us (me, my niece and my sister) together. It's like Hart to Hart. When they first met it was murder. Our version is Rose to Rose.

We walk in laughing as if we are at the park. Randall was so far from my mind all day. This was the first time he wasn't on my mind since I met him. Maybe if I had taken the time to think about him I would not have had a meltdown. Why couldn't our relationship be more than church? He would have made today so much easier.

I can see him in the distance. He is talking with the other Deacons. He is wearing jeans. As a matter of fact, they all are. I guess church is relaxed on Wednesdays. Good to know.

Damn he is a sexy man. Something makes him laugh and he notices me. He stops his laugh immediately. Sade is talking to me. I hear her but I am focused on him. Once I get closer he bows.

"Good evening Deacons," I nod respectfully.

They all speak--but he does not. I am a little shocked. Actually, pissed. *Did he not speak to me?* I turned and scan the surroundings. *Is his wife or girlfriend around? What the heck?*

"Hey Randall." I greet him again.

"Good evening Ms. Rose," he says stoically.

Oh no he didn't. I initiate the hug and whisper in his ear this time (I made sure my lips touched his ear) and I will admit it was a little seductive. "I will see you immediately following service are we clear?"

"Yes Ma'am."

"Nice," Sade mumbles.

I know exactly what she is referring to but I ignore her muffled comment. I sashay away. We walk into the sanctuary. The usher is beginning to know me. She points to my empty seat. But I tell her there are two of us. She scans the aisles. I offer to sit in the seats directly behind Randall. The usher obliges.

I was engulfed in a deep prayer when Randall came in and apparently he was distracted by my empty seat until he did not notice I was behind him. I don't think he recognizes me in street clothes. I am praying silently as Pastor Hunter is praying and I have no clue how much time has lapsed. Something kicks my foot. I look over. It is Sade getting my attention. I am sure I looked perturbed. She shoots her eyes in Randall's direction-- he's directly in front of me. He is scanning the room fiercely. I know he is looking for me and even my niece can tell he is looking for me. Was it that obvious? I have to pull up because I don't know what his deal is. I am not trying to be caught up in some BS, and especially not at church. He steps out in the aisle and starts to scan the room. Then he turns around and looks Sade directly in her face.

Now, of course she is protective of me and I can feel this is going to be a long ride home. I think I am going to be the one under the interrogation lamp. She looks at me quickly then turns her eyes away and folds her hands. I turn my head.

She leans in and says, "What's going on?"

"Service is about to begin."

She looks like she could slap me. So I shrug my shoulders. "You know what I mean girl!"

"What?"

"Who is that?"

"Who?"

"The man in front of us!" She almost touches his back. "The one you had a non-verbal attack with right after you tongued his ear in the vestibule. That one."

"Him?"

"Yes Danielle. The young, fine Deacon who you hugged on the way in when you didn't hug anyone else. The Deacon that made it a point to find you when he walked in the room. The Deacon we happen to be sitting directly behind deacon. That Deacon Danielle!"

"Oh, just one of the Deacons." I respond as coolly as I can.

"Just one of the Deacons? I'm supposed to believe that? You got me bent. Come on Dani!"

"What? It's Auntie to you thank you ma'am," I spoke sternly. I was grown and I was not going to be chastised by a child I practically raised.

"Right now you are holding out so until you tell me who he is, you are Danielle."

He knew we were mumbling. He sat sideways in his chair.

No she didn't. I refuse to let her do me today. I am the adult here. I look her dead in her eyes and put my finger up to my lips and said, "SHHHHH!"

You could see her blood boil. I knew it was on. Deacon was sitting sideways in his chair, almost as if to be able to see and hear me. Or I am being overzealous? Then it came. I knew something was going to happen but I didn't know what.

Sade reached over me and tapped his shoulders. "Excuse me, Deacon, what is your name?"

"Deacon Washington," he smirked. I am sure it confirmed we were talking about him.

I looked straight ahead.

"Can you pass Danielle a Kleenex and tell me where the ladies room is?"

This little heffa. As soon as he was back paying attention to Pastor Hunter I leaned real close to her ear and said, "As soon as we get outside I am going to kick your arse."

"Danielle!" she said loudly.

He turned around. I faked a sneeze.

"God Bless you Ms. Rose."

He did it again. He called me Ms. Rose.

Sade leans in and said, "You should not curse in church." Now my blood was boiling. Sade diligently watched him the entire service. He took the money back to count it after service. But before he walked out, he stood shoulder to shoulder to me and said, "Don't leave."

It was enough for Sade to notice something happened.

"Oh hell naw Auntie!"

"Watch your mouth."

"What's going on?"

"Nothing."

"You're lying in church."

"You cursed in church."

"So! You did too. I'm going to ask him."

"I don't doubt that you will."

"You just wait. I'm getting to the bottom of this. Wait until I tell Mommy you are holding out. You are dating Mr. James." All I could do was laugh. It was a shame we thought that much alike to bring up Mr. James. *This was going to be a long night. Why did I bring her?* We walked into the vestibule and he was coming from the opposite direction I was expecting him from.

Randall walked up and sternly said directly to Sade; "Tonight it is your job to make sure she gets some rest. She works too hard." He bowed and said, "Be blessed and be safe. Good night." He hugged me and grabbed my hand while he spoke in my ear and said, "Three more days my love." Then he swiftly walked off. I stood there looking crazy and Sade had a look on her face that said, "What the hell just happened?" Randall intercepted her interrogation. I was glad about that--but I was pissed about his behavior.

Sade and I talked and laughed all the way through dinner. We went home then kicked back and watched a movie. I was not tired. I needed to go think privately, so I said good night.

"Don't make any noise when you leave at dark thirty AM."

"If you don't like my noise go home."

"This is my home too. Are you and the Deacon trying to put me out?"

"What?" There was no mention of Deacon since we left the sanctuary.

"You heard me. Auntie you've got to admit Deac is fine. I have never met a young, nice-looking Deacon. Don't you think so?"

"Nope." I lied.

"Nope! Are you blind and crazy? I know him from somewhere. I can't remember where."

"Heck no. I do not think he is fine. I think he is super sexy. Oh my God I am so attracted to that man. Lord Help me." I said dramatically.

My niece laughed. "He is helping you all right. I knew something was up. Auntie he is digging you!" She stressed.

"Why do you say that?"

"Did you see how he scanned that room? The way he sat so he could see you. I saw him when we walked in. He was laughing then he stopped right away and concentrated on you. Where they do that at?"

"I don't know what his deal is." I said coyly.

"You haven't asked him?" she emphasized the word you.

"Kind of."

"You haven't called him?"

"I don't have his number."

"Ask for it."

"I can't in church; that is too aggressive, and besides I don't know if he is married."

"WHAT? What do you mean?"

"I have never seen him talk to anyone and the ring on his finger could be any kind of ring. You know Mama said never talk to a man with a ring, a print of a ring or a ring tan line."

"His wife has never been around?"

"I don't know."

"Did you look him up?"

"No."

"Auntie everybody is on Facebook, Twitter, and Instagram all day--except you. I am shocked you haven't used your detective skills. Stalk his ass. You slipping. He got you straight tripping boo."

We crack up. "I am not going to stalk the man."

"Why? Because you're in church? I say stalk him in the name of the Lord."

"Now you are turning me into a church stalker."

"What have you got to lose? He likes you Auntie--I can tell. I think he may be a little shy since he didn't say much around me. I say go for it. He's fine as all get-out. I see where the body shots are going to be coming from," she laughs. Tell me what he looks like with his clothes off. Y'all gone need a lot of oil. You know, for the "laying on of hands." I like Church Stalker. It fits you." By this time Sade is cracking up.

She's making me laugh, too—and I'm doing a bad job of hiding it. "Shut up!" I threw a pillow at her and went to my bedroom.

I laid there and thought of Randall. *Why did he behave the way he did? It is so confusing. I do not understand or know anything about him. How am I going to get to him outside of the church? God, what is going on? Are you tempting me? I don't know what to do! Speak to my heart.*

I always get up early--no matter what time I fall asleep. God is an on time God. He spoke to me. "Remember the church announcements. Women's conference tonight. Go!"

Oh Lord. Are you setting me up for failure? Is this going to be a Word for me? Will I meet his wife? I am going to follow your directions.

■■■

I change my entire wardrobe. This courting process with Randall is a lot of work. I normally wear what I pick the first time. I decide to change just in case I do not have time to come back home. Crap! Sade is parked behind my favorite car. I got to pull the "big girl out." No problem. She hasn't moved in a week or so anyway, so she was due for a drive.

Work was better. Not great, but definitely not like yesterday so I made it through a lot easier. Being preoccupied definitely helped. Randall had always walked me to my car before. I think today I may take Sade's advice and ask him—"What's the deal?"

I walk into church and Randall is absolutely shocked to see me. He steps out of formation. "Good evening Ms. Rose—it's a pleasure to see you two nights in a row. Did you get some rest or did you try to work yourself to death?"

I said nothing.

"Are you okay?"

"No."

"What's wrong?"

"Let's walk."

He reached back and grabbed his Bible. He takes my hand and we commence to walk. I looked down at our hands touching and think, *really, Randall?*

"What's up Danielle?"

"You tell me."

"What do you mean?"

"What was with last night's antics?"

"I do not follow you," he says.

"You were short and different and you did not walk me to my car." It was my turn to be short. I was still irritated.

"I apologize, but you had company to walk with you. I assumed you would be fine."

"You know what they say about assumptions. They make..."

"Watch your mouth. We are on." He stops me from potential embarrassment.

"Is this a game to you?" I counter.

"No it's not and that's why this does not make sense to you right now because I take this and you seriously. Really! What brings you to service two nights in a row?"

"Two sour days."

"I hope to change all of that one day." We were at our seats. He waits for a few moments and then he grabs my waist and speaks in my ear. "I am on duty. I wasn't expecting you. Enjoy. I'll be watching you."

Service was great. I looked for him afterwards. I could not find him. I stalled; still no signs of him. I proceed to my car just as confused as I was when I walked in. Then I notice someone directing traffic. It was Randall. He was right beside my car. What were the chances? I jumped in and let the masses go before me so I could talk to him. Once the lot appeared pretty empty I pulled off. I pulled so close he looked down at his feet. *Nice shoes*, I think to myself. But all I say is. "Hi."

"Hey." He did not recognize this car. "Promise me you will get some rest."

"Promise me we will talk outside of here." He may be fine, but he's still not off the hook.

He leaned in, kissed my neck gently, and said, "I promise. Three more days, my love. Be blessed and be safe until we meet again." I rolled my window up and drove until he could not see me then stopped and sat there. I was so perplexed.

■■■

Friday while at work, critiquing the work done below my satisfaction, I think, *Jesus Christ. Each step I take makes things worse. I have to figure something out. I cannot have a totally horrible week. What can I do? There is something going on tonight at the church. I don't even know what--but I know to be there at seven.*

Traffic was a beast. I really wanted to change clothes. I kick my Goodyear boots off and throw on my Stuart Weitzman's. Then I think, *I hope these shoes don't hurt my feet. I have been in a half-structured building walking and climbing makeshift stairs all day. Not to mention I'm late! I HATE TO BE LATE!*

I am checking voicemails, texts, and emails using two of my three phones when I approach the glass church door. I glance up and do a double take. *Why is Randall at the door?* He opens the door and leans out.

"No communication or electronic devices, ma'am."

I throw up the one-minute finger. One minute turns into five or longer. I am listening on one device. Typing and responding on the other. He leans out of the door again. It was a nice night. I could have been out there all night and worked. I thought, *I'll pick up dinner and sit on the deck tonight and continue working.* "Five more minutes please," I say sweetly.

"The countdown begins." He checks his watch.

He walks away, and sure enough, in five minutes he comes back. I hand him all the devices. Three phones, a set of keys, an earpiece and an iPod.

He looked at the contents and said, "Any more contraband?"

"I think that will do it." I didn't mention the camera I had in my bag.

"Where are you going?" Randall asked.

"To the ladies' room. Do you mind?" I pretend that he's too concerned.

I went in and used the restroom. But, I really wanted to check myself. It was a long ride and a long day at the jobsite. I surely wasn't expecting to see Randall as soon as I got to church. I came storming out so fast and didn't even notice him waiting for me. "Slow down. Don't be in a hurry for everything." He spoke calmly.

"I know. I hate being late." I tell him.

"It's fine. Stop! Slow down. Get it together. And do something with all this mess." He points to all my devices. Make sure they are all turned off." He handed me my stuff like it was on fire.

I checked them all. "Yep-all clear. Powered down."

"Why do you need all that?" he asks disgusted.

"Work."

"Did you get some rest?"

"No. I raced here."

"When was the last time you got some real rest?"

"When I was nineteen." I said sincerely.

"What time did you get up this morning?"

"Before four."

"What time did you go to bed? You didn't leave here until after ten."

"One-ish."

"That is not enough rest. It's unacceptable," he said matter factly. "You need to take better care of yourself."

"What time did you get up?" I challenge him.

"Same time as you. I have to be at work early."

"Okay. And your point?"

"I need for you to get some sleep." he answers seriously.

"Unlike you, no one is home other than me so I have time to work excessively."

"What makes you think someone is home with me?" Randall asked.

"That ring on your finger and your strange behavior."

"Are you asking if I am married?"

"Yes; as a matter of fact, I am."

"Yes, I am. I married my wife at a very young age. We were expecting and I thought I was doing the right thing by making her my wife. Not so. She has not agreed with me on anything since then. She does not like my job. She feels it makes me travel and work too hard. She was not happy when I chose to worship here. She prefers I worship where I was stagnant spiritually. I was not growing and learning there, so I moved on. She does not support me in anything. By the way, she does not attend church here."

"I'm sorry to hear that."

"Why?"

"It sounds like you were trying to do the right thing."

"Yeah, I did what I thought was best for me, her and my son. I get my butt beat daily to provide and she has no respect. She does not work, did not work, and has never worked. At this point, I'm not focused on what I would lose by leaving her, but more so what I will finally gain--peace, love, joy, and happiness. The money means nothing to me. I would rather be happy. This is not what life is about. My son is in the middle of this madness and I want to set a good example for him. I want to be loved and show love. I have not been able to do that."

"I'm sorry."

"No need for you to be sorry. I am glad I met you. You do not know it, but you have been my motivation to make some changes. I want to get to know you but under the correct terms and pretenses."

I speak sternly to clarify. "You are not doing this for me. You are doing this for yourself. Are you not going to try to work it out with your wife?"

He purposefully ignored my question. "If I must confess, I am doing this for us. Now Sunday is first Sunday and we wear black. With that being said, guess what?"

"What?"

"One more day till we meet again, my love."

■ ■

Sunday arrives. I intentionally wear ivory.

"Ms. Danielle, you look beautiful as always. I appreciate you wearing the hat. Promise me one thing." Randall speaks to me as soon as I arrive in the lobby.

"What is that?"

"You will wear a hat every week."

"You will have to buy some hats, pay some cleaning bills, and pay for some hair appointments before you can make that request," I tell him.

He reaches in his pocket and pulls out two crisp one hundred dollar bills. "Consider this the down payment and don't you dare not take it. We will make a scene." He threw the bills in my bag. "Did you forget black?"

"No. I am rebellious like that."

"Oh really?" He rolled his eyes and laughed.

"Yep."

He hugs me long and tight and speaks in my left ear. "We have an audience and I don't care. You look beautiful when you are rebellious."

I reply, "And you look handsome and sexy as always. Deacon Randall." He is startled by my remark. His body instantly tenses. He does not know what to do. I let go. "Come on before we're late." Randall is still speechless. As we get to the threshold of the sanctuary I say, "We're on."

WEEK 8

Tuesday

I hit the track and worked out until I felt my body giving out. I walked until I felt like my feet were numb. I begin to walk a little slower. I decide to respond to emails, texts, check my voice mails, and return a few calls while I let my feet cool down. As I am in the middle of a conversation, some dude on the side of the track is trying to get my attention. *Doesn't he see I am busy? What a jerk! Just work out and leave me alone!* Then he begins to run on the grass and not the black top. He is pretty quick, I must admit. *What a show-off!* Of course, I pretend I'm not impressed. *So he can run fast—so what?!* I continue my business until I realize the lights have come on and he, along with one other man are the only two left on the track other than me. *This isn't safe at all—I've got to get out of here, and quick!* I call Paige so I can talk to her until I get to my car.

Wednesday

My feet are in bad shape. I even wore Cole Haan flats to the office. Leigh looks at my feet and laughs.

"Shut up!" I yell playfully.

"I am laughing with you. Girl, stay on your fitness mission so you can win the man of your dreams," she encourages me.

"I won't be fat or lonely forever. You may want to try it." I give her a wink.

"Oh, low blow Dani," Leigh responds with mock hurt.

"Make it happen, Leigh," I tell her, laughing. I make it my business to wrap up and get out of the office on time so I can make it to Bible study.

I walk in and there Randall is waiting as if it was a scheduled date. I really hate when people know my routine, but for some reason it's okay this one time.

"Good evening Ms. Danielle. How was your day?" He greets me.

"Excellent now," I smile. "And yours?"

He smiles from ear to ear and replies, "The same. You look wonderful."

"I should look tired."

"Yeah, you should."

"Why did you say?"

"Never mind."

"That's a cheap shot," I tell him. He quickly interrupts.

"We are on. We will talk later."

What did he mean? Immediately after service I grabbed his arm and asked, "What was that comment you made earlier all about?"

"You worked hard and late last night. You should be tired." Randall was very matter-of-fact.

"Says who?"

"I say."

"How do you know?"

"I saw you."

"You saw me where?"

"Let's just say I am your protector. Kind of like a guardian angel--except I'm a little rough around the edges."

"Where did you see me?"

"At the track."

"At the track?" *STALKER!*

"Yes."

"You were there?"

"Yep—and you would probably relax more if you left the gadgets in the car. You have to be able to observe your surroundings. If you didn't have the gadgets you could get a good work out in so you won't have to be there after the sun goes down."

"You were jumping rope." I realized that I had seen him at the track.

"Yep--and you refused to speak. How rude!" Randall said jokingly.

I was uneasy. "Do you make it your business to stalk women at a high school track?" I ask him.

"Only you," he answers, as if his response is reassuring. "I made it my business to see you outside of church, per your request. I need to ask you a question."

"Shoot," I say.

"What has you so stressed that makes you walk so hard and long?"

"My job."

"What do you actually do?" he asked as if he did not know.

"I build buildings."

"You build buildings?" he questioned, amazed.

"Yes."

"You are the receptionist for a contractor and order materials?"

"HA! That's cute, but wrong! I'm an engineer."

"Who do you work for?" He already knew the answer to the question.

"Sanders, Carmichael, Morrison, and Shwatz."

"Oh really!"

"Have you heard of them?"

"Who hasn't?"

"I guess you're right."

"How long have you been there?"

"Eleven years. My first and only job and now I am trying to make partner."

"I'm shocked. I never imagined you in a man's world. What kind of buildings do you build?"

"I design five-star hotels; something you may not know about. And skyscraper office buildings."

"That was below the belt. Where did you go to school?" His questions kept coming.

"I received my Bachelor's and Master's from Tech."

I am concerned about Randall's comments, but I expect these responses from insecure men that have a problem with successful women. I assure him, "I work with your type every day."

"My type? I'm not intimidated. I'm sure I can still beat you pound for pound. I am sorry to offend you or upset you."

"You didn't upset or offend me. I am secure in who I am and what I do. I think the only insecurity I have right now is trying to figure out who you are." He ignored my statement.

"What is your favorite project?" Clearly, Randall was trying his best to ignore what I'd just said.

"The Smythe Royale Hotels in Belize and Dubai."

"Why? What is so special about them?"

"I designed them from outside in. They are kind of my personal sanctuaries. I love them."

"We will have to go one day." Then he laughs continuously.

"What is so funny?" I ask.

"Mrs. Washington, you never cease to amaze me. I would have never imagined you to be as heavy in the construction field as you are. All I can see is you in your five-inch high heeled Timberlands and pearls at the jobsite." He laughs to himself.

"You think you know me well. Is that an insult or compliment?" I ask him, a little peeved.

Randall smirks. "It's a compliment, girl. You are too ladylike and girly to be on a jobsite."

"You see a girl slap a girl," I remind him.

"That's second time telling me that."

"I think we will have to battle this out in the ring."

"You name the time and the place."

"Are you this rough and brutal with your clients?"

"You ain't seen nothing yet. It's always thrilling to introduce myself as Dani Rose. The guys are usually not prepared for a woman to show up."

"Why do you work so hard?"

"I don't have a life and I have worked hard to get to where I am. Besides, I take pride in what I do."

"I understand that. Do you think it requires all the work you put in or are you an overachiever?"

"To whom much is given much is required." He had been scripturized.

He gazed in my eyes with all sincerity and says, "I want to make you smile forever."

How do you respond to that? I stared. *He is so attractive to me. He looks the same every time I see him. I can't really decipher his age. He has kept himself up very well. I don't know if he's in his twenties or thirties. I have a feeling he is younger than me. Whatever he's doing it works. He looks like a little boy all the time. Not even a young man.* I watch him in service when he is not watching me. He sits the same. His reactions and expressions are the same. There is so much sex appeal in a man—especially a man praising God. *Danielle! Remember he is married. If you look lustily with your eyes you have committed adultery. Forgive me Father.*

We arrive at my car in silence. Randall speaks up. "There is so much about you, Danielle Rose that I do not know and want to learn."

"Like what?"

"Virtually everything. You work a lot, you like boxing I think and that's all I know."

"By your choice," I tell him. His face shows he agrees.

"Three days until we meet again, my love," he says. I get into my car and head home alone.

Sunday

Sunday doesn't come quick enough. I was wearing a hat this morning. Randall was pleased. We exchanged our pleasantries and then walk a few steps. I ask, "By the way, who won the fight last night?"

"Floyd."

"Dang! I hate I missed it."

"Long night? Hot date?"

I laughed. He was either prying or being sarcastic.

"What were you doing?"

"I was planning on going out to watch it, but you know."

"You better say you fell asleep."

"No. I began to work. I couldn't stop in the middle of what I was doing."

"You didn't miss much."

"Maybe it was better live. Front row action. Ringside!"

"Nope--still boring," he said, exaggerating his words.

"How do you know?"

"I was there live on the front row." He said it as if it were no big deal.

"Shut up!" I say in disbelief.

He pulls out two stubs. One said Sugar Shane Mosley vs. Floyd Mayweather at the MGM Grand. The next stub was a Delta red eye flight back to Atlanta. He ushered me to my seat and took his. I was perplexed. I cannot wait until service is over. Never mind. I am going to the ladies room now. I grab my phone and run to the restroom. As soon as I type Randall's name in my search engine, he calls my name.

"Ms. Danielle, are you okay?"

I swing the door open as hard as I could and stomp past him. *He will not initiate conversation outside of church, but he follows me to the ladies room.* I look down on my phone and see his name pop up with over ten pages of hits. It is moving slow. I am not getting any reception inside of here. Why hadn't I googled him earlier? *That damn Sade. Why didn't I listen to her?*

He catches up to me and grabs my arm. "Why are you so upset?"

"Who said I was upset? Why did you travel to Vegas and travel back in less than twenty four hours?" I demanded.

"It's my job."

"Who the hell are you?"

"I needed to be back because I wanted to see you."

I look down at his hand touching my arm. He got the hint and let it go.

The entire sermon I grind my teeth-a sure sign my body is aware of my anger. I was aware I was doing it so I would constantly exhale air through my cheeks to avoid my teeth clenching. I ground my teeth so hard my head and jaw hurt. I was going directly to the gym and work this out. But first, I need to take my time and look through the results I found online.

▪▪

After the benediction, I walked out so fast Randall was barely able to catch up. By the time he did, I was closing my car door. He stood there trying to say something but I pulled off.

This is going sour extremely quickly. First, he is married and then he has this secret job he has yet to tell me about. I am not getting involved in this mess. I pulled directly into Starbucks and spoke so loud on the drive-through microphone I startled myself.

"My apologies, I will take a venti white mocha, fat-free with whip please," I told the barista. It's not the happy go lucky sixteen-year-old coffee shop employee I'm mad at. Truth be told, its' not even Deacon Randall Washington I'm upset with. I am pissed with Danielle Rose. *Stop getting yourself in these pickles*, I tell myself. *The man is married so why do you care who he is? Enjoy the eye candy and keep it moving. That's it!*

Why in God's name did church become complicated? Then clearly, as if he were sitting right next to me, God spoke. "Where else do you go quite often to meet decent, eligible men?" I heard the Lord ask. I spoke right back in my head. *Come on, God. I am surrounded by men all day every day.*

"Dani, would you pay any of those guys any attention? You are there giving them a hard time. You would not even notice if someone was flirting or not."

I can see, and I think I would notice a flirt, Lord.

"What about the electrical contractor?" God asks.

What about him?

'He is single. The nice looking guy in legal at the firm? The owner of the building in Chatsworth? There have been tons of nice eligible bachelors that I have sent your way. You passed them up," God said.

Name them again, God.

"Now, just as I have tested Job I am testing you."

Why?

"You'll see. Walk by faith and not by sight. Doing right can be very painful. Remember my servant Job," God reminded me.

I was silent all the way home. No music. No phone. No noise. I walked in and went right to the closet to change. I didn't even wash my make up off. Being as anal as I am and a workaholic, I logged into the laptop in my bathroom. I googled Randall again. I did not know where to start. *This is going to be longer than I expected.* I take a seat on my chaise with the laptop in my lap, took a deep breath, and clicked the first link.

WHAT THE HELL!!! HE IS A BOXER???? I click and click and click and read and read and read. *OH MY GOD!*

His entire life is written here in black and white. There are disadvantages to being famous. I see his birthday. I calculate really quickly. He is thirty years old. *No way!* His high school sweetheart became pregnant and he married her. They have one child together. No other children, which means no baby mamas as far as I can tell. He owns a gym and is involved in numerous business ventures. He is an activist for this and a philanthropist for that etc. Why did he feel the need to hide this? He owns a plane. There is a street named after him in this city. He bought the county new fire engines.

And he had the audacity to talk about me. He has some nerve. His Facebook page is an informative website itself. I scan the page to see who he is friends with and who he talks to. A lot of other celebrities, athletes, Pastors, Pastor Hunter and other people that don't ring a bell. There are tons and tons and tons of pictures--but not one of his wife and child. There's no information on his family. I go to Media Take Out, OMG, Necole Bitchie, Gossip.com, Daily Coco and I don't find any gossip about him. I do find where he blogs daily.

I wring my hands. *What am I gonna do?* I send the link to his Facebook page and his website to Sade, sit back, and wait for her to call. As I expected, her ringtone makes my phone sing. I press the button to answer the phone and she is already talking.

"Auntie D, What the hell is going on? Is that "Deacon? He's a boxer? How did you find out? Heavy, middle or light? Does he still fight? Did he tell you? What did you say? What are you going to do? Hello? Are you there?"

"Yep, I'm here." I'm just as shocked as she is.

"What's going on?"

"I googled him and this is what I found."

"Are you going to call him?"

"No, I left him at church."

"What happened?"

I told her the entire story. I said "Pookie, I need to think. I'm going to the track."

She said, "Me and Mommy are coming over."

"Bye." It was one of the most pitiful "goodbyes" I had ever uttered. Most chicks would be kicking their heels because they had met Randy "Hooks" Washington, known for his hook punch, according to the reports. I was the exact opposite. I was not thrilled.

Why hadn't he told me? Can I trust him? Then again, he was, in a way, behaving Biblically: "Don't let the right hand know what the left hand is doing."

I got to the track. My phones were on my hip and not being juggled from hand to hand. My iPod was on my arm and Babyface rang out in my eardrums as loud as the volume would go and it still was not loud enough. He sang "The Loneliness." The best depressing song I've heard in my life.

I walked slowly. I don't have a clue how long I have been here. I realize I still have makeup on when I wipe my eyes and pull back a hand full of eye shadow. I don't even care. I wipe it on my clothes. I didn't even pull my hair up or wear a hat. No wonder the sweat is pouring in my face. Who cares? I'm just looking forward to taking a shower—a shower I don't want to cry in. That would really piss me off. But honestly, I have nothing to cry for. We were friends. Nothing more--obviously. I'm actually glad.

The same old faces were at the track. No one new. Then there he was—the chocolate man with the heavy accent.

"Hey beautiful."

Normally when he said this it made my day. Not that I was interested in him, but the fact that someone who had no clue who I was and paid me a genuine compliment always made my day. He saw me every day at my worst and still thought I was beautiful. Little did my ripped dark chocolate-complexioned friend know that he helped me through some rough days. Mentally, emotionally, and spiritually.

"Hey man!" I said in a friendly tone.

In the heaviest accent ever, he said, "You need to tell him to not call you during this time. He should know your schedule. If he is that insecure tell him to come out here." I shook my head at him and smirked a little.

"Okay friend, I will," I tell him. He was used to seeing me with a phone tightly secured to my ear.

I round the shaded side of the field and notice a guy in a suit. Who does that? The closer I get the more familiar the stripped suit looks. It was Randall. I walk right past him as if I did not see him. I walked the entire lap and he never moved. As I came around again he approached me.

"Excuse me Danielle; I knew I would find you here. May I have a minute with you?" he asked.

I look back and around as if there was another Danielle close by. I pull my earpieces out of my ears. I fold my arms, put most of my weight on one leg, and say as sharply as possible, "Go ahead, Mr. Randall or should I say Randy Hooks Washington? You have exactly one minute."

"Danielle, I am sorry. My intentions are not to hurt you. I hope you can understand. I am doing what is best for you first and then me. I don't want you to know Hooks first. I want you to know and love Randall. Hooks is my job. I will not have that job my entire life but I will be Randall forever. One day when Hooks passes the torch, I want you to be happy with the real me and not the celebrity version of me. My work is not my life. God is first. Then I hope to have a family--that will be second. Hooks is how I make a living. Some would say I'm good at it. Some might say I have done well and achieved great things. Others may disagree. Some may even think my job is barbaric and that I'm unworthy of the benefits I receive. But I work hard. I hit hard. I get hit hard and I fall hard. I have fallen in love with you. I want nothing on this earth but to make you happy. I am sorry I didn't tell you."

Before I could respond, he continued.

"People either really like my job or hate it. Most women hate it but will do whatever it takes to reap the benefits. I have to protect myself. I told you my situation. My wife hates it but she reaps the benefits as if she takes the hits. We have been in an ugly divorce for years. She has prolonged it and prolonged it. I haven't fought in four years. I have been trying to mentally and spiritually prepare. I think she is waiting on the next fight to get half of the rewards. I will gladly give her half if she walks away now."

"Since I met you I have been training and I feel I am mentally ready to fight again. It is a job that takes your strength, athletic ability and one hundred percent of your agility, mind, and body. You have to be ready in all of those categories. If not, you will fail. I have not been mentally prepared until I met you. I swear I was going to tell you when the time was right. I wanted to tell you everything at once. About my wife, my son and my job. I did tell you about my wife early because I felt I needed for you to understand that it was not you but me. I am attracted to you. Hell, as I said before, I'm in love with you. I think you are smart, intelligent, beautiful, God-fearing and extremely hard- working. I did not want you to lose faith or trust in me by spending time with you before my divorce was final."

"I did not want you to think I was that kind of person. You know, an indecent man. I wanted the timing to be right. But I can't lose you now. Promise me you'll understand and forgive me. I swear I only want to do things in decency and in order."

He paused. We locked eyes. I waited for him to move his eyes so I could tell if he was lying or not. He did not move them. We had a contest. I was not giving in first.

He grabbed my hands from their folded position and held them. He kissed them both and put them up to his face. I never said a word. I would even bet that I didn't blink.

He lowered my hands. I pulled them back, backed up and walked away as if nothing happened. I continued to walk and listen to Babyface. I thought about each word he said. I walked for another two hours at the same slow pace. He sat on a bench and never moved.

He was still dressed in his church clothes. I saw him put his face in his hand a few times. I finally decided I needed some water—and needed to leave.

I began to exit the track. Randall was a nice distance from me when he realized I was going to my car. As I was walking, I could hear his dress shoes hit the pavement behind me rapidly. Once I got closer to the parking area I could see his Rolls Royce parked next to my drop top BMW. I really wanted to say something but I had to hold my ground. I made sure I looked the car over as I slowly walked past. Never giving apparent notice to the Metropolitan Blue Drop head Phantom Coupe with the Light Crème Leather trimmed in Fleet Blue with Ash Burr Veneer sitting on twenty-one inch wheels trimmed in the Metropolitan Blue enamel with the Teck Deck, Embroidered hooks and W's in the headrest and the Brushed Steel Bonnet. The rims were clean the interior was custom and fabulous. Those hooks were hot the way they wrapped around the W. The tag said it all, HOOKED! The Phantom was beyond hot. It was FLAMMING! But, no I didn't notice it at all.

The first thought that ran thru my mind was that I was HOOKED. It wasn't the car that had me hooked. I don't think this is classified as a car. More like an extreme luxury travel medium. It wasn't the tailor made suit or the Presidential Rolex. I could finally see the ring. It was not a band it was a championship diamond ring. I could see the design of the diamonds in the shape of boxing gloves. I did not exemplify any expression. I could never show him I was impressed. The truth was, I loved him—, and I was glad he loved me, too.

He reached over his seat and gave me a banana and a bottle of water. He raced to open my car door. I had no choice but to chug the water no matter how mean I wanted to be. As soon as I got ready to open the water, he twisted the cap off and gave it back to me.

We stared at each other but said nothing. He leaned down. He was much taller when I wasn't wearing four-inch heels. He hugged me so tight that he almost lifted me off the ground. He is very slender but extremely strong and fit. I like that!

He kissed my neck repeatedly and gently. I know it was salty and sweaty, but he didn't care. He put his lips directly on my ear. He made such a sweet, desperate plea: "Danielle, I am so sorry. I beg you to forgive me. If only you knew how much I love you. How much I think of you and how I need you in my life. I prayed to God for you. I hope you will understand. God bless you until we meet again." It felt like a weight was lifted off him.

We stood there. Me in his arms. My arms to my side. I do not know how much time elapsed. I backed up and got in my car. I pulled off with him standing there in his suit. I felt like a Mac Truck had hit me. Why and how had I fallen in love so quickly with a man I really didn't know? And he's married!

When I got home, Paige and Sade greeted me at my door. They had already been on the internet looking Randall up. I could see paper on the printer. We did not talk about him at all. We ate zebra cakes, Doritos, peach soda, ice cream floats and sat on the couch like the three stooges and watched the Golden Girls marathon. They spent the night with me. We are such a dramatic family. In "crises" like these, we need each other.

WEEK 9

Monday

I arrive at work and Leigh says immediately, "We need to talk."

"I know." I say solemnly.

"Five minutes?" she asks.

I nod. I walk in my office and a huge bouquet of flowers is sitting on my desk. Leigh was behind me. "Told you we need to talk," she reiterated.

"If you were in town yesterday instead of globetrotting you would already know the story," I tease her.

"Well everyone else is still asleep so enlighten me," Leigh says, smiling.

I pulled up Randall's website and move back from my computer. I noticed he blogs his daily regimen, along with inspirational thoughts and poetic musings. Sunday's report read:

> I failed her. I disappointed her. I hurt her. Therefore, I hurt too. Until she heals, I remain in pain. Please forgive me my beautiful Rose.

Monday's read:

> I am not myself. I will be incomplete until my Rose blooms again.

Of course, I have to go into details with Leigh.

"I don't know about this. He is still married," she said.

"You're right. He is no big deal." I was trying to convince myself by saying it out loud.

"Are you sure Danielle?"

"Yeah I'm sure."

"Then what are you upset about?"

"That he didn't trust me enough to tell me his story. It's history now."

"I mean, when did he have the time? I am sure he was shocked you did not know who he was. He probably thought you did and had an agenda. You know he still has to protect himself."

I roll my eyes. "Come on Leigh. He is a boxer. Who can beat him or screw him over?"

"You know as well as I do that once these guys "make it," tricks are after them. Church makes it no different. He was feeling you out first." Leigh had a point.

"I'm very disappointed that I didn't pick up on who he was. It never crossed my mind. I'm really devastated."

"Oh D, don't be. Talk to him and hash this out. What do you want to do?"

"I don't know since he's married."

"I'm shocked you didn't get any more details than what you have. That's definitely not like you."

"Damn, Sade said the same thing too." I try not to slip into more confusion and gather my thoughts. I want to get back to the focused, logical woman I am.

"Well one thing is for sure," I tell Leigh. "I will make him my friend on Facebook and he will be under my radar. I will get you all in on this and we will dig up anything we can find. If there is some dirt, believe me, we will find it. It's on now."

"Danielle," Leigh interjected. I knew I was about to get a serious lecture from her if she referred to me as "Danielle," especially about something other than work. "Think about at least responding to him."

"I don't have his number."

"No worries. That problem can be resolved in a matter of minutes."

"He has not offered me his number so I am not calling."

"Danielle!"

I roll my eyes.

"Stop being stubborn."

"It's pointless," I counter.

"Did you give him the information to send you a card and flowers?"

"Nope. I did tell him where I worked."

"Step out of the box. It does not have to be square. It can be octagon, triangle, or even a circle. You know, you design boxes and none of them are square or the same." I hated that Leigh was making sense.

When we get back to the office foyer from getting a snack, I could tell from the way the receptionist smiles that something was going on.

"Thanks D!" Someone yells as Leigh and I walk down the corridor.

"Yes, you are welcome," I say. "Thanks for what?" I mouth to Leigh.

"I'll find out what's going on," Leigh answers.

She returns to my office minutes later.

"I don't think this is going to go away as easy as you think it is."

I'm exasperated. "What now?"

She steps in the door with a bundle of chocolate roses-- white chocolate, dark and colored. "He sent hundreds."

"Hundreds? Wow!" I'm genuinely shocked.

"I take it he doesn't know you don't eat junk?" Leigh asked.

"I don't think it's me he is impressing now." I go back to being slightly irritated.

"He is smart. I will give him that. Get to those around her to get to her," Leigh reasons.

"Two can play that game." I tell her, devising a plan as I speak.

"Danielle, don't you dare."

"I wouldn't eat those if I were you," I tell Leigh. Where did they come from?"

Leigh rolls her eyes at me. "I don't think the man would send thirty dozen poisoned roses with his name on it. I love the way he thinks. Who has time to find out who makes chocolate roses and have them sent in less than twenty hours? Oh, by the way there's a card. I am going to get a camera and take pictures. This will be the first picture at the reception."

"What reception, Leigh?!?" I scream.

She yells in the distance, "the wedding reception. I'm ready."

I open the card slowly. It is a simple card that the florist would attach. The front side is a bouquet of white roses and baby's' breath. The other side read: Roses for my Rose. Loving you, Randall.

It was written in what I assume is his handwriting. Nice hand writing I might add. *I am a little jealous his looks better than mine. He has more time to write. I draw. I bet he can't draw. Randall. Oh Randall. Does he realize he is not just "Randall?" He is huge. It's not that simple. He is Hooks Washington. Even if he wasn't married, this is a big step and a lot of responsibility. This has all started off wrong. How do we fix this?*

"Oh Randall. I can see me loving you too." I whisper to myself.

Tonight was my regular routine. I left work late, then hit the track for a few hours and had a wonderful powered meal. Life is good!

Tuesday

I was back on the grind. I was in the office before six. *Wow, why do I have so many messages?* I checked them at midnight. Three message from Randall. He is playing hardball.

A few hours go by. Leigh walks in. She is so not a morning person. Ten minutes later, she appears in the doorway. "The fighter is on the line," she says, completely unenthused.

I look up over my glasses. Leigh knows exactly what that means.

Leigh returns to the line to talk to Randall. "She is unavailable--may I please take a message?"

"No thank you. I'll try back in an hour," Randall responds.

I have to deal with her all day and now him calling every hour. I should have called in sick.

In one hour he was in the lobby of the building. Security escorts him up the elevator. I see them from a distance. Then I hear his voice.

"I'm sorry; I am not prepared to sign autographs today. If anyone can get Ms. Rose to talk to me I will be more than happy to give you memorabilia, which is better than an autograph."

We make eye contact right before I slam my door.

He waits most of the morning in front of Leigh's desk. I refuse to leave my office. Finally I have a meeting and I have to use the ladies' room. I have no choice but to leave. He stands and walks behind me. He does not utter a word. I hand him my drawings and files while I go into the restroom. I come back out, grab my things from him, say "thank you" and proceed to the executive conference room.

I start the meeting off. Leigh is there taking control of the drawings and the PowerPoint presentation at my cues. We have done this so many times until we could do it in our sleep.

Late as usual, Mr. Sanders walks in. "Excuse me, Danielle."

"Yes, Mr. Sanders." I reply annoyed. He knows how I feel about tardiness. Nevertheless, I can't really say anything, since he is one of the founders of the corporation.

"I know I'm late again and you despise tardiness but I wanted to introduce someone I ran into sitting outside this very room. Randy Hooks Washington." He said with enthusiasm.

Oh, God.

"Oh come on in Mr. Hooks," he said.

"His name is Deacon Washington," I murmur to myself.

Leigh makes eye contact with me and assures me it is okay. "Keep it moving," her eyes state. Everyone in the room is elated and speaks to him.

"I'm sorry to barge in Ms. Rose. Please forgive me." Deacon Washington replies.

I nod. Mr. Carmichael looks as if I have appalled him by saying nothing more to the "Champ."

Randall got my nonverbal message. "I'll be leaving now."

"We wouldn't hear of it," Mr. Carmichael replies. "You are our guest. You may want Sanders, Carmichael, Morrison, Shwatz, and one day, Rose, to facilitate a venture for you. A boxing arena locally would be a value to the city. I am sure D would love to have that added to her tremendously long and impressive resume. You should check it out over lunch."

I roll my eyes so hard I think I gave myself a migraine.

"It would be my honor to add impressive accomplishments and accolades to Ms. Rose's achievements. I have a few in mind. However, I am not sure she will accept my proposal to lunch."

I stop right then and grab my Blackberry to text Leigh, Paige and Sade. This was sickening. I speak, "Leigh you should be getting a text." I pause. "Right about now" as the lights on Leigh's phone light up. She overlooks it. I throw my eyes to the phone to indicate that I need her to check her device promptly.

> Y'all would not believe this SH*%. Deacon has showed up to my office and is sitting in my presentation. WTFH?

She looks at the phone and says in a professional tone, "Are we ready to proceed?"

The heat was on. Randall was the celebrity. I should be watching him work— not the other way around. I'm completely annoyed. "Anyone else have anything to add?" I ask abruptly with my arms folded. One hand goes up. I reply, "Go ahead," as rudely as possible.

"Never mind, let me research it a little more before we debate," the colleague relents.

I point my finger at him in mock confirmation and say, "I would suggest you do that, Tom. After you have gathered what you need, do not hesitate to bring it to the next meeting."

"Anyone else? Going once. Going twice. Wonderful. Looks like I have the floor again."

I see, from time to time, that the guys lean in and whisper to Randall. He nods. I don't conclude the meeting as I would normally do. I open the door and say, "good day, gentlemen. Leigh will take questions and wrap up this nonsense." I exit and I can hear him behind me. I walk down the hall. I speak without turning back. "Do you have your bodyguards with you today, Mr. Hooks?"

"It's Randall and I like to think I can handle myself."

"Good day," I nearly shout and slam my office door. I can see he is sitting in front of Leigh's desk. She and I email back and forth.

Please talk to him again, she emails.

No! I respond.

He is very nice, and FINE! She types. In person he looks nothing like he does on television. Do you like him?

I take a deep breath before I tell her the truth. I think I may love him.

Leigh pleads with me. Speak to him Dani. He has been here for hours. He hasn't gone to the restroom or answered his phone. He hasn't moved at all.

I suggested, Ask him if you can get him anything, and show him where the restrooms are.

She obliges. "Excuse me Mr. Washington, may I offer you a beverage or snack?" Leigh asks him.

"No thank you I am fine." Randall answers politely.

"There are some magazines there if you would like. Some of Danielle's accomplishments are in the leather bound book. The men's room is down the hall on the left and if you need to use the internet, telephone or any other services there is an office on the right."

"Thank you, but I should be fine." Randall assures her.

He doesn't want anything she emails back. Please just talk to him, Leigh begs me again.

I feel odd reading his blogs while he sits just a few feet away from me. His blog for Tuesday at 4:50 AM read:

You can't win the fight unless you step into the ring. I'm going in.

I think to myself, *Did he ask for me or did he pop up? I think he just showed up!* I make up my mind. *Until he asks for me I will not be speaking to him.*

Minutes pass. My phone, email, and texts are at an overwhelming number because Leigh has informed Sade and Paige that Randall is still here. Leigh has somehow turned her webcam around and we are all watching him. I am sure they are taping this as a blackmail tool for a later time. Or as Leigh would say, "This is for the wedding video."

"Excuse me please," Randall speaks.

"Yes Mr. Washington?" Leigh responds, delighted

"Do you know where I could purchase this book?" he asks her.

"I am not sure. Let me find out." She said fully knowing the answer to the question.

I can see she is at her desk talking. She calls my office. "Ms. Rose."

"Yes?"

"The gentleman would like to purchase the Engineers Hall of Fame. Would we have extra copies here or should I order additional copies for him?" She turns to Randall. "How many copies would you like, Mr. Washington?"

"What is the required purchase quantity and the cost?" he asks.

"Tell him one thousand dollars per book." I say to Leigh through the phone.

"Huh?" she responds, in shock.

"You heard me." I say adamantly.

"Ms. Rose says one thousand dollars per copy."

"Tell her she is selling herself short. I would have paid more." Randall smiles slightly, pulls out his money clip (a diamond boxing glove), and peels off ten hundred dollar bills.

I storm out of my office. "Mr. Washington, you can have the book." I tell him with a mock of professional confidence. I give him back his money and I hand him my business card. The card with all my cell numbers and email addresses. I notice he doesn't leave a number on any of his voicemail messages, but the phone number he called from showed up on the caller ID. Handing him the business card was my way of giving him permission to call me. However, he did not give me his information in return.

"Thank you kindly for the book and allowing me to observe your work. It was interesting and greatly appreciated," Randall says warmly. He hands Leigh two hundred dollar bills. "You are in charge of lunch and dinner," he tells her.

He turns to me. "Ms. Rose I will see you at the track tonight. I won't be late." Randall was being sarcastic about my earlier outburst. He grabs and kisses my hand.

"Leigh can you tell me the name of the gym Ms. Rose is a member of?"

She spits the name out without giving it a second thought.

I roll my eyes. "Bye, Randall." I say, holding back a smile.

"Good day," he replies.

Leigh waits until he enters the elevator. She knows I'm peeved, so she starts apologizing. "What was I going to do, D? He can kick my ass you know." We both laugh. Leigh says in a serious tone through her smile, "I think he's sincere, Danielle."

"I think he is being a show-off now," I tell her.

"I disagree," Leigh counters, trying to encourage me to see a different point of view.

"We'll see," I mumble skeptically.

"When are you going to speak to him?" Leigh asks wondering how long this charade will go on.

"Tomorrow at church."

"Promise?"

I "promise" her, with my right hand lifted like a girl scout.

Leigh and I somewhat follow Randall's instructions concerning the $200 he gave Leigh. We grab lunch and put the change in a ceramic jar we used to call our Emergency Comfort Food Fund, but this time we refer to it as the Hooks Fund. We will probably eat lunch using this money for the rest of this month and part of the next month, considering we don't get to eat often around here, much less eat out.

The night flew by, as my nights always tend to do. I curl up in bed around midnight, click the remote to turn the TV on and open yet another laptop. This time I was not looking at drawings, plans, or emails. I went directly to Randall's Facebook and Googled on another tab. I went back and forth between the Facebook page and Google results. I notice he has added more content to his blog. He wrote:

Today, I understand what it means to turn the other cheek. In my world you can never turn the other cheek, or it will get jabbed. After today, I am aware of the fact that I may not always come out the winner. Just as in boxing, you have to pick and choose your battles. You would not choose to go in the ring with a fighter you know is better than you are or much larger than you. You would not go into a fight unprepared. You have to weigh the pros and cons before each fight and strategize. Most of the time I have someone else doing this for me and all I do is throw punches. But today, I had plenty of time to sit back and strategize. I need to jump in the ring at just the right moment. That moment didn't occur today. I simply sat back and watched my opponent. At the end of the day, I walked away. Just like the lyrics of the song, The Gambler. You got to know when to hold 'em, know when to fold 'em, know when to walk away and know when to run. Today, I walked away. Tomorrow however may prove promising. I will get up and try it all over again. It's the fighter in me. I hope that the God in her will give her the strength to forgive me. I will be waiting and watering my Rose until it blossoms again. I am fasting and praying that tomorrow I will be given her forgiveness. With all My Love, Randall

Oh my! That was deep. No one has ever written anything so eloquent to me or about me. *God help me. Be a light unto my feet and a lamp unto my pathway. What am I supposed to do? Speak to me Lord.*

I send the blog link to the girls and put my hand on the answer button of my phone. I count down a few seconds, and sure enough they begin calling. It was way after midnight but their house sounds like its early afternoon. There is so much noise in the background that there have to be more people in the house than just Paige and Sade. Paige says, "You have to do something Sissie."

"I know," I tell her, slightly wishing Randall would go away, even though I had to admit I was flattered by some of his gestures.

"He is not going to go away." She was reading my mind.

"I can see that. This is way more than I bargained for," I admitted to Paige. "Why hadn't he shown more interest, opened up, and told me all of this before now?"

"I don't know, but he sure is sensitive to be a fighter," Paige observed.

Sade chimes in, "Deacon is a lover not a fighter. First off, he's handsome. There is hope for other Deacons. Secondly, he is a fighter. Third, he is a sensitive writer. Not to mention he's rich, D! I mean, seriously paid."

"Bye y'all," I get ready to end the conversation. I really don't know what else to say about the matter.

"That's your crazy child," Paige jokes with me.

"Na ma'am. I am only the Auntie," I tell her, laughing.

"Get some sleep I'll talk to you bright and early," Paige said.

"Okay." I say, a little tiredly.

"Sleep tight," Paige says hopefully.

Sade chimes in with, "don't let the bed bugs bite." She always has to get a final word in.

■■

There was no rest for the weary, me being "the weary." I researched Randall like I was doing a dissertation on him. His Facebook and Twitter pages were active all night, indicating that he was online. I learned he owned a plane. His home was not far from the church and was equipped with all the finest amenities, including a helicopter pad. MTV Cribs had the inside of his mansion featured three years ago, and the pictures were available online. I pulled up all the photos and magazines he had been featured in and sent Leigh an email to order copies from the respective printers.

She responded, Go to bed!

I replied, I love the internet.

It was confirmed and verified by online gossip columns that Randall's wife left the house almost four years ago and there is not one picture of him with anyone since then. Not that I found any of them together before then. A legal separation would be public information. Who can I get in the legal department at work to pull this record? *Forget it, I'll go to the courthouse and get it myself. If the separation is true, I may calm down some. But why didn't he come clean from the beginning?*

It was twenty after three in the morning. He is still responding to messages. Neither of us can sleep, obviously. Well I might as well make good use of this time. I put a DVD in of Chalene's Turbo Jam. I hook (what a choice of words) my laptop up to the television monitor and clip my microphone on. I pump the volume as loud as it can go and begin to work and work out at the same time. Who cares that the neighbors are asleep? They'll get over it. My emails begin to pop up on the screen. I respond with voice commands. Then I log into the network and start designing and redesigning a project I'm working on, all via voice commands. *This building is going to be the best yet if I have another sleepless night.* Screen 4 shows Randall's blog.

It was ten after four. He writes:

Today is strength training. It will be more mental than physical. My body is ready but my mind is all cluttered. Thoughts of her fill in the gaps.

Wednesday

I shower, dress, and pull out of the driveway. To work I go. Well, I actually never stopped working from the time I got home last night. In the car I am dictating some notes for Leigh to add to a proposal. I arrive at my office and start working on another project. Surprisingly, I manage to call Sissie at our regularly scheduled time.

She and Sade both pick up. Sade is never awake at this hour. What did they think happened last night? Randall rode in on a white horse and swept me off my feet? Too late. He has already done that-except he was in a Phantom.

"What are y'all doing?" I asked.

"Checking on you," Paige said.

"What are you doing?" Sade chimed in, with a bit of slyness in her voice.

"I'm being exceptionally productive at work," I say in an authoritative tone.

"BS!" Sade said. "What time did you get there?"

"A little while ago!" Almost two hours ago, actually, but they don't need to know that.

"Liar!" They both yell.

"I will not be harassed!" I tell them in mock anger.

"It's not us harassing you. It's the Deacon," they both say.

"No fair. I'm being double-teamed!" I hang up the line. We have a family rule: double-teaming each other is not allowed. Two of us can have one opinion and the other a different viewpoint but we can't jump on the lone one. We have to be fair and discuss the matter diplomatically. Since Sade and Paige were teaming up on me, I had the right to hang up.

■■■

The day is going as well as could be. My lack of sleep has not kicked in yet, and Randall has not left my mind. I leave my blinds open so I can see Leigh's desk and he has yet to show up. I am almost disappointed. Then at a quarter to noon, I hear a lot of commotion outside of my office. It sounds like silver and china rattling together. Like Big Mama's china cabinet was being moved—with all the contents inside. I ignore the noise. Then there is a knock at my door. "Come in, please," I say pleasantly. Three chefs appear. "What in all the world?" I said. Cart after cart after cart of food.

"Mr. Washington was not clear on your favorite so we have provided them all," one of the chefs explains. It looked like I was a judge on an episode of Iron Chef. Leigh was (embarrassingly) at my office door with a camera. I mock-blackmail her by saying, "Remember who pays you." She puts the camera down long enough for me to make the ugliest face possible, and snaps another shot.

"UGH!" I yell.

The chefs rattle off an extensive menu that seemed like it would have taken days to prepare. A platter full of ramekins filled with varieties of tuna and beef tartar drizzled with olive oil and presented with toast points and a hot pepper coulis, lobster tails submerged in chardonnay white pepper butter, black garlic escargot with herb butter, a large platter of salad made from arugula, candied cayenne hazelnuts, fragrant seasonal berries and pearl onion with a truffle oil vinaigrette, white asparagus with artichoke hollandaise sauce, an entire rosemary and merlot-marinated prime rib ready to be sliced, along with macadamia crème brulee with a white chocolate ganache, and an exquisite arrangement of the most exotic fruits and vegetables, both in and out of season.

I'm astonished. "Wow, guys this is beautiful. You have done an excellent job. Mr. Washington has outdone himself. I am very pleased," I tell the chefs.

"Thank you, Madame. Can you please tell us your favorite foods so we will have this in our files for future events?" The chefs are extremely professional and friendly.

"Oh. Well…" I begin to rattle off a list of foods. They take notes. It was almost like an interview. They sat me down, lit the candles, and laid the linen in my lap. I was served on fine china. I am sure the candles were a safety violation. But who cared.

After the questions one of the chefs said, "Leave everything here and we will be back to pick up the utensils later and pack the remaining food for your travel home." As they were walking out the door one of the chefs hands me a note.

The first thing I think is, *this better not be a bill!* It's a note from Randall.

My Dearest Danielle,

I hope this food nourishes your body just as you nourish my soul. Be Blessed.

Loving You, Randall

I admit. I cried. I'm not sure why. I guess because the notes and blogs have been beautiful and I'm crying tears as a sentimental response. Maybe because he is married and all of this is pointless and my tears are an indication of my disappointment. Then I came to terms with the fact I was crying because I felt the same way about him that he did about me.

Leigh came back in the office rambling excitedly. I throw one hand up as if to say "stop." She sat down immediately and handed me a Kleenex. I held my face in my hands sobbing. She knew not to take a picture at that time. But I have a feeling she somehow managed to get a shot.

"Okay, I have it together," I sniffled.

"What are you going to do?" Leigh asked.

"I'm going to talk to him tonight. Hopefully, we can formally exchange numbers and talk cordially, but openly and honestly. I want to start over from scratch. I wish I could start all over from the moment I left the house that Sunday morning on my way to church."

Leigh's eyes were full of concern. "Well, what's done is done—but that doesn't mean you can't start creating something new. Why don't you cut out of here and get ready for church? I think you need some air. I'll bring the rest of the food over later."

"I think you're right," I tell her.

"But, what are you going to say?" she asks.

"I will have something figured out by seven. First things first, I'll tell him we need to talk as soon as possible, and not at the church, my office or the track where I work out. I'll leave it up to him to pick a place we can go right away. Then I guess it will flow from there. But I'll have some bullet points in my mind that need to be addressed."

Leigh smiles. "I'm sure you will not show up empty-minded. Do you need a slideshow to present to him?" she teases.

"Oh, stop it!" I smirk at her and grab my handbag, collection of phones and iPod. I never leave home, or anywhere else, without these devices. I don't take anything else with me. No files, no folders, and not even that stupid laptop.

"Spondivitis Friday?" Leigh asks with excitement.

"It's a date!" I tell her.

"Dinner is on you." She announces proudly. I know how much I pay Leigh and she is well capable of treating me to dinner.

I quickly respond, "Excuse me?"

"Gotcha! Just kidding," she laughs.

I soften. "No, it's my treat. Call the crew and schedule it with them."

I leave the parking garage. I feel like I'm in a whirlwind because the air in my car is blowing so hard. But my mind is so preoccupied I don't even turn it down. I pull up to the house, kick my shoes off, and plop on the couch. No noise. No television. No work. I have not done that in years. I close my eyes and rest.

I am startled by snoring--then I realize it's me and my neck is leaning over in a way that is not humanlike. I look at the clock on the wall and only fifteen minutes have passed. I guess I'm tired and more exhausted than I thought. I should be. When was the last time I really slept? I close my eyes again and dozed off. When I open my eyes again it is five thirty. I have slept four hours in the middle of the day sitting up with my suit on. I jump up, shower, and change. By the time I'm done I hear thunder and lightning outside.

"The devil is a liar. Come rain, hell or high water I am going to be in the house of the Lord tonight," I say out loud to myself. All I can do is sing as the tears well up in my eyes: "Shower down. Shower down. Send your spirit Lord. Rain on us. Breathe on us…"

I stop at that moment and thank God for the rain. In my world, the rain is usually seen as a negative thing. That means concrete can't set and tons of tradesmen can't do what they need to do that day. But tonight, the rain was what I needed. If I was not on my way to church I would go run in the rain. Feel it on my skin. Take it all in. It was storming hard and the lightning was shockingly bright. I get to the lot and feel so bad for the parking lot ministry standing out there in the elements making sure we park safely. My friend taps my window. I roll it down. "Hi."

"Good evening."

"It sure is--if you're a duck. I'm sorry you have to be out here." I tell him sincerely.

"Oh it's no problem. The Deacon has requested you pull around to the back and park where they instruct you."

"Oh okay." *That was nice. The deacons are doing their best to prevent us from getting wet. How sweet.* I see the other deacons with umbrellas escorting women and children in.

As I pull around to the side I realize I have never been back here before. There is no one else coming around. Maybe people stayed home tonight. I see one of the deacons pointing to a spot. By the time I shut the engine off, he's at my car door with an umbrella. "Thank you," I say sweetly.

"Are you doing alright today, Ms. Rose?"

"Yes, thank you--and you?"

"I'm wonderful. Thank you for asking. These deacons will escort you to your seat."

"Thanks." *That was weird.* "Hi," I said to the new set of deacons.

"Hello. Deacon Washington sent us to make sure you arrived and parked safely."

"Thanks," I say with appreciation—and a bit of confusion. We walk in silence. I really could handle it from there but I dare not say a word.

Service went on as scheduled. The power blinked in and out. The praise team kept it moving as if nothing had happened. The air went out but we still worshiped. Pastor Hunter gave a powerful word. His message was so appropriate for the stormy weather. He emphasized that you will have storms in your life, because Jesus said, "In this world, you will have trouble." The message was on point--but most of all, the Spirit of the Lord was evidently present. Randall on the other hand, was not.

I tried not to be obvious as I looked for him. But I was really concerned.

As we dismissed, one of the Deacons met me back in the same place, opened the umbrella, and began to walk me to the car. I broke the silence.

"Where is Deacon Washington?"

"He is unavailable tonight."

"Unavailable!" I did not mean to say it out loud or as harsh as I did.

"Yes."

"What does that mean?"

"Duty calls."

I gave him an extremely exasperated look and proceeded to walk faster than him. My heels were clicking on the pavement and splashing water everywhere. But he managed to stay up with me and not one drop of rain touched me. He opened my door.

"Thank you." I was curt.

"You are most certainly welcome."

"Give Deacon Washington my regards." I tell him sarcastically.

"I most certainly will," the deacon replies, ignoring my sourness. I felt like I was at a funeral home instead of a church parking lot. I was so disappointed. What did "unavailable" actually mean? Was he unavailable for me? For church? For what? I was trying to call the girls but the deacon who walked me to the car was still standing around—waiting to send me off safely, I guess. I pull up slightly and he moves out of the way. I rush to get Paige on the phone.

"Hey girlie."

"Conference us all in," I tell her. She got Leigh and Sade on the line.

"Hey." Leigh is in.

"Hey, what's up?" Sade is on ready to hear the latest news, as usual.

"We all here?"

"Yep." Sade replied.

"He dissed me. Again." I tell them.

"What do you mean?" Leigh asked.

I tell the story. There was silence.

"Maybe he had to work or travel today," Leigh said. She is always too nice and forgiving.

"Maybe he just dissed me," I say adamantly. "On to plan B."

"And that is?" Paige asks.

"I don't know yet but I will call you back when I figure it out."

"Okay," they all respond.

I race home in the monsoon. I throw my handbag on the nearest chair and jump online. I immediately send a friend request to him on his social networking websites. I pop a DVD in and work out. I am glad I got that nap in. It is eleven o'clock. Too late to eat. I'll drink a protein shake. I search for my notebook where I wrote the number that appeared on my caller ID. I check the car and then I remember I left my notebook and my laptops at the office. Mental note, never leave it again. I search every search engine. I finally call information.

"Four-one-one, how may I help you?" A deep voice states.

"Can you give me the number for Randall Washington in Sara Hills, GA.?" I think there may only be one house in Sara Hills. His. They may have even made this county and city up just for him.

The voice said, "Can you repeat that?"

I repeat. There was silence. "Hello?" I want to make sure the operator is still there.

"Yes ma'am I'm here."

"Can you give me the number please?"

"No ma'am the number is private." He said in disbelief.

"Damn! Sorry! Thank you." I hang up the line. I bet the operator thinks I am a dumbass. Who calls and asks for a celebrity's phone number and expects it to happen? I pull up Hooks Gym. There is a number. I dial it.

"Hooks Gym," a voice answers.

"Randall Washington, please."

"Mr. Washington is not here."

"Can you give me a number where I can reach him?"

"You can leave a message. I will have him return your call."

"When will he be back?"

"At four AM ma'am, but he will not be available to take calls at that time. You will still need to leave a message."

"Why is he not available?"

"He is a busy man, ma'am."

"Can you contact him and have him contact me immediately?"

"What is this in reference to?"

"It is personal." There is a long pause. My irritation is growing. "Can you or can you not?" I ask impatiently.

"Who is this?" The voice on the other end of the line asks.

"Danielle Rose."

"Ms. Rose I will let him know you called."

"Can you call him now?"

"We are not allowed to call him at this hour unless there is an emergency. He should be getting his rest."

"Well I know he is not because he is blogging as we speak."

The voice doesn't respond.

"This is an emergency," I reiterate.

"Yes ma'am. Do you have a way to contact him?" The voice asks.

"Who am I speaking with?" I inquire.

"JJ."

"JJ you will regret this conversation."

"I am sure I will Ms. Rose. Have a nice night." And he hangs up the phone.

"UGH!" I throw the phone across the room. "DAMN! DAMN! DAMN!"

Randall blogs:

> Today has been a very painful day. Misery has set in. My will to fight has dwindled. I think I'm in a losing battle. I could not face my opponent. I was a coward. I stood back in the shadows and let the opposition have the victory. This is the first and I hope--the last time--I will feel defeat. I am glad for the rain today. It rained on the outside while my heart rained on the inside. God comfort, keep and strengthen me to continue this battle. Be blessed until we meet again. Officially missing your presence, Randall.

The phone rings. "Yep," I answer.

"Auntie he's blogging," Sade informs me.

"I am trying to get to it." I lied. I had already read the blog entry.

"We are such stalkers," Sade said.

"Well, we're not good at it. I tried to call information and get his number."

She laughs loudly in the phone. "What? How did that go?"

"Not well."

"DUH!" she teases.

"Then I called the gym."

"And?"

"No luck."

"We'll try again tomorrow."

"Yep."

"'Night."

Thursday

I can't get to work fast enough. I think JJ said he would be at the gym at four AM. It is twenty after four. I know it is too early to call someone but Randall isn't just "someone." And anyone who knows me knows I am at my best early in the day. This would probably be the best conversation we will ever have.

I grab the number. I reverse look up. It is a landline. I dial it. I get voice mail. I leave a message.

"Hi, Randall. It's Danielle. I have received all of your gifts and I cannot thank you enough. You really did not have to do any of this. I am flattered that you have placed so much thought and effort into each gift. You will never know how much this means to me. However, your presence was missed last evening. I tried to call the gym but I was unable to reach you, and I wanted to make sure you were okay. I sent you a few friend requests and emails last night but you did not respond and you were clearly up blogging. I hope this message reaches you in good health and spirits. We need to talk. Please call me. Be blessed. I look forward to your call. Thank you again."

No call. No email. No blog. No response. At ten o'clock the UPS deliveryman knocks on my door with a package. I sign for it and say "thanks." This is not unusual so I think nothing else of it and throw the box across the desk. Later in the day I decide to go thru my mail. I get to that box. As soon as I open it gift cards fall out. "WOW!" I almost shout. There is a note too.

My Dearest Darling Danielle,

I have seen you work in the boardroom and on the track. I have also seen you worship. You are not afraid to sweat. You give everything your all. I would like to be your everything. I would like to give you my all. I will understand if you tell me that this is impossible right now. I am doing everything in my power to change things. In the meantime I wish you health and peace. I have provided a way to contribute to that. I know you will not spend an entire day away from the office. Therefore; I have given you thirty gift cards to the spa in your building so that you may take an hour a day to relax, release, recharge and think of me.

Danielle, I am constantly thinking of you. Mere words cannot contain my thoughts and feelings. These expressions of love show a minute morsel of the way my heart feels. I want nothing more than for you to be happy and healthy. I hope you will enjoy these daily. I have included the menu of the services for your review.

Yours Truly, Randall

"LEIGH!" I shout through my office door.

"Yes ma'am?" She runs to the office.

"Look."

"What in the world? You know damn well you are not going to go." Leigh is both shocked and delighted by Randall's gift.

"I am going to make it my business to try to go daily," I tell her.

"Come on, don't flat-out lie," she taunts me.

"I said I am going to try. I want to say this for the record. I am so impressed with his outpour of gifts and blog entries. He has no recourse for displaying his affection verbally. Not only does he type it online but he writes it in the most beautiful notes." Today's letter was sent on embossed linen stationary. We both look at each other and say in unison, "Where they do that at?" Clearly Leigh and I are impressed.

"A boxer with embossed stationary. Only in Atlanta." Leigh shakes her head, smiling.

I thought out loud about all my celebrity crushes that could possibly do something like this for their love interests, TI, Nelly, and President Obama. I feel like I'm being treated like a queen. Then I quickly remember that Randall is married.

Leigh and I share a laugh about my celebrity boyfriend fantasies before she returns to her desk, and we work intently for the rest of the day. I call the spa. The attendant says she has an opening at 5:00 PM. That works for me.

I still haven't heard from Randall. I've read so much about him, I feel like maybe I should start calling him "Hooks" like everyone else. I haven't spoken to him in four days, even though he's been in my presence at least one of those days. Both of us can't be stubborn. But who should break down?

The masseuse at the spa asked me not to work out today. Not what I wanted to hear. But I knew my body needed rest.

I laid down at a decent hour. I am relaxed enough to not think of work but not enough to drift off to sleep. *I am going to breakdown and buy that sleep number bed if that is the last thing I do. I wonder if Randall has one. Probably not, since he's up, too. I am sure he has the state-of-the-art everything in his mansion.*

It's three fifty-six in the morning. He blogs:

> I will not grow weary in well doing. I will press on. This is nothing. I have handled worse storms and larger battles. This too shall pass.

How are we both on the same page with being weary? I think. *Maybe because we both need sleep.* I send another friend request and message to him. I change the subject line. Maybe that will get his attention. I can tell he has yet to read the other emails I sent.

Friday

I get to the office and leave another voicemail. This one simple. "Randall, hi it is Danielle. I am sorry. Please call me, we need to talk immediately."

No response. This is going to be a long weekend. I am glad we have Spondivitis' planned for tonight. I have a few services lined up for Saturday at the spa. I'm kind of excited. I should be busy with non-work related events. I called the gym.

"Hooks." A man picks up.

"Is Mr. Washington there?"

"You just missed him."

"Will he be back?"

He laughs. "Hooks does not pass this way on the weekend."

"Oh really?"

"He observes the Sabbath and he does the Lord's work on Sunday."

"Can you relay a message?" I ask.

"Monday."

"Monday? Can you call him now?"

"Only of it is urgent."

"This is urgent."

"Go ahead with your message."

"Will you have him call Danielle?"

"Ah, Ms. Rose it is a pleasure to put a voice with a name."

"I'm sorry?" I had no idea other people knew about me.

"I will let Mr. Washington know you called."

"Who am I speaking to?" Click. Dial tone.

Not again. Who are these guys who work for him? I am riding over there Monday. The mailroom clerk interrupts my thoughts. "You have something for me?" I ask.

"Ms. D, I sure do."

"Hand it over," I say playfully. The clerk drops a bundle of cards on my desk. I frown. "What is this?" I open the first one. It is an engraved note card.

Card Number 1: I will not go down without a fight.

Card Number 2: I will keep trying.

Card Number 3: I don't give up easily.

Card Number 4: I will be the last man standing.

Card Number 5: Love is patient.

Card Number 6: Patience is a virtue.

Card Number 7: I'm Hooked!

Card Number 8: I need you.

Card Number 9: In order to construct a building the foundation has to be strong and solid.

Card Number 10: Talk to me please.

Card Number 11: I will dig my Hooks deeper.

Card Number 12: You can win.

Card Number 13: I'm sorry.

Leigh rings my desk. "Yes," I answer.

"You have Attorney Daniel Khrittyleberrg on the line," she informs me.

"Who in God's name is that?" I ask.

"An attorney."

"No s**t, Sherlock," I laugh.

"You asked."

"Who did I piss off this time?"

"There is no telling," Leigh says, partly serious.

"Send it." Once the line rings I answered "Danielle Rose."

"Ms. Rose."

"This is Danielle Rose. How may I help you?"

"Hi, this is Attorney Daniel Khrittyleberrg IV of the Law offices of Khrittyleberrg and Sherwinterman."

I think to myself *who let you name the firm that? And are there four of you?* "Yes, what can I do for you today?" I say into the phone.

"I was trying to get your email address, as I wanted to forward some documents over to you."

"Let me transfer you to my legal department."

"I am sorry. These are personal documents compliments of Mr. Randall Hooks Washington."

"I would never say any legal document is a compliment. What is this pertaining too? Is he having me sign a prenup?" I ask.

"Not at this time. I am glad to see we are on the same page. I can make arrangements to have those drawn up. Who is your legal counsel?"

"That won't be necessary. I am surprised you are calling me since Mr. Hooks and I are not currently speaking."

"I will draft a preliminary document for your review. In the meantime, these are documents Mr. Hooks would like you to retain for your records."

I give him the email address and physical address. "In case I have any questions or problems with receiving the email please give me your contact information," I tell the man. I knew I was not going to have a problem with getting the paperwork because the documents were populating as we spoke. This was strange. I liked the fact that Randall was about business but I was beginning to wonder what this was really all about.

I scan through the papers. There's a divorce petition, marriage certificate, Randall's company information, his shareholder details, balance sheets, documents pertaining to his nonprofit organization and property deeds. A detailed biography of what Randall does and what charities he is affiliated with, along with what he gets paid for each event are also included. I immediately check the divorce petition. It is dated four years ago. He initiated the petition. The very last attachment read:

Ms. Rose,

Mr. Washington would like for you to have a copy of his personal information. He wants to show you he has nothing to hide. This information is confidential and should remain that way. If you have any questions, do not hesitate to contact me. I will be requesting a meeting with the soon-to-be former Mrs. Washington and her legal representation to demand closure and settle the divorce. Mr. Washington has asked that you be included in all further communication. You will need to be present for the final discussion of the disillusion of Mr. Washington's marriage. Expect a meeting notification from me late next week.

Have a good weekend.

Sincerely,

Mr. Daniel Khrittyleberrg, Esq.

Khrittyleberrg and Sherwinterman

Attorney at Law

CC: Hooks

I leave Randall another message before I leave the office. Still no response. I will admit--I deserve that. *I'll talk to him on Sunday and make sure to leave a message after I leave the spa tomorrow to thank him.*

Saturday

Saturday was my day of "routine." Not too unlike any other day in my life. I work until the wee hours of the morning. I go to the gym and lift a few reps. Then it's time for my hair salon appointment. I manage to slightly deviate from my routine and squeeze in a spa visit. Then I head over to Mikey's. Physically, I feel good. Nothing work-related was causing me obvious stress, and my body wasn't overly drained from exercising, but my mind was completely bombarded. I could not think straight. Well, actually, all of my thoughts were about Randall. Every time I closed my eyes I saw him. Every time I heard a voice I heard him. I needed to speak to him. I needed to figure out a way to get him out of my system. This could not be good. I practically laid my head on the bar.

Mikey asked, "You okay, mami?"

"Yeah, papi. I'm fine."

"You look like you lost your best friend." Mikey announced, concerned.

I give him a half smile. "Not exactly. You're still here. Actually, I do feel like I lost my best friend—or worse."

"What can I do to help?" Mikey walks closer to me and asks.

"I don't know yet," I tell him.

"I can kick his ass." Mikey offers.

"Who said it was a "he?" Besides I don't think you could." Mikey did always know how to make me laugh.

"It is not a woman, is it?" Mikey jokes.

Normally I would have given Mikey a piece of my mind for saying something like that. But all I said was "nah." He put the back of his hand on my head to check my temperature in jest. I laid there like an ailing puppy.

"You want to talk about it?" Mikey asked.

I shook my head "no." Then my phone rang. I didn't move. I knew it was Leigh from the ring tone.

Mikey picked up my phone and answered. "Hola Chica," he said to Leigh. "What's up with mami?"

"No se. What's wrong?" Leigh asked.

Mikey stared intently at me while he answered Leigh's question. "Well, for one she has her big head lying on my bar and is scaring my customers away. She's getting oil sheen all over my restaurant furniture. It's just not sanitary," he joked.

"Put her on," Leigh instructs him.

Mikey hands me the phone. "Yeah." I never lifted my head from the bar.

"You okay?" Leigh asks me with a hint of urgency in her voice.

"Yeah."

"What's wrong?"

"I don't know," I tell her.

"You sure?"

"Yeah."

"Would it happen to have anything to do with a married boxer?"

I didn't reply.

Leigh was really trying to cheer me up. "I'm at the mall--you want to meet me?"

"No." I must really be sad. Any woman who passes up the mall has got to be sick.

"I'm coming over," Leigh says, partly warning me that she's on her way.

I hang up the phone. Mikey slides a saucer in front of me. Without looking, I know the saucer has a grilled cheese on it, and there's a cup of strawberry milk beside it. Mikey knew me so well. I ate the grilled cheese sideways, since I still didn't have the strength or motivation to lift my head. I bent the straw over and over in the strawberry milk until I realized I was going to have to lift my head to drink it. Mikey was such a good friend. Why did I feel this way over a guy that I really didn't know that well? A guy who was married. Leigh showed up perky as ever.

"Hey girl," her voice sounded like sunshine.

"Hey," I said, with no enthusiasm at all.

"You sick?" she asked.

"Yeah."

"Lovesick, I think," Mikey chimes in.

I roll my eyes at him and slam the empty glass down.

"You know what, Dani?" Mikey says in a harsh tone.

"What?"

"You have no home training!" he tells me. "You just can't serve some people drinks in glasses," he says in mock disappointment, loud enough for me to hear. He looks at me with a slight smile and says, "You need to be served out of a bowl on the floor, or a trough outside."

I flip him the bird in the middle of his sentence.

Leigh laughed. "I think she may be coming around," she says to Mikey.

She turns to me. "Did you call him?" By "him," she was referring to Randall.

"Nope."

"Why not?"

"It's no use."

"Let's try." She says both emphatically and encouragingly.

I scan through the contacts in my phone until I get to Hooks Gym. I dial the number. A man picks up. "Hooks Gym."

"May I have Mr. Hooks please?" I ask.

"You sure can when he gets here on Monday, Ms. Rose. Have a great weekend," the man answers.

I wanted to scream. "Thank you," I say through clenched teeth.

"You're welcome. We'll talk to you Monday," the man says assuredly.

I can't hide the aggravation on my face. "I don't know if this guy is being sarcastic or not but he sure did call me out."

Leigh interjected with an optimistic point of view. "The gym employee's responses may mean Randall doesn't have women calling there, or Randall has to have mentioned you if the guy knows your name."

Maybe Leigh has a point. I try to snap out of my funk. I hang out with Leigh at Mikey's for the rest of the day. Then I head home to prepare for tomorrow. I don't think I slept a wink that night.

Sunday

Why has it been raining lately every time I'm going to church? It's storming harder today than it was Wednesday. My parking lot friend doesn't even stop to say hello. He simply points me to the back of the church. There is a deacon waiting there who signals for me to park under the canopy. I pull up and he opens the door. *Is this valet service?* I went from parking in the field, to the pavement, to what is apparently the VIP parking lot of the church. The thunder roars. I follow the deacon's non-verbal instructions. Not only do I not have to get wet I do not even have to walk a mile to the door of the church. God is still looking out for his children after all.

Service is wonderful. Pastor Hunter preached in a way that was practical, impressive, intelligent, and heartfelt. *What am I supposed to do about getting back to my car,* I think as I head toward the door after service. I see one of the members of church security speaking into the communication device on his wrist. First, I look back. Then I keep my eyes on him as he walks. As soon as I get close enough to touch the glass of the church door, the man pushes the door open and my car appears. The deacon exits my vehicle so I can get in the driver's seat. "Where is Washington?" I ask him.

"I'm sorry?" He pretends not to understand my question.

"You heard me!" I was tired of playing games. "Where is Deacon Washington?"

"I'm not sure if he's here or not."

I ask again, emphatically. "Where is he?"

"I don't know," the deacon tells me again coolly. "His orders were for me to valet your car."

"Why don't you know?" I inquired clearly peeved.

"I guess the same reason you don't," the deacon retorted.

I look him up and down and read his nametag before I respond. I need to remember his name to complain about him later. "And what reason would that be?" I ask him assertively.

"He didn't tell me and apparently he didn't tell you either." The deacon is very matter-of-fact and devoid of emotion.

I ignore his coy attitude. "You tell him to contact me immediately!" I nearly scream.

"If he is not here I won't see him until Wednesday," the deacon informs me.

"Find him, email him, text him, fax him, write it in the sky, or send a message in a bottle for all I care. Just get the message to him. Immediately!" I'm so frustrated until I am shaking.

The deacon stands there as I pull off. Once I'm out of view he pulls out his radio. He calls Deacon Washington. He clicks on but says nothing. "Washington?"

"What did you do to her?" Randall asked.

"I don't think I did it. I think you did," the man tells Randall, all the while maintaining his levelheaded tone

"It looked like she ripped you a new one," Randall smirked.

"I think she did." The deacon had to admit that I completely told him off.

"Sorry! Thanks man, I owe you one," Randall tells him.

"Front row seats to your next fight is what you can owe me."

"You got it," Randall replied.

"Ten four," the deacon says before signing off.

All night I worked--and worked out. I used all my energy keeping myself busy so I didn't have to try and figure out why Randall decided not to see me today. First thing tomorrow morning his gym will be receiving a call from me. Again!

WEEK 10

Monday

I stroll into the office a little later than normal, especially for a Monday. It was actually twenty after six before I made it to work. I couldn't seem to motivate myself to get out of bed. This week is starting out all wrong.

I also couldn't decide if I wanted to show up this early at Randall's gym. After all, he did show up to my office unannounced and uninvited. I don't really see why it should be a problem for me to do the same to him. His gym is a public place. My office was not. I thought about it a little more intently and decided against the idea-- for a few reasons. For one, it may make me look desperate. Or, an unannounced visit to the gym may seem pushy. And truthfully, a move like that was a little stalker-like. Plus, I didn't want to come across as a troublemaker. Once I walked into the gym and saw Randall face to face, what was I even going to say to him?

Spending time mulling over the situation with Randall served as my justification for taking my time getting to work this morning. I stopped by Starbucks and treated myself to a delightful breakfast full of caffeine and calories. I picked up something for Leigh. As always, I was still the first one to the office, even though I was running behind according to my own schedule. Leigh came in, thanked me for her breakfast and we worked diligently all morning.

As soon as the clock struck nine I wanted to call Randall--but I remembered Mama Rose's rules. "Never call before ten," she used to say. Her reasoning was that calling someone before that hour of the morning was rude. Then again, the gym was a business, so 9:00 AM wasn't too early to call. I knew for a fact the facility was open and someone was there to staff the phones. Promptly at 10:00 AM, I dialed the number of the gym, put the phone on speaker, and shut my office door.

JJ picks up. "Hooks Gym."

"Good morning, may I speak to Randall please." I try to add a tone of nonchalant refinement to my voice.

"He's in the ring right now," JJ tells me.

I pray for strength to resist my urge to vehemently stalk Randall. At the risk of sounding obsessive, I ask, "Do you know how long he will be?"

"Wait a minute," he says.

I could hear the movement, the music, and noise in the background.

I hear him ask Randall, "Hooks, Ms. Rose wants to know how long you will be?"

"HUH?" Randall sputters in between breaths.

"Ms. Rose said how long?" JJ repeated.

Randall seems confused and a little unnerved. "How long for what?" he asks. He was not accustomed to being questioned, much less in public and by a woman.

JJ explains further. "How long are you going to be in the ring? By the way she called you Saturday, too."

Why was Randall just now getting the message that I called Saturday? Obviously, JJ didn't realize I could hear him.

"Ask her if she is in her office," Randall instructed.

I think, *where else would I be on a Monday morning?* But before I could answer, JJ replied to Randall. "Yeah, she's at work." *How could he answer for me?* I wondered. Then I remember. *All he had to do was look at the caller ID. From now on, I'll only contact Randall on my cell phone.*

"Tell her I will call her when I'm done," Randall ordered.

"I heard him but tell him he still didn't answer my question," I tell JJ.

"She said you didn't answer her question," he repeated.

"What?" Randall scoffed. I was holding him accountable. He was pretending not to like it.

I decide to let the issue rest—for now. "Never mind JJ," I say. "Thank you and have a good day."

"Oh, you too Ms. Rose," he replies impressed that she backed down from her questioning.

I didn't get a call from Randall all day. I tried to brush it off, but I was disappointed.

Tuesday

I woke up--or got up. I don't think I got a wink of sleep. I immediately go online. Randall submitted a blog at 3:15 that morning.

> Life is funny. It can change from day to day. You will find yourself up one day and down the next. I'm not sure where I was recently but I am well aware that I'm not there anymore. Something has changed in me. Yet there are still things and people trying to keep me in the same spot. I've got to break free. I want to be free. I need to be free. Free to live. Free to love. Free to be me.

I reach for the phone. "Good morning Leigh," I say, in almost a whisper.

"Good morning." she replies groggily.

"Get everyone on the line, please."

"Now?" she asks. I can tell my request woke her up a little more.

"Yep."

"Oh gosh," she mumbles, anticipating a crisis.

"It's not that bad," I assure her.

"It better not be this early in the morning," Leigh retorts. "Those of us who aren't morning people can't take that much intensity right now," she informs me.

A few minutes later I hear, "D, we are all on the line." Paige was her normally cheerful self.

"Log on to his blog," I say.

"Umm okay," she answers me slowly, not knowing what to expect.

"Auntie, it is too early for this. Tell us what it says," Sade chimes in.

I don't have the capacity to deal with anyone else's irritation right now. "You're not doing anything else." I tell her. "We need to analyze this. Why would he take the time to write like this but go out of his way to avoid me?"

"Maybe because he is married and lovesick?" Paige offers.

"Lovesick over you-- a demanding and annoying morning person. Is that possible?" My niece offered.

"Maybe he is poetic and has nothing else to do in the middle of the morning. You two will make a great couple. I think you're both vampires." Leigh joked-and somewhat defended Randall.

"Do either of you sleep? Ever?" Sade asked.

"Please call him, Dani." Leigh pleaded being the peacemaker.

"I have--numerous times. I don't know what else to do. I am so confused. He's just too weird. I'm not talking to him anymore. It's settled. Thanks, ladies. Therapy is over." I've made up my mind. I think.

Sade expresses her frustration. "Y'all woke me up for this? Auntie, I'm going back to sleep. Call me later. Like when the sun goes down."

"I expect attitude from a hater," I retort.

"Look who's calling people "haters," Sade teases. "Besides, I'm sure you'd rather be at work than at home in bed—like me."

I shoot back. "Why do I even bother with you? Yes, I would rather be at work being creative than wasting my day away in bed." *Unless I was in bed with a certain boxer,* I think to myself.

Sade sees through my attempt at insulting her. "You love me and can't live without me. You want me to blog about you tonight too? Will that make you feel better?"

I let out an exasperated sigh and announce that I'm hanging up on the entire conference call.

I hear Leigh yell, "HEY!! What did I do?"

"The good suffer with the bad," I yell back.

Before I get off the phone, I tell Leigh, "Make lunch plans for you and I and dinner reservations for the four of us."

Wednesday

I can't believe it's raining again. Why has it been raining on the days when I want to attend church? I'm not sure what God is saying, but I'm trying my best to listen. I'm curious to see what type of antics Randall will be up to today. I haven't gotten a gift, email or call from him in days. He's really strange. Why would he go through all that trouble to get my attention and convince me to trust him, and then suddenly stop communicating with me once I try to give him a chance? I'm trying not to let my curiosity and wounded pride get the best of me. But, I have a feeling I'll be stalking him before the weekend is over.

∎∎∎

By the time I pull up in the church parking lot the rain has reduced to a light drizzle. The parking lot crew doesn't give me any special instructions. *Wow, Randall is really tripping.* I pretend I don't notice that I'm being treated like a "regular" church member after getting so much attention from the deacon's just days before. I pull in the normal spot the attendant assigned me a few weeks ago. I am kind of disappointed. So, Randall gave me all this specialized treatment for nothing? I'm beyond confused.

Church was active and exciting from the moment I stepped in the door. It was like walking into the club and hearing your favorite song-it's a sign that the rest of the night is bound to go well. Maybe it's not the best comparison, but that's the way I feel about church. Even when I come into the sanctuary and no music is playing, I feel a change in my soul upon entrance. I can't explain it. Church service was miraculous. No one was sitting in the seat across from me, which was a drastic change, but I was so spiritually full and inspired that I didn't allow Randall's off-putting behavior to get me down while I was worshipping.

I start to feel a way I never have before. Something comes over me. The only explanation I have is that the Holy Spirit decided to inhabit me. That's when it happened. Pastor Hunter extended the invitation for those in the congregation who wanted to become members of the church. Before he could step down from the pulpit, I was already at the altar. I could not contain myself. I had been waiting on the right time and confirmation that this was the church I should join. I basically laid my entire body across the altar. I knew I needed to straighten myself up but I couldn't move. It was like being asleep and hearing what is going on around you but not being able to move.

I think I feel a sheet over my back. I hope I am not showing any skin—or my underwear. Then I decide I don't care. Everyone here has seen both before. I still can't move. All I can do is rock back and forth and cry. I don't even know if I am the only one at the front of the church or not. I feel someone come down to my level and realize that it's Pastor Hunter. He is praying for me. I still can't move. I feel as if I am having an out-of-body experience.

I try to get up, but I need help. My eyes are so red and damp that I really can't focus. The congregation is repeating the prayer of salvation. I can't muster enough strength to say the words with everyone. I am holding two people's hands and I can feel a Kleenex in one of my hands, but I don't know where I got it. I also feel someone holding me steady by supporting the arch in my back.

Did something happen that I don't remember? Is everyone at the front of the church to officially join, or are these people here to help me?

I look down at the floor and see four sets of dress shoes along with my own feet. It's rather strange that, besides me, only men would decide to come to the altar today. I know one of the pairs of dress shoes belongs to Pastor Hunter because he is in front of me. His hand on is my forehead. But I am not sure about the others.

He says to the other men, "Please escort this sister to the back so we can continue to pray for her."

I reached down to grab my things from the floor and another arm reaches with me. My eyes are still blurred but I can clearly see the diamonds from the man's Rolex and the ring. It's Randall!

Where did he come from? Did he just get here? When I stood up, he grabbed me and passed my things to the other ministers standing next to me. He brushed my hair back. I still couldn't see clearly. Once we got beyond the doors, he took his handkerchief from his pocket and wiped my face. I could not speak. He barked something to someone. The next thing I knew a bottle of water was at my lips.

I don't know if I was walking funny or couldn't keep my balance, but Randall took me in his arms in a single swoop. He brought me to a room where the other ministers were. There was a nurse asking if I was okay. I was, but I was still pretty out of it. I will definitely remember this day—as the day I couldn't remember anything. Once I completely came to, I spoke to Randall first and then to everyone else.

"Hi. I have missed you," I said. I was bluntly honest and didn't care.

"Hi, my love." Randall responded warmly but was startled by my comment.

"I'm so sorry," I tell him. I was sorry for the fact that he had to tend to me after my spiritual experience. I was sorry for giving him a hard time. I was sorry for not understanding him and for trying to force an explanation out of him when he wasn't ready to give me one. But we could talk about that later.

"You're fine," Randall assures me. "We just want to make sure you feel okay."

"Yes, I'm fine," I say softly.

Randall looked at me intently. "If she's alright, I will let you all tend to her from here." I could hear the uncertainty in his voice.

"I'm okay. Really." I say although I was not sure I was.

He leans down to whisper in my ear. "I have missed you too and don't ever scare me like that again."

What did I do to scare him? I will make it my business to ask him later. I exchange information and talk with the intake ministry leaders in the room. I have no idea how much time has passed. I feel good, revitalized. I feel even better now that I've seen and spoken to Randall. I'm not sure where we're going to go from here, but I'm looking forward to finding out.

The ministers and I adjourn our small meeting. I still feel refreshed—just a little disoriented. I stopped to purchase the CD of tonight's sermon. I walk slowly to my car, trying to digest everything that has happened tonight.

Someone has blocked my car in. I snap out of my daze long enough to be aggravated. *I tell you the truth. The devil is busy.* I am a moment away from getting upset. *Just relax, Dani. Remember what just happened in there.* I walk in front of the humongous Hummer that is preventing me from leaving the parking lot and jump in my car. *While I sit here I might as well make the most of it,* I think to myself. I pull my iPad from the seat next to me, hit the voice mail buttons, and get to work. Twelve minutes have passed. Honestly, I could go on like this for another hour or two, but why should I have to? If this person has not moved their vehicle in five more minutes I'm getting out.

I temporarily lose track of time. Six more minutes go by. *All right, Danielle,* I say to myself. *Time to get this taken care of.* I hop out of my car. This time I walk around to the back of the truck. I should have known. The license plate reads "H2." I'm pretty sure this is Randall's truck. Why didn't I think of that before now? I lock my doors and head back toward the church. I ask one of the parking lot attendants if they know where Randall is and point to his Hummer.

"No, but I'm sure he's in the building somewhere," the man tells me.

"And you have no idea where in the building he could be?" I ask skeptically.

"Ask security or one of the other deacons." I can tell the attendant is getting impatient with me.

"Thanks," I say dryly.

I walk up to another one of the deacons. "Excuse me; do you know where Randall is?"

"Deacon Washington?" He corrected me quickly, as though I was not permitted to refer to him as Randall. Little did he know I had more permission than anyone did.

"Yes, Deacon Washington," I responded, trying to be as respectful as possible.

"Let me check," the deacon tells me. He pulls out a two-way radio and turns his back to speak into it. "Deacon Washington what is your location?"

What was this guy thinking? I could clearly hear him. Maybe he thought I couldn't. I could also hear Randall's voice coming over the radio. "I'll be done in fifteen minutes. Continue to work until I get there, please."

"Thanks," I say to the deacon as I roll my eyes. I sit down and observe my surroundings. I know Randal can clearly see me but I can't see him. He could see me earlier, too. Why is everyone so secretive around here? Was he watching me Sunday, too? He is such a stalker. I'm starting to like it.

The building has cleared out. I probably look stupid sitting here looking around. I guess I'll go to my car. I get ready to stand up and Randall appears out of nowhere. He gently puts his hand on my lower back.

"Are you ready, Mrs. Washington?" he asks sweetly.

I laugh. "You better stop saying that. People are going to start believing you."

Randall seemed fine with that notion. "By the time they believe me they'll have a reason to."

He looks a bit disheveled. His jacket is unbuttoned. His tie is loose. His shirt is outside his pants. His eyes are blood shot. I ask him, half-joking, "Did you get in a fight?"

He snaps his head in my direction and takes my hand. I almost feel like he is pulling me instead of walking with me. After a few seconds, he answers. "Yeah, I did--with you."

"Oh really?" I ask.

Randall sounds exhausted. "Yep, it's been an extremely rough week."

"I'm sorry to hear that Mr. Washington," I say with deliberate concern in my voice.

"I am hopeful that things are going to look up," he proudly tells me.

"I hope so too, for your sake."

He quickly changes the subject. "How was your day?"

"I won't complain," I say.

"You can if you need to."

"Well thanks. That is so nice of you." I smile.

"You're welcome," he responds.

Now is the perfect time to express my appreciation. "Speaking of thanks, I am flattered, overwhelmed, and so grateful for all the things you did this past week."

His tone is sincere. "It's no problem. I hate the circumstances behind my reasoning for presenting the gifts the way I did, but I think it was well worth it."

"Oh, you think so?" I ask.

Randall responds. "You're here, right?" He had a point.

"So, that was all a ploy?" I inquire. I really wanted to know.

"I wouldn't call it that," Randall said.

"I call it stalking if you want to know the truth." I said.

"I call it love." I could tell by Randall's tone that he was sincere.

I smile, "You would be proud of me. I have been to the spa several times."

"Yeah, I know," he told me.

"How do you know?"

"I know everything." That both scared and excited me.

"How do you know? Do you see my daily actions or do people tell you?" I had to know.

Randall was honest. "Both."

"STALKER!" I accuse him in jest.

We were at our cars by now. "I thought you were going to push my truck out of the way," Randall laughs.

"Why did you block me in?" I ask him.

"So you wouldn't leave without me." It was refreshing that he was being so matter-of-fact.

"Couldn't you have just asked me not to leave you?" I said.

"I could have, but you could have said no. You couldn't say no with my truck in your way."

"Wow. You need help!" I laugh.

Randall smiles warmly. "I think my help is on the way."

"I'm glad," I tell him. I knew his words carried much more weight than he let on.

"Go get some rest," he advises.

"I did earlier."

"WHAT! Systems were down? Bomb threat in the building?" He jokes. By now he knows what a workaholic I am.

"Shut up!" I roll my eyes, but my smile says that I'm flattered by his concern.

"Come here." He pulls me close and hugs me so tight. Then he says, "You smell good. You're turning me into a punk."

"I'm pretty sure you were like that when I met you," I tease him.

"Get some rest," he laughs.

"Look who's talking," I remind him. "You're the one up all night blogging, running or working out at the crack of dawn."

"And you call me a stalker after you intimidate my staff?" he counters.

"And what do you mean by that?" I asked sarcastically.

We both laugh. "Good night my love," Randall says endearingly.

I bury my head into his suit and speak in a near-whisper. "Good night Randall."

"I'll see you tomorrow," he assures me.

Randall backs up his vehicle to let me out. As soon as I pull out he blinks his lights at me as a non-verbal good-bye.

I walk in my front door and sit back in the same place I did earlier. I fall asleep right away. I wake up at 2:00 AM and check Randall's blog. No new posts. I refuse to believe he's asleep. I lie in my bed until I doze off again.

Thursday

At 6:00 AM I check Randall's blog again. Nothing. I get dressed and hit the road. I arrive at the office way after eight. I haven't gotten to work this late in years. The light on my office phone indicates that I have messages.

How can I have messages this early in the morning? I just checked my inbox a few hours ago. The first message was apparently left at 2:55 AM

"Danielle, it's me Randall. I know it is late but I wanted to say thank you. I would like to start over and get to know you. I was so engulfed in your presence tonight that I forgot to congratulate you on accepting the gift of salvation and finding a new church home. I'm sure I speak for the entire church staff and congregation when I say we are delighted to have you. I'm so glad we are equally yoked. I hope blessings are bestowed upon you in more ways than you can ask or imagine. Good night."

I saved the message--after I listen to it a few times. Randall left the second message at 4:10 in the morning.

"Hi Danielle, I'm sorry—I know it's early. I work out at this time every day. I hope this doesn't bother you. Yes, I admit, I'm stalking you. I wanted my voice to be the first one you hear today—and every day. Have a great day. I also wanted to get permission to buy you a present. I'll see you soon."

I listen to the message until I have it memorized. *Show me a sign if you want me to go through with this, Lord,* I pray silently. Then I remember. Randall has sent me a number of presents—now all of a sudden he wants permission?

I check my emails and Facebook. Randall hasn't left any messages. Interesting. I go through the motions of the day. I'm particularly energized. I guess that's what sleep will do for you. I go home, change, and go to the track to work out. It's pretty crowded today. I fiddle with my gadgets and turn on the music I want to hear while I exercise. My playlist starts with DMX. Just when I start to relax, I hear a voice say, "You're late!"

"Says who?" I retort.

"My clock," Randall quips.

"I didn't know I was on a schedule," I tell him. Then I realize that he has his entire gym staff with him. *What is he up to now?* Randall continues going through his normal exercise routine. A member of his staff wraps his hands and ties on his boxing gloves. He does his drills in the center of the track, in the grass. He continues the rest of his routine—jumping rope, running, sprinting, and push-ups. So he really brought his entire gym to me. Well, that's one way to show me that he wants to spend more time together. I guess.

My chocolate-skinned friend is at the track as well. He can't wait to speak up.

"Beautiful, if you tell him to stop calling you can get home quicker. Every day it's the same thing with you. The dude is clearly scared you're going to get even more beautiful and leave him for me. Tell him to man up."

"Will do," I tell him with a smile. He talks a lot of trash but he really motivates me. I look in the parking lot and there's a nice Range Rover that I assume is Randall's. There's also a van completely covered with an image of Randall in the parking lot with television monitors. The tag on the van says HOOKSGYM.

As I turn the bend I can see the tag on the Range Rover says "LFTRGHT." I assume that means "left right." It makes sense in the boxing world. It looks like the gym employees are really wearing Randall out. *How much of this is he going to do in this heat?* I wonder. *And he calls me a workaholic. I can see, once again, this will be challenging. Two overachievers may not fare well together.*

After a few miles, I can hear someone running toward me. I look at the ground to see whose feet are approaching me. I look to the right—he walks to my left and starts speaking.

"Drink some water so you won't dehydrate," Randall instructs me.

I reach for the water he hands me and he speeds off. It feels like I'm on foot and he's in a Lamborghini. Before I could get halfway around the track, Randall was passing me again.

He yelled, "Why are you way over there?"

"Huh?" He was moving too fast for me to answer. I count lanes to see how far I've walked while my pedometer records the steps I've taken.

He flew by me twice in the time it took me to briskly walk one lap. I didn't feel like running. It always tired me out. But I was going to have to in order to keep up with him.

"Hey, can you come closer in?" he asks.

"Why?"

"So I can run on the grass while you stay on the blacktop," he reasons.

"Good idea," I tell him. I probably should have been on the grass, too, so I could put less pressure on my knees. By now, I think the people at the track are starting to figure out who Randall is, but are afraid to approach him.

We continue exercising for another hour. He threw punches, jumped rope, and rode a bike around the track so fast it made my head swim.

"Ms. Rose let's wrap it up," a guy jogged by and said to me.

Randall and I walked side by side. He was in his lane and me in mine. He finally broke off from me to go check in with his team. The closer I got to Randall I realized the gym staff was scrutinizing him and logging his results—taking his temperature, checking his pulse, recording his weight, etc. As soon as a gym employee removed the last piece of tape from Randall's hands he took his shirt off.

I could see the toned muscles in his back. Nice. I'm not even sure how to label the muscles. All I know is that each part of his strong back is chiseled and expertly defined. And that I could imagine my arms wrapped around it. When Randall turned around I was closer to him than he measured. He was pulling the shirt over his waist. I'm sure my face held a stunned expression that I couldn't seem to get rid of. After all, I was looking at a live Ken doll.

■■■

"Thick or thin?" he asked.

"Uh, thick...?," I replied, clearly showing my confusion. My thoughts started to run wild. *Well, I hope it's thick,* I say to myself. *Thick, long, strong, and hard.* I smile slyly to myself and try to start thinking innocently again. *Get your mind out of the gutter,* I say to myself. Randall continues with the questions.

"What flavor?"

"Huh?" I respond. I wanted to say, "Whatever flavor you are," but I restrain myself.

"Smoothie or juice?" he clarifies.

Oh, that's what he meant by "thick or thin." "Smoothie," I tell him.

"What flavor?"

"Umm vanilla."

Then a guy behind a mega blender asked me, "Do you want me to add anything else to your smoothie?"

"No," I answer.

"Are you allergic to anything?" he asks.

"Nope," I respond gingerly.

Obviously the "smoothie guy" made it onto Randall's payroll due to his attentiveness. "Is there anything particular you like so I can be sure to keep it on hand?" he asks me.

I rattle off a list of answers. "A fat burner, stress relief supplement, antioxidants, energy boosts, immunity boosts, multi-vitamins, flax seed and a fiber blend. But if you must know the truth I would rather have a T-bone steak with a white pepper crust, medium rare, with garlic and cumin accordion potatoes."

The man smiles. "I am not sure that is still classified as a smoothie. I'll see what powdered additives I can conjure up."

He hands me my smoothie and then dumps at least fifteen different powders into the blender for Randall. And to think he had the nerve to talk about my request.

I think, *so, my request was too much for you to accommodate?* But instead I simply reply, "Thanks."

"Dinner for champs," Randall declares as he raises his smoothie cup in a toast to me. Our cups touch and he raises his to the man behind the blender.

"Where did you park?" Randall asks me.

"Over there," I point in the direction of my car.

"Let's go," he responds.

We begin to walk toward my car. Tonight I was in my King Ranch F350. Randall was clearly shocked.

"This is yours? You truly amaze me, Ms. Rose."

"It's my work vehicle. I never know what kind of terrain I have to travel on," I say coolly.

"What am I going to do with you?" he asks playfully.

"Love me for who I am," I answer. I'm only partly joking.

"I already do," he says, with complete sincerity in his voice.

"Be careful what you claim," I warn him.

Randall pretends not to hear me. "Should I consider this our first and second date?"

"What do you mean?" I ask.

"Well, on our first date, we exercised, but that was fifteen minutes ago. Now we're on date number two. We're having dinner outside."

"You're either being very clever or really cheap," I tell him through my laughter.

"Well, I haven't had the opportunity to formally take you out."

"Sounds like you have a problem on your hands, Mr. Washington," I tell him jokingly.

"Not for long," he tells me, with a smooth calm in his voice. "May I call you sometime and take you out?"

"Will your entourage be present?" I retort.

"Are you requesting me alone?" He quips back with a boyish smile.

"Is that a problem?" I ask. I could continue this banter all night.

"Well...sort of," Randall says hesitantly.

"Why?"

"I'm really not that kind of guy on the first date," he tells me

"It won't be our first date. It will be our third." I remind him.

"These dates are adding up quick, according to both our calculations. Tell you what—you pick the day and time, and depending on the place, I'll let you know whether the entourage needs to come along."

"Okay let me ask this before we go any further," I say. My voice has a note of seriousness.

"No, let me get your numbers before we go any further," Randall counters.

I reached in my truck to get a business card and he says, "No, this is not business. I have your business card." We exchange personal numbers and emails, storing the information in our mobile devices.

"By the way, what are you always listening to on that iPod?" Randall inquires.

"All sorts of stuff," I tell him.

Randall isn't satisfied with my answer. "Such as?"

"Music, Spanish, the Bible, Italian, books, movies, etc.," I say.

"You're such a nerd," Randall laughs, nudging me.

"Thanks. I'll take that as a compliment. And since we're complimenting each other you're definitely a jock—and a stalker."

"You're so kind," Randall said sarcastically.

"Can I ask my questions?" I try to get back to getting the answers I need from him.

"Originally you said one question. Now it's plural?"

"It depends on your answer to the first question," I tell him.

"Shoot," he says.

"Does your entourage travel with you everywhere?"

"Yes--but necessarily. It also depends on the venue. They may very well be there but you and the average person probably won't notice. If you're asking will they be with us on a date, then that is definitely a possibility. If the date is in a large public gathering place, I have to be honest and tell you that they'll be there. I hope this doesn't make you change your mind about going out with me."

"I see you wouldn't be able to handle yourself without your team," I respond, slightly exasperated.

Randall is unmoved by my irritation. "Don't ever think that," he tells me. "These can kill a man," he informs me putting up his fists. "I'm not even supposed to fight the average man—my skills should be reserved for competition with trained fighters. I have a group of men to travel with me to handle the average rowdy dude who thinks he can take me. I really feel like I'm going to need a lot of assistance when it comes to dating you. My payroll just went up when you gave me your number. Now, I not only have to protect myself, but I have to worry about you and your pissed off clients. This is going to make me gray prematurely."

I feel the need to be clear. "My clients are not pissed off. I can handle them, thank you!"

Randall isn't convinced. "I have seen you work and that mouth of yours is fierce. Let me protect you. Please."

I wanted his protection--but not from clients. In general, I wanted all of him. Truthfully, I wanted him the moment I laid eyes on him. I pushed those thoughts from my mind temporarily. I still had more questions. "So why did you fly Delta back from the fight when you own a plane?"

"You said one question," he said seriously. Why was he so secretive?

"Correction. I said I would have one question, depending on your answer." I remind him.

"So what answer did I give that warrants this question?" he asks.

"You said depending on the venue you would need your entourage. I'm sure you'd need protection in Hartsfield-Jackson Atlanta International Airport. Wouldn't it have been easier to take your own plane?"

Randall nodded. "You're right. I did have someone travel with me. I took my plane on the flight there with a group of my guys, but I flew back on a Delta flight with just two guys. It was more economical that way."

"Were you being economical or cheap?" I inquired.

Randall disregards my question—probably because he knows I'm being flippant. "What you should be concerned with is the reason I flew back at all."

"You had to be in service," I said practically. I knew that wasn't the only reason.

Randall smirked. "True. But why?" He was prompting me to admit the real reason we both knew he flew back. I wasn't going to break that easily.

"Because it's your job?" I guessed in mock innocence.

Randall's response was quick and direct. "WRONG! Because I needed to see you."

He said the word "needed." I really paid attention to that. But I was still suspicious and wasn't at all finished with my line of questioning.

I looked into his eyes. "Why didn't you tell me who you really were-- and that you own a plane?"

"I didn't tell you I own a yacht or a helicopter either," he retorted.

"Nor did you mention the gym, two restaurants and the mansion," I point out.

Randall laughs. "Now who's the stalker? Go home and get some rest. That means no work and no working out. I'll see you tomorrow." He takes my hands and pulls them around his waist and hugs me with an amount of passion I decide I like. He lays his neck on the side of my neck. I can feel his breath. His voice becomes a faint whisper when he says, "Good night."

My eyes are closed. I'm afraid that if I speak my voice will crack. Instead, I lay my head on top if his head. He sighs. I exhale.

"I'm not playing--get some rest," he scolds me.

I'm still not ready to completely surrender, though I do enjoy the way he's doting on me. "And what are you going to do? Work out?" I ask.

"I actually think I'll be able to sleep tonight for a change," he tells me.

"WHAAAAT?" I tease.

He grins widely. "Yeah."

"No blogging?" I inquire.

"Get in your truck, stalker!" Randall yells playfully.

∎∎

I drive home under the speed limit. Way under the speed limit. I lay my head on the headrest and picture Randall driving home, too. Then I start to think back. *This guy really doesn't know me,* I remind myself. *We exchanged numbers for the first time just a few minutes ago, even though we've been interacting for weeks. Either he is really crazy or really sincere. And I'm hoping all of this is a display of his sincerity. After all, he's gone through so much trouble. He sat at my office for hours, sent me roses, arranged for me to have an extravagant lunch, and has showered me with gift cards. He even makes sure the deacons at church personally escort me, and has written so many notes and blogs displaying his feelings. And today, he practically brings his entire gym to the track. Should I believe his explanation about him and his wife? He may be telling the truth about the divorce, but there are always three sides to every story—what he says happened, what she says happened, and the actual truth.*

I shower, change, and work on a few light projects until I fall asleep.

Friday

I didn't work out before heading to the office this morning. I get to work around 5:00 AM. Contrary to my morning routine, I don't check my emails and voicemails until I'm in my office. Of course, the light on my phone is blinking. I sigh and hit the button.

I hear Randall's voice. "Good morning my little Rose. I hope you slept well. Sorry to disappoint you by not blogging last night, but I slept well because of you and I hope you did the same. It was a pleasure spending time with you yesterday. I hope we can do it again tonight. By the time you get this message I'll be in the ring. If you need me you can always have them interrupt me. I need to give you a full list of names, numbers and other contact information you should keep on hand at all times. I'll explain later. Have a good day and I'll talk to you before lunch. See you tonight."

By the end of the message I'm grinning from ear to ear. My face is hurting, and I enjoy it. *I love this man,* I say to myself. My phone rings. "Danielle Rose," I answer warmly.

"Soon to be Danielle Washington." It's Randall!

I smile again. I try to collect myself so that he doesn't know just how pleased I am. "Hi!" I say excitedly. I stand up from my desk and try to push my door gently but it slams shut while I twist my blinds down.

"Hey." I can tell he's smiling too.

"Got your message," I tell him.

"So?"

"So what?"

"Do we have a date?"

"It depends." He knows exactly what that means.

"No the entourage will not attend," Randall assures me.

"Well then, maybe we do have a date," I tell him.

"Maybe?"

"Until you respond to my friend request on Facebook, I'm not going on a date with you." I still need him to let me know I wasn't making a mistake by trying to get closer.

"Did you send me a request?" he asks.

"Yeah, otherwise I wouldn't be asking you to respond to it," I retort.

"When?"

"A week or two ago."

"Really?"

"Yes, really?"

"Huh. Let me call you right back," Randall says.

"What?"

"Sit by your desk."

"Umm okay."

"I'll call you back," he assures me. "Give me a minute."

We hang up. Randall hits a number on speed dial.

"Hooks Gym," a voice answers.

"It's Hooks!" Randall speaks urgently into the phone.

"Hey Hooks. What's up?" Mimi replies.

"I need Vardo Yen."

"Everything okay?"

"Yep." He is short with his responses.

"Hold on please."

A moment later, the line is picked up. "This is Vickie Young."

"Your name is not Vickie Young."

"Mr. Hooks your name is not "Hooks" either," Vickie retaliates playfully.

"Vardo Yen who let you in this country?" Randall pretends to threaten her.

"Vickie Young is American. People can say it and spell it. And you, sir, are Randall Washington—not "Hooks,"" she reminds him.

"Whatever. Check my Facebook page. Did you deny access to Danielle Rose?"

"I'll have to check," Vickie says.

"Do it while I'm on the line," Randall says urgently.

"What's the deal?" she questions knowing Hooks can do the same from his phone.

"Her request needs to be accepted immediately."

Vickie pulls up Randall's Facebook profile. "Yes, I see her and I have about thirty other people we need to discuss," she tells him.

Randall is getting irritated, but tries to be patient with Vickie. "I'm not asking about the thirty others. I am only asking about Danielle. I will log on and respond. I will always respond to her personally. The others we will discuss when I am in the office. As a matter of fact I'm thinking of setting up a private personal page. How hard would that be? You can continue to manage the other pages, and I will have my own page that I take care of myself."

"Sure, Mr. Hooks it won't be that big of a deal. But why would you want to do that?" Vickie asked. She thought to herself, *who is Danielle, and why does he want to create a page just to talk to her?*

Randall seemed pleased with Vickie's answer. "That's what I like to hear. Let me speak to Danielle first and see how she wants to handle this. She may not be interested at all." He ignored Vickie's question about why he wanted to set up the private page intentionally.

"Interested in what, Mr. Hooks?" Vickie probed.

"In she and I maintaining a Facebook page," Randall answered.

Vickie was both confused and intrigued. "Why would she need to help you maintain your page?" She asked as if there was more to his request.

Randall quickly realized that the situation was too complicated to explain. "Never mind," he said.

He decides to change the subject. "I'll see you when I get there. Anything else I need to know about?"

"I guess not," Vickie says.

"Log out of the Facebook account so I can get in," Randall tells her.

"Which one?" Vickie asks.

"All of them. Bye."

Randall hangs up, taps the table, and waits impatiently to give Vickie enough time to log out. He logs in and scrolls through the friend requests. There's my request—just like I told him. It was sent two weeks ago.

"Dang! I hope she didn't think I was avoiding or rejecting her," Randall says under his breath.

He accepts the friend request immediately, then opens a second window and goes to twitter where there's a notification waiting for him from me there as well. He accepts this request as well, followers her back, and picks up the phone.

My office phone rings. "Danielle Rose," I answer.

"What time shall I pick you up?" Randall asks.

"Why?" I inquire.

"Because I did what you asked me to do," he responds.

I'm not impressed. I'm actually a little confused. "And?"

"Therefore, we have a date," Randall half-explains.

I smirk at the phone receiver, as if he can see me. "I don't think that was what I said."

Randall countered, "I do believe that's what you said. You weren't going to go out with me until I responded to your friend requests, followed back, and I've done that."

"Oh really?" I ask. Actually I knew he'd accepted my requests before he called. All of my mobile devices chimed in unison to notify me as soon as Randall clicked the 'Accept' button. I just hadn't had a chance to respond. "Let me check," I tell him coyly. There is silence on the phone for a few seconds.

"So?" Randall says anxiously.

I decide to make him sweat it out. "I don't see anything yet," I tell him.

"Whatever, you see my acceptance," he tells me, not at all moved by my failed attempt at playing hard-to-get.

"Yeah, I do. I guess you have yourself a date," I respond.

"If I had known it was this easy I could have skipped all of the hard work I put in last week," Randall jokes.

"All the butt-kissing you mean? No, that definitely worked in your favor," I tell him.

"So now I am a butt-kisser?"

"Did I say that?" I ask innocently.

"Yeah, as a matter of fact you did," he laughs.

"Oops. That was a slip of the tongue," I joke.

I like the fact that we're laughing together. "What time will you be ready?" Randall asks me.

"That depends. Where are we going?" I respond.

"To your favorite restaurant. Which is…?"

I appreciate his gesture, but remember his workout regimen. "You're the one on a liquid diet," I tell him. "Where would you like to eat or drink?"

He answers in a rather gentlemanly tone. "I'm taking you out, so you pick where we dine. What's your favorite restaurant in the city? Or out of the city? We can go wherever you like. You just name the place."

I'm smiling pretty widely by now. "Oh, I meant to ask you, do you fly the jet also?"

"I refuse to answer that question," Randall says. I can hear his smile.

"I'll take that as a yes," I laugh. I hear him laugh softly too. Nice.

"Pick a place," he repeats.

"Pano's and Paul's or Ruth Chris," I tell him.

"Is 8 o'clock okay?" he confirms.

"That's perfect. I will meet you at the gym at eight. Gotta run." I hang up. I feel accomplished. I've been sweet, accommodating, just a little difficult, and appeared to be very busy all at the same time.

Randall on the other hand, is a little confused by the fact that I hung up so abruptly. *Did she hang up?* He wondered to himself. *That's a little strange. And why did she say she'd meet me at the gym?*

I had him right where I wanted him.

"Leigh!" I yell from my office.

"Yes," she answers as she bursts through the door.

"Call Tammy and make a five o'clock hair appointment for me tonight," I tell Leigh. "And stress to her I have to be out by six thirty. I have somewhere to be."

"Would this "somewhere" be on a date?" Leigh asks, grinning.

"Shut up!" I yell, grinning just as widely.

■■

I race to the salon after work. I feel like a high schooler going to her first prom. I call Sade. Before she can say hello I call her name. I'm just too excited. "SADE!"

"Yes, Auntie. What's up?" she asks.

"I have a date with Deacon Washington," I tell her, trying to play it cool.

"What the hell?" Sade yells through the phone.

"Yep," I laugh.

"When?"

"Tonight. Well, not really a date. We're going to dinner."

"Where?" Sade asks.

"I don't know. Either Pano's or Ruth's. What should I wear?"

Sade ignores my question and simply says, "I'll be over later."

My hair appointment goes as planned. I pull into my garage, and as promised, Sade is there. I walk into the house and it looks like a dressing room at a fashion show. Clothes are everywhere.

"Big hair, Auntie?" Sade asks skeptically.

"I thought it would be sexy," I tell her, touching my strands to make sure they're still in place.

I look at all my outfit options and the three that stand out the most are the coral Herve Leger strapless bandage dress, the Gucci cap-sleeve dress with the side wrap and leather belt, or the black sleeveless dress with horse bit detail on the shoulder and the high heel platform Gucci sandal. I like the coral ensemble but I think I'm leaning towards the black sleeveless dress. Black is classy and safe.

I get dressed and head toward the gym. There are still a ton of cars in the parking lot. I'm not going in there with this dress on. I call Randall.

"Hello," he answers.

"I'm outside."

"Why? I'm inside," he jokes.

"I know."

Randall laughs. "I guess you were serious about meeting me here."

I think to myself, *did he think I was joking?* "Are you coming out?" I ask.

"Yes."

A few minutes later Randall opens my door. He holds my hand while I exit the car, he grabs me and hugs me tight. He smells good. He looks great. He is wearing a khaki linen suit and loafers.

"You look absolutely beautiful. I feel underdressed. I'm driving," he says with a smile. He escorts me over to his Mercedes S 600 and we head out. I can tell from the direction he's driving in that we're headed to Pano's. Good selection; I'm pleased with that. As we enter the restaurant, I start to wonder if they will accept us without reservations.

"Hello, Mr. Hooks your table is ready," the host says.

"Thank you," Randall responds politely.

"Is this your first time in our establishment?" The host asks.

"I haven't been here in years. My date chose this as one of her favorites," Randall answered.

We sat and the maître d' asked, "Is there anything special I can get for you tonight?"

Randall looks at me and I shake my head "no." I don't want to be too much trouble. I'm stunned that he took the time to make reservations. Then again, I don't know why I'm shocked. *And why is his wife leaving him, again?* I think. But I simply smile and say pleasantly, "I think we're fine."

Once we were alone at the table, Randall looked at me and whispered "Sorry!"

"For what?" I whispered back.

"For causing attention."

"I know it's not your fault and I guess if I'm going to spend time with you I had better get used to it," I tell him in an understanding tone.

The waiter approaches our table. "Thank you Mr. Hooks for dining with us this evening. May I take your order?"

"Our dining here was at the suggestion of the lady," Randall says motioning to me, indicating that the waiter take my order before his. "Ladies first, always," Randall reiterates.

"I will have Pellegrino with a hint of grapefruit syrup to drink and the basil-crusted, pinot noir-infused lamb chops with baby asparagus. Oh, and please add a sprig of mint to my beverage," I say politely.

"What other vegetables are on the menu?" Randall asks.

The waiter is prepared with a very detailed response. "A vegetable melody with broccoli, cauliflower, zucchini sautéed in truffle oil and a lime cream reduction. We also have asparagus-both green and white, cauliflower with red onions and white pepper, steamed baby carrots with orange blossom honey, squash on a portabella mushroom bed and steamed edamame with pink Himalayan sea salt. The next time you dine with us if you tell us your preferences beforehand, we will have them prepared for you when you arrive."

I'm impressed.

Randall responds to the waiter's extensive description. "We will both have Pellegrino or Perrier to drink- please leave the tops on the bottles. I'll have the Salmon, grilled plain. No sauce, oil, or seasoning added. I'd also like a double portion of vegetable medley and the asparagus. Steamed only. Again, no oil and no sauces please."

We have an excellent conversation. The wait staff and a few of the guests walked by our table a few times to get a glimpse of the Champ. Who wouldn't want to? He's nice looking and very charming.

I know for a fact our food came before the people who ordered before us. The wait staff placed the plates in front of us and the waiter who took our order asked, "Can I get you anything else right now?"

Randall looked at me and I shook my head.

He looks back at the waiter and says, "This will be fine for now. Thank you."

Randall reached for my hands and he blessed the food and the hands that prepared it. I peeked out of one eye to watch the crowd. All eyes were on us and you could hear nothing but him praying and me breathing. I think the whole entire restaurant stood still and motionless.

After he finished his prayer he tells me, "Do not touch anything."

I look at him cautiously and think, *Huh? Why is he being weird?* He pulls a thin box out of his pocket. He opens the box and places what looks like a tooth pick in every item on both his plate and mine. He checks the time. Then he pulls out what looks like a knife or digital thermometer. He scans the device over my plate and his. I watched in intrigue and confusion. He checked the toothpicks he'd placed in our food, then puts them back into their case.

I ask him, "Is everything up to par?"

"Yes, I think so," he says calmly.

"What are those gadgets you have?"

Randall can tell I'm a little taken aback by his actions. "I'm sorry but I have to check everything," he tells me. "I have to make sure no one is slipping me anything that is harmful to my health or against the rules of the game. I'll also be checking your food to make sure no one wants to hurt you because of me. I don't think you are in danger but I would rather be safe than sorry. Does that make sense?"

"So how does it work?" I inquire.

"These sticks are used to detect any type of chemical, substance, herb and other food item that I'm not allowed to have. The sticks will turn a different color if they detect a harmful ingredient in the food. The colors will give a general idea of what the substance or chemical may be. The device can pick up chemicals, substances, odors, herbs, oils, glass, metal, liquids, and anything that is harmful to me. It will pick up the slightest herb and reject the dish. I will show you all the device's capabilities in full one day. It's amazing."

Now I wanted to know more. "Has it previously picked up things that were a threat?"

Randall was very matter-of-fact. "No, I wouldn't say it has picked up any "threats." It has sensed some things that I choose not to eat. But I try to always be safe. The machine can pick up bacteria also. The staff members at places where I eat regularly usually will escort me to the kitchen so that I can scan my food there. That way, no one else in the restaurant knows what I'm doing, and if there is a problem with the food, I can get it resolved before my meal hits the table. Then, I simply take my food to the table myself. The restaurant staff members are familiar with the devices, and they know that when I bring a group to dine with me, we'll be scanning each dish plate, and piece of silverware that comes to the table."

I nod in understanding. As Randall continues this is getting interesting.

"I hope and pray that no one would ever try to intentionally hurt me. I trust God for protection, but I still have to be careful. There's always a chance I could be unintentionally harmed. For instance, bacteria from food or other substances can enter my body at the wrong time. Not that any time is the right time, but it can cause me to have to take doses of medication that would raise suspicion with the boxing association. I'm sure you probably think I'm a complete freak. But this has become a natural way of thinking for me. It is all in a day's work. The same way you scrutinize the materials needed to construct a building is the same way I scrutinize what I put in my body."

I was finally beginning to understand. "Oh, so that's why you're always drinking your meals. I'm not scrutinizing you for anything. You have to do what is necessary to take care of yourself."

"So do you," Randall tells me.

I give him an understanding smile. His remark let me know that he understood my need to be guarded sometimes. "Well, thank you. And, no, I don't think you're a freak. Do I think you carry a science lab around with you? Yes. Just don't leave all those tools and instruments around me. I'm way too inquisitive. I'd be testing everything from plants to paper to concrete with that portable lab of yours."

Randall laughs. "You're such a nerd. But I like it. I like everything about you. Did I tell you how gorgeous you look tonight?"

I grin. "No, I don't believe you did," I say flirtatiously.

"You look beautiful." He said with sincerity.

"Thank you--and you look handsome as always."

He continues flirting. "I can't keep my eyes off you."

I think to myself *same here*. But instead I jokingly responded "You're not an eyesore, either."

He snickers. "Thanks. I've gotten used to seeing you in church clothes. And since I've visited your office, I have an idea of what your professional attire looks like. But this...this is especially nice. Even nicer than you usually look."

I remind him, "If my memory serves me correctly, you were also wearing a suit when you came to my office."

Randall nods. "That's true. Other than that I have only seen you in workout clothes."

I pretend to be embarrassed. "Ugh, you would have to see me at my worst." I roll my eyes in mock disgust.

Randall gives me a knowing look. "I want to see all aspects of you. Except hurt. I never want to see you hurt."

He is making my heart melt. I ask him, "Why didn't we meet years ago? You seem to always know what to say. Why is that?"

"Because I like you, Danielle," he answered practically.

I smile. "Thanks Randall. I like you too." I notice he eats most of his vegetables but picks over the salmon. "Is it good?" I ask.

"Yes, it is delicious."

"So why are you picking over it?"

"I am watching what I eat."

"Yes, literally," I tease him.

He laughs.

"Well since you've already inspected the food, why are you watching it so closely now?" I inquire.

"I have to keep my weight leveled. However, if you keep me working out outside all summer I'm going to be underweight."

I scoff. "I had you outside?"

"Yes, every day at the track," Randall reasoned. "I thought the spa gift cards would relax you."

"Oh, they do--but I still have to work out."

Randall looks confused. "So why do you still need to work out? Why do you have to exercise for such a long period of time?"

I grin at him. "Look who's talking about excessive exercising! I work out the way I do because I'm thick and trying to tone my body and slim down a bit."

Randall is shocked. "THICK??? By whose standards--*Cosmopolitan*?" He holds up his pinky finger to indicate that he already thinks I'm slim enough.

I appreciate the compliment, but I tell him, "No, by Danielle's standards. I need to make some physical adjustments. Besides, you have healthy eating habits and you're very disciplined. My habits are all over the map. So I have to do what is necessary to keep myself looking right."

"I like you the way you are but if you feel the need to kill yourself go right ahead," Randall tells me. "Don't worry about me out there, sweating like hell," he jokes.

I laugh. "You don't have to come out there."

"Oh, yes I do," he quickly responds.

"Why?"

"It is a legitimate way to see you."

"Why do you need a reason?"

He touches his ring finger. I start to recoil, even though I don't mean to. My upbeat mood is instantly spoiled. He senses my reaction.

He slides his chair closer to the table and reaches for my hands. "Danielle, I am so sorry to have you in this predicament. I'm doing everything in my power to resolve this situation. If you don't want to see me until my divorce is finalized I will completely understand. I won't like it, but I know you have to take care of you and do what you think is right. But I had to let you know how I feel when I had the opportunity. I don't foresee someone like you being available for long."

I look down. Little did he know but I had been available for longer than I cared to think about. He gently pushed my chin up. Someone snaps a picture. I anticipated Randall going into a rage. He didn't flinch. He was not distracted at all. I keep trying to tell myself that we're just two friends having dinner. But in my heart I want more than to be his friend—and we both know that.

"Tell me what I need to do," Randall asks earnestly.

I don't know what to say. It's one thing to read his blogs and letters, but it's totally different to hear his sentiments in person. I'm speechless.

We stare at each other. He has a child-like look of disappointment on his face. I cannot speak; I know my voice will crack if I try to say anything. I push my chair back from the table. Randall releases my hands. We get up from the table at the same time. I grab my clutch prepared to head towards the ladies' room.

"Did I say something wrong?" Randall asks concerned.

"No, not at all," I tell him, even though it's clear that I'm flustered. "Excuse me," I say with as much confidence as possible. I needed to go splash some water on my face and try to clear my head.

The waiter promptly appears to pull my chair out further so I could walk to the restroom.

"You can take your seat, Mr. Hooks," he tells Randall in a pleasant tone. As Randall sits, the waiter escorts me to the ladies' room. "Please don't let anyone in," I tell him.

I'm refreshing my face with water at the sink when a woman walks in. I think to myself, *didn't I request that no one come in here right now?* I just need a moment to myself. The woman speaks to me.

"Excuse me Mrs. Washington. I am sorry to bother you," she says.

Before I knew it I say "Yes?" without correcting her.

"Some staff members and I wanted to know if it would be okay for Mr. Hooks to sign autographs. We really don't want to bother you all, but it's not every day that we have the Champ in for dinner."

I give her a friendly smile and kept up the façade. "If dinner is pleasant tonight we will be back regularly until we all know each other by name," I tell her.

She smiles and turns around to go notify the rest of the staff.

I interrupt her movement by asking, "How many people are we talking about?"

"At least fifteen staff members have asked for an autograph, but we have over fifty people dining with us tonight, and I'm sure some of our patrons would like an autograph as well. But I have to make sure my son gets one first," she smiles.

I tell her, "Mr. Washington is a really nice guy. But I'm not sure how he feels about spending the rest of his dinner signing autographs."

I saw the woman's face drop before I could completely get the words out. I try to reassure her. "Let me call him and ask," I tell her.

I'm pretty sure Randall will think I'm being silly, but I don't want to put him on the spot. And honestly, I'd never seen him sign an autograph so I'm not sure how he feels about giving them out. After all, I don't even have one. I grab my phone from my purse, speed-dial Randall's number and put the phone to my ear.

Randall sounds panicked and nearly shouts. "IS EVERYTHING ALL RIGHT?" he asks me without saying hello.

I speak quietly and calmly. "Yes, I'm sorry to startle you, but we have a slight issue."

"I'm coming in," Randall states.

I stop him quickly. "Oh, there's no need for that. One of the wait staff asked if you'd be willing to sign autographs."

I whisper to the waitress. "If he says no to signing autographs this evening, I'll send you one later for your son."

She smiles and high fives me. "I'll be the best mom in the world," she laughs.

I had just made a promise to this woman and had no idea how I was going to keep it. I almost forgot Randall was on the phone.

"WHAT?" he yelled in response to me asking for autographs on behalf of the waitress.

"I'm sorry," I tell him.

"Sorry for what?" he barks before I finish my sentence.

"Asking you to sign autographs."

"Is that all?" Randall can tell I'm still bothered by our conversation at the table.

"Yes." I try to sound settled.

"You're not ditching me at the table and trying to make me look bad, are you?" he asks in slight panic.

"Not if you sign the autographs," I bargained.

"Okay, then come out." he said relieved.

"Okay."

I can hear him smiling. "And hurry up--I miss you," he says sweetly.

The waiter was still standing at the door. He is well aware of what is going on and was trying to read Randall's expression during the entire exchange. The waitress looks at me hopefully.

"He says he'll sign some autographs," I tell her.

"Yes!" She hugs me tight. It felt good to know that one little phone call resulted in something that fifty people would most likely remember for years. At that moment I began to develop a different type of respect for Randall. For his title, his position and his kindness. It is unbelievable that a man's signature would make so many people so happy. I felt myself falling for him even more.

The waitress and I walk out of the ladies room as the waiter holds the door open for us. Our body language suggests that we've been friends for years. I tell her, "Come over, and shake his hand."

Randall and the waitress shake hands. He is very engaging and pleasant. He even talked to her about her son and invited her to visit the gym. "I'll make sure he gets a gym pass," Randall assured her. "What's your son's name?" The waitress told him. Randall smiled and said, "Consider it done."

He motioned to the waiter. "Can you send the valet in, please?"

The waiter was taken aback by Randall's request, since the valet usually remains outside. However, the waiter knew that the only proper response was to oblige Randall. "Yes sir, Mr. Hooks,"

I thought to myself publically his life as Hooks is extremely complicated and lavish. Hooks is the person most people know and relate to. However, the real person Randall no one ever acknowledges. At that moment I sympathized with others like Queen Latifah, LL Cool J, TIP, and Puffy. They have real names that most people forget. Dana, James, Clifford, and Sean. They have lives that are constantly intruded upon by fans and foes alike. My thoughts were interrupted.

The valet sprinted to the table and said, "How can I help you sir?"

"Could you look in the trunk of my car and bring me about fifty photographs?" Randall instructs him.

"Right away, sir."

Before the valet goes to fulfill Randall's request, Randall stops him, "By the way, what's your name?"

"Tyler—and I am a huge fan," the valet happily answers.

Randall smiles. "Thanks, Tyler."

Tyler came back and hands Randall the photos. Randall motions for him to sit at our table. "Pull up a seat, son," he says warmly.

He wrote a long message on Tyler's photo and hands him a gym pass. "See you next week at the gym," Randall tells him.

Tyler is beaming. "Oh, for sure! Yes sir! That's what's up! Thank you! Are you preparing to leave? I can go cool your car off."

Randall nods. "That will be fine." He motions once again for the waiter.

"Will you and the lady be enjoying dessert, coffee or tea, sir?" The waiter asks.

"No, caffeine and sugar are both off limits for me," Randall answers. He nods to me. "Unless you care for some?" He looks in my direction.

"No thank you," I say politely. I was in shock that I passed up an after dinner cappuccino.

Randall picks up the autographed photos from the table, including one for the waitress that includes a lengthy note. "Could you send the waitress back over? These are for her and the staff. It has been a pleasure," he informs the waiter.

The man smiles. "We are pleased you enjoyed your dining experience."

Randall looks at me. "Anytime she is pleased I am pleased." He hands the man the pictures, along with his credit card to pay for the meal.

The waiter refuses the card. "That won't be necessary, sir. We have been instructed to charge tonight's meal to the house."

Randall lets out a laugh that suggests his sincere gratitude, but says, "I insist."

The waiter also insists. "Mr. Washington, I have orders from both the owner and the chef not to charge you for tonight's meal."

"Send them both out," Randall instructs the waiter.

The restaurant owner and the head chef approach the table together. "Was everything satisfactory Mr. Hooks?" The owner asks.

Randall smiles. "It has been a pleasure. I would like to pay for our meals, but the gentleman tells me this is not necessary," he says, nodding to the waiter.

"Yes, that's correct," the head chef confirmed.

"Well, I'm not sure if I would do that if I were you," Randall smirks.

Both the chef and restaurant owner look concerned. "Why not sir?" They both ask.

Randall looks in my direction. "The lady has informed me that she anticipates dining here weekly and I know you are not going to extend this courtesy every week."

"We would be honored to have you dine with us weekly," the owner says, smiling.

We all laugh. Randall responds, "Don't be surprised if my staff, nutritionist and dietician all show up here during my dinners to provide the chef with instructions, meal suggestions, silverware and plates." His tone is pleasant but practical.

The chef looks shocked. "Are you serious, sir?"

Randall gives him a knowing look. By now he is used to the fact that most people won't understand how careful he has to be. "I'm afraid so," he tells the chef. "This is something that has to be done in establishments where I dine often."

The head chef smiles and nods. "We would be delighted," he tells Randall.

"Thank you," Randall says as the men walk away.

Randall turns to me and asks, "Are you ready?"

I smile.

Embarrassed, he asked, "What did I do?"

"Nothing." I say. I was fascinated by his charisma, but didn't quite know how to articulate my thoughts at the moment. Randall pulls out his money clip and places a $100 bill on the table right before we walk out of the restaurant. We get into the car and Randall hands a $100 bill to the valet. As the look on the valet's face turns into a blissful grin, Randall says, half-jokingly, "Don't get used to it. Your tip won't be the same next week."

The young man is not fazed by Randall's warning. He smiles and says, "Thanks Hooks! You'll see me at your gym bright and early."

I'm even more pleased with Randall. The grin on my face is proof. "Thanks for dinner," I tell him warmly.

"No need to thank me," Randall says. "By the way, what do you have planned for tomorrow? And don't say you're working out."

I laugh. "Well, let's see…I can't say I'm going to the salon, because I went earlier today. So actually, I don't know what I have planned for tomorrow. What's up?" I rarely have a day that isn't planned, and I'm sure I had something important to do, but I really wanted to spend more time with Randall.

"I wanted to check out the game," he admitted.

I nod. "That will be cool. I guess that means I'll be meeting you at the gym tomorrow," I respond.

Randall smiles shaking his head. "I guess you're right."

Meeting him at the gym is the safest bet, I reason with myself. *I don't trust him—or myself—to behave if we meet at my house.*

Randall is making some conclusions of his own as we drive away from the restaurant. *It's very impressive that she continues to treat me like an average date and is not willing to let me pick her up,* he decides in his head. *I respect that, so I won't push the issue. After all, we're already in a delicate situation, so I'll let her call the shots,* he thinks to himself.

We arrive at the gym. "Are people still here?" I ask Randall.

"Yep, all night."

"I may have to get a membership here," I tease.

Laughing he asks me, "So you can work out all night?"

Sarcastically, I ask, "Yep, will you give me a pass?"

Randall shakes his head. "Heck no! You won't kill yourself at my gym!"

"No fair!" I pretend to pout. It was time to bring the night to a close. "I had a nice time--thank you again for dinner," I say sweetly.

Randall nods and smiles. "Thanks for suggesting the place," he returned. It was great."

"What time should I be here tomorrow?" I ask.

"Before seven," Randall tells me. "The game starts at eight. I'll show you around so you'll know where everything is and how to operate the equipment when you come back to work out at some ungodly hour," he jokes.

I roll my eyes playfully. "That was below the belt. This is not my first time in a gym," I tell him.

Randall gets out of the car and comes to open my door. I get out of the Mercedes and we stand face to face, awkwardly staring at each other. He pulls me closer to him. I instantly felt my sweat glands go to work. He wraps his arms around my waist and hugs me. If I wasn't carrying my clutch in one hand I would have wrapped my legs around him. Thank God for cumbersome accessories. I choose to be more appropriate and simply put my arms around his neck.

"I better let you go," Randall says gently. I know he meant that in more ways than one. I wanted to beg him not to, but I remain quiet instead.

He continues to hold me even though he's just acknowledged that we should probably stop. "A day will come when I won't ever have to let you go. Mark my words," Randall seductively whispers into my ear.

I laugh softly. "Watch what you ask for," I warn him.

Randall looks into my eyes. "I know exactly what I am getting. The angel I've prayed for all my life. This is only a test." He moaned and threw his head back in exasperation. "This is going to be hard but we can do it. It will take discipline. However, right now, I don't want to let you go."

I sighed unintentionally. "I feel the same way," I confess.

Randall kissed my neck slowly and passionately. Little did he know that was my "spot." I really needed him to stop but I wanted him to keep going. I leaned back on his car and arched my back. I knew I had to take control. People may be looking out of the window. I grabbed his face and kissed his cheek gently. Randall's mouth opened in complete shock. I smiled, kissed his left cheek and said "left" and then his right and said, "Right. Good night." His eyes were closed when I pulled back. He opened them very slowly and didn't care that I was staring at the blissful look on his face. He blinked and attempted to compose himself before pulling me back to him.

"Do me a favor," Randall says softly.

"Okay," I answer.

"This is something you must always do," his tone turns serious.

"Umm okay," I say slightly confused.

"Let me know you made it home."

"Okay," I respond, relieved. That was easy. Not what I wanted to hear, but easy.

"Lock your car doors while you're driving and cut the alarm on as soon as you get home," Randall instructs me.

"Yes sir." I give him a playful salute.

"I'm serious," Randall says lovingly. "I'll be worried if you don't."

I look at him knowingly. "I will."

Randall took my hand and walked me to my car. "Good night, my love," he said as he opened the door for me.

"Tomorrow, and any time you come here, park next to my car," he instructs me.

"The parking spot says 'reserved'." I point out.

"I can read. It is now reserved for you."

"What if someone else is already parked there when I arrive?" I ask.

"Double park," Randall answers simply.

I get in the car and roll my window down.

"Do you have gas?" he asks.

"Yep."

"Let me see."

"I have a full tank!" I laugh.

"Check my blog as soon as you get up," he tells me.

"Go to bed!" I playfully instruct him.

He replies, "I will if I can ever stop thinking about you long enough to dream about you. Do me one more favor, please."

"Yes?"

"Consider what I said at dinner."

"Will do. See you tomorrow," I tell him as I start my car.

"I can't wait," he says through a huge grin.

I pull off. I look back and see Randall watching the car. I am overjoyed. I told the girls I'd conference call them after the date, but I need some time to myself to relive the night in my mind. I never roll my windows down. Especially when I am wearing my best. Tonight was different. I wanted to feel the air—it was soothing, and was helping to lower my body temperature. Randall had been standing entirely too close to me. He definitely made me excited. I open the moon roof and ride in silence the whole way home. I walked in the door and called him right away.

Randall answered on the first ring. "Are you home?" he asked.

"Yep." My alarm was still buzzing. My shoes made a clicking noise as I walked across the marble floor. Suddenly, the noise from the alarm stopped.

"Set it again," Randall tells me.

"I did," I tell him. The alarm buzzed again. "What is that noise?" I ask him.

"I'm running," he tells me.

"Now?!" I ask, surprised.

"Yeah," he says practically.

"Where?"

"By the gym."

"Why didn't you tell me you were going for a run? I had my workout clothes in the car," I reply disappointed.

"You just had dinner and it wouldn't have been a good idea."

I tease him. "Why are you running? Are you purging your vegetables?"

"No," he laughs.

"Then why?" I was wondering if he felt he said too much at dinner. Did I offend him by not answering?

"I needed to get some air."

"Is something wrong?" I ask concerned that I had done or said something wrong.

"Nothing is wrong." He paused. "I was just a little too close to you and I need to calm myself back down."

I silently scream and do the happy dance excited that he felt the same way I did. *Go Dani! Go Dani!* I yelled on the inside. I clear my throat and calmly ask him, "Is that a good thing or a bad thing?"

Randall laughs a little. "You know very well that it's a good thing. Just bad timing."

"I'm sorry," I said in the most understanding voice possible, even though I'm not apologetic at all.

"It's a good thing--and it's not your fault," Randall assures me.

"How much longer are you running?" I ask.

"Another hour--or until I cool off."

"I think a cold shower is usually the cure for your—condition," I tell him. I think to myself, *I may need to go take one myself.*

"I'm going to do that too," Randall tells me. "If I don't, it's going to be a long night."

"Be safe," I say sweetly. I really wanted to talk to him until we both fell asleep like sixteen year olds, but decided against suggesting it, since we were both hot and bothered.

"I'll text you when I get in for the night. I don't want to wake you," Randall says.

Inside, I'm screaming, *Wake me! Please, wake me!* "I'm hoping you'll get some rest," I say to him.

"I can't. I'll be stalking you all night. But I won't hold you any longer," Randall insists.

His statement sounds a little haunting, but I know he is only trying to be sweet.

"Good night Danielle," he says softly.

"Good night Randall," I respond. I know my sleep will be especially sweet tonight.

Saturday

I thought I would rest peacefully throughout the night. Instead, I woke up several times, checking to see if Randall blogged. Finally, he posted.

Tonight was more than I expected. You never know how much something is missing from your life until you're around the things you want. I thought I was whole and complete. I am learning that I was only fooling myself--I am neither whole nor complete. However, I believe I've found the perfect way to change my life for the better. I am not yet where I want to be, but I am glad I'm not where I use to be. And, I'm definitely glad I'm not with who I used to be with. I am a changed man!

Randall is such an emotional guy, I think. He is so in tune with his feelings. I shouldn't be surprised. Any man who is not fearful of worshipping God the way he does is definitely emotionally secure. This is a bit of a contradiction, since he's a professional fighter.

After I read Randall's blog, I lie in bed and stare at the ceiling. I don't stay on my laptop to read the latest news, check out online business reports, or even to check my emails or the weather for the day. I don't even check my phone to see if I've missed any texts or calls. I just lie there. And think.

Then I remember that Randall was going to text me when he arrived home. I jump and reach for my mobile devices. There are no messages from him on the iPhone. I check my Blackberry and see an unopened message with Randall's name beside it. It was sent at 3:20 this morning.

I am done running.

I'm home. I showered and I am going to lie down. I enjoyed dinner. I hope tonight was the first of many. I'm counting the hours until I see you again. Thinking of you. Sweet dreams.

I can't sleep. I'm going back to the gym. Call me when you can.

5:45 AM

Crap! I forgot I'd put my phone in silent mode during dinner and forgot to change it back to regular mode after we'd parted ways.

I usually never miss a text, let alone two—and I was really looking forward to those messages. *Pull it together, D!* I tell myself. *You go on one date with the guy and completely lose your train of thought.*

I'm definitely not telling the girls about this mishap. They'd never let me live it down. I look at my phone for the time. It's 5:56 in the morning. I wonder if it's too early to call Randall. *Use your home training, Danielle*, I try to convince myself. But my desire to talk to him got the best of me. *I know it's early, but he texted me first*, I reason. Before I can talk myself out of it, I hear Randall's voice on the other end of the phone.

"Hello," he answers the phone like it's the middle of the afternoon.

"Hey," I say a little hesitantly.

"What are you doing up?" he asks.

"The same thing you're doing up," I tell him.

"Why can't you sleep?" Randall inquires concerned.

"I never can," I say. "What about you?" I ask.

"I hardly sleep either. I have a lot on my mind," he spoke honestly.

"You wanna talk about it?" I offer.

He hesitates. "Would you be offended if I say no?"

"No I wouldn't," I tell him warmly. But truthfully, my feelings are a little hurt.

"It's not that I don't want to share personal information with you," Randall assures me. "I just don't know where to begin. I don't know exactly what to say or how to say it. Besides, I don't think you have that much time."

His explanation makes me feel a little better. "That's shocking. You're usually good with words," I say.

Randall lets out a half laugh. "I think there are too many words going through my head right now. I can't think straight."

"Well if you want to talk, I'm here any time," I add.

I can sense his smile when he says, "Thanks for the offer. Once I get all my thoughts together I will let you in on everything."

I'm satisfied with that response. "So what are you about to do?" I ask.

"Hang out at the gym. Punch some bags, I guess," Randall says.

"Not this morning," I tell him. "I'm coming to get you." I'm a little surprised at my own boldness.

"What?" The shock in Randall's voice is apparent.

I can't back down now. I blink hard, take a quick breath and say, "I'll meet you in forty minutes at your gym."

"What? Go to bed," Randall scoffs.

I won't hear it. "I'll see you in a minute," I tell him, and hang up the phone.

I hop up out of bed, throw on some khaki shorts and a tank top. I spritzed some perfume on and put on a little John Hardy jewelry. I slid my feet into my Gucci sandals, grabbed a matching belt to put around my waist, secured a baseball cap on my head, and grabbed my handbag and car keys. Keys to my Porsche, might I add. It's my latest purchase. It is everything a driving machine should be. Fast, four doors, black, a Porsche, and I love it. Of course, triple black and the license plate reads SKYHI—a nod to my love for designing skyscrapers.

I pump the volume up on my stereo, open the sunroof of my Panamera, and hit the highway. I wonder if the State Patrol would be out this early. I quickly decide that I don't care. I just want to get to Randall as soon as I can. I push the gas a little harder. I get off the exit for the gym and am driving into the parking lot within minutes. Then I remember the instructions Randall gave me to park in the reserved space, so I do. I reach for the door and hear the electric buzzer signaling that the lock is unlatched before I can put my hand on the handle. I'm a little startled.

Obviously someone other than Randall was expecting me. As I enter the gym door I can see him running down the stairs. The way he moves is so athletic. And by "athletic" I mean sexy. He walks up to me and spins me around.

He yelled back to the other guys in the gym, "I'm gone. I'm riding with her. If something happens to me it's her fault," Randall jokes. "Tell King I'll be back shortly. I have no clue where I'm going." He pushes the door so I can exit the gym in front of him. It's still dark outside. Not quite the crack of dawn. My favorite time of day. The city I built is still quiet. If they ever rename this city the new name should include Rose in homage to me and the Elder Rose, my father.

I smile at Randall, "Hey," I say flirtatiously.

He grins. "Hey. I'm glad to see you," he says as he kisses my neck.

I realize the neck kiss is "safe" for him and allows him to show affection without being inappropriate—or so he thinks. He has no idea how turned on it makes me. I take a second to compose myself. "Do you have your science kit?" I joke.

"Do I need it?" he raises his eyebrow.

I grin slyly. "I believe so."

"Pull around to the back," Randall instructs me.

He gets out and takes a good look at my Panamera. "Wow! Who sold you this car?" he asked fascinated.

"What?" I respond, pretending to be offended.

"Do you know what to do with this?" he teases.

I smile at Randall while rolling my eyes. "Any day you want to run it let me know," I tell him.

He shakes his head and laughs. "You are wild--you know that?"

I wink. "You ain't seen nothing yet," I respond.

"That wink of yours is going to get you in trouble," Randall playfully warns.

Randall goes to his car to grab his "kit." We pull out of the gym parking lot and I drive through town. Surprisingly, he never asks me where we're going. Since it was so early, the streets were clear. I point things out about the buildings we pass that I've had a hand in constructing. He seems genuinely interested. We pull up to our destination. Randall, ever the gentleman, got out of the car to open my door. We walk hand in hand to the restaurant after Randall opens the door for me.

"Ms. D!" The man behind the bar greets me.

"Good morning," I sing.

"Who do you have there?" The man behind the bar asks through a mischievous smile.

"Oh, just some roughneck I picked up," I joke.

"He looks like a fighter," the bartender observed, without even looking up from washing glasses and restocking shelves.

"That's what they tell me," I say.

"Do you believe it?"

I look Randall in the eyes while I answer the bartender's question. "I'll have to see it for myself."

The bartender continues. "I heard he's decent. He's won a few bouts. I would put my money on him."

"'Decent don't cut it where I come from," I respond.

"Well you know what you got to do," the man answers.

Randall interjects. "Hello, people! I'm standing right here—listening to you two talk about me," he laughs.

I smile and make a formal introduction. "Randall Hooks Washington, meet my favorite short order cook and my best friend, Mikey." I lean over the bar and give Mikey a kiss on both cheeks.

Mikey turns to Randall and confirms. "Did she call me a short order cook?"

Randall shakes his head. "I think she did. Good to know I'm not the only one getting insulted here," he says through a laugh.

Mikey extends his hand to Randall. "Nice to meet you, Mr. Hooks."

Randall smiles. "Call me Hooks." The men shake hands. "How did you meet this busy body?" Randall asks.

"I ran into her and saw she needed help," Mikey tells Randall.

I promptly interrupt. "Oh, now it's my time to be insulted," I say with mock agitation.

"How long have you known her?" Randall wanted to know.

Mikey smiles. "Come in one day when you have time. I can give you the low-down on Danielle," he says, nodding in my direction. "I've known her for years—we've been friends through college, clubbing, dating, crying, successes, and failures. You name it, and we've probably worked through it—right here at this bar."

Mikey turns to me. "Did Mr. Hooks pull you away from your weekly hair appointment?" he frowns.

"Kinda sorta," I tell Mikey, laughing.

"You should never ever miss your hair appointment if you know what I know," Mikey teased.

I jokingly dismiss him with a wave of my hand. "He took me out last night, if you must know," I tell Mikey. "And for your information, I went yesterday so I don't need to go this morning," I retort, rolling my eyes.

"How Christ-like of you," Mikey says sarcastically. He turns to Randall. "You're disappointing me, Hooks. You should have messed it up for her," Mikey quips while winking at me.

Randall grins. "All in due time," he proudly responds.

"Goodness, you two! Give me a break," I say loudly.

Mikey laughs. "Alright. Are you having your Saturday usual?"

I nod. "Yes. I'm not sure what the Mister is having. Just make sure you make the food on your most sanitized equipment and serve it on pristine plates, because he's going to check everything."

Obviously Mikey doesn't take me seriously. He ignores what I say about Randall's obsession with cleanliness and says, "What can I get you, Mr. Hooks?"

I interject before Randall can answer. "He doesn't eat. He only drinks liquids."

Mikey answers, "Well, it's too early for alcohol, and that's not appropriate for a fighter, anyway. But if you keep hanging around this place, you'll start drinking all day. Don't worry; I have a solution. I call it my 100% Hangover Cure. I think you'll enjoy it. Unless you want what Danielle is having. She always gets four egg whites scrambled soft and a cranberry juice.

"Actually, I think I want citrus juice today," I tell Mikey.

He gives Randall a surprised look. "Wow, you've definitely got your "hooks" in her. She hates citrus!"

"'Hooks'? That was soooo clever Mikey," I said facetiously. "I drink citrus juice sometimes." I stick my tongue out at him.

"Yeah, when you're sick," Mikey says, rolling his eyes at me.

I laugh. "Shut up! Just give Randall the "special." Make it an extra-large. I hope to never need another one in life."

Mikey nods. "One 'Hangover' coming up."

"Mikey, lay the vegetables on the counter first and bring me the blender and the glass," I say. Mikey lays everything on the counter and Randall pulls out his kit and test them. Mikey is amazed.

"It's good. Run it," Randall says with approval in his voice.

"You two belong together. You're both so meticulous!" Mikey comments.

Randall and I laugh and sip our juice while I eat my eggs and we hang out at the bar exchanging banter with Mikey here and there. The restaurant is starts getting packed.

"We'd better head out," I tell Mikey.

"See you bright and early Monday Ms. D," Mikey says. "And bring 'the roughneck' back when you can. Nice to meet you, Champ." Mikey smiles and shakes Randall's hand again.

Randall whispers to me, "You didn't pay."

I chuckle and turn to Mikey. "Mikey, he says I didn't pay."

"She never pays," Mikey explains. "She has a running tab here. You're welcome to settle it for her. Or, I can just call the police on her like I do every day," he jokes.

I give Mikey a look of fake disgust. "Go to you-know-where, Mike." I jab him with my elbow. I explain to Randall, "Mikey and I settle up once a month. I've been coming here for years. I remember when he opened this place. We've been friends ever since. I have spent a lot of time at that bar." I quickly reminisced. "Did you enjoy yourself?"

"It was good," Randall replies. "I don't think I've ever juiced those particular vegetables together before."

I smile. "Good. This place is open twenty-four hours, so we can come back any time you want."

We head to the car. Randall opens my door. We talk and laugh the whole way back to the gym. I was hoping he couldn't tell I was riding slow and taking the long route to prolong our time together. Or, maybe he noticed and he didn't mind. Either way, I was having a great time.

When we arrive at the gym, Randall turns to me and says, "Thanks for breakfast. It was a nice surprise."

"You're welcome. It was just juice," I say humbly. "I mean, it's not like I cooked you a meal. Besides, I didn't even have to pay." I was really trying to downplay our morning together for my own sake. I was enjoying myself, but I was still trying my hardest to keep at least some of my defenses up.

Randall chuckles. "You're a mess," he tells me. "And you can cook a meal for me any time. But, of course, that would require me coming to your house."

"No it doesn't," I say quickly. "You've heard of Tupperware," I tease, smiling.

Randall bursts out laughing. "You're hilarious. Go try to get some rest," he tells me.

I smile. "I'll see you in a few hours," I reply.

"I can't wait," he says warmly—with his eyes and his mouth.

I get home and honor Randall's request from the night before to text him when I arrive safely. I also thanked him for going to breakfast with me in the text.

He responded,

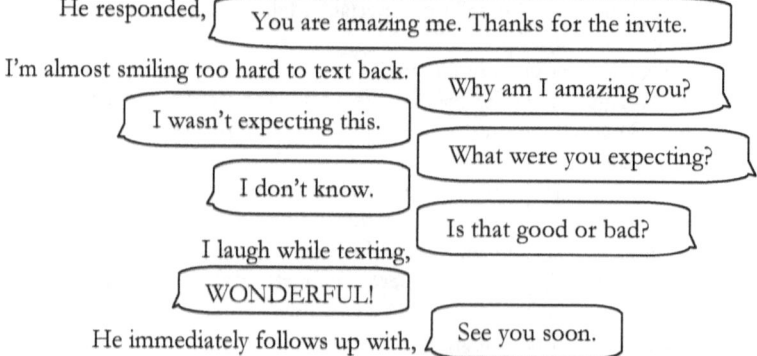

You are amazing me. Thanks for the invite.

I'm almost smiling too hard to text back.

Why am I amazing you?

I wasn't expecting this.

What were you expecting?

I don't know.

Is that good or bad?

I laugh while texting,

WONDERFUL!

He immediately follows up with,

See you soon.

I lay on the chaise in my bedroom and, per Randall's orders, I actually do get some rest. I sleep for a few hours. Both my iPhone and Blackberry are resting on my chest. The devices ring numerous times, slightly disrupting my sleep. I press 'ignore' each time. Then it dawns on me. Those calls are probably from the girls. I realize that I never checked in with them last night after my date with Randall. I answer the next call and quickly respond. "Hey, dinner was great. Went home last night alone-don't worry. Check the blog. I picked him up this morning and went to Mikey's. Taking a nap. Going out with him again tonight. Everything's cool."

Paige replies, "Are you asleep?"

"Yeah," I respond.

I can hear the taunting in Paige's voice, "How out of the norm for you! Okay, call us back later."

I wake up around 1:00 PM. I never sleep that late. I call the girls and make sure everyone is on the line before I start relaying information.

Everyone tells me they've already called Mikey and gotten all the details from him. Sade asks me, "How were you and Randall together at 7:00 AM?" I give a brief summary of the early-morning conversation Randall and I had. I also inform the girls that Randall has invited me out tonight to watch the game.

"We'll be over," they say in unison.

"Okay," I say cheerfully.

We all decide I should wear my Rock and Republic jeans with a white tank top and a T-back studded vest. Oscar de la Renta studded platform sandals, my Sobe LV clutch and a chunky black and silver bangle to complete my outfit. My makeup is dramatic yet flattering. My coif is perfectly styled. I feel like I'm getting ready for the prom again, and the high-school star quarterback is my date.

"Do you even know where you two are going?" Leigh asked.

"Nope. I didn't ask," I tell her.

She smiles slyly. "Have fun!" she responds. I realize that's both a suggestion and a command.

Sade takes a look at my complete ensemble and says, "I am borrowing that outfit, Auntie."

I laugh in her face. "I don't think so," I tell her.

Sade smirks. "We'll see about that! Just make us proud tonight. You could elevate the whole family to celebrity status if you behave yourself," she jokes.

I push her playfully. "Shut up!" I laugh.

Of course, Paige has to give her speech as well. "Remember to behave like a lady," she says. "Don't do anything you'd be ashamed to tell us about. What date is this, again?" she asks as if she is not keeping count.

I give her a half-smile. "According to me, I'd say it was about our seventh. But technically, we're not going on a date. We're just two friends hanging out. Randall is married, and I can't date a married man. If he were divorced, tonight would definitely be a date. After all, it's been quite a while for me, if you know what I mean."

Sade screams and covers her ears in disgust. "Auntie, please!" she yells. "That is way too much information!"

"Whatever!" I laugh.

"Just do it, Auntie!" Sade teases. "Get it over with!"

I shake my head. "You are so hot in the pants. I am staying celibate," I assure her.

Sade continues taunting me. "Don't be such a church lady. Take a walk on the wild side."

"Been there done that," I quickly inform her.

Leigh confirms the levelheaded advice Paige provided. "Keep yourself together," she encourages. "You can do it," she says with a wink.

I pretend not to know what she means. "Do what? Get with him--or stay celibate?" We all laugh. "Heaven knows I want him," I admit dreamily.

"THAT IS NOT WHAT I MEANT!" Leigh screamed.

"I know," I admit, laughing. But it's what I'm thinking--and what my body is saying. "Don't worry. I'm cool. There will be no kissing and no touching. The fact that he's married is helping me maintain my self-control. Because if he wasn't, I'd definitely be his baby mama after tonight."

Of course, this prompts the girls to sing their own version of the 50 Cent hit. "Have a baby by Hooks, be a millionaire," they all sing, taunting me.

I shake my head. "Just lock up when you guys leave," I say in between scoffs.

"We ain't going nowhere," Paige replies.

"Well, have breakfast ready when I get back," I reply.

"Wow! You plan on being out that late?" Paige asks.

"Just kidding!" I say quickly. In my mind I wasn't kidding at all.

I arrive at the gym. Randall meets me at the door. I was glad I picked the outfit I did. He was dressed casually as well. Casual for him, anyway. I still thought he looked dashing in his, Coogi shirt and white Air Force Ones. Anyone from the ATL knows it is mandatory for all ATLiens to always have a fresh pair of AFO's on hand. If you don't then you are not a true ATLien. And most definitely not from the SWATS!

"Hey my love," Randall says casually.

"Hi, sweetie," I say coolly.

"You okay?" he asks warmly.

"I'm good-and you?" I respond.

Randall's smile is sensual and warm. "I'm great now that I'm with you."

We hug. All my talk about self-control is almost out the window until he says, "They're bringing my car around now."

This time, his car is a Maybach 62L sedan in Antigua white with Vesuvius black leather and black piping interior. The license plate read SHOTIME. This doesn't help my attempts to be less attracted to him at all. "You're out of control," I tell him.

Randall laughs. "I know. I was hoping you could help me."

We ride in the backseat as the driver takes us to our destination. I realize midway through the trip where we're going, and mentally kick myself that I didn't associate Randall with this place before. *The girls are really going to be pissed with me,* I say in my head.

We pull up to a club/sports bar called Heavy Weights. I'm sure he owns the establishment—I don't even have to ask. We're in front of what looks like a metal garage door. The door isn't moving. The driver calls Randall, even though all he has to do is turn around and speak to him. Randall answers the phone and says, "What? Okay." Randall makes another call on his cell phone. "Hey what's up with the garage door?" he asks the person on the other end. A moment later the door opens. It looks like we've pulled directly into a room in the restaurant instead of the garage.

The attendants inside are apologetic. "Sorry! We didn't know you were coming out tonight, Hooks," the guy tells him.

Hooks is gracious and jokes, "Y'all got it locked down like Fort Knox up in here."

"What's the occasion?" They ask him. This gives me the impression he doesn't visit his own sports bar often.

"Does a man have to have a reason to come to his own spot?" He asks. His tone suggests that he is getting slightly annoyed.

Everyone, including the driver and valet, answer him with a unanimous, "Yeah!"

Randall ignores their response. "I'm watching the game," he tells them dryly.

"What's up with the Bach?" The valet asks frowning.

Randall scoffs. He's well aware that the valet is asking on behalf of everyone in the garage. "Damn, y'all ask a lot of questions," he says. He grabs my hand and shoots a look to the guys that warns them not to embarrass him while I'm around. Obviously everyone didn't get the hint.

The bouncer yells, "Who's the girl, Hooks?"

We look at each other. He turns to the bouncer and uses my line, "If you see a girl, slap a girl."

I grin slightly and nod my head in agreement with his response. You can tell from the way the attendants were behaving that Randall wasn't being his normal playful self because I was around. Now was clearly not the time to ask why.

He gives me a tour of the place. He shows me his office, and his hangout area, which is larger than the average person's home. *I can't ever bring Sade here,* I think. *She'll try to move in!* "Why do you have so much space just to 'hang out'?" I ask him. "Do you come back here by yourself, or is this where you bring the groupies?" I was being jovial, but I really wanted to know whether other women frequented this place.

Randall looks me in the eyes. "To be honest, I don't think a female has ever been back here. Not even you-know-who. I don't think she's been in this place period. This was something I built once she left."

"Left? Huh? Left to go where?" I ask.

Randall gave me an irritated shrug. "She just left and took my son. When they returned I had practically packed up everything in our house and asked her what she wanted to do. She said I should know what she wanted to do. She moved one way and I moved another. It is four years later we are still at odds. We rarely speak. However, I am extremely active in my son's life. She and I do not need to communicate constantly in order for me to be a good father. We can't seem to have a civil conversation with one another, and having a lawyer present doesn't seem to be helping, either. I honestly have no idea what she wants from me. She's the one who walked out on me, and now she doesn't want to make the dissolution of our marriage legal. I'm not sure if it's a money issue, or if her pride won't let her officially divorce me. But apparently there is something that is causing her to be very difficult."

I try to process the information Randall is giving me. So, is he saying that his estranged wife has never lived in the house he currently lives in? I can't help but ask him, "So what did you decide to do with the house the two of you shared?"

"There hasn't been a full-time occupant in the home for four years, and I moved out when she moved out," Randall replies. "I refuse to sell it until she signs the divorce papers." I don't want to live there anymore, and she would never be able to maintain it. I've had a number of offers from very interested buyers. The home has been used for a number of things; movies, commercials, and summer vacation rentals. So the property has definitely been put to good use. I can tell you're thinking pretty intently about this," Randall observes.

I give him a smug laugh. "Oh, you think you know me that well already?"

Randall looks at me intently. "If this is making you uncomfortable, we don't have to talk about it."

"It doesn't bother me," I assured him. "Actually, it may be important for us to discuss."

"Will this help you in deciding if you should trust me and wait for me to resolve the matter of my divorce?" he asks.

"Maybe." That was the most honest answer I could give without becoming a puddle of emotions. Now was not the time.

"If that is the case, then ask as many questions as you want," Randall said. "As a matter of fact, I can get her on the phone so you can speak to her as well."

My eyes widened. "That won't be necessary," I say quickly. "That would result in way more drama than I have the energy for these days."

Randall nodded that he understood. "Well, is there anything else you want to ask me?" he asked gently.

"How do you feel about it?" I questioned. I really wanted to know where his head was on the matter.

"I just want this whole ordeal to be over. I want to write her a check and say 'good riddance.' I don't want to be lonely and unhappy the rest of my life."

"I feel you," I tell him. "Where exactly did things go wrong?"

Randall was blunt. "Our first mistake was having unprotected sex. When we found out we were having a baby, I thought marrying her, and making us a family was the right thing to do. I pursued boxing after we got married. She hated it. I can't actually recall a happy time in our relationship, to be honest. Once my son got older, she and I had less and less to talk about. Our child was—and continues to be—the only reason we're in each other's lives in any capacity."

I nodded understandingly. Randall continued. "It's been four years. I've prayed about the situation and received pastoral counseling. I've reached out to my estranged wife several times to try and rectify the situation. I don't know what else to do except continue giving her the necessary funds to take care of our son. I'm ready to move on with my life, and I think I've found the right person to do that with," he said, looking into my eyes. "I hope you feel the same."

I didn't say anything. I still had so many questions.

Randall quickly changed the subject. "Okay, I won't bore you any more with those details," he said. "Let's have some fun. I'm glad you came." He gently places his hand on my arm. "Any time I'm with you my heart skips a beat or five, I get butterflies in my stomach, and I can't think straight. It's more intense than the feelings I get when I'm preparing for a fight."

I smile. "You're such a softie," I tease him.

Randall can't help but grin as he puts his arms around my neck and we walk down a corridor of metal doors. All kinds of pictures and memorabilia, along with monitors showing the activity on the other side of the wall, adorned the corridor.

I looked at him and said softly, "Randall, I feel the same way."

He leaned down and kissed the top of my head. He gave me a look of concern and asked, "You ready for this?"

"I guess so." I said hesitantly.

"We need to have a long conversation about how you feel about being in a relationship that will also be in the eye of the public."

"Okay," I respond. This is starting to sound really serious. And not the good kind of serious.

"Let's do that tomorrow or one day next week," Randall says assertively. "I need to give you something during the discussion."

"Okay," I agree this time even more cautiously.

"I'm sorry being with me involves all this hassle. But, unfortunately, it comes with the territory." He smiles alluringly. "If you don't feel comfortable here, we can always go to your house or mine and find…something to keep us busy." He raises his eyebrows and starts to move closer.

"Yeah right!" I exclaim, laughing. I figured the only way to act like I didn't want to make love to him for hours on end was to treat what he was saying like a joke.

Randall smiles. "We're on," he jokes, as the last metal door opens. He already knows everyone will be staring at us. I swear a light flashes as we walk through the door; probably someone taking a photo.

There's still 45 minutes left until the game comes on. The place is full, but not quite packed to capacity. The bouncer hurries over and rushes us to a table fit for royalty. The table overlooks the entire establishment. There is an impressive display of fruits and vegetables on the table that looks absolutely delicious. I was expecting chicken wings, fries, and peanuts--standard sports bar food. It should have occurred to me that health food would be on the menu. After all, this was Randall's place. I'm still thinking about our conversation from a few minutes ago. *Well, if nothing else, at least I'll lose a few pounds as a result of being in this…situation*, I figure. I really like Randall, but my mind is reeling from all the challenges that would come from being with him.

Randall interrupts my thoughts. "Which team are you rooting for?" He leans in and asks. We are sitting pretty far apart, which means that the people in the bar will think we're either just friends or on our first date. I'm not sure that's the impression I want to give. But that may be best. I can see people at nearby tables trying to snap pictures of us with their phones without being too obvious. I even recognize one of the men from church working security. I'm guessing he's a part of Randall's team. Suddenly I have a question. I lean in to ask Randall.

"What do you want me to call you, and where can I communicate with you openly?"

Randall smiles. "I want you to call me your husband. I want you to communicate with me everywhere."

I laugh and roll my eyes. "Randall, be serious," I tell him. All of my stomach's butterflies made their way to my heart and started dancing. I tried not to smile so hard.

Randall reaches for my hand. "I know there are a few challenges on my part that need to be worked out. Please be patient with me. Our day will come," he said sincerely.

"Seriously?" I ask. I truly wanted to know what the future held for us---and what he wanted me to call him.

"You can call me what you feel comfortable calling me," Randall responds.

"Great. I'll call you...Deacon," I tease.

He laughs. "If that's what you wanna do."

I quickly had a vision of us making love and tried hard to push it out of my mind so that I could focus on the conversation. "How about Randall?" I ask.

He nods. "I'll take it. And how should I refer to you?"

"Queen. The High One. Ms. Rose. Your Royal Highness. Ma'am. Anything along those lines," I say with mock pretention. The full smile on my face made it obvious that I loved joking around with him.

"What about Mrs. Washington?" His tone was serious. He was talking about marriage again.

"It depends on what the rock looks like," I retort quickly.

"I don't think you'll have to worry about that," Randall says with confidence touching my hand.

I try hard not to grin and quickly change the subject. "And to answer your question, you can call me whatever you feel comfortable with also. My friends call me D," I tell him.

"D? Oh really? Am I a friend?" Randall asks. I know he's trying to gauge how I feel about him.

"Or Dani," I say casually.

"How about My Love or My Rose?" His tone was romantic.

I smile. "As long as you don't call me Ms. Rose or Ms. Danielle," I say.

"Even at church?" Randall is slightly surprised.

"Even at church," I reply.

We observe the view. Some of the employees come over to check on us. We snack on the fruit and vegetable spread and have great conversation. I lean in and ask Randall, "Where is the ladies' room?"

He motions for a guy to come over. "He'll follow you," he tells me. The man waits for me to stand and walks closely behind me.

Damn, I can't even go the restroom by myself around Randall! I think. It never occurred to me that I'd be getting all this attention as a result of being associated with him. When I arrive at the restroom, the man knocks on the door and announces that a male is entering the restroom. He clears all the other women out of the area. He comes back to the entryway and tells me, "Take your time. No one else is allowed in until you come out."

As we're leaving the restroom, I see one of Sade's friends.

"Hey Auntie! What's up?" The girl greets me. Most of Sade's friends call me "Auntie."

The bodyguard quickly stands in between us.

"It's okay," I tell him quickly. "She's cool." He ignores me and scans her anyway. She rolls her eyes. I shrug in return.

"Hey baby," I say to her warmly.

"Where's Sade?" she asks me as if she is supposed to be with me.

"At my house," I reply.

"Who are you here with that requires I be patted down for speaking to you?" The girl asks, partially joking.

I try to keep my facial expressions cool and neutral. "Just a friend," I respond.

Sade's friend laughs in my face. "Auntie, come on!" she almost shouts. "You're not fooling anyone."

"A friend," I repeat.

"What baller are you hanging out with?" she probes.

"I said a friend," I tell her again.

"Okay church lady, keep it on the low. I want to be like you when I grow up," giving me a look of both suspicion and admiration.

I laugh. "Oh yeah? It's hard work," I warn her. "I'll see you before I leave," I say, giving her a motherly touch on the arm. "Stay out of trouble." I already knew Sade would show up within an hour. I am sure she'll be driving my car, even though she knows I don't want her to. Not to mention the fact she has her own ride. If I wanted her to come I would have invited her. Kids give you no privacy. I walk over to the bar with Sade's friend, order her a drink, and get a cranberry juice for myself. I remind her again to behave and walk toward Randall.

He stands up and says, "Dang what took you so long?"

"I ran into one of Sade's friends."

"Who?" Randall asks.

"My niece Sade. I saw one of her friends here," I explain.

"Oh okay. I thought you left with the body guard and I was going to have to mess him up." Randall leans against me playfully.

I shake my head. "You always want to fight," I tell him.

"Not true. I'm a lover--not a fighter."

"Whatever," I say, smiling. "I'm sure my niece will show up now," I warn him. He looks surprised and confused. "Why do you say that?"

"Mark my words," I assure him.

"You think so?"

"Oh I know so."

"It's cool," he tells me. I love how easygoing he is. It helps me not to be so irritated.

"They're so nosey." I say, shaking my head.

The game was starting. The place gets packed, but everyone watches quietly so they won't miss a play. At certain points in the game, the silence is broken by roars, cheers and taunting. I realize there is a DJ, spinning music at the commercial breaks. I look around the room trying to see where he is. I finally locate him. Impressive.

"I didn't know you had a DJ here," I say to Randall.

"Me either," he whispers.

I get ready to ask another question, but don't want to take more of his attention away from the game. He raises his eyebrows to show that he's ready to engage with me. "Never mind," I say, shaking my head.

"What were you going to ask?" he persistently inquires.

"Nothing, I just remembered this is your first time on this side of the metal door."

"I'm sorry, I'm not a big partier," Randall explains, slightly apologetically.

I smile and touch his arm lightly. "No need to be sorry. You are who you are."

"I don't really think you are much of a partier either and it maybe cramping your style." he assumes.

I just smile understandingly. Little did Randall know there was a time I opened up the club and shut it down. Those were the days, but I'm glad they were gone. I was glad "he" was gone, too. "You can't really work and party," Randall continues.

"Says who?" I ask. I open my Sobe and pulled out my Blackberry and iPhone to log into my email accounts.

Randall stops me immediately. "Oh, no you don't—not tonight," he declares, snatching the phones from me and slid the devices across the table.

How rude of him, I start to think. Then I realize his determination to have my undivided attention is admirable. I had to admit to myself that I need a man with a strong personality. Otherwise, I'd be in charge—just like at the office. Allowing Randall to exhibit his masculine strength began to prompt more sexual thoughts in my mind. You can easily be submissive to a man that is strong easier than to a weak will and weak-minded man. I blinked a few times to bring myself back to reality. I glance over to see Randall watching the game and I envisioned us like this more often. I'd love to spend more time with him. I'd love to be with him every day. I confessed to myself that I really liked this guy.

I heard the beat to my favorite song. I turn to Randall and say, "Well, are you coming?"

"Coming where?" he asks obliviously.

I pointed to the empty dance floor.

He responded, "Have at it."

I jump up and tap the bodyguard to let him know where I was going. I was the first one on the floor. Obviously, no one came there to actually dance. It took a few minutes for people to start moving. Fine with me. I had no problem dancing by myself. Then, Sade's friend headed to the dance floor to join me. I had an instant crew and we were about to step it up. They all paced and jumped in on the same foot. It was Cupid Shuffle time. By the time we got to verse the floor was crowded. Security came over to stand next to me.

Sade's friend yelled to me, "Auntie who is that?"

"Don't know," I told her. I didn't feel like answering her questions. I just wanted to dance. Truthfully, I didn't know who he was other than Randall's bouncer.

"BS," she retorted.

The commercial on TV was ending, which meant the crowd would be focused on the game again. The DJ announced he would pick the song back up at the next commercial break.

I look over the crowd to get the security guard's attention and indicate I'm going to the bar. I grab two bottles of water and ask the bartender to leave the tops on. I pay the bartender, head back to my seat and hand Randall one of the bottles.

"You can't already be tired from dancing, as much as you work out," Randall teases.

"Oh, I'm not," I tell him confidently. "Just staying hydrated." Out of the corner of my eye, I can see Sade's friends have noticed I'm sitting with Randall. Oh, boy this will get interesting.

"So you think you can dance, huh?" Randall continues with his taunting.

"Is that a challenge? Just let me know, because as you can see, I've got my crew with me," I say, tilting my head toward the girls. "All I have to do is give them the word."

Randall laughs. "D, don't even try it. I keep my crew close by at all times—you know that. All I have to do is push this red button." he points to his watch.

"Do you even know what you're asking for?" I ask him, giggling. "My goons got goons."

He gives me a mock-serious face. "You will not clown me in my establishment."

I raise my eyebrow. "So, how far down the block do we need to go to be off your premises? Or do you own the block too?"

Randall lets out a laugh and shakes his head. "You talk so much trash."

I stare at him, indicating my complete lack of fear. "If you can't handle it, just say so," I respond with a wink. "I never back down."

He pulls me closer. "I think we both know that's not all I can handle."

"Watch it, Ali." I say through a flustered laugh.

He looks at me longingly. "First you insult me, now you give me the highest compliment. Every fighter wants to be compared to Ali."

"Well, I guess sometimes we have to 'break up to make up'," I said softly.

Randall looks intrigued. "Are you insinuating we are in a relationship?"

"I don't think that is what I said," I reply coyly.

Randall whispered in my ear. "Is that what you want Danielle?"

"Does it matter?" I asked. I didn't mean to kill the mood, but I wanted him to realize that his marriage, is not as emotionally trivial as he tried to make it seem. It was still a major obstacle.

The crowd starts roaring in response to the game, and we can't hear each other over the noise. When I look up the bodyguard is preparing to stop someone from getting closer to us. Oh, no! Is it one of Randall's crazed fans? I look closer and realize that it's just Sade. I look at my watch. Yep, this is about the time I said she would show up.

The security guard looks at Randall. Randall looks at me. I finally nod and wave my hand, letting security know it's (barely) okay for my niece to come through the crowd.

Security scans her and allows her to access the booth.

"Hi," Sade says gingerly as she approaches us.

I roll my eyes, look at Randall and say, "I told you."

He laughs a little. "You sure did." He turns to my niece and says pleasantly, "Hi, Sade," before checking his watch.

"Hey Mr. Hooks," Sade replies. She continues aggressively, "what's up?"

"Nothing. We were chilling." I answer her, in a tone that indicates how I'd like some privacy.

"On a date." Sade states, without asking if this is actually the case.

Randall and I both say, "Nope."

She looked at us both in complete disbelief, and then decided to change the subject. "Who's up?" Sade asks Randall, pointing to the TV screen.

She and Randall begin to talk like they have known each other for years. I know this situation will become more complicated if they actually start to get along with one another.

Sade looks down at our array of vegetables and fruits at the table and makes a face of disgust. "Umm...I'm about to order some real food," she announces. "Do you guys need anything? I mean, I know you two don't get out much, but this is not what people order when they watch the game," she scolds, pointing at our plates.

I ask her if she needs money.

"Nope," she answers quickly.

Randall interjects. "What would she need money for?" he inquires.

"Oh, she's about to order some food," I inform him.

"And?" he looks confused.

"So...she has to pay for it," I reply.

"Did you pay?" he asks me in disbelief.

"Yeah." I was a little surprised by his questions. He continues his interrogation.

"What did you pay for?"

"A drink, a juice and two waters," I answer.

He grabbed my arm and said with slight firmness, "Come with me."

He told security, "Watch the table, we'll be at the bar." Then Randall asks me, "Who did you pay?"

I pointed to one of the bartenders dressed in black.

He motioned for the bartender to come over. She looks petrified. You could tell Randall didn't come here often, and when he did, it wasn't usually to socialize.

"Yes, sir?" The bartender said nervously.

Randall nodded to me. "Whenever she's here, her bill is on the house."

The bartender's eyes grew wide. "I apologize," she said to Randall. She stares me in the face, and I can tell she's trying to memorize what I look like. Then she went to the register and gave me a twenty-dollar bill.

I smiled and slid it back across the bar for her tip.

Randall turns back to the bartender and says, "Let everyone know, and we will have a meeting next week to confirm. Have a good evening and keep up the good work," he ends his statement with a smile, which immediately eases her tension.

"Thanks. Enjoy Mr. Hooks," she replies.

When we turn around, I can see everyone talking—about us. After all, Randall has his hands on my waist and is leading me through the crowd. His guys had a series of questions and comments concerning us.

"Man, who is that Hooks is with?"

"We don't know."

"When was the last time he was out here?"

"What is going on?"

"She has been at the gym and I heard he was working out with her."

"You think she's the one?"

"I haven't met her."

"Where did he meet her?"

"We don't know but he must like her."

"He has to if he's comfortable being in public with her."

The game is almost over. I danced to a few more songs. I had a blast. He whispered in my ear, "Are you ready?" My body jumped involuntarily. I'm beginning to think Randall is noticing the strength of my attraction to him. He put his lips on my neck and said, "It's getting late."

He tries to bring innocence to the conversation with his words, but his tone is still alluring. "I need to get you back so you can get some rest. We have to be at church at 6."

I turn my head quickly and notice just how close our lips are. I try to move back slowly and give myself time to form the words in my mind before speaking. "You have to be there at 6," I correct him.

He closed his eyes, sighed, grabbed my hand, and said, "Let's go."

I motioned to Sade so she could see us walking out. "You're leaving now?" she rushed over to ask.

"Yep, bring my car back in one piece," I tell her.

She playfully rolls her eyes. "Who said I was in your car?"

I respond with an eye roll of my own, kiss her on both cheeks, and say, "Be safe, Sade. No drinking and driving." I could only hope she was truly listening.

Sade gives Randall a hug and tells me, "You be safe, too, Auntie. Text us when you get home." Then she turns back to Randall. "Watch her," Sade says to him. "She has eyes in the back of her head and she's a workaholic."

Randall gave her a smile and a smug, "I know," he told her. He motioned to a nearby bodyguard to let him know that he should keep an eye on Sade and her friends for the rest of the night.

We walk down that long corridor and head back towards the Maybach. Once we get in the car, I prop my head on the headrest and reach for his hand.

"What are you wearing in the morning?" he ask.

"Huh?" I replied, surprised.

"I'm sure you laid your clothes out before you left. What are you wearing?" he asked again.

"What color, you mean?"

"Yes."

"Yellow," I reply.

"And what other color?" He inquired not feeling yellow.

"No other color--all yellow," I said.

We held hands the entire way back to the gym in silence. When we pull up next to my car, Randall jumps out and opens my door. He walks me to my car and says, "You know the routine."

I smile. "I'll text you." We hug without rushing to let go.

He said in my ear, "I told you I would have a good time. I hope you did too."

"Yes I did and I wish…" I let my voice trail off because I'm not sure I should finish my sentence. I get in my car and roll down the window. He leans in. I looked him directly in the eye and say, "I wish things were different." I figured that was the best way to put it. I texted him when I got home.

He responds:

> Good night. I'll see you in the morning.

> Thanks for everything! I'm home. Sweet dreams.

An hour later I start thinking about tomorrow and text Randall again.

> Do you have plans for tomorrow night? We're going to a play if you want to join us; it starts at 6:00 PM. Let me know.

He immediately replies.

> Of course. Thanks for the invite. Now go to sleep!

Sunday

I arrived at the church a little earlier than normal. For some reason I felt very nervous, like I was meeting Randall for the first time. I sat in the car fidgeting for a few minutes, trying to gain control over my emotions. *He's just a friend*, I think to myself. *And besides, this is church, not your first prom. There's nothing to be nervous about.*

I stepped out of the car, walking slowly and deliberately as I felt my body temperature rising involuntarily. My breathing was intense and rhythmic. I step into the foyer cautiously. I don't see Randall. Maybe I arrived too early.

"Excuse me, Ms. Rose," one of the deacons said.

"Yes?" I respond a little stunned. I quickly regain my composure and say, "Good morning."

The deacon is pleasant but unfazed. "Good morning. Deacon Washington would like for you to wait right here." he pointed to a chair.

"Oh okay," I replied while taking my seat.

The deacon stood with his back to me, practically covering me. I look around the room and take in my environment. I don't see anything suspicious. I people-watch for a few minutes until I see a pair of especially nice men's dress shoes walking in my direction. I stood up as Randall got closer. I let out a small sigh that I hope he didn't notice. He was such a sexy man.

"Good morning," Randall said in a polished tone that indicated he wanted to use the proper decorum at church.

"Hi," I said, trying to match his approach.

"You look nice," he says with a smile.

I blushed. "You look handsome as always," I tell him.

He blushed too which made me grin. He dropped his head and said, "Thanks," through a satisfied smile.

"Why are you blushing?" I asked him.

"I'm embarrassed," he said still smiling.

"Why?"

"I don't know."

"You shouldn't be," I assured him.

"I know," he nodded. "But I am."

"Is it because I said you're handsome?" I asked.

Randall shrugged boyishly and said, "I guess so."

"Well, you *are* handsome." I give his arm a subtle touch for emphasis.

He laughs nervously. "Stop it. You are really embarrassing me. I'm supposed to be complimenting you—not the other way around."

"Says who?" I ask grinning at him.

He smiles and points to his headset as someone announces the time in his ear. "Let's go. We're on."

We walk so close that our arms touch. We were obviously close enough to be holding hands (which I think we would have both preferred), but that would have raised too many eyebrows.

Then I realized why Randall asked me what color I was wearing to church today. He was wearing black pants, a yellow shirt, a black vest with a yellow back and exquisite cuff links. *He looks appealing,* I think to myself. *Men really underestimate the effect a tailored suit has on a woman.* Randall walks me to my seat and goes to his.

Pastor Hunter's message was wonderful--as always. At the end of service when the pastor instructed us to hug the person sitting to the left and right of us, Randall leaned his supple lips onto my ear and said, "Wait for me," as we embraced.

"Anything for you," I said with a smile.

My response caught him off guard. Randall grinned wide. "That's good to hear," he responded. He sped off so quickly until he was almost running. I hung out in the vestibule waiting for Randall to finish up church business. I chat with some of the church members as they are on their way out. It really helps to pass the time. Before I know it, Randall walks up to me and hands me a CD. "You ready?"

"Yep," I say gingerly. "But you know I can walk to the car by myself," I tease him.

"I'm aware of that," Randall replies emotionless. "But it would be less than chivalrous for me to allow you do that. Plus, your walk to the car would be lonely."

I laugh and quickly brush my shoulder against his. "I guess I can't argue with you on that. But I do have a bone to pick with you. You tricked me!" I smirk.

Randall's face shows innocent surprise. "How?"

"I didn't know you planned on matching me," I say, pointing to our clothing.

"Oh, that," Randall replies laughing. "I figured it was best to just ask which colors you were wearing instead of trying to guess."

I nod, indicating that I understand his point. "Are you planning on us matching every week?"

Randall shook his head. "No, I'm not expecting anything--but I think everyone else is." As we walk, the two older women who commented on our outfits in previous weeks greeted us. They immediately proved Randall's point.

We get to my car. He asks, "So, what's the deal for this afternoon?"

"The play starts at six," I tell him. "The girls and I are going."

He touches my arm. "I don't want to impose if this is supposed to be 'girl's night'," Randall says in an understanding tone.

"You won't be imposing at all," I tell him warmly. We're going to see Deron Cloud's 'The Child Support Man.' I think it's going to be pretty entertaining."

I can see Randall feels more comfortable with the idea. "What time shall I pick you all up?" he asks gentlemanly.

"I don't think so. We'll meet you. You are not that slick," I say, laughing. I knew he was trying to find a way to end up at my house. I wasn't ready for that yet.

"At the gym again?" He correctly guesses rolling his eyes.

"Yes. Is five o'clock okay?" I ask.

"Five it is. I can't wait," Randall says, winking.

"I'll see you then. Now back your little feet up before I run over them," I say flirtatiously. Although, I can clearly tell his shoe size is over a 12, which makes me smile.

I text the girls. | Meet at my house at 4:30. |

Sade starts critiquing my outfit as soon as she arrives. "Auntie, stop being so conservative," she critiques.

"Shut up," I playfully snap. "And since you think my outfit is so conservative, don't try to borrow it later."

Sade rethinks her criticism, "Well, I definitely wouldn't wear the jacket with the rest of the outfit," she says, a little more lovingly. "You can't be conservative and sexy at the same time, Auntie."

"Yeah, we're gonna have to agree with Sade on that one," Leigh and Paige say in unison.

I roll my eyes. "Thank you for the input ladies," I say as I point towards the door.

Sade laughs. "Auntie, I've been put out of better places."

"I am sure you have with that mouth of yours," I retort.

"I had to get it from…somewhere," she teases, looking directly at me. Unfortunately, I can't argue with her. We hop in the car and laugh all the way to the gym. A large part of the car-time hilarity comes from Paige, when she asserts, "where is Randall going to sit? It's my turn to ride shotgun, and I'm not giving it up. I don't care that he's a professional fighter or not," she informs us defiantly. Paige's statement reminds me that she hasn't met Randall yet. The girls and I try to give her some quick pointers on what to say when he comes to the car.

"I know how to act!" Paige shouts defensively.

"Yeah right," we all mutter through laughs.

We arrive at the gym. I park the car in the space that had a simple RESVERED sign on it last week. This week, there's a rose intertwined into the word "reserved." I was impressed. I made a mental note to thank Randall for this later—but I didn't want to do it in front of the girls. I was hoping they wouldn't notice the new addition to the sign, but Leigh speaks up.

"Umm excuse me Danielle, what's up with the rose on this parking sign and the hook on the other sign? I don't think that's a coincidence."

I try my best to play dumb. "Huh?" I mutter.

I open the car door and by the time I get one leg out of the car, I see a set of feet by my leg. I look up to find that Randall and I have once again dressed in the same colors.

He smiles pleasantly and leans into the car. "Hi ladies," he greets everyone warmly.

"Hey, Hooks," Sade sings.

"Hi Mr. Washington," Leigh replies, grinning.

Of course, Paige has to state her observation out loud. "You're much taller than I expected."

I give her an exasperated look before turning to Randall. "Randall, this is my annoying and *sometimes* sophisticated sister Paige. You can clearly tell she is Sade's mother."

He extends his hand. She grabs his arm instead and walks him away from the car, but is still talking loudly enough for me to hear her.

"Excuse Danielle's manners," she tells him. "Let me ask you, what's the meaning of the parking sign?" she blatantly inquires.

Randall looks back to make sure I noticed the sign. I give him a wink and a smile. He replies honestly, "I wanted to make sure Danielle has a permanent parking spot whenever she's here."

In chorus, all the girls repeat the word "permanent" in an intriguing tone of voice.

I shake my head and smile. Thankfully, the limo pulls up.

Randall speaks up. "Ladies, I hate to break up the party but we will be riding in separate cars."

I look at him as if to ask, "*Who made that decision?*" Then, I come to the conclusion that riding separately may be a good idea. After all, I'm sure the girls will have a discussion about the parking sign that I didn't want Randall to hear. Honestly, I didn't want to hear the discussion right then, either.

They rode in the Hummer Limo. Randall and I rode in the Maybach with a driver.

"I wasn't expecting this," I tell Randall. "We could have all gone to the play in the same car. I was fine with driving."

He rubs my hand, unfazed. "Sit back and relax." His suggestion was both soothing and imperative.

I let out a deep sigh. "I am pretty impressed with the sign," I admit.

"I hoped you would like it," Randall replies, smiling. "I wasn't sure what color the rose should be, so I ordered a white one, pink one, a yellow one, and a red one."

I smirk. "Well, if you're indirectly asking me the meaning of rose colors, then you may have selected the wrong one. But that's okay. No one will know what it means, anyway."

I could tell he was making a mental note to research the meaning of roses. "If you want that color rose on the parking sign to stay there, I'll use the rest of the roses at the restaurant," he says.

"You're not there that often," I remind him.

"I've never had a reason to go there often. Now I do. We have to eat," Randall replies casually.

"Well, you actually go there to drink smoothies and snack on fresh fruit. I think I am the only one of us who actually eats," I taunt him.

"Oh, stop it," he laughs heartily.

We arrive at the play and are escorted up to the playhouse from the underground parking lot. The usher takes us to our seats—which are much better than the ones I originally reserved. I wonder how in the world Randall had time to make these arrangements.

He leans over and hands Sade and envelope. He tells her, "You're in charge of the public relations department tonight."

"Huh?" she responded confused. I have to admit, I wasn't sure what he meant either.

"I will not be signing autographs this evening," Randall said coolly. "You can give these to the people who request an autograph."

Sade opens the envelope to find five hundred glossy five by seven signed photographs. "Hooks, I'm selling these," she tells him matter-of-factly.

Randall throws up his hands. "Like I said—you're in charge. Do what you think is best. Just use the money for a good cause." He looks at the bodyguard and driver and gives them simple instructions. "Please make sure no one takes pictures tonight. I just want to have a regular night out with friends," Randall orders politely.

The men nodded, almost as if they were going to enjoy turning Randall's fans away.

Randall turns to me and the girls and says, "Ladies, can I get you all anything?"

We all place orders for sodas and water. Randall, the driver and the bodyguard disappear to get our beverages.

Paige leans close to me and whispers, "I like him a lot." An unusual comment for Paige.

"Me too," I whisper back.

"He's nothing like what I expected. I see how you misconstrued who he was," Paige continues. "I think he's a great guy."

"I concur," I tell her, smiling. Then reality sets back in. "But..." my voice trails off.

"But what?" Paige asks.

"He's still married." I sadly confess to her.

Giving back my same tone she ask. "So what are you two going to do?"

"We're just going to be friends for now, until he's able to get a divorce," I reply, sounding slightly defeated.

"I hope this works for you Dani," Paige says sincerely squeezing my arm.

"Me too, Sissie. Me too." She can see that I really mean it, but chose to lighten the mood a little.

"Don't get all mushy on me," she teases, pinching my cheeks. I smile and swat her hand away.

When the play ends, we make our way through the crowd and back to the car. It's obvious that people want to ask for autographs, but they are intimidated by the bodyguards. If Sade sees anyone looking especially disappointed or looking at Randall for more than a few seconds, she hands them a picture.

Randall is holding my hand and pulling me slightly to hurry us away from the crowd. Sade is in front of us, walking side by side with one of the bodyguards; Leigh and Paige are behind us with another bodyguard. The other two men assigned to protect us are racing to the car doors to open them before any fans have a chance to talk to Randall.

Once we get to the car, Randall says, "Ladies, would you like to grab dinner?"

"Yeah," we say in unison.

"Where to?" The driver asks. Of course, I direct the driver to Mikey's.

There's no place to park the limo when we arrive at the restaurant. "Just pull up to the curb," I tell the driver.

When we all walk in, Mikey yells, "Well, look what the cat dragged in! And just so you know, if you park a car on my curb, it becomes my car," he teases.

I roll my eyes at him. "Just fix our food," I say, laughing.

"Did you call an order in?" Mikey asks, trying to appear indignant.

I ignore him. "You know what we all want."

He looks over to Randall and says. "You are going to ruin your reputation hanging out with this bunch," he warns him with a smile.

Randall smiles back. "I'll take my chances." The two men shake hands. After we finish eating Randall looks over at me and announces, "It's getting late."

I nod. "Thanks for the ride, the sign, the play and dinner," I tell him.

He shrugs and grins. "I didn't do anything. This was all your idea."

Back at the gym, Randall and I share a short but intense hug (people are watching) and the ladies and I get in my car.

"You can kiss her in front of us," Paige speaks up.

He leans in closer to me, but addresses Paige's comment and says, "That will certainly happen one day—but not tonight."

The girls and I talk and laugh all the way home. Once I enter the house I text Randall to let him know I've arrived safely.

> I'm home-thanks again. My girls really like you. So does Mikey. And that's a HUGE compliment.

> I had a lot of fun with them too. I'm glad they like me but what do YOU think of me? That's what really matters.

I decide to evade the question and reply, Are you home yet?

No

Are you on your way home?

Well I wasn't but I guess I should be.

I inquire further, And why were you not on your way home?

I wasn't sleepy yet so I was going to punch a few bags at the gym.

I text him imperatively. GO HOME!

Will do.

Less than an hour later, I've showered, flipped on the TV and was logging onto my email accounts when Randall texted me to let me know he'd made it home.

And you didn't answer my question.

I responded coyly as if I didn't know what he was referring to. What question?

Do I need to call you?

I continue playing coy. Are you threatening me?

No but I would like an answer.

I can tell he's laughing. Yes

That's not a complete answer.

I can feel the warmth in his message.

I can't quite put the words together right now. But eventually I'll answer your question in detail.

What's the hold up?

I want to make sure I respond appropriately.

Good night.

I can tell he wants to know what I'm thinking but doesn't want to push me. Randall posts a blog at 3:46 in the morning. My phone beeps to notify me that his post has been published.

I've never known this side of life. All these years I thought I was at peace, but now I realize I was fighting--physically, mentally and emotionally. These past few weeks have shown me that I only need to fight inside the ring—not in life. I miss real life. I miss real friends. Real family and real fun.

I text him after I read his newest passage.

> Hopefully I can help you live a "real life"
> one day. I hope this answers your question.

Week 11

Monday

Monday was an intense day at work. Nothing went as planned! It was so stressful that Leigh and I tapped into the 'Hooks fund' and went out to lunch. Randall called a few times. I took the opportunities to tell him how much my day sucked.

"I'm sorry. Is there anything I can do?" he kindly offered.

"I wish there was," I answered. I quickly followed up with, "No presents please." Seconds later, I thought to myself, *why did I say that? Who doesn't want presents?*

"Will I see you this evening?" Randall asked.

"You know where I'll be. Gosh, you're such a stalker," I tease him.

I sensed the concern in his voice. "I hope your day gets better."

"I can't imagine them working me any harder," I tell him, letting out an aggravated sigh.

Randall laughs. "Well, you know what the Word says. A man that works hard eats. That applies for women, too."

"I guess you don't work hard since you never eat," I retort. I managed to get through the day. Around 4:00 PM, I told Leigh it was time to go. She almost fainted. I went home, changed into my workout clothes, and was at the track by 5:30. As usual, I was working while walking, checking emails, and inputting important tasks on my calendar. Randall and his crew hadn't arrived yet. I actually got more done on the track than I had all day in the office.

Around 6:15, the vans pulled up. When I passed by Randall I told him, "You're late!"

Randall scoffed. "Well, hello to you, too," he said then asked. "How long have you been here?"

"Long enough to think you weren't coming," I tell him.

He points at my mobile devices. "Give 'em up," he says squarely.

"What!?" I ask, trying to play innocent.

Randall rolls his eyes at me. "You know."

I try to run from him. He grabs me. My heart jumps out of my chest. He reaches out his hands for my phones. I give him one.

He shakes his head in disapproval. "The other one, too," he demands.

I hold the device close to me. "I won't look at it," I promise. Randall ignores me and continues to outstretch his hand. I take my time, but finally pass the phone to him. "Can I at least keep my iPod?" I ask.

He smiles and nods. "You can keep that. Do I need to search you?"

"You're so mean," I pout as I walk away to continue my workout.

"Have a good walk," Randall says sweetly.

"So you want me to just walk for an hour without anything else to keep me occupied? How boring!" I'm slightly aggravated, but I know Randall is trying to get me to establish more balance in my life. *And yes, you can search me.* I think to myself.

"You've had way too many distractions lately," Randall says seriously.

"I know," I tell him thinking that he was the major distraction.

"You can't concentrate," he continues.

"I'm fine."

"That's obvious," he says, giving me a quick glance.

I laugh at his comment, hoping I'm not blushing as he takes off running.

As I walk around the bend closer to Randall and he says, "You may want to let your 'friend' know that I'm a lover---and a fighter. I do fight. I can fight and I will fight!"

I knew he was referring to the African guy that I always engage in friendly banter with when I'm on the track. "I detect a little jealousy," I respond with a smirk.

"I detect a little disrespect," Randall retorts, eyeing the guy. The man has been shamelessly looking in my direction since he got to the track.

I continue to walk the track and get to a point where I'm close to my "walking buddy." He trots up to me and says, "I think your...love interest is getting upset," he says, trying to hold back a laugh. "He's not that insecure—is he?"

"Oh, stop," I say, trying to laugh it off. "You're a mess."

"Be careful.....I think he is a stalker." he winks and sprints away.

I take a few more steps before Randall runs up to me. He gets close enough to me to say sternly but softly, "Tell your boy to back up before I have to f**k him up." The authority in his voice is both attractive and jolting.

"Wow!" I say, startled. "I don't think I've ever heard you speak in this tongue before! I thought you said you were a lover. Leave the trash-talking in the boxing ring," I tell him.

Truthfully, I was elated that Randall was so jealous. He stayed by my side to walk a lap around the track with me. When we passed my "friend," both men were silent. Randall felt sure that he'd gotten his message across and started to run a little ahead of me. I could see the TVs playing on the sides of Randall's van. I walked up to my car, selected a CD, and put it into the van stereo so I could hear it while I completed my workout.

The upbeat sounds of Justin Bieber made me pick up my speed. Then I hear Usher's voice on the next track, which motivates me even more. And of course, no playlist is complete without a song or two from my favorite rapper T.I. By this time I was warmed up and maintaining a steady pace. The music was helping—but honestly, Randall's display of manliness was especially effective when it came to today's workout.

Apparently, Randall looked at me long enough to see that I was running instead of jogging or walking briskly. He turned to a guy from his team and said, "Stop her, please," in an annoyed tone of voice.

Randall's trainer, whose name I think is King, comes up to me. He grabs my wrists and puts a pedometer device on me before running off. I can't help but slow down a bit. I stare at the device as though it's a house-arrest bracelet. By the time I encounter Randall on the other side of the track, I've slowed down to a walk, thoroughly confused as to why I'm wearing this small monitor. I throw up my arms in irritation once I get a few feet away from Randall to show him that I'm both aggravated and perplexed by this gadget.

He laughs. When I get close enough to hear him, he tells me, "It's for your protection."

"Protection? From what?" I inquire.

"Don't take it off," Randall instructs me.

Randall has officially thrown my workout off. I continue walking and get close to my African workout buddy. The man is on the side of the track doing abdominal exercises. As if he needed to. "You should work on your abs," he tells me.

I shake my head. "Not today," I tell him.

He glances at Randall, "Maybe another day, huh?" he says with a little scoff.

I ignore him and continue on. Randall is suddenly right behind me on my right; his trainer appears on my left.

"Danielle," Randall says sternly. I look back at him.

"What part don't you understand?" Randall asks.

"About...?" I respond with my brow creased.

"About that friend of yours," Randall answers, nodding toward the African runner.

"Would you relax?" I say rolling my eyes. "You seem angry. We're all just here to work out."

"I'm not angry," Randall said softly. Maybe he was trying not to be angry, but he was clearly bothered.

"I told you, save that aggression for the ring," I reminded him.

"You're not prepared to see how I operate in the ring," Randall retaliates.

"Oh no?" I ask. "And why is that?"

"Just trust me on this one," he responds bluntly. "It's something you're not ready to witness."

"Oh, please," I laugh. "I could take you in the ring myself," I tease him. "Any time." I sucker punch him in the arm and increase my pace so I can run ahead of him.

King shows up again, at my side. "Are you tired yet?" The trainer asks.

"No," I tell him. He completely ignores me.

"Well, you should slow down if you plan on running a little longer," he instructs me.

"Okay," I mumble. I feel like a child being forced to take direction. I know Randall is trying to protect me (or so he says) but I'd like my work out to be a little more enjoyable.

I run past Randall again and stick my tongue out at him. After a few minutes, I hear a lot of noise behind me and see that Randall and his crew have gathered on the track. When I get back around to them, I stop abruptly.

I can't believe what I'm seeing. Randall is creating a makeshift boxing ring—right there in the grass! I continued to run around the track, shaking my head. Suddenly, I hear a beeping noise. It's the device on my wrist. I try to ignore the alert, but to no avail. Randall "magically" appears right next to me.

"Can't you hear it beeping, Dani?" he asks pointing to the device.

"Sure do," I reply with mock enthusiasm.

"The device sounded to indicate that your heart rate is up," Randall tells me.

"Okay," I say not seeing his point.

"That means you need to slow down," Randall says in a fatherly tone.

I'm slightly irritated. "How can you even hear it from over there?" I ask.

"I can't," Randall explains. "King's monitor registers your heart rate. That's how I knew your workout was getting too intense. You can't run this hard for this long. Not until your body gets more accustomed to working out that way."

"I'm fine," I respond, a little defensively.

"Yes, I know. It's obvious to everyone," Randall says with a flirty smirk but implying it is also obvious to the runner too.

I'm not in the mood for his flirts. I change the subject. "What's up with the boxing ring in the middle of the track?" I question him.

"You challenged me to a fight in the ring—did you not?" he inquired, smiling a little wider.

I roll my eyes. "So, am I to understand that you're always prepared for a challenge by traveling with items that can create a boxing ring no matter where you are?"

He rolled his eyes in return and retorts, "Don't you always travel with a laptop or electronic device of some sort?"

I scoff. "I'll take your extremely sarcastic answer to my question as a "yes.'"

Even though I didn't want to fully admit it, my body was getting a little tired. I slowed down my pace. Randall and I began walking side by side toward the 'boxing ring.' He jumped in and started throwing practice punches with King. I sat on the grass for a few seconds before someone from Randall's team offered me a lawn chair and a bottle of water.

"Hey, jump in," Randall says, motioning for me to come into the ring.

I look around and point to myself. As if he could be talking to anyone else.

"Yeah you, trash talker," he answers laughing.

I climb in the ring without saying a word.

"Let me show you how it's done." I can tell Randall is going to enjoy "teaching" me how to box.

He stood behind me and put his wrapped hands around my arms to guide my punches.

I said, "Where I'm from this ain't how we fight."

"I can't imagine you ever fighting," he says gently admiring my hands. A huge contrast from his aggressive boxing moves.

I laugh a little. "Little do you know, I had to fight a lot growing up."

He looks shocked. "Really? What was your strategy?"

"Cover with the left jab and then hit em' with the right. Then keep hitting until I knock my opponent out!" I tell him.

"In that case, I'm sure you won your fair share of fights," he says. "But I know you started a few of them, too."

He turned me around and said, "Stand here." Randall proceeded to give me a lot of helpful pointers on boxing and self-defense. My wrist heart monitor began to beep. Randall's trainer looked up from his laptop when he heard the alarm. Randall and I both clearly knew what was going on. He was too close to me and my heart rate shot through the roof. Actually, I think his increased, too. I felt--and could see--the change in the structure of his shorts. I was glad to know I wasn't the only one who was slightly embarrassed. Only the two of us knew what was actually happening— thank God. We laughed and fell to the mat, laughing like guilty children.

"Told you I would win," I say through my laughter.

"Who said you won?" he chuckled.

"You're on the mat aren't you?"

"Not because you won," he assures me.

"Well, how come, then?" I ask.

"Because your monitor was going off," he says, nodding toward my wrist.

I look down slyly and remind him, "I think your antenna was up, mister."

He put his glove over my mouth and we wrestle like two lion cubs engaged in play.

His trainer interrupts us. "Guys, what are you having for dinner?"

"I'll take my usual," Randall says, almost out of breath.

We climb down from the ring and his crew untapped Randall's hands. I look at the process in disbelief. "Dang, that's a lot of tape."

"Yeah, I know. You don't want me to break my wrist, do you?" He asks with a wink.

"I sure don't," I tell him with a smile.

We walk arm in arm away from the track. After today, I've developed a new love for boxing. We get to our cars. Tonight Randall is in his silver-colored Chevrolet Silverado. Of course the plate reads HVYWGHT. He let the tailgate down so we can sit on the back and drink our liquid dinner, stare at the stars and engage in conversation. Everyone else has left the track but us.

I surprised myself by saying out loud, "I feel like we should be making out." After our romp in the ring, it was hard to keep denying our physical attraction to each other.

Randall was a little surprised too—pleasantly so. He said, "You feel like it?"

"Yeah, we are here at the high school like school kids."

He sighed. "Well, I feel like it too--and God knows I want to--but we can't."

"I guess you're right. We're too sweaty anyway."

He laughed. "And on that note, we should leave before we both get into trouble."

I knew Randall was right—even though I didn't want him to be. I wanted to kiss him. But I knew the affection wouldn't stop there.

He opened my car door. "I'll talk to you until you get home," he said.

"Are you going home?" I ask.

He looks at me a little strangely. "Where else would I go?"

"To the gym." I say sarcastically.

"The gym, church, and home are the only places I go," Randall replied with a shrug.

"So are you going home?" I inquire again.

Randall begins to confess. "Actually, I was planning on going…"

I knew it! He was headed to the gym. "HOME!" I interrupted him quickly.

He feigned disappointment. "I guess I'm going home."

I give him an approving smile. "Drive safe."

"You too."

He closed my door. I pulled off. I really wished we were going home together.

Tuesday

I arrived at work before the sun rose. I was working steadily by the time Leigh arrived. "We called you all night!" Leigh said, both irritated with me and relieved that I was all right.

"Oh sorry. I didn't even check the messages. I was working out." I was uncharacteristically nonchalant.

"All night?" she asked suspiciously.

I nod slowly. "Kind of."

"I don't want to know any more," she said, shaking her head rapidly and throwing her hands up.

I laughed. "It wasn't like that. We hung out at the track talking."

Leigh winked. "Umm hmm. I believe you."

At 9:20 AM I got a text message from Randall.

> Good morning I need to see you as soon as possible. I also have something to give you.

> Good morning. Okay.

> I'll call you.

My office phone rings immediately after I get the text. "Dani Ro," I answer.

It's Randall. "Hi Danielle. So, this present I have to give you isn't the type of gift you're probably expecting. You may not even appreciate it, but I need you to trust me."

Well, he had certainly taken some of the fun out of receiving a gift, but I knew he was serious. "I'll meet you at the gym at six," I tell him. When I get to the gym, a couple of the men from Randall's training team are unwrapping his hands. Once he sees me, he says, "Hey" cheerfully and walks over to give me a bear hug.

"Hi," I say warmly, returning his embrace.

"I've missed you. Come into my office," he replies, walking just ahead of me.

His "office" was the size of a condo. He pulls out a box. I open it. There is a watch inside.

"Let me explain my gift and give you a few instructions," Randall says. "It's actually a tracking and monitoring device."

"What are you, some type of international spy?" I ask him jokingly but I was really thinking this is stalking!

He doesn't even crack a smile. "Seriously, Dani. I wear the same type of device."

I still want him to lighten up. "Well, I must say, I'm a little disappointed. After all, this is a far cry from a Presidential Rolex like the one you wear on Sundays."

Randall continues with his explanation noting I pay close attention. "I hope this fits. The large dial is the functioning clock. You can also use three other dials. The green dial is the locator. When you touch this green button, it sends your location to me and to the security team. The yellow dial illuminates when the device cannot locate you. If you are too far underground, on a plane or in a vaulted room or any location where you can't easily be detected, the device won't send a signal. If you press the red button on your watch, this will send a signal to me and the security that you're in trouble. Either the yellow or the green arms of the watch will light up once you activate the red button. If the watch arms are green, it means we're able to locate you. If the arms turn yellow, this is a sign that we can't find where you are. The closer our team gets to you, the faster the red dials will move."

"If you're in immediate danger, press the red button three times. It will notify the nearest police station. If you're home or at work and don't want to be located, press the green button until it beeps. The arms will stop moving, showing that your location can no longer be detected. Press the button again and the arms on the dial will begin to move once you're active again. Did you get all that?"

I was a little dazed but tried to take in everything Randall was saying. "Umm…I think so."

Randall showed me his wrist. "My watch is like yours, except I have six dials. I have three dials for emergency purposes, and now I have your three dials to track your activity. You can wear the watch I just gave you every day. It's water-resistant for as deep as three hundred meters."

I guess Randall could tell that I started to look concerned, so he continued explaining the reason for his gift to put me at ease. "I've never had to use mine in an emergency before. I hope you never have to either, but I'll feel better if you would oblige me by wearing this. I didn't know if you wanted a necklace, belt, charm bracelet, or watch. I can have whatever you want made. If you want this with a metal band instead of leather I can have that arranged."

I smile. "I think this is fine. It looks like something from an *Inspector Gadget* episode, but its fine."

He chuckled softly. "I hope that's a good thing. Oh, one other thing--I need to program your phones."

Again, I'm surprised. "With?" I ask.

And once again, Randall goes into a thorough explanation. "When you're texting me to let me know you're home or notifying me of your whereabouts, I need you to copy this address. The message then goes to a transmitter that will be able to track you if necessary."

I can feel myself rolling my eyes. Randall quickly continues talking. "I know this sounds crazy and annoying. I'm not trying to invade your privacy. I want to make sure you are safe. I know you leave out very early and I want to know you're okay. I will not use this for any other purpose other than to monitor your safety. You don't have to wear it if you don't want to. But I would feel much better if you do so."

My face sent the message that I still wasn't sure about all this. "You can try it and tell me what you think. Tell me if you like it or you hate it or you wish it did this or did that. Whatever you want, I can make happen," Randall said assuring.

"I'm not sure if mine works now that I have added your device to mine. I've worn this device for more than a decade. This leather band is longer than a wristband, so you can wear the alarm system on other parts of your body like your neck, waist, thigh, ankle, or underneath your clothing. For instance, if you were somewhere like an awards dinner and you didn't want to wear this watch with your dress you can move it to another location on your body. However, you would need to have it on so that the device can work to accurately transmit a signal while you're in a public place. If you encounter an unsafe situation, simply pull up your formal clothing and press the panic button. If you find yourself in danger, I think having to pull up your dress for a few seconds would be the least of your concerns." He hands me a long leather band and emphasizes what he told me a few minutes earlier.

"If you don't like it and want to order something else we can. Just please, try it out, and tell me what you think. We can have other pieces made. Say for instance you want the device to look like a phone or earpiece, we can definitely do that."

My intuition promptly notified me that his wife didn't have one of these safety devices, because he wasn't as concerned with her safety as he was mine. I was flattered now instead of shocked and peeved. Plus, I liked electronic gadgets and Randall knew that. However, my intuition also informed me that I needed to make sure my feelings of flattering were warranted. "Who else have you given a safety device like this to?" I asked him.

"I have one, and so do my bodyguards and security," Randall responded. "My lawyer and accountant can also gain access to the data on these devices via the Internet."

I was satisfied with that answer. I played with my new present all night to learn how it operated. I felt like a child on Christmas night.

Wednesday

I worked out to a DVD before heading out for work. I stopped by a site to see how things were coming along, then headed to the office. I looked at the watch Randall gave me all day. I guess I wanted to make sure it was really working. But, I didn't really know exactly what I was looking for.

Randall and I talked several times throughout the day. He asked if I liked the watch and if it was working fine. I texted him to ask if he could tell my location when I got to a site downtown. He responded by telling me the street I was on, along with the directional coordinates. The device even worked when I got in an elevator below ground at the construction site.

I decided that I liked this gadget. I left work at a decent hour to make it to bible study. Pastor Hunter's message was just what I needed to hear—as it often was. After the benediction, Randall hugged me, rested his face on my forehead, and said, "Wait for me." I waited in my normal seat. I noticed King, Randall's trainer, was there. I wasn't sure if he was there to observe me or simply came as Randall's guest. Either way it was fine. When Randall returned back to where I was sitting, he looked exhausted. "Hey, what's wrong?" I asked.

"I think I'm tired," Randall said between pants.

I looked at him closely. "Your eyes are red."

"Are they?" he asked surprised. "I better get some rest tonight."

"Promise?" I asked.

Randall nodded obediently. "Promise."

I wanted to make sure he was serious. "No blogging, no punching, no running?" I inquired.

He was so tired that he squatted on the side of my car and leaned over in the window while muttering, "I feel like a punk—,and it's all your fault."

I laugh. "Oh whatever. Even though you may be tired, you're looking especially tasty. Chocolate-y, even," I tell him flirtatiously.

"I know," he grinned. "I've been getting a lot of sun lately. There's this chick that has me out chasing her in the sun. She seems to like warm weather," he responds with a wink.

My smile is as wide as can be. "Is she worth it?" I ask.

"Oh, absolutely," Randall replies quickly. "But I own a gym. I don't understand why she won't work out there."

I raise an eyebrow. "Have you invited her?"

"I thought it was clear that she is invited anytime. What is mine is hers." The look in Randall's eyes is especially caring.

"Does that hold true for the Maybach and the Phantom?" I ask laughing.

"Umm…" Randall answers playfully.

"Oh, you have to think about it?!" I say playfully pushing his shoulder.

He laughs. "I'm tired--but not that tired."

"You said what's yours is mine," I tell him with a shrug.

"Yeah but those two cars? I don't think so," Randall says, shaking his head.

I pretend to be hurt and whine, "Well, why not?"

"You don't want to drive either of those," he tells me.

I remind him of his words again. "You did say what is mine is yours. Correct?"

"Let me just buy you a Bentley or a Benz," he offers. I knew that he wasn't bluffing either. But I had to hold my ground to prove a point.

"No. Let me hold the Bach or the Phantom." I turn away from him slightly to indicate that he should be trying harder to make me feel better. Just then, one of the church members walks by.

"Deac, she got you outside begging on your knees in your suit," the guy says, laughing as he walks by.

Randall chuckled. "I know. I don't understand why she treats me like this," he says, shooting me a pitiful look.

The guy smiles. "Man you got to do better. You are making it hard for the rest of us."

"And I am begging to buy her a car!" Randall tells the man, trying to form a masculine alliance.

"For what?" The man asks. "She's riding pretty clean now. What does she want, man?"

What a loaded question. Randall and I look at each other and try to keep from bursting into laughter.

Thursday

Work was going well. I was stuck in my office designing plans, but I didn't mind. All of a sudden, a meeting request pops up on my calendar for Thursday at 6:00 PM--a meeting with Pastor Hunter. *Wow, what is this about?* I wonder. *Maybe it's normal for the pastor to want to meet with new members. But he definitely didn't give me much notice. He wants to have a meeting less than eight hours from now!* I look at the meeting request again. *Well, maybe I can reschedule the meeting if I need to, I reason.* I accept the request. *After all, how bad can it be?* I think to myself. *He probably wants to know about my involvement at my previous church and encourage me to be more active in ministry.*

I arrive at the church at a quarter till six. "Good evening," I say to the church clerk.

"Good evening. May I help you?" The clerk replies.

"I'm Danielle Rose--here for Pastor Hunter."

The clerk smiles. "Sure, right this way. They're expecting you."

"They?" I ask.

"Yes, Pastor Hunter, and Deacon Washington."

Whoa. What is going on here? I pull my phone out to make sure I didn't miss the fact that Randall would be at this meeting. I don't see anything in the meeting request pertaining to 'Deacon Washington.' My mind immediately starts filling with questions. What is this meeting actually about? I almost felt like cancelling, but it was clearly too late.

I had spoken to Randall several times before today, and he never mentioned anything about a meeting with the pastor. Things were happening too fast for me to try to sort them out now. I walk into the room where Randall and Pastor Hunter are sitting. Both men stand to greet me as the clerk announces my entrance.

Randall looks just as surprised as I am, which makes me think he knows less about this meeting than I thought. He takes both of my phones from my hand and gives them to the clerk. "We'll pick these up on the way out," he tells her. I was irritated with this, but decided not to show it.

"Good evening." Pastor Hunter said.

"Hi." I responded shortly.

"Let's pray," he says gently.

This is getting stranger by the minute. The pastor clearly has very little to say to me, and I don't remember Randall saying hello. I've been called into lots of offices before. I've even been called before a judge. But I've never been called into a pastor's office. What does all of this mean?

Pastor Hunter starts praying. "Father, we come before you humbly, thanking you for your grace and mercy. We are grateful for all that You have done. We thank you for this day and for the opportunity for us to fellowship in Your name. Father, we ask that you dwell among us as we come together for the business of the Kingdom."

I opened my eyes slightly and peek around. I was waiting on someone to say that this was all some sort of practical joke. I tapped Randall's foot as a non-verbal way to ask him what this was all about. He looked at me shrugged his shoulders. I rolled my eyes. He may not have known all the reasons for this meeting, but I was convinced he knew more than he was telling me.

I missed the last few sentences of the prayer. The next thing I heard was the pastor saying "Amen." Randall echoed the pastor with an "Amen." I waited silently with my eyes open, trying to figure out what was happening. Then I realized the prayer was not "complete" until I said Amen also. "Amen," I muttered.

Pastor Hunter observed the matching confused looks Randall and I had on our faces. "Neither of you were aware that the other was going to be here?" The pastor asked.

Randall and I looked at each other again before he answered. "No, I didn't know she was going to be here," he told the pastor. I could hear the shock in Randall's voice, which made me a little less peeved with him.

Pastor Hunter continued. "Shocking, I thought you two would have had a discussion. I guess you're wondering why I called you two in today."

"Yes, as a matter of fact I am curious," I said, rather curtly.

Pastor Hunter turned to me and replied, "Well, I want to talk to you about your relationship."

"With whom?" I replied abruptly.

He sat up in his chair and pointed at Randall and me. "With each other," he answered. I was pretty sure my shortness caught Pastor Hunter by surprise. I was hoping it occurred to him that this meeting caught me by surprise.

"We aren't in a relationship," I told the pastor coolly. It was clear, however, that I was annoyed.

Randall intervened. "Let me handle this," he said, looking at me. He turned to Pastor Hunter and said, "Pastor, we are friends."

"I just wanted to confirm that," Pastor Hunter said with a slight smile. "I'd also like to counsel you two."

Now I was more than irritated. I was upset. "Why didn't your meeting request say anything about counseling?" I asked the pastor. Turning to Randall, I said, "And thanks, Deacon Washington but I can hold my own-- even with Pastor." I cut my eyes at them both. I could sense that Pastor Hunter found my attitude a little amusing.

The pastor ignored my question. "Guys, I just want to make sure you all are doing things decently and in order. I think you two are great people and I want other people to look upon you the same way. Deacon, you hold a great position here in the church, and Danielle, I am looking forward to what is yet to come from you. I have contacted your former Pastor and he was very saddened to lose your membership, talents, and gifts."

Now the pastor was looking directly at me. I was nervous to hear what he would say next. "I've reviewed your engineering accolades and they are remarkable. I can tell from Hooks' new positive disposition that you've made a great impression on him." I was beginning to soften up. But I was still skeptical about this meeting. Pastor Hunter kept talking. "Hooks, I can clearly understand why you would be attracted to Ms. Rose. She's beautiful, smart, and God-fearing. And Ms. Rose, what woman wouldn't fall for Hooks? Ms. Rose, I know your affection for Randall is sincere and that you have no ulterior motives for wanting to get to know him. I just want to make sure that you all are following the Word of God in terms of growing closer to one another."

"We are," Randall responded, nodding his head. "Pastor we are friends. Nothing more. We are following the Word," he said reassuringly.

Randall looked at me. Mainly because he knew I really wanted to comment on the "nothing more" statement he had just made. But now was not the time.

I spoke up. "Pastor Hunter. Randall and I are friends. I am aware of Randall's situation and I have to trust what he has told me is accurate in his divorce petition."

Randall nodded his head in confirmation before talking to the pastor again. "Pastor, I have shared with Dani everything I've disclosed to you. She has a copy of the all the divorce information. I have been extremely open and honest with her. Yes, we have hung out. We enjoy each other's company and yes, I would love to be more than her friend. As a matter of fact, I would love for her to be my wife. I am working diligently to resolve my divorce. What do you suggest I do?" he asked.

I decided that Randall made up for his previous comment about us being "nothing more than friends." I actually wanted to squeal with delight about the fact that he had basically told the pastor he wanted to marry me. But it was too early to let my guard down. After all, Pastor Hunter reiterated some serious issues that Randall and I still had to deal with.

I had definitely softened and wanted to let Pastor Hunter know that I was no longer aggravated, now that I understood the nature of our meeting. "Pastor, I appreciate your concern. The fact that you wanted to talk to Randall and me says a lot about how seriously you take your leadership position. However, I feel that this may be more of a conversation for you and Deacon Washington."

"Well, I wanted you to be here as well. I want to know how you feel," the pastor responded.

"Feel about what?" I asked.

"About you and Deacon Washington," he said casually.

I could feel myself blushing a little. "I'm not sure what you're expecting me to say. But yes, I like Randall. I like him as a person and as a potential mate." I had to be honest. I was in church, and I was talking to a pastor. I couldn't just blatantly lie. "I think Randall is a caring man. He has a great sense of humor, and yes, I'm attracted to him."

I could see Randall trying to minimize his grin, which made me want to give him a huge hug. But again, I had to restrain myself. I continued talking to Pastor Hunter. "But yes, Pastor, I do understand that Randall is still married. That's why we're only friends. We have not been intimate. Randall has been the perfect gentleman and hasn't made any unfriendly advances toward me. We haven't even kissed." I couldn't believe how honest I was being. But since we were having a meeting about our situation, I figured I might as well be as forthcoming as possible.

I went on. "Honestly, Pastor Hunter, I would like for things to be different between Deacon Washington and me. In addition, yes, Randall's attorney has provided copies of all the divorce petition information. I have spoken with his attorney. All I can do is be his friend until things change. I sincerely want Randall to do what he feels is best for his family and am not trying to selfishly sway his decision. If Randall were to tell me he and his wife decided to reconcile, I would definitely be disappointed—devastated, even. However, I would hope for the best for him and would not stand in the way. Pastor, you said yourself that I am a God-fearing woman. That means I know enough to know an intimate relationship between Randall and me would not be appropriate at this time. Yes, it is a struggle. I am being completely transparent here, and I will tell you it is difficult, Pastor. On one hand, I am very impressed by the fact that you wanted to meet with Randall and me. But on the other hand, I want to make sure I'm not being judged or having to defend myself for something that hasn't taken place. No, I am not perfect. Yes, I have sinned and fallen short of the glory of God. Every time I see Randall, I sin because I lust with my eyes. I repent and ask God for forgiveness and I try it all over again the next day. And every day, it gets harder for me to resist Randall. What is there not to be attracted to? What about him would a woman not like? I am sorry that I feel this way. I pray for strength daily. I ask God to strengthen my strength."

I sit back in the chair as if I have taken control of the meeting. I let out a deep breath and look at the pastor with a smug grin. Who does Pastor Hunter think he is, calling a meeting as though he's about to chastise me? I wanted to clearly convey to the pastor that he'd never get away with trying to make me look foolish, even if his "exposure" was cleverly disguised as concern. But once again, this was not the time.

Both Randall and Pastor Hunter were shocked at my soliloquy. Randall looked at Pastor Hunter and then moved his chair so he could look directly into my eyes. He said, "Danielle, I feel the same way. Actually, I love you." Obviously, we both had a lot to get off our chests and it was now confession time.

Pastor Hunter interrupted abruptly. "Deacon, let me stop you right there," the pastor said hastily, leaning over almost tearing up his desk to indicate he didn't want Randall to say anything else that may incriminate him.

"What exactly is holding up the divorce?" The pastor asked.

Randall shrugged and said, "Pastor, my wife is delaying the divorce intentionally and I have no idea why!"

"What has her attorney said?" Pastor Hunter inquired.

Randall let out an aggravated sigh. "A bunch of garbage and excuses. I can show it to you later," he told the pastor.

I reach for my cell phone. "Actually, Pastor, if you hand me my phone, I can forward the information to you." Randall reminds me the pastor's assistant has my electronic devices.

Fortunately for Randall, I have a solution. I reach down in my bag and pull my mini laptop out. I log on. "Pastor what is your email address?" I ask, unfazed by the stunned looks I could feel from Pastor Hunter and Randall. The pastor told me where to send the document and I quickly forward it.

He does a quick scan through the email and exclaims, "Wow!"

Apparently Pastor Hunter's response triggers an indignant bout of irritation in him. Randall has been so patient about and surprisingly agreeable about the whole divorce situation. But the meeting with the pastor and my confession of my feelings for him prompt Randall to put his foot down.

"You know what, Pastor?" he started. "This has gone on too long. It has interfered with my life and my happiness. I am demanding the divorce be final by the end of the month. Then, I hope you'll give Danielle and me your blessing."

Randall comes closer to the pastor's desk and presses the speaker button on the phone. He dials a number and listens to it ring a few times before the call goes to voicemail. He hangs up and calls the number again. A young boy's voice comes through the phone.

"Hello?"

"Hey son," Randall replies.

"Hey dad," the voice answers.

"What's up?" Randall asks.

"Nothing." And by "nothing," Randall's son meant "everything." He went into detail about everything from school to friends to sports. Randall listened intently, relishing the sound of his son's voice. Pastor Hunter watched the conversation transpire with his hands folded on his desk. I looked down at the floor to avoid staring at Randall. But I was listening. Intently.

Randall smiled, but took on a more serious tone. "That's great, son. Where is your mom?"

"Watching TV."

"RJ, I need to speak to her please," Randall says sternly.

"Hold on," the boy responds cheerfully.

"Thank you," Randall answers warmly.

Minutes pass. It seems like hours.

All of a sudden, I hear a woman's voice say, "Hello" rather abruptly.

"Tameka," Randall responds

"What!" she nearly screamed.

Randall tries to keep his cool. "I have no need for small talk with you either," he tells her. I have never heard that tone of voice from him before. He continued. "I am fed up with your games, Tameka. You will need to sign the divorce papers before the end of this month. Take this as your last notification. You'll need to get the utilities activated in your name on the first day of next month. You'll also need to get your own insurance."

She disputed him by shouting words and phrases that were difficult to understand. Randall had no problem deciphering her words.

He spoke to her again in this new controlled but angry voice of his. "I am not doing this with you. Get the papers back to me as soon as possible."

"Whatever," Tameka responds before hanging up.

Randall turned to the pastor and me and pointed to the phone. "Do you see what I have to deal with?" he asked aggravated.

Pastor Hunter gets ready to respond. I sense this may need to be a private conversation between the pastor and Randall. "Do I need to leave?" I ask graciously.

Randall said quickly, "No, you're fine."

The two men talk about previous conversations they've had concerning Randall's wife. I listened. Then Pastor Hunter turned to me and said, "I hope I haven't offended you. I do hope you understand my position and my concern."

I looked up and nodded at him politely. But he understood through my body language that I was still perturbed.

Pastor Hunter asked me, "If I told you why I wanted to meet with you and Randall, would you have come?"

I wanted to say, "Hell no," but instead I calmly responded, "Probably not."

Pastor Hunter nodded. "My point exactly. Sometimes as your spiritual father I am going to have to chasten you and step on your toes. If I didn't, I wouldn't be doing my job. I hope you understand this is for your good, and for Deacon Hooks' benefit as well. I want to make sure you are both acting in a way that lines up with the will of God."

I give him an insincere smile. "Thank you for looking out for us," I say. "I appreciate it." Truly I did.

"Let's close with prayer." Pastor Hunter was careful to make his voice sound especially comforting and reassuring. The three of us hold hands around Pastor Hunter's desk.

I squeeze Randall's hand hard. I'm halfway hoping I break at least one of his fingers. Although I know that is wrong of me. His fingers are his livelihood. I'm still convinced he knew something about this meeting and didn't tell me.

As we are leaving the pastor's office, Randall asks, "What day can you go with me to see Daniel?"

I'm puzzled. "Who?"

"Daniel Khrittyleberrg."

"Who is that?" I ask.

Randall looks me square in the eyes to respond. "My attorney." I could tell he was a little aggravated that I didn't remember this bit of information, considering I had just pulled up the email containing the attorney's name with the email about his divorce proceedings in Pastor Hunter's office.

I tried to soften the conversation. "You pick the day," I told him. "But why do you need me?"

"I want you to be involved," he responded practically.

We had arrived at my car. We knew we were being watched so we hugged quickly and I pulled off. As usual, I couldn't sleep. But tonight, I couldn't stop thinking about the meeting that had taken place hours earlier.

Friday

I woke up in an extremely good mood. It was Friday—the end of the week. I was actually excited. As usual, I got to work before the sun was up. Surprisingly,

I was also thinking of a thank-you gift to send to Randall to express my gratitude. Even though I still believed he knew something about our meeting with the pastor beforehand, I could tell Randall was very serious about being with me.

I started searching online for the perfect gift. I wasn't sure what to get. I looked at music, books, event tickets, jewelry, clothes, shoes, and I still couldn't decide. Then I realized shoes and clothes were out, because I didn't know his measurements.

Something told me to check the Louis Vuitton website one more time. Then I saw it. The perfect gift. I would run over to the mall to pick it up as soon as it opened—in four hours. I decided I would get him the Champs Elysees Collection. I figured the Champ collection was fitting. I was hoping I could call Randall *my* 'Champ' pretty soon. I printed the page so I could use it as a reference when I went to the mall. I was having a hard time choosing between the black cuff links, the tiepin, or the Champs Gris tie. I wanted to hear Randall's voice, but it was still early. I looked at the watch device he gave me to double-check the time. I called anyway. Before I could stop myself, I heard the phone ringing in my ear.

"Hooks Gym," a voice answered.

I thought quickly. I was sure I had called Randall's personal phone.

"Good morning," I said slowly. "I'm sorry to call so early. I wanted to speak to Randall."

"Is this urgent, Ms. Danielle?" The voice asked.

I took a deep breath. "Actually, no."

"He is running now. Can he call you in an hour?"

"Sure, that will be fine."

Apparently Randall had taken a break. The voice said, "Wait one moment." I could hear him talking to Randall. "Hooks, Ms. Danielle is on the line. Should I tell her to call you back later?"

"Ask her if everything is okay," Randall responds. I knew he was looking at his wrist device to make sure there was no distress signal.

I could tell Randall was outside. I was sure I'd called his phone—not the gym. I was still confused.

"He said are you okay?" King asked me.

I tried to sound as calm as possible. I didn't want Randall to worry. "Yes, tell him I am fine. All I wanted was to tell him good morning and to have a great day."

"Gross," King replied. I snickered. I could hear him giving Randall the message. "Hooks, she wants to say have a good morning and a great day."

The smile in Randall's voice came right through the phone. "Tell her I said thank you. Tell her the same to her, and that I miss her dearly."

King came back to the line and asked me in fake disgust, "Did you hear that? I am not repeating it."

I laughed. "I heard Hooks talking but I could barely make out what he was saying." Of course I heard Randall clearly, but I just wanted to give King a hard time. Plus, I wanted to hear Randall's sweet message one more time.

King took a belabored breath and replied, "He said, Thank you. Same to her and I miss her dearly." he sighed heavily. "You've turned our heavyweight champion into a push-over," he told me.

"I didn't mean to," I answered, smiling.

King's voice was stern but playful. "Well make sure you help me keep him in the heavyweight category. We've worked hard to get him here."

"I'll do what I can," I assured him.

"If he keeps running like this every day he is going to fall back into the middleweight or lightweight category."

"How long has he been running?" I asked.

"We started at four."

"Four?" I checked my watch. It was 6:18 AM.

"Yep, we were running together. Now I'm in the truck driving beside him."

"Oh my Lord." I knew Randall was running primarily due to nervous energy.

"Tell me about it. He is going to have to stop before traffic begins."

I was getting a little concerned. "Will you make sure he calls me?"

"Will do."

"You have a good one too, King."

"Thanks Ms. Rose."

■■■

Leigh drags herself in the door and to her desk. "Good morning," she mumbles.

"Hey, mall at ten," I say cheerfully.

"Why so early?" she grumbled caring less about my field trip.

"Got to get Randall a present," I reply as I walk back into my office.

Leigh pulled at my blazer. "Oh no you don't, ma'am. Start explaining."

"There is nothing to explain," I say casually. "He has been so nice until I thought I should reciprocate."

"Reciprocate?" Leigh repeated, raising her eyebrow.

"Is something wrong with that?"

"You mean other than you lying? No," she replies.

"What am I lying about, Leigh?"

"Well, for starters, let's talk about that watch on your arm," she quips.

I stare at the device. "But how am I lying?" I ask again.

"Is it new?" she inquires.

"Huh?"

"You heard me. Is it new?"

"As far as I know."

"What in the hell does that mean?"

"It's from Randall," I tell her.

"You all are exchanging presents? Sounds like more than friends to me," she told me. I was having a hard time ignoring the judgmental tone in Leigh's voice.

"Technically, it is not a present," I tell her.

"What the hell is it?"

"It is a tracking device?"

Leigh's mouth dropped open. "A TRACKING DEVICE? Why would you need a tracking device?"

"In case I am in danger."

"You got those two feet, that big mouth, that bat and the blade you carry. We won't even get to what is in your bag, Madea." Leigh was practically yelling.

"Seriously?" I ask her.

"I am so serious. Why do you need it? Other than the fact that you two are stalking each other."

I try to explain the reason I'm wearing the wrist device calmly. "He feels it is for my safety since I'm out early and late by myself. He also gave me the watch in case we are ever together and someone may try to harm me to get to him."

Leigh shook her head. "That is complete BS. He gave you that watch to keep tabs on you—'friend.'"

"I'm not paying you any attention," I tell her, scoffing.

"That's because you're too busy allowing yourself to be tricked," Leigh answered.

I look directly at her. "Leigh, just be ready at ten so we can go to the mall." I continue talking to Leigh as I head to my office. "While you're busy telling me how naïve I am, could you call and make me an appointment at the spa today?"

Leigh didn't miss a beat. "And while we're on the subject of you being naïve, did you give him some?"

I stopped at my office door and turned around quickly. "Say what?" I asked, indignant.

Leigh shrugged. "Just asking."

■■■

The rest of the workday was a drag. My phone rang the very moment I returned, and all throughout the day. I was anxious to give Randall his presents. We spoke several times throughout the day. I told him we needed to talk right away. I could tell he was uneasy, but he agreed to meet me at the gym.

I had to admit I was a little tense too. I was looking forward to the spa appointment Leigh made for me. My massage was nice. I needed it. I don't know why but Randall really makes me nervous, even though we've spent lots of time together. I guess I feel so jittery because I like him. I have to admit, I was glad Randall was a little nervous too. For once, I felt like I had the upper hand.

As soon as I walked into the gym, King escorted me to Randall's office. I forgot just how awesome this office was. It looked more like a condo than an administrative space in a gym.

Randall came from around his desk and hugged me right away. He had a look of concern in his eyes and asked me, "Is everything alright?"

I smile, "Yes, everything is alright. How are you?"

"Fine," he said hurriedly. He didn't come across rudely, but I knew he wanted me to tell him why I was here. He caught himself and attempted to readjust his attitude. "How was your day?"

"It was good—how was yours?"

"Great," he said passively.

"Really? Great?" I asked.

"Yep," he replied.

"So why did you run for so long this morning?" I asked him.

"I felt like I needed to," he answered.

"Why?" I didn't want to pry (too much), but I really was curious.

Randall looks at me. He's trying really hard not to get aggravated. "It clears my mind and it gets me in shape. Also, it's my job."

"You seem a little upset," I say softly.

Randall makes his tone a little gentler. "No, I'm not upset. I'm just wondering what it is you want to talk to me about. I hope it doesn't upset me—but I have a feeling it will."

"Well, I hope not!" I say with a wide grin.

Randall gives me a smug grin. "We'll see."

"Relax," I say sweetly while passing him the shopping bag.

A smile spreads across Randall's handsome face. "What's this?"

"A thank-you gift," I tell him.

"For what?"

"All of the nice things you've done for me."

He sits down on the couch next to me. He looks in the bag and shakes his head. "You didn't have to do this," he says warmly. It's not even my birthday."

He opens the bag and takes the lid off the box. He looks at the gifts intently and thanks me after picking up each one. Randall lines all the gifts up on his desk and stares at them with an elated look on his face. Then his elation turned into a bit of disdain.

I touch his arm. "Are you okay?" I ask.

"I'm just trying to remember the last time someone gave me a gift for any occasion, let alone a "just because" present," he tells me. "Usually, the gift-giving thing is the other way around for me," he shares.

I was happy to finally see Randall pleasantly speechless. After all, Randall is a man who has everything. He also has the power to buy anything he wants, but was completely flattered that I thought enough of him to pick up a few items for him to express my gratitude. I actually had to fight back tears. I wasn't expecting him to be so touched.

Minutes pass, and Randall doesn't say a word. He stares at his desk. I stare at him. He stares at me. I keep trying to blink back tears. Just as one was about to drop from my eye, Randall gently grabs my neck and softly kissed my forehead. This was definitely not a "we're just friends" kiss. It was warm and sensual.

"Thank you so much Danielle." Randall's tone was soft yet strong. "I'm at a loss for words. I really thought you were coming to tell me you were never going to speak to me again after our meeting with Pastor yesterday. I actually called Pastor Hunter to tell him that you'd probably tell me you wanted me out of your life. I wish I could tell you just how much you mean to me, but that wouldn't be appropriate right now. I hope you can see why I tell you that you make me weak," he says with a grin. He nudges my arm and continues. "You're a hazard to my health," he jokes. "I may as well retire if you're going to keep doing things like this. Make me a promise."

I try to hold my head down so Randall can't see me crying. He lifts up my face and cups it in his hands while gazing into my eyes. My tears come from both joy and sadness. I'm happy that I've made his day, but sad that we still can't be anything but friends.

Randall wipes my tears with his fingers. "I can see this is as hard for you as it is for me," he says. "But just promise me that you'll allow us to stay friends. I don't want to cross that line. I don't want to hurt or disappoint you. I have to admit, I don't trust myself, so I'm going to need your help. I don't want to be your friend. But I have to do the right thing. If I ever get out of hand, please correct me. Can you promise me that?"

This situation was getting increasingly difficult. The man of my dreams was wiping my tears away and asking me to keep him in the friend zone because he's still married. Why did I have to pick this time in my life to be so serious about doing right by God? Christianity is very complicated, especially in situations like these. I may as well go to the club, sleep with whomever I want and go home drunk every night after drinking tequila shots off the chiseled chest of some 20-year-old if I can't have Randall. God was truly testing me.

I decided right then that I needed to back away from the situation immediately before either of us got any more attached. I nodded in response to Randall's request. This made the tears flow faster. Randall wiped my face again. We sat back on the sofa and I fell back into his arms. It all felt so right. We just sat there, motionless, for over an hour. I finally broke the silence.

"I'm glad you like the gifts. I should go."

Randall nodded. "Thank you so much. I think that may be best right now."

■ ■

I needed some air. I was having a hard time breathing. Randall and I walked out of the office solemnly. Every eye in the gym was on us. It was obvious I had been crying. Randall had a pitiful look on his face as well. He walked me to the car and we embraced. We held each other as though it may be the last time we'd ever hug. I got into the car, and he closed the door. "Drive safely," he was all he said.

I got to the edge of the lot, put my hands in my face, and sobbed. *WHY?* I couldn't help questioning God. Randall was practically perfect. And I couldn't have him.

I went home. I didn't go to the gym. I didn't stop by the track. I didn't even work. I showered, put on my sweatpants, and threw myself across the bed. It was seven o'clock on a Friday night and I was lying across my bed all because a boxer, a *married* boxer, had knocked me out, so to speak.

I couldn't sleep. I went from the bed to the chair, then back to bed. Then the phone rang. It was Randall's ringtone—"Winner" by Jamie Foxx, Justin Timberlake and T.I. I wasn't sure how fitting that song was now.

"Hello," I answered sadly.

"Throw on some jeans and a tee. I'm picking you up in twenty minutes," Randall answered.

I wiped my eyes and tried to shake myself out of the half-sleep I was in. "What time is it?"

"10:01."

"Where are we going?" I asked.

Randall ignored my question. "Be ready in twenty minutes."

"Twenty minutes?"

"Jeans and a tee." Randall hung up.

I was still a little bewildered. I didn't have much time to prepare. The "spontaneous date" outfit I usually have on standby clearly isn't the right choice according to Randall's attire instructions. I open my closet door and stare inside. I look in the mirror. I see dark circles under my eyes and notice my profile included a little water weight. I shouldn't have skipped the gym today.

I glance at my clock. I only have 19 minutes to get ready! I go to the jeans section of my closet and frantically push hangers out of my way to find the pair I want, even though I'm not sure what jeans I want to wear. I was having a minor panic attack. I couldn't decide between my Seven for Mankind, CJ by Cookie Johnson or my Ed Hardy jeans. The Seven jeans were new, the CJ jeans fit me better, but the shirt I usually wear with my Ed Hardy jeans was quite flattering. I didn't even have time to consult the girls. I kept checking my home monitor to see if Randall pulled up.

I decided on the Glory Sequined Boyfriend jeans by Cookie Johnson. Now it was time to find the perfect top. Should I wear a t-shirt or a halter-top? Then I remembered Randall specifically asked me to wear a tee. I scan through my collection of Henley's. They had just the right amount of cleavage and any color would be appealing. I have 11 minutes left.

Jeans on. T-shirt on. Now it was time to decide on shoes. Why was this so difficult? I never have problems putting my look together. I guess I was nervous because I really like Randall and I had no idea where we were going. Should I go with flats, heels, or wedges? Heels were definitely the sexier choice. But should I try to be sexy? No. He's still married. I decide to go with wedges—a safe middle ground because I want to be sexy while still being appropriate shoe.

I remember that I didn't plug in my curlers! I get out my flat iron and unwrap my hair. I give my hair a few carefree curls and apply a little eyeliner. Should I carry a handbag or a clutch? I decide to grab a clutch. I put on a little lip-gloss and take a deep breath.

Time's up! Randall calls. I try to tell myself to calm down. It's not working very well.

"Hello." I try to sound as though there aren't a million butterflies floating around in my stomach.

"Hey." Randall's tone was upbeat.

"Hey."

"You didn't tell me how to get in the gate."

"You hung up too quickly," I told him. "Hold on." I had to do some fancy phone tricks to get the gate open since he was not calling from the call box. I heard it buzzing.

"Thanks." He hangs up. I take a few more deep breaths.

I knew I still had about three minutes before he reached my door if he stopped at the signs and obeyed the traffic laws. I swallowed almost an entire bottle of water then stopped. *This is going to make me have to pee* I thought. I checked the full-length mirror. I wanted about 15 more minutes to spruce up a bit, but I didn't have it. I splash some Rumeur by Lanvin on my neck and wrists and brushed my teeth carefully so I wouldn't mess up my lip-gloss.

I look up at my monitor. "Oh no he didn't. He is such a show off." Actually, he is not and that is why it is so shocking. He is very calm and reserved. But the 599 GTB Fiorano Ferrari in my driveway was a bit shocking as it growled in my driveway. It was a beautiful car. I'm going to love riding in it tonight. But I'll love the company even more. What was even more shocking than the car was the guy standing at the doorbell. He is legit. He is sincere. He is a multi-millionaire boxer. He is a man of God. In all reality he was just a plain guy. He was a normal guy standing there wearing a crisp white t-shirt, dark jeans and Air Force Ones. How did he know that I thought a white t-shirt and Air Force Ones was just as sexy as a pinstripe suit on a guy? He was wearing an Atlanta Braves baseball cap too, which gave him a bit of a "bad boy" look. I felt myself getting weak. I sighed. I mentally confessed two things to myself. The first thing was we were both so hood even if we didn't show it on the surface. And secondly, this was *going to be a long night*.

I snap as many pictures as I can from my surveillance monitor so I can email them to the girls along with the selfies I took. I didn't have time to get their approval before Randall showed up, but at least they could see what I was working with on the date. I click on the buzzer to talk to Randall. "I'll be right there," I tell him.

He looks stunned and steps back from the door, trying to figure out where my voice came from. I knew he also wanted to know if I could see him. Once again, I felt, briefly, like I had a bit of the upper hand. Randall would never figure out how the intercom gadgets worked.

I think about changing purses but decide against it. I throw a piece of gum in my mouth and apply some more lip-gloss. I let out one more deep breath. "Let's do it," I whisper, smiling into the mirror. I disarmed and reactivated the alarm. I could see him through the door, even though the light was dim. He smiled. "Hi!" he said excitedly.

"Hey you!" I thought my face would break from smiling so hard.

"You look beautiful." he hugged me. "You smell good too." He laid in on my neck, which reminded me, again, that this would be one long night.

I smiled. "You smell pretty wonderful yourself, Mr. Hooks. I touched the chain around his neck. It was the one I bought for him today. "Thank you again," he said grinning. He held my hand and we walked down the cobblestone to his car.

"I figured you hadn't had dinner," Randall explained.

"No I haven't, but it is 11 o'clock," I reminded him.

He looked at his watch. "Not quite. I haven't had dinner either."

"You got me out of bed for a juiced piece of fruit?" I teased.

"Oh you were in bed?" He questioned mischievously.

"Kind of."

"Were you asleep?"

"No. I couldn't sleep."

"Me neither."

"Why?" I asked.

"I was caught off guard earlier and I felt like I was a little rude and insensitive so I wanted to make it up to you. I feel really bad. I don't want you to be upset or disappointed in me."

I touch his arm lightly. "I'm not. I actually understood how you felt."

Randall let out a sigh of relief. "Well, I hope you feel the same way too."

"You know what?"

"What?" Randall's innocent act wasn't convincing at all.

"You are full of surprises," I tell him.

"Surprises? Like what?"

"Like pulling up to my house unexpectedly."

He pretends to be offended. "How dare you say that? I have manners. I called you and told you I would be at your door in twenty minutes."

I laugh. "Okay. I'll give you that. The surprise is that you came to take me to dinner at this hour after I had a meltdown earlier. It's also very surprising that you would show up to my house in this car. Also, I don't recall giving you my address."

Randall intentionally ignores my last comment. "I wouldn't call it a meltdown. I think we both expressed our feelings without saying a word. It's a difficult situation. But I'm going to work it out. Just hang in there with me please." he pauses for a few seconds. "And yes you did give me your address."

I gasp and playfully punch his arm. "No I didn't."

Randall explained. "When you accepted the watch you gave me permission to access your address. I see you have it on now."

He had a good point. I didn't think of that. "You are such a stalker." That statement definitely contrasted with the girlish giggle I let out.

He pulled me close to him and hugged me again. *Now would be a nice time for my neighbors to be outside. Where are they?* I thought to myself. Then I remembered that I should probably watch what I ask for. I exhale loudly. I'm sure he heard it. He was too close to my body again. I had to keep the conversation flowing. "So where are you taking me?" I ask.

He sighed and released me from his embrace. He knew exactly what my sigh meant. "To eat. I hope you're hungry."

"Yep." I was hungry alright. I walk around the car to get to my side. I purposefully walked around the back of the vehicle to see the vanity license plate that I knew was there. Randall didn't disappoint. The tag read LB 4 LB. Pound for pound. He was a fighter to his core. So was I.

We cruise the city, talking and laughing and singing the songs on the radio. We passed by Mikey's. We pulled up to the Cheesecake Factory. I looked at my watch-- the one he gave me. I'm sure they're closed by now. Randall gently pushed my arm down to stop me from checking the time.

The valet opens to door. "Right on time Mr. Hooks," he says with a smile.

"On time for what?" I said, looking puzzled as another valet came to open my door.

The man started to open my door but Randall stopped him. "Don't you even think about it," he said to the valet.

The man grinned. "Yes sir."

Randall opened the door and I winked at the valet guy as he reached for my hand. "I saw that." Randall looked the guy eye to eye and said, "I'm watching you," in a joking tone. Who really wanted to joke with an undefeated middleweight and lightweight champion? Obviously these valets were familiar with Hooks.

I winked again. The guy laughed.

"So y'all think this is funny," Randall said, laughing. He looked at me and said, "What am I going to do with you," and linked my arm to his.

I laughed as we walked into the candlelit restaurant. This was one of the busiest restaurants in town and right now it was almost silent. You could see diners preparing to leave and servers waiting to go home. I wasn't sure what was happening.

"This way please," the hostess instructed us.

All of the tables were pushed to the side and there was one table in the middle of the floor. It was set elaborately. The flower arrangement was humongous and the candles looked to be about five feet tall. The table was long. We would be sitting extremely far away from each other. I assumed Randall chose this seating arrangement so that our meal would be considered dinner and not a date. He pulled my chair out and we both sat down.

Someone whispers in my ear. "You did it big this time baby girl. Remember if you don't want him I will take your leftovers." Harold and I both scream from surprise. I turn around to see the waiter's huge smile. We hugged and jumped in a circle like we hadn't seen each other in years. Just a few days ago, Leigh and I had come here for lunch and Harold was our waiter. Harold had seen me through some interesting times. He was the waiter for some of my best dates—and some of my worst. He's been my waiter for everything from blind dates to girls' nights. Harold also knew sometimes I'd pig out, and sometimes I'd just order a water with lemon.

I tried to gain my composure. I was holding my chest as I introduced Harold to Randall. "Harold, this is Randall Hooks Washington. Hooks this is my favorite waiter in the world."

"Nice to meet you," Randall said pleasantly.

"The pleasure is all mine," Harold said as he extended his hand.

I slapped it down. "Behave." I knew Harold just wanted to see how strong Randall's hands were.

"I will. Don't want to get my ass kicked," he said, pretending to flick his hair as he swayed to the other side of the table. "What's the deal with these chairs?" he asked. Harold tapped my shoulder. "Get up, honey," he instructed me. He moved my chair to the middle of the table. "Strong man, move your chair over there," he warmly instructs. Randall and I were now still sitting across from each other and were much closer to each other. I liked this arrangement better. Leave it to Harold. "I know you two are not on a "date." But anyone that rents a restaurant out and brings a woman is, technically, on a date. I don't care what anyone says. That goes for you too, Mr. Hooks," Harold said, laughing. It was interesting how everyone always felt the need to respect him by saying Mr.

I yell, "We are not on a date," as Harold walks away.

"I know honey," he says in a playfully patronizing tone. "Are you ready to eat?" He motions for someone to come help him reposition the plates since we moved the chairs.

"For the gentleman?" The waiter stands by the table to take Randall's order.

Randall interrupts. "Take the lady's order first, please."

"I'll have grapefruit juice with a splash of pomegranate in my famous De'lite nonalcoholic cocktail," I tell the waiter. Harold comes back to the table with a basket. "Here's your bread, Ms. D. With honey butter—just the way you like it." He uncovered the next dish. "Your crab cakes. Ahi Carpaccio. Asparagus with hollandaise, and the food you can't live without--bistro shrimp pasta."

"AHH!" I yell. I clap my hands in delight. "Who is responsible for this?" I ask. I could see the wait staff peeking around the corner grinning with satisfaction. "OH MY GOD! This is great. This is so great. Bump a diet." I was squealing like a little girl. I leaned over an empty spot on the table and whispered to Randall, "For real. Who is responsible for this?"

Randall made a clamping motion with his lips and pretended to throw away the key. He'd done so many nice things for me, and each one was better than the last. He had to have talked to the right people to find out what I liked. He had to do some research to make sure my favorite waiter was here. I was falling for him even more. I wasn't sure if I would be able to keep the promises Randall and I made to Pastor Hunter just 48 hours ago. I wanted to burst into tears again. This time, I was elated. Harold's voice interrupted my thoughts.

"Sir, the Thai Lettuce Wraps, Firecracker Salmon Rolls, Carrot Corn Chowder, and an open-faced turkey burger with a double side of steamed vegetables. Last but not least, an Arnold Palmer. Sugar-free, of course."

"WHAT? Who ordered that?" I was astonished.

"I did!" Randall answered, laughing.

"NO WAY!" I screamed.

"Yes way!"

"You've got to be kidding me," I giggle. Every time I had been out with Randall, he had some type of smoothie or bland item that was good for his fitness regimen. I looked at the wait staff. "He eats actual food?" I asked, pointing to Randall.

The staff nodded playfully as the chef and manager made their way to the table. "Is everything to your satisfaction?" They asked us.

Randall looked at me. "Yes. Thank you for asking."

I felt like everyone's eyes were on us. I looked at all the plates around Randall and whispered to him, "Are you going to eat any of that?"

"I'm going to try to eat all of it," he replied.

"When was the last time you had solid food? Or fried food?" I asked.

Randall grinned. "None of this food is fried. Let's just say grace so I can eat."

We held hands and he blessed our food, the hands that prepared it and thanked God for our many blessings. I opened one eye slightly during prayer to find that everyone in the room had their heads bowed and eyes closed. I liked it. I don't think they did it out of respect for Randall but due to reverence for God. It made me smile, though. Randall could hear the smile in my voice when I said "Amen."

He pretended to give me a suspicious look. "What are you laughing at?"

"I'm laughing at you. You're claiming that you're going to eat food?"

Randall uses his device to scan his food and waits for the results. He looks at the manager and chef and nods his approval. They both give Randall an understanding grin and walk away from the table.

We both dig in.

"Here, taste this." He passed me a salmon roll.

"Umm good! You want to taste mine?" Randall looked up deviously. I laughed so loud. "I left myself open for that." I honestly didn't mean to be flirtatious. That time. But the thought has crossed my mind.

Yes you did, Randall thought to himself trying to remember and remain in his place although his manhood was challenging him to respond and react.

"Your food still looks healthier than mine," I tell him.

"Yeah I see. Do you have something that isn't fried or white? Is there a vegetable on your plate?" Randall pretended to scold me.

"Excuse you," I said, acting as though I was offended. I passed him a piece of tuna with my fork. I was expecting him to take the entire fork. Instead, he leaned over the table and ate the piece of food from the fork. "That's really good," he said in a relaxed tone that indicated he was talking about more than the food. "Can I have some more? I'm not sure if it's part of my diet, but what the hell."

I said, "It is fish. I'm sure it's safe for you to eat."

"Maybe not," Randall shrugged.

"Says who?" I asked

"King—and my nutritionist."

"Oh, King." I said smugly.

He laughed. "You have a beef with King?"

"I wouldn't tell you if I did," I said, laughing.

"Well do you?"

"No! Actually, I like him. He has your best interest at heart."

"I would hope so and I hope it always remains that way."

"Speaking of which, does everyone always do what you tell them to do?" I really wanted to know.

"Like who?"

"Like King and JJ." I point around the room to indicate that every person working in the restaurant seemed like they wanted to please him, too.

He said, "No one does what I tell them to do."

"Oh really? What would you call it?" I asked, laughing.

"They do what I pay them to do."

"So is that the secret?"

He shrugged. "No, it's not a secret. I wish I could get someone to do what I told them to do."

"Who do you want to obey your orders? And what do you want them to do?" I was curious.

Randall stared at me lovingly. "Well, for one thing, I would get Tameka to sign the divorce papers immediately. And as you can see, I can't even pay her to do what I need her to do."

I touched his arm. "Who would voluntarily give up such a good guy like you?"

"She clocked out many years ago. And flattery gets you nowhere, Ms. Rose. Nice try, though. But you don't have to worry. I'm going to pay for the meal and take you home, as promised." he winked.

Some nosey person in the room snickered. We both looked in the direction of the sound. Then my phone chirped. It was a text from Sissie.

Hey, you okay?

Where are you we haven't heard from you?

You are not answering the phones!

I could tell she was worried. I texted right back. She probably thought I was lying.

At Cheesecake Factory with Randall.

It's closed.

Not tonight ☺ I'll text you when I can. Smooches.

Randall and I talked, ate, and laughed. I was shocked that he really ate most of his food. He actually ate all my tuna but I didn't mind. The chef offered to make us more, but the table was so full of other delicious dishes that I politely declined.

Then a sterling silver cart arrived. *Where did the Cheesecake Factory get a fancy piece like that?* I wondered. There had to have been over 50 slices of cheesecake on the tray. Harold didn't even have to ask me what I wanted.

"We've got red velvet—my favorite, and Oreo cheesecake, which I know is your favorite," he said with a grin. "The house favorite is white chocolate. What would you like, sir?" he asked turning to Randall.

Randall stares at the tray. "None of these options are low-fat," I tease him.

The chef chimed in. "Actually, there is a specialty dessert for Mr. Hooks. It's sugar-free, low-fat and contains no whipped cream or skim milk." The chef rattled off a long list of ingredients that, in my opinion, no longer qualified the dessert to be cheesecake. It sounded more like cardboard.

"I'll take that one," he said. While I was thinking *I am dessert.*

Harold placed one dessert in front of Randall. I had three.

Randall was not about to make me look like a pig. "No sir," I said, shaking my head. "You will have some of this cake."

Before the night was over my shoes were off. We were sitting side by side eating off my slices of cake. The restaurant staff was wrapping up the leftovers. I didn't know what I was going to do with more than 40 pieces of cake. I didn't even know where we'd put it on the ride home. I checked my watch. I checked his watch to see if his was spinning also. "We should let these wonderful people go home," I said nodding to the wait staff.

He said, "I think you're right."

As we stood up the manager said, "You don't have to rush. Take your time."

I nodded politely. "Oh, I think we should go. We've held you up long enough."

"We're fine, I promise," he replied.

"We'll definitely be back," Randall assured the staff, as he pretended to jab Harold.

Harold dodged the playful blow and said, "I can't wait, darlings."

Randall reached in his pocket and gave the manager his Black Card. He came back with the check to sign. I tried to read the bill but Randall was writing too fast. But I could tell from his hand movement that the tip was four digits—before the decimal.

"Thanks Randall," I said sweetly.

"It's nothing. As long as I see you smile." His voice was soft and delicate. He passed something to Harold. I'm sure it was an extra tip so Harold wouldn't have to split with the other waiters.

The valet guy was on the bench dozing off. He jumped up and went to go crank the car when he heard us approaching. I know he was disappointed all he got to do was crank it. I would have been.

We get in the car and he begins to pull off, then he stops abruptly. I look at him as if to ask if everything is okay.

"You have me so discombobulated that I forgot to ask you what I really wanted to ask you," Randall said.

"No, I can't marry you," I giggle.

He laughed. "You are such a mess. And one day you'll be able to. What do you have planned tomorrow?"

I smiled. "You don't have to worry. I don't have a date," I assured him.

"I'm glad to hear that." he turned to look into my eyes. I could feel my heart melting.

"I have an event at the Georgia Aquarium tomorrow and I wanted to know if you could come. It's casual—nothing fancy. You can even invite the girls if you want."

"Okay." I made sure my tone was bubbly. "What time?"

"After 2:00 PM," he said. "It's an all-day event, so it will be going on until 9:00 PM or so."

"I'll be there, and I'll invite the girls," I told him. "You won't look like a player with four ladies around you, will you?"

He winked. "Let me worry about that. You wanna stop and see Mikey since we're just a block away?"

"Yep!" That really made me happy.

As soon as we walked in Mikey started with his antics. "You keep hanging out with Rif Raff," he told Randall. "Hooks, if you want your reputation to stay clean you shouldn't be out this late with this trouble maker," he taunted, pointing to me.

I pretended to be hurt. "Mikey who loves you other than me?"

"No one I guess," he replied, chuckling.

"I rest my case. Zip it!" I punch him in the arm.

We sit down and Mikey starts making fruit drinks for Randall and me.

"D, can I talk to you a minute?" Randall asks suddenly.

"Yeah what's up?"

"I want to discuss the card you gave me today."

I had forgotten about the card. It read:

My Dearest Randall,

Your random acts of kindness have made an everlasting impression on my heart. I could never repay you, but I wanted to give a little happiness back to you, since you've given so much to me. I am very flattered that you've taken the time to surprise me on numerous occasions. Your generosity is beyond belief. I'm not sure what I did to deserve this, but I'm grateful.

I'm so glad we met. God places people in our lives at the right time for the right season. You've spoken to these dry bones. I hope I've served a purpose in your life. If it is in His plan for us to be together, I gladly accept that. I hope it is God's will for us to be one. But if we don't end up building a beautiful life together, know that this is God's doing and not mine.

I hope that all your wishes and dreams are fulfilled. I pray that God continues to bestow blessings upon you that you don't have enough room to receive. You have been blessed. You are a blessing. I am blessed we met. I am praying for you, your health, your safety, and your happiness always—until we meet again.

Miracles and Blessings,

Your Rose.

"Danielle, I read your card." Randall's voice was a whisper but I could hear his appreciation.

I smiled.

"I have to admit it was the nicest thing anyone has ever done for me," he confessed. "I'm really torn up on the inside. I can't think straight right now. I couldn't sleep and I'm surprised I was able to eat. I don't even know where to start. But, I do want you to know that you don't have to buy me presents. It's really not necessary."

I chuckled. "I hear you. But, I could tell you the same thing. Except I like presents." I just wanted to lighten the mood. For now, at least. Randall smirked.

He continued. "Danielle, as much as I want to spend time loving you and spoiling you and getting to know you, I think the right thing to do is wait. My deepest fear is that the wait may take too long for you, and you'll end up moving on. And if you do, I can completely understand that. I'll support whatever decision you make. I just want you to be happy. This whole divorce ordeal has been going on for four years now. I don't know if it will take four more months or four more years for it to be resolved. It's unacceptable for me to ask you to wait for me. I'm stuck between a rock and hard place. It wasn't this difficult six weeks ago. You said that God brings people in and out of your life for a reason. I believe you've come into my life to motivate me to accelerate my divorce and not let it linger any longer. The whole situation has put my life on hold for four years. And, I haven't fought in the ring at all during this time, because I wasn't mentally prepared for the battle. But yet, I could get into the ring and fight any opponent right now, and I'd feel at ease, even though I haven't been training intensely."

I thought to myself, *what have you been doing? Did you not really want a divorce?* Instead of responding, I let Randall continue.

"Tameka and I aren't equally yoked, and we've never been. She doesn't respect my career choices or any of the major decisions I've made for my life. The goals I've set for myself spiritually are nowhere close to what she wants. Honestly, it has made me feel stagnant. I've tried to hold on to the marriage and do the right thing. But Tameka was the one who walked out on me four years ago. And she didn't even give me a reason. She just left and never looked back."

He continued, "The divorce petition is not for irreconcilable differences. The petition is for abandonment. Which is what she did. There was no infidelity in our marriage that I know of. Tameka just really hated the fact that I am a boxer. She couldn't care less about my health and well-being and the great habits I've adopted to be prepared to fight. She was never interested in my work and never pretended to be. Even though what I do is physical, it takes a lot of mental preparation. I wasn't able to fight Tameka and fight in the ring."

He finally takes a breath. "I'm so sorry," I tell him.

"No need to be sorry," he told me. "Things happen for a reason. I hate to say it, but I'm glad this is happening. I wished it would have happened years ago, but apparently now is the time. If my marriage had officially ended earlier, I may not have met you. Everything will work itself out. The process may be slow, but it will be okay."

"Are you sure you're making the right decision?" I ask. I really wanted to make sure Randall was thinking clearly.

He looked at me with a determined expression. "Believe me. I'm sure."

Mikey interrupts our conversation by yelling from across the bar. "No serious conversation or work-related topics are allowed," he teases.

"Mikey, you make me sick!" I scream back.

"And so what?!" he shrugs.

"I demand respect in this place," I tell him, hitting the table with my fist.

"I'll show you respect," Mikey retorts, laughing.

"Oh really?" I laughed.

"You talk a lot of trash when the fighter is with you. Come in alone and talk trash." Mikey was always pretending to threaten me.

I flicked my hand in his direction while sticking my tongue out at him.

"I'm not worried about you, Mikey. It's the other dudes in the streets I'm worried about," Randall chimed in.

"You need to be worried about them," Mikey answered. You've got a heartbreaker on your hands. The only problem is she works too damn much." I couldn't even argue.

It was four in the morning the next time I looked at my watch. I didn't want to leave, but I knew we had to go.

"Bye my Mikey," I said sweetly, blowing him a kiss.

"See ya D."

"I may be back tomorrow."

"Why don't you just get your cardboard egg sandwich now?" he joked.

"I'll be back after my salon appointment."

"What time do you go to the salon?" Randall asked.

Mikey answered for me. "Six in the morning. Unless she works out first, then she goes to the salon at eight. You should know this by now, Champ. Danielle has a routine. Just put all her activities in your phone until you know her schedule by heart. If you can interrupt her schedule, you're officially the man. No matter how much of a champ you may think you are, you're not a winner until you can get this one to break her routine," he said nodding at me. "I don't even know how I got to be a part of her schedule, but I'm so glad I did. I love Dani. She always has my back. She's definitely my angel."

I punch Mikey in the arm. "Stop getting mushy on me. But I love you, too."

Randall gives Mikey a knowing look. "We'll talk later," he said. Mikey smiled and nodded.

"See ya in four hours," I say, winking at Mikey.

"Hey, why didn't you tell me you needed to leave?" Randall asked.

"It's cool. I'll sleep under the dryer. It is not like I'll be able to sleep after a night like this anyway." I touched his hand and said, "Thank you for everything."

He blushed. "You're welcome."

He liked looking me in my eyes. I loved it. It gave every bit of him away each time he did it. I could see right through him. It was like a mirror into his soul. I hoped I was the only one that could tell. Randall was always so transparent with me. I just hoped it was sincere.

We pulled up to my house. He jumped out and opened my door. We both walk up extremely slow; I didn't want him to leave. I couldn't however invite him in, even just to talk, especially after the conversation we'd had with Pastor Hunter last night. I could hear my Big Mama's voice ringing in my ears, "Ain't nothing open after midnight but legs," she used to tell me. And honestly, I didn't trust myself.

We got to my door and I fumbled with my keys for a few seconds. I opened the door and ran to disarm the alarm before it made any more noise. I wanted him to take the initiative and come in behind me, but he was a perfect gentleman and stayed right outside the door. I went back to the door and used every ounce of willpower I had to tell him goodnight.

His smile was radiant. "Goodnight," he said. His voice was so warm I wanted to snuggle up next to it. I had to keep the moment upbeat without getting in trouble.

"You have beautiful teeth," I said. Randall dropped his head in embarrassment. I reached for a hug. Our embrace was so secure and comforting, even though I was on one side of the door and he was on the other. His cologne filled the space of our hug like a warm blanket. I pressed my lips against his cheek. He kissed my ear.

I felt a rush of panic and excitement. Then he kissed my forehead and placed my head on his chest. His heart was beating a thousand times a minute. He was so strong, but still so human and relatable. He had needs just like me. His heartbeat the same way mine did. His gesture showed me that he wanted me to feel his heart. Completely. That was when I became sure. Randall loved me, and I loved him too.

"You know what to do when you get home." I told him.

He laughed lightly. "Who said I was going home?" he answered quickly.

I had to keep things jovial. If I didn't, I'd be making him breakfast in a few hours. "Well I think the last call at the strip club has been made. So it's either home or the gym for you. I would suggest home. I hate to tell you this but you don't live at the gym."

He flashed his beautiful teeth at me again. "Yes ma'am."

I could tell he was impressed that I cared enough to send him home. I went inside and threw myself on the chaise with all my clothes on. I looked at the ceiling as the moonlight came through the windows. I put my phone on my chest and checked my watch to make sure I was still online. I had just a little over an hour before I had to be at the salon.

A text made the phone vibrate. It was Randall.

> Are you asleep?

I wanted to add a smiley face but didn't want to be too suggestive.

> No

> I'm calling you.

> Okay

Immediately my phone rings. We talked up until he pulled into his driveway and I arrived at the salon.

"Get some sleep Randall. You have to be somewhere later," I tell him gently, even though I didn't want to end our conversation.

"I can't," he said. "I need to do quite a few reps right now to look my best and combat the food from last night."

"Sorry," I say. "But I'm glad you enjoyed yourself."

He laughed. "If I look bad it's your fault."

I told him goodbye and looked forward to daydreaming about him under the dryer.

Saturday

I texted the girls.

> Deacon Washington has invited us to a photo shoot at the Georgia Aquarium today after 3:00 PM. Cancel all other plans and be there. That's all I know.

After the salon, I run a few errands and then got ready for the Aquarium. I have no clue what I'm going to wear. I decide on my black legging-style jeans and a multi-colored top. After all, I may need to be picture-ready.

But I hope not. Clearly, Randall and I aren't ready for that yet. Well, we are but…I stop myself before I become mentally exhausted. I do NOT need my face all across a gossip tabloid. I don't ever want to be called into the pastor's office again. I didn't like that one bit. I purposefully told the girls to show up an hour later than the time I was arriving so I could check out the scene. And Paige would be even later than the time I gave, anyway. I pulled up to the Aquarium and realized I had no idea what to do next. Where was I supposed to be? I call Randall.

"At the next light, pull into that driveway," he tells me. "There will be a valet there waiting for you. I'll send someone to escort you to where I am."

He hadn't even said hello when he picked up the phone. I decided to check him on that. "Hey Randall. How are you?" I said a little curtly.

"Sorry I didn't give you details about where to go earlier. I think I'm a little nervous," he said.

"Nervous? For what?" I ask.

"Nervous that you were coming."

That melted my heart. I felt the same way. "You knew I was on my way. You were tracking me," I remind him.

He admits it. "Yeah, so I would know when to send someone for you."

I laugh. "Umm hmm. See you in a minute."

I pull up and sure enough there is a guy waiting for me. I exit my car and see a nice drop-top Bentley parked next to Randall's Phantom.

"Good afternoon ma'am," the man says.

"Good afternoon," I answer politely.

"There is a gentleman waiting inside the door for you."

Oh holy crap. I walked in and see Pastor Hunter. I feel like I'm being set up again. I need to text the girls and tell them there's been a change of plans. I felt like Pastor Hunter was about to assign me to hell right then and there.

"Ms. Danielle," Pastor Hunter greets me.

"Pastor," I nod.

"Good to see you."

"Same here," I said dryly.

"You're right on time. I think they're waiting on us to begin."

I still didn't know what we were doing. We walked a few feet to where Randall was seated. His eyes were closed and he was wearing a boxing robe. He looked different for some reason. Maybe he had professional makeup on.

I heard a voice say, "Ready in eight minutes, Mr. Hooks."

He opened his eyes. "Let's do it," he said. When he saw me his face lit up. Pastor Hunter noticed it and looked right at me. He gave me a smirk. It was almost a smile, until he remembered he had recently chastised me.

As I walked closer, Randall got up, walked over to me, and hugged me. "Thank you so much for coming. This means a lot to me," Randall said. I looked back at Pastor and smirked back. *I win* I thought to myself. Randall spoke close to my ear. "This is very important and I want you to be a part of my life and every event, no matter what it is." I looked back at Pastor Hunter again and smirked. That was two points for me, in a matter of seconds. The pastor gazed at me as if he could read my mind and knew what Randall said. I felt like I was in a competition, but I wasn't quite sure why.

Then Randall transformed from his sensitive self to Heavy Hitting Hooks. "Come on fellows. Huddle in," he said to the men around him.

I stood back to see what was going on. I saw JJ, King and a few other familiar faces from the gym circle around Randall. The makeup girl and cameraman joined the huddle as well. Randall stepped out of the circle and gently pulled my arm. He guided me into the circle with him and held my hand. I saw a flash. Someone was taking pictures, as I had anticipated.

"Grab you neighbor's hand and let's pray," Hunter said. He transformed also, from Tre, Randall's friend to Trevor Hunter the renowned Pastor.

Randall pulled me closer and raised his right hand. Pastor Hunter came closer, too. I could tell that his voice was louder. Another camera snapped. I think it was directly over our heads.

Pastor Hunter placed his hand on Randall's forehead. Randall tightened his grip on my hand. The more Pastor Hunter prayed the tighter his grip got. Then I felt it slipping. I realized Randall was going to his knees. Hunter went down with him. I stood directly behind Randall. King pushed in closer. The cameras flashed from everywhere. King took my purse and held my hand while putting a little pressure on it, to indicate I should kneel also. Then Pastor Hunter began to pray for the others in the room. It was like he had been given a list. He prayed for the makeup artist, Randall's trainers, the animal trainers, the camera crew, the director, the staff, the visitors in the building who had no clue we were there, the medical staff, the family and friends surrounding Randall, and lastly the animal Randall was about to take pictures with.

He prayed for the animal's behavior. He prayed the animal would not display fear and would not see Randall as a predator. He prayed for no person to ever be harmed inside these walls—not today, not tomorrow or forever. The atmosphere was set. I was glad Pastor was there, after all. Even if he did give me an uncertain look. He had Randall's best interest at heart and honestly, mine too. He is a man of God and follows the precepts and principles of the Word. He was definitely someone I needed to keep on my team. So, actually I had two champions who truly cared about my being, and they both loved the Lord.

The prayer was ending. "In Jesus' name, Amen." Pastor Hunter said.

I could see people wiping tears from their eyes. Some probably have not been to church in quite some time. They had no clue they would have a spiritual experience today. Everyone who was part of the prayer needed and respected it. Pastor Hunter always knew what to say to touch people's hearts. His words were always relatable, no matter what walk of life a person was from. As I looked across the room, I could see that every cameraman that had been taking pictures was teary-eyed.

Randall had gone from being on his knees to lying prostrate. Pastor Hunter, King, and I stayed still. I didn't know how long we'd been praying. But we didn't move until Randall moved.

Randall sighed and his body heaved. He attempted to lift himself up and fell back on his face. Hunter got down with him and continued to pray. I was on my knees but I couldn't make out the prayer clearly. King was down on his face also. JJ was standing straight up in a protective stance. No one else in the room moved. There was no other noise besides the murmurs and prayers coming from Hunter and Hooks. I subconsciously held my breath. Moments later Randall lifted his body up. King pulled him up to his feet. As soon as Randall's feet hit the floor he swooped me up and placed my feet on the floor. He said, "Are you balanced before I let you go?"

"Yes," I replied.

JJ motioned for men to come in while they sprinkled Randall's face with water and handed Pastor a cloth to pat Randall's face. The makeup artist cringed from the other side of the room. At least half an hour of her work had been ruined. As they were patting Randall and pumping him up he reached for my hand and gave a nod to Pastor Hunter before taking me to my seat.

Randall took me to a couch just a few feet from where his chair was. Pastor Hunter had a chair next to the sofa. There were refreshments on the table and all around the room.

JJ handed me back my purse. Randall kneeled in front of me. "Are you okay?"

"Yes," I said. I was a little shaken and didn't know what to expect, but I was okay. I think.

"If you need anything, get King or Vickie," he instructed me, pointing in their direction. "Thanks again for coming. It means so much to me. You will never know how much. I gotta get to work."

Randall turned to Pastor Hunter. "Pastor, are you staying all day? I have a quiet room reserved if you need to go study or make some calls. Help yourself to anything. Don't forget dinner tonight."

Pastor said, "I will be right here."

Randall clasped his hands together and smiled. "Y'all enjoy." He immediately changed his energy level. It was like Dr. Jekyll and Mr. Hyde. It was a transformation I had not seen in him before. He went from praying prostrate to a full fighting stance in a matter of seconds.

The area we were in was like a dry spot in the ocean. We were surrounded by water and all types of exotic fish. I hadn't had time to see all the beautiful sea creatures, but I knew there was an array of them. Above us, and to the left and right there walls of tanks filled with beautiful creatures.

The lights dimmed and flickered and all of a sudden the glass boxes filled with what I would call sea monsters. These animals were much too large to be classified as fish. Then I saw trainers in the tanks in scuba gear. Randall was nodding and listening to the men giving him directions. Then it happened. He took the robe off. *Good God!* I had never seen his chest before. Even at the track he changes shirts so quickly that I can't get a full view of his chest or abs.

Pastor Hunter saw the expression on my face before I could change it. He smiled so hard that he turned his head away from me, hoping I wouldn't see. I giggled like a thirteen year old. I turned back to Randall and saw that he was wearing a chain with a black diamond pendant and what appeared to be Speedos. I hoped there was a protective cup inside to shield him from the ferocious sea animals in the tank.

Basically, the man was ten feet away from me, nearly naked. And I liked it. King handed him his trunks. They were royal blue and had the word CHAMP across the waistband in sparkling letters. I was still not sure what was going on. I'm usually more aware of things, but Randall completely caught me off guard last night and this was way more intense than a fancy dinner. And looking at his body with the pastor standing right next to me was pure torture. God was testing me.

The cameras started to flash. The scuba-geared divers prodded the creatures up to the glass. It was like taking baby pictures—a long and slow process. The fish have to be in the right place at the right time. That gave Hooks time to pose while he was waiting to get in the tank. More torture for me.

After what seemed like hours Randall came over briefly and asked Pastor if he was okay and if he needed anything. Then he leaned over me. "You good?"

"Yep."

"Boring huh?" he asked apologetically.

I smirked, but tried to hide it. It wasn't working. "No not at all."

"If you want to walk around fell free to do so."

"I will."

"You hungry?"

"No, I'm good."

"Where are the girls?"

"I told them to come at three."

"Oh!" Randall sounded disappointed.

"You okay?" I asked responding to his disappointment.

"Yeah. I'm fine. I'm worried about you," he whispered in my ear.

I said, "Pastor Hunter is right there." The pastor's protective stance made me feel like my dad was watching me while I was talking to a boy. *Well, Pastor Hunter is our spiritual father,* I thought. *So I guess he's just doing his job.*

Randall sensed what I was feeling. "Why did I invite him again?" he joked.

"To keep you in line," I replied. Well, now that I've seen Randall's body, Pastor Hunter was clearly there to keep me in line.

"Yeah, you're right," Randall replied with a smile.

He bounced up with exuberant energy. I saw the change in his energy again. He was so calm around me, but ambitious when it came to his work. Randall had a focused and determined look in his eyes. "Duty calls. I'm in the ring with another champ."

He pranced away then turned around and came back toward me. He leaned his neck down so I could take his chain off. "You're in charge of this," he said once I had the necklace in my hand. It was heavy. "Watch out for Pastor. He may try to steal this," he laughed.

Pastor heard him and laughed. "Give her the keys. That's what I really need."

"You don't need my keys, big baller," Hooks yelled back at Pastor. "Besides, I think she may fight you for them."

Pastor formed his hands into small guns and pointed them at Randall.

I turned to Pastor. "That's right. I might be able to take you. I've been training with the champ," I say, nodding to Randall.

"You'll need lots of training to take me down," Pastor Hunter said jokingly.

"Don't make me take you to the mat too," I laughed.

Randall grinned, "Don't listen to her, Pastor. I let her win."

Pastor and I exchanged fighting gestures. Then he disappeared in what seemed like a glass wall. I was trying to figure out what happened when my phone buzzed. It was the girls. I looked at Hunter.

"What's wrong?" he asked.

"I need to get my sisters."

He said, "Vickie can help you with that."

I got her attention. She told me to tell them to park in the same location that I did and she would meet them. When the girls walked in Pastor Hunter and I were on the edge of our seats. I'm pretty sure this was the moment pastor realized why Randall asked him to come today. Randall was inside the aquarium now. The scuba team was guiding him toward the glass. I stood up to get a better view. Randall smiled, but I could see from his expression that he knew this feat would be easier said than done.

I shot a panicked look to King, JJ, and Vickie. They all seemed calm. I looked at Pastor Hunter and his expression matched mine. I guess he and I were the only two who were freaking out. The girls walked over to where I was standing. I pointed to the aquarium. I was too stunned to speak.

All Pastor Hunter had to say was "Beloved..." and extended his hands. The girls and I formed a huddle with him and began praying. I felt the room stop, just as I had the first time we prayed earlier. But this time, the prayer was different. We were all intensely concerned for Randall's safety. After the pastor petitioned God to keep Randall secure, we all confirmed the prayer by saying "Amen."

"Did you know he was getting into a tank with an octopus?" I asked the pastor.

"No," he said seriously.

"Me either." I was stunned.

"Hooks is crazy," Pastor Hunter said matter-of-factly.

Sade said, "Hooks is sexy is what he is. Even if he is in a tank with a big smelly fish. By the way Auntie, what is that around your neck?" Sade always knew how to lessen the shock of a situation. She also knew how to be nosey.

Out of the mouths of babes. They call it exactly like they see it. Nothing more or nothing less. All she saw was a sexy man, with great abs in a tank with a big smelly fish. We saw a human named Hooks in a glass box with an animal that had real hooks with danger written all over it. "Randall took this off before he got in the tank and asked me to hold it for him." I touched the necklace softly and tried to hide my distress.

"Nice," Sade said while staring at the tank.

The girls sat on the sofas and chairs with me and Pastor as we all watched in amazement. This was a long process. They had to make sure Randall had enough oxygen. The diving team also had to make sure the octopus behaved and was in position for photographs and video footage.

Around half past four the aquarium staff motions to the tables to indicate the food was being served. I got up and so did the girls. They sat at the tables where the food was. I walked over to King.

"Is he wearing his watch?" I asked King.

He could tell I was concerned. "Yes, that's what I am monitoring."

"Where is it?"

"It's on his waist. You can wear yours like that, too," he said with a smile.

"What does it read?" I was curious.

"His heart rate. It's steady but different. It's not elevated, but it's in a different pattern than normal. He was warm in the water but his temperature is back to normal now."

"Is he scared?" If he was, we felt the same way.

"From the looks of it, he's not too frightened," King tried to assure me.

I wasn't convinced. "You get him out there if he's afraid. Let me see." King showed me the device he was using. I had no clue what I was looking at. I walked away from King and I stood directly on the glass of the aquarium. I put my hand up and the Octopus flowed right to me. Randall put the opposite hand up on the glass and I put my other hand up to meet his. A fish suctioned itself to the glass to meet my hand.

"Stay there," a photographer said. "Don't move. Can you get the shot without her?"

"No," was the reply.

"Take the shot. We'll edit her out." Then I heard a cameraman say, "Roll the cameras!"

"What's going on?" I asked. Then I realized what they saw. The fish was not pleased with someone in the tank. The animal did, however, respond to the motion of my hands. The photographer and cameraman shot for over 20 minutes. After they were finished they allowed me to take a look at a cut of the footage. One of the cameramen said to me, "You can have a seat. We're taking the Champ out for a break."

I sat down. When Randall walked up I said, "I wasn't aware that you'd be doing...this," I told him. "Was this the original plan?"

Randall nodded. "Yes, it was. I didn't want to tell you because I thought it would freak you out. I'm already scaring myself a little bit."

I was surprised. "Are you? You're hiding it well." I patted his arm.

Randall turned to King. "What are my numbers?"

King yells some numbers back to him. "How do you feel?" I ask.

"Okay. I want to take a shower but no need if I am jumping back in there," Randall joked. "I would get close to you but I'm sure I smell like hell." If he did, I didn't notice.

"What is all of this you have on?" I asked him.

"These are safety blankets for hyperthermia."

"What was the water like?"

"The temperature was a shock when I first got in but I acclimated quickly just like in a pool. When I came out they hosed me down with some chemicals and cold water. So that's why I have these blankets on."

"You want something to eat or drink?" I ask him.

"I do but I'm going to wait," he answered laughing on the inside at the volume of questions.

"Do you need to use the restroom?" I didn't mean to act like his mother but I had to be inquisitive.

"No, I think I am fine," he said with a laugh.

King came over to us. "Thanks for helping the Champ," he told me, motioning to Randall. "The next part is going to be intense. If you need to look away or step out, it's cool."

I had just calmed down. Now I was getting scared again.

Randall turned to the pastor. "Trevor, you okay?"

"Yeah, I'm good," the pastor responded.

"You need to go study," Randall respectfully instructed him.

"I do, but I don't want to miss you in the aquarium with an octopus. I'll stay. My wife is coming down in a little bit and I'm sure she'll make me go study when she gets here."

Randall noticed the girls had arrived. He flashed them a smile. "My favorite ladies." He made sure he said it loud enough for them to hear. Then he leaned toward me. "But you're my absolute favorite," he said.

"What's up?" Sade greeted Randall.

"Hey Hooks," Paige said with a smile.

Randall nodded at them. "I would hug y'all but that wouldn't be nice at this point," he laughed.

Paige holds her hands up. "Stay back," she tells Randall. "You smell like the sea."

"Keep it up and I'll make sure you get in with me," Randall tells her with a wink.

King calls me over. He's talking with the producers. I walk over and try to take in what they're saying.

"Ms. Danielle, we're going to need your help on a few things. I know you didn't come to work but it looks like you can keep us where we need to be."

I was happy to help. Anything for Randall. "Okay," I said.

"We may also need your friends and Pastors help to," King said. "We're going to put five additional monitors on Hooks. We'll need to watch him very carefully during this next round. I need someone to monitor his levels, and I need you to stand on one side of the tank like you did before. Just stand wherever they tell you and I'll get someone to stand on the other side of the tank as well," King explained.

King kept laying out the details to let me know what was about to happen. "There will be ten trainers in the tank in case it gets dangerous, but we are keeping Hooks calm from the outside. If there is any increase in his heart rate we will pull him out of the tank. He's wearing a hoist and there are glass partitions waiting to be lowered to separate the animal from him if need be. We have someone in the tank ready to inject the octopus with a sedative if that becomes necessary. In this case, we have to realize the octopus is the proven champ. Hopefully, Hooks will assume this title as well once the match is over."

I try to process everything King is saying. I wave for the camera crew to come over. I lean in and ask them in a tone that is gentle but demands an honest answer, "So, what is really about to take place here?"

They all look scared to say. I search for Randall and see him standing with JJ. JJ is pouring water into Randall's mouth. A team of people is applying something to his skin. I don't know if the substance is meant to repel or attract the octopus. No one has answered my question. "Let's not all speak at once," I say, trying to control my agitation.

One of the men finally answered me. "He is going to box with the octopus. The Champ vs. The Champ." The octopus' name was The Champ.

I gasp. "OH HELL NO!" Who signed him up for this BS?!" I try to contain myself. "Excuse me, Pastor," I say, turning to Pastor Hunter.

Pastor stood with his arms folded like he wanted to know the answer too. He wasn't even offended by my angry outburst.

"Well?" I said, pressing the men for an answer.

"Is it safe?" Hunter chimed in.

I heard one of the men answering the question, but I had stopped listening. I yelled to Randall across the room. "Hey!"

He held up his hands to try and tell me it was okay. I motioned with my finger for him to come here. Now!

He scurried over to me. "I guess you know what's next," he said.

"Yes I heard," I said, almost yelling. "Are you crazy?"

"Some may say. It will be a piece of cake. Relax." His tone was extremely calm, given the circumstances. He motions to his guys. "Give her a monitor too," he tells them, pointing to me.

I was too nervous, scared, and angry to let anyone else get close to me. "I have my watch. I don't need another damn monitor. What I need to know is how you plan to box with an Octopus--and why?"

Randall touched my shoulder. "It's no big deal."

I look him dead in his eyes. "You need to pick your battles wisely. Do you want to box with an octopus or fight with me?"

King flips the screen (I forgot he can read my heart levels as well) and said to a man nearby, "Give her a water. She is rising."

At this point I was livid. "Damn right I am!" I turn sharply to Randall. "Let me speak to you for a minute." We start to walk off. "You too, Pastor Hunter." I made sure I was loud enough for him to hear me as Randall and I separated from the crowd.

"Me?" Pastor Hunter was a little stunned. I didn't have time for niceties. "Yeah you! Duh!"

Randall tried his best to calm me down. "Dani, it is cool. Believe me, there's no way they're going to let anything happen to me. They would kill the fish first."

"How do you know that?" I snapped.

"I would like to think I'm more valuable than the animal," Randall said. "Come over to the tank and let me show you." He explains how they are planning this stunt. I could tell he had been in the tank and heard the rundown of the stunt numerous times.

"Who do you think is faster? Man, fish, crane or shooter?"

Randall's voice was pleasant but resolved. "I'm leaning on God."

"Don't get spiritual on me now." I said.

"Now would be a good time to pray," Pastor Hunter said.

"You got your oil Pastor?" I retorted.

"Didn't know I needed it," he replied. I knew he was shocked by my sudden change in attitude. But I couldn't help it.

"What kind of Pastor travels without it? Hold on." I grabbed my bag and took a long breath. I fumbled through my purse to find my oils. "Frankincense, Myrth, or Boaz?" I ask.

"A girl that comes prepared," Pastor said, winking at Randall. "I love it."

How could he be joking at a time like this? "Don't play with me Pastor. I WILL go to the trunk and get the Alabaster Box."

"I'm going to anoint you too while I'm at it," Pastor said sternly. Obviously I needed it right now.

"Do what you have to do Pastor. Just make sure I get a double portion of your anointing." I instantly started to get excited. I guess there was something about a man and an octopus that got my blood pumping. I held up the oils and got the attention of the trainers. "Is it okay if we put this on him?" They recognized the oils and nodded that it was safe. "Are you sure?" I just wanted to double-check.

Paige was watching this whole exchange. She looked at the others and said, "What in the hell is she doing?"

"Who knows," Leigh said, unfazed considering this was Danielle's normal work behavior.

Pastor prayed and anointed Randall. After we all said Amen he took his oily hand and put it on my forehead. "Help her Lord," he said simply.

"Hallelujah," I responded in agreement.

Randall went straight over to King. King put a monitor on both of Randall's ankles and wrists. King held up another one and Randall shook his head to indicate he didn't want it.

"What's that?" I yell to King.

Hunter laughed. "Get em' girl," he said. He was enjoying watching me be so protective.

"A monitor for his chest, and I have one for his neck," King responded quickly. He knew I wasn't playing.

"Put it on him," I ordered.

King shrugged. "He said he didn't want it."

I rolled my eyes at Randall. Randall reached for the monitors King had in his hand, but quickly changed his mind.

Pastor Hunter whispered to me, "You almost had him."

Randall turned to the crowd surrounding the aquarium and said, "Be right back." Randall whispered to me in stern voice, "Behave, girl!"

Sade heard him and turned to the girls. "Now, he should know by now that she's not going to behave." The girls nodded and laughed.

I stood with my arms folded. My shoulder was touching Pastor Hunter's. King was trying to give us monitoring instructions. I interrupt.

"Wait a minute," I said, holding up my hand. I grabbed my bag again. People laugh at how heavy my handbag is, but it pays to pack a variety of items in there, even if I don't need all of them every day. I pulled out my iPad and my mini laptop and logged on. "Where do I need to go, King?"

The Pastor was impressed again. "You're ready for anything. What else you got in there, girl?" he said.

"Let that big fish make a wrong move, and you'll see what else I have in this bag," I tell Pastor Hunter. "I don't have time to sedate creatures. I hope you have experience-eulogizing animals, Pastor. If not, today could be the day you learn how."

Everyone looked at Pastor as if he was responsible for her behavior. He said, laughing, "Today is my first time meeting her." The people around returned his laughter, since they knew he was joking. He turned to me. "You can't come in these people's establishment and threaten to shoot their animals!"

"Humph!" I responded with lots of attitude. I couldn't even get the words out to explain how scared, surprised, and nervous I was.

King gave us instructions. I gave one computer to Hunter, Paige, and the other to Leigh and Sade.

"Danielle. Give me your watch," King said, holding his hand out.

I hurriedly took it off my wrist and King linked my watch to Randall's monitors. My eyes widened. "Wow! It can do that?"

King seemed unfazed by my astonishment. "Yep. Now listen to me."

"OKAY." I fixed my gaze on him so I could take in his every word.

"When your levels are up, the watch will vibrate. When Randall's levels are up, you'll feel a pinch from the device. The higher his heart rate gets the harder the watch will pinch until you feel a shock. If we see you flinch, we'll snatch Randall out of the aquarium. You got it?"

I nodded. "Got it. But why am I getting shocked?"

"Because he will stay in there and endure the shock. He will not allow you to endure it. It's on me and you, girl," King said with a nervous grin. We high-five. Then

I heard a tapping sound. Everyone turns around. Randall throws his hands up to show he's ready to start.

"We're ready," the production crew yelled.

The lights went off. Everything moved very slowly. Then I saw a person in scuba gear floating through the water and holding the octopus. I have to admit it was a pretty animal. Then a few more trainers floated up slowly and took their positions as everyone outside the tank stood still. Then they placed the Octopus on Randall's back. It clung to him immediately. The camera flashes were so fast and numerous that I couldn't stop blinking. I'm surprised they didn't startle the octopus. I was vibrating but I think the darkness and the flashing caused the increase in my heart rate, because it caught me off guard.

The watch was not pinching me. That was a good thing. I was extremely close to the glass. I don't know how the cameramen weren't getting me in all their shots.

They changed the position of the Octopus and took more pictures. I wondered how could they do all of this in a way that would edit the scuba tanks out of the picture. But I didn't have time to think about that right now. There was an octopus wrapped around the man I love. The creature seemed small, but once they placed the arms around Randall's body the octopus's arm span expanded. I felt like Randall could defeat the animal if he needed to, but I wanted to be completely sure. Randall and the octopus wrestled for about half an hour. Then the lights came back on and the scuba crew took the animal away.

King nodded to everyone in the tank and yelled, "Good job, crew. One more round."

I looked at Pastor. My expression made it clear that if he were not here, I'd be using some very choice language right now. He knew I wanted to say something.

"Go ahead," he said with a smirk.

I shook my head. "If I say what I really want to say, you'll have to meet with me in your office and hold a special prayer vigil just for me."

He laughed.

King walked up to me. "Dani, your levels went up a bit. Do you want to see what the numbers were and check out Hooks' levels?"

I looked at King. "Oh my. I did get a little stressed." King played the footage back and was mixing my heart levels in a split screen right next to the footage of Randall fighting the octopus. At all points, my heart rate was higher than Randall's. Each time one of the octopus' arms touched Randall, my heart jumped. And it was documented.

I walked to the glass. "You good?" I asked Randall. Maybe if he could convince me that he was alright, I could calm down.

He threw his thumb up.

They were changing the glass in the tank and it looked like they were sedating the octopus and attaching the animal to something. I guess they were taking precautions in case the octopus got riled up. Then there was a countdown. I was directly in front of the tank. Hunter was on the right. I was supposed to be closer to the left. I was too enthralled to move.

The underwater team positioned the Octopus. I think the trainer was a woman. She waited a few moments before she let the creature go.

I could see she was patting the animal on its soft side to soothe it. All I could think was, *if that octopus gets out of hand, everyone in here is having calamari for dinner.* The trainer let the octopus go and backed up.

Everyone waited in silence. As the octopus floated Randall shifted from foot to foot. It was just like he was in an underwater ring and moving in slow motion. Finally, he threw what looked like a delayed punch in the animals' direction. And in midair the Octopus "punched" back.

"Wow," I said out loud.

Hunter stepped back from the glass.

Randall threw another punch. The octopus punched back. Then the fight got faster. Each punch was countered with another. Randall was gaining more and more confidence. He started to bob and weave. The octopus was, however, a worthy opponent. No matter what type of punch Randall threw, the animal seemed to mock it. It was a good show, I had to admit. Both "champs" were doing well. At some point the animal got a little restless and threw a few swats just to get Randall away from him. The trainers didn't like that and pulled at the animal's strings.

Then when the octopus was bored and tired, he reached out his tentacles and grabbed Randall in what looked like an embrace. The watch pinched me. That meant Randall's heart rate was going up. I held my arm up to get King's attention.

"CRAP!!" I screamed. The pinch subsided. Damn. I didn't come here for this. That was not a pinch. That was a labor pain. I took a deep breath, breathed an apology to God for my unladylike language, and started praying for Randall's safety.

The crew almost knocked me over with their cameras. It was an awesome, impromptu photo and they had to get as many shots as possible. Randall flashed his brilliant teeth at the flashing cameras. Then the nicest thing happened. The octopus laid his head on Randall's head. That was the shot.

Whew. I was glad that was over. I could relate to the way the eight-legged sea creature felt. I was exhausted, too. I laid on the couch a few feet from the aquarium. The scuba crew pulled Randall out but I didn't see him. The next thing I knew an hour had passed. I had fallen asleep and woke up to see Randall back in the tank, dressed in a tuxedo. I blinked a few times to make sure I was awake. The room was quiet.

Paige was at the foot of the couch doing what she always does. Reading. Sade was sitting on the floor right in front of me to slyly break my fall in case I fell off the couch while engrossed in texting and looking at my laptop. King and Vickie were monitoring me and Randall. JJ was up at the glass. Pastor Hunter was in a chair with a table pulled up to him to create a desk. He had a concordance, an Apple laptop, an iPad, and a notepad in front of him. Leigh was taking all the pictures she could. She always had her camera with her. I was surprised the camera crew didn't have a problem with that.

"Hey, sleepyhead," Paige said, nudging me.

"What time is it?" I asked groggily.

"7:30," she replied.

I was confused. "In the evening?"

"DUUHH!" Sade said, giggling.

I thumped her in the head without even thinking about it.

"What's going on?" I asked the girls.

"You mean other than you snoring?" Sade asked sarcastically.

"Hush!" I replied, shoving her. I turned to Pastor Hunter.

"Pastor, was I snoring?"

"I don't think it's wise for me to answer that question. But if my sermon includes a snoring analogy tomorrow, you'll know why," he said with a light laugh.

I smiled. "Your sermon should be about Jonah and the great fish tomorrow, but that's just a suggestion. I won't tell you what to preach about."

Sade turned to Paige. "Now I know there was no way she was sleeping," she said, finally nudging me back.

I was still confused. "What are you talking about?"

Paige gave me a suspicious glare. "You were clearly playing possum. Pastor changed his sermon subject to the story of Jonah while you were supposedly sleeping. How else would you know that?"

I stood up and did the happy dance. "That just means I'm in the flow," I said, grinning. The girls got up and joined me in prancing around the sofa. It doesn't take much for us to have a party.

One of the men around the tank said, "Mr. Hooks it looks like your family is partying without you. Just hold on for five more minutes. We'll wrap up and let the chef know you'll be ready in thirty minutes."

Vickie yells, "I got the chef covered."

The man continues. "You've done an excellent job Mr. Hooks. I can't wait to have you back again. And please bring your family again. The crew has enjoyed working with you, even though the day has been pretty long." I assumed the man was one of the executives at the aquarium. He walked over to Pastor Hunter, extended his hand and said, "Thanks for coming out. Your work is appreciated. It has truly blessed us all."

Hunter replied, "To God be the glory," and gave the man a friendly smile.

We paused for the interaction and went right back to dancing. Then I noticed Pastor Hunter's wife was in the room. I went and introduced myself and pointed out who everyone was and said, "They are all crazy." She joined us in our party without thinking twice.

It didn't seem like it took a long time for Randall to get dressed. While we were dancing when Randall came out. He was wearing jeans, a plain white tee, and Air Force Ones. He was carrying a LV duffel bag and some shirts over his shoulder. JJ was pulling the LV Pegase luggage bag. Randall passed a shirt out to everyone. That man is so sexy even if he did just exit a tank full of sea monsters. As a matter of fact, that made him sexier. He looked exhausted.

Randall grinned widely while he gave the t-shirts out. "A whole day's work for a few t-shirts. Don't ever say I don't love you guys. I spent all day in a tank fighting an octopus just to get y'all some dinner and t-shirts. What a day!" The girls giggled and congratulated Randall while thanking him for the shirts.

Randall motioned for us to come over to the table. "Let's eat." He leaned down in front of me and I put his chain back on his neck.

I realized he had done all of this for free. I am sure he had to pay his crew. But he got just what he said—a bundle of shirts and dinner for his time, work, and courage. He donated his time and talents in a dangerous situation and still covered the cost for his crew to be there all day. His generosity had impressed me once again.

The staff opened a door and brought in more elaborate tables filled with food, along with the chef. We ate in the same room as the exotic fish. The lights dimmed and gave the setting a romantic feel, especially since neon lights were coming from the aquariums. The fish looked beautiful. I could see the jellyfish glowing. It was breathtaking.

We ate until we were all full. Even Randall ate his uncooked vegetables until he was stuffed. Needless to say, no seafood was on the menu. We all started to say our goodbyes as the crews packed up their equipment.

"See you at dinner tomorrow Randall," Paige said, waving goodbye to Randall.

Leave it to Paige to mess stuff up. Who in the world told her he was coming to dinner at my house?

"Dinner where?" Randall asked.

"At D's. We have Sunday dinner there. Swing by after five. There will be some good eating and family fun."

Randall smiled and nodded. "See you then."

I wanted to smack the grin off Paige's face. She knew good and well I hadn't invited Randall, and she knew why I hadn't invited him.

Everyone else was gone except Randall and me. We sat in front of the aquarium, watching the brightly colored fish swirl through the water without a care in the world.

"We haven't discussed our attire for tomorrow," he said.

I was surprised he used the word "our." "What about it?" I asked with a laugh.

"You've picked the color the last few weeks. Now it's my turn."

"Okay. I hope it is green," I hinted.

"Nope," Randall shook his head. "Black and gray."

I frowned.

"I want to wear my new tie," he pleaded.

"Oh, okay. I guess." I rolled my eyes. We looked at each other lovingly.

"Hey make sure you're extremely careful when you're traveling alone," he said.

"I will. That goes for you too," I replied.

He smirked.

I touched his arm. "No, I'm serious. Unfortunately, we live in a cruel world where glamour and glitz is more important than a human life. Make sure your radar is being tracked and your personal antennas are up. People will see you and have no clue who you are but will follow you and try to jack you for something they see, like your watch or shoes. And if that happens, just give it to them. Don't risk your life over things we can purchase again. That goes for the Phantom, too. I would hate to lose you period, but I especially don't want it to happen unnecessarily." After everything that happened today, I couldn't bite my tongue when it came to my concern for him.

Randall rubbed my shoulder. "You know I hate to lose, and I definitely don't want you to lose me."

I smiled.

"I really appreciate that, Dani. Now you see why I've provided this tracker for you. By the way, I meant to tell you it registers your heart rate, pulse, temperature, etc."

"Huh?" The heart rate I knew about. But my pulse and body temperature? Wow!

"Yep, I can also tell when you are nervous, upset, excited, and even sick."

I shook my head. "You are a freaking stalker."

"No, I'm just concerned about you," Randall corrected me. "I'll do what it takes to make sure you are safe."

"Can you tell when I am ovulating and menstruating?" I asked just to throw him off.

He looked stunned and embarrassed.

I prodded. "So can you? No need in shying away now."

"Umm, I had not thought about it but I am sure I can," he said slowly in thought.

I rolled my eyes. "Figure it out and let me know the dates so I can be prepared."

He brought me to his chest with one arm and kissed my forehead. "You're crazy. That's why I love you."

He said the words. I am not sure how he meant it, but he said it. We were walking to our cars and both stopped suddenly. I don't think Randall meant to say that he loved me out loud. It made the moment awkward even if we were in the middle of clowning around. But the worst part was I couldn't say it back, even though I wanted to. It would just make things more difficult. He was still married. Once those words are said, you can't take them back, and our dynamic would officially change from friendship to relationship. Yes, that was what I wanted, but it couldn't happen right now.

I think we both felt the same way. Two people that could do anything they wanted, when they wanted—except be together. Sure, I could ignore my spiritual beliefs and do what my heart wanted, but I knew I'd feel guilty. I had to do things the way I knew God wanted me to. So my choices right now were to be Randall's friend, wait for him to get a divorce, or walk away from the situation altogether.

Sometimes following God made life more difficult. I had been walking with God a long time, and obviously, the same was true for Randall. After all, he was a deacon! And he was a deacon in the traditional and Biblical sense. He didn't just have a title. He invested his time and talents in the church and gave back to his community. He was called to do that work, and I could tell he loved it. Whenever I see Randall in the sanctuary, I can easily picture him becoming a minister. I wouldn't be surprised to learn that he's been allowing Pastor Hunter to mentor him in preparation for pastoral ministry. And if that was Randall's goal, I prayed God would allow it to happen.

I respected Randall. I respected his position at the church and his moral point of view. We were both on the same page. However, our bodies sometimes informed us that they had a different agenda. But so far, we'd been successful at resisting temptation. And I was starting to get the feeling that these monitoring watches Randall and I wore were somehow tracked back to Pastor Hunter. To be honest, Pastor Hunter kind of had me scared to do ANYTHING that looked bad. I was sure he had eyes in the back of his head. I realized I had been daydreaming and not paying much attention to Randall.

"Are you okay?" I asked.

"Yes, are you?" he replied.

"Not really." I said as I looked at the ground.

His voice sounded panicked. "What's wrong?"

I paused. "Can I ask you something that I've been wondering about for weeks but never thought it was the right time to ask?"

"Anything," he said. "Shoot."

"What is your motivation behind your blogs?"

Randall hesitated. "I'm not sure what you're asking. But I think you're the motivation."

"I need more details," I say shyly.

"I think they speak for themselves," Randall told me sweetly.

"No, they don't," I disagreed.

"Well, what do you want to know?" he asked willing to clarify.

"Honestly?" I replied.

"Of course," he said.

"Who are you talking about in your blogs? Who do you want to read the blogs, and why are you writing them?"

"Wow! That's a loaded series of questions," Randall said with a nervous laugh.

"Well?" I look into his eyes and wait for the answer.

"I'm talking about you and I'm writing for you to see. You're the whole reason why I write those blogs."

He turned his back to me and I moved in front of him. He looked down and I could tell he didn't want to talk about it anymore.

"Oh no you don't," I tell him. "I want answers. You need to talk to me and be man enough to look me in the eye. At least tell me why you don't want to keep talking about this. You can't just shut down like that. If you'd understand it better in boxing terms, the bell didn't ring to end the fight. We're still in round one. So you're going to have to fight like a man or step out of the ring. It's up to you."

I had never spoken to Randall in such a stern tone. I didn't think he was being rude. I could just sense that I'd touched a nerve and he didn't want to take the conversation further. But I needed to know.

He looked me in my eyes, held my chin, and said just as sternly to me as I said to him, "I am not trying to be rude or uncooperative. Neither am I stepping out of the ring. This is a conversation I cannot have with you right now. I answered your questions. I will express the rest of my feelings on my blog before service in the morning. But for now, we need to end this conversation. This is too deep for either of us at the moment. But trust me, we will have the conversation when the time is right. Are we clear?"

Did he just ask me if we were clear? Who does he think he is? "Actually, we're not clear, Randall," I said with displeasure.

"I'm sorry, Danielle. That's all I can give you right now. I will respond to your questions in more detail when I can better express myself."

I huffed.

"Are you angry?" he raised his brow.

"No," I snapped.

"Danielle, I can't say too much or do too much now. I don't ever want to hurt you. Just please let me do what I need to do."

I was disappointed. "Good night Randall." I opened my own door, jumped in my car, and closed the door behind me before he could do any of it for me.

He leaned down over my window. "Drive safely," he said softly.

"You too. Go home and let me know you made it home. I am not upset." I was lying. But I didn't want him to feel bad.

"Are you sure?"

"Yes." All I was sure about was that I was getting tired of not being able to be with him.

Randall was talking to himself as he walked to his car. *Damn, I really messed up. I know she's pissed at me. I can't let any more of my guard down now. I can't let Danielle see all of me until this nonsense with Tameka is final. How is it that a person makes your life miserable for years, walks away, and still manages to destroy your happiness? This has to end immediately.*

I texted Randall when I got home. I cut the oven on to start making brisket for tomorrow's dinner. I ran to my closet to figure out what to wear to church. I jumped in the shower and heard the text alert on my phone. I dried off and saw Randall's text.

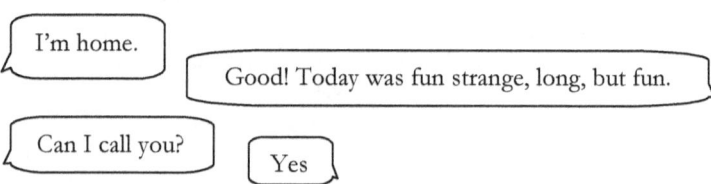

I'm home.

Good! Today was fun strange, long, but fun.

Can I call you?

Yes

The phone rings immediately. "Hey, what's up?" I answer.

"I just want to tell you thank you again for coming today and make sure it's okay that I come to dinner tomorrow.

I smile. "Oh, you're welcome and it's not a problem at all for you to come to dinner."

"Are you sure?"

"I'm positive. I have some water to spare."

"I do eat food, you know," he said with a laugh.

"Really?" I joked.

Randall really wanted me to know that he was sincere. "Do you understand and accept my apologies?"

"Everything is fine," I told him. I tried to add some assurance to my voice.

"I don't feel like you're being honest," he told me.

"I'm being as honest as I can," I said.

"I'm not sure how to take that. But on a lighter note, you were great today," he responded.

I blushed. "No, you were. That was awesome. I can't wait to see the final production."

I could hear Randall smiling through the phone. "I'm glad you mentioned that. Will you accompany me to the preview of the commercials?"

"Sure," I said happily.

"Great."

"Get some sleep," I tell him. "I'll see you in a few hours."

"You too." We both held the phone for a few seconds, not wanting to hang up. After listening to him breathe and feeling myself weaken, I ended the call.

Sunday

I was not waiting for Randall after church today. I was planning on skipping right out the door. I also had a feeling I'd get in my car after service, admit that I was being childish, and go back inside. But being stubborn was worth a try. I walked out of the sanctuary after the benediction.

"Have a great week," one of the hosts sang as I neared the door.

"Thank you—same to you," I said pleasantly.

Then one of the parking attendants stopped me. "Slow down," the man said.

"OKAY," I replied. Now was not the time to fight.

"Aren't you going in the wrong direction?" The attendant asked me.

I squint my eyes. "Not that I know of. Is there something I should know?"

The attendant shrugged. "I guess not. Have a good day, ma'am."

As soon as I went to push the door it was pulled opened for me, which startled me. I didn't see anyone on the other side. I looked back. The parking attendant was standing at his post, motionless. I slowly walk through the door. I felt like I was in a haunted house. Suddenly a body appeared from behind the door.

"Ms. Rose," Randall crooned.

I jumped and almost cursed. "Deacon Washington!" I stopped to catch my breath.

"You okay?" he asked placing his hand on my back. "How are you out of breath with all the exercising you do?"

I finally had enough air to speak. "I was out of breath because you scared me!"

"How did I scare you?" he asked.

"Look at you," I said flippantly.

"Oh no you didn't," he laughed. I couldn't help but laugh, too.

"I meant because you were standing behind the door. Most normal people don't do that."

"Who said I was normal?" Randall asked. He had a point.

"Other stalkers may think you are normal," I responded.

He was laughing. His smile was mesmerizing. Another door opened and I could see Security looking in our direction and possibly speaking in his ear. Randall motioned toward the men and I could make out voices in Randall's earpiece. I had been set up. As soon as I got ready to tell Randall that I knew he was up to something, a woman walked through the door and stood shoulder-to-shoulder to me. I looked at Randall. Immediately my attitude changed. His expression didn't give me the impression that anything was wrong. He didn't even act like he knew the woman.

I looked her up and down. Actually, I mean mugged her. I was prepared for "whatever" to go down. It took me a second to remember that I was at church and not in the old neighborhood.

"Deacon," she said, addressing Randall.

"Yes ma'am," he replied, in a voice he'd never used with me. Then I recall that this was his tone of voice when we first met. That's the voice he uses with the general public. When he talks to me, his voice is softer and much more playful.

"I need to speak with her for a moment," the woman said, referring to me.

I looked at Randall and widened my eyes. I tensed my body and reached into my bag in case I needed a weapon. "Excuse me?" I said harshly to the woman.

"Yes. I'm taking your bag," she said calmly.

"What?" I almost screamed.

She repeated herself. "I'm taking your bag."

I forced my body to relax. Since Randall didn't give me the impression that he knew this woman, I calmed down. I thought it might have been Tameka. I hoped no one had been looking at the security monitors to see me behaving in such an unruly manner at church.

He twirled me around and said, "Let me see what bag you have." Noticing my hand in my bag he responded. "What were you going to do? Cut the woman?"

"I didn't know. It didn't look like you had my back," I said, slightly less tense.

The woman was waiting for me to comply. "I'm sorry. I just want the bag."

I looked at Randall. "Are you just going to let this happen? You're going to let this woman take my bag?"

Randall was cool. "Yeah, give her the bag," he told me. He turned to the woman and said, "Ma'am, you can take it."

I put my hand on my hip and got in his face. "Are you planning on buying me another one?" I ask enraged.

"I'll buy you two," Randall promised. "Bless the lady with the bag."

"You're supposed to be on my side," I say eyeing him.

"I am on your side. That's why I'm buying you two new bags," Randall answered.

I looked at the woman. "Ma'am, I'll give you this bag, but the bills come with it."

She backed away. "Never mind," she said.

Randall was still trying to make this happen. He said, "Ma'am, don't worry about the bills. Take the bag."

"Oh, stop it," I tell him.

The woman said "Deacon, you, and your wife look nice. Have a good day. I will see you all next week."

Then I realized we did look nice. I could see our reflection in the glass door. We looked good individually but we looked better together. He was just the right height for me and we coordinated well. I was wearing my black and gray suit. Black skirt with the gray jacket with black piping and a two toned black and gray hat Mr. Smith made for me. I was wearing my black and gray peep-toe pumps. He was wearing a charcoal gray suit, black shirt and the Gray Champs tie I gave him two days ago with the tie clip.

His hair and face freshly shaved. I swear he had Vaseline on his teeth they were so sparkly. His status just changed. He has been attractive, handsome, fine, and sexy but at this moment he was hot! I could imagine waking up to that. He was talking and I could see his lips moving but I was daydreaming about being with him all the time. I have no clue what he's saying.

It was probably best he didn't have time to pay me much attention in church today. When I walked in he was running through the vestibule. I knew it was him, even though I only saw his back. He turned and held up his finger to tell me to wait a minute. But my stubbornness pushed me to go have a seat before he could get to me. I saw him peek through the door to check to make sure Pastor was seated and everything was in order. I could see his profile in the security booth behind everyone. I hadn't seen him up close until now. That was a good thing, because I wouldn't have been listening to the sermon at all had I been anywhere near all this beautiful manliness in the sanctuary. Randall interrupted my thoughts. I was almost mad at him for doing so.

"Are we still on for dinner?" he politely asked.

"Yep. I told you that you were welcome to come," I reminded him.

"You sure I'm not intruding?" he wanted reassurance.

"You are, but I don't mind," I joked.

He smiled. "I'll see you around five."

"Do I need to get anything in particular for your diet?" I ask him.

He shook his head. "You don't have to make anything special for me," he said nicely.

"Are you sure?" I was trying to be as sweet as possible, since I'd been so short with him hours before.

"Yep," he assured me.

"You need directions?" I ask with a giggle.

He rolled his eyes. "Very funny. But that reminds me, can I ask you a question?"

I knew what was coming. "Now?"

"Yeah now," he laughed.

"Shoot."

"Why did you turn off your locator last night?"

I didn't have an answer. I had no explanation other than the fact that I was being a bitch and didn't want to feel like he was controlling everything after he didn't answer my questions the way I wanted him to. I looked at him and raised my eyebrow. I knew he knew the answer to his question. He leaned in to indicate that he couldn't hear me responding. I still had nothing to say.

He hugged me. I knew he was waiting for an answer but I pursed my lips.

"I thought so," he said with a smirk.

"So are you walking me to my car or not?" I ask.

"Yeah, come on."

"On second thought, I can handle this. You've already given my bag away. You may give my car away too."

He ignored me and we walked side by side. He opened my door. "Get in the car. You know what to do. Until five my love."

He closed the door and took off running. He looked so damn sexy in that suit and even sexier running. Dark colors looked great on him. Hell, any color worked well on him. "DAMN," I whispered to myself. I realized I was still on church grounds and took a long breath to center myself. "Hey, Deacon," I said, rolling the window down.

"Yes baby."

Did he just say baby? I tried to shake it off. "You may not want to run in those dress shoes on this pavement."

Raising his eyebrow he asked, "Why?"

"If you fall we may have to call 911."

"Am I going to hurt myself?"

"No. The paramedics will have to come resuscitate me from laughing so hard." I couldn't let my guard down completely.

"Go away," he said chuckling.

"Bye," I sang.

"Bye Sweetie." Why is he using these terms of endearment with me? He was just making everything more difficult!

I sat there watching him walk away long enough to see someone flash their lights at me. *Oh crap I'm holding up traffic.* I pulled up and over into another parking space. I pulled my list out of my bag. I needed to see what was on my grocery list to determine which store I needed to go to. I decide it was better for me to go out of the way to DeKalb Farmers Market to get the freshest fruits and vegetables. All the produce I needed wasn't available in my garden.

I heard a tap at my window and looked over my shoulder. A concerned deacon was at my window. "Are you okay?" he said through the glass.

I smiled to let him know I was fine. "Yes, thank you." Geez! I couldn't even look over my grocery list without Randall sending his colleagues to check on me! I decided to turn my locator back on before Randall freaked out.

My front door opened at 4:20 PM. The girls were really early! Paige made no effort to hide their intent. "We were trying to beat Hooks here," she said unapologetically.

"I should have known," I laugh.

Sade looked around the dinner table. "Auntie, where did you order all this food from?" she joked.

I ignore her. "Girl, check the cake in the oven," I tell her. "Before we even start no one touches the cupcakes. Those are Leigh's."

"Yeah, so hands off, little girl," Leigh said, swatting Sade's hand before she could get to the desserts.

"Y'all are a trip," Sade quipped. "And I wish you people would stop calling me 'little girl.' How many times do I have to say it? We're all the same age."

We hung out and laughed while the girls helped me finish setting everything up. I looked at my phone to check the time.

"OKAY, I've got 13 minutes before he gets here," I say. "And I know he's going to be right on time. He may even come a few minutes early. Let me go get ready."

"I'm coming, too," Sade said.

I look at her skeptically. "I don't think I need any help."

"From the look of those sweatpants and head scarf, you do," she joked.

I pretended to be indignant. "How do you know Randall doesn't like me in a scarf?" I asked.

"Oh, excuuuuuuse us," the girls tease me.

"Yeah, maybe he does like you in a scarf. If that's all you're wearing," Paige said naughtily.

"Paige!" I throw a pillow from the sofa at her.

She covers her mouth as if she is ashamed, which couldn't be further from the truth. "Oops, did I say that out loud?" she asked.

Leigh nudged Paige. "Don't try to play innocent now," she said with a laugh.

"Must be the wine," Paige reasoned, looking down at her glass with a sly grin.

I shook my head. "Y'all are crazy," I told them as I walked to my room. I went to my closet and grabbed a pair of jeans and a Henley. Sade, who I didn't realize had followed me, let out a disapproving sigh. I turned around. She quickly shook her head and passed me the tightest jeans in my closet. They had to be the tightest ever. I practically needed the jaws of life to get those pants off! Then she threw me a low-cut racer back tank with studs around the collar.

"No ma'am," I told her, shaking my head.

"Auntie you're at home. You can wear it," she said, shoving the clothes in my face.

"I know what you're trying to do," I told her laughing. But I obliged. As I was lying on the bed trying to get into my skin-tight pants, the phone rang. Sade picked it up before I could get to it. I knew it was Randall.

"Auntie, how do I let him in?" she asked grinning.

I stick my tongue out at her and snatch the phone. I walk into the restroom and lock the door behind me before Sade can come in.

"Hey," I say into the phone.

"Hey. I'm at your gate," Randall said cheerily.

I press a series of buttons and put the phone back to my mouth. "Now, you know you're not obligated to stay long. You can leave any time you want. Just ignore my family. They are nuts. I'm working on getting help for them," I say with a nervous chuckle. I had no idea what the girls would say to Randall now that we were all on my turf.

Randall laughed. "Chill, they're good people." He seemed to be really relaxed. Hopefully that would help me calm down.

"We'll see if you still feel that way after dinner," I told him.

"OKAY," he laughed. "I'm pulling up now."

I walked out the bathroom and through the room toward the front door. The girls were all standing in the living room with ridiculous grins on their faces, like we've never had company before. I gave them a grimacing look and pointed my finger at them. "You better be on your best behavior! Understood?" I barked.

"Whatever! Open the damn door," Paige snarled.

"Are y'all just gonna stand there looking stupid?" I ask. "Look busy!" Instead they came closer to the front door. It was made of glass so I know Randall saw them all, standing in a line looking like devious schoolchildren who were just waiting to misbehave.

I opened the door. "Hey!" I noticed I had too much excitement in my voice. Or maybe I was just jittery.

"Hey," he said, handing me a bouquet of roses, a bottle of non-alcoholic wine, and a regular bottle of wine. "I didn't know what to bring. You didn't give me any instructions," he said with a wink.

"I didn't know you needed instructions—or if you would follow them," I tell him with a laugh.

He was walking extremely close to me as we went through the foyer to the family room.

The girls had positioned themselves in a number of inauthentic positions. One was pretending to text someone on her phone, one was acting as though she was reading a magazine the other was channel surfing.

"What's up, ladies?" Randall said, trying not to laugh at the show the girls were putting on.

"Hey," Paige said, as casually as she could. Sade got up to take the wine from my hands and Leigh grabbed the flowers to put them in water. The both said hello to Randall politely.

I roll my eyes and smirk. "Have a seat," I say to Randall. "Make yourself comfortable."

"I plan to," he said softly.

Paige was putting the wine in the wine chiller. Leigh was checking the sweet potato pie. They were doing well so far. Randall still hadn't sat down yet. Once everyone else was out of the room, he came up behind me. So close that I could feel his warm breath on the back of my neck. He started speaking. I wanted to faint into his arms.

"Let that be the last time you greet me without a hug," he said. "No matter where we are." I tried to decrease my wide grin and grabbed his hand. I led him back to the foyer, stood slightly on my toes so I could reach him and hugged him with a little too much passion. Both of us let out a pleasurable sigh. I had never hugged him without heels on before. He was taller than I thought. This, of course, made him even more attractive.

I heard the girls clearing their throats to let us know they saw us. I didn't turn around because I knew Leigh had a camera. Before I could warn Randall, I heard the flash.

Paige said to the two of us, "Enough, break it up. Get a room," she smirked. I think we were both embarrassed, but didn't want to let each other go. I held his hand back to the family room.

"What is that wonderful smell?" Randall said.

Sade chimed in. "Dinner that Auntie picked up from some hole in the wall. Make sure you scan it." I jab her.

Randall laughed. "Oh, I will."

I answer him with a grin. "Herb crusted beef brisket, garlic roasted red potatoes, collard greens, sautéed eggplant, fried corn with bell peppers, pound cake, cupcakes, sweet potato pie—and some other extremely healthy food just for you."

"Oh really?" Randall asked, impressed. He turned to Sade. "What is she planning to feed me?" he pointed at me.

"Some garbage from her garden," she said, rolling her eyes. He laughed again.

I said, "I've roasted some vegetables for you. Eggplant, bell pepper, tomatoes, and mushrooms. I also tossed some mixed greens and made a fruit salad for you. Sade forgot to mention we're also having cornbread, but I'm sure you don't want that."

I could tell he was surprised. He was probably wondering how I had the time to do all this. His expression also indicated he appreciated me going out of my way to make sure he had a great meal.

"By the way Hooks, all of the vegetables are from Dani's garden out back." Paige reiterated.

"Even the mixed greens and mushrooms?" Randall asked

"Yep," she said grinning at me like a proud sister.

Randall rubbed his hands together. "So, when do we eat?"

"Three minutes—we're just waiting on the cornbread to brown." I headed towards the dining room. Everyone stops in amazement. Usually my dining room is completely off limits.

"Y'all eat in there?" He asked looking at the picture perfect room.

"NEVER!" They yelled.

"Then the kitchen it is," he said. Even though I was trying to make the dinner as special as possible, Randall wanted me to feel comfortable.

We all sat down. He grabbed my hand and before I could ask, he began blessing the food. I peek during prayer and see him staring at me. He winks. I smile. He continues praying.

We ate and laughed for hours. I was glad everyone was having a good time. Everyone was indulging in all the calorie-filled fare on the table except Randall. He sat at one end of the table and I sat on the other. It was like we were the man and woman of the house.

Sade had a chunk of cornbread on a side plate that had so much honey butter dripping from it that I wanted to take it for myself. Just as I was thinking it, a fork reached over and took the bread from her plate. We all looked over at Randall and laughed. He had crumbs all over his mouth. He grinned with a closed mouth.

"Oh hell no!" she said. She went over to Randall's chair and pretended to try and take the cornbread out of his mouth. He clamped his mouth shut tight and fought her off with his arms. We laughed hysterically.

"Get your own cornbread!" she yelled. "Don't you know better than to steal food from a hungry woman?" she playfully punched him in the arm.

"I couldn't resist," he said, after swallowing his food. "I haven't had cornbread in years."

Sade pointed to the table. "There's a whole pan over there. We have it every Sunday. Get your Boo to make you some low-fat cornbread. I am sure she'll figure out how--just for you."

Randall gave her a disapproving look. "Low fat? That defeats the purpose."

"The next time you steal off my plate you will be defeated," Sade retorted, rolling her eyes.

Leigh reached for her camera to capture the moment. It was the perfect time for Randall to steal her brisket.

"Leigh, he got you!" Paige yelled.

"What?" Leigh looked back and saw a huge piece of meat on Randall's fork and dived at him.

She was a second too late. "You have no manners," she told him, chuckling. "Where is that type of behavior acceptable?" she pretended to scold him.

"At Danielle's table," he said with a grin.

"I'm not responsible for this," I say quickly shaking my head.

"I think next week everyone should eat what I eat," Randall suggested.

Did he say next week? Was he inviting himself back to dinner? This was both great and not so great.

"Sorry to inform you Randall," Paige chimed in. "But Danielle only sets aside every other Sunday for us.

She has no time for us the other Sundays. She goes to church, the track, and work." Randall gave me a disapproving look.

"A girl needs her rest," I said, shrugging.

"Maybe you can convince her to change that," Paige said to him.

He folded his hands as if he was begging and looked at me with sad, pleading eyes.

I shook my head no.

"Please," he said.

They all joined in. "Pretty please?"

"Wow, you guys are ganging up on me now?" I was only partly offended.

"We'll cook," Sade volunteered.

"Cook what? Raw vegetables?" Leigh said with a scoff.

"I'll cook," Randall said. "Or I'll at least send the chef," he laughed.

I looked at all of them. "No. No and NO!"

Randall laughed. "Is that your final answer?"

"Yes!" I said showing him my fist.

"Aww, man!" Paige said, folding her arms.

"We tried," Leigh said with a shrug.

"Danielle, why would you deny your family a decent meal on Sundays? What do we need to do to make this happen?" Randall's voice was playful but sincere.

I widened my eyes. "Randall Hooks Washington!"

"Yes ma'am," he said sweetly.

"Eat your dinner," I said firmly.

He widened his eyes and looked around the room at the others. He opened his mouth to protest some more, but decided against it.

We all ate dessert and headed to the couch. For the first time, I didn't rush to wash the dishes. I just wanted to relax. Hooks picked up the remote.

"NO ESPN," Leigh warned.

"What about BET?" he suggested.

"Let's see what's on," she replied.

We watched a few movies before Sade spoke up.

"Karaoke time!" Sade announced grabbing the microphone that was connected to the karaoke machine.

"UGH!" I sighed exasperated.

Paige held her hand up. "Stop it, I say. You are obsessed with karaoke. No Gloria Gainer tonight."

Of course we all had to participate. In karaoke, that is. We had a blast. We all took turns singing solos and then there was the group number: "We are Family" by Sister Sledge. We changed the lyrics and could barely get through the song for laughing so hard.

Then we realized it was after 10:00 PM. Paige joked, "We're never going to be invited back," she said shaking her head.

"Why?" Randall asked.

They all looked in fear.

I answered Randall. "Because they know they're past curfew."

Randall looked at the girls. "Dang, two meals a month and a curfew. Danielle runs a tight ship around here. Let's clean the kitchen so we can go before we get put out."

They all jumped up. Everyone took a task. Everything was clean by 10:45.

"Let's ride," Sade said to the girls.

We all walked to the door.

"Umm that means you too, Mr. Hooks," Paige said loudly.

I could tell from Randall's body language that he had planned on staying a few extra minutes after the girls left. But he was being called out, so he got up to leave, too.

"Oh, okay," he complied.

We all hugged and kissed like it would be months before we saw each other again, even though most of us would see each other again in a few hours.

Randall and I hugged for a long time. "I really enjoyed myself today," he said into my ear. "I hope I'm invited back next Sunday."

I smiled. "I enjoyed it too. Sorry my family is so crazy. And next week is still off limits, so don't get any ideas!"

We were really close and his lips were on my neck. My eyes were closed and I suddenly felt a tug. He was being snatched away.

"Come on," Sade said, nudging Randall toward the door. "Wii Bowling and salmon dinner next Sunday, Auntie," she said to me. "4:00 PM."

Before I knew it I was agreeing, then I caught myself. "Nice try Sade."

Sade turned to Randall. "Try to work on her this week, Hooks. Help us all accomplish our goal of having Sunday dinner next week."

"That's not fair," I yelled as Sade walked to the car. I watched the girls and Randall pull off like they were my children going off to college for the first time. I sat on my porch steps for a few minutes and reflected on the day. My phone rang and jolted me out of daydreaming.

Where was my phone? I hadn't used it since I let Randall in the gate. I knew Randall was calling because I could hear the ringtone. I didn't get to the phone fast enough. My phone beeped to let me know I had received a voicemail. I called my cell phone from my house phone. I followed the sound to get to my cell and called Randall back.

"Hey," I said

"What, your boyfriend came by that quick?" Randall joked.

I smiled. "Are you jealous?"

"Do you need to ask?" he quipped.

"Why didn't you call the house phone?" I ask him.

"I don't have your home number," he told me.

"Huh?" I could have sworn I'd given him my home number.

"Nope. I don't," he said again.

I thought about the fact that I didn't have his home phone number either. "Do you want it?" I asked. I knew my question had several meanings.

Randall didn't hesitate to respond. "Of course. Does this mean I'm a keeper if I get the house number?" he asked.

"I don't think so but nice try," I teased him.

Randall laughed, "Well, I tried. You want to call me from the house phone so I'll have the number in my phone or give the number to me once I get home?"

"I'll hang up and call you from my house phone," I tell him.

I grabbed my laptops, house phone, cell phone and a natural fruit juice and head to the deck. It was a nice night. I could get some work done and listen to the crickets. How peaceful. Randall and I talk briefly before I start getting my work done. He posts a blog at 2:13 in the morning.

> Today was beautiful. Family entails the most important earthly relationships a man can have. I miss family time. I have found a family that I want to be a part of. I hope they accept me with open arms. I plan to one day officially call these people my family, and to make their home my home.

WEEK 12

Monday

I went to bed late but woke up early. That was nothing unusual for me. By the time I got to the office, there was a message blinking on my phone. That was also not unusual. I was so pleased to hear Randall's voice.

"Good morning my love. I want to thank you again for dinner and your hospitality. I hope we can do it again. This coming Sunday would definitely work. Just wanted to let you know I'm thinking of you, and I hope you have a wonderful day."

I was both elated and perturbed. Why did Randall have to be married? I'd asked myself this question a thousand times. I felt like I was being cursed. What did I do to be in a situation like this? It was torture. I jump up from my desk to go fill my cup with water before I call him back. I needed some time to collect myself, even though we weren't face to face. I took a few deep breaths and dialed his number.

"Hey," he said with an upbeat tone.

"Hey," I answered with a sigh.

"You made it to work yet?" he asked sarcastically.

"Funny," I replied dryly.

"What does that mean?" he pretended to be innocent.

"You can tell where I am," I reminded him

"Yeah I can but I'm not checking the device right now. I'm actually on the mat. And you thought I was a stalker," he said, trying to sound like he was hurt.

I apologized. I didn't mean to interrupt his workout. "Do you want to call me later?" I ask.

"Yeah, but I really want to talk to you now," he admitted.

I giggled. "Oh how sweet. What's up?"

"Nothing in particular. I just wanted to hear your voice," he said in one of the sweetest tones I'd ever heard from him.

I was flattered—but skeptical. "You wouldn't happen to be sweet-talking me into having dinner Sunday, would you?"

He laughed. "Not at the moment. But I do plan to put sweet-talking into action before Sunday."

"Why?" I ask.

"I'm taking my son camping this weekend, and I'm going to need a good meal when I get back."

"CAMPING?" I asked, surprised.

"Yeah, what's wrong with camping?"

"Other than the fact that you have to be outdoors? Nothing, I guess. Well…there is the tiny matter of not having electricity, running water or indoor plumbing."

"Those are all the things I love about camping." His voice was relaxed.

"Oh, well have fun then." I shrugged but forgot he couldn't see me.

Randall's voice sounded sheepish. "Well, I wanted to ask you to join us at the lake."

I was shocked. "You and your son?"

"Yes."

I hesitated before answering. "I don't think so."

"Why?" Randall sounded as if he had no idea why I would decline.

"For a few reasons," I tell him calmly.

"Can you name them?" he challenges me.

"Yes, of course," I tell him. "For starters, do you own a palace on the lake?"

Randall sounded a little caught off guard. "Why did you ask that?"

"I just told you how I feel about camping. So I'm sure the accommodations are pretty stellar if you're asking me to be out in the wilderness."

"There is no palace there," Randall said with a laugh.

"Well what would you call it?" I ask. I knew his camping arrangements had to be especially fancy.

Randall's voice was smiling. "You really want to know?"

"Yes."

"I call it a lake house."

"I'm sure you're being modest," I scoffed.

Randall kept pressing me for an answer. "So will you come?"

"I don't think so, Randall." I was flattered by his invitation, but it just didn't feel right. Not yet.

"Why not?" he asked. "You can stay in the lake house the entire time if you want."

"Well, even though I'm not a huge fan of being outdoors, that's not the reason I don't think I should come. But I can't tell you how to raise your son."

Randall sounded disappointed but I knew he understood. "I'm listening to your opinion and I do value it from here on out."

I knew everything Randall was trying to say. And, again, I was flattered. But I had to use my better judgment. "I think it's inappropriate right now," I reiterate.

"I understand but I want you to realize I'm asking you for a reason. It's imperative that you meet him," Randall tells me.

"I will meet him. I'm excited to meet your son. Now is just not the time. You have to remember that you're in the middle of a divorce. I don't want to make anything worse. So, it's best if I hold off on doing anything that could make the situation more complicated."

"I see what you're saying," Randall told me. "I wish your answer were different, but I understand."

"I also think you should spend some quality time with your son," I respond. "You haven't mentioned him much lately and I'm sure he misses you a lot."

"You're right," Randall said with a laugh. "You've had me so mesmerized lately that I haven't thought about much of anything else."

I was blushing like hell on the inside. "Mesmerized huh? So do I get a pass this time?"

"I want you to change your mind between now and Thursday," he admitted.

"Now you know I am not missing work," I tell him, trying to sound as practical as I can.

"You are aware that when you become Mrs. Washington, you'll miss days of work sometimes—right?"

"Why?" I asked. He chose not to answer me.

"Just think about coming. We won't bother you. We'll be too busy tubing, fishing, grilling, hiking and doing other guy stuff. It will be quiet and peaceful. You may get some work done." He was really making this hard for me.

I sighed. "Randall, I really appreciate the offer and even though I really would love to join you, I don't think now is the best time. But I promise I'll go to the wilderness with you one time, and one time only! Just not now."

Randall sighed, too. "I'm disappointed but I am glad there's hope. My son and I spend a lot of time there. I actually like camping a lot. It's really relaxing and it gives me a chance to spend long periods of time with my son. When you do decide to come, I hope you like it so much that you come more than just once. I think you'll love it!"

"Well, now I would feel like I was intruding on your father son time," I tell him.

"Nice try," Randall responds. "You know I want you to be there."

"Honestly, I don't want to intrude on your father and son time," I tell him. "I'll miss you while you're gone," I was really trying to soften the blow.

Randall's voice sounded a little more upbeat. "Well, that's good to hear," he said. "I'll miss you too. I'll have my phones and they both get reception at the lake house. So, you may not have time to miss me," he teased.

"Your phones work up there?" I was surprised.

"Yep."

"You'll still be busy tubing and fishing with your son, though," I reason.

"If you call, I'll answer," Randall promises.

"I'm going to hold you to it," I reply.

"Will I see you after work?" he asked.

"If you want," I tell him.

"Of course I want to see you. I want to see you all day every day. I want to marry you," he answered. He sounded so sweet. I was starting to feel guilty for not going on the camping trip. But I knew I was making the right choice.

"You are so unpredictable," I say with a sigh.

Randall laughed. "I hope you always think that."

"I hope you always stay this way," I said.

He sighed. I knew he wanted to say more, but we both had to get our day started.

"Have a good day. See you soon."

"Thanks, you too. You have less than eight hours to go," I reassure him.

"You sure?" he asked.

"Yes," I laughed lightly. It was unusual for me to pull an eight-hour day but I couldn't wait to see him, either.

"Bye, my love." Randall's tone was like a glass of cool water on the hottest day. Refreshing and necessary.

"Bye," I sang.

I had a great day. I couldn't get Randall off my mind. I wondered if this is the way love was supposed to be. It was raining again after work. I decided to go to Hooks' gym instead of the track or my gym. I pulled up to my assigned parking spot. I just sat there and stared into space for a long time before getting the courage to go inside. I was shocked that I hadn't seen Randall yet. One of his guys greeted me at the front desk.

"Good evening Ms. Rose. How was work?"

I smiled. "Hi, it was good."

"What can we do for you this afternoon?" The man asked.

"I was planning on working on arms and abs."

"Let me show you the equipment."

I was at the gym for over 40 minutes and still didn't see Randall. I was getting worried and upset but decided to keep my cool. I worked out a little longer. I took in my surroundings carefully. I noticed I was being watched as well. But, that was to be expected. I worked out for about two hours before packing up my things and preparing to leave. I had lingered around long enough. As soon as I stood up to leave, the man who welcomed me into the gym showed up next to me. He asked me if I wanted anything to drink.

"I'll have water," I say politely. The man leads me around a corner to the gym's juice bar. I see a familiar face behind the counter. It was the man Randall brought to the track to mix his nutritional drinks. We exchanged grins.

"How are you Ms. Rose? I see you decided to stay out of the heat today," he said.

"Actually, it was the rain," I say with a laugh.

"Will you be having your usual?" he asks.

I shake my head. "And do you have anything that will help me get a good night's sleep?" I ask.

"I do," he says with a nod.

"OKAY, add that to my 'usual' please," I tell him.

"You got it. Is it for here or to go?" he asks.

"I will take it with me if you don't mind," I said.

"No one ever wants my company," he joked, holding his head down.

I smiled. "Then make it for here."

He put my smoothie in a glass that is usually reserved for fancier drinks and topped it with fresh fruit. I grabbed my wallet out of my duffel bag and handed him a twenty-dollar bill.

He leaned real close into to me. In a low tone that was both jovial and somber he whispered, "Are you trying to get me fired?"

"No, why?" I was shocked by his question.

He nodded to the $20. "Your money is no good here."

"Well, consider it a tip," I tell him with a grin.

"Oh, so you really are trying to get me fired," he chuckled.

I gave him a knowing look. "I definitely don't want to do that," I told him as I put the money back into my wallet. "You have a good night."

"Here, take a water for the road. You'll need it." He places a Voss bottle on the countertop.

"A plastic bottle is fine," I tell him.

"No substitutes for the lady of the house," he replied without hesitation.

Randall's staff was trained well. I laughed at the thought, but he didn't even crack a smile. That made me nervous.

"See you tomorrow," he said with certainty. He worded it like a statement, but I took it as a question.

"If it rains, I'll be here," I tell him.

I walked toward the door. Once I got to the desk, a person I'd never seen before turned to me and said, "Good night, Ms. Rose." I was a little caught off guard, but said, "Thanks, good night."

I got to my car and popped my trunk. I threw my gym bag inside the trunk and jumped into the driver's seat. I opened my bottle of water and stared at my name on the parking spot sign. I was really disappointed Randall didn't show up the whole time I was at the gym. I felt like he was in another part of the gym and didn't bother to come say hello. I looked down at my Blackberry, scanned the emails, texts, and missed calls. I hit the voicemail button to listen to any messages I had missed. Randall hadn't tried to contact me at all. I laid my head on the steering wheel. I was trying to recuperate from my workout while thinking of all the possible reasons why Randall was a no-show.

Then I heard a gentle tap on my window. I looked over. It was Randall. I reached to open the door, almost knocking him over. He moved back to let me out of the car.

"You're done working out?" he asked shocked.

"For the night," I answered, trying not to sound aggravated. He looked sad.

"I thought we would have finished at the same time," he told me, pouting.

My suspicions about him being at the gym the whole time were correct. He was dripping with sweat. "Are you done?" I asked him.

"No, but I wanted to see you before you left," he confessed.

I felt a little less irritated. "What were you doing?" I asked him. I knew he was working out. But what I really wanted to know was why he took so long to come see me.

"I was working out on my aquatic fitness system."

He clearly didn't realize I was trying to indirectly chastise him for making me wait two hours to see him. But I decided not to be sarcastic. "No, I mean what held you up?" I asked in the nicest tone of voice I could.

"Nothing," he said. The look on my face indicated that his answer was incorrect. "I mean, I was letting you work out," he said quickly. "I thought you would have looked for me before you left," he mentioned as if I was wrong.

I guess we were both sending each other cryptic messages in order to avoid an argument. However, I was done beating around the bush.

"I thought you would have been at the door to welcome me, since you invited me," I point out.

"I'm sorry. I figured you were okay." Randall sounded apologetic.

"I was okay and I was well taken care of. However, it is more hospitable for the person who invites you to their home to greet and entertain you instead of the servants."

Randall sounded hurt. "That's below the belt, Danielle."

I knew I had hit a nerve. He called me Danielle. I stared at him, deciding to let my eyes do the talking.

"Dani, don't look at me in that tone of voice," he said almost pleading.

"I'm trying to figure out what rules we play by," I said flatly. He knew exactly what I meant.

"I just got out of an aqua machine. I didn't think you wanted a wet hug," Randall responded. He still looked dejected.

"You're wet. I'm sweaty. So what?" I asked. I suddenly hoped no one was around to hear. My last sentence could clearly be misinterpreted. Randall grabbed me and squeezed me hard; all the while, his mind raced. He wanted to but there was no way he could reveal his true thoughts to her.

I can't tell Dani that I intentionally avoided her. My feelings for her are getting stronger. I wanted to work out with her. But I have to put some distance between us—no matter how difficult it is. After being at her house Sunday my attraction toward her has intensified. This is so challenging. I have to be strong if I'm going to get through this. I can't show any more vulnerability. I don't want to hurt her and I definitely don't want her to get angry with me.

I had to break the tension the best way I could. I slowly pulled away from Randall and said, "I'll let you get back to your workout."

"You don't have to," he said affectionately.

"Well, you're already soaking wet. And I know one of your trainers is probably waiting on you."

"Have you had dinner?" Randall asked.

"You're hilarious," I quipped.

"What?" Randall pretended to sound innocent.

"You know I already had a protein shake," I told him, shaking my head, and trying not to smile.

"Is that all you're having?" Randall inquired.

I shrugged. "That's all I was offered," I replied.

"Well, do you want to get something else?"

"No, I'm fine," I said with a grin. "What are you going to eat?"

"I'll have what you had," Randall replied.

"Okay," I say as I open the door to get back into my car. Randall got lost in his thoughts again as he backed away from the car.

It took all I had to say good night to her. I wanted to tell Danielle I loved her right then and there. I wanted to tell her I needed her. I wanted to beg her not to leave me and ask her to become my wife. But I knew I couldn't. There are so many legal reasons that are stopping me from expressing my true feelings.

Randall shook his head slightly to remind himself to snap back into reality. "I'll call you," he told me. "Please don't turn your locator off."

I blew him a kiss and said, "Until we meet again," before pulling off.

Randall drifted off into his thoughts again. He sat on the curb in front of the special parking sign he made for Danielle, watching intently as she pulled off. He had no idea how long he had been sitting outside. JJ came outside and jolted him out of his daydream.

"Hooks, you want me to cut the machine off?" he asked.

He wiped his forehead and took a deep breath. "Yeah, man. Sorry to keep you waiting. I got sidetracked."

JJ smirked. "No problem. You need anything?"

"What time is it?" Hooks asked him. Clearly, he had been in a daze.

"Ten o'clock."

"Oh. I'll see you tomorrow whenever you get here," he told JJ. He didn't want him to think he had to get up in the wee hours of the morning on his behalf. After JJ told him the time, he figured out that he had been outside for over an hour, thinking about Danielle and going over the conversations he wanted to have with her in my head.

"I got to go back in before I leave." JJ told me.

Randall nodded. "I'll be in there in a minute. I need to get my phone. I'm sure she's called by now."

JJ was always so helpful. "You need me to bring it?"

"Nah, I need to get up anyway."

I checked my phone. Just as I thought—Danielle texted me to let me know she was home. I felt my muscles relax. But my mind continued to run wild with the things I wanted to do with and for Danielle. But I couldn't do any of them right now. I stayed at the gym all night. I didn't have the strength to go home—especially to a huge and lonely house. I wanted to be in a place where I knew friends of mine would eventually surface. That was better than being home alone.

It was ten minutes before 4 AM. When King got to the gym, I was already dressed and ready for my workout. I hadn't been to sleep at all. I left Danielle a voicemail at 2:00 AM and another at 3:30 AM on her work phone. She had been all I could think about for the past few hours.

"What are you doing here?" King demanded.

"Waiting on you. I hope you got a good night's sleep," I replied quickly. I didn't want him to think I had spent the entire night at the gym, desperately thinking about Dani. But he thought it anyway.

"No, you didn't," King said, shaking his head and laughing at me.

I couldn't help but laugh, too. "It's gonna be a rough morning," I told King.

"Not for me," King said. "I'm bringing the truck. I'm not killing myself out there with you, man. I stay outside of the ring—, which means I don't have to work as hard as you. You're getting weak, Hooks. You're letting that girl get to you. You've got to start getting more sleep. Get it together or I'll ban her from the gym."

On the other side of town, Danielle was fast asleep, completely unaware of the fact that I wouldn't be able to rest until she was in my arms forever.

Tuesday

My eyes popped open at 3:45 AM. I debated whether I should squeeze them closed again or just get up. I decided to get up and spend some time in prayer. After about an hour, I also decided that I would not check Randall's blog or look at my emails, texts, or voicemail notifications. I was trying to trick myself. Obviously, if I had received any messages from Randall my phone would have beeped. If I didn't hear the beep, the phone would have shown an indication light. I saw nothing.

I cruised into the office around 5:45. I sat there staring into space for an extended period of time. I couldn't figure out what I needed to do. All I could think about was what I wanted to do, and that was to spend the rest of my life with Randall. I thought long and hard until tears welled up in my eyes.

Why did I meet a man who is perfect for me yet married to someone else? I covered my face, as if someone were in the office with me. My temperature was rising. I turned my watch off so Randall wouldn't worry. I didn't want to lie and tell him I was working out in case the monitor showed my temperature levels. I wanted to call Randall, but it was too early. I was always hesitant about calling him. Besides, the last thing he said to me was, "I'll call you later."

I checked the messages on my office phone. There were four. Two messages from Randall, and two from people in the office. Randall's 2:00 AM message said, "I was just thinking about you and realized I didn't say goodnight. Goodnight. Sleep well." He left a second voicemail at 3:30 AM. "Good morning," his voice said. "I wanted to redeem myself for not saying goodnight last night. King and I will be hitting the asphalt in a few minutes. I'm not sure how long my workout will be this morning, but I'll be sure to call as soon as I'm done. Have a good day my love. Until we meet again."

■■

I worked as best as I could. It was close to 4:00 PM and Randall still hadn't called. I was determined not to call and I was not going to his gym today. I stood my ground—about not calling.

I wasn't planning on going to Randall's gym—until I got closer to his exit. It felt like the car jumped off the highway on its own and into the gym parking lot. Pulling into my parking spot at the gym reminded me that I had been working at my firm for quite some time and hadn't made partner yet, much less gained my own parking spot. Yet, here I am at Randall's gym, and I'm technically just his friend, but I have my own spot, labeled with my name. I hated that I had to admit Randall was still just my friend. But alas, that was the reality.

I took my time getting out of the car. I checked my iPhone and Blackberry before stepping outside. I walked into the gym slowly. I had a sinking feeling Randall was going to avoid me again.

"Good evening, Ms. Rose," a man's voice said.

"Good evening," I replied sweetly.

"How are you?" The man asked.

"Fine, thank you," I said.

"Are you sure?" he probed.

"Yes I am," I said with a nod.

"Did you have a good day?" The guy inquired.

"Not really, but I won't complain." I responded.

The man gave me an understanding nod. "I could tell by watching you cross the parking lot that your day was a little difficult. I'll let Mr. Hooks know you had a rough day. I'm sure that's reason enough for a night off."

I shook my head. "Oh, don't bother him," I said. I was thinking to myself that had Randall called me today, as he said he would, my day would have been better. I went further into the gym and headed to the locker room to change into my workout clothes.

The man stopped me. "Wrong, Ms. Rose," he said.

"I'm sorry?" I was confused. This was the locker room I always used.

The man explained. "You are headed in the wrong direction. Mr. Hooks would like for you to always use his private facilities."

What a jerk, I thought. Why did Randall always have someone else do his work for him? I turned to the man sharply. "Tell Mr. Washington that until he can talk to me himself I will act like a guest and use the guest facilities. Thank you."

The man tried not to smile. "I take it Mr. Hooks is not in good standing with you at the moment," he observed from my response.

"Let him know -if he wants to talk to me he has to do it himself. Thank you kindly," I reiterated. I was somewhat abrupt. I didn't mean to be. But I was too upset for niceties. I turned around and walked to the women's locker room. I changed my clothes and turned off my locator before heading to the workout machines. When I was done exercising, I went back to the locker room, got my things, and walked toward the door. I didn't even stop to order a juice or protein shake. My keys were in my hand and I was ready to leave.

The woman at the front desk said. "Are you leaving?" Almost as if she hoped I would say no.

I threw my hand up and yelled, "good night." I didn't hear her response. I clicked the lock, threw my stuff in the front seat, and backed out of the parking space.

Two can play that game. I went home and blocked Randall from my mind. Out of sight out of mind.

Wednesday

I hopped up early this morning to get my work out in since it was church night and I was NOT going back to Randall's gym until he could at least display a decent degree of hospitality toward me.

I started checking my messages when I got to the office. I saw Randall left a voicemail at 3:50 AM. What was the deal with him and the wee hours of the morning? I immediately thought, *maybe he's especially active in the morning. If his boxing skills are any indication of the...other things he can do, I'm impressed. And all I know is I'll be satisfied.*

I tried to calm myself down. As upset as I was with Randall, he was still very likeable. There was no denying that. I listened to his message:

"D, good morning. I wanted mine to be the first voice you hear. I also wanted to tell you to have a good day."

Why was he playing games? I was tired of his antics. I called him back as soon as the message ended. He didn't answer. I left him a voicemail. Randall was dangerously close to getting on my bad side. I don't think he was fully aware of that. I tried to sound as controlled as possible in my message.

"Deacon Washington, this is Danielle returning your call. I see you like to leave messages. Let me give you the number where you can reach me. It seems as if you always call my office in the middle of the morning. That would be fine but I seem to think your early morning calls are a little passive-aggressive and serve as your way of avoiding me. You can catch me on my cell all day every day. I would appreciate you calling me there."

Work was busy. I had meeting after meeting. Leigh and I were drained. I made time to make a spa appointment. When I left the spa, I was a little more relaxed. I needed to be as peaceful as possible to avoid giving Randall a serious attitude at church this evening.

He really did not need to meet the other side of me. I also had to remind myself he was not my man and he is married. I tried to stay calm all the way to the church. By the time I pulled in the lot and closed my eyes for a minute to gather my thoughts, my phone chirped, indicating I had a voice message. How did I miss the call? I keyed in my password and the voice I heard was Randall's.

"Danielle, I have received your message. I am unclear about the tone of your message. It was not as pleasant as I would have liked. I hope I have not offended you. I did tell you I am a morning person and that I planned to call you every morning before I work out. If this presents a problem and I should no longer continue to do so let me know and I will regretfully oblige. I hope that you will get your day off to a better start tomorrow. I hope you have enjoyed service. God Bless until we meet again."

That little snot! He was intentionally trying to leave a message while I was in service. I was completely pissed. I called him back immediately. I do not know if he sent me to voice mail or if the phone automatically directed me to voice mail. Either way, I wasn't happy.

I gulped my water. Then I closed my eyes tight trying to avoid blowing a blood vessel. I exhaled and inhaled numerous times. I could feel the steam rising from my nostrils. I reclined the seat back and rested for a moment. Suddenly, I jumped up and got out of the car. I got to the door of the vestibule and exhaled. Before I could put my hand on the handle the door was opening. "Good evening," one of the greeters said heartily.

"Good evening." I spoke quickly and moved pass the greeter without wasting time.

I walked right up on one of the other deacons and tapped him on the shoulder. "Hey, where is Deacon Washington?" I knew my approach was rude and abrupt but I needed him to let Randall know that I was very angry.

"Hey. Umm I do not know if he is here or not," the deacon replied, caught off guard.

I tried not to roll my eyes. "Can you find out?"

"Well is there anything I can help you with?"

"Yeah can you find him and tell him Ms. Danielle said he is a coward and that is putting it mildly." I was trying my best not to yell.

The deacon's eyes bulged and he spoke slowly. "I see. Let me find Washington and I will let you tell him yourself."

"I will be right here waiting," I replied with my arms folded.

"Do you want to have a seat?" he asked.

"No I will stand. I don't want to get too comfortable," I snipped.

He looked so confused. He started to walk away and then he turned back, examined the look on my face, and kept moving. I looked at my watch. I had eight minutes before service was starting. I waited patiently. He reluctantly walked back toward me with news he clearly didn't want to convey.

"I'm sorry he is off today," the deacon told me.

"Off?" I asked bewildered.

The deacon explained further. "He is not on the schedule for tonight."

"What?" I was appalled.

The deacon clearly didn't know how to respond. "We are not expecting him." That's all he could manage to say.

"Oh yeah?" I held my finger up to stop him from talking any further.

I pulled my Blackberry from my purse. I was still holding my finger up. I pressed a button to speed-dial Randall's number. No man who was programmed into my phone was going to treat me with disrespect.

His voicemail came on. I proceeded to give him a piece of my mind. "Randall Hooks Washington! This is Danielle. Your behavior has been unacceptable these past few days. I am disgusted and shocked. I guess I'm on your schedule only when it is convenient for you. I see that church falls into the convenience category also. I'm sure I will hear your reply to this message in the morning. You know, since you're a morning person. If you happen to be hiding in the building I am for certain you can see where I am and which deacon I am with--and my level of frustration. I am going to my seat now. You know where to find me."

I hung up the phone and went inside the sanctuary. I sat in a different spot than usual. The room looked completely different from this view—and by "point of view," I mean where I was sitting and how I was feeling. After service, I raced to the door.

I had a strong feeling Randall was at church. I walked to the parking lot. I couldn't find his car. But I still wasn't convinced that he wasn't there. I huffed to my car and turned the locator off. I checked the messages on my phone and turned my devices off. I can't recall the last time I turned off my phones. All this foolishness with Randall reminded me why I had stopped dating and dedicated myself to my work. From now on, I decided to devote all my focus to my career again. I worked intensely throughout the night. I was too stressed, upset, and hurt to sleep. Working didn't make me feel better. I don't know when I started fooling myself into thinking that spending all my time at the gym and the office would stop me from feeling any pain in life. Clearly, I had been fooling myself, but I had to keep the delusion going. I didn't check my emails, social media pages, texts, or voicemails for the rest of the night.

■■■

Tonight, I wasn't at the church. I was on the other side of town, sitting in my recliner, in the dark, with my iPad in my lap, trying to figure out why Danielle was so upset with me. I was also trying to figure out how long I could go on like this. It was unhealthy and disturbing for Danielle and me to have this type of interaction and attraction.

I knew what I was doing by dodging her. I knew why I was doing it. I was trying my best to avoid getting my feelings too involved—and I was attempting to spare Danielle's feelings, too. But it wasn't working. I was doing more harm than good, but I didn't know what else to do. Or when to do it. I just wanted the idea of having Danielle as my wife to become a reality. It was simple—but so very complicated.

Thursday

It was somewhat quiet at work. I stayed to myself and did my best to look extra busy. I decided I was going to the spa today. I needed to relax. I had to gain control. I needed some me time. Not work time. Not family time. Not agenda time. Today was going to be Danielle time. I liked to call these days D Day, and I was very clearly in need of one.

Once I got home, it was going to be my couch, remote, the take-out, and me. I was already debating whether I should have pizza or Thai food. I was determined to forget about Randall's phone call this morning. He left a message on my office phone that simply said, "Good morning, Danielle. Have a great day."

I attempted to call him back, but hung up four times before noon. I intentionally left my locator at home that day—and I hadn't turned it back on. My phones were still off as well. If he wanted to contact me, he knew how. Leigh was his best option. I didn't know if he called Leigh or not. She hadn't mentioned it, and I didn't ask.

I left the office at 3:00 PM sharp to go to my spa appointment. Visiting the spa really helped me to unwind. I wasn't sure if it was the tea or the massage, but I felt so great I purchased all the spa products the masseuse used, along with the tea I was drinking.

When I got to the reception desk to pay for my items, the woman behind the desk placed my items in a bag, handed the bag to me and wished me good day. "But I haven't paid for these yet," I told her.

"Oh no ma'am. You are already taken care of," she replied with a grin.

I was only partly perplexed. "How?" I asked her.

"We have your husband's credit card on file."

I was too relaxed to discuss the matter further. "Thank you. See you next time." I said.

She nodded. "Have a good day Ms. Rose."

I thought about the fact that she clearly didn't notice my last name was Rose, not Washington. Yet she believed "my husband" had paid for my spa visit. But I guess it didn't matter.

I stopped by the car wash on my way home to get my car in good shape. Since I was in such a fine mood, I figured my vehicle should reflect that. I still couldn't decide what to eat; I ordered both Thai food and pizza on my way home. I stopped by both restaurants and continued my journey to the house. I couldn't wait to eat and relax some more. Then I did something I hadn't done in a while. I lit candles, drew a hot bath, and stayed in the tub for as long as I wanted. I got out, toweled off, and got ready to be glued to the couch for a marathon of my favorite shows.

Friday

The soothing feelings of the day before had worn off. I woke up with a vengeance. I was mad at Randall and mad at myself. I had worked so hard avoiding this feeling and I walked dead into it. I decided I was going to continue taking time for myself. Today I would get a manicure and pedicure. I would treat myself to sushi afterward.

He left a message--as usual. As soon as my voicemail recording informed me that I had two messages, I knew they were both from him. His first message was at 3:55 in the morning. "Good morning," he started. Then there was a long pause. "Danielle, I've been busy training. I promise…" I hit seven to delete the message before hearing the rest of him. He left a second message at 4:19 AM. "Danielle, I hope you understand and aren't angry or upset with me. I'll explain everything to you later. You're in my thoughts and prayers—as always. I hope you have a wonderful day. I look forward to seeing and talking to you soon. If you would, please activate your watch. I'd really appreciate it. Again, I miss you. Until we meet again."

After listening to my voicemail options, I decided to press nine and save the message. I appreciated the message. But at this point, I really felt like he was being a coward. At one point, he was stopping at nothing to get my attention. Now, he was doing all he could to avoid me. But yet, he left me a heartfelt voicemail every day. I didn't understand his behavior, and I had stopped trying to.

I've had enough of his bipolar disorder. I had no idea what he was thinking or where this behavior was coming from. Did I do something to upset him? Was he politely trying to blow me off? This confirmed my reason for being a workaholic— once again. At least at work, I had more control. I was in charge.

"Leigh, let's go." I yelled.

"I'm not done." She barked back.

"Yeah, you are."

"You must have a date," she said, gearing up to tease me.

"Yep, with a lady and a nail file," I replied sarcastically.

"And what are you doing after that?" she inquired.

"Chilling."

Leigh squinted her eyes at me. "Yeah right. You're rushing out too quickly. You wouldn't happen to be "chilling" with a handsome boxer, would you?"

I thought of Randall quickly. But I couldn't dwell on it too long. "No ma'am. And he's not all that handsome. Kind of dusty looking if you ask me."

Leigh burst out laughing. "Liar!" she said pointing at me.

I had to laugh. "You're right--he is sexy as hell."

Leigh and I talked and giggled all the way to our cars before telling each other good night.

I dropped the top on my car—something I never did this early in the day when the weather was so warm. I also hardly ever left work this early. But it didn't matter. I was pushing myself into a good mood as I continued to commit myself to spending more time with myself.

After my Mani/Pedi, I drove home. Then I asked myself why did I have to stay in the house all night. A night on the town was in order. I hit the shower and stood in the closet trying to decide what to wear. Jeans, dress or a halter? I had no clue. I didn't even know where I was going. Randall was heavy on my mind. I couldn't shake him. I spotted a red dress in my closet and immediately thought of that old Johnny Gill song. "Put on your red dress…"

"Perfect," I said out loud, grabbing the dress from the hanger. I looked at three pairs of shoes before settling on a pair of Stuart Weitzman's. I made up my face with a slightly shimmery eye and a red lip. I was pumped up. I went to the kitchen, drank a little veggie and fruit juice for energy, and headed out.

Originally, I planned to grab some sushi. But as I turned onto the highway, a new idea came to mind. I decided I wanted tapas. I pulled up to Luckie Lounge, mingled, flirted, and walked back to my car. The next stop was Shout a great tapas and full-plate restaurant. The ambience was right and the guys were definitely in the place. And as much as I was enjoying myself, I still couldn't stop thinking about Randall.

I left Shout and went to Strip, another great restaurant for mingling, enjoying great drinks, and soaking in the atmosphere. A live jazz band was playing. I was a little jealous of every couple I saw in the restaurant. I suddenly felt a little uncomfortable and kept checking my phone, as if I was getting important messages.

I went up to the outdoors bar and ordered a glass of lemonade with fresh fruit. I listened to the jazz band for over an hour. I felt my feet giving out when a guy asked me if I wanted a seat. I gladly accepted.

Then one of the members of the band encouraged the guy to ask me to dance. I was hoping he wouldn't so I could give my feet a break. No such luck. But I had fun dancing.

"Thank you for the seat—and the dance," I told the guy.

"You're welcome," he said courteously.

I went to the bar and had another round of tapas. I was still thinking about Randall, although I was truly enjoying myself. I had forgotten how much fun I could have. Yes, I was alone—but it was by choice. After leaving Strip, I went to Copacabana so I could really party. I danced all night. My feet went numb. Had I known I would develop an urge to dance for hours, I would have worn a completely different outfit. My dress was completely sweated out.

At 2:00 AM I figured it was time to leave. The valet pulled my car around and when I jumped in, I checked my phone. I had eleven missed calls. Randall had called, of course, and there were a few calls from Sade and Paige, along with some numbers I didn't recognize. I will check my voicemails and texts in a minute—after I arrive at Mikey's.

He pretended to look at the clock on the wall in shock. "What day and time is it?" he asked.

I laughed. "Hey Mikey."

"Where you coming from, mami?" Mikey was so nosey!

"You're such a hater!" I yelled.

He was relentless with the teasing. "What corner did you work tonight?"

"I had a night on the town," I said pretending to swat him.

"Where is the Champ?"

I shrugged. "The punk, you mean? Who cares?"

Mikey creased his brow. "I know that tone. Trouble in paradise. I'm glad he is on the hot seat and not me."

"There is no paradise. He is just my friend," I said flatly.

"Umm hmm." Mikey responded as he handed me my Shirley Temple.

We chatted for a bit and I left. After all, I did have a standing 6:00 AM hair appointment.

Saturday

I went home and showered. I arrived at the salon early. I really didn't know what to do with myself after I left. I had already been to Mikey's and had breakfast. I couldn't believe I didn't have a full schedule.

After giving it some thought, I decided there were two things I'd love to take care of by Monday. I went to the office. When my phone chirped, I looked down to see the time. It was almost four in the afternoon. I had spent a full day in the office, which wasn't my original plan.

The distraction was a text from Randall. What are you wearing?

I didn't want to be inappropriate or put too much thought into my answer, so I texted, Lavender. How are you?

Where are my manners? I'm great thanks. How are you?

WHAT? I'm working.

Yes I had a few things I wanted to work on.

I wish you would find more time to relax. I will one day.

Promise? Promise.

Do you want to do anything later?

> Depends on how long I'm at the office.

> Don't stay long.

I didn't reply right away. I was actually a little insulted. Randall had done everything in his power not to see me the past few days. And now he wanted to do something? I did want to see him, but I didn't want him to think he could only see me on his time. I decided I would decline his invitation.

He texted.

> How is white linen?

He was trying to coordinate our outfits for church the next day.

> Is that what you're wearing?

> Yes

I took a deep breath. Obviously, it was impossible to be thoroughly upset with Randall for more than 72 hours.

> White linen it is.

Sunday

I was a little distressed when I arrived at church. I didn't know how to address this whole situation with Randall. I had to keep remembering we were only friends. So, maybe I would ask him what was going on with him—as a friend.

I didn't see Randall. It was his idea to wear white linen today, and he was nowhere to be found. He may have very well been at church—and in hiding, as he'd been the past few days. I wasn't going to wait for him after service like some desperate groupie.

Church service started and Randall was not in his usual seat. In the past, I would have gotten up and walked out long ago. Instead, I looked away from the seat where Randall used to sit and exhaled.

I was really in tune with Pastor Hunter's message today for some reason. When he stepped onto the pulpit, I could tell something was on his mind. He stood there, saying nothing, for a few minutes. I prayed for God to give him strength to preach a message that would inspire and impact the congregation. Finally, he spoke.

"There are some in here who have received an eviction notice. You have to be out of your homes by tomorrow. But because of your faithfulness, today your needs will be met." Three ladies walked to the front of the church. A man came up with his wife and children. The members of the church began to lay alms at the feet of the people standing next to Pastor as he spoke again. "Deacons, please take your place at the altar."

I was searching in my wallet for some cash to take to the altar when a whisper tickled the top of my spine.

"How many families are up there?" Randall asked.

I was both irritated and relieved to hear his voice. I still couldn't figure out why he'd been so reclusive lately. "Four," I whispered back.

He reached into the pocket of his linen pants and pulled out his wallet. He removed four $100 bills from the wallet and handed them to me. I turned to protest, but he shot me a look that warned me not to dispute him right now.

I took his cash along with the money I took from my wallet and walked to the altar. I noticed Randall walking to the front of the church as well, laying money in front of the families. We made eye contact. He winked at me. I tried hard not to smile but failed. He winked again. I looked behind me to pretend I thought the wink was for someone else. His expression told me to be honest.

After everyone had given alms Pastor said, "Deacon Washington can you please take this to the back and count the collection? Find out what each family needs and we will divide it up amongst them so that each of their needs will be met." Randall grabbed the basket and looked back at me longingly before he disappeared.

After service, I walked right out the door directly to my car. If Randall wanted to talk to me, he knew how to get in touch with me.

Week 13

Monday

I woke up at my normal time. I saw that Randall blogged last night but I was not interested in what he had to say. I continued getting dressed. Once I was in the car, I noticed I had a text and voicemail. I refused to listen to or read them. I knew I was being mean and stubborn but I didn't want to keep torturing myself by loving someone I couldn't have right now.

Once I arrived at my desk the light on my phone flashed, informing me of the five messages I had. How did I have five messages when I just checked them a few hours ago? I was reluctant to check them. All five of the message could have very well been from Randall. But I did have a client coming in today and I needed to make sure the messages weren't of a professional nature.

I exhaled deeply. I grabbed a pen and paper to jot down the messages just in case. Even with all the modern technology I preferred, I was still a little old school. First message: "Good morning Danielle, I hope this message finds you in perfect health and spirits. Have a blessed day."

"Ugh!" I let out a sigh and hit the button again to hear the next message. It was from a client who wanted to let me know he was providing breakfast, but wanted to know if the caterer needed special admittance into the building. The next message was from Leigh, informing me the caterer would be here at six to set up. The fourth message was from Randall. "Danielle, there are some things I really need to speak to you about if you would not mind giving me a call this morning. King and I will be running until seven. Feel free to stop by the gym if you have time--or call me anytime."

I wouldn't be stopping by. The last time I went to the gym Randall acted as if I didn't exist. I wouldn't let that happen again. There was one more voicemail. It was also from Randall. "Danielle, I wanted to really know if you could accompany me to meet with Daniel Khrittyleberrg. I need to meet with him tomorrow. Please let me know your schedule or you can have Leigh call me, Vickie or Khrittyleberrg directly. Thank you for your support."

I made a note to have Leigh call Khrittyleberrg direct. Once I was done checking the messages I sent Leigh an email to call Daniel Khrittyleberrg and find out the time of the appointment. I would see if I could join the meeting via teleconference or conference call. By all means, I didn't want to physically be there. I asked Leigh to find out the location of the meeting, but not to mention that I would be attending remotely. I asked her to send an email to Randall Washington and Vickie Yardo confirming my "presence" at the meeting.

Leigh was bright enough to know that if I was referring to Randall as "Randall Washington," I wanted to avoid him. She was also wise enough not to ask me why. She and I had been friends a long time, and I knew she wasn't afraid to tell me when I was being immature. I knew she sensed there was a reason for my stoic behavior.

The rest of the day went smoothly. I was too busy to even wonder why. The breakfast my client provided was delicious. My colleagues in the office mentioned this several times. I heard a number of my coworkers saying that we hadn't had food like this in the office since Hooks provided a meal for us. The client heard the remark a few times and asked some of my colleagues if they were referring to Hooks the boxer. I quickly stuffed a strawberry in my mouth.

My client turned to me and asked about Randall. "How do you know each other?" he asked.

I swallowed my fruit slowly and stood erect and confident. I said in the most professional tone I could muster (and with a clear mind and heart, since I wasn't lying). "He and I worship at the same church."

Leigh almost choked. She could tell from my tone I was trying to end the conversation before the client had the chance to ask me any more questions. But he wasn't getting my hint, because the inquiries kept coming. No one noticed that I didn't answer any more of his questions.

Finally, Leigh interjected and informed me she was scheduling a meeting with Randall right now for tomorrow.

A meeting for which my presence was requested. I glared at her. Just for that, she was coming, too. I cleared my throat. "In the meantime, let's get back to the business at hand," I said. "I will inform Mr. Hooks that you all are fans of his." My cell phone rang. It was Randall. I slid the phone across the table to Leigh for her to answer.

Her grin was huge. "Danielle Rose's office—hello Mr. Hooks," she sang as she excused herself from the conference room. Leigh was in big trouble when this meeting was over. I could see from the window that her conversation with Hooks was a question-and-response type of banter. However, the discussion was getting a little longer than it should have. She should have told Randall that I was with a client right now and would return his call later. We had a rule. We always left a small part of the blinds open so we could see each other's silent cries for help if necessary. I looked away. She was on her own.

It seemed like 15 minutes had passed. My group of colleagues was just as anxious as I was to find out what was taking so long. I was making a presentation to a securities technology corporation. Their new facility had to be extremely secure and state-of-the-art. The new building would be the site where my clients impressed future customers. A lot of detail had to go into the building, and extensive research was required to install the right security system. There were several different sets of plans—all of which needed to be stored and saved. However, only one master set of plans was to be used, but the general contractor would never know which set was the correct set without my guidance. The blueprints were like those for a Federal Reserve or casino—top secret.

As I was presenting I realized that maybe I could get with members of the Randall's crew to get input on some security options they would use. I made a quick written note in between breathing deeply. Finally, Leigh rejoined us. The meeting went well past noon. Everyone left pleased. I was drained. I went to my office and leaned back in my chair to recharge my mind. I sat for a moment while Leigh checked her messages at her desk. I could tell she was forwarding them to me because my voicemail number kept increasing.

Finally, she walked in. "I think that went well."

"I hope so," I answered, still trying to catch my breath.

She smiled. "This will be a nice project. You get the letter of intent and I will book it."

"I am considering going down to the county tomorrow to have a discussion about some of the secret panels and exits for the building. I need to make sure before I fully sell this that we are not ignoring any codes."

"It's no different from the basic building plans for casinos, right?" Leigh asked.

"That's what I want to confirm but remember none of the casinos are in Georgia. They don't operate under Georgia's code."

Leigh nodded. "Oh, that's right."

"Let's be prepared to spend tomorrow down there," I told her.

Leigh shook her head. "I think not."

I cocked my head to the side. "Excuse you?"

Leigh smiled slyly. "You are meeting with a boxer and his attorney—remember?"

"No. We are meeting with a boxer and his attorney via webcam while we are at City Hall." I informed her. Leigh locked her gaze on me. "Are you purposefully planning this City Hall meeting the same day as your meeting with Randall?"

I tried to avoid looking her in the eye. "No, but it could not have happened at a better time."

She responded quickly. "Liar."

"Well, I can go downtown and you can go to the meeting," I shrugged.

"I will and don't ask me anything about it."

"Don't forget where your help comes from," I said shaking my head.

"You either," she shouted as she slammed my office door.

I worked until I could hear the custodians running the vacuum on my floor of the office building. It was time for me to go. Especially if I was going to get any day light at the track. I needed it. I needed to transform from Dani Ro in the boardroom to Danielle the little girl that needed love. I needed to think. I needed to try to figure out why men were so confusing. This was one reason why I made it my business to stay clear of them—men, that is. It was so much easier that way.

I arrived at the track in just enough time to get a few laps. I left that stupid tracking device at home. I planned to do the same thing tomorrow, and every day after that. When I got back home, I got a text from Randall.

> I hope all is well. I will see you tomorrow. Good night.

I didn't respond. At 2:19 AM he blogged.

> There are times when trying to do right means the good you do will be spoken of negatively. But you have to continue doing what is good. Never stop doing what is right—even when it hurts you. Even when it hurts others. You will prevail. I hope you know it.

Tuesday

The words in Randall's blog made me sick to my stomach. I couldn't even explain why. *Why can't he just say what he has to say to me? Why does he put his feelings in a blog that the entire world can read? If he and I have issues, then we should discuss them.* I texted those sentiments and got ready to send the message to Randall. I changed my mind and decided to roll over and go back to sleep.

A few hours later, I waited at the office for Leigh to arrive. I was determined to spend all morning at City Hall. I needed to have all the building plans reviewed so I could work on the final changes for the project this week. I also needed to continue avoiding Randall and fooling myself into believing I didn't love him. I drove. Leigh checked her messages and worked the entire ride there. Once we got to City Hall, we went directly to the office space and got right to work. Leigh spoke to the inspectors and engineers in the office.

"We have a ten o'clock meeting--we will need to step away and come back here after the meeting—if that's okay with you?"

I knew I was going to have to redesign a few of these pages just in case someone had memorized the plans. I had headed enough casino projects to know how this whole security thing worked.

At 9:40 AM, Leigh excused herself to a smaller conference room to set up for the teleconference. Technology was incredible. But could also be a beast if used maliciously. Randall had not called or texted. I was glad I chose not to be physically present at the meeting. At 9:56 AM Leigh walked back into the room. She was typing a message on one phone and had the other to her ear. She motioned to me that the meeting was about to be live.

I turned to the engineers. "Excuse me guys. I'm not sure how long this will be. Can I track you down as soon as I'm done?"

They nodded. One of the inspectors said, "Of course, Ms. Rose. We'll be around."

I smiled and nodded. "Great. Lunch on me, guys." I walked into the room confidently—as if I were hosting the meeting. My hands were full, so Leigh put one of her phones down to help me put everything I was holding on the table.

"Good morning," I said in a sterile but slightly friendly tone. "Thank you for including me in the proceedings."

"Let the record show the meeting began promptly at ten o'clock AM." Daniel Khrittyleberrg recited the date and all the other legalities while his assistant took dictation. It seemed like fifteen minutes of legal preparation. I flipped through my phone and emails while he spoke. I was forcing myself to look busy. Leigh and I exchanged kicks under the table. I put my phone on the silent setting. Then a strong kick came from Leigh. It prompted me to look at the screen to see Randall standing up and walking out of the conference room with a phone to his ear. If it was a game he wanted that is what I would give him. I was winning.

Leigh tapped her phone to let me know to check mine. I could see it lighting up but I didn't look at it. Randall re-entered the conference room he was in. He remained standing on one side of the room, still holding his phone. He turned his back to the camera and Leigh and I exchanged kicks again. I smiled radiantly and looked over at Leigh. She recognized my expression. It was the look of victory.

Then Randall spoke. "Danielle," was all he said. I hesitated to respond and pretended there was a bit of a bad connection. Leigh was holding back her laugh.

"Yes?" I responded.

"I am calling your phone."

"Now?" I asked pretending not to know.

Randall's tone was serious and pleading. "Yes."

I looked down and picked it up. "Hi Mr. Washington," I said, treating him as if he were a business associate.

He began to walk back out the door and said, "Step outside of the room, please."

Leigh was feverishly texting me as I began to exit the room. Once we had both stepped away from the people around us, we were silent for a few seconds.

"What's with the BS Danielle?" Randall asked harshly.

"I am not following you." I said stern and abruptly.

"Why are you on a webcam?" he inquired sounding hurt.

"The same reason why I was asked to join a meeting via voice mail. If I am going to be dealt with like that then I need to treat you no different than I treat my clients. If I show up to YOUR GYM, where you invited me, and you do not show up then I am clear that we are associates. I do not mix business with pleasure. You have initiated the client relationship and I am rolling with it. Two can play that game."

Randall sounded like he wanted to yell. "This is not an F'ing game."

"Well, two can be in the ring, then," I retorted. "Sorry for using terms you're not familiar with."

"Why do you think I invited you here?" he was furious.

"Your voice message did not state the reason you invited me to the meeting. And since I'm on the other side of the door, I guess I won't find out why you asked me to join this meeting."

Randall sighed. "You are being extremely and unnecessarily difficult."

"I am practicing what you preach. You have been extremely and unnecessarily rude to me. I am following your lead," I spat.

He was shocked. "Rude. What do you mean rude?"

"I am under the impression that you have gone out of your way to avoid me. And if that were the case then it is all good. I know how to stay out of sight."

Randall's voice became gentler. "You are wrong--that is not the case."

"Well until your actions show me different, then this is what I will presume and this is the reaction you'll get from me. And I am being rude—to my clients. I'm actually supposed to be in a meeting. The people on your end are probably accustomed to your discourteous behavior—because you pay them." I hung up the phone and re-entered the room.

I was in my chair kicking Leigh under the table before Randall came back into the room. "Sorry for the interruption and delay. What did I miss?" I said brightly.

Randall stood up in the back of the room. He had one hand in his pocket and was texting with the other. I still had the phone in my hand. I slid it directly across the table to Leigh. She read the message Randall sent and slid the phone back to me.

> I don't think I deserved that.

I held the phone in my hand, placed my other hand over my chin and listening intently to the information being conveyed at the meeting. I scanned the room to see who was present. A spreadsheet appeared on the screen. I couldn't see it that well, but I could make out a 10-digit figure at the bottom of the sheet. My phone lit up in my hand again. I didn't look at the message, I handed the device to Leigh.

Randall interrupted Khrittyleberrg. "Danielle. I am texting you. Leigh give her back her phone. Respond to the text or step outside and finish the conversation."

Randall backed up from the telephone speaker and moved toward the door and Khrittyleberrg continued his presentation as if nothing had been said. I didn't move.

> Ask her to respond to my text.

Randall was texting Leigh on my phone to get me to respond.

I glanced at the phone in the middle of the table and looked back at the screen where the teleconference was taking place. The discussion was concerning the amount of money that would be offered to Tameka to settle the divorce. I still wasn't quite sure why I was attending this meeting, due to Randall's most recent behavior. But it was interesting nonetheless. Randall texted me twice more, but I didn't answer. I sat through the remainder of the meeting in silence. Randall huffed and barked orders the entire time. He never sat down. He nervously rattled the change in his pocket while texting me.

Once Khrittyleberrg adjourned the meeting, I stood up. I let it be seen that I was handing Leigh my communication devices. I spoke to the monitor. "Thanks for the invite guys. This was very informative. Let me know if there is anything I can do to assist in this process. Mr. Washington, forward all documents via email or certified mail, please."

"Umm hmm," he murmured with both hands in his pockets.

"Best of luck to you and you are in my prayers. You surely need it," I replied.

Once the teleconference was over, Leigh muttered, "Bitch."

"With a capital B," I said, adjusting my blazer.

"I haven't seen this side of you in a long time." she was almost sympathetic.

I exhaled slowly. "I know."

"Are you going to tone it down?" she pleaded.

I shook my head. "No. I'm making sure he knows I'm serious."

Leigh let out a nervous laugh. "He has no idea what he started," she confirmed.

"No he doesn't. Did you see that balance sheet?" I asked. I didn't want to talk about Randall anymore.

"Umm yes," she said, holding up a copy for me to see. "And I would advise you to let the attitude go."

I smiled and touched her arm. "You wouldn't be a good friend if you didn't. But I have to take the money out of the equation and look at the whole situation and Randall's behavior."

"The love of money IS the root of all evil," Leigh agreed. "But I think he has enough money to pay his wife—and for behavior lessons," she teased.

We both laughed. I didn't respond to Randall's continuous texts for the rest of the day.

Wednesday

Hours had gone by, and I hadn't received any calls, emails, texts, or voicemails from Randall. He also hadn't blogged. Now I was getting concerned. But what was I supposed to do? I went about my day as usual. Or, as usual as I could. The weather was ugly—it fit my mood. It stormed pretty much the entire day. But that wasn't going to stop me from getting things done—and neither was Randall.

I left work and headed to church. It felt like I was paddling a boat with all the rain that was outside. I finally pulled up in the church parking lot. None of the deacons came outside to greet me. I sat in my car and debated whether I wanted to even go inside. Due to the rain, and all. I heard a tap on my window. It was King, holding an umbrella. A deacon soon came behind him.

My mood changed immediately. If King was here, that meant Randal wasn't far. I opened the door and King spoke to the deacon. "I have her taken care of," he said.

"Thank you," I said to them both.

"You are welcome," the deacon nodded.

King led me to the front door. I went to my seat alone. Service started. By the time it was ending, I thought Randall would have shown up, but I didn't see him. Did he really think I would believe King came to the church by himself? Now he was insulting my intelligence. This was silly. Silly of both of us. And I didn't like it one bit.

King walked me back to my car. It was raining harder than when I arrived. The rain was a good thing. No one could see my tears. I drove home and did not even notice the horrible weather. I was too preoccupied with Randall's behavior. I finally fell asleep. I slept all night in my clothes on the chaise.

Thursday

I am so stressed and worried over this situation with Randall. I really don't know what I've gotten myself into. Randall was acting like someone suffering from bipolar disorder. One day, he was totally into me. The next, he acts as if I don't exist. I had to move on. I couldn't continue to stress myself over a married man. I needed to focus on other things, like my pending partnership at the firm. I didn't want any more drama, and it was clear Randall came with drama. I remembered my last relationship and vowed to never welcome those feelings into my life again.

I decide to hit the gym when I leave work. My gym, not Randall's. I didn't want to look desperate, even though I was. I desperately wanted to be OKAY with everything that was going on. But right now, I wasn't.

Work was actually enjoyable. Except for the fact Randall didn't call, text or email all day. I was really angry about it, but I didn't breathe a word to Leigh.

I left work and raced to the gym. I looked around. The coast was clear—no Reginald. I hadn't been here in months, and the last thing I wanted to do was run into him. My trainer was there, and she and the other friends I had made at the gym acted as if I had been gone for years. I had. It felt good to be missed—and that no one was feeling sorry for me. Being in a familiar environment lifted my spirit and motivated me to give my all to my workout.

Randall wasn't in the forefront of my mind, but I was still thinking about him. I was determined to push him out of my thoughts permanently. It would be difficult; it would hurt. But hopefully, going through the pain of forgetting him would be more beneficial to me than to try to continue loving him.

I was pushing myself beyond my limits today. I kept telling myself if it didn't hurt it wasn't working. As I was working on my legs, I heard a voice. My heart sank. There was nowhere to hide. I knew it was him. I tried not to move in hopes that he would just walk out. Of course, he didn't leave.

"Hi D," Reginald said.

"Hey," I replied, trying not to sound rude or anxious.

"What's up?" he tried to make small conversation.

"Nothing," I answered immediately.

"What brings you out here today?" he continued.

"It's a gym," I retorted smartly.

Reginald scoffed. "Yeah, I know that. But we didn't think it was a gym you were still a member of. You haven't been here in months. But I can see you're still going hard at it."

Who was "we?" I looked over to see him and a few of the guys from the gym. Reginald was wearing a white t-shirt, jeans, Air Force Ones, a baseball cap and the necklace with the cross pendant I'd given him. Damn he looked nice. He had gained a few pounds of muscle. He looked very different, but I couldn't put my finger on it. His muscles were especially built now. Clearly, I was enjoying the view. It looked like he was training for a bodybuilding competition.

"Can I get a hug? I haven't seen you in a while," he reminded me.

I stopped and allowed him to embrace me. He smelled wonderful. It felt like we were the only two in the entire gym. I pulled myself away from the hug and continued my workout as if Reginald wasn't there. Who called him to tell him I was here? I find it hard to believe that he coincidentally showed up. He wasn't even changing into workout clothes. He came over to my workout space and started talking to me again. I kept thinking how unfair it was that he looked so great. Why did he have to be wearing all the things I liked? What was God trying to tell me?

"How long are you working out?" Reginald probed.

"Don't know," I quipped. He still wasn't getting the point. I wasn't going to budge.

"What are you doing when you leave here?"

"Don't know," I repeated.

He sounded a little sad. "I thought maybe you'd want to hang out," he offered.

"Nah," I replied casually.

He wouldn't give up. "Well what night is good for you?"

I laughed. "I don't know."

"Ride with me across town so we can talk."

"Not now, I have to finish this workout."

"I'll wait for you." (That was such a loaded statement. And he knew it).

"No, I will be sweaty. Besides, I have to run."

Reginald smirked. He was probably thinking he liked me sweaty and couldn't wait to be the cause of that sweatiness. I had to focus. I could tell he really wanted us to spend time together. But I shook my head. He knew why. I couldn't fall for the "take a ride with me" routine. He would change my whole mindset. I couldn't cry anymore for him. My heart wanted to embrace him again and work everything out. But my mind wouldn't let me give in. I felt so conflicted. I wondered again, who called him to tell him I was at the gym. Before I could think, I looked at his necklace and asked him to give it back to me.

"I would if I could," he told me.

"And why can't you?" I asked sincerely.

"Someone special gave it to me."

That necklace was the last present I gave Reginald before he broke my heart. I had spent a fortune on it. And I had given it to him just because. I presented it with some emotional speech about how the necklace was a symbol for God's covering and protection and that I wanted God to keep him always. His response devastated me. It hurt to even bring up the memories again. I remember calling him shortly after the breakup asking him to return the necklace to me. He politely told me he couldn't give it back, but that he would pay me for it. I threw a tantrum and faxed him the receipt for the jewelry.

He clutched the necklace again. "I really need this cross," he told me. "If you take it, you'll be taking away the best part of me. You'll be taking a part of my history—a part of my life. But again, I'll pay you for it."

My face was void of emotion. "Well, I may let you keep it, then," I told him. "You need as much Jesus and prayer as you can get. But I will take the cash."

Reginald was stunned. "Did you just say I need Jesus?" he laughed.

"Yes, and you know you do," I replied.

His tone immediately got softer. "What I really need is you, Danielle," he confessed. We had a short discussion about it. We didn't talk about mutual friends, family or include any small talk in the discussion. I still didn't want to get too sucked in. It was nice to feel wanted—but how long was that going to last?

Finally, Reginald said, "I have to run. You sure you don't want a ride? We can talk some more, squash all that drama from the past and I'll buy you dinner."

I smiled slightly and shook my head. "No, thanks," I told him. I could buy my own dinner.

He threw up his hands. "All right—I'm leaving. Call me if you change your mind."

"Bye," I said without stopping my workout. Then I softened as I saw him head toward the door. I knew I was being cold and I really didn't feel like being angry anymore. Or maybe I really wanted to forget about Randall. Or maybe it was a little of both.

I walked up to him. "Hey, Reginald," I called out to him.

He turned around, grinning widely. "Yes, ma'am," he replied.

"Don't I get a goodbye hug?" I asked. He gave me a half-hearted embrace. "It was good seeing you," I said, with a hint of closure in my voice. I had to end this chapter in my life for good. The last time I saw Reginald, my blood pressure was at unacceptable levels. This time I felt much healthier. I knew I wouldn't give in.

"Thanks, D," he replied, giving my cheek and forehead inappropriately sensual kisses. "I hope I didn't leave a mark," he said mischievously. "I would hate for your new boyfriend to go crazy."

"He likes to fight," I answered as I held Reginald tighter. I was standing on my tiptoes, kissing Reginald's cheek repeatedly. I didn't realize how much I missed him until right then. If only he had apologized. If Reginald had tried to make up with me before, Randall may not even be in the picture right now. He pulled back abruptly and stared at me.

"Can I call you later?" he hoped she would oblige.

"You probably shouldn't." I told him.

He stared into my eyes again. "Are you sure?"

"Yes, I'm sure."

"You can change your mind at any time. I pray that you do. It will make my life much better. And I hope it will make yours better, too."

"Thanks for the offer Reggie," I communicated with a smile.

"Hey, you're welcome," he told me. "Thanks for being cool—and for being you."

I couldn't manage to say, "You're welcome." I wasn't sure what he meant by thanking me for being "cool." I stood there staring out the gym window as Reginald pulled off. I was getting confused again. I stood in that same spot for a while. Then finally, I sat down right where I was. I was deep in thought. I laid on the floor looking up at the ceiling until my trainer looked down at me and said, "You want to call it quits for tonight?"

I nodded yes and took my time getting up and leaving. I was solemn all the way home. When I got home, I tried to work. I tried to sleep. I tried to watch television. I thought about calling Reginald. Instead, I called Randall--he didn't answer. I couldn't figure it out. Was Reginald showing up a sign that he was the one? Randall was married. How crazy is this I am tied up mentally and emotionally with a married man? I needed help. It made no sense that he would show up out of the clear blue. What did this all mean? After all, Randall was close to getting a divorce.

Friday

I woke up and checked my messages, texts, and emails. Still nothing from Randall, however, there was a voicemail from Reginald. It was obviously clear he was up to his old tricks again, calling in the wee hours of the morning, surely an attempt to catch me at my weakest. Humph, what Reginald failed to realize is that those weaknesses have become my strengths and I'm at my best at this hour. I decided to not get myself worked up by checking my office voicemails or Randall's blog; that would have to wait until I got to work. Right now, all I needed was a little "liquid nitrogen," better known as coffee, in case I needed it for the day ahead.

Randall blogged at 3:56 AM and Reginald called at 3:50 AM. They were both trying me. "You can run but you can't hide" was truer than ever for me. I had done everything in my power to avoid the way I felt. I was not successful. My emotions were always present, no matter where I went. Just like God is always present. Randall had been running from me all week physically and I had been running from him emotionally. Just because he was out of sight didn't mean I had stopped thinking about him. Absence made the heart grow fonder. Obviously, he felt the same.

His blog read:

> Out of sight out of mind has not proven to be true. I thought if I stayed away from her, my feelings would change. My heart would forget. But absence makes the heart grow fonder. The more I am away from her the more I need her. I desire her. I crave her.

I stared blankly at the screen for a very long time not knowing exactly how to respond. This whole situation was strange and unclear. There was no way I could respond to either of them at this time. Instead, I made up my mind that this was my Friday and it would be an easy day for me, responses would have to wait.

■■

Hooks phone rings and displays Pastor Hunter's picture "Hello, what's up Pastor?"

"Yo, what's good? I wanted to come over, throw a few punches, and get a work out in. You around?"

"Yeah, I am here all day. What time you coming through?"

"I am on my way now." Sensing something in his friend's voice he asked, "What do you have planned today?"

"Nothing much," Randall solemnly replied.

"You wanna hang out? It's been a minute." Tre offered.

"That's cool, I don't have plans." Randall replied both obliging and a little miffed.

"I was thinking about going to look at some new whips," a passion both men shared. The idea of a possible new ride sounded appealing enough to lighten the mood he was in, "Let's do it." Randall said with a bit more enthusiasm.

One thing was for sure, Pastor Hunter wasn't your traditional preacher. He was cool and kept it real at all times. Even the way he dressed didn't fit the profile of a "regular preacher." You wouldn't find him wearing a normal three-piece polyester suit, like most pastors. Instead, his clothing style consisted of the likes of Coogi to Black Label Lauren to Armani, and from Gucci to Louis Vuitton and everything in between. He was hip to the hottest gear. He rocked the hottest kicks, the freshest bling, knew the best hooks and he drove the tightest whips. Of course, the First Lady kept him right. She is the perfect example of a great helpmeet.

He was considered a role model in the community, not only because of his title, but because he was relatable. He had a talent of speaking the word to any person on their level; this was his calling and he was definitely blessed. There wasn't anyone he couldn't reach. He could breathe life to the dry bones of the seasoned saints and to the saints fresh out the womb. His ability to connect with all kinds of people also made it easy for him to relate to the youth. He was a positive figure for the young people, showing them how they could succeed legally and successfully by the word and work of God. He spoke the truth to them, not to kill their dream, but honestly letting them know that not everyone was going to be an athlete, a rapper, or singer. His goal was for them to discover and live their God given purpose in life.

He and Hooks worked out, threw punches, and then showered. Once they dressed and met up again Randall asked, "Pastor what's next on the agenda?"

"You tell me," said Pastor.

Sounding a little uncertain Randall said, "You wanted to hang."

Now all set on a different agenda, Pastor Hunter replies, "Let's go to your office for a minute and talk."

Randall walked in first and took his seat at the chair on the opposite side of the desk. Pastor Hunter sat right next to him.

"What's on your mind Pastor?" Randall said.

Raising his eyebrows as if Randall should know what's up by now, "You tell me Deacon."

"You wanted to talk." Randall said, knowing full well where Pastor was going with all of this.

He chuckles, "Yeah I did. I want to talk about Ms. Danielle."

Randall sighed hard. I was trying not to think about her. Not that my effort was working, but this definitely wasn't helping.

"It is not as bad as you think," Pastor Hunter reassured him. "I just want to know what's going on. I am not trying to be all in your business, but I am trying to help you friend to friend and pastor to parishioner. RW, you're a deacon of the church and you have to set the same examples required of me."

"I'm not sure what you want to know Pastor," Randall said clarifying he was speaking to Trevor as his pastor at this moment instead of as his best friend.

With concern in his voice, Pastor Hunter continued, "Is something wrong or going on? I have noticed that you've been staying away from the sanctuary. Did something happen? This is why it is not good to mix these relationships out of order."

"Yeah, I have been hanging out in the shadows and surfacing only when I need to," Randall admitted.

"What's up with that?" Pastor Hunter digs further.

Feeling uneasy, Randall says, "It's hard to explain."

"We have all day, as I remember correctly; you said you didn't have plans"

Randall, not being a man of many words, knew he could talk to his friend honestly, "I have been trying to distance myself from her."

"Why?" Pastor Hunter asked.

"Man, to tell the truth, my flesh is weak." There, he said it.

Pastor quickly replied, "Well if that is the case you are doing the right thing."

"Let me rephrase this," Randall said. "It's not that I've done anything I shouldn't have, and believe me, man to man, I damn sure want to. It's been more of an emotional thing than physical. No doubt, I have the physical aspect under control right now, but if I don't get the emotions in check, the physical is going to take over. I've been trying to back up to keep her emotions out of the picture too. I mean, I want mine to be clear but I am more concerned about hers. My feelings for her are growing stronger daily and I can't help but to hope that the feelings are mutual. I can't sleep or eat and all I do is think of her. Danielle energizes me, encourages me, and I know, bottom line; she is the one for me."

Shaking his head, Randall continues, "My hands are tied though, and I can't do anything, until I get this divorce behind me. Man, I wouldn't have imagined feeling like this, seeing my life like this; not that it's a bad life; it took some turns I didn't see coming. Hell, I never saw a boxing career in my future either, football maybe. Tre' I see her in my future. I'm feeling crazy man; I can't fully focus on it, fully commit, or confirm it yet. It is killing me inside and I don't know how to handle this. To be frank, I really want to get away for a few months and clear my head and come back refreshed."

Understanding how his friend is feeling, Pastor Hunter agrees, "Why don't you do that?"

Shaking his head no, Randall says, "I can't. I'm afraid."

"Afraid of what?" Pastor asked.

"To leave her. I NEED to be here with her. If I'm out of sight then I might be out of her mind. I couldn't handle that. I figure I can try to stay back just a little, but do just enough so she won't forget me."

"What do you think is going to happen?" Pastor asked.

Randall replies, "I am hoping this divorce is final and I can do whatever I want."

"And what is it that you want Randall?"

"I want to court her and marry her. Marry her quickly."

"Are you sure?" His friend asks.

For clarity, Randall asked, "Sure about which part?"

"All of it," Pastor Hunter said.

"Pasa a brother is growing weary. You got a wife at the house. You are in the promise land. I am still in the wilderness." They both laughed.

"As your Pastor, you know I have to encourage you and keep you on the right path. If you're feeling like you state, then you're right, you do have to let up a little. This type of relationship has the potential to be damaging. I suggest that I counsel you through this transition. I'll be your spiritual advisor during this process and we can discuss setting up counseling sessions until this divorce is final."

"As my Pastor, honestly, what do you suggest I do?" Randall asked with hope.

With a sly grin, Pastor Hunter says, "Don't grow weary in well doing. If you faint not the promise land maybe your reward." They touched pounds and laughed. "So how long are you going to be a pop in Deacon?" Pastor Hunter inquires.

"I'm not sure, hopefully not too long. All I know for certain is that I have got to pull up."

Pastor Hunter asks with concern, "Hooks, are you sure it's not just *your* emotions? What about her emotions, has she mentioned what she's feeling?"

Looking down, Randall answers, "No, not yet, and I'm trying to keep it that way for the moment."

"That may be the best judgment, but let me ask you; how long do you think you are going to be able to play charades?"

"Pastor, why do you make it sound like I am doing something so bad? The way I see it, I'm looking out for both of our best interest. That way no one gets hurt and our friendship is not ruined."

Pastor Hunter interjects, "No, I think if you were to take all of your feelings and emotions out of the equation *that* would be the best interest. Of course, in order to do that you just might have to stop talking to her for a while."

As if thinking aloud, Hooks asks, "Why would God send her to me if she was not for me? All of the women I see at church, in my gym and in passing, yet none of them have captured my attention. Not one. And of all the men at the church, how is it that she's attracted to me?"

"Are you saying God sent her to you?" Pastor asked with skepticism.

Hooks replied in total confidence, "Yes, Pastor, I am."

"How do you know it was God?"

Looking Pastor directly in the eye, "I *feel it* in my knower," he replied.

Pastor Hunter continues the line of questioning, "What if your knower is wrong?"

"God is never wrong Pastor, I've prayed for my life to change and to begin anew, a refreshing. Danielle is whom He sent. I'm sure of this."

"What if you are supposed to just be her friend? What if she is simply assigned to be the architect of your next project and not your wife?" Pastor asked hoping to help Randall think about all of the many possibilities God may have allowed Dani in his life.

Hooks replied honestly, "I guess I will find out after the honey moon is over."

Always the one to offer the best thought out advice, Pastor Hunter proceeds, "If I may suggest, you probably should change your strategy."

Hooks replies, "Why do you say that?"

"Friend to friend. You are probably pissing her off. Perhaps she's thinking you are blowing her off and being rude."

I hadn't thought of that. Then I remembered Danielle's attitude during the meeting with my lawyer. It was all starting to make sense. "I guess I need to figure out a new plan," Randall said with a sigh.

"That was your first free counseling session," Tre joked. "But you're going to have to come up with a new plan on your own." Pastor Hunter teases with his friend, but with all sincerity attached.

Laughing, Hooks throws his hands in the air, "Aww, come on man; we boys. How you gone leave me hanging like this?"

His friend shrugs his shoulders and says, "I can't get in it. All I am going to say is don't lose your swagger or get swagger jacked."

"Wow, really? That's all the advice you got?" Shaking his head and laughing, Hooks tells Trevor, "And you want me to keep coming to you for counseling?" he joked. "You are wrong for that!"

"Let's go check out some rides." Pastor replies and stands up.

"Alright. Leave your boy hanging." Randall says once more, jokingly, in hopes that his Pastor and friend would give him advice on forming a new plan.

■■

On the other side of town I never bothered to turn my locator on and while I was home resting, Randall was still out with Pastor Hunter having real talk.

Saturday

I followed my regular schedule of course. I went to Hooks gym, but this time I brought my trainer with me. She worked me over and then said with a sly smile, "I see why you have been ditching me. You have been too busy with the boxer boy."

Playfully rolling my eyes, I tell her, "Shut up Ms. Dot." Ms. Dot and I have worked together for years. She and I clicked from the time we met at Smith's. She is an avid fitness trainer with quite an impressive résumé. She has won several fitness contests and trained numerous stars around town. Not that I ever planned to enter a contest but I liked her work, the sister is bad. Ms. Dot was also a woman of God. Literally. Ms. Dot is a Preacher. I loved her dearly.

The remainder of the day went as it usually did, spa, hair salon, and Mikey's. For some unknown reason, Randall and I had become distant suddenly. I couldn't figure out why and I hated it. I decided I was going to go with the flow of things with him and follow his lead. I was at Mikey's when he called.

"Hello." I answered dryly.

"Hey," was his reply with a little too much dead air.

"Yes."

"Are you at Mikey's?" he asked.

Randall was fully aware of my location, as I had turned my locator back on and within ten minutes, he was calling. It's almost pathetically hilarious to hear him ask me where I am when he knows damn well, where I am. Surely if he wanted, he could check his phone or laptop and locate me at any time. Obviously, I had his attention.

"Randall, you can see where I am." I replied.

"Are you alone?"

"No, Randall, I am never alone."

"Do you want some company?" he continues.

"I am not sure how to answer that."

"It's simple a yes or no." Randall said.

Wanting to make myself clear, I told him, "Yes, I would like to have company with a person that wants my companionship but no I don't want company with someone who is a fair weather friend."

"I'll be there in five minutes," was all he said, and hung up the phone, which was so Hooks.

As soon as the call ended, I could hear his engine roaring. He was in the Audi R8 Spyder with the tag that read HOOKS. I didn't have to look at the door because I already knew he was there. I heard the door open and remained cool. Mikey was on the other side of the bar in a friendly debate with a regular customer.

"CHAMP!" Mikey exclaimed.

"What's up Mikey?" Hooks says.

In typical Mikey fashion, he replies, "Just doing your job entertaining D. Next time let me know when I am back on detail. I thought you were permanently relieving me of these trivial duties."

I thought to myself, *Mikey has such a big A' mouth. I am going to talk to him about his behavior as soon as I can. Some stuff is between us and not to be shared. Butt clown.*

"Man, I know. I am going to do better real soon and I will have you off duty PERMANETELY," Randall said proudly.

He stood directly behind me. I did not move, didn't even blink an eye. I was determined to ignore him, just as he had ignored me for nearly two weeks. When he cleared his throat, I continued a text. He was not going to receive the satisfaction of knowing that I would stop at the drop of a dime for him. Before I knew it, he was picking up the entire stool. He turned it around facing him. Sat it back on the floor and said, "Hello."

Being stubborn I know, I threw my hand up waving a quick hello but never looked up from my texting. This time he picked me up out of the chair and stood me on the floor.

"Do I have your attention now?" he asked softly.

Little did he know he had my attention all along but I wasn't going to make this easy for him. "It did not require all of this. All you had to do was address me. The world does not stop because you appear after two weeks." I said sarcastically.

He hung his head. "I deserve that." Hooks replied honestly.

Now ready to let him have it, I continued, "You actually deserve more and I plan to give it to you."

He smirked. You can tell his mind went to left field. "I hope so," he said alluringly.

No he didn't, I looked up with the eyes of death.

"Sorry." he said trying to hide a smile.

"What can I help you with today?" I said, trying to sound as if this was just an ordinary meeting.

"What?" he said as if he didn't hear me correctly.

"What do I owe the pleasure to and for?" I asked sternly.

"I wanted to see you Dani."

Looking him up and down, and still wanting to give him a hard time, "Hmm, that's strange."

Rubbing his head, Randall looks over to the counter, "Mikey, it's going to be a long day. Get me a strong tomato juice please."

Mikey nodded. "You got it, Champ."

He took my handbag and passed it to Mikey across the counter, then reached down and took a hold of my hand and led me to a small table in the corner. I slid in the booth and he slid next to me. I was not expecting him to sit on the same side. He put his lips up to my ear and whispered, "Forgive me." He placed my right hand in his hands and placed them on his face. He covered his face and we sat like that in silence for a few minutes. The silence was disturbed with Mikey placing his vegetable juice on the table; it was in a tall martini glass with a carrot and the leaves coming out of the top for garnish. Then he placed a plate of fruit and a glass of fresh squeezed grapefruit juice in front of me. Randall looked up as if to say thanks to Mikey, then pushed his juice away and nodded at Mikey to indicate that was all he needed for now.

I broke the silence. "Are you okay?"

With his face still covered, Randall said, "Danielle, I am glad you asked. No, I am not okay. This is very difficult and frustrating for me. I'm not sure what to say, where to start or know how to move forward. This is killing me. Please know that this is not who I am. It is hard to do what is considered right when your heart tells you to do something totally different. It isn't easy to be patient and wait. It's as if when you try to walk the right path, obstacles continue to get in the way. Life is difficult and I'm learning that some battles you can't win by fighting." He never uncovered his face.

"Is there anything I can do?" I asked with concern and sincerity.

"Please just be patient with me. I know this is selfish, rude, and even disrespectful for me to ask this of you. But I have no choice. You can say yes or no and I will understand. I assure you though; I am doing all I can. I want to do more, but right now, I can't. I want to see you. I want to be with you every day but I have to limit myself."

He paused. He took one hand and drank his juice. He held my hand tightly with the other and looked me in my eyes. "Danielle, promise me you will never allow me to step outside of the boundaries."

I didn't respond. I let him continue to speak.

"Right now I do not trust myself with you. My flesh is weak. My mind is weak and my heart is weak. Do you understand what I am saying?"

I still did not respond.

"I want you in a way that a married man should not want another woman. I want you desperately. Day and night. Even if I were a single man, I'd still have to control my feelings; and right now, I'm trying to do right in the sight of God. Dani," he continues, "If you should wait, as rude as it is to ask of you, be prepared to get married quickly. I'm afraid my flesh is far too weak for a long courtship and engagement. We are going to get married in the Chapel."

I respond assuredly, "Oh no sir, you're going to wait until I walk down that aisle taking my sweet little time."

"I am not going to be able to do it," he said, "You may want to reconsider. Are you aware that you *will* marry me?"

"No, as a matter of fact I am not," I said.

With as much certainty as I had given him, he replied, "You *will. As a matter of fact, you* might as well go ahead and pick out the ring and the dress now. Although, this is too long of a wait for me; it's much sooner than you would ever think."

I was shocked. We both sat in silence. I certainly didn't know what to say at this point so I picked up a pineapple.

"Let's go." he said breaking the silence.

"Where are we going I asked," putting the fruit back on the plate.

"To get a tie," he said.

With raised eyebrows I asked, "A tie for what?"

"To match what you are wearing tomorrow," he responded.

"Oh you are showing up tomorrow?" I said with a little too much surprise in my voice.

"Don't give me a hard time," he said. "You know my heart."

"You know Randall, actually I don't," I said.

We stopped in the middle of the restaurant. He lifted my chin. "Dani, are you not aware that you have your hooks in me? Are you not aware of how I feel about you by now?"

I shrugged my shoulders. I knew, but I needed to hear him confirm it.

"That's bull! You have got to be blind. How in the world does everyone know except you?"

"I just don't," I whispered almost like a little girl.

He looked around the restaurant and said, "Can you all tell that I love this girl?"

People were so amazed he was there that they would have agreed with anything he said. Needless to say, we went and picked out a tie. I drove myself just to be difficult and to let him know I was not jumping at his beck and call.

As we were walking back to the valet to get our cars I asked him, "What do you have planned for tomorrow?"

"Nothing. I was hoping dinner at your place," he suggestively replied.

"I won't be there, I told him. I will be at Atlanta Motor Speedway and wanted to know if you'd like to come?"

"I can't," he replied without hesitation.

He just acted as if he was free for dinner, then when I suggest something I wanted him to do with me, he immediately said no. It hurt my feelings; it's not like I ask him to do very much. I was glad we were at our cars so we could disburse.

The girls were spending the night at my place tonight. We were going to have a quick breakfast after church in the morning before I went to the race. They were coming to church basically to chastise Randall for not talking to me; that's my girls for you. Initially I wasn't sure if I should tell them, never mind, since he called me, however, I changed my mind. We were still not cool as far as I was concerned.

Sunday

It was a challenge for four women (three of which are not morning people) to be at church, dressed early and on time for service. They were not aware that the Deacon and I had spoken and would be dressed alike, as if we were an item.

I had it all planned out. I would park in a different location, come in a different entrance, and sit in a different section of the sanctuary. With there being four of us, I figured Randall would not see me. Unfortunately, my plan was interrupted when the parking lot guy directed me in my normal spot. UGH!

Maybe he won't be at the door, I hoped, as I slowly approached the entrance. Low and behold before, my foot could step in the door, he was there. He was caught off guard by the crew.

"Ms. Rose," he said sarcastically, I'm sure due to me ditching him last night. Then the crew stepped in behind me.

"Ladies. What brings you all out this early Sunday morning? Good to see you. Especially you baby girl," he said acknowledging Sade's presence.

"It is a public meeting place. Correct?" I asked, this time I was the one being sarcastic.

He gave me the look as if to say that if we were not in church, it would be on.

It didn't take long, Sade picked up on it immediately. "Are y'all dressed alike?"

"No." I lied. *Lord please forgive me for lying in church.*

"Yes." He corrected looking at me as he spoke to Sade.

I rolled my eyes so hard it gave me a head rush. Leigh and Paige both eyed me at the same time.

"Do you all have a printed schedule because no one informed us of the color for today?" Sade said.

Smiling, "No we met yesterday and decided on Royal Blue," he expressed with pride.

"Oh really now." Paige whaled and looked over at me suspiciously.

"Yeah, we coordinate every week," Randall added.

Sade and Leigh both said, "COORDINATE!"

"Oh, we were not aware," Paige commented in an exaggerated mock surprise.

UGH! I thought. *They ALL talk too much.*

He and I were exchanging some very hostile looks. I walked into the sanctuary quickly and angrily. The deacon was right on my tracks and caught up with me, ignoring all of the Ushers motions. He placed one hand on my lower back and grabbed my other hand into his own. I attempted to jerk back, but he gave me a vice grip squeeze like Mama Rose would give, which indicated, try me; and as with Mama Rose, I decided not to.

He directed us to his side of the row and seated us so I would have no choice but to sit next to him. He put his bible in his chair, gave me an ugly look, and then left the sanctuary. I think I was in trouble and to top it off, my feelings are hurt that he wasn't going to the race with me and didn't bother providing an explanation. *I will not ask him to do anything else that's for sure*, I thought.

Praise and worship began. He appeared next to me. I did everything in my power to avoid him. When Pastor Hunter instructed everyone to hold hands across the aisle, I held my hand open. It felt as if all eyes were on Randall and me. It made me a bit uncomfortable; however, surprisingly he seemed to enjoy this kind of attention. It wasn't just my crew doing the staring, but the Pastor and others. He finally took hold of my hand and stretched me across the aisle. I did not look in either direction to my left or right. I did not want to face any one. Once the prayer began he jerked my hand to get my attention. I opened my eyes but refused to look in his direction. He let my hand go and dived into my ear and spoke.

"What is your problem?" he demanded.

It wasn't *what* he asked, but rather *how* he asked. It was the wrong way to ask me anything, especially when I could not really answer like I wanted too. I looked up and Pastor was looking dead at me. I did not flinch. He asked again.

"Do you hear me speaking to you? What is wrong?" he continued on. I motioned in front of us. He looked and saw Pastor had his attention directed toward us. The entire service he talked to me. At one point he practically turned his entire body around facing me. I talked back just enough to answer but not enough to hold conversation. After all we were in church.

There were a couple of things I noticed. One, he did not have on his ring and two, he had done an excellent job in matching my attire, which he hadn't seen beforehand. I told him royal blue. He wore a navy suit, with a French blue shirt and a royal, light blue and French blue tie with sapphire cuff links. He looked quite nice. His navy shoes were perfect and added nicely to his entire look. He looked handsome, as always. Whether in jeans, slacks or a suit he was always on point. I could hear the girls whispering. However, I did not entertain their nonsense. When the collection had been gathered, he prepared to take the money to the back, but before he moved he said, "I will see you before you leave." It was not an option.

I must have looked suspicious because he then leaned over and told the girls "I am taking the money back do not leave."

That was a cheap shot. The benediction was given and I had every intention of sneaking out. As we walked towards the vestibule the questions came, just as expected.

"I did not know you two dressed alike." Paige took the lead with the questions as expected. "How long has this been going on?" she continued.

"Huh?" I said, looking around for an instant distraction. At that very moment he showed up. *Thank God.* I was happy to see him for two reasons. One, I loved him and two, I needed to be rescued.

"Ladies, what do I owe the pleasure?" He asked as he clapped his hands.

"Hey Randall," they all chimed.

"I'm glad to see you all. Are we on for dinner today?"

Each of them looked a little confused. Sade said, "Umm, Auntie is going to the race."

"So does that mean we will not have dinner?" Randall attempted again with raised eyebrows and a sly smile.

"Unless you can talk her into it." Sade directed as she nodded her head in Dani's direction.

He looked at me, "Don't even try it," was my immediate response before he could even get the question out of his mouth.

"Why not?" Randall pressured.

I rolled my eyes. "Well, for starters, I'm going to the race and afterwards I'm going to be too tired to prepare a dinner. Secondly, if you were going to the race with me, as I so graciously asked you to begin with, then we'd be having dinner together anyways."

He huffed.

Paige said. "Well dang; play fair kids."

I stomped off.

"Danielle," he said sternly which was the first time I had ever heard him speak that stern to me. It caught me so off guard that I stopped dead in my tracks. He caught up to me quickly, then said real close in my ear. "I am not sure what's up with the attitude, but it will be addressed when you leave the race. I will meet you at your house regardless of the hour."

I felt a little perturbed that he spoke to me in that tone; however, I was relieved all at the same time; considering the fact that he hadn't spoken much to me all week. I felt better knowing that he actually noted and addressed the issue.

"Uncle Hooks," Sade said to break the tension, "what's up, where you been for the past two weeks?"

He smirked and laughed out loud, his nervous response whenever he was caught off guard or put on the spot. He was not prepared for that. I'm sure he wasn't expecting them to "jump him" at church, and from the look on his face, he definitely wasn't expecting the attitude I was giving him.

"I have been laying low all week. It looks like Auntie is a little frustrated with me." Then he winked at me.

"More like perturbed," I said still full of attitude.

He cut his eyes real tight at me and grabbed my hands as if he wanted to hold it but instead he squeezed it extremely tight. I raised one eyebrow in return.

"Does anyone have a clue why Danielle is pissed at me?" he solicited.

For some reason I felt like he found this humorous and found joy in my behavior. They all looked at me as if they were silently questioning if it was acceptable to tell him, but said nothing.

"Let's walk." I said. He looked like he really wanted this resolved.

He looked at Leigh, knowing she was the nicest of the crew, and the peacemaker. "What's up Leigh?" he said to her.

"Hey Hooks." Leigh replies in her normal chipper tone.

"What I do?" He probed. "Help your boy out." His voice was almost pleading.

"Well Randall, I think she feels as if you've avoided and ignored her these past few days. I'm sure you've been busy and it was unintentional."

He turned around to me, "Is this true?"

"Can we talk about it tonight?" I asked.

"Y'all wanna go have breakfast?" he asked in hopes of continuing this conversation now verses later.

"I really have to run," I acknowledged checking the time.

"Let's just get something from the drive thru." he offered.

"You can't leave right now Deacon." I continued in my stance to not give in and do what Randall wanted.

He pulled me to the side again. "Danielle, I don't know what's going on with you today and don't understand why you're being so difficult. This is getting to be annoying."

"What do you mean?" I said, as if I didn't really know.

"Why are you calling me Deacon?" he said.

"Oh, excuse me, but is that or is it not your title?" I huffed. "Like I said; you can't leave now Deacon."

Looking a little more frustrated, Randall stated, "We are just picking up. They won't be ready for me for another thirty minutes. I really want to clear up this misunderstanding with you before you go to the race."

"Yeah, I know but it will have to wait." I mentioned coolly.

"Danielle, why are you ticked off with me?" he asked again as we continue through the maze of cars in the parking lot.

As we finally approach my car, I'm prepared to get in when he yells, "Shot gun!"

"Ah man," Sade yelled, "You wrong for that Uncle Hooks!" she laughs.

There was something about her calling him Uncle that made his day and you could clearly tell. I couldn't even bring myself to protest his lil' intrusion, although I was secretly glad he did. We drove down to the restaurant and he said, "Park, we'll go in."

We ate quickly, laughed, and enjoyed the fellowship. When we took him back to the church, we parked in the back. There we sat, like a couple of teenagers on a date not wanting it to end.

"Danielle, call me when you get in your car after the race, this way I can meet you directly; no matter the time. Also, please keep your watch on and activated." He knew my tactic; the watch would physically be on my arm but not tracking me.

You could hear the chuckles. As I drove back to the house I was really shocked I didn't get any static from the crew; not even about dressing alike. I changed quickly and headed out to the speedway. On the way I realized I did not bring my sunscreen and had to make a quick stop at the nearest convenience store to get some.

Once I arrived at the speedway, I layered the sunscreen on, caught up with my group, and went in for the race. It was a hot day, perfect for such a good and exciting race; I love Nascar. After my favorite driver was named the winner we rolled out to a brag dinner. This was a fun-filled day for me, even if it was still work. During dinner I begin to feel a little itchy paw. I made the assumption it was from the rubber hitting my skin, or possibly it could have been from the sun, the anger, or the excitement. I had my locator on. Before we left the restaurant I texted Randall.

> Hey I am at dinner. I am not feeling well. Do you still want to come by or can we meet tomorrow? Tomorrow would be better.

The first thing Randall did when he received the text was check the locator. Not that he didn't have any trust or was stalking, but he was trying to find out what was really going on. Now he was the one feeling as if she was blowing him off. *Is this an eye for an eye?* From the locator, she was about seven miles from the speedway. What he couldn't tell, however, was if she was with someone, if she was hungry or was just buying time to allow the traffic to die down before heading out.

> What time are you leaving there?

> I am waiting for the check now so I can pay and leave.

> I will be at your house when you get there.

His response caught her of guard. > Oh! Okay. *I guess he missed the fact that I said I didn't feel well.* I can't explain it but my skin feels hot like I may be having a heat stroke or something. *Relax, D. Get you a glass of crushed ice, take a cold shower and chill for the rest of the night.* I turned my satellite to the jazz station. The first voice I heard was that of Ella Fitzgerald and the timing couldn't have been more perfect. Maybe he is the reason why I feel like I have fever.

As soon as I pulled to the gate, I notice Randall is parked over in the shadows, waiting. *OMG, he's serious. Why is he in that Maybach? My neighbors are going to think I went from being man-less to a tramp overnight. Every time he comes he is in a different car. F what they think.* Technically, it was still Sunday and he must still be in the Sunday car. I flashed him and let him go thru the gate first. He drove extremely slowly or perhaps it was me and I was just in a hurry to get home. I pulled into the garage and stepped out.

"Go in and get yourself settled. I will wait," he uttered.

Why is everything with him an order? "You don't have to wait out here Randall, you may come inside."

"It's fine." *I need to stay outside and as far away from you undressing as possible,* he thought to himself.

I walked right up to him, gave him a hug and a soft and gentle kiss on his cheek. From the look on his face, I could tell he was not expecting that and I wasn't sure if I may have overstepped my boundaries. He looked nice as always. Better yet, he looked sexy, as always, and he smelled tantalizing. *What was this man doing to me?* I stepped back slowly with my eyes looking down and walked away.

I went inside and quickly shut the alarm down. I ran to the bathroom and flicked the water on and began my hunt for the Benadryl or anything to stop this itching. I took a quick birdbath in semi-freezing water, since I didn't want anything to touch my skin. I grabbed a pair of leggings and a long racer back shirt. Semi-cute but a quick lounging outfit.

As I walk back out of the house, there he is, sitting on my front steps with his iPad. I sit next to him, extremely close; so close until I was almost on his lap. "Hey sexy," I say in almost a whisper.

He laughed his famous nervous reaction laugh and leaned over on me.

"What are you doing good looking?" I continue in the flirt. He looked over as if he didn't know what to say.

I leaned down over his shoulder. The image on his iPad looks like a big graph to me. He explained it as some sort of virtual program showing him and an opponent. If he threw a punch it showed the opponent's most likely next move. Some would call it a game, but technically, this was his job, so I called it work. "Oh working are we?" I teased.

"No just looking at some techniques," he replied.

Was there a technique he didn't know? "Are you learning anything?" Looking at this app made me realized how technology had taken fighting or boxing to an entirely different level. I guess I could say the same as it related to my work and drawing.

"Yeah, how not to get my A-S-S kicked," he spelled the bad word.

"Let's go inside it is hot out here," I said.

"It's not hot!" He flicked his finger across the pad and checked the temperature.

"Well, I am hot." Okay, maybe that didn't come across exactly how it should have and for a first, I wasn't "hot" in that sense of the word around him. I don't know which I prefer.

He swiped the device again and on the screen appears my name, all my logistics, and heat index information. "You are cooling down," he said without skipping a beat.

"So you say," I said before I knew it. I thought *S-H-I-T* to myself.

He laughed again, this time not out of a nervous habit, but because I made him laugh. I liked that I made him laugh. "Yeah, you are. Check it out," he said. This conversation stimulated a few questions. *Was she heat hot or HOOKS HOT and what was causing this naughty girl behavior when earlier she refused to entertain me?*

He pulled the iPad closer to me and BUYAH... there on the screen showed my temperature from the entire day. I saw where I was steaming in church. You could see when we talked my blood pressure, temperature, and pulse rate went up. It relaxed out at another point and then my temperature spiked again during the time I was at the race. It seemed to have dropped some while at the restaurant but it declined during my shower.

He said, "You see right here is when it fell off," pointing to the figure on the screen. "So you can understand why I was determined to come over?"

"No," I replied.

"Apparently, I had you upset earlier, and something appears to be wrong now. Are you okay?"

"No, I feel a little exhausted I think. How often do you study my temperature?" I curiously asked.

"I won't trouble you long. I know you have had an exciting day in the sun. How was the race?" He purposefully ignored the other question.

"Well, since you *didn't* come," I emphasized, "I got to entertain and be a company woman all alone. But you know my driver won. YEAH BABY!"

"I saw. Check this." He swiped again and there were the race highlights and interviews. He could see my excitement. "This is nothing," he said. "Wait until you are next to me while I am being interviewed before or after a fight; you'll then have a total different level of excitement. The adrenaline is different for racing and fighting. I can't explain it," he said.

We continued our discussion about the race. I felt like a fifteen-year-old sitting on Mama Rose's porch courting... then he sprung it on me.

He lifted my chin and spoke. "You know I am doing all I can?"

"All you can for what?" I said.

Looking me directly in my eyes, he continues, "For a lot of things actually."

"Like what?" He was always so stern and direct. Right now he was being vague or this itching was effecting my listening.

"Like. Like. Like," he stammered. "It's difficult. I am trying not to allow myself to get closer or attached to you. I am trying to do right with you, in the sight of God, the church and my fans. It is hard because I love you all, I need you all, and I want to please you all. I am not in the right position right now, so I can't be entitled to the freedom to do what I want to do."

I was getting sleepy. So sleepy. The Benadryl was kicking in.

"You okay?" he probed.

"I think the Benadryl is kicking in," I told him.

"You took a Benadryl?" he asked.

"Yes," I reply, holding in a yawn.

"Why?" he asked looking concerned.

"I feel a little itchy paw."

"Itchy paw. What is that?" *Girls are so strange.*

"Itchy. Maybe too much sun or rubber hitting my skin."

"Did something bite you?" he asked. "Why didn't you get a box seat? Because you are stubborn and want to sit there in the heat and see it all, feel it all and hear it all." he answers his own question.

"Nothing bit me that I know of."

"Well the Benadryl should work it out." Then he swiped that pad again. He began to type.

"What are you doing?" I asked.

"I am sending this to King and the Doc. I need for them to let me know if they see anything strange here and if we need to go to the emergency room."

"EMERGENCY ROOM! I am not going to an emergency room." He was speaking bad words to me as far as I was concerned. He cut his eyes at me. I said to myself, *I guess I will be going to an emergency room if they say I should.* "Let's go in," I tell him. I really wanted to go inside by this point.

His phone rang, "It's King, hold on." he told me. "What's up?" he spoke into the phone.

"What's wrong?" King asked.

"She refers to it as an itchy paw." King must have said something because he looked at me and laughed. "She took a Benadryl," he continued.

"Gotcha. Get Doc on the line." He listened and said, "Okay. Okay. Okay. Okay. Will do. I will call you if I need too. Do you think you need to come over now?"

"Just watch her all night." Doc said.

"I can't stay all night." *Did he just give me permission to stay all night,* Randall thought to himself. "Can you put this in writing and call Trevor?"

"Why?" Doc asked.

"She is not that kind of girl and I am a respectable gentleman. Let's go in the house," he said to me.

"Y'all are outside?" Doc asked.

"Yeah, I just found out what was wrong and called you all. Shut up. We are going in now."

We went inside and sat on the couch. He went to the kitchen and got some ice. I laid down. He put crushed ice in my mouth and in a cloth. He placed the cool compress on my forehead and I think I feel asleep. He was on the other end of the couch when I opened my eyes holding my feet and swiping away on that pad. I jumped. He jumped.

"You okay?" he asked.

Sleepily I reply, "Yeah, I guess I dozed off."

"It's cool. Why don't you get some rest and I am going to leave. I will text you when I get home. You do not have to text back but please just keep that watch on. I will call you or come over here if I need to." he said. He got up to leave and placed his iPad in a nice Gucci cover.

"DANG! That is a sweet cover. When did you get that?" I felt like crap but I knew I was still fine if I recognized the G's.

"Umm. You like it?" he asked looking at it.

"WHAT?? It's a Banger!!!" I exclaimed.

"I didn't even think to get you one. I will pick you up one if you like. You want black or brown?" he asked.

"Both! I excitedly told him. I may need to see the black one first. Now that is HOT!"

"I will bring it over tomorrow so you can see it," he said.

"Oh you have both?" I asked. He laughed. You could tell he was not accustomed to being in a relationship because those were items you always picked up in doubles. One for him and one for her. "OH HECK TO DA NAW!" I was too excited about this case.

He kept laughing. "I thought you were sick?"

"I am not that dog gone sick; that case is enough to make a girl like me feel much better," I laugh. By now we were on the steps.

Shaking his head he said, "Go to bed Danielle."

He didn't have to tell me twice. "Sir, yes sir." I saluted. I was sleepy and giddy. I was slurring my words although I could not tell.

"I am not playing," he ordered.

"I know when you call me Danielle you are not playing," I tell him frowning.

"Good night my love. Feel better. Call me if you need me. I mean it. Until we meet again. May God watch over thee and me while we are apart."

We embraced. *OH MY GOD! I can really fall for this man.* I locked the door, powered up the alarm and headed for the bed. I made sure the phone was under my pillow, all three of them. It was a wrap. I was not planning on thinking, just dreaming. I was hoping I would be alert long enough to hear his text, but that didn't seem like it was going to happen.

WEEK 14

Monday

It didn't happen. I was not alert when he texted. My eyes did not open again until a quarter after three. When they did, I was confused, didn't know where I was or how I got there. I sat straight up in the bed and tried to get my bearings together. Once I felt a little like myself again, I grabbed the phones and sure enough, he did text.

> Good night my love. I hope you feel better. Call me if you need me. Otherwise call me in the morning. Sweet dreams.

I fell back on the bed. *Why couldn't he be free to be with me?* I just laid there for a minute looking up at the ceiling. Finally, I had to pinch myself to make sure this was real. *Was this truly happening to me?* I felt a little strange and decided that maybe I should just go workout. *Should I do a tape or the treadmill?* I got dressed in workout clothes but when I leaned over to tie my shoes I felt light headed. *I had better wait until later. I did take a Benadryl or two last night.* I took off the workout clothes and got dressed for work.

When I looked into the mirror, my face looked puffy. *Maybe I needed more water. Maybe I slept too hard so my face is a little puffy.* I just didn't look like myself; even after the boatload of eyeliner and mascara, I painted on. *Dang. I had better wear my glasses today. Why does my face look like this?* I tried to put on my rings and bangles but I was so swollen; therefore, I opted not to. I quickly left the house before I was too tempted to lie back down.

I felt like crap! I was so groggy that I did not bother to check his blog, my emails, or voice messages. Instead, I pulled out of the driveway and headed out. I couldn't help but to keep looking into the review mirror trying to figure out what was wrong with my face. *Maybe Starbucks will help.* I drove into the Starbucks drive thru to grab a caffeine fat loaded treat. It was the least I could do if I had to look ugly all day. Besides, as sleepy as I was I need the jolt. Maybe it would shake me loose. I grabbed Leigh a treat too.

I arrived to my office and parked the Bemmer crooked in my favorite spot. It was a much-needed relief to park and sit myself down somewhere. *I should come back to life once I gulped this Carmel Macchiato*, I hoped. Nope! It didn't work. I was still broke down. After thirty minutes or so, I had gained enough strength to call Randall.

"Hello." he answered.

"Hey Babe."

"How are you?"

"Umm. Sleepy. Did you drug me last night?" I asked jokingly.

"With ice?" he asked with laughter in his voice.

"Yes." I replied.

"I won't ever tell," he teased.

"Well, I sure hope that if you did drug me with ice, you took full advantage of me too; and I liked it and you plan on repeating it again tonight."

You could hear him blushing. "You think I would do something like that?"

"Which part? Drug me, take advantage of me, or repeat it?"

"You are a mess," he laughed.

Well I hope that you would do so. I thought to myself. *Here it is I've drugged myself up and now I am tripping. I need to shut my mouth before I really say something out of the way.*

"I may one day. Why did you go to work if you were sleepy?" he asked.

"I'm a crazy over achiever," I confessed.

"I love it," he said.

"You love it or me?" He gave the infamous laugh. I really wanted an answer.

"I answered because I wanted to hear your voice and make sure you were all right. I am still running though. Can I call you back in an hour?"

"And you call me an over achiever? Carry on. I will speak to you later." I held the phone while he clicked off.

I attempted to start my day, but could not focus enough to read the emails. I was typing and falling asleep. I decided to lay my head on my desk for a while. *I will be able to hear the commotion when the others begin to arrive.* So I thought. I did not hear anything until I heard Leigh yelling.

"Danielle, are you okay?"

I swear I felt like I did years ago after too many spirits the night before. "Yeah, why are you yelling?"

"Because I've called your name four times. What is wrong with you?" Leigh asked in alarm.

"I felt like crap last night so I took a Benadryl, but now I can't seem to shake it. I stopped and got a Macchiato but it isn't helping. By the way, yours is over there with your oatmeal."

"Thanks. Which oatmeal is mine?" she asked.

"They are both the same."

"I am going to warm them up. Maybe you will feel better after you put some food on your stomach," she said then walked out of the office.

"Good." I knew I had at least ten minutes to lay my head down again, but I swear it seemed like it took Leigh two minutes to go and come back.

"Here," she said, placing the oatmeal on my desk. "Did you eat yesterday after being in the sun all day?" she asked.

"Yep, we went to dinner."

"Did you have a beverage?" she was not insinuating I was hung over but more like someone slipped something in my drink.

"No I am not hung over. I was feeling bad at the restaurant. I went right home and took a Benadryl shortly before Randall got there." I reassured her.

"Randall got there?" she asked in surprise.

"Yes." I said.

"And?" she asked waiting for the details.

"That was it. He wanted to talk to me but I do not think we ever did." I said.

"What hurts?" she asked.

"Last night I was just itching. Now I don't know. I feel weird."

"Let me pull out the Heat Stroke Safety Information." She retrieved the pamphlet from the first aid box. She went through all the symptoms, but I didn't feel like I had any of those.

"Sit up and eat your oatmeal," she instructed.

I struggled to lift my head up.

"OH HELL!" Leigh screamed.

I was so tired I could not speak quickly enough, but my heart was pounding fast just from the sound of Leigh's reaction.

"Oh my goodness, your face is three times the normal size."

"What?" I said, attempting to touch my face to size it up.

"I'm calling the doctor. What is your dermatologist name?" she asked observing my face.

I wasn't going to give it to her, but before I could react, she reached for my phone and started scrolling. I did not have the strength to argue and from her actions, I don't think I had a chance.

"If they can't get you in you are going to emergency," she stated.

"Damn, everyone wants to send me to emergency," I slurred.

"Who else?" she asked.

"Randall wanted me to go last night. He called his doctor."

"Why didn't you go Danielle?" Leigh said sounding frustrated at this point.

"I didn't need to," I said.

"I'm calling him and cursing him out next. Why didn't he take you?" she said as she put the phone to her ear.

"I didn't need to go." I thought I had already answered that question one time.

"And he listened to you?" she rolled her eyes. "Ugh! MEN! Were you slurring like this too?"

She was talking on the phone and all I could hear was "She will be right over."

"Let's go. Where is your purse?" she asked.

We headed to the elevator. I heard her speaking as soon as the door closed.

"This isn't Danielle, it's Leigh, Hooks." She didn't sound like the nice Leigh either. I was giggling under my breath.

"Hey what's up?" he replied.

"Dani is sick. That what's up? What did she look like last night?"

I heard nothing.

"Apparently," then she lost the call in the elevator.

We made it to Leigh's car and I was so glad because all I wanted to do was take a nap. She must have ringed him and it went straight to voice mail. She tried several times.

"Dani," she called out to me.

"Yep. I can hear you," I said. Why was she yelling?

"How does that watch work?" she inquired.

"What do you mean?"

"I need to get in touch with Randall," she spoke frantically.

"Okay." I pressed the buttons until the red dial began to spin. I didn't feel like I was in danger but I was too weak to disagree or disobey Leigh. Finally, my phone rang. It was his ringtone.

"He is calling," I told her.

Leigh answered. "Hooks!"

"What's wrong?" he asked remaining calm.

"What did she look like last night?"

"Fine. Why?" he asked now sounding alarmed.

"Her face is three times the normal size. I am on the way to take her to the dermatologist. She is extremely incoherent. She can't stay awake. Did she only take one Benadryl?"

"Leigh, I can hear you and yes I only took one." I said. I pulled the mirror down to see my face but I could not see anything because my eyes were so swollen.

Randall said, "I'm on my way to pick my car up from the gym, then I'll be there shortly. Hold one moment; this is the alarm service calling about her watch." A few seconds later, he clicked back over. "Keep the alarm on so I can know where to a find you all. I will see you in a minute. She just called me two hours ago and said she felt fine other than sleepy."

"She lied," Leigh said. "We will see you in a little while." Her tone relaxed a bit.

We arrived at the dermatologist office, but I could only see light. The nurse said, "Danielle what did you get into?"

"I don't know." I said slurring.

"Come on back. The doctor is not here yet but let me let you lie down."

I think I was asleep before she could exit the room. She came back with my chart and started asking questions. *Why wouldn't everyone just let me sleep?*

"Danielle, has any information changed?" The nurse inquired.

I held my finger up and shook it no. I never opened my eyes. I was not capable at this time.

The nurse continued, "What did you eat yesterday?"

I pointed at Leigh.

She spoke. "We had breakfast but all she had was a parfait and fruit."

"What kind of fruit?" The nurse asked.

"She had raspberries, strawberries, blue berries, apples and plain yogurt."

"Have you ever had a reaction to berries before?" she then asked me.

Once again, I waved my finger no.

"What else did you eat?"

"Funnel cake. Salad." I slurred.

"What was on the salad?" The nurse probed.

I threw my hands up. They were asking too much.

"Danielle, I need to know what was on the salad." The nurse insisted.

I hesitated. It was taking a lot from me. "Spinach, tomatoes, onions, grilled chicken."

"Any mushrooms?" she asked another question.

I shook my head. *Am I allergic to mushrooms? No!*

"What kind of dressing?"

"Vinegar." I could not even get vinaigrette out.

"Any peanuts?"

I shook my head no.

"Where did you have it?" She needed answers to give the doctor.

I struggled to speak the name of the restaurant. This time I wasn't sure if I was just tired or if it really hurt me to speak.

"I am calling the restaurant," she said. "Where did you get the funnel cake?"

I pointed at Leigh like I was driving.

"At the speedway?" Leigh asked me.

I nodded yes.

"I wonder what kind of oil they used," the nurse said out loud as she made notes on the chart.

I pointed at Leigh the receipt was in my bag.

"Did you have anything else to eat?" The nurse drilled.

"No." I reached for Leigh's hand. At this point, I'm pretty sure that it actually hurts to speak.

I heard my phone ring. Leigh answered, "Hello," she said. "Who? Oh hi. We are here. The Doctor has not arrived yet."

She listened. "Okay. Excuse me, what is the number here?" Leigh asked the nurse to give to the caller on Danielle's phone the information.

The nurse rattled off the number that Leigh repeated in the phone. Then she informed the nurse, "Her doctor will be calling for an update."

"I will go let them know at the front desk. I am also going to get what I need for the skin test to see if she had an allergic reaction. Danielle, do you have any rashes?"

I shrugged my shoulders. I really didn't know. I didn't last night and I was too sleepy to check before I left the house.

"Undress and put this gown on. I will be right back. Do you need help undressing?" she asked.

I did but I pointed at Leigh. She was still on the phone. I was lying flat and doing a poor job trying to pull my clothes off.

"Doctor is Randall on his way?" Leigh asked into the phone. "I will see you two when you get here. I need to help her take her clothes off."

We waited a few minutes more. Then the nurse arrived and looked over my skin from head to toe. "I do not see any rashes," she confirmed. "Do you know if you have any allergies Danielle?" she asked a groggy Danielle.

I shook my head.

"The doctor is pulling up now. As soon as he gets in we will do the skin test. Can you use the restroom?"

I shook my head yes.

"Great, I'll need a urine sample and then I am going take a blood sample just to make sure we do not miss anything."

Both women helped me off the table and walked me to the restroom. My entire backside was exposed, but who cared. When we got into the restroom and the lights were turned on, I moaned. The pain was intense, absolutely brutal to my eyes. I wondered why she needed urine but I was in too much pain to ask.

"Can you do it on your own?" Leigh asked.

I shook my head yes. However, I was wondering if I was going to be able to catch some urine in a cup considering I could not see the cup I was holding. *I think I did it.* "Leigh," I called out.

She opened the door. "You okay sunshine?"

"Umm hmm."

"Are you finished?" she asked.

"Yes."

"Good job," she encouraged.

She walked with me slowly and patiently back to the table. I could not see anything. I felt my face getting tighter and tighter. There was no doubting it Leigh was a true friend. Here she was holding my urine, of all things, and helping me through this; considering I had no clue what was going on other than I was sleepy. She was handling business on behalf of my health.

The nurse came in and said, "Danielle, I am going to take some blood now. You will feel a stick." As soon as the needle touched my skin I heard the door open. I thought it was the doctor, but it was Randall. I could still smell his soap. He had rushed to take a shower and then raced over to the doctor's office. It was true what they say; when you lose one sense, the others automatically kick in. I could smell everyone in the room. He kissed my forehead.

"Hey Leigh."

"Hey Randall." I could tell she was pissed. Her tone was harsh.

He spoke to the nurse. "Good morning."

She spoke back, "Good morning to you sir, but unfortunately not so good for our patient here."

She looked up and noticed him immediately. "Oh my word! You are, you are," she stammered.

"Yes, I am," he confessed.

"You are the boxer," she said with enthusiasm.

"Yes I am, and right now I am concerned. Danielle, why didn't you tell me you didn't feel good this morning; actually last night?"

I held up my hand.

"She can't really speak, her face is too swollen." Leigh said abruptly.

"I can see," Randall retorted with his back turned to Leigh.

"She looks as if she's been in the ring with you!" Leigh barked.

"I don't think so. This would be light if she was in the ring with me." He was joking but he said it ever so seriously.

I threw up my middle finger. I mean seriously, here I am laying around with a face the size of a globe and they are cracking jokes. What are friends for?

"How much more blood do you need to take?" he asked as the two doctors entered the room.

"Ms. Rose," my doctor said, not realizing it was a room full.

"Mr. Washington," Hooks replied with his hand stretched out to shake the doctor's hand. "You must be the patient here for my colleague," the doctor said.

"That is correct. I spoke to him last night when she stated she didn't feel well," Randall replied.

"Danielle, can you see?" The doctor asked.

I shook my head no.

"How long have you not been able to see?" he continued.

Randall spoke. "She could see clearly last night. She drove herself to work this morning, stopped at Starbucks, and then called me. So somewhere within the last few hours she has swollen like this. I fight for a living and I gotta tell you, my face has never taken a lick like this before."

Listening to Randall's words about my condition was enough to put me in panic mode.

"The Benadryl may have worn off. She may have counteracted the reaction last night."

"Danielle, I am going to swab your skin numerous times. Okay?" The doctor replied in a very calming voice.

I nodded yes.

Randall held one hand and Leigh held the other. He leaned in close. "Are you okay?"

I leaned my head on his head. I took my hand from his hand and pointed at my throat.

"What's wrong?" he asked gently.

I opened my mouth like it was dry and thirsty.

"Nurse could you please get her some water?" Randall's doctor asked.

Not being able to see, it was amazing how my other sense really kicked in. I could identify everyone in the room by smell. I could hear them shift their weight from one foot to the other. I could hear Randall placing his hand in his pocket, the doctor checking his phone and Leigh swallowing really hard.

"Did you call Paige and Sade?" Randall asked Leigh.

"No let me do that now," she said. When she reached into my handbag for my phone she pulled out the sunscreen I bought the day of the race.

Randall's doctor said, "Let me see that."

Leigh must have passed it to him. "Danielle, did you use this sunscreen yesterday?"

I nodded.

"Where did you use it?" he asked.

I motioned all over my body by waving my hand in a circular motion in front of me.

"Did you use it on your face?" Randall's doctor asked.

I put my hand over my face.

"She was itching last night. I think she may have broken down the rash and now the reaction has kicked in," Randall's doctor observed.

The nurse came back with the cup of water. Randall held my back up touching my bare skin as I tried to drink. Not one drop fell down my throat. It fell completely out of my mouth. I looked down. I tried to open my eyes. I realized I could not swallow.

"Ahh. We have it," the doctor said and they both left the room.

Randall placed my hand into Leigh's as she was on the phone, and he left the room as well. I was struggling so hard to see, but it didn't work. I was living in darkness and it seemed like forever before they returned.

"Danielle, we are going to give you a series of shots. I am going to need both hips and both arms. We are giving you a steroid, anti-inflammatory, antibiotic and a pain killer."

All I could do was roll my body over. It didn't matter who was in the room at this point. I remembered nothing; not even the multiple needle sticks. I was out like a light.

"I think she is all done. She will need to be monitored over the next twenty-four hours however. I am going to prescribe her a few medications. Although she may still be swollen when she wakes up tonight, she shouldn't swell any further nor be in pain. If you notice swelling, difficulty breathing or difficulty swallowing, take her to emergency," the doctor instructed.

Randall's physician said, "I will be seeing her a few more times throughout the day. We should not have any more issues Doctor."

"If so do not hesitate to call me. I want to make sure her esophagus does not swell and present a problem," the doctor stated.

Randall said, "Doc you said when she wakes up tonight?"

"Yes, she will be asleep for at least eight to ten hours if not longer," the doctor replied.

"So she will not be able to work tomorrow?" Randall asked.

"Definitely not and I would prefer for her not to have any outside activities until after I have seen her next week," the doctor stated.

"I need that in writing please," Randall said.

"You need a doctor's excuse?" The doctor asked for clarity.

"No, I need a letter from you addressed to her stating that she is not to work or workout outside. Otherwise, she will think we are lying," Randall explained.

"Doctor, Danielle is not going to believe any of us if we tell her she cannot work when she wakes up. As a matter of fact, I am inclined to leave her here so you can inform her of the bad news yourself." Leigh added.

The doctor smiled and said, "Oh I see. We have a worker bee on our hands. I will write the letter. Who has her cell phone?"

"I do," Leigh answered.

"Good, I will leave her a message also. Shall I demand she stay off work for a week?" The doctor asked.

Randall and Leigh laughed; they knew Danielle all too well.

"That will never happen; she will never go for being off an entire week," Randall said.

"All right, how are we going to do this?" Leigh asked.

"Do what?" Randall asked in return.

"Get her back home etc.," Leigh said.

As if he had already thought it out, Randall said, "Simple. I will take her home and pick up the prescriptions. Not a big deal."

"What are we going to do with her car?" Leigh asked.

"Is it still at the office?"

"Yes," Leigh replied

"Are you going to the house or back to work?" Randall inquired.

"I'm going to go back to work. I'll need to wrap a few things up, get her computers and a few other things she may need from the office."

"Did you say computers?"

"Umm yes. Dani carries around quite a few. Why, I don't know? She has the Sony, the Mac, the Dell, the iPad, and the Gateway that she carries. She is something else and actually works off all of them at once. All I can say is you have to see it to believe it. Have you seen either of her offices at home or work?"

"No, I have not. Doesn't she work off the phones also?" Randall enquired.

"Yes, Dani has a system that works well for her. You can find the internet up on one, emails on another, and the programs and software packages she's using on the others. You can safely say she is a company girl. She loves what she does, loves her job, and does it well," Leigh said.

Randall shook his head in agreement and said, "I can tell. Well, if you bring her car home, my driver will take you back to pick up your car. Will that work for you?"

"That will work fine, my friend. Either way it goes, she is going to freak out anyway, so it doesn't make that big of a difference. Are you going to stay with her all day or do I need to get Sade to come over?"

"I am going to stay with her but you can get Sade to come also. That would make me feel better. I would hate for her to freak out that I am at her house." Randall said.

"I will call Sade now and have her go to the house. She has a key and knows how to unlock the code so she will be able to let you in."

Randall asked, "Where do I need to pick up the prescription?"

"She uses the pharmacy that sits right on the corner as soon as you exit the highway. Everyone there knows Dani. Lisa is the pharmacist, she'll be able to help you," Leigh answered.

"Do I need an insurance card?"

"No, you should not; they have it on file."

"If there is a problem I will pay for the prescription."

"You can do that if you need to and she will handle it tomorrow. She does however carry a yellow visa from work specifically for medical cost in her wallet."

"Don't worry about it. I will pay for it. I am sure she will be pissed about that too."

Leigh laughs, "Oh yes, you are learning her oh so well Hooks."

"Well I sure hope that is a good thing," he replied.

Looking over at Dani, Leigh sighed then asked, "Now how in God's name are we getting her to the car?"

Randall got up to leave and said, "Let me go pull the car to the curb."

While Hooks went to go move the car Leigh and the nurse got Danielle dressed then Leigh called Sade and Paige. "Paige, hey it's Leigh."

"Hey girly."

"I'm calling to let you know I am at the doctor with Dani."

"So, is she pregnant and having an abortion because she does not know who the father is?" Paige joked longing for her baby sister to have some drama.

"Umm no!" Leigh said laughing.

"She is so straight laced now and no fun. What's wrong? Is she okay?" She said dryly in mock disappointment that her theory was not true.

"Kind of sort of. Right now she is snoring like hell. She's been given a painkiller. She apparently had a reaction from sunscreen she used yesterday at the race."

"See, she should have stayed home and cooked for us," Paige said. "What do you need me to do?" she asked a little more serious now.

"Hooks is here and he is going to take her home. He wants Sade to come over to watch her though."

"Sade pick up the phone. Auntie is sick." Paige called out to her daughter.

Sade picked up the other line and immediately started with a stream of questions, "What? Auntie is sick? What happened? Where is she? What's wrong? What's going on? Somebody tell me something now!"

"She had a reaction to sunscreen at the track yesterday." Leigh said.

"Did she take a Benadryl?" Sade said. "I told her not to go to that race."

"Yep actually that is what probably kept her from going to the emergency room last night. Her face is really swollen though."

"Send me a picture!" Sade said with excitement.

"I will do no such thing!" Leigh barked. "She is snoring and passed out Sade."

"Leigh you have to send a picture. As a matter of fact video it. We have to have this footage. She always gets us," Sade begged.

"No Sade. I am not doing that. I think you've forgotten, but I do have to work with her you know."

"Leigh do you remember when I had that reaction to the hair color and she ragged me for weeks? Come on!" Sade pleaded and enjoying the idea of a good payback.

"You can do it when you get there," Leigh said.

"She may wake up. You have to do it now," Sade continued.

"I'll think about it." Leigh replied to Sade. "Are we ready?" she said to Randall as he entered the room again.

"Yes," Randall said.

"Hey, Sade meet Randall at the house. We are about to get Dani into the car."

"RANDALL?" Sade shouted.

"You are correct," Leigh replied without hesitation. "Are you on the way to meet Randall so he can get into the house?"

"Yes. He doesn't have a key?" Sade asked under her breath but they both heard her.

"You call us back immediately Leigh. I am not playing!" Paige ordered.

"Will do ladies. Thank you," she said then disconnected the call.

"Sade is on her way to meet you at the house," Leigh said.

"Cool," he replied.

Leigh was still heavily concerned. "How are we getting her to the car?"

"Why don't you go ahead and gather her things and get her checked out. I'll take care of everything else," he said.

Leigh was very thankful Randall was there. Considering the fact she was not a "morning person," he made this whole ordeal a little easier to handle on such an early Monday morning. She was looking forward to returning to her coffee too, as she hadn't had the chance to enjoy a good cup yet. She paid the co pay and returned back to the room.

"Hooks, here is the card for the prescription." He looked at Leigh and at the card and frowned, as if he was insulted. "Okay then," she shrugged and she put the visa back in Dani's wallet.

"Are you ready?" Randall asked.

"Yes! Let's go. This is more than enough excitement for one morning. Leave it to Danielle!" She turned to walk away and looked back and realized Randall was carrying Danielle. *How romantic*, she thought. *Too bad Dani isn't even alert to know*. She had a quick remedy to that problem however, and she pulled out her camera and began snapping shots. She snapped shots all the way to the car. Once they got to the Range Rover she switched the camera to record and began recording Hooks putting Dani in the seat as if she was a rag doll.

Looking back as if he could sense being watched, he asked, "Are you taking pictures?"

"Shh. Recording," she whispered.

He closed the passenger door but Leigh opened it again. Dani was snoring so loud, completely out of it. "Good footage," Leigh said with laughter in her voice.

"Get in," Randall said. "We are driving you to your car."

She got in the back but leaned over the seat with her camera. "Dani how do you feel?" Nothing. "Danielle!"

"HUH?" A groggy Dani muttered.

"You feel okay?" Leigh asked as she recorded.

"Yep, real good." Dani slurred.

"Are you going home?"

"Nope! I am going to work," Dani replied quickly.

"Oh okay. You talked to Randall?" Leigh continued.

"Yes."

"You like him?" Leigh asked.

"Huh?"

"Do you like him?" Randall asked this time.

"Yes, no, maybe," Dani said.

"Which one?" he asked. She stopped responding. They were making cheap fun at Dani's expense. He dropped Leigh off at her car. "Leigh what is your number?" She gave him her number. He called it right then. Once it rang he spoke. "That's me lock me in."

"Got you. I will call you later," Leigh hung up.

"Dani."

"Huh!" she said aggravated this time.

"I hope you feel better," Leigh said caringly.

"Umm hmm," she replied annoyed.

"I love you."

She rolled her head over and threw up one finger. Whatever that meant.

Hooks pulled off. Once they were half way down the street he grabbed her hand, pulled it to his face, and rubbed it against his cheeks. Then he kissed it over and over again. He felt so helpless, she wasn't feeling well, and he couldn't do anything about it. He was also pissed with himself for not making her go to emergency the night before. He realized then that from that moment on he had a responsibility to take care of her. Even when that meant making her do things she didn't want to do but what was in her best interest. In this case, what was best for her health. First order of duty was for her to go to bed at night.

This time with Danielle felt so right to him, so natural. Why couldn't this be his life? Why couldn't she be his wife? *I have to do everything in my power to keep her.* He pulled up to the red light and just watched her sleep. He took a picture with his phone. When he pulled into the pharmacy parking lot he parked and stared. He laid his head back on the headrest and closed his eyes. He meditated and thought. He had plenty of time. He could not get in the house anyway.

"Danielle, can you hear me?" he asked. She did not respond. He checked her seat belt. Got out, locked the door, and cut the alarm on. He really did not want to leave her in the car alone. He came back to the car to wait on the prescription. After twenty minutes he went back in to pick it up. They pulled up to the house and as soon as he got out Sade opened the door. She had the phone up to her ear.

"Uncle Hooks. Let me help you," she said.

He was stuck on being addressed as Uncle Hooks. He liked it. "Hold the door for me please," he ordered.

She opened the passenger door and when she looked at Danielle's face, she said, "Oh my God. Auntie!" a little louder than she meant to.

"She will be fine," Randall assured her.

"Are you sure?" She growled at him as if this was all his fault. "Let me call you back." she said angrily to her caller.

"Yeah. Pain killers, not enough food and very little sleep will lay you out like this," he said. He lifted Danielle out the car like she weighed ten pounds. "Sade get her things."

She grabbed Dani's purse and the prescription then ran to the door to hold it open.

"Where should I lie her down?" Randall questioned.

"Can you take her to her bed?"

"If that's where you want her."

"Is she heavy?" she asked.

"Not really."

"Can you carry her further?"

"Show me the way."

She led him to Danielle's bedroom. Once the double doors opened he could not wait to lay her down. This was where she slept or didn't sleep. He looked around. It looked just the way he had imagined. It was so her. Sade began to take her shoes off and he leaned up against the column. She was so beautiful to him, inside and out. Looking at her laying there, it was confirmed how his heart truly felt. For the first time ever, he felt butterflies in his stomach. Sade began to charge Dani's phones and put her bag and keys in their respective locations, all the while, Randall stood right there watching her sleep.

"Can you hang this up?" she asked him as she passed him her suit jacket.

He looked around and went to what he assumed was the closet. He walked in and surprisingly said, "What?"

Sade stopped what she as doing and followed behind him. "What's wrong?" She yelled.

"Is this a closet or a small department store?" It was extremely organized. Everything had a place and there was a place for everything.

"That's what you screamed for?" she asked perturbed.

"I did not scream," he said.

"Umm huh. So you say," she smirked and walked out of the closet.

"I didn't," he said again to convince himself didn't scream.

"You are tripping. I am sure your closet is one hundred times this size. It probably makes that closet look like garbage," she laughed.

"I don't think so," Randall replied.

"We shall see," Sade said rolling her eyes.

He stood there looking at the suits, handbags, shoes, belts and all the other clothes. He didn't know where to start. He wanted to walk around and get a closer look, but didn't want to seem nosey. So he stood where he was and got a good look at everything. He noticed all of the hats and wondered why she did not wear them to church every week. *She needs to be wearing these*, he thought.

He stepped outside the double doors and spoke. "Excuse me."

"What's up?" Sade answered.

"Any particular reason for the chairs and the mini bar?"

"They are chaise lounges and the refrigerator stocks water and juice. It can get hot in there trying to get dressed. Sometimes it can be considered a strenuous job just trying to figure out what to wear. Of course men would not know anything about that. You all throw on a pair of jeans and a white tee or pair of slacks, a shirt, and tie, then it's a wrap."

"Not true."

"So true," she said, clearing her throat and looked him up and down.

It was then he realized he in fact had on jeans, a tee, and Air Max. "I was in a hurry to get to the doctor's. You may be right but this is overboard," he said pointing to the closet.

"Let's leave right now and go check your closet." Not that she really wanted to see his closet. She really wanted to investigate his house. Did the wife actually live there? What remnants had she left behind? Was the house a male's touch, a woman's touch or clearly a decorator's touch? So many questions could be answered just by viewing his house. Was it his house or his home?

"We can do that, but not until we know she is alert and feels better," Randall proposed.

"If your closet is in any way off the hook then it is on." Sade said.

"It is not. Well it was built like that. I didn't have anything to do with the design of my closet. It looks like this house was designed around the closet."

"Yeah right," Sade said, rolling her eyes again.

"Okay what's up with the TV's?" he asked this time deflecting. "Ugh! One is a security monitor, one her computer monitor and the other we watch while we are in here chilling. And before you ask, yes, that is a tea station, makeup and hair station. We do drink tea. A lot!" she emphasized.

Looking a little confused, Randall asked, "Why in the closet?"

"I just told you," she said. "We spend a lot of time in here getting outfits together and getting prepared for the events of the week. It can be stressful."

"What is so stressful about it?"

"Auntie likes to have the right look for the right function or client or anything. And it is stressful for me because I am trying to get her to change her style and give me the majority of what's in this closet. One day I am going to be successful. Just wait until you have the chance to invite her to a function that causes us to sit here and drink tea. Then you will appreciate this closet."

"Wow, I didn't realize it was this serious," Randall said.

Sade gave him a look that told him she was in fact just that serious. And he should understand how immaculately he dressed. "Not to mention she is an architect. It is surprising the closet and the kitchen are not bigger than the entire house," Sade said.

With mock surprise, Randall said, "Who said they are not?"

Shaking her head in agreement, Sade told Randall, "Yeah, you're right, they are pretty big. But let me be the judge after I see that monstrosity you live in! I am sure gargoyles are on your mailbox and you even have to use a golf cart to go check the mail."

They both laugh. "My kitchen is not huge," Randall stated neither confirming or denying the other statements.

"Umm hmm, why should it be? All you need is a blender," Sade joked.

"SHUT UP smarty pants!" Randall laughed.

"Am I lying?" Sade asked in a serious tone.

"Well I do not really cook. But I can. I just don't eat much," Randall said.

With a smirk on her face, and turned up lips, Sade said, "Ah ha! So then it is true!"

"No it is not," Randall unsuccessfully tried to persuade.

Rolling her eyes, Sade replied, "Whatever. Let's get out of here before Auntie D wakes up and thinks I am showing you her secrets. She will have a conniption!"

"No she won't," Randall said.

"Humph, oh yes she will," Sade said. "I can hear her now. You let Randall in my closet and I had shoes on the floor and blah blah blah."

They laughed. It was eleven o'clock now. It seemed like an entire day had passed. "So what do we do now Hooks?" Sade asked.

"Watch her I guess," he replied.

"I don't think so Uncle Hooks," Sade said. "We are not about to watch sleeping beauty sleep. She probably wouldn't be okay with that anyways. Knowing Auntie she ain't even really asleep. She's probably watching and listening to us right now. Ole Inspector Gadget." She laughs then leans down really close to Dani's face but she does not move at all.

Randall grabs her arm. "Leave her alone. Let her sleep."

"I'm sure if it were the other way around and it was one of us laid up like this; she would be aggravating the snot out of us," Sade said and laughed.

"You are probably right but we will get her once she wakes up," Hooks said.

"All right! It is just me and you. Do you know what time it is?" Sade asked with a big wide grin.

"No I don't," he replied earnestly.

"Time for me to whip up on you," Sade said as she threw him a Wii controller.

"Oh you think? Come on then little girl let me kick your butt a few times and then send you for lunch," Hooks said.

"Talk is cheap. I won't tell anyone that I beat you," she said confidently.

"I am sure you won't because it ain't happening," Randall mocked.

"I'll just post it on your Facebook page. BUYAH!" She threatened in a teasing way.

Randall didn't appear to be moved by the trash talk. This is what he did for a living. All day! Every day! He looked at Sade and calmly and just as confident said, "Get the game started."

"What do you want to start with?" she asked.

"Pick your poison." Hooks said.

"All right then, tennis it is." Sade smiled as if she had this one in the bag.

"Tennis! UGH!" he responded.

"Thought so!" she said. They battled a couple of matches. All of which were very close. They tied. She won two matches and he won two matches.

"Sade, let's change this lame game," Randall said, growing bored of tennis.

"All right now that you've warmed up let's hit bowling," Sade said.

"Run it," Hooks ordered.

She killed him the first game but the second game was more challenging. "What's wrong Hooks? You don't bowl?" Sade ridiculed.

"I have lanes in my house; of course I bowl," he replied.

"Well you just might want to get some practice in next time," she said smartly.

"You have a lot in common with your aunt; you know that?"

"Like what?"

"Trash talking!"

"She did raise me. But you know what I like to say?"

"What's that?"

"If you ain't first, you're last. In the words of Ricky Bobby. But you wouldn't know anything about Ricky Bobby." Sade said.

"I wake up in the morning and I piss excellence." Hooks perfectly quoted.

"Oh, so you are a Ricky Bobby fan?" Sade said with surprise. She was forced to be since Danielle was such a NASCAR fan.

"Kind of sort of. What now?" Hooks said, putting down the controller.

"I'm getting a little hungry now. What's up with lunch? I am sure there are enough vegetables in there for you to drink, but as for me, I was thinking more like Chick-Fil-A."

"That sounds good. Are you going to pick it up?" Randall asked.

"I don't think I have a choice, unless you got the Chick-Fil-A delivery power. It wouldn't surprise me, since it seems as though you have the power for everything else. Make that happen," she snapped.

"Such a smart mouth for such a young lady. The boys can't get anything past you," Randall perceived.

"I hope not," Sade replied.

"Well they better not." Hooks said, sounding just like a protective uncle. "Just let me know if something pops off."

"All right," Sade said with a smile. "We will have them dealt with."

"Pick up some soup for Danielle. Here is some money," Randall said as he reached for his money clip.

"I have money; what do you want?" Sade asked him.

"Okay, you baller you," he teased.

"I can cover Chick-Fil-A. Worst-case scenario; I'll have to use Auntie D's Amex that's in my wallet. BUYAH!"

"If that is the case then let's go have a steak at Ruth Chris." Randall said jokingly.

"On you," she said. "What do you want?" she asked again.

"I think I am going to have a liquid meal."

"That figures," Sade replied. "You probably carry them with you."

"Correct. Never leave home without them." Randall said smiling.

"You need anything else?"

"No, but what do you think Danielle will want when she awakes?" he asked.

"A Birkin Bag."

He rolled his eyes at the hint. But he did take note of the suggestion.

"She will probably need some grease to soak up the medicine. I will get her nuggets. I will stop and get her some vegetables and potatoes also," Sade said.

"Cool," Randall said.

As soon as Sade left the house, he went straight to Danielle's bedroom. She was sound asleep in the exact same place he left her. He watched her chest to make sure she was breathing. He noticed her face was going down a little; at least her eyes were not as puffy. He went to his car to get his camera. *She will hate me for this today but she will love me for it later*, he thought. He came back in and began to take pictures. She did not move. He wondered if she slept that still all the time. She looked so peaceful. No makeup. Nothing fancy. Just herself. He liked that.

He stood next to her, watching over her until his phone suddenly rang distracting him. He jumped. It was the gym. He got ready to leave the room until he realized she was sound asleep and could not hear him. Instead he stepped in the closet and looked around again. Then quickly moved back to the room. "Hello."

"What's up?" JJ said on the other end.

"Everything all right down there?" Hooks asked.

"Yeah, we were trying to check on your girl."

"Say what?" Randall asked, surprised by JJ's response.

"We are checking on Danielle?" JJ restated.

"Who is we?" he said a little perplexed.

"All of us. King told us you stopped your work out to go to the hospital."

"It was the doctor's office," he corrected disgusted at how quick a story could be misconstrued.

"Wasn't she sick last night?" JJ asked.

"Yeah."

"Why didn't she want to go then?"

"Stubborn." Hooks replied short and curt.

JJ continued, "You and your girl are both stubborn. How does that work?"

"Why do you keep saying my girl?" Hooks asked.

"Because she is." JJ replied.

Getting a little more annoyed, Randall said in a higher tone, "You know damn well she ain't my girl."

"We can't tell."

"Again who is we? You didn't answer the question the first time," Hooks said.

"All of us. If she ain't your girl then you are slipping because she should be," JJ declared.

"I guess I am slipping then," he replied annoyed.

"She is definitely something to make you stop training."

"She is my friend," he nearly yelled.

"So you say she's just a friend," JJ switched up the lyrics to Biz Markie's song a little bit, trying to make light of the situation, but still concerned.

Hooks took a deep breath and said, "I am concerned and for the record circumstances only allow her to be my friend."

"So are we. Therefore, we will continue to monitor her." JJ said.

"I got the point," he said pissed.

"Why are you so upset?" JJ asked.

"I'm not," Hooks lied.

"Are you upset because your girl is sick?" JJ said being a pest.

"SHE IS NOT MY GIRL!"

"Whatever," JJ replied calmly.

"Later," Hooks said as he clicked off the line. He was furious. Not that he called. Not that they were concerned. Not that they were monitoring her bracelet. Not even that they called her his girl. He was pissed at the fact that she was not; and he so desperately wanted her to be.

"This is some BS." He murmured. Then he laughed. He thought about what Sade had said and wondered if Danielle was playing possum. If so he would be embarrassed. Hopefully, she was not. He leaned in real close. "Danielle." She did not move an inch. Her eyelids do not quiver. She was sound asleep. He sat at the foot of her bed and sent a text to everyone at the gym.

The text simply read.   JERKS!!!

Then he put the phone back in his pocket. He did not even hear Sade enter the house much less the doorway of the room.

"Hooks!" she yelled. He jumped. "You are pitiful," she said shaking her head.

"What I do?" he asked innocently.

"She ain't going nowhere," Sade said. "She is asleep. Come on out of here and eat or shall I say drink your lunch. I got you something."

As he followed behind Sade, he said, "I am not pitiful. I just walked in there. You know, you really should stop creeping up on people."

Giving Randall the side-eye, she said knowingly, "I bet you have been in there ever since I closed the door. You watch dog."

"Get off me. Why is everyone ragging me because I am making sure she is fine?" Randall said.

"More like possessive and stalkerish," Sade replied.

Ignoring her comment, Randall simply told her, "Let's eat."

"Get your magic wand out," Sade said with a smile.

"Why?" Randall asked curiously. He could never tell what Sade might have up her sleeves.

"I got you some juices from Arden's Garden and some flowers and balloons for Auntie. You can lie like it was your idea to get them." He frowned at the word lie. Sade noticed the look and said, "Oh you would want to. You will earn brownie points dude. Major points," she reassured him. "Roses are her favorite. Of course!"

He agreed to the lil' white lie in this case and said, "That's what's up. Let me go to the truck."

"Hurry back they may go bad or get hot or ferment or whatever juice does," she called out.

When Hooks returns, he scans his juice; they talk and enjoy their lunch. Afterwards they retreat to the couches to watch a movie. Around three o'clock Sade's phone rang.

"Hey, Sade its Auntie."

"Hey Auntie?" she said like the ringtone and her name on the screen didn't already give it away.

"Hey," she said dry and wearily.

"What's up?" Sade asked.

"I feel like hell warmed over," Dani replied.

"Whatchadoin?"

"Trying to figure out how I got in my bed."

"Oh you at home?" Sade asked.

"Yeah."

"You don't know how you got there?" Sade asked, while trying to hold in her laughter. "It is kind of early to be hitting the bottle don't you think?"

"Actually, no," Dani said.

"What is the last thing you remember?" Sade went on.

Dani sighed, "I remember Leigh taking me to the doctor, whom by the way, I am going to fire her for that. Then it seems like I heard Randall or saw him. I must have been dreaming. By the way what time is it?"

"Three eighteen," Sade replied.

"DAMN!!! I have been asleep all day?" Dani yelled.

"I guess so. You want me to come over?" Sade continued.

"You not busy?" Dani asked.

"Nope. I'll be right over. Don't get out the bed by yourself, you may get hurt." Sade hung up the line, looked over at Randall and said, "Watch how hard headed she is Uncle Hooks."

Not even ten minutes later, Dani came into the living room.

"Hey lil' girl," Dani said to her niece.

"OOO Auntie you look like hell," Sade said, covering her mouth in mock surprise.

"Thanks heffa," Dani said rolling her eyes.

"Hey Randall."

"Hey Babe."

Suddenly taking a double take, Dani realized Randall was actually there, "OH CRAP! What are you doing here?" she asked.

"I brought you flowers?" he said like a little boy.

"Huh?" she said looking confused.

"And balloons," Sade chimed in with a wide grin across her face.

"What time is it?" she asked trying to figure out what was going on.

"Three thirty."

Dani looked around, a little more confused than ever and asked, "What is going on here?" They both laughed but she figured it out. "You were already here you little snot."

"Yep." They laughed louder.

"You were going to let her trick me Randall?"

He threw his arms up in a gesture that said you got me. "How do you feel?" he asked.

"Like a fool right now."

"Why Babe?"

"I am standing here looking stupid and confused. You guys are funny."

"You look fine sweetie," Randall said.

"I'll be back," she said as she ran off.

"Hey, where are you going?" Randall asked.

"Auntie?" Sade called out.

"I am sure she is going to the department store slash salon back there," Randall said.

"HATER!" Sade yelled.

"I am not." Hooks yelled back calmly.

"Yeah you are. Let me go check on her. I'd rather get my cursing out done in private. I'll scream if I need back up though," Sade said and she got up from the couch.

Laughing, Randall said, "Got you covered."

Danielle was brushing her teeth when Sade stepped in the doorway. "I am going to strangle you!"

"Why?"

"What in the hell is going on here?"

"What's going on? Ha! You tell us. You are the one that went to a race and ended up two heart beats away from dead."

"WHAT?" Dani asked in alarm.

"Are you really unaware?" Sade asked.

"Yes. What's going on?" Dani persisted.

"Hold up. HOOKS!" Sade yelled. Nothing happened. She screamed.

"Damn! Sade what is wrong with you child?" Dani asked, still looking confused.

Instantly, he stepped in the doorway. "You rang?" he sang.

"I love it," Sade said. "He follows good instructions. You may be a keeper after all." He smirked. "Please tell Auntie what happened to her."

"Well Babe, it appears you had a reaction to the sunscreen you used yesterday. It was actually causing you to swell. Your face was about five times larger than it is now. Had your face continued to swell it could have very easily caused your esophagus to close and your oxygen would have been cut off," Randall explained to her.

"You would have died." Sade interrupted boldly.

With her hand over her heart, Dani asked in disbelief, "WHAT?"

"Yes," they both replied in unison.

"From sunscreen?" she asked in disbelief.

"Yes. The doctor gave you a series of shots and some prescriptions to fight this. You will be fine my love," Randall told her.

"Good Lord," Dani replied, not believing what she was hearing.

"Yes, you scared us."

"I am amazed this is from sunscreen. Either way Leigh is still getting fired. Matter of fact let me call and fire her now. She started looking for her phone."

"Leigh helped you," Randall said.

"Umm hmm. She can put that on her resume too." Dani said still looking for her phone.

Sade raised her eyebrows at Randall and put her finger to her lips to say shh.

"Take it easy D," he said wanting her to remain calm.

Cutting her eyes at him, Dani told Randall, "You should have gone to the race with me."

"One thing is for sure right now, you won't be going to any race, outdoor activities, or any other sun related functions until this is resolved." Randall said with authority in his voice.

"I guess you heard that!" Sade instigated. "That means walking too."

"We will see about that!" Dani said ready to dismiss the instructions already.

"I bet you wish you had that indoor track in here right about now." Sade murmured.

"Oh is that right?" Dani barked at Sade.

"Well, let me break the news to you now Ms. Rose Washington." Randall began. "You will not be going to work tomorrow, neither will you be working out today, and walking is out of the question too."

"Says who?" Dani asked, as she stomped away lifting her blouse and exposing her camisole as she headed to change.

"I just said so," Hooks said calmly.

She peeked her head around the door, looked at his face, and knew this was not the time to dispute. "I feel good!" This was all she yelled. "And who has been in my closet and why?"

He ignored her question. "Sade and I will be here all night to confirm you follow Doctor's orders."

"Oh no Sade will not be here all night." Sade said. Hooks looked at her like WTH? "Now that she is feeling better Sade has a date," Sade continued. "One swollen up Auntie don't stop no show." she whispered, "I told you she would know someone was in that closet."

"You are not leaving me here with her all night," Randall said nervously.

"Sorry Uncle Hooks, but you are on your own."

"I can't stay here with her. It is not good, right; you know what I am trying to say?" He stuttered.

Looking him up and down, Sade said, "You might get lucky."

He blushed.

"Sade I can hear you," Dani called out.

"She can hear extremely well," Sade confirmed.

"I see. Isn't the shower running?" he asked.

"Yep."

"I am not staying here with her all night ripping me because she can't work. Call Leigh or your mother. Get somebody on the phone." Hooks ordered.

Sade started making calls.

"Randall!" Dani called out again.

"Yes."

"I can hear you too. I will handle you once I am out," she shouted through the closed bathroom door.

He had lustful thoughts. "I am going back in the living room," he uttered.

"Doesn't matter. I will find you there. Don't leave." she warned him.

"I wasn't planning on it but I may have a change of plans," he said. He sat next to Sade. "How does she do that?" he whispered. He was scared to speak too loud. He looked around the room to see if she had any devices that help her hear so well.

Sade put her hand over the phone. "Do what?"

"That bionic woman hearing," he said looking around as if Danielle would appear any moment.

"She has eyes like that too." She told him then removed her hand from the phone to continue her conversation.

"Well damn. Nothing gets past her." Hooks mumbled to himself.

"NOTHING!" Sade agreed in the middle of her phone conversation.

He flips the remote while Sade continues on the phone.

"All right we are all set. The ladies will be over to relieve me once they are off work. I will be on my date. If it sucks I will be back, but don't wait up," and she winks.

"You may want to bring the little punk by here. I would hate to have to break his neck!" Randall said sounding fiercely serious.

"I would but Auntie don't play that."

"Play what?" he asked.

"Strangers at the house." she said seriously. "Actually, no one comes to the house."

"Bring him to the gym. I will meet y'all there. Who is this dude?" Randall questioned.

As soon as they began to discuss the details of Sade's date, Dani appears looking fresh and revived. Not quite her normal self but much better than five hours ago.

"Why y'all sitting so close? What is going on here? Did some school kids come by and trash this room?" she asked all three questions in one breath.

"Glad to see you are feeling good Auntie D."

She rolled her eyes.

"You look better D," said Randall.

"You are on my S list." Dani barked just as Randall's phone chimed.

He pulled it out and checked it. It was a text from Danielle. It simply read

PAYBACK!

"What is this?" he questioned.

"My nasty gram to you." she said fiercely.

"Whew. I am glad I was not on the nasty gram list." Sade said happy it was Randall and Leigh this time.

Dani, looked over in her niece's direction and said, "It ain't over yet."

"Ahh man."

"You will be all right. So what's up? What are we doing? How are you all entertaining me since I can't eat, work out, or go in the sun," Dani rattled off pissed.

"The doctor's orders were the rest of the week."

"What week?" Dani said in shock.

"This week." Randall answered, knowing she was about to have a fit.

"It's Monday!" Dani said.

"I know." Randall replied. He could feel the fit coming on now.

"Ain't no way in H-E-L-L," Dani said.

"Well if you are still swollen tomorrow, you're definitely not."

"Cow manure." she said then crossed her arms in front of her chest.

"What?" Sade looked up from texting or whatever it is she was doing, unable to control her laughter, fell onto the floor rolled around and holding her stomach. "Manure Auntie!" Sade repeated amazed Danielle would use the word manure.

"Yeah. Manure." Dani repeated still enraged.

They hung out for the next hour or so until the other two ladies arrived. Once they got there Danielle lit into Leigh. "Leigh!" she yelled.

Leigh's eyes got big, "Yes ma'am?"

Sade looked at Randall and Paige. "Here it comes."

"You know I love you?" Danielle started sweetly.

Leigh said, "I love you too, just like a sister."

"You know I got to go ahead and fire you now don't you?" Dani said still in that sweet singsong voice.

Shaking her head no, Leigh said, "You know that is not what Jesus would do?"

"Good thing I am not Jesus," Dani graciously replied.

"Danielle, you know you hired me to look out for your best interest."

"And you have done an excellent job. I will be sure to write you a wonderful recommendation letter," Dani expressed void of emotion.

"No ma'am, you will do no such thing," Leigh said. "I refuse to accept being fired, because I was doing my job by looking after you."

"I think you are being a smarty," Dani realized.

"Well, I love you too." Leigh said to her friend.

Dani rolled her eyes and addressed them all. "All of you guys make me sick."

"That's my cue," Sade said. "I am gone on that note."

"Curfew is at midnight." Hooks said calmly. They all looked at him. "By the way, Danielle I told her she needs to bring the little punk by here so I can meet him."

"Okay." Dani said without hesitation. No one could believe that she simply said okay and looked at her like she had to be high on drugs or something. "What's for dinner?"

"You feel like eating?" Hooks asked, pleased.

"Heck yeah! I'm starving!" she said while frowning that he would even ask.

"You want to go get something?" he asked.

"That will be fine."

"Okay, go get dressed. I'll take you to grab something to eat," he volunteered.

"Can you help me?" she replied mischievously.

He looked immediately at the other two.

"Don't think about it." Paige said while Leigh folded her arms.

"Don't listen to them." Dani whispered and pulled him to follow her. They both peeked around the corner. Once they were out of sight she leaned up against the wall and pulled him to her. He was a little stunned and not sure how to react. She threw her arms around his neck and kissed his cheek. "Thanks for everything. You really did not have to be here. I truly appreciate it."

"It is not a problem. I would have been awfully upset if no one had informed me. I am glad they did and I am glad to be here." Hooks professed.

"You are very special Randall Hooks Washington."

"You are too Danielle Rose future Washington."

That brought a smile to her face, "I like that," she confessed.

"I do too," he admitted.

He laid his head on her shoulder. "Get dressed before I have regrets. Besides, the mother hens are around the corner timing us," he joked.

"We have five minutes," Danielle whispered seductively.

He got the joke and laughed. "Please give me more than five whether I use them or not."

"If I give you all the time in the world are you coming?"

"I am definitely coming if you just give me all the time in the world."

She picked up on his word play. "You are making this difficult."

He laid his head back on my shoulder. "No, you are the one making this difficult; with you being this close to me. I have been fine all day. Now, go throw something on and let's go eat. I need food to settle me down after this." He let me go then grabbed me again. He then held his arms up as if he had touched something flaming hot. I was hot to say the least, but how did he know it. I begin to wonder if the doctor had given me something that made me all of a sudden very frisky to say the least. His facial expressions let me know that I was putting him in a very awkward position. I slowly moved to the bedroom and closed the door behind me.

I leaned on the other side of the door and swallowed hard. Once I got myself together I ran to the closet. *Oh hell no! I know Sade didn't have him in my closet and I have these shoes out of the boxes everywhere. I am going to kill her.* I looked in the mirror. I looked like crap. No need in putting on make-up now; the damage was already done. I grabbed a maxi and threw it on, flat sandals and dumped my stuff in my Speedy forty. Hopefully, no one would notice I have my computers with me. I sprayed some perfume, lined my eyes, and glossed my lips. *This will have to do.*

I opened the door and begin to call Randall when I realized he was sitting right there on the floor where I left him. "Hey." He looked up. "Why are you sitting there?"

"Waiting on you," he said.

I pointed to a chair three steps away from him.

He looked over, "Yeah, I know."

I suddenly remembered they mentioned the doctor had given me a prescription, so I asked, "Do I have any medicine?"

"Yeah, you need it?"

"If you don't mind," I replied.

"You can't take it until you eat," he informs me.

"Really?"

"Yeah."

"Seriously?" I asked.

"Yep."

"Can I have it?" I asked.

Randall looked at me suspiciously, "After you eat," he told her for a second time.

"UGH! Come on."

"Do you really think you are that slick?" he said with a knowing look on his face.

"Yes, I do." He knew good and well I would ditch the meds if I had the chance to do so.

"Dani, this may be news to you, but you are not that slick ma'am."

"You are mean," I whined.

He grabbed me by the neck in a bear hug. "Let's go."

"Y'all ready?" I asked. They nodded and made motions to the door.

"Let's do it!" I said with enthusiasm. You would have thought this was the first time in my life leaving the house. For me it felt like life.

"Babe," he said.

"Yes." They looked at each other.

"Put this in your purse," handing the meds to her.

Just that quick I had forgotten I had my laptop and iPad in the bag. I opened and let him drop the meds in. As soon as I got ready to turn the alarm on I said, "We ready?"

"No," he replied.

"Why not, what's wrong?"

"Not until you leave those devices home," he said home. I like the fact he referred to my house as home.

"Exactly what are you saying?" I said.

"You heard me," he articulated clearly.

The ladies laughed and snickered. I could tell they were enjoying this. I put on my pity-me-face, "Please. I have not worked all day," I said sadly.

"Fine. Come on." he gave in. It was much easier than debating with her.

We got into Randall's truck and had originally planned to go get pizza. Then it occurred to me that Randall probably wouldn't eat there.

"Let's go to Mikey's please." It was safer there for Hooks to eat.

He looked in the review mirror.

"I am not staying out with you all night. Some of us have to work tomorrow." Leigh stated with conviction.

"Then you are fine. Remember I fired you today," I shot back.

"I have to catch your slack since you are at home playing sick," Leigh fired back.

"You do that but first thing Wednesday you come and pack your desk."

"Oh crap!" Paige screamed startling everyone in the truck.

"What?"

"I forgot to call Mikey back. He is going to rip me a new one."

"He will be fine."

We talked during the whole ride there. When we walked in Mikey greeted me, "Why are you alive?"

Puzzled by Mikey's strange questions, Dani responded with, "What?"

"The last report I heard they had embalmed your face." he joked.

Rolling her eyes, "Why am I your friend?" she questioned aloud.

"That is what I heard."

"I'm sick Michael."

Mikey, being the jokester he always is continued, "What? You are admitting it?"

Shaking her head and deciding to ignore her friend's taunting, "Fix me soup and a grilled cheese," she demanded.

Winking his eye, Mikey replied, "I didn't ask to take your order." Then he proceeded to take the rest of their orders.

We all ordered, fellowshipped and ate. Mikey and I were best friends with a love hate relationship.

"Baby, girl. What else can I get you since you are a little under the weather?" he asked in a sweet tone.

"I think I am fine, thank you, but I will take a sandwich or something to go. Considering I'm going to be confined to the house, I'll need something I can eat in my bed. A sistah don't want to be drugged up, home alone and hungry," I said.

"You know I got you babe." Mikey said as he retrieved their dishes from the table.

A text came into my phone. I looked around to see if it was safe to check it since the masses flipped when I started to check emails earlier. Randall, the screen read. I looked over at him, but he did not look my way. I hit the button to open but I never moved my eyes from him.

> I planned to spend the night to make sure you are safe if that is okay with you. I won't bother you or sleep. I will be up watching you instead of being at home thinking of you.

I put the phone back in my purse. On the ride home he asked, "Do you all mind if I stop by the gym?"

"It's cool," Leigh said.

"That will be good. I will get a chance to at least see it, since I'm not allowed to work out." Dani hastily replied. Looking over at her girls as if she could read their minds, she said, "Don't get excited ladies. There are no cute guys there. They are all like King. Typical jocks."

We pulled right up to the curb. He did not even park in a space. He got out of the car and opened Paige's door directly behind him, Leigh's and then mine, as he held my hand to escort me out. We walked in the front door.

"Hooks, Ms. Rose, Ladies." Mimi greeted us.

"Hello," we all replied.

"What's up Mimi? Anything going on?" Hooks asked.

"No, not really," she said mildly watching me.

"Can you get Dani her smoothie and whatever the ladies want?" he asked then he ordered. "I will take my usual to go please. Actually, make it two for me; my breakfast one also."

"Sure. We are glad you are feeling well Ms. Washington." Mimi said wondering why Hooks would want his breakfast smoothie in advance and to go.

"Thank you so much." Dani replied tapping Randall on the shoulder. Instead of responding he grabbed my hand and shrugged his shoulders.

"Ms. Washington show us around please." Paige said, smiling innocently. I knew I was going to get ragged about this for a long time.

We hung out while Randall did whatever it was he needed to do. Once he finished, we piled back into the truck. Looking at Danielle, he asked, "Where is your bag?"

"Under my feet," I said.

"Let me see the medicine," he said in that commanding tone he issues regularly.

I handed them to him and watched as he took one out of the bottle. He then handed me back a pill and the smoothie. I took the medicine, leaned back and from there, I do not even remember the ride home.

Before I knew it, I heard Leigh say, "I will call you in the morning."

"Love you Sissie," I heard Paige say.

The next thing I recall it was one AM and there was a light on in my room. Before I realized what was going on, I heard pecking. I looked over to my right, and there he was, busy on his laptop. I said, "Excuse me."

"Yes sleeping beauty?" he replied looking at his monitor.

"What are you doing?"

"Hanging out and watching you."

"Hanging out huh. It looks like you are working to me."

"Not really," he said.

I rolled my eyes at him, "BS."

"How do you feel?"

"High. Did you take advantage of me?" I asked.

He blushed, "Not this time."

"Well damn. What does a girl have to do to get taken advantage of?" I said in a playful disgust.

"Just wait," he replied.

"Okay. Do you know where my sandwich is?" I asked suddenly hungry.

"I figured you would be hungry," he said. He went into the kitchen then brought the sandwich to me. I do not think I finished eating it. When I woke up again it was four forty three. I jumped out of the bed.

Tuesday

"Where do you think you are going?" Randall spoke more than questioned.

"To the mirror to look at my face, brush my teeth and get ready. We are running." I replied.

"Now?" he asked. "I take it you feel better?"

"Good morning. Yes, thanks to you," I said.

"After our run I will come back and juice us some fruits and vegetables."

Shocked he said, "From sick to running. What next?"

Smiling, I replied, "Did you really think I was going to let you keep me down long?"

As he walked out the door he asked, "I kept you down?"

"Yeah you did," I replied.

"More like sunscreen and Dale Jr. kept you down."

"Hater. Blame it on Junior. I bet he is faster than you," I shot back.

"Not by foot," he replied with confidence.

Randall went to his truck to get his bag and Danielle retreated to her closet to get dressed for their workout. To make sure they stayed hydrated they drank a bottle of water and of course they had to ensure iPods and heart monitors were set. He double-checked her watch to make sure it was in monitor mode so he could review her results later. He assumed JJ was up watching also. Little did he know, Dani had her phone on and had already checked messages. It was early but it was still hot outside. They got to the front step and did a few stretches.

"So where do you want to start?" Dani asked.

"I was thinking we could begin to the right and just continue until the sun comes up." They walked down the driveway adjusting and setting their gadgets.

"What are you listening to?"

"Kilo," Dani replied smiling.

"KILO ALI?" Hooks asked surprised.

"Yep, hype music."

He laughed. As soon as both of their feet touched the edge of the driveway they waited just as if there were cars in the street. Seeing there was no traffic in the way, they picked up the pace. A nice jog. Nothing too fast and not to slow.

"You can leave me at any time," Dani reassured.

"This will be fine," he said. Even in his regular workout Hooks always started out this way then gradually picked up the pace. Danielle had no idea her trailing behind him was not an option Randall wanted. He wanted to jog or walk right next to her. Side by side for as long as she wanted to.

He was running and doing what I assumed were boxing moves. I figured he was probably occupied enough to where I could check my phone and send a few emails. I pulled my phone out and got through the first email and reply successfully. I was on the second message, hit reply and suddenly the phone disappeared. I pulled my plugs out of my ears astonished. He had the phone. "UGH!" I put the plugs back and said as loud as I could, "I'm never running with you again!" I shouted and sped up.

Hooks laughed at her outburst, "Who cares!"

I turned around but continued running backwards. "YOU! That's who!" I yelled.

He laughed again. I ran ahead of him for quite a while. Actually I ran in front of him a lot longer than I thought I would have been able to. I wanted to check my heart rate. I didn't want to fall out while having a temper tantrum. I knew he would notice I was checking it though so decided I would leave well enough alone. Surely if it's too high something would happen. It would pinch me; he'd get a call from NASA, the Secret Service or somebody. All of a sudden he shot by me. Catching me a little off guard, I said, "What the?"

I looked back as if someone was behind me. When I turned back around he was doing what I did. He was running backwards with my phone in his hand as if he was making a call. "Can you keep up?" he taunted.

"Who are you calling?" I asked.

"I am on a conference call with Antarctica, Greece, Thailand, and Moscow," he pretended.

"Wow. Impressive. Does everyone understand each other?"

"I am the interpreter. It is going to be a long call."

"Good luck!"

He turned around and ran at a very fast pace. I knew he could not stay on my pace for too long and there was no way I was going to attempt to keep up with him. I was able to check my heart rate and it was fine. The Benadryl and other crap they injected me with had not affected me other than laying me out yesterday. I was not taking that mess again today.

Once I reached the hill, a beautiful scenery laid before me, a sunrise. All that was missing was me on the beach chilling. At the top of the hill the first car finally passed us. He was sitting on the curb. "Do you want go another round?" I asked.

"Only if you can handle it."

I took off running again. This time I knew I was not going to be long, probably less than an hour. He came next to me and we ran side by side.

Once the subdivision began moving around he asked, "Are you ready to call it quits?"

"I guess so since we have to stop at every driveway," I replied. We slowed it down and walked back to the house. The neighbors blew and one heffa even had the nerves to stop.

"Hey Dani. Girl, I haven't seen you in forever," she said to me, but eyeballing Randall.

Giving her the side eye, "Good morning," I said in a monotone voice. I do not think she even noticed. I knew she was stopping just to be nosey. I hope she recognized him.

"Let's get together this week," the neighbor added.

"Sure, call me. I'll be around," I replied.

"Hi!" she said to Randall.

"Good morning. Have a blessed day," he replied as uninterested as he possibly could be.

Nosey heffa, I thought to myself.

"Nosey neighbors?" He asked as she drove away, obviously picking up on my tone.

That is putting it mildly. I wanted to tell him that for as long as I've lived here I hadn't had a gentleman caller other than Mikey. I once thought about inviting someone over just to impress the neighbors. Since girls are the only ones to ever visit. I didn't want the neighbors to get the wrong idea and believe that I actually liked girls. However, most of them knew who they were anyway. HOW LAME!

But don't grow weary in well doing, God immediately spoke to me. *You waited and look now. Not only do you have a gentleman caller. But you have a Champion Boxer running the streets of your neighborhood with you and he is madly in love with you.* I thought to myself, *go God*!

We walked back up to the front door where he laid out on the steps. I turned around to make sure he was okay. He was playing. He pulled me down to sit next to him. I felt refreshed. My lungs felt great and my heart was pumping. I was sweaty but I was next to the man of my dreams, so it didn't matter. I was in Ms. Rose's neighborhood and it was a beautiful day in the neighborhood. Oddly, I really didn't miss work. *Maybe I could do this after all*, I thought. I understood why he ran so early in the mornings and for so long. It refreshed you, got your blood pumping, cleared your mind and lungs. *Yeah, I definitely could do this.*

"You ready to shower," I asked?

"Wow, I got to watch you sleep last night. I was allowed to run in your neighborhood, although I was not introduced to any neighbors," he threw in, "and now I get to shower?" He jumped up and started running in place. "Come on unlock the door before you change your mind."

I laughed. I knew he took my comment as lets shower together although he knew I meant separately. But my body and his screamed together. He went his separate way like he had been there thousands of times. I went my way. I hit the remote and turned CNN on through the house. I finished before he did. I put on khaki shorts and a yellow boyfriend beater. I sprayed my favorite fragrance.

I decided to make veggie omelets with egg whites for breakfast. So I went to the kitchen, turned on the skillet then pulled out my cutting board to chop fruit and vegetables. I juiced some of the fruit and I sliced the other and placed it in a bowl. I turned the camera station and could see the bathroom door was still closed. Yes, it could be considered as snooping, but then again this was my house, so technically it wasn't snooping. He was not ready and I was glad because I needed a few more minutes.

I had the tablecloth on the table that was out on the deck. The juice and fruit were now laid out. My laptop was set and so was his. *Gosh, I need to run and cut fresh flowers for the table and the plate.* After I finished setting everything I could hear him coming down the hallway. *Shoot, maybe I have gone overboard and overstepped my boundaries. This maybe a little too pushy and saying too much.* You could tell I had not had a man over in the morning. EVER! *Too late. Can't take it back now.* He is standing behind me. *I really wish he would just go ahead and grab me, hug me, sweep me off my feet, and make passionate love to me.* I thought wishfully.

"Wow, Danielle. You have outdone yourself," Randall said with random thoughts running thru his mind.

I smiled from ear to ear, but he can't see me because he is behind me. "That is your second wow this morning."

"Do you go out like this every day?" he asked sounding a little impressed.

"Actually, most of the time I do."

"Really?"

"Yep."

"Seriously?" he asked.

"Well, when you have to do it by yourself you treat yourself the way you want to be treated," I replied.

"D, why are you by yourself?" It was a question he really desired an honest answer to.

"I am not sure," I answered honestly. "Have a seat you don't have to stand," I said trying to get off the subject. Instead he slapped me with another tough question no doubt.

"Is it by choice?" he continued clearly wanting to learn more.

"Not really. I would not like to be by myself but it has been this way for so long now until I have grown accustomed to it. Don't get me wrong, it's not as though I would not be grateful to have someone in my life, but I also know how to live without. I needed to learn that. It has made me stronger, wiser, and successful," I said proudly.

"I had to do the same. I had never been by myself. It was a huge adjustment. It took me a long time to figure it out, understand it, and accept it. You mentioned successful. Why?"

"Can you bless the food and I will answer your question?" I interrupted.

He took my hands. "Gracious Father, we thank you for another day and for all the things we have been given on this day. We thank you for your love, mercy, and kindness towards us. We thank you for the food that has been prepared for us on this day (he squeezed my hand); we pray that it is nourishing to our bodies. God please bless the hands that prepared it. We thank you for

Danielle's health, friendship, and fellowship. We pray that you lead us and guide us in the proper direction you would have us to go and in the decency and in the order of your will. In your son Jesus Christ name we pray." We both said Amen and held hands for a moment longer. It was an awkward moment, which I thoroughly enjoyed.

Finally, I let go and said, "Dig in."

"Hey, why you got eggs and I didn't?" he asked.

I held up my plate and reached across the table and scrapped over half on his plate. "Don't you touch that until it has been okayed by your science kit," I instructed.

"I think I am cool," he laughed.

"Oh helicopter no. You won't get sick and blame that on me. Get the kit!" I instructed.

"Are you serious?"

I gave him a glance over and said, "Heck yeah. PETA won't be after me."

This time, he is the one that gives me the glance over and says, "That is for dogs D," as he stands up to go get his kit.

"Well whoever comes after people that harm boxers. The National Don't Harm The Athlete Association. NDHAA. President King," I said.

He laughed, "You are crazy."

I sat and waited for him to return before even touching my food. When he returned he said, "You could have started without me."

"Then you would say I am rude. Are you trying to set me up?"

"NO," he said as he scanned everything.

"Is it good?" I asked.

"Yes. Just like I thought. Eat. Back to the question."

"Why do I think I am more successful?" I asked, as if I had forgotten the question.

"Yes," he replied.

"Well, honestly relationships can be lovely, wonderful and all that, but also a hindrance," I said. "I think I was more distracted than anything else. A lot of it was unnecessary drama, which of course is always a distraction by itself. I also did not put a hundred percent into my work. I found myself doing other things that seemed important, like trying to build a relationship, but he was not. Truthfully, we both were still in the stages of our lives where we wanted to hang and party. Since that part of my life is now over I have put one hundred and fifty percent or more into my career. I didn't before because he was just as important as work. If not more important."

"More like two hundred and fifty percent," he said under his breath.

"Excuse me?"

Acting like he didn't hear me or understand, "Huh?"

"What did you say?" I asked.

"Nothing."

"I heard you; two hundred and fifty percent."

"If you heard me then why did you ask?"

"I was giving you time to retract the statement smarty," I said.

"Sorry."

"Even at two hundred and fifty percent it has paid off," I said. "If someone had told me so, I never would have believed I could have done it without him. I needed to know I could and I did. So right now I am busting my butt to make partner and possibly one day have my own firm."

"Wow. You are very ambitious. Do you think you diverted that energy?" he asked.

"A little of both," I finally replied. "I had these desires from day one but I also had a desire to have a family." I said somewhat sadly.

He picked up on it. "Had? What is that about?" he asked.

"Well, I still have the desire, but it is just not as strong as it was then," I said.

"Why do you think?"

I simply replied, "No prospects at this time."

"So you say." I could tell that it disappointed him that I felt that way and had not considered him a prospect. This had been the happiest day of his life, one that he could see this in his future. Running or strolling with his wife, having breakfast on the deck daily before they separated and started their days work.

"It's true," I said.

He then asked, "So why aren't you dating?"

Taking a deep breath, "Well for starters, you have to be somewhere to meet people. They usually don't just walk in the office or knock on my door at home. To be honest, when I am out, I am so preoccupied with work or something until if Mr. Right did walk up I've probably been much too busy to notice or address him. It is partially my fault. Besides that, as motivated and ambitious as I am Mr. Right would certainly have to be the same or okay with me being this ambitious."

"I can understand you there coming from a relationship where the person had no desires or motivation. What happened with you and the other guy?" he was dying to ask.

"Life I assume."

With a slightly puzzled look he asked, "What does that mean?"

"We grew up and apart. Or rather I grew up and he grew apart."

"I know that feeling all so well. Tell me more."

"What do you want to know?"

"Everything. I know nothing personal about you," he brought to my attention.

"My ex and I have known each other our entire lives. We were boyfriend and girlfriend at five years old all the way until our twenties. I did have one other boyfriend when we were on a hiatus, sad to say," I replied.

"I have you beat. Tameka was my girlfriend through high school and during my college years and look at what happened."

"I guess you are right," I said.

"Let me rephrase that. She was my wife and we had a child while I was in college. At least you didn't get that far out there."

"No doubt, I guess it could have been worse. Not saying your situation is worse or bad." I clarified, not wanting him to think I was passing judgment.

"It is," he said honestly.

"No. It is what it is," I told him.

"So why did you break up?" he then asked.

"Same story I think every girl has at some point. I was at one place in life and he was at another. He was at the strip club, gambling and chasing the shortest skirts. Needless to say they were not mine. Girls mature differently from boys, you know that. He waited until we got grown and got crazy, I guess you could say. Which I guess is better than him getting crazy after we had gotten married. One day after having enough of the alleged tricks, late strip club nights, drinking, partying, and gambling I asked him what were his long-term goals and intentions with me. He politely said and I quote, "If you asking if I want to get married then the answer is no. I do not think I will ever get married."

His eyes got big and he replied, "Wow! What did you say?"

"I didn't say anything at all. It was a repeated punch in the face as far as I was concerned. I felt as if I had wasted all those years and this dude never had intentions beyond being a boyfriend."

Frowning, he asked, "Did you say punch?"

"No, I said a repeated punch. I was at his house when he said it and once I left, I never returned. That was it for me," I reminisced.

"So what did you say?" he asked again.

"Like I said, I never said anything at all."

"How did the break go?

"For me that was the break up. When he said he never intended on marrying me that was all I needed to know. My intentions were different. Could I have handled the situation differently? In hindsight yes. But hindsight is always twenty-twenty. Should I have handled it differently? Yes. I also think he should have too." I thought out loud.

"Do you ever wish you had married him?" he continued.

"No, absolutely not! Do I think about how my life would have been had we married? Then I have to be honest and say yes, sometimes I wonder about that."

"Do you ever feel like you might have made a mistake?"

I replied, "By wasting so many of my good years? Yes. By leaving, no." I laughed at the thought. "The way I see it, if a man had no intentions on marrying me after dating me for double digit years, then I cannot see what would possibly change his mind later. I was sad and disappointed originally. I thought my life had come to an end; boy I had wasted so much time. Time I will never get back. I chalked it up as a lesson well learned. If we were still together I think we would be just that. Still together. Nothing more and maybe less. That is not what I want. I am not interested in being any man's permanent Boo. I want the works; I deserve the works. You know, the four-bedroom house, three cars, a dog, two and a half kids, husband, picket fence, music lessons, soccer practice and family vacations. The works."

Randall was shocked by the responses. *That was all she wanted and some guy missed the opportunity*, he thought. *Well, you know the saying; one man's junk is another man's treasure.* Randall knew without a shadow of a doubt he had run up on a treasure. He was at the right place at the right time. The parking lot guy could have radioed anyone, but he didn't. She owned more than three cars herself. Her home was larger than most. All she required was the bare minimum as far as he was concerned.

"I think you have surpassed that alone," he said. "You have the wrought iron fence and five cars yourself. In a gated community I might add. Instead, would you settle for an eight bedroom house, a jet, a yacht, as many cars and kids as you want, a step son, a life where every day can be a vacation and maybe like a small time boxer for a husband?"

"That would be nice but." I thought to myself. *Are you serious? This isn't just nice. This is like having your cake and eating it too with a bowl of ice cream and cherry on top. This is every girl, woman, trick, and groupies' dream. You damn right I want it!*

"I know the but," he said with a nervous look on his face.

We both knew what the conjunction alluded to. "Do you?"

He touched his ring finger.

"I was thinking about the small time boxer. I am more into big time winners." I wanted to lighten the mood, although he was correct in his thinking.

He laughed.

"Okay, your turn," I said. "Now tell me your story."

"You know most of it. Tameka was my first girlfriend in high school and that has been a wrap. I have not had one since. Pretty lame huh?"

"I have only had two boyfriends," I reminded him.

"You are a step ahead of me. Tameka got pregnant early on. I originally went to college on a football scholarship. I had the option for academic scholarships as well but I chose to go to a big football school. If it had not been for sports, I'm not sure if I would have ever made it to college. If it had not been for college I would probably have ten baby mamas. I probably would not have married Tameka. I would be married to the streets. Who knows, I guess in a way it was a good thing but overall it was a bad thing."

"Tameka and the baby lived with my parents," he continued. "Her mother sort of kicked her out. My parents had high hopes for me and made the decision that in order for me to stay in school and stay focused; they would help to care for my son. Needless to say, Tameka came along with him; they were a package no matter how much my parents tried to remove her from the picture. She stayed home and raised him. She never went to school, worked a job, or volunteered. She never really partied or hung out either though. To tell you the truth, I can't tell you what she has done over the last thirteen years. She has not learned to cook, bake a cake, gone on a field trip or anything. I can't explain it. I thought I was being a man and a good father by marrying her, but it was clearly a mistake. Both were a mistake, having a child I wasn't able to care for without the help of my parents and marrying the child's mother. If I had waited I would have learned that although we had a baby together we had nothing else in common. We had grown apart and what we had was just "puppy love.""

"I was a good student athlete. I stayed out of trouble that many I knew found themselves in while in college. I do not know if I was just lame or if I was a little more mature since I was a father and had quickly become a husband. If anyone would have asked me fifteen years ago if I was going to be a boxer, my answer would have been no. It was never my original intent. I wanted to be in the NFL. I would have taken the NBA, MLB or I could have even been a runner. But, as you can see, boxing chose me."

"As a child I spent a lot of time at the boys and girls club in the neighborhood. I was a little smaller than most boys my age and have always been very thin. The competitive spirit in me learned to work on my speed so I could beat them. I would jump rope and other training techniques that fighters do. There was a ring upstairs in the club and sometimes I would venture there and just watch. Before you knew it, I was passing towels and getting water. When it was discovered I was fast, one thing led to another and before long I was training to be a boxer. If you think going in the NBA's chances are slim to none, then boxing is even slimmer. For that reason, I was never interested in boxing. I only worked on it because no one else would let me do anything else. The more I did it though, the more I realized it helped me; so I continued. It has been a long, hard, fun, and worthwhile journey. I do not think I would change any of this," he paused.

"Continue," I smiled.

"In high school I wrestled. I also fought a few big organized fights. Some were underground and I made a lot of money for a high school boy. But, while I was in college I spent a lot of time in the ring because it helped me on the field. My name has not always been Hooks; it was Speed. That was the name I got way back while in Boys and Girls club. They would have me racing cars if it had been up to them. That named followed me. You'll see when you meet my family they still call me Speed or Speedy. I ran track in college and even tried out for an Olympic team," he said.

"Oh wow," I said unaware. "What happened there?" I asked intrigued.

"Honestly, they told me my talents were not in running. They didn't think I was serious. I was fast and I probably could out run anyone on the track, but my talents were better suited in other areas. Not only that, but I think because I had so many talented people working with me as a child they helped me to clearly recognize my strengths and develop them. The foundation they instilled in me has become my life."

"Then what?" I asked, totally engrossed in his story.

"Well during and after college I tried everything. I was married, working a corporate job and trying to make it. After no one accepted me for NBA, MLB, etc. I kind of gave up."

"You gave up?" I asked stunned. He was so not the give up type.

"Yep, I kept working out and when I least expected it happened. The guy at the gym asked me if I was interested in fighting. I said naw man. He said it would pay you. I still wasn't sure if I was interested. When I thought about it more and the circumstances at the time, you know, we needed a new car, in our first apartment and struggling. The guy told me it was a paying fight. My first question was is this a legal fight? He said that it was and would give me details within a couple days. I told Tameka that same day. She told me it was stupid and she has yet to change her mind. I took it upon myself to fight. My first paid fight; I was nervous, scared, and upset. That was when I got the name Hooks."

"How?"

"The headlines read, 'A new comer with a fierce Hook.' The rest is history. Before I knew it I was Hook and some way an S has been added. I would not change any of this part of the story because it showed me the awesome powers of God in the process. The day I fought I came in as RW Speed and it has now evolved into Randall Hooks Washington. All I remember is hard work," he said.

"Now that the foundation has been laid and the work has been put in, I want to live a life. My life. Like you, I want the happy things. The stuff that makes work worthwhile. I would like to know that after I have been punching bags or avoided being punched that there is someone at home that loves me, respects me and the fact that I fight for a living. It is not barbaric, as I was often told. It is what I do. I did not mention one important aspect of all of this."

"What?" I asked.

"Trevor and I have been friends since third grade. He has been the one that has been there for me from day one. I have watched him evolve into who he is today and he has watched me. Without each other, God and the Boys and Girls club in our lives I have no idea of what in the world either of us would be doing. He has been my support and has made sure that I have stayed focused and in line and in the will of God."

With a newfound respect and admiration, I looked at him and said, "After all of that all I can say is wow Randall. I am happy for your success. I hope one day it all comes together for you. I pray you have the life you so desire within the will and the plan of God."

"Thanks Danielle. That means a lot to me. I wish the same for you." At that very moment they were both wising for a life with each other. "While we are on the subject. D, I want to talk to you about something," he said.

My heart started to beat faster. It took me a moment to reply. "Umm okay. Please, go right ahead," I said nervously.

He did not say anything.

"What's up?" I asked feeling a little anxious.

"I need to know how you feel about something," he said.

"Okay shoot." I was very nervous by this point. My palms were sweating. I could feel the sweat running down my back. The goose bumps that were previously on my arms as a result of him telling me his life story had now simmered down.

"I was thinking." he paused.

"Is it that difficult?" I said jokingly.

He looked down. "Actually it is," he said.

Rubbing his hand, "Sorry," I said.

"Dani, I have not considered fighting in over four years as a result of all that's happened in my life."

"Okay. Why?" I asked.

"My mind was not where it needed to be."

"So," I responded.

"So, I think I am where I need to be now," he replied.

"Okay, and where exactly is that Randall?" I questioned.

"I think I am ready physically, mentally and emotionally."

"Well, that's great. So what's the next step?" I continued with the questions.

He said, "I am going to Vegas to meet with the National Boxing Association."

"What do you need to do there and how long to do you think you'll be gone?" I inquired.

"Well, because I haven't fought for the past four years I'll need to have a physical of course. They'll do a drug screening and numerous other tests. The rest will consist of discussions on why I left and why I want to come back," he responded.

"When do you leave?"

"Actually, I'll need to be there tomorrow."

I shouted, "Tomorrow!" Before I knew it.

Lifting his hands in a gesture as if to say calm down, Randall said, "I know it is sudden D. My plans were to discuss this with you on Saturday when I met up with you but the time never was right. When I came by on Sunday you fell asleep. Monday you were out of it and so here we are on Tuesday."

Blank stare, "Wow!" I said.

"I'm sorry if this came as a shock, I certainly didn't want to do that, but I do want your open honest opinion," he said sincerely.

Yes, I was in shock, "I, I, I don't know what to say," I stammered.

Randall's eyes pleaded, "Tell me how you feel about it. I really need to know. D, I want you in my life forever and if this is the deal breaker, I need to know now. Maybe that is where I went wrong before," he said looking down. "I didn't have a proper discussion before I started making big decisions. If you are uncomfortable I want to know so I can make the right decisions before things go too far."

Looking him in the eyes, "Randall I can't tell you whether you should do what your heart desires or not," I said. "This is a decision you'll need to make."

"Yes you can and it is important for me to know," he countered.

"Randall, you must take care of yourself."

"And hopefully one day I can take care of you too, if you'll allow me."

I retorted, "I totally understand, but we are not at this point right now."

Solemnly he said, "I pray that we will be."

"I would feel horrible if I told you not to do something that I know is your passion," I told him.

"Danielle, I am not asking you to make a decision. I am asking you to tell me how you feel. Do you think you can support me in my decision? Would you be there for me? Could you see yourself on the front row cheering and praying at the same time? Could you stand the sight of me with a black eye, busted lip, or broken ribs? Will you understand my diet and fitness routine? Will it offend you if I have to use my science kit everywhere I go? Can you handle the paparazzi? Can you handle our lives constantly being in the public eye and sometimes scrutinized? Can you handle traveling with a bodyguard all the time? Will you understand when we are shuffled in and out of places like a herd of cattle? Will you understand red eye flights? A lot of responsibility comes with me and most people think it is glamorous but it may not always be."

He continued, "Look Danielle, I realize I've asked a lot of questions. You have to put some thought into this. I do not know what your answers will be, but I had to ask them of you first. I want you be prepared. If get a call and I'm told that I'll fight on Saturday, I don't want you unprepared or uncomfortable."

"This is all so sudden. I have not given it much thought. I mean, I understand that you are a fighter but I have never thought about how I would feel to see you fight. Sure, you have your bodyguards, King and JJ, but I have never given it much thought that they may have to be with us everywhere we go. I don't know why but I haven't thought of it. When I see you, I just see a guy, not a headliner. I guess I need to consider all of this though," I said. "I can tell you however, no matter how I feel, I want you to do what is best, and what you think is right for you. I want you to be happy Randall and if that is fighting then by all means fight."

A look of relief was on his face as he said, "Don't just say it to soothe me."

"I am not. You need and deserve to be happy. I would hate for you to tell me you no longer wanted me to design. I would be devastated and more than likely very resentful. I'm sure I would always remember it and hold it against you forever. No sir, I could not live with that on my conscious," I said while shaking my head. "The way I see it, if a person loves you and what you're doing as a career choice is legal and moral, then they should learn to love what you love as well."

"Are you saying you love me?" he asked hopeful.

"What I am saying is I will need to see you in action. I know how excited I get watching Floyd, Shane, Holyfield, and Tyson and I do not even know them personally. I am really feeling Devon Alexander too," I added. "But I am partial to Andre Ward."

With a light chuckle he said, "You will meet them all."

"What I'm saying is, as excited as I get watching these fighters, I have no clue how excited I will be to see someone I know and care about fight. I'm sure it will be very intense for me. Maybe even stressful."

"Are you saying you love me?" he repeated.

"I am saying that if I love you then I will support you and love you whether you are winning or losing. If you come out beaten and scarred, then I guess, I will have to deal with the stress of watching the event. It may be nothing to see Floyd take hits, although I can't recall Floyd taking hits. However, it may be totally different to see someone I love and care for getting hit and there is nothing I can do about it."

"I hope that I do not get beaten and scarred," he commented. "I kind of think I may need to be aware of how you are going to act or respond. I can't imagine you'd faint or cry or anything like that, but I still wonder your response. I'm thinking that you would probably be hanging on the rope yelling and screaming," he smiled at the thought. "And although I would like if you responded that way, I'm not so sure if others would approve."

"Well Randall, I cannot promise that I will behave," I laughed. "You may need to sit in those shoes to see how difficult it is to sit still. Now if you are asking me if you have my blessings, then go get em' tiger! Make me proud. Whatever you do, give it your all and do your best. That is all I can ask for."

"I really hope I make you proud in everything I do. Will you promise me one more thing?" he asked.

"I promise to support you in all you do," I offered.

"Will you promise that if anything makes you uncomfortable you will talk to me about it immediately? Anything!"

"I promise." I agreed.

"Let's shake on it," he demanded.

I responded jokingly, "Dang, you don't' trust me? What about a pinky shake and shedding of blood?"

"By the way, King is my trainer and JJ is my manager, promoter, and trainer. I have another set of guys that are my body guards," he corrected me.

"Another set of guys? Try telling King he is not top-flight security. Do you have your personal Paparazzi too?" I teased.

"Oh please change the subject," he laughed.

"Why couldn't you come to the race?" I asked feeling as though now was a good time to ask since he did say change the subject.

"For events like that I have to have protection. When you asked, it was too short of a notice for me to properly get everything in place. I would have needed a little more time to make arrangements for parking, security, etc. You have to understand I want to go wherever you are but I can't if I don't prepare. There are tens of thousands of people at those races and I can't just walk through the gates like I would like to," he explained.

"You can't be like the rest of us ordinary people," I replied.

"I would not say it like that," he said.

Changing the subject once again, I said, "I have also noticed you are not wearing your ring anymore."

"You are very observant."

"Yes, I am." I raised my eyebrows.

"What?" he asked suspiciously.

"You know what." I replied.

"No. What?" he asked again.

"Do you care to elaborate on why you are not wearing it?" I asked. I wanted to know if his divorce was final or not. Maybe that is why he had been distant. Was he having second thoughts of his divorce?

"Only you Danielle," and he shook his head.

"Only me what?" I said in a high pitched voiced. "I will not be the only person noticing you are no longer wearing a fifty carat ring anymore."

"You are stupid," he said jokingly. "It is not fifty carats. It is not a wedding band either."

"I am fully aware of that. But you were wearing it as a cover up anyways," I remarked snidely.

"Says who?" he barked.

"Tell the truth!" I said while giving him the, you know I'm right look.

"Well, I was wearing that ring in replace of my wedding band. I do not think anyone has ever noticed. If they did they did not mention it. Right now I am anxious for this divorce to be final and I have taken the ring off in preparation," he said.

"What do you mean?" I asked confused.

"I do not want people to think I divorced one day and started dating and remarried the next day," he replied.

"So?" I needed him to elaborate.

"So I took the ring off now so that when the divorce is final and I start dating you officially, people won't think badly of me. Most people have no clue that I have even been separated for years, so it may seem a little inappropriate. I really want to do things in decency and in order. So I guess you can say that I will be ring less for a minute."

"Wow. You have put some thought into this," I was a little surprised.

"I have and I am excited about it."

We sat in silence as we finished eating and entertained ourselves via our respective gadgets. Breaking the silence, "Hey, what do you have to do the rest of this week?"

"Work. Catch up on work. I guess that is all I have to do. I will be lonely all week since you will be gone." I gave him a sad face.

"I did not say I will be gone all week. Maybe one day, maybe more, depending on what they say and how it goes." he said pitifully and frowned. "What do you want to do for the remainder of the day?" he asked knowing that he needed to do something to make up for his future absence.

"I have just the thought." I said excitedly and stood up to walk away. He grabbed his phones, science kit, and laptop. "Leave all of that here. It will be fine unless it rains," I instructed.

Looking at the sky, "it doesn't look like rain."

"And you don't look like a fighter either." I replied, smiled, and walked down the deck stairs. He just sat there watching, not knowing what was about to happen.

"Hey wait up!" he yelled while catching up to me, "Maybe you are not as fast as you think you are."

He moved so quickly, I had to do a double take. "Wow Edward Cullen," I said.

"Who?" he asked completely unaware.

"Never mind," I said. I was more team Jacob from the Twilight series anyway. Jacob was more of the bad guy type.

On the way down the trail he observed as I stopped at a shed, pulled out a bucket and a few drivers.

"I didn't know you live on a golf course," he said.

"I do not. I am not that wealthy. I cannot afford the greens and the maintenance."

We arrive at the green. "Pardon my error. I did not know you had a golf course in your back yard," he corrected.

"I do not. It is a driving range," I said with enthusiasm.

"Not from the looks of it," he challenged.

"Well I added three holes but I rarely play them," I confessed.

"Why not?" he asked looking puzzled.

"I can't play," I replied.

"So what are we doing?"

Swinging my club, "we are hitting."

"Really?" he asked in sheer amazement.

"It's a great stress reliever and exercise," I told him.

"What is with you with the outdoor activities and exercise?" he asked.

"Look who's talking Boy Scout of the year," I joked back.

"We can do all of this inside you know."

"I am sure at the Hooks Mansion you have an indoor course, but it defeats the point." I swing and suddenly a digital board lights up, telling how far the ball was driven and how fast.

"Not bad for a girl," and he swings. He was pretty impressed and amazed. She was such a girly girl and here she was nailing a ball across a field. The question still remained. Could she handle him fighting?

"Same to you," I said checking his range and speed.

"How often do you come out here?"

"A few times a week, every week all year long," I replied.

He then asked, "Exactly when do you refrain from outside activities?"

"As long as it is over thirty degrees then I can do my regular activities," I state.

Looking concerned, he said, "Thirty degrees is too cold to hit balls and walk or run outside."

"Oh but I like. I love the feel of the cold air going through my lungs. Once I cut the lights on out here it warms up; and not to mention, I have on enough clothes to keep me warm," I said. "Besides, I can't have an indoor nine hole course at the house, a roof track or a property large enough for a walking trail like you," I teased.

"Neither do I but it's nothing that can't be done," he replied.

"I know. I have designed a beautiful indoor track for my house. But the city would not allow me to build it. I should have done it in the original plans." I replied. "But I am sure you could add it to the mansion." We swing at the same.

"Good Lord! That was awesome!" he yelled.

"Thanks dude," I reply.

"Wow!" he said.

"That is not my speed it is yours. My Brookstone meter can only measure one hit at a time," I said.

"You did not get that from Brookstone. I am glad you told me it was mine otherwise forget boxing; I would have been spending the next few days upping my distance. You can't just out do me like that." She hit again. "So why don't you use the treadmill?" he asked preferring she changed her routine.

"I have a full gym in my house, and I hate the treadmill. Besides, I need the scenery. I need the movement and actually I need to be outside the house. Otherwise, I think about numerous other things I could be doing other than working out. Don't get me wrong, I do use it, but it is not my favorite. It is bad for your knees also."

"So you would rather walk on asphalt?"

"Actually, I would rather walk on rubber," honestly I replied. "I'll even take hardwoods. I think I prefer being outdoors because what I really want is the movement and scenery."

"You have the television and iPod," he observed.

"I can also work," I said with a smile. "I have a voice activated system that allows me to walk and work."

He raised his eyebrows at the thought of my gadgets, shook his head, and said, "Huh? I should have known."

Returning the look he gave me, I replied, "I don't think you have room to talk mister."

Changing the subject, he asked, "Why don't you play?"

"Play what?"

"Golf," he said.

"Oh, I'm not good at it." I confessed.

"So what are you doing?" he asked.

"I'm just killing some balls and letting out frustration. If you go through my balls you'll notice they have names, faces and projects on them," I said laughing.

"If you can drive you can play D."

"Hmm, I'm not too sure. For some reason, I can't seem to judge the right amount of force for the distance. The firm continues to tell me I would increase my business if I played golf with the guys. Not interested." I added.

"You can learn. It will take some time but, just like with anything, it comes with practice."

"Do you play this sport well also?" I asked, expecting him to confirm that he did.

Hesitantly, "I guess, but I am more of a contact kind of guy. Let me show you how to judge."

We walk over to the holes. "Take a shot," he said. I did and I was short.

"Try again," he ordered.

I tried again, but this time I was too long.

"Here, let me help you," as he came over next to me. He took a shot. "On point."

"I can't do it. I need an equation." I said sincerely.

"EQUATION?" he reiterated with a slight chuckle. "A female with a driving range that is not a golfer needs an equation? I doubt that. Let me show you." he said again this time standing right behind me.

Lord help me, I think as he stands so closely. When I take the club and stance myself my back touches his front. *Talk about contact.* I almost collapse. *OMG, I swear my underwear is now moist.* I took a long hard breath in the attempt to get myself together.

He turns his face over my shoulder. "You ready?" he ask.

"No," I replied.

"Let me help you." This time, he places his hands over my hands and swings the club over my hands. My arms go back with his and then his come over my chest. I can tell from the way the flag rocked that we hit it. *Or did he just hit it. Never mind!*

I fall out onto the grass. *I know, a cheap way to get him off my back; literally get him off my back.* He has no choice but to fall with me. The grass is plush and thick just like I like it. The way in which we've fallen, somehow I've landed lying on his arm. *This feels so perfect; I really hope he doesn't ask me to move.*

"Will you teach me one day?" I quietly asked.

"I sure will. One day when you can stay away from the office," he said in a joking voice, but I knew he was serious.

"Play hooky? I don't think so." I said with authority.

Laughing, he said, "I am shocked you have left the phones and laptop for this long."

Honestly feeling surprised and proud of myself, I said, "See I can do it," and then smiled.

"Do you want to?" he asked.

I looked him dead in his eyes, "sometimes I do," hoping he understood I meant that for him. We both laid there in the grass a moment longer as the sun shined in our faces. Finally, I broke the silence and asked, "If you could write your life; what would the story say five years from now?"

Without a second guess, he replied, "I would be a handsome married gent with beautiful kids, happy, healthy, and looking forward to a long life," he replied.

I couldn't help myself; I roll all over the grass laughing. By this point, I'm now off his arm and he's leaning over me. Playfully, he put his hands over my mouth. I tried to scream as he said, "What's so doggone funny?"

I threw my hands up.

"Say what?" he demanded.

I held my hands up motioning that I couldn't speak. He removed his hands and I released a laugh.

"Hello." he said impatiently.

"Okay, okay, okay! Let me get myself together," attempting to compose myself. "I am laughing at what you said," I told him.

"I know that but why?" he asked.

"Everything you've said is currently true Randall," I replied.

"Huh?"

"You are handsome, you are married, you do have one child that I know of, and living a long life." I told him.

Looking down, "I see." he said disappointed.

"You see we have to be careful of what we ask God for. He gives us exactly what we ask."

"I did say happy," noticing that I left that part out of my observation.

"Yes, you did. But you did not say anything about her being happy too," I said.

"Okay, I get it. I can see where you are going with this," he said. "So I need to be more specific."

"Not necessarily with me, but most definitely with God," giving him a look.

With now a look of understanding verses disappointment, Randall said, "Now that my five year goals are a bust what about yours." he smiled.

Returning the smile, I said, "I told you I want the family, children, husband, everyone happy, healthy, mentally, physically, emotionally, spiritually and financially. I wish the same for my family and my friends," I added.

"I am surprised. You didn't say anything about your career," he stated.

"You didn't either and neither did you say anything about the ministry."

"What about it?" he asked reluctantly.

"You didn't mention your future pastoral desires." I said.

Acting as if he had missed something in the conversation, "What do you mean? I am not quite following you," he admitted.

"It is not me you should be following, but the calling that is upon your life." I was referring to his blogs. They were more like mini sermons hidden inside of words disguised as daily inspiration.

He knew exactly what she was referring to. He had heard the spirit of the Lord telling him years ago and in his heart he knew Danielle was simply confirming it. He had been ignoring the calling for a few reasons. For one, he knew that with Tameka on his side he would not be an example of the word. Second, he also thought that with a divorce under his belt he would never be able to do it.

"Why did you say that?" he asked desperately.

"It's crystal clear that is the path you are headed. Don't miss your calling Randall," I said. "One thing is for sure; God will wait on you, nudge you, tug you, and push you until you have done his will." They laid in complete silence for nearly thirty minutes. "Let's go back and get some water."

Randall was still confused and wondered how the previous conversation changed in such a way. This was confirmation to something he was not ready to accept; or so he didn't think. They walked back to the house. He tried to act as if it didn't faze him, but it did. Approaching the house Dani asked, "What kind of juice would you like?" He stayed on the deck checking his messages while she juiced. "These are in no comparison to the ones at the gym," handing him a glass.

"I'll be the judge of that. So what are your plans while I am gone?" he probed.

"No doubt, I will be playing catch up."

"I will miss you," he said sadly.

My heart beat a little faster, "We will see," I said coolly.

"This will be the first time I won't be able to stalk you." he joked.

"Ah ha! So you are admitting you are a stalker?" I teased.

"Not really. I have a few things I need you to do this week in my absence. Think you might be able to help?" he asked.

"Sure, okay." I said and pulled out a notepad and pen.

"I need for you to keep that watch on and monitored at all times," he began. "I need for you to use the treadmill this week while I am gone, just in case you are not feeling as good as you think you are," he said.

I stopped him right there. "This sounds more like I am grounded," I said.

He ignored my comment and continued, "I will also need for you to go meet the people I told you I would have you meet, okay?"

"Umm okay. What's up?" I asked.

"These are people you will eventually meet anyways D. You let me know the time and I'll have them to meet you at your office maybe or the gym; whichever is better for you," he said.

I thought, *WTH*, but answered, "Umm okay," as he continued.

"Since I am leaving tomorrow do you want to do something tonight?" he asked.

Smiling widely, I said, "Yep. Dinner and a movie. My treat."

Looking at me as if I had two heads, he replied, "Both are fine, but your treat is completely and totally unacceptable."

With a little pout I said, "But I owe you. Now don't dispute me and go ahead and pick your favorite restaurant. What time is good?" I asked.

"Six or seven. I will pick you up." He got up and gathered his stuff to walk out. We embraced. "I shall see you later my love."

"Thanks for everything," I smiled. "Sorry to be a pain."

Winking, he said, "Not a problem babe, I enjoyed every minute of it. Besides, I am sure that was the only way I will ever be invited to sleep over."

"Umm, it's not considered a sleep over when only one sleeps and that is because of the medication you drugged her with! Speaking of which I am flushing immediately," I yelled out.

Laughing, "You feel better right?" he asked.

"True," I replied.

"Well, I guess that's all that matters," he said getting into his truck.

I went back inside to continue checking my emails and work remotely from home. Around half past three I called it quits. I'm sure; Leigh was relieved, as I had bugged her enough for the day. I walked into my closet and laid on the chaise lounge while trying to decide what to wear for my date with Randall. I wasn't sure what restaurant he'd choose so I didn't quite know how to prepare. I decided a sundress would work but then found myself wondering if he had chosen a twelve star restaurant; and in that case I'd be under dressed. I decided it would be better to call instead of guessing.

"You changed your mind?" he answered.

"Well a better offer came up," I teased.

"Say what?" he shouted.

Laughing, I said, "Just kidding. I was trying to get dressed and needed to make sure we were not flying to the White House for dinner."

Wow, that's actually a good idea, he thought. He had never done the Pretty Woman thing. Tameka could have cared less, but Danielle, on the other hand would like. He wanted to make Danielle happy and purposely took in a mental note that would be their first real date after the divorce. "Not tonight. Barak and I could not coordinate our schedules. Very, very, very casual is the attire."

I immediately thought of JJ's Rib Shack. "Are you taking me to JJ's Rib Shack?" I asked.

He laughed being familiar with the famous rib shack. "If that is where you want to go?"

"I have not been in years," I said.

"Me either."

"I won't shock you tonight, but that will be on our schedule to dine one day," I said.

"Shall I pick you up now?" he asked.

"I am not ready yet. Are you?"

"You were calling this early makes me think you are a little excited," he said.

I teasingly replied, "Negatory! Why would I be excited about going on a date with you when I had the Champ watch me sleep last night? Dude, get over yourself." I laughed.

Randall noticed she had never called him Champ before. It sounded and felt different coming from her than from everyone else. With others, Champ came across as a title, but coming from her it was a name that made him feel good. It also felt as though it gave him the confirmation he needed that she may just be okay with him fighting again. He desperately wanted to fight. It was in his blood. It was all he knew. He knew that by committing himself to boxing, it would help him get through the divorce and the idea of starting over fresh. If it weren't boxing, he would surely obsess over something else. He chose his passion, boxing.

"Babe, I'll see you at five forty five," he attempted.

"You said between six and seven," I reminded him.

"Put the work down Danielle and enjoy the night. It is my last night in town and I want to spend it with you," he said in a tone that alluded it was not open for further discussion.

Liking the way that sounded, but still needing a little more time to get ready, I said, "Six forty five."

Laughing, he replied, "You drive a hard bargain D. You're on."

"Hey!" I yelled, hoping he didn't quickly disconnect the call.

"Yep." He was still on the line.

"Thanks again!" I said, as I clicked the line off. Feeling all mushy in my heart, I just laid there and daydreamed. I couldn't remember the last time I had felt this way, it felt good and I wanted this feeling to last forever.

• •

At six thirty seven Randall was already at the gate and ringing my phone. *Why is he always before time? I need six more Baptist minutes to add the finishing touches. Either I am still a little swollen or I need some more sleep. My face is puffy.*

"Hey there," I answered.

"Are you ready?"

"Not quite," I answered honestly.

"Well, you'll just have to go as is," he said bluntly.

She buzzed the gate open for him. He pulled around but apparently, realized what she said and gave her a few minutes before he rang the bell. It was actually six fifty one. *Impressive,* she thought and smiled. His timing could not have been better. She was complete. Lips extra glossed. She liked the way she looked and no longer thought she saw the puffiness she previously saw. She was dressed very comfortable and casual. Hopefully, it was appropriate and she was not going to meet his mama; they definitely had not discussed that. Although she hated flats, the ones she wore seemed to work well this evening. *I must still be high if I like these shoes on my feet. We will see how they do after a few hours.*

She shut down the alarm and could see him through the door and the redness from the car. She opened the door and completely overlooked him as if he was not even there. She dropped her bag, jumped off the few short steps and walked directly to the car. She placed her hands on her hips and walked around it several times. *This is unreal.*

"What's wrong?" he asked.

Putting her index finger up to her lips, "Shh," she said. He was clueless. She ran her hand across the car and felt as if she really wanted to pinch herself to make sure she wasn't dreaming or in heaven. Reality hit her for the first time; she was hanging out with Randall Hooks Washington! This was serious! This was a different league than what she was used to. He was major. The game had been upped, she couldn't deny that. He tried to walk over but she held her hand out as if to say stay back. He didn't really know what was going on and went to sit on the steps to wait. She then kneeled down and stood back up, but he could not see her on that side of the car. He stood up off the steps then came around behind her and spoke.

"Is everything okay?" he asked in a quiet voice.

"NO!" she yelled.

Totally confused at this point and looking every bit like it, "Why? What?" he stammered with his words.

"I have had enough of this," she yelled again.

He was startled. "Enough of what?" he asked desperately not knowing what to do.

"YOU!" she said firmly.

She had really caught him by total surprise and he stepped a few feet back to give her some room. However, the more he stepped back, the closer she walked up to him. She was extremely short compared to him today; it was the flats. She took a mental note, *do not wear flats again.* She folded her arms and took the stance. "GODLEE BATMAN! WHERE DO YOU GET THESE TOYS?"

He was speechless. He remembered her saying he was out of control. "I swear I only have a few more at home," he attempted to reassure her.

"A few more?" She blurted out in disbelief. *Did he really just say a few more?* "This is mad stupid crazy! You need help you know? I have got to find a therapy group for you or something."

"Talk to Pastor Hunter then. He is the one that had me out looking at whips with him the other week and well, I came home with this," he replied.

Rolling her eyes, "You and Hunter are going to make me snap," she said. "No one just casually comes home with a right hand drive, next year's model, fire red V8 Vantage Roadster with Chancellor red leather seats; inserted with monogrammed silver stitching, black and red carpet with matching stitching, monogrammed seat belts, graphite black piano trim, not to mention, with every upgrade known to man. Open the door."

All Randall could muster was, "Huh?" As he stood with a bewildered look on his face.

"It wasn't a question. Open the door."

"Do I have to?" he asked shyly.

"Yes."

"Let's take the Porsche," he said referring to one of her cars.

"Nope," she replied.

Still confused Randall stated, "I am sending this back tomorrow."

"No sir," I said still walking around the car in disbelief.

"Yes ma'am, I am sending it back."

"Humph, no sir you are not getting off this easy. Besides, you can't send it back," I said.

"Okay, you are right. I had to order it. It was at the gym when I got there today," he said.

"Please let me drive it," I gave in smiling.

He laughed.

Catching what he said, "You have been to the gym too and not home?" I ask.

"I went home."

"Randall!"

"Danielle."

"Just open the door," I stated.

"Okay, get your bag."

"Not until you open the door," I said.

He slowly opened the door and then turned quickly.

"I knew it! I knew it! I knew it!" I couldn't help but to yell. There it was, stainless steel personalized sill plates with HOOKS and boxing gloves etched right in them. It was beautiful and I'm positive that it cost a fortune.

"See, I knew I should have gotten some red roses or something engraved instead," he mumbled.

"No, what you should have done was not gotten this car. I would hate for you to be jacked. Knowing you and Pastor Hunter that is probably platinum and not stainless steel," I replied.

"No it is not. And like who is going to jack me?"

"Me!" I replied. "I'm taking this and the Phantom. No more cars Randall!"

He was impressed that she cared what he did with his money. "What else can I do? I can't buy you diamonds?" he asked.

"Nope, no diamonds either Randall. If I leave it to you, I will have to wear a brace to hold my wrist up."

Actually, Randall was thinking more on the lines of a diamond ring, but it gave him a much better idea. He should start with a bracelet first though.

"If this is your hobby sir, you really need something else to do. I am enrolling you in basket weaving and pottery classes first thing tomorrow." I joked.

"Get your stuff!" Randall playfully snapped.

"You just wait. Don't be rushing me. I am admiring this beauty," I said as I continued to take in the beautiful masterpiece before me.

He replied, "Thank you," as if I directed the statement to him personally.

"Not you, the car!" I shouted. "You know what Randall; you need to get Pastor Hunter on the phone."

"I will do no such thing. He has not seen it yet. I will probably ride by his house later on," he declared.

"Ugh!" As Dani stomped off to get her things she turned back and said with one hand on her hip and shaking her head, "Why didn't you get the One 77 or the Carbon Black?"

Smiling and thinking to himself, *this woman knows her cars*, he told her, "You need to do more work. I could not decide on Carbon black or Fire red. We can ride by there and pick up a black."

Racing to get her things, "You better have that top down when I get back."

He did as he was told. He was very impressed with Danielle. What person wouldn't be? She was homeboy cool but soft, gentle and feminine. Most guys had no clue of the specifications of this car. But she knew them precisely and she was a girl! He liked that.

Dani came back out the door and like a little girl, jumped down the steps. She was more excited than he was. "Let's see what these four hundred and twenty horses can do. If we can't go zero to sixty in less than five seconds we want a refund," she said out of breath.

Looking at her in disbelief, he said, "I am not messing with you Danielle."

"If you scared say you scared." Her tone changed to serious "Why buy a car that goes over a hundred and eighty miles an hour if you can't confirm it?"

Smiling, Hooks simply said, "Put your seat belt on girl."

"Now look a there. I have a hook wrapped around my heart. How cute."

"I am always protecting you," he graciously added.

"Can I keep this car while you are out of town?" She ignored his sentiments.

"NO!"

Pouting, she lied, "I won't drive fast. I promise!"

"I don't believe you."

Shrugging her shoulders, "Oh well, I tried. " Where are we going?" she asked excitedly.

"Sit back," he replied nipping her questions in the bud.

"I gotta perfect idea. Let's go to the speedway," Dani said.

"I don't have helmets crazy. Besides, you should have had enough of the Speedway."

We were going north in what seemed like a long way. "Are we going to a different state?"

He laughed, "No. I am glad to see you feel better."

"Me too," she said. "Initially, I was concerned I might still appear to be a little swollen, but after you pulled up it hasn't crossed my mind since." She pulled the visor down to check her face and yes it was still puffy. They exited the highway. She had no clue where they would be going. They turned into a plaza across from the largest mall in the city surrounded by all sorts of other establishments. Suddenly, she looked up and there it was! All she could do was just layback in her seat. He shut down the engine, got out the car and then came around to her side to open the door. As he reached for her hand, she did not reach back.

"You okay?" he asked concerned.

"OH HELL NAW!" she replied mesmerized.

He laughed her laugh. He knew exactly what she was referring to. "Sorry, but you said my favorite place; you did not specify."

"I said to eat."

"And you will eat," he politely confirmed.

The enormous sign read JUICE IT with all kind of fruits and a hook that dangled the words.

"OO you make me sick!" she yelled laughing.

"Well D, you said my favorite restaurant and that you are paying," he reminded her.

We walked in and right smack in the middle one table stood out from the others. It had linen, flowers, and fruit lined all over it.

"Our table is ready," Randall said sweetly, holding out his hand as if to lead the way.

"You make me so sick," she said, still taking in what was occurring.

His juice was on the table and my fruit was there. The place was the Fat Tuesday of juice.

"Man cannot live by juice alone," I teased.

"It's fruit. Eve, you will not trick me," he smartly replied.

I rolled my eyes, "Oh now I am Eve?" I said.

Mini cocktail glasses with dangling metal labels to identify the different juices were brought out to us. There had to be at least twenty-five juices. I tried them all. Some I liked, some were strange, and some I didn't like. We hung out for a while and I paid a whopping $14.78. Wow, what a date! I must admit, I was full. *Oh boy, I know I am going to be up peeing all night*, I thought to myself.

"What do you want to do next?" he asked.

"I thought you were going to see Pastor Hunter?"

"I am but I want to make sure I spend time with you before I leave," he confessed unashamed.

Smiling, "What time do you leave tomorrow?"

"Around eleven."

"Are you flying charter?"

"No Delta," he replied.

"Why is that?" I asked.

"Sometimes it is more economical. There will be over ten of us but it is just easier. I can't afford to fuel the plane. We rode in my gas money on the way over here," he joked.

"You got that right," I said but thinking. "You got time to catch a movie? I don't want to keep you out too late." However, I wasn't quite ready for this date to end.

"Let's do it," he said.

After the movie he drove me home. I must admit, I did not want to leave him nor that darn car. We got to my door and it could have been the scene from Hitch.

He didn't want to leave and I didn't want him to either. I fumbled with my keys after I finally found them. We lifted heads at the same time. His lips were a mere millimeter away from mine. He closed his eyes.

He whispered, "Remember the promise."

I blinked out of my mini captivated trance. "What promise?"

"You remember." This was not a good time to bring up promises. But I had too. It was hard enough staying with her for a night. He thought, *I am about to leave her and God knows I want to kiss her, bad! Passionately and deeply. But I can't. I know in my heart if I kiss her right now, I will not be able to stop.* He never opened his eyes. He sat on the step. "I am going to get myself together for a while," he said while he desperately wanted permission to kiss her. "You can go in if you need to."

I reached for his arm and pulled him up to me. I embraced him. It was hard for me too. "Go home Randall. God knows I will miss you," I said.

"I will miss you too." He gave me that smile and dunked his head in my shoulder. He put his lips to my ear. "Good night and God bless you my love. God watch between me and thee until we meet again."

"You know what to do when you get home," I reminded him.

"Yep, but I am going to stand here until I hear your alarm on," he said.

I reached in my pocket and gave him a penny. I placed it in his hand and closed it and said, "Good luck." It was a good luck penny.

I turned on the alarm, as I was asked then went to take a shower. I could not stop thinking about him so decided to give him a call to tell him, thank you, nice car, and good luck.

His phone rang Dani's ringtone, "I'm sorry," he answered.

"For what?" I said surprised by the way he answered.

"Sitting in your driveway," he replied.

I looked at my monitor and he was there with his head rested on the seat. "Hey you are messing up my seats!" I yelled.

"I can't leave just yet. I don't ever want to leave," he admitted.

"Then don't," I replied.

"I can't stay either," he stated honestly.

I was caught a little off guard and his comment floored me. Why couldn't he just do wrong one time? He knew best, for there would be no turning back. "I wanted to tell you thank you," I managed to say. Knowing he was just outside, I wanted to go to the door, but I could not. I too, knew if I did there would be trouble. There would be no way to erase the wrong. Besides, this could very well end up being bad luck for his trip, and that would be bad for us.

"You treated me," he said in a quiet voice.

"Well, I love the car," I said.

Smiling, he replied, "I think I do too."

I then told him, "Good luck on tomorrow. Go get em' Champ."

"Thank you. You don't know how much that means to me. No one knows I am going but you, the crew and Hunter," he said lowering his head.

"Your secret is safe with me," I assured him.

"It is not really a secret. At least I don't think so," he replied.

"Go get some rest Randall," I instructed and he pulled off.

It was early for me. I was going to attempt to get at least a thirty-minute tape in and hit the drawings for a while. I didn't want to stay up too late and risk not being fresh in the morning and ready to handle business. I was also trying to figure out what I could do to get my face to completely go down.

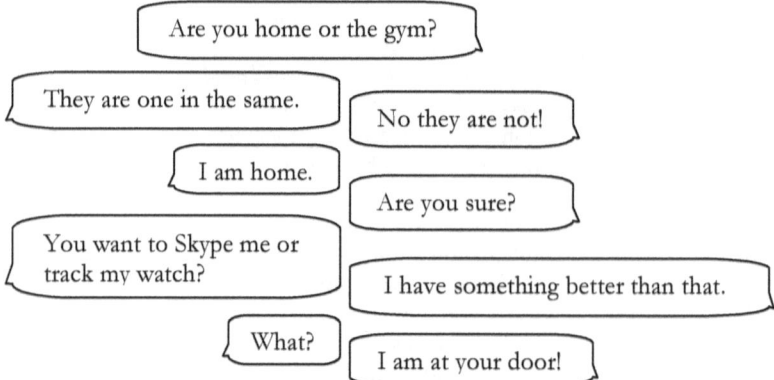

He sat patiently. *She could not possibly be at my door. She has never been to my house.* His phone rang.

"Hello," he answered.

Trying to hold in the laugh I said, "Did you fall for that?"

"I knew you were not at my door," he replied.

"No you didn't." Of course he didn't believe she was at his door, but he sure hoped that she was.

"What are you doing?" he asked.

"Chilling. And you?"

"Just walking around looking crazy like I have never been here before." He replied.

"That is because you spend most of your time at the gym," I said.

"I told you why I'm always at the gym didn't I?" he asked.

"Why?"

Being transparent he said, "It is lonely here."

"Get a dog," I replied upbeat.

"Hey, that might not be a bad idea," he said engulfed at the thought.

"I was just kidding Randall. The dog would never get any rest. It would have to be a German Shepherd or a pedigree along those lines. You know a dog that wants to work and not just be man's best friend."

"I do not work all the time," he said sounding a little offended.

"Right," I said sarcastically.

Proudly he said, "I did not work at all today."

"You went to work," I reminded him.

"No, I went to the gym," he said.

"That's work."

"No it is not. It is leisure."

"Oh really?" I asked with sarcasm in my voice.

"Yes," he replied.

"Seriously?" I continued, trying to figure out how he would consider going to the gym to be anything other than work for him.

"If you don't believe me call the gym and ask anyone," he said.

"Whatever."

Changing the subject, he asked, "Are you ready for tomorrow?"

"Yeah, it is just another day in the neighborhood for me. What about you? It is a massively huge day for you!" I said enthusiastically.

"I am excited and a little nervous to tell you the truth," he acknowledged.

"What can I do to help?" I asked sincerely.

He replied, "Pray for me."

That put a smile on my face. "I'm on it doggone it."

"Thank you so much for your support. That means a lot to me," he said.

"I haven't done anything yet," I said.

"So you think," he replied.

"If that is the case then you are welcome," I said. "Are you packed and ready?"

"Nope, not at all," he replied.

"What is your flight information?" I asked.

"Good question. Do I need to let you know or provide you with my itinerary?"

"Umm that would be so kind of you. And by the way, where are you staying?"

"Take one guess."

"Never mind." Embarrassed I admitted, "That was a dumb question."

"No it was not."

"You are right. You could have a mansion there or own a hotel." I didn't put it past him that's for sure.

"No to both," he laughed.

"Well go pack your things. Send me the itinerary and call me later if you feel like it," I said.

"Will do. What are you about to do?" he asked not wanting to get off the phone.

I wanted to say chill but I knew that was a lie so I came clean. "Check out some revisions on some drawings and work out," I answered.

Shaking his head, "I should have known."

"Good night Randall"

"Good night D."

●●●

I tried to stay up but apparently I dozed off. I awoke to find I had all kinds of lines all over my drawings. Boy was I glad to see I had saved the document before I fell to sleep. Looking at my phone, I realized I had a few messages from Randall; however, I rolled over and didn't bother to check them. It was pleasure enough knowing they were there.

At two forty I felt a buzz. I opened one eye to see what was going on and realized he was blogging.

I have not even left her side and I already feel lonely and lost. How did I make it all these years without her? She may not be what or who I want her to be but she is my best friend. A friend I love. A friend I need. She has taught me so much in so little time. It was no accident we met. We were in the right place at the right time. Waiting, searching, longing, hoping, and praying for each other. I am so glad I found you or rather you called out for me. I thank you for all that do. God Bless you. I am here for you too.

I shot back one quick text.   Thank you! I feel the same way too.

Randall was flabbergasted. *Dani was up and responded.* He did not know how to reply, so instead; he cheated by leaving her a message on her work phone. He thought to himself, *she brings out the best in me; all the qualities I hide from everyone else, my sensitive side.* He quietly lay back in his chair and went to sleep.

Wednesday

It was morning although the sun wasn't up yet. I jumped up quickly, as if I were running late and got dressed. Since being away from the office the past couple days, I wanted to be at my desk getting it done by five and I had exactly one hour to make it happen. *You can't even get a good cup of coffee anywhere in this city this early. I will ask Leigh to pick us up a cup.* It puzzled me that he didn't respond to the text. *Is he getting these blogs from a Shakespeare book? Is he really writing these blogs himself? If so I love these soliloquies.* I pulled out the berry to check my messages and there it was. A big smile appeared across my face as I listened.

"Hi sweetie, I am about to call it a night. I got your text but I didn't want to text back because you should be asleep. I wish I could see you before I leave. I wish I could hold you or take you with me. Please be prayerful and stress free in my absence. I hope to see you in a few days. I'll try to log on to check out service tonight. Be good. Keep that monitor on. You have the numbers if you need me. Thank you for your support and encouragement. With all my love."

That man really knows how to get to me, I thought. *Am I being punked? Where are the cameras? I wonder how many days are we talking about; I guess we will wait and see.* I check the watch and it appears to be functioning properly.

I texted Leigh around six.

Bring coffee. We will be hitting it until time for service. Get ready.

Thank God for service.

I am sure the last thing she wanted was to bust our butts after she had been covering me for two days.

I texted him.   U up?

Instead of a quick reply, he called back immediately. "Do you ever sleep lady?" he asked as I answered the line.

"Nope, we got stuff to do. You ready? Let's get it done baby!" I told him excitedly.

He laughed. "I hope I have that energy in a few hours when I need it."

"You will be fine," she encouraged.

"Thanks," he said, looking at his watch. "Right now I am waiting on somebody, anybody to pick me up."

"What do you mean?" I asked, not believing what I thought I heard. "NO ONE IS PICKING YOU UP?"

"Calm down," he laughed. "I have someone picking me up, but you know me, I want them to come now. I'm sure they are coming at the last minute just so I won't have the time to stop by the gym to check everything out and leave my final instructions," he reassured her.

A little more relieved, she said, "Leave them alone Randall."

"Give me a minute to check their location real quick and I will give you a call right back," he replied.

Leigh arrives with latte in tow. "Hey friend," she says.

"Hey girl."

"How do you feel?" she asked with concern.

"One penny short of a million bucks," I replied.

With a straight face, she asked, "Where is the penny?"

"I gave it to Randall for good luck."

Smiling now she said, "That was nice of you."

"Do I still look a little puffy to you?" I asked.

Squinting her eyes while observing her friend's face, she replied, "Yeah, but nowhere like it was on Monday. It's okay friend."

"I am hungry," I said starving. "Did you bring food?"

"Sure did. I brought oatmeal," she said.

"Yeah baby!" I ate as she sipped her latte and walked to her desk. I was in a zone of my own. Over two hours passed and I hadn't even noticed it. I heard a very light knock on my office door, I answered, "Yeah." I heard nothing. "Come in," I said, never once looking up or moving from my drafting table. I could hear someone come in and I could smell them, but they never said anything and neither did I; busy in my workflow, I kept right at it.

I could hear the door swing open again and this time I heard Leigh say, "Whoops sorry."

"Un huh," I replied, once again never turning around. A few moments of silence passed and as I was erasing I said, "Jesus."

"A name above all names," someone behind me said.

I spun that stool around so fast and jumped off like he had been away at war in Vietnam and this was the first time I'd seen him since. "Oh my God what are you doing here?" I flung my arms around his neck. Not even thinking about the fact that I was at my office and technically he was still married. *Dang, I just left him less than ten hours before so why I am I so excited to see him?*

He was smelling so good and looked even better. He had on a pair of black slacks with a black and white striped shirt. I love stripes. You could tell his suit jacket was probably left in the car. His face was clean-shaven and smooth as a baby's butt. His haircut was skinned to the bone. *When did he have time to do all of this?*

"I told you I wanted and needed to see you before I left," he answered.

My heart melted right there. "Are you going to be late?" I managed to say.

"No worries. I just had to stop by and hug you before my flight."

Grinning from ear-to-ear like a little girl, I said, "That is so sweet."

"I have to be honest; my stomach has butterflies fluttering like crazy. My sweat glands are on overload and I can barely speak. I am flat out nervous, but it is all good and all worth it," he said being transparent.

"I wish I could go with you or give you a good luck and good bye kiss." I said staring into his eyes.

He stood there so calm; had he not just told me that he was nervous, I never would have known.

"You can do both," he replied.

"Did you do this on purpose?"

"No, I really did not know how I was going to make this happen," he said, referring to his surprise arrival.

"No I meant did you come here to make me nervous since you are nervous?" I asked.

I do not know if I was nervous to see her, to leave her or to meet with the association. "Why are you nervous?" he asked.

"You just do that to me," I said shyly out of embarrassment while dropping my head.

He tilted her head back up so he could see her eyes, "Hey, you do the same to me," he confessed.

Leigh bust the door open. "Five minutes Hooks," she said with authority.

He shooed her away without looking back. We just stood there. I was holding his hand and swaying it. Neither of us knew what to say.

"You do know there may be a press conference and all of this may be televised at some point?" he asked.

"I hadn't even considered that," I said. Having a celebrity on my team was new to me. Well, to the rest of the world he was a celebrity, but to me he was just Randall, a regular guy that I had a huge crush on.

"I will call you in advance if I can, and if you do not mind, King or JJ will keep you posted. Vickie will also be a point of contact along with other members of my team that will send emails or texts providing updates."

"I better get Sade on ESPN alert," I said.

"Yeah, if I may suggest, you may want to subscribe to their minute by minute news and have it playing here and on your laptops," he replied.

I reached for the nearest phone, my iPhone, to call Leigh. "Leigh can you please subscribe to ESPN on all of our cells and emails for news alerts? Also I'll need for all the monitors in the building on ESPN for the remainder of the week," I instructed.

Before she could respond, the door opened. I assumed it was her and hung up. "HEY! SORRY!" Instead it was Mr. Shwatz. I dropped Randall's hand quickly as if Pastor Hunter was at the door.

"Mr. Hooks, good to see you again." He nodded, "Dani," addressing me.

"Thank you Sir. Same here," Randall said.

"I see you travel in style Mr. Hooks."

"Thank you for allowing me to come in," Randall obliged.

My brows touched together. I had no clue what they were discussing.

Mr. Shwatz looked over to Danielle and said, "I apologize for the interruption Dani, I hate to disturb you, but I need that space for at least thirty minutes then you may have it back. I have a group scheduled to arrive from China in ten minutes."

"No problem," Hooks said. "I will move it now. It's all yours and thank you for your approval," he added.

Randall grabs my hand to lead me out of my office. "Let me get that for you," Mr. Shwatz said as we walked toward the elevator and Leigh jumped in. As he put his key in to turn the elevator he said, "Good luck Hooks. You will do fine."

Where are we going, and why are we going up, I thought. As soon as the elevator doors opened, I knew exactly where we were going. To the roof. *He flew a helicopter here?* As we began to climb the stairs to the roof I could see at the top what appeared to be his two bodyguards. We arrived to the top where it was loud, windy, and noisy.

"No hell you didn't!" I said loudly over the noise while smiling on the inside.

"Yes, I did. That is how much you mean to me. I detoured my route and landed on the roof of your building just to look you in your eyes and say goodbye," he said over the noise. He hugged me so tight that the guards moved in. Leigh was standing at my back and they were standing at his. His lips lay on my neck.

I spoke, "God be with us together and apart."

"Amen." He agreed to the simple prayer request.

One guy said, "Twenty seven seconds." He let me go. Just like a scene from a movie, he ran towards the open door and jumped in. The guys followed behind him and shut the door. The helicopter gently lifted off the roof and I thought to myself, *I knew this landing pad would come in handy someday.*

Our hair was flying all over our heads like crazy. I could still see him looking down at us with his hand on the glass. The further it lifted up the further I moved towards the mark until I could no longer see his face. I turned back at Leigh and handed her my phone and yelled, "Text him now!"

"What do you want me to say?" she screamed back.

I wanted to say I love you but I chose not to. As one helicopter went to the right and spun around to go back in the direction of the airport, the other one landed right as I backed up from the X. As it touched ground I put my hand on the door.

I had no memory and felt discombobulated. I tried to yell to Leigh to ask, "What are their names?" but she could not hear me over the propeller. Instead I said "Good morning and welcome," as the door opened.

"Thank you Mrs. Rose it is such a pleasure."

"It is Ms. The honor is ours. How was the flight?" I was yelling to the top of my lungs. Leigh handed me the phone for my approval of the text to Randall before she submitted. I could not ever fire her. Who would take the time to learn me well enough to be able to send a personal text for me without me ever speaking a word?

I conversed with my client while we walked to the conference room. I did not go get my things. Leigh brought in my items and the others in attendance followed her inside. My game was on. I put on a very impressive stellar performance; I could sell pork to a pig right now! The presentation went over fabulously to say the least and I did not even get a chance to sweat. Once I unveiled my model deign they all stood admiring it. They conversed amongst themselves and completed a wire transfer right on the spot. They asked if I would be available to travel to China to design a building there.

"It would be my pleasure," I beamed. I was delighted to be asked to travel and anticipating going. What an accomplishment it would be to say that I designed a building there? I would love it for nothing else but for the bragging rights. Normally, this process takes weeks, days, swooning and tons of man-hours. What a delight! Not to mention I was down for two days. If I had been up to par I would have worried myself to death and never had this kind of outcome for sure.

I texted Leigh while we were still in there.

> Celebration time! Lunch on me today! Nails and Feet.

> Thank God!

She texted back instead of speaking aloud. I knew she carried the weight these last two days and I owed her big time. That was why I loved her. Not only was she a damn good assistant but truly my friend.

We accomplished all we set out to do for our little victory celebration. I even snuck in a shampoo before bible study. I pulled into the lot at the church at six fifty six. Not good timing, but excellent compared to all the tasks I accomplished for the day. Besides, the church hall monitor was not there. However, as soon as I walked in the door security announced, "You are late."

"I won't even ask who told you to say that but technically I still have one minute. Give me a break." I really wanted to say, "Dude, as fabulous of a day I have had don't start with me."

"Can't do that. I would not be doing my job then. I am doing it all in love," he replied with a genuine smile.

"So you say."

"I will be your escort tonight," he continued.

"Really?" I stopped and gave him the once over. I looked him up and down and back up again.

"Yes. And to think you were about to stand me up," he said.

"I do not need an escort, body guard, or date. I think I can handle walking in the sanctuary by myself," I replied.

Clearing his throat, he said, "That is not what Mr. Hooks seems to think."

Just as I figured, "If Mr. Washington told you it was Monday today would you believe him?" I asked sarcastically.

"Ms. Rose you are under my care tonight regardless," he was serious.

"Seriously?" I said, smiled, and shook my head.

He held his hand out to allow me to lead but also indicating that he was going to remain behind me. I kind of threw a silent temper tantrum and walked to my regular seat. He sat in the seat Randall normally sits in.

After service was over and Pastor Hunter gave the benediction the bodyguard quickly demanded, "Come with me. Pastor Hunter wants to see you."

What now? I thought. *What is he planning on jumping on me about this time? I am sure it's because I had an overnight guest. Whatever! I'll just take it like a champ.* I felt as though I had been escorted like I was going to see the warden. I waited in line until after everyone else spoke and then I spoke.

"Hey Pastor Hunter."

"Hey, beloved. How are you?"

"Marvelous and yourself?"

"I'm blessed. I wanted to make sure Hooks made it," he said insinuating I had confirmation.

"I am sure he did, but I have not heard from him just yet." I looked at security, "Did he make it?" I asked.

"The trackers showed earlier that the plane made it to the tarmac safely," the guard reported.

"If you talk to him tell him to buzz me no matter the time." Hunter said.

"I will if you relay the same message," Dani replied.

"Why don't we get together tomorrow?" Hunter suggested.

Pastor Hunter's tone threw me off a little so I asked, "Is that a question?"

"It is a question before the command," he said smiling to smooth the rough edge.

I must have had a strange look on my face or something.

"I just want to talk to you," he ensured.

I looked at the bodyguard as if to say, "*Help me.*"

His return look stated he was off duty for me for the evening. "You are on your own tomorrow," he smirked.

"What good are you?" I asked with an ugly face. *This is the main person I need protection from.*

"What time is good for you?" Hunter inquired. He was obviously not letting go of this.

"Send me a meeting request please," I replied.

Pastor Hunter gave a slight smile and said, "Will do. Be safe."

Top flight walked me to my car. "Do you have the numbers to text when you get home?" he asked.

I sighed, "Yes, I have everyone's number to text," I said.

"Keep you monitor on," he instructed.

"Okay." *Geesh, how many times am I going to hear that?*

When I got home I texted everyone including Randall. Later in the evening I sent him a text saying.

> I miss you. Good luck and Pastor said call him if you have a chance. I am here for you.

I received no response. I had a lot of work to do. My mind, however, was thinking of Randall and what Pastor Hunter wanted to talk about. *Scary!* I could not sleep but I tried. *How in the world is a girl supposed to sleep after a man lands a helicopter on the roof of her building?* He was an amazing man; that fact couldn't be denied.

Thursday

I woke up antsy and the day seemed to go by extremely fast. It was getting closer and closer to the time for my meeting with Pastor. I still had not spoken to Randall. I was curious and wanted to know the how, what, why and everything in between. Not worried, but a little concerned. When the time came I showed up to the church promptly.

"Greetings," the person at the desk said in a chipper voice.

"Hello. I am Danielle Rose here to see Pastor Hunter," I said.

"Of course," she replied with the same enthusiasm and escorted me back.

I walked in his office prepared to shake his hand but to my surprise as he was holding my hand he walked around his desk and gave me a respectable hug.

I sat in the same seat I sat in the last time I was in his office. This office was nice. He was nice. But I did not like being there. Had I initiated the meeting, I'd be at ease; however, it was very intimidating when he did it. Pastor was like a father. You couldn't lie, flinch, or do anything. You might as well have been under a swinging light in a white room, with a cigarette burned table, 1960's chairs and a 2-way mirror being interrogated.

He sat in the chair next to me but at this point, I wasn't sure it made me relax or more uncomfortable.

"I brought you in today to talk to you about Randall of course," he began. "I can tell you now, I can understand this is not what you may want to hear nor is it one of those messages I want to convey either. Even Randall himself, didn't want to hear this I might add. What I'm going to share with you may be a little painful, but it hurts me also because I think that you two are both great people." Clearing his throat, he continued. "Honestly, I would love to see you two in a different situation, however, the situation is what it is and we have to deal with it face on. Although I would like for both of you to be happy, I would much rather you do what is right in the sight of God; and if doing what's right means being obedient and sacrificing your happiness, then that is the right thing to do. I would be doing you a disservice if I did not tell you to not jeopardize doing the right thing for happiness. Always do the right thing and happiness will fall into its respective place. I hope you are not thinking that he is doing anything wrong because of his sporadic behavior. He is trying to separate himself but also remain in the picture as your friend while being as far away from you as physically possible. It is less painful and brings less temptation. However, he is having a real hard time just being your friend. Please understand he wants to do what's right in the sight of God first and with you. I foresee a bright future for him as a man, a father, a boxer, and a man of God. He has to keep his mind and eyesight right. I see bright and wonderful things for you as well, in your career, your growth, your family, and your walk with God. I would hate for these things to be ruined, destroyed, discredited, not shone upon or diminished for you or him based upon something that is not and assumed."

He paused as if waiting for a response; however, I gave none.

He continued, "I informed him to pull up, pump his brakes, hold his horses, and stay back. Your relationship needs to be friendly and Godly. He did inform me that he spent the night at your house because you were ill. He said you slept in your bed and he sat up in a chair all night working and watching you. From what I understand that for the majority of the night you were not even aware he was there due to the medication you had taken. I commend him on doing that as a friend and also for being able to do that in the house of the woman he cares deeply for. To obtain this platonic relationship is difficult for him. Your relationship must remain friendly and Godly Danielle. We have to do what is right and consider how it looks and appears in the eyesight of others."

"You two may know what happened, but the people on the outside do not know. You must consider the fact that you both are in the public eye. Why, I see your name in the paper every day; and he is in the public eye under a different light. I have to tell you, I pray for you two daily. My prayers include your safety, health, happiness, your ability to discern and the increase of your vertical relationship. I do not want you to hinder, block, or delay a blessing by being disobedient. Please don't misunderstand, I am not chastening or judging you or him for that matter. I just have to be obedient myself and tell you what the Lord has instructed me to say to you two."

"I brought you two in separately for a reason. I am not sure if you know it or not but Randall and I are friends. I am not only his Pastor. I am both. I take off my Pastoral hat for him. So with that being said, please understand that we talk much more than I'm sure you may imagine and about WAY more stuff than you think. We were friends before I became a Pastor and he became a boxer. He may have already told you that. So you can say I have insider information. It is not bad. But I can't advise him on something even if it is good for him but it is not right for his situation. I hope you understand. I am having this conversation with you as a response to the conversations I had with him."

Pastor could tell that Danielle was taking this all in. "I can guess your concerns," he said. "He is one hundred percent Randall today and then he clocks out tomorrow; and these are most certainly valid concerns. He does this because he feels he can't control himself so he pulls back. I can even give you several examples where you all may have hung out strictly as friends and the next thing you know, he can't sleep, eat or do anything the next day. I am not ratting him out or putting him on front street but it's just obvious to all of us that are close to him. We can see his happiness but we can see his pain also. It's no secret how he feels about you. If you'd ask him he'd tell you himself. When these days occur he is hopeless and he backs up. This is the only way he knows how to regain composure and control. Then there is the other way he gains control. To fight again."

"Women are different. They know how to be a friend and stay a friend even when they are attracted to that person. Some people can go to the strip club and save souls. I for one do not think I am strong enough to do so; therefore, I don't go. He is saying the same thing. He is not strong enough on a daily basis to do the things with you that he wants to do and still remain your friend in his heart and in his mind. We won't even talk about physically."

"I want you both to be happy. If another gentleman comes along, he's single and treats you right then of course go for it. You still have to live life. I did however want to explain his behavior. He is trying to do the right thing. I am not defending him. I am just telling the truth. His situation may seem different. He may seem single; however, he is married no matter how it looks. Yes, she has abandoned him, but we still must acknowledge that she exists and we have to deal with it. She may not be around but we know where she is and who she is and that fact alone must be honored and respected. It may be his choice, her choice, or a mutual choice; either way we have to respect her position until legalities are complete. Whether we like it or not."

"A few years ago he told me he would never fight again. He did not have it in him anymore and he did not desire it. His drive was gone, his zeal was gone, and his tenacity and fight was gone. But now you have come into his life, the zeal has returned and he has the desire to fight again. We owe this to you Danielle. I owe that to you. The boxing world owes this to you. We have been waiting on this for what seems like a lifetime and have greatly anticipated his return to the ring, him pursuing his passion. You may not realize this, but, should he ever mention that you are the reason he came back to the sport, you'll become a celebrity. Who knows, a book will probably be written and so on and so forth. I personally would rather he hold off fighting until all of this is final. Your name would be mentioned and we don't want that. I do not want you to be in the public eye with him at an event like that just yet. We live in one of the few states where the wife can sue the mistress or alleged mistress. Now I know that you nor Randall may not consider yourself the mistress, but the attorney's and the public will relay this differently to the determent of both of you."

"He is ready and wants to court you. He respect you, values you and what you think. He considers you a great friend. He has not worked out at this level in a long time. Yes, he has stayed fit and in shape, but he has not been at this level of preparation in a long time, if ever. Has he been prepared to fight before he met you? No, I'd have to honestly say he has not. Has he mentally and physically prepared like this before? Once again, no, he hasn't. His walk with God has taken a shift too. I think you have brought something different to him. I see him totally different than he was at the beginning of the year. We all see it. He even sees it. He wants you to meet his parents, his friends, and his son. He wants you to become intimately active at his gym, his restaurants, and his businesses and in his life. He declines and does not accept a lot of public functions because he is not really a public guy. He is a very humble person; then again, he would not want to go alone anyways. Now he has someone that he is excited about and has someone to go with that would actually love to go and be a support to him. He wants you to be an active and integral part of his life. I am the one saying no. I think the timing is wrong. Someone is going to misconstrue it to your disadvantage. A picture is going to be taken at the wrong time exemplifying something more than what it is. We don't want it for him or for you. You are a business professional, just as he is, and you do not want or need your name discredited."

"I do not think your intentions are wrong or to harm him in any way. If I did, I would let him know. By the same token, I do not want either of you to find yourself in a bad situation, that's all. I hope that this works itself out and loses its pain. You know this is my job, my duty and responsibility to tell you the right things biblically and morally. I know you may be adhering to them but we need to make sure the public can see it. That is the public outside and inside these four walls. I love you both. I love you both dearly. I want the best for you two. Do you have anything you would like to add or say?"

I had been waiting for my opportunity to speak, "Yes, as a matter of fact I do," I said.

"Oh, I'm sorry go right ahead."

"WHAT IS UP WITH THE ASTON PASTOR?" I broke the intensity.

Clearly confused, he replied, "HUH?"

"You heard me," I gave a mischievous look.

"I am not sure what you are asking me," he said.

Giving him the side eye and I was not about to let him off the hook. "You are very clear on what I am asking you. Don't play with me. Let's lay it all on the line. What is up with the Aston?" I asked again.

He threw up his hands and burst out laughing. "I don't know what to tell you. You have the man so confused until he just drove up and drove out," he said rolling with laughter.

"Oh helicopter no! I am chastening you now. What's the deal?"

He put his hands together in a praying and forgiveness gesture and said, "Please forgive him for he know not what he do," then laughed.

I cleared my throat.

"What?" He asked, pretending to be confused.

I cleared it again.

"Forgive us. Please forgive us for we know not what we do," he corrected.

"Father I stretch my hands to thee no other help I know. Will you help these two to and fro?" I replied.

He laughed so loud until his assistant knocked on the door to check up on us.

"Come in," he said between a laugh.

His assistant looked at him then to me and asked, "You okay Pastor?"

"Yes, I am. Ms. Rose is off the chain. She is praying for me and Washington," he said while trying to regain his composure.

With a knowing look she said, "Oh Lord, what did they do this time?"

I waved my hand at her and said, "Girl, those two together are unstoppable. They are out of control." I laughed.

"Hey! Wait just a minute!" Pastor interjected. "I heard you wanted the car and LOVED it."

"That's right, and don't you even think about it mister. That one and the Bach are mine!" I yelled while pointing my finger at him.

"I thought you wanted the Phantom?" he said.

With a shrug of the shoulders I replied, "Okay, since you don't want it I will be greedy and take them all," I said.

"You bought a new car Pastor?" His assistant asked shocked she didn't know about it.

"Actually," he started.

I rolled my eyes before he could complete his sentence.

"Deacon Hooks bought a new car," he said cautiously.

"I don't even want to know," his assistant replied. She was fully aware of how these two guys rolled.

"Why didn't you get one Pastor?" I asked. As I sat back in my chair and folded my arms.

He raised his eyebrows and replied, "Huh?"

Once again he got the look from me. He already knew what it meant. He had been married long enough to know that look. He began to speak, "Umm, first lady said I could not."

"Umm hmm, just as I thought!" I screamed out.

"Oh no, I hate I told you that. The bible says it goes both ways. I have to be submissive to her too," he quickly added.

"Umm hmm. So you let your boy get in a world of trouble?" I asked.

"If first lady ain't happy ain't no one happy. A brother got to keep the promise land open. Hooks is still in the wilderness. He can do whatever he likes." he replied with a chuckle.

"So y'all think," I said, rolling my eyes.

"Oh let me get him on the phone. Sounds like I just heard a whip crack his back." Pastor Hunter joked.

"Oh well, do what you need to do Pastor," I said with sass and threw my hands up like what?

His assistant said, "Girl get Pastor."

I could understand why they were such good friends. Pastor was cool. Here it is he called me into his office to lay down the biblical law so to speak; yet we were able to remain calm, cool and still laughed in the end. One thing's for sure however, if this goes any further, when the two of them are hanging out, spending will be limited. They both have the tendency to go overboard on any and everything. As I sat there thinking, I became a little distracted, or rather a little blinded by the bling of Pastor's ring and chain.

"It is nothing wrong with it. I actually love that they love what they do and reward themselves appropriately, but Aston's, Lambo's and Ferrari's are a little over the top don't you think?" I replied.

"And by the way Ms. Danielle I see what you drive, how you roll, the bags you carry, how you step and I heard you live pretty well," Pastor threw in.

"Yes, that's true. I work hard too Pastor. Girls can have swag and be bosses too you know."

"So you understand then?" he replied.

"Humph!" I couldn't even say anything else to that. He was right.

"Check your phone let's see if our boy called," he said.

"It's in the car," I replied.

"Why did you leave it in there?" he asked with curiosity.

"The last time I was in the judge's chambers they got taken so I avoided that all together," I said snidely.

"Oh, okay," he smiled and checked his own phone. "No call, but you may have one. We're calling," he said and pushed the button to call Randall's line.

Apparently, he did not answer. "RW, it's Tre. Ms. Rose and I are trying to figure out what's going on. I need help. I am getting beat up over here man. Hit us back. I am praying. Be in peace," he hung up.

I was thinking, *Tre. Tre? Oh, Trevor! I got it.* We talked and laughed for a few more minutes and before I knew it I was completely relaxed and had forgotten that I was in Pastor's office. When his phone and email suddenly chimed, he waited until I was finished and said, "Excuse me." He pulled out his phone again.

"I think we have a message," he said. "You got your laptop? I do remember that you carry those around."

I reached on the side of my chair and had the laptop open before he could even get to his desk. "Where are we going?" I asked.

"ESPN."

I got to the website first, a commentator was talking in the background, and there were tons of pictures of Randall. I did not have my phone so I shot an email to everyone. TURN TO ESPN NOW!

The reporter spoke, "It appears the National Boxing Commissioner has just entered the MGM Grand and has gone into a closed door conference room. We are aware that Hooks Washington was seen here earlier today. This could be coincidence or this could be the start of something big. I think the boxing community is hoping for the latter," he added. "Could Hooks be considering stepping back into the ring? He has not been in Vegas since his last fight four years ago. This would be a long awaited come back folks. Wait a minute, here is Daniel Rice who has been here for the last few hours," he reported.

"Good evening." The slideshow stops and a guy appears live in the MGM Grand. The girls are dinging my email accounts off the hook, but I can't even look at them right now. I am trying to get my DVD and jump drive both to record this. I finally send an email; somebody better be recording this.

"This will be what all boxing fans are waiting for! Hooks Washington was seen here earlier today with his entourage, trainer, promoter, physician, and a host of others. Several hours later the boxing commissioner arrived. From the looks of it Hooks has put on weight. We are not sure at this moment if the weight was intentional or not. We cannot decipher how much weight. The scales will reveal that but we are certain and confident that he could go either way; middle class or heavy weight. Either way, we wish him luck and look forward to seeing him back in the ring. Coming to you live from MGM Grand in Las Vegas. We will continue to bring you live updates as they develop. Back to you in the studio."

I was in shock! I know this happens and it's his job, but this was my first time seeing or hearing his name live since I met him. I really didn't know how to respond. They started showing earlier footage of him being herded through the hotel.

Pastor Hunter looked up and said, "See what I told you? He has only been there a few hours and they have already camped out to see him."

"He wanted you to go but I would not allow it. Remember what I said; it was best. No one would have thought this meeting would turn into a production. They may not be able to snap his shot but they would find a way to get your photo," he said.

I had not considered his public life for all I saw was him personally and at church. This was going to be different and to be honest, I wasn't sure if I was ready for it. I mean, I can handle it, but ready was another word. I had never dated anyone that was a public figure. If anything, I had been featured on my buildings a few times and was more of the public figure.

"Pastor you are right," I said. "I think it would have been a disaster had I been there. I'm more than positive the tabloids would run wild with it."

"Yes, you better believe they would have. RW has never been seen or pictured with anyone other than his wife. The last four to six years he not been seen or photographed with anyone other than his crew. I do not know which they would enjoy most, him boxing or him dating. You don't want to put yourself out there. Next week they will be stalking your building trying to wait for him, but finding out about you instead," he said.

"Have patience. I know it is not fun travelling with guards all the time and it can be a bit annoying. You will have to be on your best game. You surely don't want to have to do that with a Mrs. hanging over your head. I'm sure in your heart, you know this is the right way," he continued.

"It is but Pastor can I tell you something?" I asked.

"Anything."

"This is as Randall's friend not my Pastor," I told him.

"I am his Pastor too," he said.

"Wow Sherlock," I said sarcastically.

"Watch it," he advised.

"I like and care about Randall a lot," I said looking down. At that moment I knew I had said too much and I had not even started. "I know it is bad and I know it is a sin; and I cannot make an excuse on how it happened. I don't know what to do. I cannot go a minute without thinking about him. I need him just as much as he needs me," I said.

"He knows how you feel. Pray and ask God for forgiveness. Go in peace and sin no more," Pastor replied.

"How do I do that?" I asked.

He stared me right in my eyes and swallowed hard. He made the face I have seen in the pulpit hundreds of times.

"I must confess I do not see how I am going to be able to shut it off and walk away as if I don't care about him," I said with all honesty. The tears begin to fester in my eyes. This was difficult. It was not in the plans to come here for him to make me cry. I know he was not trying to. I wasn't going to do it, but it hurt. "Pastor I have; or rather, we have not done anything wrong. We are two broken people that accidentally found each other lost. I was not looking for him and I do not think he was looking for me. We were content with our boring, dull, lonely lives, and our work. Why has this happened?" I asked, not necessarily expecting an answer.

Pastor said, "We do not know if this is God's work or Satan's. We will have to run on and see what the end will be. I am glad to hear you have done what is right. I want you to keep it that way but do we need to go to the word?"

"No." I said like a three year old.

"It is right there in your bible. Lust of the eye. Lust of the flesh," he said.

I held my head down. "Did you have this conversation with Randall?" I asked.

"Which time? Which day?" he said.

"And?" I said, hoping he'd share.

Shaking his head, he replied, "And he is just as stubborn as you."

I laughed, that made me feel a little better. "That may be true for me but not as true for him."

"Oh no, trust me. He is stubborn. He is like an old mule," he said.

Laughing, I said, "No he is not. He is very disciplined."

"Until it comes to you."

I gave him a suspicious look.

He pointed to his chest, "Would I lie to you?" he asked.

I raised an eyebrow.

"Don't push me cause I'm close to the edge," he sang out the verse from an old school Grandmaster Flash rap song.

I doubled over in my chair laughing hard.

"Alright Danielle, let's get out of here. We can sit here all night. I know you are going to go home to work out, put in some work, and hope he calls," he said.

"Pastor don't take this as being disrespectful," I said cautiously.

"Yes ma'am," he replied, calm and cool.

"Shut up!" I said. We were at the door. "Good night."

"Come back tomorrow for more confessions," he called out.

"You ain't ready for my confessions. You will step down out of the pulpit dealing with me," I warned him.

"You know what to do," he said.

I looked puzzled.

"Now who ain't ready?" he said. "Keep that monitor on and text whoever you are supposed to text," he reminded me.

I gave a salute, "Yes sir and thanks for making me feel like crap on a stick," I said.

"My pleasure," he smiled.

I rode home in silence. There were so many missed calls, texts, and emails until I was going to need to be sitting down by my computer when I began responding.

When I got home, I went through the emails and texts. He had not called, texted or blogged. I didn't know how I felt about that. It really did not matter at this time though since my mind was cluttered with ESPN and Pastor Hunter anyways. It was so cluttered that I could not sleep. I lay there all night until I could not take it any longer.

Friday

I was so glad it was Friday. I was quiet pretty much the whole day. Not because of Randall, but everything. I stayed to myself. By noon I knew that I would be cooped up all day. I felt the need to digest all of this and come up with a plan of action.

Around two, I went to the spa and told Leigh to lock up. Catching her off guard by my comment, she did a double take. Before I could finished my services I thought I heard her voice calling me. I thought, *am I dreaming?*

"D!" Leigh called out.

I turned my head to the other side and squinted my eyes, "What's wrong?" I asked.

"Nothing," Leigh said. "You have a delivery."

"Oh yeah? Who is it from?" I asked.

"I don't know."

"Well what are you sitting there for? Open the box," I said jubilantly. It was the iPad covers for my two iPad's. I knew who it was from because we discussed it.

"You ordered this?" she asked.

"No, they are from Randall," I said.

"From Randall," she stated and not asked. "How do you know?"

"We discussed them. He had one, but I wasn't really expecting one myself, much less two," I said excitedly; I was almost done. It felt odd receiving gifts from someone that sort of disappeared from my life. Honestly, I didn't know what to make of it. Maybe I was being dramatic; after all, it had only been two days. *He did land his helicopter on the roof of your building. What else do you want?* I asked myself.

I decided to pop in today and get a shampoo instead of tomorrow morning. Thank God she was able to squeeze me in. Afterwards, I went to the crib, ran the neighborhood, and chilled on my deck. Actually, I chilled all night. I looked at those iPad covers quite a few times, taking them on and off several times. I wondered was this a special order or would Gucci accept returns. *"I am taking this back first thing tomorrow. I will not be bought! JERK!"*

For the remainder of the night, I did nothing at all; not even watch television or complete any work related project. I chilled and surfed the net until I got the bright idea to scrub my house spotless. Let's just say I started with great intentions but it only lasted for an hour or so. I simply could not get myself together or motivated and sadly, my phone never rang one time. I was left in peace; however, I am not sure it was the right day for solitude. I think I may have needed some noise, some company, or something else to do.

ESPN shows shots of him all day. Up until this point he had yet to confirm or deny why he was in Vegas. Actually, he had not spoken to the cameras at all. I had never seen this side of him. I always saw the talkative side. Although he is extremely talkative he is also humble. For the past few days however, he was completely speechless. He said nothing at all. He had not even displayed that beautiful smile I was accustomed to having the pleasure of seeing from him on the regular.

Just when I felt like I was either getting it together or wearing myself down from trying, it happened, he blogged. It was twelve fifty eight AM my time.

> Hard work pays off. It is mandatory to survive and to succeed in life. It's mandatory for love. It completes your purpose. I have worked hard in everything I have done and do. Now it is time for me to live and complete my life with my lovely wife.

My heart sank! *What in the whole wide world did that mean?* I quickly went in the house and popped open a bottle of wine. Sade was calling. "I saw that mess," I answered.

"You okay?" Her voice was full of concern.

"I guess so," I said but I wasn't really.

"He may be speaking of you Auntie."

"Yeah, and he very well may not be," I replied.

Sade reassuringly said, "Don't worry. I think he is."

Not being too optimistic about the situation I said, "It must be nice to be young and naïve. Thanks child."

I sat on the floor in the dark with my back against the wall and while the television continued to play his clips. I have to admit that I was hurt. To be honest, I think I kind of expected for him to need me more while he was there. I had even practiced my words of encouragement, but now I'm facing the fact that he didn't need me after all. Maybe I wasn't as important or as relevant as I thought. Maybe I was only important in Atlanta and not Vegas. There was no denying it, I was so very sad. *How did I get myself in this predicament? Why am I sad over a married boxer? I was probably just springtime to him.* So many thoughts ran through my mind. I rest my head on the wall. When I awoke I was surprised that I had slept the entire night on the floor.

Saturday

I wished I hadn't drank the entire bottle of wine because I felt miserable the next morning as if I had a hangover. At least I had an excuse to feel the way I felt, however, it wasn't a hangover feeling. My body felt more like it had been hit by a Mack truck on a set of railroad tracks, then drugged down the track until the train derailed into the ocean, after swimming and coming close to the shore I was bitten by a piranha and waddled my way to the sand where the heat blistered and wounded me to decomposition. Yeah, one could say that I felt pretty bad. I have only felt this way once before in my life and I had promised myself that I would never feel this way again; and I'll be dammed if I didn't. Talk about being pissed off with myself. My promise was that I would never allow anyone near my heart again. I thought immediately of Patti Labelle, If You Ask Me To lyrics. *But he didn't ask me too*, I thought. I had done so on my own and right now I was pissed at Danielle. Right then and there I vowed his would be my last time coming out of my shell and getting hurt.

Once I was able to get myself together, I got in a good hard work out. Before I knew it time had passed and it was early afternoon. I was in one location and my phones were in another so I didn't know if he called or not. I made up my mind I was not leaving the house until it was time for me to go to work on Monday. I hadn't eaten nor washed my face for that matter and it was cool. I convinced myself that after Monday I would be back together and everything would be okay. *This too shall pass*, I thought. I understood that this feeling wasn't the first time but hopefully it would be the last. I was on the deck with my iPod going when I heard her speak.

"Tee, where are you?"

I didn't respond. *She will find me one way or another.* Sade came to the deck and took a seat.

"You been here all day honey?" she asked concerned about her bestie.

I nodded.

"Why?"

I didn't have any words so I simply shrugged my shoulders instead.

"You feel better?" she asked implying that sulking was useless.

I shook my head no.

I could tell she felt a little awkward and speechless. Not really sure what to say so her next question pertained to one of our favorites, "you want to eat?"

Again I shook my head no.

"I'll cook," she offered in her chipper voice obviously trying to cheer me up.

I cut my eyes at her.

Disgustingly she asked, "What are you listening to?"

I clicked the remote to take the headset mode off and Patti Labelle, If You Ask Me Too blared in the air.

Sade looked at me as if I had lost my mind and yelled, "YUCK! Who listens to that? Who still has that? Matter of fact, who is that?"

She asked me so I gave it to her; my moto. Give the people what they want. I replied, "It is Patti Labelle." Then I went into a long discussion about the songs meaning and lyrics. I am sure it was information she was dying to know.

She looked puzzled and walked in the kitchen. After what seemed like forever and a lot of noise rattling she came back with two bowls of ice cream. Sorry, correction, two bowls of loaded ice cream. Whip cream, hardened chocolate, caramel, cherries, nuts, and the works. She sat mine next to me. I looked over at it and decided I couldn't let it go to waste. I had to share with her in my sorrow. It was what family and besties did. Therefore, I dug in.

The music was still blaring as we went through the playlist I had derived this morning. They were all old love songs made before Sade was even born. These were all the real love songs; the kind that made you depressed and made you say, "Ain't no way nobody can love like that."

"Auntie, if I was allowed to curse I would right about now and never stop," Sade said out of the blue.

"Why?" I asked confused.

"Because we have been calling you all day and you have not answered; that's why. I mean no response at all." Shaking her head she continued, "Auntie that shiggy ain't cool. I've been worried like hell. Now I got to sit over here on this beautiful day listening to this, this, this, ugh, noise coming from your iPod," she said with disgust. "Where did you get this stuff anyways?" she barked.

That did it. One thing was for sure, I was not going to sulk in misery and get cursed out by a child. I jumped up with no shoes on and handed her a club and headed towards the driving range. *No need in staring at it. Maybe if I hit a few rounds I will let off some steam.*

"Oh hell no! I'm not going out there!" she yelled. If we are going somewhere, let's go to the pool," she suggested.

Pointing to my hair, I said, "can't do, fresh do."

"Okay then let's go see Mikey," she said excitedly.

Frustrated I responded with, "UGGG!"

"Oh come on Auntie," she tried to soothe me with her words.

"Come on Sade," I said back sarcastically.

Sade knew how to win this one, "The only way I will come and hit with you is if I get your phones."

I threw my hands up. I knew how to pick my battles wisely. She ran to my bedroom and found them. One phone had a half-dead battery. By the time she made it to me I was sweating from hitting a few rounds. Little did I know she had responded to over half the texts while she was in the process of retrieving the phones. She had taken it upon herself to respond to Randall's text and the ones from the people at his gym. *That little snot.*

> Uncle Hooks. It's me Sade. Call me or text me when you can. Auntie Dee is not available.

I soon felt a little better after we hit a few rounds and finally ready to talk, "Hey, Sade?" I said to get her attention.

"Yes ma'am," she replied dryly and unamused. You could tell she was over my pitiful tail.

"You want Church's Fried Chicken?" I asked sweetly.

I knew Auntie was down if she was requesting that but I was not going to pass up the opportunity. "HELL YEAH!"

With more enthusiasm than I had for the last two days, I said, "alright, let's do it baby!"

We were headed to the car when Sade looked me up and down, apparently realizing how I looked she pointed at me then back to the front door and said, "negatory. You gonna go back inside and wash your face and take off them, them, them, them Daniel Green's. What age will I be allowed to curse?"

Looking down at myself I had to agree, "Oh yeah. I need to do something with myself. And as for age? NEVER MISSY!"

"A bra would be nice too," she called out to me as I headed back to the house.

"Really, okay! I'll meet you in the car," I said joyfully.

Timing couldn't have been more perfect. Just as I turned around to go back inside Randall texted.

> Is she okay?

> No! She is not. She is upset with you I think.

> Can you talk now?

> Not really we are about to go get Church's Fried Chicken.

> WHAT THE???

> Told you!

> What is wrong? He asked concerned.

> You haven't called.

> I do not think she realized it would be this difficult.

> You were only supposed to be gone for a day.

> I really can't call. They have me in boot camp. I texted and called her numerous times today when I could sneak and do it. She didn't respond.

> She has not looked at her phones since yesterday. I got them when I got here.

> I wasn't expecting them to keep me. I don't know when I will be home.

> I think reality has set in.

> Reality of what?

> That you are married and that she cares about you a lot.

It stabbed his heart. *Out of the mouths of babes.*

> Did she say that?

> No. But the fact that you haven't spoken to her is not what would push her to this limit. It has to be a combination of it all.

> What limit?

> Despondent.

He sat on the floor. King asked, "What's wrong?"

"Nothing," Hooks lied. "Can you track down Tre?" He waited before he responded back to Sade again.

> DK.

> Are you staying with her all night?

> Stay with her until I can call or write back please.

Sade was concerned that Danielle would bust her texting Randall back and forth.

> BTW, what was she doing a little while ago?

> Driving range.

Randall immediately thought, *she's knocking the cover off some balls. I should have known her levels were rising and dropping sporadically.*

> Stay by your phone and hers.

> HELP ME! I can't take another sad song.

> SORRY! So Sorry!

She came out and hoped in the Porsche. "Hey, let's do like we used to do," she said.

"When we were teenagers?" Sade asked.

"When I was a teenager and you were a toddler."

"We were teenagers together," Sade replied fiercely.

"You are right."

Sade smiled, "I love it when I am right. I am right all the time, but it is just getting you to admit it is the challenge."

"You make me sick," I teased.

"Let's eat in the car and ride?" she stated, or rather asked, hopeful.

"YEAH BABY!" I yelled. She knew that eating in the car was definitely off limits any other time.

Grinning from ear to ear and feeling a tad too excited, "Let's do it," she said enthusiastically.

"We getting a nine piece, okra, plenty of sweet cakes and a double order of jalapeno poppers."

"My treat," Sade added.

"Today is looking up already!" It was a shame that a box of free Church's Chicken was making me this excited.

"Auntie, you want to go to Mikey's tonight and hang out?" Sade asked.

"Umm maybe," I said. I really didn't want to. Saturday night was his biggest night and I wasn't sure if I wanted to be in the crowd. We ate and rode until we could not eat anymore. When we got back to the house Sade plopped on her favorite couch and me on mine. I laughed.

Curiously Sade asked, "What's so funny?"

"That was good and fun!" I said.

Sade retrieved the phones and asked, "You ready to start calling people back?"

With a blank expression, I replied, "Nope. Why would I want to do that? You can tell me who called."

She rattled off everyone including herself.

"Who texted?" I asked.

Sade read both texts and emails. Two texts stuck out to me. The texts from Mikey and Randall.

The one from Mikey she read, "Mami you stood me up today for the rough neck. I'm jealous."

"Text Mikey back and tell him I did not stand him up. The roughneck is traveling."

Mikey hit right back. Sade read, "Oh so you just stood Papi up?"

"OMG, really Mikey! Please respond to him no I did not."

Sade said, "he responded I'm crushed."

"Tell him you will always be my first love Papi."

Sade read back, "He replied. BS. BS. BS."

"Text back what does that mean?"

"He said, I knew you would get all booed up and forget about me," Sade laughed.

"I will deal with Mikey's jealousy later. Read the next one please." I instructed.

"It's from Randall," Sade said while looking over to check my reaction.

"Okay." I took a deep breath, closed my eyes, and expected the worst.

Sade began reading the text. "Hey. I hope you are doing fine. Thanks for your support. It means a lot to me. I am in boot camp. I will call you back or text when they allow me too."

She sighed. "He texted again four hours later. If you can, call me now, otherwise I will be back at it in ten minutes." She sighed again and said, "Auntie eleven minutes later he texted again. I miss you. Take care. He also called seven times Auntie." She looked back at me waiting for me to tell her what to say back to him, but I didn't respond.

Apparently I took too long to say anything so Sade took it upon herself to reply to his text.

> Can you talk now?

> No. Everything okay?

> Yeah, hit back when you can.

I still didn't say a word. Instead I got up off the couch, turned the corner in the hall, and asked, "Are you coming?"

"Coming where?" Sade asked in suspense.

"We are going to Mikey's."

"YAY!" she said with a lot of enthusiasm.

I got dressed and we headed out. When we arrived Mikey was not in his usual spot behind the bar. I walked behind the bar, unnoticed, and stood behind him while he gathered some spirits.

"What's this mess you are talking?" I asked.

He turned around surprised to see me standing there. Shrugging his shoulders he said, "I'm just saying."

I crossed my arms in front of me, "Saying what Mikey?"

"Don't act like you don't know," he said. "You stood me up."

Uncrossing my arms and looking down, I replied, "I've been home all day."

"Why didn't you answer? So unlike you," he asked with sincere concern.

Mikey was my good friend and knew me better than I knew myself half the time. He knew if I was not working or sick then I answered that phone; at the bare minimum I at least responded by a text. He also knew the only other reason I would not answer my calls was because I was hurt; more than likely by a man. A fighter man to be exact. Mikey had been down this road with me before and it wasn't an easy journey. I am sure he didn't want to go that route again with me, just as much as I didn't. You could both see and hear the emotions on his face. That was the reason I showed up tonight. I needed him to know that I was good. At least for now anyway.

Suddenly distracted, he yelled, "Sade get from behind my bar before I go to jail!"

"I'm making me a drink and Auntie a Danilicious," (Grapefruit juice, pomegranate juice and Cîroc) she replied.

"I was in a funk Michael," I replied still not looking up to meet his eyes.

"The champ dumped you?" he asked without emotion.

Finally looking up I said, "No."

Raising his eyebrows, he asked, "Why are you in a funk" Then his eyes got big and he whispered, "Wait a minute, are you knocked up?"

Playfully hitting at him, I said, "No Michael! He can't dump me because we can't date and we can't date because he is married." *There, I said it.* "So this is why I am in a supercalafragalistic funk."

"Is that all?" he asked as if he were irritated.

"Yes, that's all," I replied.

"Hell, I thought something was wrong with you," he said, as if this were just some minor issue. "And get Sade from behind my bar before I go bankrupt from the drinks she is making."

"Sade!" I yelled.

"Relax Auntie; I heard Uncle Mikey the first time. Your drink is on the bar and Uncle Mikey I opened you a Red Bull. Now if you don't mind, I am going to go flirt with my favorite DJ," she said while pointing over to the young handsome DJ. "I'll be in the booth if you need me. Auntie, you want your phones?"

"Naw, I'm good," I said before turning my attention back to the conversation I was having with Mikey.

"So you like him D?"

"Yeah. I do," I said with tears in my eyes.

"What's his wife's name?"

I thought it a little strange but I replied, "Tameka why?"

"We can make her disappear. Just say the word."

"Oh you goon!" I said and smiled at my protective friend.

"Okay, so what are you going to do?" he asked.

"You know me Mikey, I am going to work like hell to get him off my mind. What else?"

"So do you really think it will work?" he asked with skepticism.

"Yeah as long as I don't see him in church."

"You sure you don't want to see him?"

"I do but I can't Mikey," I said.

"Why not?" he asked.

"Michael, the man mesmerizes me."

"From the looks of it, apparently you mesmerize him too. Didn't this man land his personal helicopter on the roof of the building you work in? This sounds like a pretty woman ending to me. Only one problem though," Michael said and abruptly paused. "He is short a pretty woman."

"Mike!" I yelled.

He made himself laugh. "Instead he has my one and only beautiful sister."

"Aww, thanks Mike," I said.

"Now, tell me how you really feel," he said looking in my eyes.

He knows me too well, I thought. "Right now I feel like crap. I don't know what to do. It is hard to just be his friend and nothing more. Mike he makes me nervous! My hands sweat, I can't speak, my heartthrobs, butterflies in my stomach and I even get sweaty armpits. You name it, he does it. I feel like I am sixteen all over again," I said.

"Honey, newsflash. You were never sixteen. You have been grown and old your entire life. Just give him some. That would cure all of that nervousness and stuff you got going on. If it is good, he is a keeper. If it is bad, then no hard feelings."

"MIKE!" I yelled.

"Hell, give me some!" he yelled back.

I punched his arm.

Rubbing the spot where I socked him, he yelled, "Dang girl! You are too strong you need some testosterone."

"What am I going to do Mike? Real talk."

"Just be yourself. Do what is right. I have confidence that you can be in control of this situation. You can be his friend if you put your mind to it. Just be Danielle," he advised.

Shaking my head, I said, "I really like him Mikey."

"Dani, I think you love him." He laid his finger on the tip of my nose. "I think he likes you too. There is no reason for a handsome boxer to go after a little ole girl that is a fru fru tomboy on the inside; that builds buildings, but ain't giving him none. He could have been long gone, yet, here he is hanging around for a reason Danielle. If he was a hit it and quit it type guy you would know by now. Besides, I know you," he said. "If this man didn't have morals and values there is no way you would be hanging on the line. He could easily lie, build you up, feed you crap, but he has backed everything up. He has done nothing-wrong Danielle. If falling in love with you is wrong then he is guilty as charged. Otherwise, he is riding the waves just like you."

I did love him. This was the first time I really gave it thought. Mikey was the first person it was revealed to. He was right, and being true to myself; I confessed my feelings.

"No sulking at the bar. Let's have fun!" he said as he came from behind the bar. We danced and had a blast. He always knew how to cheer me up.

"Good night Mikey," I said. It was getting late and time for us to leave.

"Let me walk you out," he replied.

He walked us to the car. Just as we were saying our goodbyes a slight argument broke out at the entrance of the establishment.

"Gotta go," he said. "Text me when you get home." He kissed my forehead then walked over to the other side of the car and kissed Sade. "I love you girls."

"Love you too," we both said.

"Mikey works too much," Sade said as he walked off.

Agreeing, I replied, "Yeah, I know but he won't listen to me.

Sade looked me up and down and replied, "Ha! That's like the pot calling the kettle black, don't ya think?"

"No, I do not think so. He practically lives there, at least I go home," I rebuttal.

"That's only because you don't own the building. If you owned it you would have a suite and never go home either," she replied.

∙∙

My phone chirped indicating I had a message; possibly a picture. I could tell from the sound. "Who is it?" I asked.

"Randall."

"Open it," I said.

It took forever to load, but then out of nowhere, Brian McKnight began to sing. Find Myself In You. I got mushy instantly.

"Text back thanks. Please."

Instead she texted,

> We are leaving Mikey's she said thanks.

> Tell her hi and I miss her.

> Thanks.

> Can I call her?

> She said sure.

Immediately the phone rang. "Hold on Uncle Hooks," Sade said into the phone.

I covered the phone with my hand. "Stop calling him uncle. He is not your uncle."

"Shh. Not yet anyway," she said smartly.

I rolled my eyes. "Hello."

"Hey Danielle."

"Hi," I replied.

"I apologize for not being able to call you, however, I was not expecting them to keep me this long. It was supposed to be a meeting. I do not know if this is good or bad, but, now I get the feeling that it is bad between us."

I told him, "No," but nothing else.

He could tell something was bothering me, "Are you sure?" he asked.

"Yeah," I replied. I knew I was being very short.

"Would you tell me if you felt different?" he continued.

Once again, I answered, "Yeah." Anyone who really knew me understood these one-word answers were never a good thing and meant trouble.

"I think you feel different," he said.

"Nothing we need to discuss right now. What do they have you doing?" I asked cheerfully.

"I appreciate your concern but what is bothering you?" he asked me.

"Nothing is bothering me," I lied.

"Danielle, we have not deceived each other so far and I would appreciate it if we do not start now," His tone was stern and direct.

"Deceive is a harsh word," I replied. I didn't think I was the one being deceptive. I don't know what you would call it, but not deceptive.

"Please tell me what's bothering you," he nearly begged.

"I can't. Not right now Randall."

"Is it because Sade is there?"

"Mainly because you are there. It is nothing that can't wait until you return."

"This is extremely hard for me Danielle," he practically whispered.

"How so?" I asked.

"A few reasons," he replied.

You could hear someone in the background and then he yelled, "Give me a few more minutes," he paused and became focused back on our conversation.

"I am not supposed to be in contact with anyone," he said. "I am being disobedient by doing this. It is a disciplinary action that I am disobeying."

"Do not get in trouble," I replied sharply but flattered he would risk trouble for me.

"I don't want to but we really need to get an understanding first. Returning to the ring is hard for me. Sometimes I'm torn with the thoughts of what's expected. I am not sure how people will react or what their expectations are? Returning to a life that includes dating is new to me as well. I know it might be strange, but I have never really courted. Tameka and I were boyfriend and girlfriend and then suddenly became parents and married. We never really dated. I know that the day will come when I will have to start to do that and it is scary to be this old and have your first real date. It is scary to be your friend and just your friend only. Believe me, I feel as horrible as you do. It is hard to admit this, but right now is the first time in my adult life that I want to; just for a moment, cut myself off from God and do the worldly things my mind and heart has been telling me to do. But I can't. It is a hard fight against flesh, but even harder fighting against God's principles. If you feel the way I do, and something tells me that you do, that you are fighting against the same force and higher authority as I am."

"I'm sorry I haven't called you D, but they will not allow it. They do not want me distracted in any way. But as I stated, I am new to this. I am not clear on the rules and expectations of dating or being friends for that matter. I have never been given any instructions and haven't had any. Other than instructions for my son, the only other instructions I have ever given was for you to text me when you get home. I can and will conform if you just give me a chance though. This may be rude and I know I am over my limit on asking you to be patient with me, but please, let me finish one thing at a time. Let me get thru this and then I can work on the next problem." he paused, "All I can say is I'm sorry. I'm so sorry."

I did not respond.

"You there?" he asked.

"Yes."

"I can't promise but I am going to try to call you back later. I don't want to make a promise to you that I can't keep. The only person I can openly call is Pastor."

"I met with him yesterday. AGAIN! Do what you can," I said frustrated.

"I am not feeling good about the way our conversation is ending," he admitted. He was concerned as to why she met with Tre. Tre did not mention one word of it when he spoke to him earlier.

"Don't be. I am not trying to upset or distract you. Please do not let me do so. I would feel like crap. We will get all of this resolved once you are back. It's all good. I promise," I said, trying to reassure him.

"D, I know you well enough to know you are not telling the truth," he replied. "You are not a good liar."

"I know you have to run." I wanted the conversation to change or end.

"What are you wearing to church tomorrow?" he asked changing the subject. She was blowing him off and he knew it. Something was clearly wrong and as much as he wanted to discuss it and clear the air, his time would not allow it. This was the very reason they didn't allow him to use the phone. Because now he was distracted. His thoughts were going to be on what was wrong with her.

"I do not think I am going," I said.

"WHY?" That was unusual for her.

He said it so loud I moved the phone from my ear. "I have been out late and I think I just might catch it on streaming faith."

"The devil is a liar," he proclaimed.

"WOOWW!"

"Don't miss church because of me," he demanded firmly.

"Oh no. It is not because of you," I lied.

"So what are you wearing?" he asked again.

Sade's phone rang out that she was receiving a text. She quickly responded to the text.

"I really want to keep talking but they are going to break down this door if I don't come out. Good night my love. Relax and be blessed," he said. "We will get all of this cleared up. Don't trouble your heart and let not the sun go down on your wrath," he said calmly.

"I am not troubled and neither angry. Good night Randall. Stay focused. Most of all keep your head up. I have the faith and confidence that you can do this. You are an excellent fighter and I know you can do whatever you set your mind to and whatever your hearts desires."

"Thanks Danielle. I need your support desperately. It's the only way, other than the Grace of God, that I can make it," he said with all sincerity.

"Good night Randall."

"Until we meet again," he said then clicked the line.

Unbeknown to me, he was texting Sade.

> Make sure she is in church tomorrow. I need to know what she is wearing and I need to get my thoughts together. Stay by your phone. I only have four suits with me. Gray, black, navy and brown. She needs to wear something to match one of those colors.

> What are you saying Uncle Hooks?

> Lay her clothes out. Let me finish this next training session. I will get my thoughts together.

He opened the door and exited the bathroom. He shoved the phone in King's chest when the door opened.

"What?" King asked concerned.

"Don't give it to me again. Get Vickie on the line," he demanded.

King couldn't believe what he was hearing, "Now?" he asked in disbelief.

"Yeah, right now. I need to make arrangements," Hooks said.

"Man, you and this damn girl are going to be the death of me. I do not want any mess from you Randall." King warned as his blood pressure rose.

King never called him Randall so this was serious. "I am getting it under control."

"I knew this was going to be a bad idea," he mumbled more to himself than anything else

"What?" Randall asked.

"You getting involved with a chick," King replied heated.

She wasn't just a chick to him and he kind of resented King for saying that; although he clearly understood why he said it. Randall knew his actions affected him. If his game was off; so was King's day. It meant King had to work harder.

• •

"Auntie, what time we got to get up?" Sade asked trying not to sound too suspicious.

"I think I am going to play hooky," I said.

"No we ain't," Sade said. "Let me help you find something." She hadn't been given much from Randall to work with, but she was going to try to make it work. She found a red, black, and gray suit. She took a picture of it and sent it to him and said to Dani, "How about this?"

I told her, "I don't want to wear it," but then I remember a pair of red shoes I had and decided it would be okay since I hadn't spent a lot of time planning.

Sade set the clocks on her phones to ensure they didn't miss church. *Auntie did not sound too convincing that she was going.* At ten after one, just as Sade laid down, a text came in from Hooks.

Okay. That will be fine, it stated. Do not leave church tomorrow until you have gotten a message from me. I do not know who will deliver it

Okay

For some reason I wasn't sleepy. Sade had passed out on me a while ago. Seeing her laid out like this reminded me of when she was a little girl and I had worn her out. I keep telling her that she is still a little girl and can't run with the big dawg, but she continues to try and keep up. I smile. We didn't do much for her to be asleep already. *I might as well make myself useful,* I thought. I decide to prepare something for dinner tomorrow, presuming it is my Sunday to cook. I looked through the pantry for ingredients and thought; *I should have been doing this all day instead of trying to prepare a menu at two in the morning.* Lack of sleep pumps my adrenaline harder. *I swear I could live like this forever. Let a sister get a three-hour nap in the middle of the day, every day, a few nice cups of coffee and I am good. A little Siesta is all I need. Speaking of which, I haven't left the country in a minute. As soon as I get everything going an internet search for a European trip is next on the list.*

I looked at the suits Sade pulled out for me to wear tomorrow. I am not fond of the black and red at all. *Why did I even buy it? It must have been on sale. UGH! The stupid stuff you waste money on. I am not wearing that.* I pulled out something else and hooked it up. I returned to the kitchen to finish preparing my Sunday dinner and logged online in the process. While surfing the net, I couldn't help but to check out the sports news. There was a nice picture of Randall running down the strip in Vegas. The headline read: The Champ is back!

Hmm. I thought. I read the story below. It was all speculation. They assumed he was back since he met with the commissioner and the fact that he showed no signs of vacationing. He was with his trainers, so why else would he be there if he were not preparing to fight again? They had not seen him outside the hotel other than to run and all of those shots were at night. *Really? Is it ever night in Vegas? I think not, the sun just goes down.* Then I thought of how much I loved Vegas. I love everything about it; the lights, the noise, the shows, the people and the fun. I sighed, wishing I were there. You have got to be disciplined to live in a city like that. People say the same about the ATL; however, we do find time to sleep, unlike New York and Vegas. Let me rephrase that; the city sleeps; Randall, Paige and I are always up on duty. I mean really, if there was a clock tower in the square we would be on duty daily. Medically it's not really a good thing to not sleep. I have wondered from time to time if Paige knows when she stopped sleeping. Randall may say it was when his wife left. I too can blame it on when the ex and I split, but I think it was before then; maybe even a year before. I was probably too busy getting my mind right to rest peacefully.

To tell you the truth I don't miss sleep. Yes, I should certainly do better and I am sure somewhere, somehow, my body requires a good night's sleep. I continued to surf and check my pots. My mind drifted to the outfit I had just laid out to wear to church and it dawned on me that I might hurt Sade's feelings if I don't wear what she picked out. So I went back to the closet, looked at the outfit she had chosen and thought about how I could make myself like it? *Hey, I have a hat that will slam this. Let me run that.* I took the hat out of its box and I realized it was red, black, and gray. *I know exactly what I will do as a quick fix.* It was three o'clock in the morning when I raced to my hobby room and turned on the glue gun. I was dangerous with a glue gun; most women were. As I rambled through a few decorative boxes, I found exactly what I needed. Fifteen minutes later I had a red, gray, and black Shirley Franklin blinged out accessory. I debated with the hat. I knew it was slamming but felt like it needed to really be tricked out too, but I opted not. I figured that the suit is boring so it'll be best if I leave the hat simple too. *Who put this suit together?* I really did not like it; however, I knew my shoes and hat would make it work. I laid out my favorite rubies and decided to change my bag to a small clutch. Something told me not to do that, so I listened. It seems that every time I use the smaller clutch I end up needing something out of my normal luggage; also known as my handbag. *Since Randall won't be there I can carry my big bag with all my junk,* I thought.

Finally after forcing myself to lie down, I still could not make myself sleep. I do not think I even closed my eyes. Everything was prepared for sleep. The room was dark, quiet, but my body would not shut down long enough to relax and sleep. I wanted to call him so badly. Instead I opted for an email. It was the least I could do to encourage him. Besides, the time there was three hours behind us so I was sure he would be awake. I was going to support him in this endeavor; however, I was pulling back emotionally.

Hey, it's late, I know. I just wanted to tell you good night and that I believe in you. I think you are the Champ and always will be. I am sure they will see that too. I pray their decision is in your favor. Ignore the media. They are a pain but know they are happy and excited for you too. God Bless. I am praying for your strength, endurance and will to fight. Good night my love, Rose.

Signing as Rose made me think of my father. I never did anything personal as Rose. Only business related. It was odd to me that I did it tonight.

• •

Randall was up as well, busy making plans for tomorrow. He heard his phone chirp, but dared not to ask King if he could see it. King had already bent over backwards today to help him and this was just the beginning. King did not break the rules today because Randall was his boss, but rather because he knew Randall never asked for much that was of personal gain. He was actually happy to do it for him; normally it had always been the other way around. Randall was always doing for him and others. If allowing him to use the phone was all he asked, then what the hell. Besides, he had not known Hooks to want to go against the grain and break a rule; ever. For as long as he could remember, Hooks didn't break a rule for anything and especially not for a woman. He knew that Hooks was interested in Danielle and he really hoped she felt the same. Danielle had not only changed his fighter, but his boss and his friend. They had been together since college years. Both of the men had participated in the sport, but King wanted more of bodybuilding than fighting. He was a muscle man and so he was great at keeping Hooks right at whatever weight class he needed to be in. Like magic, he could take him down to one thirty five or up to one hundred and seventy. All Randall had to do was say the word. He was gifted like that. He knew in his heart that if his fighter was going to fight he needed his dose. Most fighters used some form of something; fortunate and unfortunately, Hooks' dose came on a stem in the form of a Rose. Danielle Rose. King was going to need her help desperately to pull this off though; at least the first battle. Once he got his confidence up he may be fine and then again maybe not. He could surely see a difference in him. And tonight what he was asking was not absolutely unacceptable. Therefore, King agreed this one time and no more exceptions until we get a yes you can fight. He knew that she was not aware of what was going on and probably needed to know. That is why he allowed it. No, he was not the boss. But Hooks knew he needed King and; therefore, he abided by his rules. This was the first time ever he had gone against them. Even when he didn't like the rules he never went against them.

He thought to himself, *it must not be urgent if he hasn't said anything. Guess I'll just have to wait until day light to see who it is. I hope it is Danielle. Who else would call or text me at this hour? Tre? If it were him he would have given me the phone.* He prayed and went to sleep for the night. Tomorrow was turning out to be a much bigger day than he had originally planned.

Sunday

Sade woke up and felt a little discombobulated. She asked, "Tee, why you let me sleep on that couch all night girl?"

"You looked so peaceful, like a little sweet angel. I couldn't bring myself to wake you," I answered.

The scent hit her, "What is that smell?" she asked curiously.

Smiling, I said, "It's our dinner."

"Oh we having some of that before we go to church?" Sade stated.

"Now?"

"Yeah now," she replied ready to dive into the delicious food Dani had prepared.

"No I can't."

"Humph," she said. "The devil is a liar. You had Church's last night. Let's do it."

"Girl, I am not messing with you. I am getting dressed. What about a vegetarian sausage?" I suggested.

"Oh no, that sounds right up your alley, but no thanks for me. What a wonderful offer though, it is so hard to refuse," she said under her breath. "What is the purpose of vegetarian sausage anyways?"

"Hush! If that is the case I'm having a protein shake," I replied strongly.

Throwing her hands up, she said, "Now that's out of the ordinary and living on the wild side."

"When will you be going away?" I asked.

"Sorry Auntie, looks like you're stuck with me."

"That's what I was afraid of." We got dressed and headed to the garage. "Sade can you drive me?" I asked.

"Oh Auntie! Why?"

"I need to look at some things," I replied.

"I will read you the Vegas headlines if you drive," she barked back. "Can you give the news and work a break for thirty minutes? I mean really, nothing has changed this early in Vegas." We pull up to the church and I grab my hat. "When did you pull that out?" she asked. She hadn't noticed the hat when we were leaving the house.

"While sleeping beauty was knocked out. By the way, you need to stay at home if you are going to pass out on me," I said.

"Ain't no need in us both being up. God had everything under control while I rested."

Agreeing I said, "You are right he neither sleeps nor slumbers."

"So what do you and your sister do?" she asked sarcastically. Reminding me that neither of us sleeps much.

"We kind of keep Him company every night," I replied hesitantly.

"Him, as in God? Like he really needs that. You two should be like super-sheroes. At least go fight some crime or something if you are going to stay up all night." she laughed.

"Maybe we do."

"Well, one thing is for sure, one of you could not keep it a secret, and the other is so far gone until it wouldn't be a secret."

"I do not know what you are referring to," I said as I rolled my eyes at her. We walked in and took our seats.

Moving in closer to me she whispered, "This is too early for anyone to digest anything."

"Let me remind you that you were the one that volunteered to come to church this early," I replied.

Sade thought to herself, *note to self; I will need to have a word with Uncle Hooks about this.*

Service began and just as Pastor Hunter had finished his prayer and we sat down, I noticed there was a gentleman standing in the isle that I swear was not there when I closed my eyes. I wanted to look back at him, but I did not. He waited a few more seconds and I could see his feet move. He squatted down next to me and my heart started to pound harder.

"Can you please come with me Ms. Rose?" he asked quietly.

Not sure what was going on, I asked, "Now?"

"Yes, ma'am now," he replied in a tone that suggested urgency.

I was uneasy and a little shocked. I felt as though something bad was about to happen. I leaned over to Sade and said, "If I am not back in eight minutes come looking for me." Then I thought *we are not in the club. Who would come and get someone in the presence of hundreds of thousands of people and take them somewhere and hurt them.* My mind wondered further as I thought of MLK and JFK and said under my breath, "Well it is possible." I felt like I needed to have my blade on me. I stood up to leave.

"Grab you things," he instructed.

I nodded in Sade's direction, "She is going to be here with them," I said.

"She is coming too," he replied.

I thought to myself, *Oh hell naw, what in the world is going on?* I whispered, "You are coming too." It came out a little louder than I expected. *So much for whispering.* I made sure to make eye contact with Pastor Hunter. I wanted him to see I was leaving with a stranger just in case something popped off.

"Looks like we are both going down together," Sade said in a comforting tone.

As soon as I exited the sanctuary doors and entered the vestibule, I looked up and saw who I thought was Randall. As I got closer, I realized it was him! I had to do a double take.

Sade said surprised, "What the…"

I stopped her before she could go any further. "Watch it! We are in church young lady," I barked. I was so confused at this point.

"Aww, a man after my own heart," she said. "What else can you say?"

I stood there right in front of him. We stared at each other for what seemed like forever, but no words were spoken. Someone removed the bag off my shoulder. I could have cried right there at that moment. I just stood there speechless. As it always happened in the presence of Randall, my sweat glands kicked in. I was glad I was sweating out a suit I didn't like. Then I noticed that he was wearing a black suit, gray vest with a red, gray, and black tie. I looked back at Sade and she returned a guilty as charged look. I smirked.

"I didn't know David Copperfield was going to show up?" she said condescendingly.

I rolled my eyes at her.

He grabbed my arm. "Excuse me," he said. "Does anyone mind if I have a moment alone with Ms. Rose?"

I know I told him not to call me that. He held my hand as we walked down the long corridor. Our fingers were interlocked. I had yet to speak. Once we got all the way to the other end he spoke, "Good morning."

"Good morning." I replied hesitantly. *OMG, he looked great*, I thought.

"I am sorry to interrupt your worship. I held out as long as possible and I really didn't want Pastor to get started. I knew your attention would be taken," he said.

I didn't respond.

"This is how much you mean to me and don't you ever forget it. I am glad you did not embarrass me and stay home today."

I could have fainted right then and there, but instead I tried to play hard and I folded my arms.

"Say something. Anything," he said.

Out of the corner of my eye, I could see King approaching the end of the corridor making sure we were in his sight. Either my heels were extremely high or he was closer to my height than I realized. I couldn't resist. I reached over and hugged him so tight and abruptly until he nearly lost his balance; he had to take his hand out of his pocket to get it together. He then placed his arms around my waist. Although he felt smaller and appeared shorter, he was definitely stronger.

"Why are you doing this?" I whispered in his ear.

Smiling, he said, "The same way you would do things at work for clients that may seem like a loss in order to gain their trust, confidence and business is the same thing I am doing in this relationship. I want to gain your confidence now. No matter where I am, what I am doing or what my situation is, I promise, I will always make you a priority from now on. I am gaining your trust and respect and when the time is right I will not have to earn it."

"You really did not have to do this." I leaned up against the wall so forcefully until I knocked my breath out. I felt as if I was in a trance. I could not believe he had done this. It was amazing; he was amazing. His efforts will not go unnoted and unnoticed.

"I didn't feel like we had a good conversation last night," he continued. "I needed to see you face to face to get this resolved," he said.

"You need to be worried about you and not about me right now Randall."

Putting my hand up to his face he said, "You are my worry. You are my main interest and concern."

"Randall you can't just hop on a jet and land helicopters every time you and I have a conversation you don't like," I said.

With raised eyebrows he said, "Says who? I can if I choose to."

Shaking my head, I replied, "Not the right answer mister. You still have rules you must adhere to."

"Lately, I have broken all of my own rules and even some from the Master," he said, looking over in his friend's direction. "I apologize for this. I'm sure King will probably never let me live this one down. Not only have I broken the rules, but I have flat out defied them."

"What makes you think it warrants this or is worth it?" I asked.

"You let me be the judge of that," he said.

"Where do they think you are?" I asked with concern.

"Where am I?" he answered my question with a question.

"At church."

"Oh well, there you have it," he smirked.

"You told them you were going to church?" I asked surprised.

"Am I not at church?"

"Well yeah, technically you are. But two thousand miles away?"

He smiled, "I didn't tell them what church I was going too."

"Omission is also a lie," I corrected him.

"I did not omit. They didn't ask. I will make a mental note not to omit in the future."

"This is ridiculous. You are out of control. You know that?" I said.

"I hope you are getting my point."

"Which is?" I asked coyly.

"I really should not have to say it. I have gone through a lot of work, organization, and people's time to be here this morning. Not to mention we are headed right back," he said.

"Randall you can't just fly across the country to make a point." I laughed an I don't get it kind of laugh.

"Oh I am sure I will hear it from Hunter. Be prepared, we may be subject to a lie detector test upon my return," he joked.

"You never answered my question," I said. "Was all of this worth it and why you are doing this?" I asked again.

"Rolls Royce has no intention on building me a half a million dollar car until I show a sincere interest and leave a deposit. Then they will build the car upon my specifications and specified time. Unfortunately, you are the same way Danielle," he explained. "You are not going to give me the time of day until I show some sincere interest."

"I think you are looking at the big scheme of this improperly. Right now you have no time to worry about what I think, how I feel or if I am accepting of your career etc. None of this is really up for discussion. You need to be focused on Randall so he can focus on Hooks. Don't worry about Danielle, she will be fine. I assure you, she will be here after you get Hooks cleared. I must say though, I am impressed. I think you have an inkling as to how I feel. Sure, you and I both know there is some unfinished business that stands in between us like a brick wall; a hundred foot tall brick wall I might add. If I told you how I feel right now it would be extremely inappropriate and totally unacceptable. Besides, all of that, I feel like I am being stalked."

He smiled. He loved the way she separated him into three people. She made it seem as if he had multiple personalities. In all honesty, he did. He was three different people at any given moment; Randall, Hooks and Deacon Washington. He had never himself thought of it like this, but it was true. None of those people ever collided to make one complete person however. Hooks was a total different breed from Randall. *Thank God*, he thought. Deacon Washington, on the other hand, had none of their qualities; he was his own person too. This gave him food for thought. *Do these people need to become one? Is this acceptable that they are three different people or is it beneficial?* Right then, although she had no clue, she had just ministered to his soul. He would have weeks of mental thoughts while training trying to understand these three men inside of him. If she had never said another word to him again, she had said a mouth full. He now understood part of her purpose in his life. It actually began the moment he met her. She inspired him to do things in just four short months that he needed to do four years ago. The reality that sometimes we do not move to the next step until we have no choice stared him in the face. She gave him no choice. As the old cliché goes, it was either piss or get off the pot. He had held the pot down long enough and he knew that he would be forever grateful for her. His mind could not wrap around a word quick enough to describe this moment. Epiphany. Yes, that was the only word that could describe what had just transpired. He knew no matter the cost, this trip was well worth the double digit thousands he spent, the restless night and the future roasting it was sure to bring.

I began to get a little concerned that he hadn't spoken in what seemed like ten minutes. I could tell he was embedded in thought. Touching his face, I asked, "Are you okay?"

"Yeah. I'm sorry. Something just came to my mind. I came here to say, I feel the same way D. I really needed to see you and make sure you understand the challenge I am faced with right now. I have a lot I want to share with you when the time is right. Everything is going so fast until I can't get it all together. I never expected that the girl who didn't want to park in the grass would have me flying a plane two thousand miles to see her for eighteen minutes." he laughed. "I tell you, God can change your life instantly. Just like that," he snapped his fingers. "I am a witness."

"So what do we do now?" I asked.

"Well, I'll jump back in a helicopter and fly back to Vegas to keep training. I'll listen to my crew dog me for this for the remainder of my life and pray that they do something that will get the attention off me. I'll also pray that God has favor upon me and Trevor does not find out I have landed a helicopter on his house of worship. I am sure I will never live this down."

"No, I don't think you will either," I agreed. "Actually, I think they taped it from the conversation I can hear." There was a crew standing not far from us and I could hear them speaking.

Randall stood in front of me looking puzzled. "How do you do that?"

I shrugged my shoulders, "I do not know. Who knows? Probably some kind of experiment my father did while my mother was pregnant or when I was a newborn which caused me to generate this animal hearing," I said shaking my head not understanding it myself.

"What are they saying?" he whispered.

"It was taped from the surveillance on the top of the building as you came in. They are planning to take a video crew up there on your way out," I replied.

His eyes got big, "Oh really?"

"Really," I confirmed.

"Seriously?" he stated more than questioned. "Grab Sade, let's go." He pulled out his phone as I turned back. He then motioned one minute. "I am calling the pilot," he said.

I returned with Sade.

"You two are flying to the airport with me," he ordered.

Sade did not hesitate, "If I go I am going all the way to Vegas. You will not leave me at Charlie Brown."

"We are not going to CB. We are going to DeKalb. You have no clothes," he informed her.

"Oh no, the devil is a liar. Give me one second to get my bag out of the trunk. Auntie said there would be days like this." She was excited and ready to go at the drop of a dime.

He looked at me. "Oh Auntie did? Days like what?" he asked looking directly at me.

"Girl stuff," I replied with a sly smile.

"Not a problem. You are still staying here with her." He leaned down in my ear and said, "I think I may be gone another week." I didn't expect that. "Once they make their decision I should not have to leave unannounced like this again. You will know personally from me before anything is ever announced publically."

I heard the keyboard playing which meant Hunter might be wrapping up.

He ran. "Let's go before Trevor shuts us down. I knew he would cut it short. No doubt, my phone will ring in ten minutes."

We all hopped in and I had no clue how I was getting back. This surprise visit was like an icebreaker for everyone. The twenty-minute flight was so much fun; we laughed nearly the entire time. King told me what I needed to help him do as Randall told Sade what he needed for her to do, and Hooks told all of us to let him do what he does. Just as he predicted, sure enough, his phone rang. He answered on speaker and pointed at Sade.

"Hooks Gym," she said professionally.

"I have no clue who this is, but I know there was not a helicopter on top of my church."

"I'm sorry Pastor," Sade said innocently.

"You are sorry it was there?" he asked.

"No, I am sorry I don't follow you," she replied as if she had no clue what he was referring to.

He sighed really hard. We couldn't help but to burst out laughing.

"Randall DeWayne Washington, land it on my roof again! Try me boy!" Hunter yelled in a fatherly tone.

"Pastor, it is technically not a roof. It is a landing pad," I corrected.

"DANIELLE! Don't speak to me in that sarcastic tone after you walked out of church!" he barked.

"Tre she is right. I wanted to make sure it works." Randall backed her up.

"Beloved." Hunter said ever so calmly. No one said a word. "Beloved," he repeated.

We looked at Sade to prompt her to reply, "Yes sir?"

"Do not let them corrupt you with their nonsense," he said.

"Tre, I am almost at the airport. I will call you once I change aircrafts."

"Why didn't you wait to take me with you?" he scolded.

"Umm, you didn't have a bag," he said while looking at Sade.

"I keep a bag with me." Trevor informed him.

"What is up with all you nomads? Jesus said bring nothing," he laughed.

"Yeah, yeah, yeah. I know what Jesus said. You have some explaining to do." Pastor reminded him.

I widen my eyes and mouthed, "Uh oh."

"You too Ms. Rose," he added.

I moved my lips to say, "SHOOT!"

"Hey boy," Hunter said.

"Yeah!" Randall replied sharp and disrespectfully.

"Run it. Make us proud. Redeem yourself for landing on my roof. Oh, pardon me, I meant landing pad Ms. Danielle." It was encouragement even during chastising.

"Thanks man!" Randall replied. As the chopper landed and touched the ground, we grabbed hands to pray. "Pastor we have touched down. Can you cover us in prayer?" We bowed our heads and Pastor prayed. When we finished the prayer Randall said, "Hold on Tre." He gave Sade a nuggie and kissed my forehead and said, "Love you girl." He looked over to the pilot and said, "Get them back to the church." He literally ran away before Sade and I could grasp the adventure. He looked back at us, got in the plane, and was rolling down the runway in the blink of an eye.

We looked at each other and laughed like two fifteen year olds. "How are we getting back to the car?"

The pilot replied, "Do you want land or air?"

We were already strapped in. "AIR!" we said at the same time.

We rode in silence during the flight back. I texted and emailed while she made calls to fill in Paige, Leigh and the rest of her crew about what just took place. As we approached the roof, I was deep in thought. I heard the pilot calling for someone to be back on the roof.

"DAMN!"

Catching her off guard she asked, "What's wrong Auntie?"

The look on my face said it all. "I get to face Pastor first."

"Oh crap! We in tro-oouble!" Sade said putting her hands to her face and opening her mouth wide in an exaggerated expression like the young actor back in the day, Macaulay Culkin in Home Alone.

"Maybe we can sneak by him," I said, not sounding too convincing.

"Yeah right." she laughed vetoing my idea.

"Can you land us at Burger King?" I asked.

"Sure thing," he said as he touched down on the roof avoiding my serious request. He did not understand the nature of the problem I was challenged with.

Sade and I looked like we were going into a haunted house as one of the Deacons helped us out of the chopper.

"Nice ride?" he asked like we had been to Six Flags or something.

"Smooth flight," I responded.

"Good company?" he smiled; or maybe he was holding in a laugh.

I cut my eyes. Where was he going with this? No sooner than the other Deacon opened the door to the roof, guess who stepped out? Pastor Hunter.

"Ms. Rose," he greeted.

"Pastor," I nodded as if nothing had taken place.

"Do we need to talk?" he asked.

"Yes we do." I said quickly. "Your Deacon is so out of line."

"My Deacon?" he asked astonished.

"Umm yes, your Deacon. Who in God's name would land a freaking helicopter on the roof of a church during service? Now that is just flat out rude. I am sure you are going to have a word with him and I would suggest you do so." I said trying to sound serious.

He shakes his head and laughs, "I just spoke to him," he said.

"Did you let him know that he is a stalker?" I asked.

"No, but what I did let him know is that he was not doing what we discussed. You can't do what we discussed if he won't do his part," he replied.

"BEEP, BEEP, BEEP! News Flash. Crazy, Stalking Deacon Alert." I said.

"That is not what I said."

"Pastor, you said look at the signs. Run if they are crazy." I started running in place really fast and he started laughing so hard until he was bent over. I was not about to get a lecture today about Randall's behavior. Forget that; I quickly switched it up. "You need to talk to your boy. Tell the truth, he is a stalker isn't he?"

"I am going to try to fly up there tomorrow and get his head right. Are you going?" he snidely asked.

"Going where?"

"To Vegas," he said.

"Pastor you are trying me," I replied.

"So are you?" he asked again without hesitation.

I stopped dead in my tracks and said, "No! Keep trying me Pastor." I threatened.

"Yes ma'am. I'll take that as a no!" he taunted.

"Is there a law against punching a Pastor?" I asked.

They all yell, "NO!"

He yells, "SECURITY!"

"Un huh, yeah, yeah get your boys. This might not be what you want!" I joked.

One of the security guys yell, "SWAT vs. SWAT!" Referring to the fact that we were both from Southwest Atlanta.

"You know how we do it," Pastor said. "We are still being recorded."

Sade said, "Auntie, I got you boo. Mighty funny Pastor talking trash now Hooks gone."

"What are you talking about? I taught the boy all he knows, so what is he gone do?" we laughed. Then he straightened up. "Do we need to talk?" he repeated again seriously as if I was going to change my mind.

"Don't know," I said.

Looking me in the eyes he said, "You know."

"If you want, but I didn't do anything," I said proudly.

Throwing his hands up in the air, he said, "Y'all make me work too hard. Both of y'all stubborn and hardheaded. I can't deal with this."

I pump my arm, "YEAH!"

"That did it. Get in my office! Why are you laughing?" he said to Sade, "You are coming too. Ring leader."

"Gheez Louise," I said. I couldn't get a break.

There I was, once again, in the principal's office. This time the culprit was in the air texting me every second.

"Excuse me," he said as he pulled out his cell phone and dialed on speaker.

"What's up?" Randall's voice came over.

"Don't you call her again," and he hung up. His phone rang immediately right back and he answered on speaker. "Yes son!"

"I'm not calling her. I'm TEXTING!" He hung up.

"Why me Lord?" he held up his hands.

I quoted Psalm 121, "Look to the hills which cometh your help. Your help comes from the Lord."

He stopped in motion. He opened his mouth, shut it, and opened it again. He laid his head down on the desk. Without looking he slid his finger across his phone and dialed another number.

"Hello," a sweet voice rang.

"Hey baby. This is going to take longer than I thought," he said dismayed.

"Everything all right?" The sweet voice on the other line said.

"No, I am dealing with Randy; and Danielle is just as bad as he is."

"I love you." she laughed.

"Pray for me." he pleaded.

"See you soon. Tell RW to behave," she said before hanging up the line.

When he hung up the phone he took an unusually long time to gather his thoughts. He lifted his head and began to speak but nothing flowed from his lips. He propped one elbow on the desk and pointed his finger with the other hand. Not once, not twice but repeatedly. I did not think he was being rude or mean but rather couldn't find the right words or wanted to make sure they came out right. I was used to this type of reaction. Mama, Paige, every teacher and anyone in between had given me this same reaction at some point in my life, my entire life.

Finally, he spoke. His finger stretched directly at me. "Don't ever let anyone make you sacrifice what's in this book." He held up his Bible. "Anyone! Never! Not even RW, beloved. You stand on these grounds and principles. Your obedience will pay off. Don't you waiver. Be like a tree planted by the rivers of water. Don't grow weary in well doing. God will see it and reward you if you faint not."

He was speechless. This was a strange situation, even for him, a pastor that has heard almost any and every type of scenario from all types of people. He had to strengthen me to do right and to chasten his friend. Either way it went, at the end of the day, friend or no friend, he had to shepherd his people. He could not stand by and ignore this. Correction, he was NOT going to ignore this.

"Beloved," he continued. "You tell Deacon Washington that he is your FRIEND ONLY! That is all he will be. If he is interested in being more than your friend then he needs to call you once he has a status change. Until then you are available and interviewing. Don't miss your Mr. Right waiting on Mr. Hooks. Now I know he is charming, humble, nice, caring, and a man of God. You may even think he is talented and handsome, but that is beside the point. Either way it goes, he is not available, but you are. You were doing so well. You ran so well. Don't let this helicopter thing distract you. Now he on the other hand is going to regret this MacGyver stunt after I finish with him." He mumbled, "Show off."

"I'll handle him tomorrow. I am going to tell him; not ask but tell him, to leave you alone! You don't want to be bothered with a married boxer," he warned.

My eyebrows rose. Was he now my spokesperson?

"Was that too harsh?" he asked.

"I do believe so Pastor," I said, trying to swallow the lump in my throat.

When Sade and I finally got in the car, we realized the time and how hungry we were. The Sirius station played Keyshia Cole and Monica's song, Trust. *How appropriate*, I thought to myself. I was hoping she didn't mention it, but so much for that. Sade turned the volume up and said, "They're singing y'alls song." *Children*, I thought. I was glad I was never one. I didn't respond. We got to the house and could not wait for the other two to arrive before we prepared our plates and dug in.

True to form, Sade spilled the beans via text before they arrived. Now, MacGyver was being called 007. You had to both love and hate your friends and family sometimes. I really did not have time to marinade on his guest appearance right now anyways. I was busy reflecting on what Pastor Hunter said or more so remembering that finger pointing, and pointing, and pointing. I could not concentrate when he called or texted. *How did I always manage to get wedged between a rock and a hard place?* I asked myself.

I was really feeling some type of way. I wanted them to leave on one hand so I could concentrate, but I also needed them to keep my mind preoccupied on the other hand. Surely if they were not there and I was left in silence, it was destined to lead to yet another sleepless night. Lord knows, the last thing I ever need is an intentional sleepless night, but so much for that. It was another wakeful night in Daniville.

WEEK 15

Monday

He had given me a set of rather strict instructions on what I was requested to do the next day. I wasn't sure if Hunter would approve or not and I was just at the point of calling the church to speak to him when it blared over my speakers and the television in my office.

"It appears that Hooks' longtime friend and Pastor from his home church in Atlanta, Georgia has arrived. Pastor Hunter is the Senior Pastor of Victory Hope Greater Faith Christian Church, the Southside's fastest and largest growing church. It's been said that Hunter's goal is to be one church in multiple locations where they are not only making members, but also turning them into disciples. Hunter is moving rapidly through the collaboration of reporters and photographers that have camped here around the clock waiting on a word from the Champ or the Association as to why the Champ is here. From a glance, Pastor Trevor Hunter looks as if he is the star at the moment. His stature is much more buffed than it was four years ago when he personally led Hooks to the ring to what we now know as, "The Last Fight." He has just as many if not more body guards than Hooks travels with."

"With this appearance it is almost certain a statement will be made. Knowing Randall Hooks Washington as we remember him and his strong faith, he will not make such a decision until it has been carefully prayed over. I'd say this gives us just that much more clarification. Daniel Rice reporting to you live from the MGM Grand in Las Vegas, Nevada."

Well that settles me calling Pastor at the church, I thought. Well maybe not. Surely, I can speak to him easier with Randall than going through the church. I have never tried calling the church, but I cannot imagine saying, "This is Danielle," and a few seconds later him picking up the line. I am not sure whose security he is rolling with but they rolling deep.

It felt as though a hundred things ran through my mind. *I wonder if Randall was aware he was coming. I didn't think to mention it and felt somewhat bad that I didn't forewarn him. As soon as he rings me again I am asking for Pastor. Then again, these guys have been friends long enough Randall probably knew his thoughts. Oh wait a minute; they spoke yesterday on the flight. He probably knew he was coming if nothing else but to chastise him on his actions. Randall is a fool for landing that helicopter on my building and then on the church. I loved it too.*

I did what I was told to do. I had instructions to go to the gym immediately after work, no matter the time. I pulled into my spot and just chilled for a moment. I really did not know what I was getting into and truth be told I hated secrets.

When I opened the door, Mimi greeted me as usual in her pleasant manner. "Good evening Ms. Danielle."

I smiled and replied, "Hi. How are you?"

"Fine thank you. Are you here to work out today?" Mimi asked.

Raising my eyebrows, I said, "Actually, I am not sure. Randall instructed me to come over."

Mimi obviously had no idea what was going on either. She asked, "Can I ask you to wait here for a minute? Let me call to the back."

She made the call. "Hey, Hooks told Ms. Danielle to come by." I was almost concerned. "Umm hmm. Okay. Oh. Oh. Oh. Okay. Not a problem." She hangs up and gives me the biggest smile. I wasn't sure if it was genuine or not.

"Ms. Rose, we are under construction on the inside while Mr. Hooks is away. Sprucing up the place a little."

"OH?" I felt myself get defensive immediately. This was my field, this is what I do, and he didn't solicit my help?

"One of the guys will come out and escort you around the back to a safe zone," she said with enthusiasm.

"Oh great." I made a mental note to ask Randall about this. The lot was packed so I wondered if the others were in a non-safe zone.

From out of nowhere, this super fine brother comes through the door. I looked twice and had to catch myself.

He walked over to me and said, "Ms. Danielle, I am Vic nice to meet you."

I reached out to meet his outstretched hand for a shake, "Nice to meet you too," I replied.

"I will be working with you tonight."

"I didn't bring my bag in."

"That's okay, you may not need it right now," he replied. "Let's go around back."

I looked at Mimi confused. "Good night Ms. Danielle. See you tomorrow."

"Thanks. Have a good one." *That was positive. Did she know something I did not know? Like I would be back tomorrow. Or was she just guessing?* I liked her assumption, but I didn't like not knowing why she assumed she would see me tomorrow. *Would Randall be back then?* I no longer had time to think about it because Vic was suddenly opening a door.

We ended up in what appeared to be a conference room; I was still clueless as to what was going on. I pulled out my phones and sent two texts, one to the crew and one to Randall. I also checked my watch to make sure it was tracking.

"Ms. Danielle, Mr. Hooks wanted you to come here for a few reasons. However, the situation has changed a little but we will make it work."

"Who?" I asked.

"Right now me and you," he answered.

"Carry on." I said wide-eyed.

He reached for a few binders and photo albums and placed them on the table. "For starters, I am one of the twelve Disciples."

"HUH?" I said, totally confused.

"Judging from your reaction, you are not aware of what's going on are you?"

"Umm, I am afraid not."

"I'm so very sorry," he stated. "I thought he may have had an opportunity to speak to you today, but he has been extremely tied up. I think it is killing King and JJ more than it is killing him. This is a lot for us."

"Us who?" I asked this time sounding a little irritated.

"Oh, his security Ms. Danielle, the body guards. There are twelve of us, the twelve disciples. Most of us have been with him since he first needed someone. Since he has been lying low there hasn't been a need for all of us to travel with him on a day-to-day basis, but we do roll deep when we need to. You probably know most of us and you have seen all of us."

"From where?" I asked.

"For starters, you have been driven by two and you see four or more at church weekly."

"I DO?" I asked, not recalling any of them off hand.

"Yes."

"Who are they?" I asked.

Winking his eye he said, "Well if you don't know, then they are doing their job."

"I take it the other four were with him when he flew in on Sunday?"

"Correct, and I am the other one."

"How did you all get together?" I curiously asked.

"This sport," he stated. "We all knew each other some kind of way from this sport. We've fought, competed, or trained with or against each other at some time. Eventually bonds were formed and when Hooks made it, we instantly had to change roles. It is coincidence that there are twelve of us though."

"Okay," I replied. I knew that there was no such thing as coincidence, however, now was not the time to dispute it.

"The faith Hooks has now is the same faith he has always had. We cover him as the disciples covered Jesus. We move when he moves. Not because of a command but out of order and respect," he said.

"Okay."

He continued, "Six went with him last week. Back here we are calling him Gilligan."

I laughed. I got it instantly.

"Four left today with Pastor and two of us are here holding it down. You catch on quick," he said. "It's a good thing you are a quick learner. My job may not be so hard after all. Something huge would have to go down for us to leave the Fort completely unattended."

Vic talked, but all I could do right now was think of Gilligan's Island and that damn song. To make matters worse, I changed the lyrics in my mind as I normally do.

"What is so funny?" he asked.

"I am thinking of the song from Gilligan's Island," I admitted.

"Why is that funny?"

"I changed the words."

He looked lost, "I do not follow," he replied.

Of course, he didn't follow. I explained, "I changed the words to fit the scenario."

"Like how?" he asked.

Therefore, I began to sing the song to him.

"Bravo. Bravo," he said as he clapped. "That was awesome! Can you sing it again?"

"I will not," I stated.

"Sit right here I need to record what we are about to do." He pulled out his phone and quickly reverted to business. "I want you to look at these pictures and remember as much as you can as quick as you can. The purpose of this exercise is to test your memory. Can you be the seer? Can you quickly see something and imprint it on your mind?" he informed me.

We completed the exercise. He then handed me a photo album and asked me to look at them closely. He also asked that I make note of the people I knew and the ones I didn't. I recognized two that are always at the church from the photos.

We went through numerous memory exercises. It was interesting to say the least. It was as if I was training to be one of them as well. He also gave me some more information on what all my watch can do. We looked at other styles and downloaded the software to all of my devices I had with me.

He asked, "May I measure you?"

"I guess so," I answered as if no was an option.

He handed me a towel and said, "I will need to touch your skin to have items fitted for you. If I measure over the clothes, it will be too large when you put it directly on your body. I know you are going to hate this question."

"What is it," I asked.

"How much do you weigh?"

Holding up my hand, I told him, "I draw the line."

"Ninety?" he said under his breath.

"Huh?"

"Ninety pounds?" he asked.

"Heck no!" I shouted.

"We need to know in order to assist you accordingly. We need to have an idea so we can make sure we factor other things in just in case something pops off," he said.

"Something like what?" I asked. You could tell my questions were annoying him.

"Anything," he answered. "If anything should happen and we feel like your life is endangered or Hooks life is in danger, then the scene will change quickly."

"Meaning?" I asked for clarity.

"For example," he said. "Let's say you two are at church, an event or his club; and after we have asked for photos not to be taken; they're still being taken we may quickly escort you two to a safe location. Let's say people start pushing to get to him. We will more than likely pick you two up and run. We have had all kinds of escapes, but nothing major has ever happened that we were not prepared for. We are strapped at all times too. Speaking of which, how do you feel about weapons?"

"I am not afraid of them if that is what you are asking."

"Great news. That's good," he said.

"I hold a license to carry myself," I added.

"Even better."

"We have some rules we are going to have to go over and I'm afraid there may be some you may not like."

"Like?" I said sharply.

"You will always need to have your monitor on. If I'm not mistaken, I believe you are getting some additional monitoring devices also. I would request that you carry handbags that can be zipped and that you keep them zipped at all times. If we have to run out quickly, I don't want you to lose anything that someone could use maliciously. I would also like for you to wear shoes that have a back at all times," he stated.

"What???"

"Ms. Danielle, if you get picked up or have to run I don't want you to lose a shoe."

"Oh wow, that presents a problem," I said. "A fashion problem that is."

"Not sure what else to tell you then. Otherwise, you will need to be able to pick them up quickly or take the chance of losing them," he said.

"We may have to take that chance. I keep a spare pair on me at all times."

"We will run with you to make sure you can run at the drop of a dime in your heels, with your coat, handbag, and all this other stuff you seem to tag along." He pointed at my bags.

"This is serious?" *Why is everyone always on my bags?* I thought.

"Yes. It is. We are not trying to scare you, but we would rather have you prepared than shocked and freak out."

"I see."

"This is all new to us also. We have never had to train a woman for this; it has always just been us," he said. "If Vickie is with us she already knows what to do and aware of when it is time to move. It will not be hard, but we want to get your senses up and on guard."

"I guess I appreciate this," I replied hesitantly. We went through a few more exercises before calling it quits.

"Well done tonight Ms. Danielle. This has been easier than I thought. Shall we convene tomorrow?" he asked.

"Do we have to?" I replied with a question.

"We probably should for the remainder of the week. Then our next task will be escape proofing your job and your home. We will have to show you some safety precautions at church as well," he said.

Feeling overwhelmed already, I replied, "Looks like this is going to be a long week."

"One more thing Ms. Danielle. I also need you to think about places you frequent and how you get there. We will probably visit them all."

I was thinking to myself, *what does this mean?* "Okay. I will do that," I replied.

"I know most of this may seem senseless and over reacting, but people may follow you and hurt you to get to him."

I hadn't thought about this, so I asked, "Do you think he is in danger?"

"No, I don't. We don't," he corrected.

Relieved, "That's good news," I said.

"We would rather be safe than sorry. Let's call it quits," he said as he grabbed my bag. "Do you always carry this much stuff?"

I replied, "Yes. Always!"

"What is it?"

"Girl stuff. Laptops, iPad's, Mini's, iPod. DUH!" *What was he thinking?* I thought to myself.

"Have you considered carrying a Pullman?" he asked joking but his face was serious.

"Not my style, but my bodyguard said I need something I can grab quickly." *Only if it is Louis Vuitton.* I thought to myself.

"You listen well," he said and smiled. "But tell me, how are you going to grab this quickly?"

I took my bag and crisscrossed it across by body. Zipped it and put my handbag on my shoulder. He looked impressed that I could make all those gadgets and weight compact and secure over my body, but this time he did not crack a smile. He was not as harsh as King but twice as serious. "Looks like you have this all figured out. Now if you eliminate some of those gadgets that would be great. I'll check around for one gadget you don't currently have that will work the ten you do have." He held the door open for me and walked me to my car. He was built too; that sure made a girl feel secure. When we reached my car he said, "You know what to do."

"Good night and thanks."

"See you tomorrow." I was not sure if it was a question or a statement. "You sure will."

"If you speak to Hooks tell him we got everything covered here," he said.

I did speak to Hooks and we talked for over an hour. He gave me every detail of his day and I shared every detail of mine. I then sent a text around midnight with the vision. I knew we did not have a lot of time, but with the four of us, I was confident we could tackle this task.

Let's get together on teleconference to put all the details in motion.

I hope they didn't get pissed. I knew it was a last minute thought and we only had a day or two to achieve it. Individually my vision was impossible, but collectively with the Wonder Twins, Super Woman and Super Girl this was a challenge we could easily handle. I hope that it would be well worth the efforts.

Tuesday

After talking to Randall all night, I was finally able to get a good night's sleep. I woke up refreshed and with one thought on my mind. *When life comes at you, it goes hard in the paint. It spares no expense. It cares less about your feelings. It breaks you down to the lowest common denominator. It ain't no joke. You either win or lose. You ride or die. It is scary but that is the way it is.*

I rode to work thinking of Randall; as if that was new. He said he was still unsure as to when they would be done with him. I missed him terribly, hoped, and prayed for the best for him. I prayed for his spiritual health, his mental health, his strength, his endurance, his will and ability to fight. I felt good after our conversation. It seemed like he felt good too. It was probably a good thing he took the opportunity to see me and that Pastor went to see him. I am sure it is distressing to be away from home by yourself, working and trying to prove yourself without being able to talk to your friends and family. Without their words of encouragement makes it even more challenging. I did not know how that felt and I empathized with him. I was glad he landed on the roof, not just for my sake, but for his sake. It helped him in more ways than it helped me. He had the chance to see his fellow Deacons, his friends, his Pastor, Sade, his home city and me; whoever or whatever I was to him.

In the midst of my thoughts, You Know You're Looking at a Winner rang so loud I jumped. "Hey," I answered the phone stunned.

"What's wrong?" he asked.

"The phone scared me, that's all," I replied.

"What? Are you on a date with your Boo or something?"

"This early? Nah."

"Well, you never know."

"My Boo tucked me in bed last night," I said.

"What? Don't make me hurt his..."

"Watch your mouth," I interrupted and laughed.

Randall continued, "I just called to say good morning. I miss you. Have a great day and thank you for believing in me."

My smile widened, and I replied, "Good morning. I miss you too. Same to you and you are welcome."

"Alright now hang up the phone. I'm all mushy this early in the morning. It is sickening, big, strong robust fighter, all mushy. I am pathetic."

"Whatever," I laughed. "Bye."

"Bye Babe."

I smiled all the way to the building. The girls and I got together around eleven. We had come to the conclusion that this could be done, although I was stretching it. A real stretch for me. I didn't like to work under pressure. I didn't operate that way, but for the other three, it was probably a normal day's work for them. Me on the other hand, I was freaking out.

Randall and I spoke several times throughout the day and we texted. After work, I went to the gym. Vic was there and took my measurements for some reason. He then gave me some self-defense techniques. It was a productive day for both of us, I must say. After two days with Vic though, I was exhausted. He had me doing a week's worth of activities in just a few short hours.

Vic seemed to be a very mild mannered guy, much calmer, rational and more tolerable than King. However, he was the same worker bee. Worker beast was more like it. I guess Randall had the right crew with him. He needed work alcoholics to be on his team because he was one himself. I am not sure I would enjoy his kind of work; it was too physical and strenuous. I am sure I could jump rope long enough to get through the childhood chant, ice cream ice cream, and hoped my boyfriend's name started with an A. In other words, I do not foresee me jumping a darn rope for hours. How boring could that possibly be? And he did it with ease and without a television, iPod or anything. Now this is where I really drew the line. There was no mistaking, this is why he did what he did and was good at it; he liked it.

I had the opportunity to speak to Randall, but we did not speak for long. I think we were both exhausted. We said good night and I crashed.

Wednesday

For some reason the day seemed extra-long. Maybe it's because I was not able to talk to him. I could not wait to leave work. I had planned to leave at a decent hour to be on time, or early, for church. I was meeting Sade at the house for our official weekly date.

We did exactly what I had planned. I left on time and we arrived at church way before time. It was somewhat disappointing considering he was not present. The regular security guys were not either. There were a few others that I have seen around, but I didn't really know them. Just as we approached our seats, Keith appeared. Praise and worship was over and Pastor Hunter was in his zone. I was sitting at full attention when Sade poked, kicked me, and squeezed my hands. "What the?" I said as I stopped writing and looked up.

She squeezed my hand again and cut her eyes in his direction. *I have taught the child well.* Apparently, he had just run in and was still buttoning his shirt. I looked over. Randall winked and smiled. I winked, smiled, and dropped my head. I was just as giddy as a three-year-old catching Santa coming down the chimney.

He nodded for me to exit the sanctuary. I bent over and tried to slide out with the Baptist finger in motion, but Keith stopped me in my tracks. I was trying to do this with as little attention as possible. Once Hunter saw him enter and exit and me trying to follow right behind him, he spoke louder. Instincts made me want to look back but wisdom told me not to.

Before I could push the door all the way open he was pulling my wrist. I looked back quickly to see who might be watching. He stuck his head in the door as if to see what I was looking at then he hugged me. We embraced. It was an intense moment for both of us.

One would have thought he had been gone for years. It was the type of hug you give to welcome a person coming back from war or prison. *Oh, he smelled good so good!* He was freshly showered and shaven. He felt different. I could not really explain it. All I knew was that I was happy to see him. His eyes were completely blood shot, as if he not been to sleep in days. Why was that unusual? He never slept anyway. But there is a difference from no sleep by choice and no sleep by force. This past week it was certainly by force. I am sure he was a little worried also.

"Hey. How are you?" I asked trying to contain my excitement.

"I am glad to see you," he said.

"Why didn't you tell me you were coming?"

"I called to tell you to wait for me but you didn't answer."

"I was here."

"I see that," he replied.

"You look great," I told him. He did. He always did.

"Thanks, you're being way too kind. I am tired, stressed and I feel like my body is about to explode. My legs are like spaghetti, my arms are weak, and I do not think I can feel my hands or my feet," he said sorely.

I took his hands and rubbed them in my hands. They were badly bruised. I kissed them and then suddenly remembered that I was at church. Glad I caught myself, as that would be considered out of line. I rubbed them again, "Do they feel better?" I asked.

"Of course," he said with a slight laugh. I knew he was tired when he didn't give that hearty robust laugh.

"Let's go back before we get detention," I said with all seriousness. I was not looking forward to getting into trouble with Pastor tonight.

We walked back in together. So much for not being obvious and getting attention. After service, Sade and I waited for Randall. He and Sade joked around. He talked as much as he could about his ordeal. He said he still didn't have an answer. "Can you get your crew together to meet at the restaurant tomorrow? They will call me with their decision. At eight our time," he said.

"Are you sure you want everyone there?" I asked.

"Yes, of course. We will party no matter what."

"I am always game for a party," Sade chimed in.

"You are not old enough to party," he said as he walked us to the car.

"Dani, do you mind if I call you once I get home?" Randall asked.

"Of course not."

"I am going to get Keith to take me to the house and I am calling it a night. It has been a long and rough week. I am glad I came to see you." He leaned in, "You too Sade," he said.

"Are you leaving now?"

"Yes. I am not on duty tonight. I made a guest appearance to only see you."

"Get some rest. I will be praying for the outcome," I said.

"Thanks babe, I need it. I did not think it was going to be this hard," he said. He hugged me lightly. You could tell his body was sore. He jokingly punched Sade in the arm and then we pulled off.

Thursday

We all met at the restaurant as we were told. Me, JJ, King, Keith, Pastor Hunter, Vickie, Leigh, and Randall were in his office. The others were in the restaurant area being entertained and eating hors d'oeuvres. We had been on our knees praying for what seemed like hours. As soon as the phone rang, the others scurried to the other side of the door. He had his back to King who was at the other side of the desk. I sat in the chair at his desk. Vickie was busy taking notes on everything and she had a camcorder on a tripod already recording. Pastor was still on his knees praying. JJ was in charge of the door.

The call was not a very long one, but rather short. He was brief and to the point. He did not say much. He spent his time on the call waiting and listening on the opposite end. The silence was disturbing. He paced back and forth; however, he never turned around to face us. Finally, he said, "Thank you for the call," and he dropped the phone. He laid his head in my lap. I picked the phone up and hung it on the hook. Leigh kept snapping shots. It was her job but it was not what I would have thought was the right time for pictures. Regardless, all the moments had to be captured. Even if they were emotional or bad. I looked back. No one murmured a word. I slid down the chair, my heart racing a mile a minute.

He grabbed my face as I tried to pull back. I could tell from his elevated breathing that he was crying. I took his face but he dropped it. "Look at me," I said, but he didn't. Instead, he put his forehead to mine and whispered directly in my mouth as if we were kissing.

"I love you so much. I do not know where you have been all my life, but I do know that I'm glad you are here now. I could not do this without you D. Please be patient towards me. I, I, I am not a bad guy," he stammered. "Please believe me when I tell you I have all the right intentions. I need your friendship and I would never do anything to jeopardize it." He paused. "I need a minute to get myself together." Other than the camera flashing, not a creature stirred. Leigh got down on her hands and knees. She was practically lying under us to get our facial shots. I was going to be the first to handle that camera tonight to review these photos. I waited a few minutes, but it seemed more like hours.

I grabbed his face again and said, "Look at me." Leigh snapped. He did but his eyes were closed. I wiped his tears. "Look at me Randall. Please," I begged.

"I can't," he replied in a whisper.

The tears ran down my face too. I sniffed. Snap. Snap. Snap. That damn camera had gotten on my nerves.

He asked, "Why are you crying?"

"I am crying because you are. Besides, you won't talk to me or look at me. What else am I to do?"

He held his head at eye level but he never opened his eyes, "Danielle, I love you," he said.

"I love you too." SNAP! I jumped. She snapped again, and again, and again.

"I love you more than you will ever know."

I said very sternly and harsh, "Open your eyes and look at me Randall!" I was so loud until the room got quieter instantly, not even a snap from Leigh's camera could be heard. Pastor stopped praying, the door opened and JJ pushed them back. He then opened his eyes like a newborn baby does and he closed them back right away. Within that split second that his eyes were opened, out fell a butt load of tears. When his fell, so did mine.

Sobbing, he said, "I, I, I'm trying."

Frantic, not knowing how to calm him or what to do, "Trying to do what?" I asked.

"Look at you," he managed to say. "I can't right now though. Please don't think I am being rude."

I grabbed his head and spoke directly in his ear. I was so choked up until I didn't think I could speak. "Speak to me Randall. Talk to me please baby," I said.

He stood up and lifted me with him. His arms were around my waist and mine were around his neck. Now my back was to the room. He picked me up and swung me across the desk. Leigh snapped and I think everyone in the room did too. I felt a little light headed and I could now see why he couldn't open his eyes. My feet knocked everything off the desk, including the monitors. He yelled, "I'M FIGHTING!"

"Oh my God. Oh My God. OH MY GOD!" was all I could say.

JJ opened the door and yelled, "We are fighting!"

I heard the champagne popping. Cork after cork. I hadn't opened my eyes, yet I knew the paparazzi must have come inside; the snapping from everyone's cameras would not allow me to open my eyes. He was speaking and Pastor was right there covering him. I think someone must have had a tape recorder or camcorder up really close to capture the sound. Finally, he pushed everyone away. My eyes were still closed. "Leigh you stay."

It was a lot to take in. As we lay out on the floor holding hands, Leigh snapped so much until she changed cameras. Then she gave us a variety of poses.

"Now don't do anything I will miss," she instructed. "Let me pick this stuff up so I can go start uploading and I will be right outside the door when you all come out. I am very happy for you Hooks, Congratulations!" she said with a smile. She put most of the stuff back on the desk. "Dee your shoes are scuffed let me get you another pair before you come out."

"Okay," I replied as she left the room. "I am so proud of you," I said as I rolled over and lay on top of him.

"Thank you."

"Congratulations!" I said. Words couldn't describe how excited I was for him.

"This means so much to me D."

"I know."

"No, you really don't," he said. "You are lying on top of me. And if you don't get down, we will miss our party and Tre. Well, Tre will have to be mad and forgive me of this," he said with a slight laugh but with all sincerity.

Suddenly, I noticed something poking me. "Ooo. I rolled off real quick. Sorry!" I said, embarrassed.

"You see what I mean about distractions? Eve."

At that, I couldn't do anything else other than laugh.

Shaking his head, he let out, "Damn!"

"What?" I asked, startled.

"I must be lame as hell to ask you to get off. Man, I should have taken advantage while I could. Here it is the first and only time I may catch you off guard and look what happens; I am distracted about being able to fight. What kind of foolishness is that?"

As he leaned over me, I blushed. He was so close, our eyes were closed, and we were breathing the same oxygen.

"F**K!" he yelled. He rolled back over on his back. "DAMN! The biggest moment in my life and I can't do what I want to do. God is really trying me," he said in frustration.

"This is not the biggest moment in your life."

"Yeah it is. The biggest and most memorable so far."

"What about your other fights?" I asked.

He leaned up again and said, "You were not there. What is the law against me kissing you and you know what again?"

I named a few, "Adultery, fornication, lewd, lascivious behavior. I can go on and on," I said.

"I am fine with all of those what about you?" he asked.

"And Pastor Hunter is like fifty feet away," I added.

"DAMN Tre. I told him not to be a preacher."

"No you did not," I said and shot him a look like he was caught in a lie.

He laughed, "You right. I didn't."

"So."

"So what?"

"So how do you feel right now?" I asked.

"I. I feel like all of my dreams and goals are finally coming true. I have never felt this good in my entire life. I need this comeback. I can appreciate it more. The first time was different. I can't explain it. I was simply a kid with a quick hand. I was an un-caged untamed fighter. Years later, here I stand with you a skilled fighter, a father, a business owner, a man of God and a fighter ready to enter the ring again."

"Goon?" I asked.

He ignored my remark and continued, "I'm back in a position to fight again. I am lying on the floor under my desk with the girl of my dreams. It's somewhat sexy I must admit. I feel like I can tackle the world right now. I'm unstoppable." he said confidently.

"Save the tackling for the ring mister," I teased.

He looked over at me and said, "Unless you want to be tackled."

"Oh no, I think we have established the answer to that," I said.

"Did we?" he said as if he was up to something.

"Yes."

"And the answer was?" he asked.

"Yes and no," I replied.

"I can't let a woman not have her dreams." He tackled me right there under the desk.

We laughed. "How is that?" he asked.

"Not quite the tackling I expected, but it will work for now." I replied.

"Eve, stop pushing my buttons," he said. "I only have on or off. You are going to make me give in now. No more talk of tackling, wrestling, sex, you on top of me and me on top of you. A brother gone slip; I'm trying to tell ya. This moment is going too good for me not to. Lawd help me! The Lord is my shepherd he knows what I want!" he yelled out.

"So what does this mean for us?" I questioned.

"What do you mean?"

"Where do we go from here Randall? How do we get there? What do we do in the meantime?" All of my questions came out at once.

"Are you concerned?" he asked shocked.

"Should I be?" I replied.

"Hell no! You should not be concerned with anything. But to answer your question, we keep doing what we are doing until I overcome this next obstacle. We keep working out and training together. We take it day by day until we can move faster and further."

"You are not going to be traveling are you?" I asked.

"No. I have no plans to fight until all of the other things in my life are straightened out. I could fight today if I wanted too, but I would rather be one hundred percent clear of the past. With my past no longer hanging over my head it will make a big mental difference to me; and I need that. I may travel to some other fights to watch the competition but it could be at least a year before I step into the ring officially. Or it could be next month, but I do not want a public announcement until I am done with her," he said. Then as if he had a sudden thought, "As a matter of fact, I think I need to mention that tonight. This announcement does not go outside this building." He looked over at me lying on his side, smiled and told me, "I wish I could explain to you how I feel right now D. Just chilling here with you is all I need."

"You may get free and get back on the scene and get all booed up," I said.

"Is that what you are concerned with?"

"Kind of," I answered honestly.

"Why do you think that?" he asked.

"Because Randall all of this will be new to you."

"You are correct. Danielle, look at me. You are the reason I am doing this."

"Why?"

"When I met you, you had no clue who I was. To you, I was just some guy. You did not see the jewels, the cars, or the gloves. All you saw was a Deacon and that is exactly how I want to be seen. When I showed up to the track in my suit, hot and sweating, I knew then you were for me. It was at that moment I knew I wanted to fight again. I had to get the desire and motivation to fight and to move on with my life. I think you have said before that we must pick and choose our battles. That resonated in my spirit. I found myself working harder, praying harder and I pushed myself. Do you think I would do all of this and walk out on you? Not a chance! You are the reason for this Dani. You have stood by me in a not so welcoming situation. You have been down with me and have proven that you got my back. Do you think I would gas up a plane, land a helicopter on the roof of a church for an eighteen-minute visit just cause? This is way more than just cause. This is way more than a pretty face, sex and anything materialistic. My heart is involved."

"Just to let you know boxing is not like football and basketball. Groupies don't flock to you. They have fewer chances to get backstage at a boxing match. At a football locker room they have up to fifty-five players from each team and fifteen for basketball. If they are good they are bound to get someone. Anyone. At a boxing match it is two of us. Typically, we have a date, a wife, or someone there. The chances are slim to none. If you are worried about me being booed up, don't! What we are doing now is about the extent of that. To be honest, this is the most I have ever been booed up anyways. People are often amazed and have no clue how Tameka and I have co-existed this long. Coexist may not be the right word," he said. "Let's just say they felt we should have dissolved before my first fight. I am the one that held on this long. What you and I are doing now I have never done before. Just chill; you don't have anything like that to be worried about. You may think I am lying, but I will tell you again; as sad and shameless as it may sound, Tameka is the only girl I have ever kissed or been with intimately. When I tell you that I am a man starting over from scratch, I am."

"Well if it makes you feel any better I am only one up on you," I said. "One long term boyfriend and one get back short term boyfriend. I think we are both in the same boat. Which may not be a bad thing at all, right?"

"So to answer your questions, I was wondering if it would be rude to like sign the divorce papers and we get married the same day. Is that legal?"

"Umm, I don't think Hunter would fall for it. Not to mention, like the old folks say let the ink dry."

"Bump that. She can sign in crayon for all I care!" he shot back.

"You are sick, you know that?" I said and laughed. "We should greet the crowd. It is your party after all. I'm making a toast; you are drinking champagne, and remember you promised to eat a burger."

"I said share a burger and I said nothing about champagne," he quickly corrected.

"You either drink it or wear it mister!" I teased. "Now can you please ask Leigh to slow down with the snapshots?" I nearly pleaded with him.

He laughed and replied, "No can do. Get used to it."

"Jerk! I hate you!"

"No you don't!"

We had to get up and get ourselves together for this party. Leigh was already back in the room snapping away with her camera. I was in the mirror attempting to camouflage my red eyes with make-up. I grabbed my phone and sent him a text.

As he opened the text he asked, "What's this?"

"It's my new ringtone for your phone," I told him.

It was TI. "What is up with you and TI? I am just about over it," he said with a tad bit of jealousy in his voice.

I smiled, "Home team baby."

"I'm about to get jealous," he said. "He and Joe gone make me snap."

"You may not want to do that."

"I'm a fix this. Let me call Tiny," he teased.

"Do what you gotta do. But you don't seem to have much luck with Tameka's." I laughed hard. That was a good one and he knew it.

He cut his eyes and said, "You are worried about groupies and I got to worry about rappers and singers. I'm keeping the lil' ring tone, but I ain't happy about it. Just make sure you are just as much of a fan of mine as you are of theirs."

"You don't have to keep it. I will still put it down for you," I said.

"My ring tone on your phone is TI too?" he asked.

I gave him a look that said he was absolutely right, "It sure is, and I am not changing it. You ready Boo?"

"Let's do it." he said. He instantly got pumped up. He went from Randall to Hooks in zero to two seconds.

"We're on." I chimed in.

Leigh snaps a few shots. I can tell she's in her creative zone as she gives us poses that look like we are together and some that involve props as if we aren't together.

"Be ready," she said. Leigh scanned us over, fixed us up, and debriefed us. I felt like we were Michelle and Barak. "I think Sade is at the door with the camera," she continued. "Vickie will be recording everything and there is the professional photographer that is going to photograph you alone, so please be ready. Oh, here change shoes," she instructed. She looked over at Randall with a slight frown and said, "Hooks, I think you may need a new shirt, this one is quite wrinkled from rolling on the floor."

"I have some in the closet," he replied.

"We will keep this one to keep the same look but it will change after these initial pictures. Ready?" Leigh asked.

He looked at me and me at him. "Ready," we said at the same time. We were holding hands with our fingers locked. He touched my nose and the door opened. The first shot was his finger swiping my nose. It felt like the beginning of a new life. I was glad I could share it with him.

He thought to himself. *I wished I were not only announcing my return but also my engagement with her.* Then God spoke to him and said, *slow it down. You can't handle but one thing at a time. To whom much is given much is required.* He mumbled to himself, "Speak Lord your servant listens."

I heard it and winked. I really wanted to know what the voice of the Lord said to him, but didn't dare ask. It was a private conversation. I leaned into him and whispered, "I'll catch you later. Congratulations my love." He pulled me back.

"Don't go," he said.

Giving him a reassuring smile and wink of the eye, I said, "Someone has to entertain this bunch before they get rowdy. Just call me the hostess with the mostess. I will be sending you an invoice sir."

He smiled the same smile he smiles all the time, and although we separated physically, we were not separated mentally. As we each worked the room, we'd find ourselves starring at the other, totally busted. I did remain busy however. I spent a lot of time with the DJ and going back and forth with the wait staff, the chef, and Mikey. The DJ kept the party crunk and the dance floor stayed pack song after song. After mingling for a good thirty or forty minutes Mikey said, "We are ready whenever you are." I made rounds with the videographer and photographer interviewing people for a memorial disc. I asked the guests to tell the camera things about Randall such as how they met, how long they've known him etc. I was sure to reiterate that this was still a secret and not to be discussed outside of the room.

Then the DJ played the theme from Rocky and I took that as my cue to ask him to the dance floor. He was shy at first. I know it I caught him off guard. I do not think he was expecting that song and it meant a lot to who he was and his struggle to get there. It's the fighter's anthem! At that moment I quickly realized I might be watching more Rocky, Hurricane and similar movies more than I ever intended. After we danced I took the microphone again and called Pastor Hunter up to bless the food.

"All right big timer. Here is your burger." I said as I handed over a burger fit for a champ.

With his eyes big as ever, he shook his head and said, "No ma'am. We are splitting a burger."

I gave in, "That's fine and fries," I said.

"I did not say anything about fries," he protested quickly.

"Ahh, who eats a burger without fries?" I asked.

"Come on D. I can't eat that," he said genuinely.

"Tell me why not?" I asked.

"They have grease for one," he replied.

"And?" I waited patiently for him to finish.

"D, don't make me do this to you?" He was referring to disappointing me by saying no.

"Okay Randall. I will give up the fries if you drink the champagne then," I said.

"What are you trying to do? Kill me?" he asked.

I cut my eyes at him and said, "No, why would I do that? I need you. Remember? You are so disciplined it's nauseating. You make me so sick!" I teased. I actually liked the idea he could stick to a plan, but I also wanted him to realize it's okay to bend the rules every now and then. After dinner I was back to working the room and he was back to mingling. Parties are always hard work. He took two bites of the burger; just enough to satisfy me.

I took the microphone numerous times during the night and even spinned on the ones and twos. We were having such a great time and enjoying the fun. When it was time for the first toast, I grabbed the mic again. I held my glass while the wait staff made sure everyone had a glass. I called out, "Someone please make sure Mr.

Hooks has a glass in his hand and it is filled with champagne and not sparkling water." When the tray came around he waved it off. "Excuse me, he needs a glass," I yelled. Then in front of everyone I didn't hold back. I expressed exactly how I felt and confessed my true feelings.

"To my dearest Randall," I began. "It is my hope and prayer that from this day forth all your dreams become a reality. May you walk away from each fight, whole, unharmed and the winner. I pray for your health, strength, and safety in all that you do. I pray the protection of God will continually surround you, to comfort and keep you on a daily basis. There is nothing impossible for you Randall because you believe it's in fact possible. May you continue to be the humble, sincere, caring, considerate, and fun loving person that you are. I look forward to your growth and maturity in your walk with God. I see big and great things for you Champ; I have faith in you. I pray you are blessed and covered from the crown of your head to the soles of your feet; every path you tread shall be blessed. The rings you battle in and the pathways of your daily journey are covered and illuminated by the light of God. This is only the beginning. You have yet to see all that God has in store for you. Eyes have not seen, ears have not heard and it has not crossed the hearts of boxers what you are about to show this world. Your cup shall be filled with plenty and prepared before the presence of your enemies. Get ready. Get ready. Get ready. It's time to rumble!" I held up my glass and motioned for him to do the same. Once he did, we all drank.

Pastor Hunter approached me and I thought he wanted the microphone so I tried to hand it to him, but he pushed my arm down and said, "We need to talk," instead.

I looked shocked and couldn't think of what I might have done wrong. I asked, "What did I do now?" I was thinking, *did I curse?*

He placed my hands inside of his and said, "You are missing a calling beloved. I am not sure if you were preaching a sermon or giving a toast."

"It was one good toast," I smiled, relieved I was not in trouble. "I am not missing a calling though. That was just my adrenaline pumping at the right time. I have a wonderful covering by a faithful man of God. I am just following his teaching."

"To God be the glory. We'll talk," he replied. He walked away, but looked at me suspiciously. I knew this was not the end of this conversation.

I walked towards Randall, but he spoke before I could, "I'm taking you home."

"Now?" I asked.

"I was," he said with the wink of an eye.

"Give me thirty more minutes. The festivities have just begun," I smiled.

Now looking alarmed, Randall asked, "Is this something that will embarrass me?"

"I hope not," I replied.

"Take your time. I'm driving you. You have to work tomorrow remember?"

"Yeah, I know. What a dumb night to have a gathering," I winked again since it was his idea.

"We can have a gathering any day you want Ms. Rose," he said.

"Like TI; I can have whatever I like." I couldn't resist throwing in this quote from his song.

"NOT what I said. I am just about sick of you and TI," he laughed.

I was on a limited time schedule and quickly realized we hadn't given Randall his gift nor brought out the cake. I also needed the photographer and videographer to get more shots. I called a quick meeting with the photo and video crew, to include Leigh and Sade. "Hey guys, I know this whole event was last minute for many of you and I greatly appreciate the hard work you're putting into capturing this great moment. I think we are going to have wonderful memories. With that being said, we have about another thirty minutes to an hour to capture. Let's run with it. From this point on I'd like to get as many candid shots as possible. Shortly I will be presenting a present and want to make sure we get that captured. We'll then serve the cake and at that point, it'll pretty much be a wrap. Besides, it is a school night." I looked at everyone and said, "Are we good?"

"Yes," they replied.

"Great, let's do this!" We left the huddle and just as any great photographer would, many of them were taking pictures of the huddle itself. I made my way to the DJ's booth to give him final instructions. The first song he played caused me to throw up the peace sign to the DJ. He knew exactly what it meant; that I needed more time to get the present and cake set up, which I had yet to see in person. Sade had brought them inside, but when she arrived I was not able to take a look at it. I am sure it was fine; however, I did want to see it first. I put in a last minute call to my seamstress/tailor and had her make a boxing robe to cover the gift. Since it was such short notice, she could only go with the measurements I provided. It was a robe I hoped he would wear in his next fight, but if my measurements were not accurate, maybe not. I was relieved to see that she arrived with a dress bag in tow while we were eating. This last minute planning ordeal was more of Paige's territory, but I gotta give it to her; she kicked it up quite a few notches today. She had spent the majority of the evening with Mikey preparing food, which turned out amazing. The meal was a formal sit down meal, other than the burger Randall and I shared. From the way everyone seemed to enjoy it, I am sure the chef at the restaurant will be adding Mikey's delights to the menu permanently.

I finally made it to the kitchen to check on the cake set up. Actually, I ran in and startled Paige. She said, "What?" in a short and quick tone as soon as I opened the door.

Raising my hands, I said, "SORRY! SORRY! SORRY!"

She rolled her eyes, "Are you sorry for rushing us or sorry for coming in?"

"Okay fine. I'll go back out. Thank you." I sweetly smiled and proceeded to exit.

I turned around quickly though when I heard her say, "You can come in."

"I love y'all." I could tell they were flustered and annoyed with me.

"Whatever!" Mikey said.

"What do you want?" Paige said in that motherly tone of her's.

"Are you ready?" I asked.

"If you are. We are just waiting on you," she replied exasperated.

"Okay. Great!" I said, clapping my hands together. "Let me take a look at the portrait."

Sade and I walked to look at the portrait. It was breathtaking. It was hard to believe that this was done in less than two days. I couldn't help but to stare at it and want to keep it for myself. It was so beautiful. I immediately kissed all over Sade, I was so impressed. I also knew that as soon Leigh and Paige laid their eyes on it, they too would fall in love. This last minute event caused a lot of pressure, I just hoped they didn't hate me for it. I did not bother to even think futuristic because I didn't want to get my hopes up. However, something on the inside of me told me that life might be like this forever when dealing with Hooks Washington.

"Sade, this is phenomenal!" I said staring into the frame.

"It is Auntie. You did a great job."

"Me?"

"Yeah."

"No you all did," I said. "All I did was state the vision and you materialized it perfectly. Thank you!"

Sade grinned and said, "There is no way he can't like this. It is a little big though. Where is he going to put it?"

"I initially thought it would be great for the gym, but now that I see it I'm thinking it needs to go in his house."

"I was thinking more like your bedroom," Sade said.

I had to laugh because she was right. "Me too. Let's go girl." We walked arm in arm with Leigh busy snapping that camera in our direction as we made funny faces. I then gave instructions to the DJ to play some light jazz after the current song ended.

I walked over to Randall. "Hey."

"Hey," he said with that smile of his. "I wasn't expecting tonight to turn into a huge party."

"It's not huge. Had I had just a little more time to plan, then you'd see huge." I pulled his arm and motioned for him to come with me, "I have a present for you."

"Oh God! Are you going to give it to me now in front of everyone?" He raised his eyebrows. "I promise you will have ample time to plan the next gathering."

"Promise! I hope you like the surprise," I said.

"I am sure I will," he replied as he followed me.

When we walked up King, JJ and Keith were stationing the photo. Everyone stood around in silence. I stood back far off and allowed Hunter to stand next to him. He reached back for me but I was moving to get in position to capture this moment with the camera I had taken off Leigh's shoulder.

The stand held the huge framed photograph draped with a sheet and a kelly green silk robe encrusted with colored rhinestones. There was even a hook in the center of the back of the robe intertwined with a cross-trimmed in white. The front left chest had the same deign as the back of the robe. It was draped over the portrait with the back facing the crowd. The seamstress also made a set of blinged out boxing gloves that hung on the frame itself. She had done an excellent job and the creativity was amazing. Although I wanted to ask him where he purchased his robes I was glad I took the chance and called my seamstress. Needless to say, she was more than happy to do it and I am sure it cost me a fortune. She said it was the first she had ever done, nevertheless, it was beautiful beyond words.

He stood there and let the cameras snap. You could tell by the look on his face he was anxious to see what was behind the draped robe. He reached for me again, but I was too busy being the photographer for this particular shot, I just had to get it. Besides, there was no way for me to be in two places at the same time considering the situation.

He put the robe on. It fit perfectly! It wasn't too long, too short and the color complimented him very well. He looked back at me and I pretended to have no clue as to how it got there; all the while I snapped the camera to capture the moment.

He snatched the sheet off and instantly, "Ahh!" filled the room. He leaned in for a closer look and it was obvious he was just as amazed as Sade and I had been. Everyone wanted to lean in too, but they gave him space to observe it.

The portrait was absolutely fascinating and consisted of over twenty-three photographs, uniquely conformed out of ninety-seven different portraits that had been cut and pasted creating a masterpiece. A few of the pictures were ones that Sade had taken herself. The first main picture was one of him in the black suit that he wore to church on Sunday. Another photo was captured as he was praying. His head was leaning down and his hands were clapped together in praying position. Sade had also captured two pictures of him while on the helicopter. The other two predominate pictures were of him to the left and to the right. Get it; left and right? Another was of him in his red boxing attire; gloves and all. There was one of him in white tee, jeans, AFO's, and a red Atlanta Braves cap. In the original picture the cap was not red, but an excellent job had been done with the picture's modification. What made the entire picture completely unique were the holograms of him all around the main pose representing different alter egos. The more you looked, the more you found them.

The glass within the frame was etched with a hook, boxing gloves, and a cross. In the far right hand corner of the glass was a red rose. The frame was a Larson Juhl original that had been made over night. It was a black frame embossed with boxing gloves on the first trimming, hooks on the outer trim and on the inner wood were crosses.

The matting was heavy and extensive. At the time in which the order had been placed it was difficult to know how to matte it because I was unsure where it would hang and I had not actually seen it. The instructions were to match the colors in the photo and I must say they did a damn good job for a twenty-four hour turn around. I was extremely impressed and I now considered them to be my new exclusive vendor. I am sure this was going to lead to tons of future photos framed. He stood there in sheer amazement.

When he looked back at me, I grabbed the microphone out of my pocket and said, "DJ give me that." There was no need in being sentimental. Truth be told, we could not even if we wanted too. There were far too many spectators, with the main one being Hunter. The DJ was right on cue with his next selection. I started walking to the kitchen just as Paige called me back.

"D?"

"Yeah."

"We are ready whenever you are," she said.

"Good. Sit down rest yourself and enjoy what is left of the night." Then I caught her right where I needed her and quickly kissed her cheek.

"UGH!" she said and dramatically wiped it off. Paige is not the emotional and sentimental type.

As soon as she did, Randall came inside the kitchen, grabbed my waist, and said, "Thanks Paige." He then planted a kiss on the other cheek.

"What's with you two touching and kissing?" she asked as if disgusted; but I noticed she did break a smile.

"I need to speak to you," he said to me.

"Only on the dance floor," I said. We walked out holding hands and looking like we were about to dance with the stars.

"Danielle, when did you have time to do all of this?" he asked.

"Today," I replied. I then realized the DJ was playing a new song. It was the most appropriate song for the night and I was going to make a mental note to knock the DJ upside his head as soon as I had a chance.

"You have done too much," he said. I could tell he couldn't believe how everything turned out.

"Says who?" I asked.

"Says me," he backfired.

"Nothing is too much for my Champ," I said sincerely and sweetly. "Besides you haven't seen the bills yet. You will be getting them," I laughed.

He laid his head on my shoulder. I waited for Paige and Hunter to come over and separate us. Just then, low and behold, TI came on.

He quickly lifted his head. "I. I am. Never mind," he wouldn't finish his sentence.

Just when TI sang the next line of lyrics, I caught him singing right along. I said, "Oh TI fan are we?" He chuckled a little then we pounded at the next line while the cameras flashed. It was as if they were waiting on a good time to snap or shall I say an appropriate time.

We both blinked. "Let's have cake," I suggested. As we walked over I continued to sing the lyrics. Mikey did a great job turning the baby booties form into a set of boxing gloves. I owed Mikey dearly; everyone actually. After everyone had been served cake I looked over to my friend and said, "Michael take that Chef's jacket off and dance with me." He did. I took the microphone out of my pocket and said, "DJ we stepping." Mikey had on his black wife beater. I took my top off right there on the dance floor and exposed my white wife beater. I took the band from my wrist and pony tailed my hair over my shoulder and we stepped until the floor was packed. Randall cut in and Mikey grabbed Paige. I said to Randall, "Hey you get First Lady and I am getting Pastor." We switched partners and somehow I wasn't surprised to see that Pastor had skills on the dance floor. As the old people say, "He can cut a rug."

We reconvened and Randall asked, "Are you ready to go?"

I said, "I think so." I made sure to grab a piece of cake for the road. Suddenly a thought came to mind, so I asked him, "By the way, if you ate cake what kind would it be?"

"You picked my favorite," he said. "Red velvet."

"Good you are eating some too then. Can we eat in your car?"

He laughed. "Sure." We gave final instructions such as to lock up, bring my car home, etc. He thanked everyone and told them they were all expected to be at work on time regardless as to what time they left. He told King he would be at the gym hitting the bag at three. "I have to get this burger out of the bottom of my stomach." Then we left, got in the car and I was asleep before we even hit the first red light.

I heard his camera snapping. "I heard that," I said.

"She sleeps," he said. "I could not pass up the moment. I am going to have to do this every day if it makes you sleep." We pulled up to my house. He opened my door. I unlocked the front door and he hugged me.

"Good night," he said.

"You are not coming in?" You could hear the disappointment in my voice.

"No, I can't," he said so sadly.

"Well, I hope you enjoyed tonight," I said. Hoping he'd change his mind and come in.

"I did. Thank you for everything. I was not expecting it. Thank you for sharing my moment, making it memorable and for hosting."

"You are welcome. It was the least I could do," I smiled.

"Had I planned it, I would have come out and said I'm fighting and that would have been that. I might have served everyone a vegetable juice, some fruit and said good night."

I laughed because I knew he was telling the truth. I said, "I bet. Leave me in charge of the public relations events please."

"I think you and da crew just got hired," he said. "Matter of fact, the next party maybe in the works sooner than you think."

"What party?" I asked excited.

"The white linen party," he replied. Hoping it would be an engagement party.

Nodding my head, I said, "Name the time and the place. I got it covered. Just do me one favor please."

"What's that?" he asked.

I exhaled deeply then said, "Give me some time to plan." He kissed my forehead good night. "You sure?"

"YEAH!" And he ran down the steps. The Benz was still running.

I closed the door and set the alarm. I put my bags down, kicked my shoes off right smack in the middle of the kitchen floor, and got a fork for my cake.

I texted the crew.

FABULOUS! FABULOSO! FABOLOUSITY! Save me some cake! Leigh take tomorrow off. Love y'all. Send us the bill.

As soon as I hit send and unzipped my pants, I realized I hadn't worked out or done any work since two o'clock. I was just about to freak when my doorbell rang.

"What the freak?" I stopped dead in my tracks. I slowly backed up so I could see my monitor. I was startled and then realized it was Randall. "OH!" I said as I ran to the door. I did not even disarm the security system. "What's wrong?" I asked immediately.

He didn't say anything. Instead he grabbed me and hugged me tight. My phone and my cake hit the floor. I heard it chirping but I wasn't sure if it was from the fall or from a text. *The security company should be calling any minute*, I thought.

"Danielle, you are so special. What am I going to do with you? I was rude to just say bye after all the work you put into tonight."

My cell phone, the house phone, and his phone all started ringing at the same time. He let me out of the embrace and I ran quickly to answer the house phone, "Hello." I hit accept on the cell too. Whoever was on the other line could hear me talking and knew to hold the line.

While I was on with the security company Randall answered his call. "Yes Tre, I am aware. I know. You are right. I am in total agreement. Yes it was. Thank you so much for your love and support, but can you extend it some other time? Now, is not a good time. I know. I know. I understand. Can you give me the lecture tomorrow? I am a little tied up," he said as he looked me dead in my eyes. He then turned his back. "TRE!"

Once I finished with the security I whispered. "Hold on," into my cell phone.

"WE HEARD THAT!" Screamed the other end. Referring to Randall's voice.

"HUSH!" I said. "What's up Diva's?"

"Hey lady?" Paige sang.

"What y'all doing over there?" Sade asked.

I whispered, "Well I locked the door and he came right back. I am not sure what's going on but he and Pastor are having a heated argument."

"Go eaves drop and call us right back," Leigh said.

"Okay," I whispered.

"Pastor ain't no joke," Sade said.

"Bye y'all," I said and clicked off the line.

Randall was still on the line with Pastor as I heard him say, "Tre. Man, I hear you. Let a brother shine one night, damn. Just one night, that is all I ask. I don't ask for much. As a matter of fact, I can't remember the last time I required anything. All I want to do is fight and be happy. Is that too much to ask? Well, ride my ass tomorrow please."

He was quiet for a moment, listening, then he said, "You are correct this has transcended to a new level and who said it was a bad thing? You have to trust me man. I am going to do right if it kills me. Where is your trust?"

He continued, "Let me just say this and then I am hanging up because I am being extremely rude. Give me the opportunity to Fup. I have done the right things most of my life and I am not asking permission to do wrong. I need for you to let me live and make the choices I'm going to make." He listened a little while longer to Pastor on the other end. "Yeah, you and I both have had a sheltered life. You married your high school sweetheart and so did I. Now I am sorry that my decision did not work out; however, I am happy that yours did. You seem to be so worried and concerned that I am going to slip until you won't even give me air to breathe. I know right from wrong man!" He looked over at me, apologizing with his eyes. "I know you are doing your job. Let me ask you this, if you were not my friend would we even be having this conversation? You know damn well that if I did anything; and I mean anything, you would be the first to know. As my boy not as a confession to my Pastor. Damn just stop riding my ass please! Not tonight Trevor. I am on top of the world and you are pulling me down brick by brick. Not tonight."

He looked at me again then said, "I am so sorry. Excuse me please."

While he talked, I sent an e-vite. It included a song once the email opened, playing Where My Girls At by the late 90's girl group, 702. It read: *Ladies be prepared for a girl's night of fun followed by a pamper me day. Pajama party at my house tomorrow night to review pictures and videos! Then prepare for a luxurious spa day, lunch and lastly the viewing of the Twilight Movie.*

He came back to the room and plopped down on the couch. I grabbed a bottle of water and handed it to him. He sucked it all down in one swallow. He didn't say anything. This was the first time I had ever seen him angry. He was fuming.

I laid my head in his lap looking directly up at him. "Randall, you know he has a difficult job. I'm sure it's not easy for him to say some things to you just as it's equally difficult for you to hear. But, he is your friend and he wants you to stay in right standing in your vertical relationship. He is right you know. Talk to him tomorrow, maybe it'll be better then. This is hard for all of us. Remember, this is his job, this is what he does. Please don't be angry." But he was.

I continued to try to soothe him. "Calm down," I said. "It is bad timing, but take a minute to walk in his shoes. You have come too far to mess up now. How do you think he would feel if he has to counsel you on doing wrong? Like a failure I'm sure. If his own boy doesn't get it, ain't no way he can relay it to ten thousand plus people. It's cool, don't be offended. This is just as important to him as it is to you."

"I am not. He could have waited until tomorrow for this though. He didn't have to do this tonight, that's all I'm saying," he replied.

"Next time don't pick a Pastor for a best friend," I said, trying to lighten the mood.

He looked at me like, whatever. "Remember he wasn't always a Pastor but I should have dumped him when he was ordained."

We laughed. I heard my door opening.

"Hey y'all," said a familiar voice.

I threw my hand up. "What the hell Sade?" I said.

"What y'all doing?" she asked like a toddler.

"Nothing," he said. You could tell from his tone he was pissed.

She looked over at me then asked, "Why Auntie pants unzipped?"

We said, "Nothing," in unison and looked down at my pants.

She put her hands on her hips like she was grown and said, "Humph. That don't look like nothing to me. Pretty damn suspect if you ask me. Why is her head in your lap anyways? Never mind, I don't even want to know. GROSS!" She rolled her eyes at us. "Uncle Hooks when is the next shing ding?" She looked over at me and said, "Auntie zip your pants and get your head up. You are busted. Both of you are nasty."

"I'll let you know. Let me go before he GPS's me. Lord knows if he mess around and shows up we will have to fight like third graders. Not to mention, I really do not feel like kicking his ass tonight and it probably would not read well in the headlines. Boxer tackles Pastor."

I whispered, "You don't have to go."

He leaned over me and said, "I am glad to have the offer, but I better. You know I am doing everything in my power right now to do the right thing and none of this is helping at all."

"None of what?" I asked, clueless.

"A few things. One, my good news." He then eyeballed me below and nodded, "Two, you here with your pants unzipped with your head in my lap and three, Tre jumping down my throat. It makes me want to be rebellious and do wrong just because. I know that is not right."

We hugged and he left. He was a little calmer when he left my house but still it was obvious he was pissed. I have to admit, I'd love to be a fly on the wall and hear the conversation between him and Pastor Hunter tomorrow.

"Sade, pull me something out to wear to work tomorrow and make sure Leigh is not coming in tomorrow. Where is my cake?"

Sade frowned, "Auntie, you are going to eat cake now?"

"Umm HECK YEAH!" I replied.

"What happened to the cake you took?" she yelled out from the other room.

"Crap! It is at the front door where I dropped it," I said.

Sade came into the room and shook her head at me, "You are pathetic Auntie. Hooks has you so mesmerized you can't even hold a plate."

I swatted at her bottom, "GO TO H."

She stopped me mid-sentence and quickly moved out of the way of the swat, "watch your mouth young lady I have virgin ears."

●●

Pastor was feeling very uneasy and needed to vent to First Lady, "Baby wake me up in a few hours please," he said as he climbed into their Grand Venetian ultra-king sized bed.

"Okay honey, but what's wrong?" she asked, knowing when something was going on with her husband. She set the old-fashioned alarm clock on her nightstand, climbed in the bed, and snuggled next to him as they talked.

Sounding concerned, worried, or maybe both; Hunter said, "I am going to meet RW at the gym around six. I am not convinced he is going to keep his nose clean."

"Why not? He said he would right?"

"Yeah he did, but saying it and doing it is two different things babe."

First Lady chose her words carefully, "I'm not asking you to give me any information, but I want you to think to yourself of a time when RW has not done what he said he would do. Think of a time in which you know he has gone against the word of God."

"What is the point of this exercise?" he asked flustered.

"Honey, why have you lost trust in him?"

Pastor looked into the darkness of the room and answered honestly, "I don't want him to be vulnerable to sin. I want him to stay the way he is."

She rubbed her husband's chest gently, "Why do you think he will not?" she questioned him sincerely.

"A lot of reasons," he said. "He is ecstatic right now. I do not think he has ever been in a position where he truly liked someone. He has never had anyone show interest, concern and care for him the way that she does. This is new to him and I am really worried about him."

"Baby what's wrong with that?" she asked.

"You mean other than the fact that he is married?" he replied reminding her of the facts.

"Oh, is that what you call it?" Her tone suggested she didn't fully agree.

"That is what it is? We need to call and address sin as sin. You know the scripture or do we need to have bible lessons?" he said.

Still she pushed a little more with the hopes of getting him to view things differently. "When was the last time they saw each other? RW and his wife."

"I don't know."

"Yeah you have to know. Think back," she said and waited for his response.

"A few months ago I guess," he said.

"Try a few years Tre. With the same determination you are using to encourage him to do the right thing; is it the same way in which you've counseled him concerning him and Tameka's situation?" she stated aggressively.

"You know I can't do that," he replied.

"Why not?"

"I can't tell a person to divorce even if I personally feel it's the best option, the right thing for them to do and they want to."

"Not even as a friend? You would not suggest it?"

Stubbornly he said, "No, I will tell him what the Bible says about divorce."

First Lady continued. She knew she had him thinking now. "Trevor, I am asking you to talk to him as a friend, not Pastor Hunter to Deacon Washington. You have to separate the two people, honey. Just speak to him as Tre and RW. Step outside the pulpit this time. Are you harping on this because he is your boy or your Deacon?"

"Babe, I have to do a job regardless as to whether we are friends or not," he said.

"That was not the question I asked," she said holding her tone.

He looked over at her and said, "You sure are taking up for RW."

"No, no sides taken," she said. "I just want you to understand why he is mad. Tonight was a big night for him and to be honest, you ruined it. You have to ask yourself if you are showing him that you trust him or if you are going overboard. You don't want it to come to the point where you are pushing him into being like a rebellious teenager. I am sure that is not what you want. Good night Sweetie. Pray about it." First Lady had spoken.

He laid there and was at a complete loss for words. That was how First Lady rolled; she said what she had to say and closed the subjects. "Good night," he mumbled back. He laid there in silence thinking about how he had now caused commotion and ruffled feathers with both of his best friends. He lay on his back and waited a few minutes and said, "Furthermore, I told him three years ago to leave Tameka after she had been gone for a year."

At that, she rolled to her other side with her back facing him and spoke. "If that is the case, then the same tenacity you are using to encourage and strengthen him to do right is the same tenacity and resilience you should have used to encourage him to depart from Tameka. That would be the right thing to do. I am happy for RW. He wants to fight and he should be awarded the promise of happiness too."

He did not reply. He felt this had the potential to lead to more than what was necessary, so he kept his mouth shut. He could not sleep at all and if First Lady had not already expressed her opinion he would have gotten up and called RW, but he didn't. He laid there and decided he would wait for six AM and then show up at the gym.

Friday

Staying up late and getting up early was totally different from hanging out late and getting up early. I was use to the staying up late. It also made a difference that we were literally celebrating. The night before consisted of me moving around, dancing, hosting, and entertaining; I was tired to say the least. Not only was I dealing with fatigue, but I did not exercise and had a burger lying in the pit of my stomach, even if it was turkey. Since I was up early I knew had to play catch up for a few reasons. One, I cut it short the day before. Two, I asked Leigh to take off and three, I did not work at all last night and I have no intentions to work all night tonight either. Or shall I say, work that much.

It was only a few minutes before four and my body was trying to tell me it had not had enough sleep. I dressed anyways. While getting ready, I heard the thunder roar loudly just as the lighting lit up the whole house. *I have never in all my days heard thunder or seen lighting like this*, I thought. I decided it would be best if I drove my truck. I got all my stuff together. I got my shirt and shoes, and then just as fast as the lightning, I quickly raced out to the truck. Once inside, I immediately pulled my laptop out and synced it to my radio. I didn't waste time and logged on right there in the driveway. I found his coordinates and then used the crack berry to locate them. "Map it," I said. Instantly I was provided with directions.

It was a monsoon! *I should have stayed home a few more minutes. If I know where this place is it is a long way away from the gym. It has to be at least ten to twenty miles away*, I thought.

He was exactly where I thought the place was. It was raining cats and dogs as I pulled up on the side of him. I rolled my window down. He was alone and was not expecting anyone.

"Good morning," I said. He looked down. "Get in," I told him.

"I am soaked," he said not wanting to wet the inside of my truck.

"Who cares? I said. "You better get your tail in this truck before I get out!" I ordered.

He jumped in and plopped down on the seat. Either he was exhausted or still frustrated. It was his moment to shine and he should not have been upset about anything. That made me feel bad for him.

"What a nice surprise," he said breathlessly.

"I'm glad you feel that way. I am a little disappointed however," I admitted.

"Oh?" he said with raised eyebrows.

"Yeah," I replied.

"Why?"

"You are twenty miles from the gym, alone and soaked."

He dropped his head again. "Yeah."

"Yeah? I was expecting an explanation."

"What part do you want to know about?" he asked.

"All of it." His behavior was worthy of a butt chewing but I let it ride since I knew he was feeling some type of way right now.

"This is nothing," he said.

"The distance or the rain?" I asked.

"Both. You might as well get used to it. It will be more intense now. A lot harder and a lot farther. I took your advice and gave King the day off; he works just as hard I do. When I am up he is up. When I train he is right there with me. He needed a break too."

"Yeah, but you are going to mess around and get sick," I said.

"I hope not, but thank you for your concern," he replied. Then he looked over at me with a hint of a smile and asked, "Will you nurse me back to health?"

"Or course I will," I said. He then faked a sneeze. I looked out the corner of my eye. "Yeah right!"

I switched the satellite station to one that was playing a song that forced me to mentally make a wish. He looked over at me and asked, "What's up with your clothes?"

I was wearing jeans, a wife beater, my hair clipped back and my Birkenstocks were in the seat with him. "It was raining and I had to get in the truck in the rain. I have my shirt back there. I did not want to get my shirt wet or slip and slide in those heels."

"You are such a girly girl," he said.

"Is that good or bad?" I asked.

There was the smile. He said, "It's all good. Now, what are you about to do?" as we pulled up to the gym.

"I'm going to go to the office for a few," I said.

"Not before breakfast," he replied. "Come in my office, I'll make you a smoothie. Breakfast is the most important part of the day."

"Anything wrong?" I asked. I thought *the only way breakfast is important is if it is with you*, but I didn't say it out loud.

"Not really. I am just waiting on Trevor to finish ripping me," he said. Instantly his demeanor changed as he remembered why he was mad.

"You think he will?" I asked.

"Think he will? I know he will. He will be here by sunlight. I have looked at his calendar and it is a free day, so I am sure he will occupy mine," he said.

I pouted, "I am sorry he is ripping you."

He rubbed the tip of my nose with his index finger and said, "It is not your fault. He is not being malicious. He just wants to keep me on track, on target and focused. I don't think his intentions are for me to leave you alone, but just to stay on my side of the line. But heaven knows; once I can cross it (he paused) it is all over."

I blushed.

"He may actually help me without realizing it. This is almost the hardest thing I have had to do. To be quite frank with no disrespect intended, I think I may have used Randall's judgment on a few occasions, which may not have been the right thing to do, but it felt right at that moment."

"Are you going to be all right?" I asked while wondering which judgments he was referring to.

"I will be fine. Thank you so much for asking. That is very kind of you."

"Are you sure?" I asked.

"Yes I am."

"Are you really sure?" I pressed on.

"Yeah babe. I think I can handle Trevor. I fight with my fist, but he fights with the Word and unfortunately, he may be winning. The fight he is having with me is over flesh, and we need not wrestle with flesh and blood. I hate when he is right and he usually always is."

"I wasn't just speaking about Pastor Hunter," I said. "Are you all right with everything?" I asked.

"You know I have not really had time to think and focus. So to be honest, I'm not sure."

"What were you doing while you were running in this storm?"

"Thinking about you and how lame I am," he smiled. "Also thinking about how am I going to tell Trevor to stay out of my business?"

"I do not foresee that happening, but hey, you know him better than I do," I said.

"Yeah."

"Maybe he will go easy on you," I said trying to put him at ease. I knew he was not looking forward to having this conversation with his friend and Pastor.

"I doubt it. You have seen him in motion."

I replied, "I know, but he only means and wants the best for you."

He looked at the clock on the screen, "You have to get to work. It is almost six," he said.

Sensing that the conversation was getting a little uncomfortable, I asked, "Are you rushing me off?"

"No, I just want you to get to work before rush hour. Plus it is raining," he said.

"Oh, good idea," I said. Anybody that has ever lived in the ATL can attest to the fact that rush hour traffic was a beast, and even more so in the rain.

"As a matter of fact, let me go ahead and drive you," he said.

"You don't have to do that."

"No problem. Let's roll," he said.

I decided to take him up on the offer. "Okay, but you need to go and change into some dry clothes first."

"Get your stuff out the truck," he ordered.

I walked out the door while he changed clothes. Seemingly from out of nowhere, who of all people do I bump into this early?

"Beloved," he said so formal and authoritatively.

"Pastor Hunter," I replied. *What was he doing here this early? This was not good.*

He gave me a suspicious look then said, "Good morning."

"Yep, good rainy morning. Have a great day." I rattled off quickly then grabbed my phone to call Randall; I was trying to beat Pastor. You could hear the shortness of breath when he answered.

"Hey babe," he answered quickly as if to say what is it.

"Change of plans. You have company."

"What?"

"Call me later," I spoke quickly.

Just then I could hear Pastor, "RW."

"Humph. Thanks," he said annoyed.

"Speedy," Hunter spoke.

"Yes?" he replied to Hunter. He then said to me, "Have a great day. Call me if you need to I am just a phone call away."

"You too," I said in case he needed me.

I went to my truck and just sat there for a minute. I wasn't sure if I should wait around a minute or what to do. I finally came to the conclusion that there wasn't much I could do here. Pastor was resilient and was not taking no for an answer. *You got to love him*, I thought as I drove off.

∙∙

"What's up Tre?" Randall started.

"What's up? Why are you wet?" Trevor asked.

"It is raining outside." he responded sarcastically.

"Yeah but you are inside." Tre replied.

Hooks could feel himself getting irritated. "Now I am? Cut to the chase."

"Danielle is here mighty early," he smirked.

"Yes, and she is welcomed any time," Hooks replied in a tone that suggested the conversation was over.

At that, Trevor raised one eyebrow.

"Look Tre. I feel like I am under a microscope. What's going on man?"

Tre replied, "That is what I want to know too," he smirked again.

"I have told you. The story still remains the same and nothing has changed since the last time I told it to you."

Tre looked him over and asked, "Why are you so upset?"

"Dog, I think you know why," he shot back.

"Not quite. What's up?"

"This is some BS Tre and you know it."

"What is?" he asked as if he had no clue.

"How you riding me dog!" he replied, getting more upset by the second.

Trevor was determined to remain calm however and said, "That's only because I want you to keep your nose clean."

"It is clean!" His voice was elevated.

"Are you sure?"

Now, he was officially heated, "I am sure for the last f'ing time!" He threw his wet shirt across the room. "I ain't gotta lie man nor explain anything to you."

"Why are you yelling?" Tre said still calm and cool.

"I am yelling because I am a grown ass man, standing here soaking wet, in my own gym, before six AM, being chastised by my best annoying pastor friend; about something I have not done and I am about sick of this!" he yelled.

Trevor looked at his Presidential Rolex and politely said, "It is six nineteen."

He gave him the look of death and walked over to the double doors. Took the wet tee shirt off and changed into a dry shirt, but kept on the wet pants. He walked out into the gym area and grabbed a jump rope and began jumping.

"RW what's up with the construction crew?" He kept jumping. His phone chirped. "You want me to get that?" He continued jumping. He had yet to miss a beat. "It's a text."

Now he is reading my texts, he thought, but he did not say a word. He kept jumping.

Trevor read the text aloud. "Hey, I am at work," he read. "Take those wet clothes off and relax. He is being a good friend. You will appreciate it later. Don't be upset. Have a great one!"

"So First Lady is mad and the promise land has been shut down. Now you mad too? I probably won't get any until you get some." Trevor said laughing at the insult.

Randall did not speak but he thought to himself, *good for you. That is what you get.*

Putting down Randall's phone, Trevor continued, "I guess nobody is talking to me. Danielle was short with me too. Sometimes doing right will make you lose friends. It is a hard road following God."

Randall kept jumping but said, "That is what you get. You are being a jerk. This is supposed to be a high for me but you are making me miserable as hell."

"I am happy for you man." Trevor said with all sincerity. He really was happy for his friend.

Randall stopped jumping. "Yeah, well you got an F'ed up way of showing it. This is the worst behavior you have ever exemplified."

"I see Danielle is the only one that appreciates me being a good friend. She is a smart girl." He grabbed a jump rope and starts to jump too.

"What's up?" King said as he walked in.

"I thought I told you to take the day off," Randall said while he picked the rope back up again and resumed jumping.

"I am off," King confirmed.

"Then why are you here?" Hooks asked.

"They called me and told me you were running in the rain so I came to find you. I see you are in good hands though, Pastor got you."

"No I didn't, Danielle did." Pastor replied expecting King to go off.

"Good. I hope she ripped him for running in the rain by himself," King said.

He threw the ropes down in a tantrum. "I've had enough!" He went to his office and slammed the door.

Trevor and King conversed and worked out a little leaving the fighter alone to throw his little fit.

●●

He calmed himself down and dialed a number from his desk phone after realizing Trevor still had his cell.

"Hello."

"Hey son," he said.

"Hey Dad. What are you doing?"

"Working what are you doing?" he asked.

"About to eat breakfast," RJ replied.

"Oh okay, that's what's up. What's on the menu?"

"Cereal."

"Cereal?" *What the...?* He thought. For what he paid Tameka she could pay a chef to prepare his sons meals.

"Yeah Dad."

"That's healthy and filling," he said with extreme sarcasm. However, he wanted to say, "Tell your mother to get up and fix you a warm healthy breakfast," but there was no need in starting another fight for the day.

"I knew you would say that dad."

"Where is your mom?"

"Still sleeping," the child answered.

"What do you have planned for the weekend?"

"Nothing."

"You want to hang with an old man?" he asked.

RJ answered with quickness, "Yeah Dad!"

"Okay, cool. Wake your mom up and put her on the phone please."

He heard her voice as soon as RJ handed her the phone and cringed, "Who is it?" she asked abruptly.

"RJ's father," he replied.

"What?" she asked not comprehending his first statement.

"I was trying to see if I could pick RJ up today for the weekend?"

"Y'all woke me up for that?" she said sleepily and annoyed.

"It is an important question since you have custody of him Tameka, I have to ask."

She sighed real heavy and said, "This could have waited until later."

"I'll pick him up at three. Put him back on the phone please."

"RJ your damn daddy's on the phone. Waking me up to ask me a stupid ass question this damn early in the morning," she mumbled.

RJ grabbed the phone and said, "Hey Dad. Can I come?"

"Yes man. I will pick you up at three."

"Okay, I will be ready!" he said with excitement.

I figured since I had Trevor breathing down my neck I might as well make the best of it. Besides, I wanted him to go with me to pick up RJ so he could see firsthand how Tameka behaves. I wished he had been in here to listen to the call. Suddenly a thought crossed my mind; *I just made a decision without consulting with Dani. I need to call to make sure she doesn't have any plans for us this weekend.*

I picked the phone up again, but realized I did not know her cell or work number by heart. Mental note, *I need to learn those quickly.* I pulled it up via AT&T.com. *I won't forget it this time. Shoot,* the automated machine answered and gave the number and dialed it automatically. It happened so fast until I didn't get it all. It was so early until I had to zero out and dial her by name.

I answered the line immediately, seeing that it was him, "Dani Ro," I said.

"Hey."

"Hey there yourself," I said.

"How are you?" he asked.

"Oh, I'm just plugging along," I said.

"What are you plugging at?"

"A justice center right now."

"Oh," he replied.

"Yeah. They want it majority glass. Not sure I agree. It is a justice center. Haven't they heard never throw stones if you live in a glass house? They are asking for tons of broken windows if you ask me. Nevertheless, I will give the people what they want."

"You do. I agree," he said.

"You two playmates haven't killed each other yet have you? I am not an attorney and neither will I assist in hiding a body. Call Sade for that." I teased, but I did hope everything was going well between the two friends.

He laughed. "Not yet, but it is real close. He better be praying for himself or he may not survive this day," Randall said.

"You two will make up by noon," I said.

"Eleven fifty probably. I wanted to ask you a question."

"Yes sweetie," I replied.

She was unaware that just calling him sweetie did it for him. It melted his heart every time she referred to him in a term of endearment. "What do you have planned for the weekend?" he asked.

"I'm not sure yet. I haven't really thought about it to make plans. Why? What's up?" I asked.

"I am asking because I want to spend some time with my son this weekend."

"That will be great. I can chill or plan a girl's weekend," I replied.

"I vote for a girl's weekend if you don't mind." *No time for another guy to interfere.*

"Cool. I will be hanging with the girls while you; Hunter and Randall Jr. have a boy's weekend."

"I think I have had just about as much as I can take from Tre to be honest," he said.

"Aww, don't say that," I tell him.

"So is it cool with you?" he asked.

"Sure!" I said.

"You need me to plan anything or do anything?" he asked graciously.

"Yep. Relax and have fun with your son. You need it and he deserves it." I answered.

"I think if we take a few days apart, Trevor will ease up off of me too," he said.

"You may be right. I feel bad that I am the cause of all of this. It's such an awkward position to be in," I said.

"It is not your fault he is a crazy, possessive pastor friend. I need to seek help for him I tell ya."

I laughed, "Leave your Pastor alone," I said.

"He is your Pastor too."

Shaking my head, "Yeah, you are right," I replied.

"Well, I guess I will let you get back to work and finish building a glass courthouse. Go figure."

"Okay sweetie. I will talk to you later. Remember what I said okay."

He replied, "I will. I never forget any words you say. Have a good one babe."

After I hung up, it dawned on me that he consulted with me before making plans and asked if it was a good time for him to keep his son. *How sweet! That was impressive of him and let's not even mention respectful. You got to love the boy.* I continued to work, then reality hit me suddenly that Leigh was not coming in today. *OH CRAP!*

I sent a text in spite of the time. I had already checked everyone's calendar, but I wanted to confirm that tomorrow is fine for the girls.

> Spa, hair, lunch, dinner and a night on the town.

Paige responded.
> Sounds like fun. Count me in.

Leigh texted.
> I'm down.

Sade hit back.
> You are not going to be booed up?

> Sade, Ihateu.com. Party starts tonight at my house.

I wanted to talk to him and see him so badly. I replayed in my mind a hundred times, him telling me that he loved me. I really needed to spend some time with him so we could discuss this. Instead I continued to draw, draw, and re-draw my puzzle piece by piece. I grabbed a scratch piece of paper and started a brainstorming list with places to setup for tomorrow. Spa, hair, lunch, breakfast, Mikey's, dinner, movies, and pottery. "What have we not done in a long time?" I asked myself. It was after ten and I had not had breakfast. *If I can just make it until lunch I will stop. I am not at a good stopping point right now.*

• •

On the other side of town Randall was preparing to spend a day doing something else. Randall and Trevor both shared an interest in getting a haircut, but decided to do it tomorrow when they would have RJ, plus it would still be fresh for Sunday. Out of the blue Trevor said, "Hooks let's go check out some whips."

That broke up the silence and tension. This was surely a rather different type of retail therapy but therapy nonetheless. Hooks replied, "I thought you would never ask! Besides, you are a whip down and I need to treat myself to a gift for being allowed to fight again."

"Let's do it."

"Let me shower and I am ready."

"Do you know what you want to look at?" Trevor asked?

Smiling, Hooks said, "I sure do."

• •

I was still in my office, but I could no longer concentrate on work. I was fully aware as to why I could not concentrate. I wanted to talk to him. Desperately! I knew he was more than likely being ostracized by Pastor at this very moment and I really wanted to intervene. But what could I really do; they were friends. The entire situation was stressful; at least it would be stressful for me. I contemplated on working from home for the rest of the day, but it would really be of no use considering he was the only thing on my mind. I needed to see him and talk to him.

We had not had the time to fully discuss what this meant for him, and I had not had the chance to tell him how excited I was for him. I wanted to spend some quality time with him. Correction, I wanted to spend every waking moment with him and every moment that I slept, I wanted it to be next to him; on his chest and in his arms. I wanted to spend the rest of my life with him.

I laughed out loud at myself. Why? Because it had been a long time since anything, much less anybody had me so distracted to the point that I could not work. I was kind of both impressed and elated. It showed me I actually still had feelings other than the ones associated with my relationship with lines and blue prints. I felt ALIVE, my blood was pumping again, and all I could think was, *God is good.* It's far more than a cliché; He brought me this far by faith. The way I saw it, even if nothing ever surfaced out of this relationship, something special did in fact happen, and I was grateful. This goes for both Randall and I. He began to breathe again and I did too. We both were merely breaths on the mirror until we met. It was clear that life itself was now moving and breathing through us. It made me think and I found myself turning my iPod to Toni Braxton's Breathe Again.

I hoped this feeling never went away and if nothing materialized from this encounter with this amazing man; I was afraid I would never be able to breathe again. The same thing that brought us breath, I hoped would not be the thing that continued to take it away, but rather keep us together. I pushed my chair back and put my feet up on my desk. I looked closely at my shoe on the desktop and began to laugh once again out loud. I saw the visible scuffs on my shoes and was reminded how I got them last night. *I will run over to the mall one day and get them polished*, I thought, but right now I wanted them to stay just like this. They were memories of last night, picture perfect memories. I leaned back in my chair, folded my hands behind my head, and enjoyed every second of reminiscing.

I am not sure how many minutes passed while daydreaming when my phone rang. Initially, I did not move, but then I realized Leigh was not there so I had no choice but to answer.

"Hello, Danielle Rose. How may I help you?"

"You already have."

"Hey you!" I said with excitement.

"Are you busy?" he asked.

"Actually, I was busy. Busy thinking about you."

"Wow! We are on the same page. I love it and I love you too Dani."

"Thanks. Same here."

"Danielle," he paused.

"Yes," I said. He still did not respond. "Is everything all right?" I asked concerned.

"Yeah, we haven't had time to have a real conversation after last night. I feel bad. I would have much rather spent last evening alone with you. I am hoping we have a lifetime of evenings together. Don't get me wrong, I enjoyed last night. Not to mention, the party was the best I have ever had and it was for the best cause so far. However, I do think you and I need to celebrate alone."

"I would like that." My body slumped down in the chair.

"Unfortunately, I have occupied my day today and tomorrow. Would you be offended if we had to postpone until Sunday or later?"

I didn't mind that he was spending time with RJ, I simply replied, "Absence makes the heart grow fonder. Besides the anticipation will be exciting."

"If my heart grows any fonder I will be in ICU."

I laughed.

"I don't really know what I wanted to say or why I called. I just wanted too."

"It's fine. I was thinking of you also. Now my only problem is figuring out what to do with three rowdy ladies for two days. Any suggestions?"

"Yeah, I have one. Magically, drop them off with Tre and RJ while you and I escape. Name the place. I will meet you anywhere."

"Sounds like a plan," I said. "A plan that neither of us can go thru with though." I laughed.

"Can you imagine all of them together looking for us?" he asked then laughed too.

"Let's try it one day," I laughed.

"I would love to be a fly on the wall for that event," he replied.

"So, what are you and Tre up too today?" I asked.

"I'm sure he will badger me all day while I will think of you every minute; so I could care less. Why don't you go home and get some rest, that would make me feel better."

"I am going to blow this Popsicle stand in a few hours. Since you are tied up I was thinking of maybe going on a date," I said.

"Oh, that will be fun. Let me know where you are so I can come break his neck," he said all matter of fact like.

I laughed and said, "Just wanted to make sure you were still jealous. And there is no need in me letting you know where I am, after all, you can track me."

"I am, and by the way, I owe you a pair of shoes. Why don't you swing by the mall and pick up a pair. I will leave an envelope at the desk for you. Please note, I said a pair. Hopefully, I won't have to mortgage my house."

"Funny you should mention that. I just propped my feet on the desk and checked them out. I think I am going to get them polished next week."

"Next week?" he asked as if he was surprised.

"Yeah. I want to look at the scuffs today. Battle scars. Or shall I say the beginning."

"The beginning of what?" he asked.

"Whatever you want to call it," I replied.

There was silence for a brief moment then he said, "I am not sure I follow you. What are you saying?"

"The beginning of the millions of times you will tell me you love me."

He spun around and sat on the counter top in his bathroom. He dropped his head. "Oh that," he said.

"Was it not sincere?" I asked.

He answered embarrassed, "It was sincere."

"You can always retract the statement," I sadly offered.

"Statements." He was right; he did say it more than once.

"Correct," I agreed. "Statements. It's only fair that you're given twenty-four hours to retract. Sometimes when we're excited and so much is going on we get caught up in the moment"

"No, I do not want to retract. I wish I could do it differently," he said.

"Meaning?"

"Over a nice dinner with just the two of us alone. And when I say alone, I mean me being alone without legal attachments. I realize that I said it when my heart was heavy and full. Not to mention it was also one of the most important nights of my life. However, I made it complete by telling you exactly how I feel. Although, I didn't want to tell you while I was under a boat load of tears."

"I would not say a boat load," I giggled.

"Enough! Embarrassing."

"Why?"

"A big old grown man crying."

"Well if it makes you feel better, it wasn't the first time I saw you cry."

"Huh?"

"I sit next to you every Sunday," I reminded him.

"I don't cry in church!" he said.

"OH REALLY?"

"Yes, Really!"

"Seriously Randall?"

"Seriously! I am full!"

"And there is a difference?" I asked.

"Yes, and as a matter of fact, I was full last night too," he said.

"Full of what?" I asked. "Love?"

"I hope you don't feel sorry or pressured to agree. Or were you agreeing because you felt sorry for me?" he asked.

I pretended as if I wanted to change the subject and said, "Is that pastor calling you?"

"Don't try to get out of answering the question!" he barked.

"You are a pushy little man!" I teased.

"Did you mean what you said? If not it won't hurt my feelings. Tell me now," he said, sounding a little more serious and desperate for an answer.

I paused for a long second. Not for the effect, but because I didn't want to sound too excited or overjoyed. This was my last chance to pull out if I ever wanted too. I had to think quickly and hard. I really wanted to tell him that I needed to think about it. "Can we discuss it later?" I asked.

"We can," he paused. "Should I take this as a retraction?" You could hear the disappointment in his voice.

"I would just rather talk to you in person. Eye to eye."

"Oh okay. Then we will have to make a way to do it Sunday," he replied.

"No Randall, you will have your son. We can do it next week," I said.

"I will make a way!" he said with his voice elevated.

I had to shut it down because I felt an issue arising. An issue I wasn't prepared for and it was going to be useless. "I meant what I said and I said what I meant Randall."

"Thank God." You could actually hear the relief in his voice.

"What?" I asked.

"I said thank God." He held the phone to his chest. "I know this is bad timing but I got to run before mother hen breaks the door down. Call me if you need me. Pick up a pair of shoes and I will call you later."

"Have fun and keep your head up," I encouraged.

"I will."

"Randall!" I called out.

"Yes sweetheart," he replied.

"Congratulations!"

"Thanks, that means so much to me."

"I am very proud and happy for you!" I added.

"Okay, we will see what you say during training and after the first fight. I hope you will still love me with a black eye, busted lip, and swollen face," he said.

I laughed. "Just come back with all your teeth. I will handle the rest."

•••

Randall and Trevor went from lot to lot looking at cars.

"What are you deciding on dawg?"

"The first one I think," Hooks replied.

"Oh okay, what color?" Trevor asked.

"I want a different color this time. No red or black."

"What you waiting on?"

"You. It is your time. Remember?"

"I got to talk to first lady. You go ahead man."

Although he wanted to, he was reluctant as well for the same reason as his friend. "Naw, man," he replied.

He gave a look as if he didn't understand what the big deal was. "Why not?" he asked unaware.

"I got to get the check first," he answered.

Now he was really confused and said, "Since when did you start waiting on a check?" Trevor knew money was not the issue. He could purchase the entire lot if he so desired.

"Since I have someone riding my back," he replied.

"Who? Me?" he joked.

"Naw, man. Danielle."

Shaking his head, he said, "You are hen pecked already?"

"I am not!" he said offended.

His response didn't matter to Trevor. He knew what he was witnessing. "Yeah you are," he said. "Wait until I tell the boys at the barber shop tomorrow," he threatened.

"Watch it Tre."

"So, you are checking with Danielle first?" he asked for confirmation.

Looking like a lil' boy he replied, "Yeah, she thinks I am out of control."

"You don't?"

"No, not really. Maybe with cars I guess, but I had no reason to be in control of anything before now," he answered.

"I am sure I will regret saying this somehow, but I like Danielle," Tre said.

"Oh do you now?" he asked surprised at his friend's comment.

"I never said I didn't."

"Well, what did you say?" Hooks asked.

"I said pull up. I'm hanging all weekend to make sure you do."

"All weekend?" he asked not really ready for the answer.

"Yeah. I think this weekend is a good weekend for you two to slip up," he said.

"She is with her girls."

"And what does that mean?"

"She is busy and I will have RJ."

He looked over at his friend and cut his eyes. "Dude, who you think you talking to? You would and could make a way. I am not new to this man," he said.

He knew in his heart that his friend was right. He replied, "I'm cool."

"You are cool? BS! That girl is everything you have needed. You can't keep your hands off of her. I can understand why. She is smart; on top of all of that, an all-around beautiful person."

"So why are you riding me so hard about her?" he questioned him further.

"Because I see what you see. We all see it. I want you to see it too, but I want you to see the brick wall named Tameka in between you two. Once that wall is moved, then I am still going to ride you. You better hurry up and handle your business man before she is gone."

He dropped his head. "That would be my luck. She has been single for four years and now that I am interested she will suddenly become unavailable."

"Yeah, and I told her not to wait," Tre admitted.

He couldn't believe what he just heard and immediately got a little heated. "You told her what?!" he shouted.

"I said if another man comes by don't miss him. Seize the opportunity."

"You said that bull for real dawg?" Hooks furiously asked.

"Yeah. Right is right and you know me? I got to tell her the right things too."

"You should have told her it was mandatory she wait for me and here you go throwing her in the arms of another man. What kind of friend are you?" he asked not really offended, but the thought of Danielle with someone else did bother him.

"So you know what that means?"

"Yeah, that I should kick your butt," he replied.

"No, that means you have got to handle your business. Let's talk about your shamelessness last night."

He did not want to talk about that. "What about it?" he yelled.

"How you gone just tell the girl you love her in tears in front of a room full of people with a camera snapping? Man, I taught you better than that. You are making me look bad. If I was living vicariously through you, honestly, I would be ticked off at myself. You have got to pull the emotions out of this and get back to the real of it."

He gave him a suspicious look. "You were supposed to be praying. How do you know what I was doing?"

"I was, but I can do more than one thing at a time."

"Tre man, you killing me bruh. Why are you my friend?"

"Hooks. If I wasn't riding you right now you would be enjoying the fruits of her labor. Your emotional state is going to lead you to intimacy."

He punched his arm.

"You may need to take it back down a little. Man that was a hard punch." he said while rubbing his arm.

"I meant for it to be."

"Tell the truth." Trevor said.

"About what?" Hooks asked.

Trevor raised his eyebrows.

Hooks knew exactly what his friend meant. "I would not right now. But last night it was a STRUGGLE for me. I could have gone through with it even with you in the next room. It wasn't you that was stopping me though, it was this legal attachment. Tameka keeps ruining my life man."

"I KNEW IT! I KNEW IT!" Hunter yelled out.

"I, I, I don't know what to do now," he said frustrated.

"Now that I know what's up. Once the papers are signed, I will still be riding you. Let me call Mama and tell her you are moving in," he laughed. "I'm serious. I have to keep all my eyes on you. You can't do this alone." He paused for a moment as if he had a good idea. "Now that I think about it, this may be right on time. I have a project I have been working on and I was trying to figure out who I was to delegate this to. I think you just bought yourself a project," he said.

"You trying to keep me from my girl. I know how to handle me. I know how to be abased and abound," Randall replied.

Rubbing his chin at that. "Yeah, we do don't we man," Trevor replied. "We have been on both sides and have gone from bologna to Boars Head. The long and hard way!" Hunter chimed in thinking Danielle was never involved.

Randall said, "Yeah man. Life has had its days with us. Ain't nothing wrong with a good bologna sandwich though, cooked just right with a lil' burn around the edges. Shoot, sometimes I eat bologna just to remind myself of how I got here. Through the power and strength of His might. Not my might, my power, or my fight. I could have been long dead in my grave it if were all up to me."

"Come on Deacon! Preach boy!" Hunter said in his church voice.

Hooks pulled it like the old pastors, sweating and spitting. "Ahh, well," and he went to preaching.

They had service right there on two-eighty-five. The roles had been switched. Pastor was the Deacon and the Deacon was the Pastor.

Once the Holy Spirit inspired service was over, Hunter said, "Randall."

He knew he was serious because he rarely called him Randall. He had called him RW ever since they were kids. He prepared himself to listen intently.

"I have three things I want you to take away from today. One, you are missing a calling. I know you have heard the voice of the Lord tell you to take it to the next level. You heard it a long time ago."

He felt the chill of goose bumps rise on his arms at that moment. "You are right Tre."

"Why are you not being obedient?" he sincerely questioned.

"Two reasons. I can't take it to another level until I get this issue right," he answered honestly.

"Jesus didn't ask for you to be right before you come to him."

He nodded in agreement. "I know, but I would hate to take on a higher title and position and I have drama. Let me get this drama done and over with. Can you see me in the pulpit and Tameka roll up acting a fool? Man and then I have to take it back to the street? Nah bruh, that might not work, not right now." he replied in thought.

"Boy, don't do it."

"I have been more than patient with her. I think that would set me over the top. Besides, how could I be expected to counsel anyone else when my own marriage is whatever it is? Let me get all of this together first. I can be a divorced Minister, but not one with a wife he hasn't seen in over a year. Honestly, I don't want to see her."

"So you are aware of this calling?" he probed deeper.

"Oh yeah. I've known it for some time now," he confessed.

"How you gone handle it?" Trevor asked.

"What do you mean?" Randall asked back.

"With fighting, Danielle, divorce, etc.?"

"I am not going to run her off before I get her. I can't tell her that yet."

"You better find out from the beginning. You had a first wife that did not understand your career. The last thing you want is a second wife that feels the same way." Trevor made a valid point.

"I agree," he said deep in thought.

"You said there were two reasons. What is the second one?" Tre asked.

"I don't want to take your shine away," Hooks replied.

"Shine?"

"Yeah. I get to preaching and you are done buddy."

"Go ahead on with that. Man, I need some HELP! Help me, please. I'm out here making it happen, but I want to go to sleep at night too. I want to relieve myself of some of these duties. Come on board man and help your boy out," he replied sincerely to his friend's joking comment.

"You have Elder," he replied.

"Yeah and I need ten of him. I need your help and his."

He nodded his head for a moment and said, "We will see."

"So do you love her?" Trevor asked, catching his friend off guard with the question.

He slowed up almost forgetting he was in the fast lane on two-eighty-five in pre-Friday traffic. "Trevor. I have never felt like this before in my life. I don't know if I can fully explain it, but I do know that I want this feeling forever. I never want it to go away. She makes me happy and I want to make her happy too. She believes in me, encourages me, inspires me and she trust me. She not only listens, but she hears me; totally feeling whatever I throw at her. She's smart and she is beautiful. You can see for yourself man; she has her own and can hold her own. The icing on the cake, she is a woman of God. I need her. I feel like I can't live without her." he paused for a brief moment, "Where has this incredible woman been my entire life? I would give her the world."

Even a blind person could see it a mile away; his friend was in love no doubt. "When you have the right person the feeling will last forever," Tre replied. There was a long silence.

"You riding to pick up RJ?"

"I can."

"I need you too," Randall replied. He knew Trevor had to see Tameka's behavior first hand to fully understand what he's been up against.

"Okay."

Once they arrive he parks in a way so Trevor will be able to see everything that happens from his passenger seat. He rings the bell and RJ comes to the door with his bag. "Where is your mother?" Randall asked.

"Upstairs asleep. Bye mom!" he called out as if this were the norm.

Randall thought to himself. *How does she even know for sure who he is with?* This was out of control and was the reason he wanted Trevor to come be a witness. Now he could prove he had not seen or had really spoken to Tameka. This is what their relationship was like and how it had been.

As soon as they got into the car. He said, "What's up RJ!" Then he quietly said, "Hooks, I see you are correct. Your point is taken."

Randall replied, "Thanks." He was grateful that someone else saw firsthand part of what he's had to deal with.

"Sorry."

"No need to be. It is what it is."

●●

I did what I hadn't planned on doing. I worked all day. I made it to the crib around five. I hadn't spoken to the girls at all, which was unusual. As soon as I rounded the corner, I could see why I hadn't heard from them. There they were, already at the crib chilling. I got out the car and went inside. As soon as I walked in, how do I say this; it appeared I walked into a war zone! It looked like my refrigerator had been raided and for the first time I didn't care. "Ladies, how did the party start without me?" I asked.

"Get dressed Auntie. We have the night planned."

"What do you mean get dressed? Girl, please. I am always ready." I took my blazer off and unwrapped my blouse to expose my wife beater and wah lah! I was ready. They all laughed. I really did want to change. "I'm not messing with y'all. I am changing." I headed to my room to get dressed.

They laughed so loud. I was missing the fun and apparently had missed most of it. I knew I had to fight the temptation to stay home and work. I felt like I really needed to stay and finish the final touches on this building I had been working on. I had to get a mock sample for an upcoming presentation next week. It wasn't quite where I wanted it, but I also needed to pull away from it. It was all I looked at all day. I found myself changing it, changing it more and then re-changing it back to the first change; this went on all day. Truth be told, I'd prefer to be in my oversized chair snuggled with my Boo. Whatsonever, my three ladies was a very nice substitution indeed. Instead, I was looking forward to our girls' night out.

"What's the game plan?" I said as I entered the danger zone.

Paige looked around at all the ladies, then back to me and said, "What do you feel like?"

"I planned for tomorrow. I thought you all had tonight covered," I answered.

"You want to wild out tonight or tomorrow?" Sade said.

Leigh said, "It doesn't matter. I am rested up and ready for whatever."

I threw up my hands and said, "Well, I am not hitting the pole tonight. It's you all's turn." We laughed. "I have to do everything. Let's hit some tapas and then check the salsa joint out," I suggested.

"Sounds like a winner to me," Paige said. "Let's ride."

I knew I didn't feel like driving tonight, besides I wasn't sure which car I wanted to take anyways. When we got to the garage I looked at Sade and said, "You pick. You driving." She shocked me by choosing the drop top instead of going for the Panamera, like I assumed she would.

"Nice choice," I nodded. As I looked at all of us I couldn't help but observe how we were so much the same. A group of modest women set to go and have a good time and enjoy the company of one another. We were all dressed in our typical attire. Skinny legs, distressed capri's, stoned pockets, low rise, tank, wife beater, halter, tube, peep toes stacked, heels high, strap around the ankles, slides, glittered, shadowed, glossed, clutched and Buckhead bound.

Anyone who knew ATL knew Buckhead was the place to be. One thing was for sure, you never went to Buckhead to post up. You went to bar hop, club hop, and hit spot after spot. It was still twilight and we had plenty of time ahead of us to enjoy the evening hanging out. Back in the day, we could go through all the astronomical sunsets and sunrise on any given night (daylight, twilight, dusk, dark, etc.). Somewhere along the way, the ex and the job retired those nights for me. Tonight however, I had to admit I missed them and I felt one coming on. This was always a good location, not too close but not too far. The best part was the fact we could always hit Mikey's up on the way back. Actually, that is how I met him on one of these nights. Sade was still a kid back then.

I hoped in behind Sade, sat back, and let my hair blow in the wind as we went through the gate. It had been a good week. In the words of Ice Cube, "Today was a good day." I laid my head back and reminisced. My Randall, my Deacon, my Hooks, my Boo told me he loved me and he has been allowed to fight again. Now, I have the pleasure of chilling with my girls, my sister, my baby girl, my assistant, my best friends and me. All the folks who have my back, my spotters. Life was good! What more could a girl want?

The ride was quiet as we were in chill mode as we rode through town. As we drove, I observed the architecture along the way as if I had never viewed it before. We arrived at our first destination and as soon as the valet opened the door, it was like girls gone wild. We were mentally preparing ourselves for a big event as we drove over. We walked the pavement to the entrance of the establishment as if it was a catwalk. Charlie's Angels had nothing on us. Once we entered, we hit the high tops and the fun began.

Around nine thirty my phone rang. It caught me off guard at first because everyone that would normally call me was with me. Then I heard Randall's ringtone so I immediately stood up and proceeded to the door so I could hear. I hit answer and quickly stated, "Hold on. I can't hear you." Once outside I posted up on a banister and gathered my composure, trying to play it cool. After all, I did not want the man to know that he always made my heart flutter. I moved my feet so he could think I was still walking while I got myself together.

"Hi," I said.

"Hey babe. How are you?" He really wanted to ask, "Where are you?" But decided against it.

"Hey you. I am good and you?"

"I'm good. I am missing you." he said sounding as if he was embarrassed to admit it.

I rolled my neck back and smiled so hard until the people walking by stopped. I waved. I said quickly into the phone, "I miss you too." It came out much faster than I meant for it to. Why on earth I felt the need to speak it so fast I do not know. I immediately hoped it didn't come across like I was trying to say it before anyone else heard it. "How was your day with the boys?"

"It was good."

"And you and Pastor? How are things with you guys?"

"Well," he said then hesitated.

"Well? Everything okay?" I asked.

"Well, he simmered down. He told me exactly how he felt."

"And how do you feel?"

"I am not sure, but I do know he has no intentions on letting up on me any time soon. I really think that once this issue is resolved he is going to be worse."

"You think?" I asked. However, my mind lingered on the statement he just made about the issue being resolved. I thought. *Does that mean he is pursing resolution seriously?*

"Yeah I know."

"Why?" I asked.

He didn't answer right away, but instead said, "Well, I know you are out. I don't want to interrupt that."

"You have time." I could tell he was hesitant.

"He knows that legally my hands are tied and I am not going to do anything stupid. But once the legalities are over he is not sure what may happen," he answered.

I thought to myself. *He has not been with a woman in four years. That can't be.* I could hear his iPod from his other ear playing Rupee Tempted To Touch. "Do you think you can do it?" I asked.

"Do what?"

"Do right?"

"Well, I have done so for this long," he replied.

"You also said that was due to legal reasons." I reminded him.

"Well yeah."

Curiosity got me, "What have you done for the last four years Randall?" I asked.

He thought that was a strange question and wasn't sure if he wanted to answer it. "What do you mean?"

She knew that it was now or never. She had no choice but to go hard in the paint. "You once said you and Tameka have been apart for four years right?" I paused, but he said nothing so I continued. "What have you done?"

The question was a shock to him, he was totally off guard and unprepared to answer her question. It was more shocking to him that she would ask and a shock that she felt the need to ask in the first place. "I have done nothing," he replied.

"What do you mean nothing?"

Now he was slightly confused, yet curious. "Maybe I do not understand the question," he said discombobulated.

"Yeah, I think so."

"Okay, so what is it you want to know?" He hoped she would be direct.

She took a deep breath and asked, "What have you being doing in reference to your needs? Physical, emotional, conversational, intimate desires and so on and so forth."

I thought that was the question she was asking, he thought to himself. "Yeah, I will make it my business that we speak on Sunday," he said concerned. He didn't think now was the time to have this conversation. He continued, "No matter what accommodations I need to make, we'll talk. We have a lot of ground that needs to be covered and it must be treaded immediately. Let me say this again. I am not sure if you were not listening the first time or if you forgot, but let me tell you a second time. I told you Tameka is the only person I have ever been with."

Oh! No he didn't second time check me, I thought. He didn't say it in a defensive tone, but in an I told you this before and I am shocked you would ask me again kind of tone. Well, since he jumped a little let me go ahead and get froggy with him. "I do remember you stating that, and if you recall correctly, I responded that I was just one up on you. Now that we have our intimate past open and behind us, let's go back to the original question." I paused long enough for the effect. I figured I would just let that simmer for a bit and then resume. "The question was and I will repeat and omit intimacy. What have you being doing in reference to your needs? Physical, emotional, conversational and so on and so forth. These are separate needs Randall and can all be filled by one person or multiple people. You are aware of that right?"

She is serious. Calm down Randall. How do you respond? Just then Trevor walked in. He threw his hand up gesturing that he was going to back out the room, but Randall motioned for him to stay.

At the same time Sade and Paige peeked out the door to check on me and to make sure I was still there. We had a rule that we were never to leave each other alone and I had already broken the rule. I think they only allowed it because of who he was. I motioned for Paige to come over and of course Sade came as well. I motioned for her to go back with Leigh, but she kept coming anyway. I bucked my eyes. I needed Sissie only. Right at that moment I heard his iPod stop.

"Danielle," he said.

I could clearly hear his tone shift gears again, but this was a question I wanted to know the answer to and I wasn't going to be shy about it or retract it. "Yes," I answered.

"I am going to say this as best as I can and hope there is no further confusion or conversation."

"I can't promise, but okay. You know what, truthfully, it's not that important. We can discuss some other time." I said backing down. *Why did I bring it up and then back out?*

"Yes, it is important. You have alluded to this before, so it must be significant to you. I am sure we will have this conversation again on Sunday. It is very imperative to me that you know and understand who I am and what I stand for. I should not expect for you to automatically know considering I am constantly having to even remind my best friend that I am not the guy everyone suspects I am. And to answer you; yes, I do know there is a difference between a physical, emotional, conversational, and intimate relationships. For right now, however, I hope we are both clear that we have two of those relationships covered with each other. The other two positions are and will remain vacant for both of us until things change." he hoped she agreed.

Trevor raised his eyebrows and folded his arms at that remark.

He didn't ask questions, but he did make a statement and a command. "Humph, what do you mean the person we suspect you are?"

"Meaning for the last four years I have detached myself from the things you are asking about. I have not involved myself with conversation, physical, emotional, or intimate relationships. That is why I was not prepared to fight. You have taught me that all of these are required and a necessity. I shut myself off from the world and basically from myself. Sure, it was probably not the best idea, but if it did not involve God or working out, it was not on my agenda. No matter how hard I worked, I was not prepared and now I understand why. I was not mentally prepared." He paused waiting for a response. "I think we need to have this conversation soon, but right now, you are out with your girls and I do not want to disturb your evening."

"No, I apologize for asking an inappropriate question." In all honesty, I wasn't sorry. This was only one of many questions that required an answer as far as I was concerned. The next set of questions was how did he get with Tameka and why did he stay so long in an unhappy, unfulfilled marriage.

"Inappropriate, no. Unexpected, yes. However, we are supposed to be able to talk about anything and everything, right?"

"I would hope so," I genuinely replied.

"We can. Just for the record, there has not been a woman in my life. Period! Not a friend, a girlfriend or a boo. A friend girl either. None! No one!" He looked up at Tre then added, "Or a man for that matter." Trevor nodded. Pastor Hunter had strong, valid biblical reasons and views on that topic. Considering this day and time Randall always felt it was important to mention it in certain conversations and this happened to be one of them. "Don't ever get it twisted. Let's just get it all clear." He threw his thumb up to Tre. "Believe me; I've waited a long time for you."

I smiled and leaned on Paige's back.

"Promise me we will continue?" he begged.

"We will," I countered.

He changed the subject and asked, "So are you having fun?"

"Yeah we are. Long night ahead!" I said enthusiastically.

"Do I need to send someone to get you all?" he enquired concerned about their safety.

"No, but thanks for the offer. I think we should be fine."

Think? That was not the word he wanted to hear. "Are you sure?"

"Positive. You do too much anyway. Check the net to locate us at any time. I am sure you even have a way to detect my blood alcohol levels along with my levels of excitement to tell if a man is around or not."

"No need. I trust you. Hopefully, it is mutual." he casually mentioned.

"It is." I whispered.

"So, what's the game plan for tomorrow?" he asked.

"I'll have the pleasure of trying to convince them to be up and ready for boot camp at six AM. Considering that we are dancing tonight, I'm not too sure how well that will be received so early in the morning. Other than that, the spa, then breakfast, hair, lunch, maybe a movie and dinner is on the agenda. What about you and the guys?"

"Gonna hit the gym around six and then go to the barbershop afterwards. Think we'll check out the car lot too and then RJ and I are going rock climbing. More than likely Tre will go home and prepare his final touches on his sermon." He took a deep breath and hesitated. "Speaking of which, let me just forewarn you to not be shocked or offended if the sermon steps on your toes. Or shall I say our toes? You know, something I learned about preachers is that they are like comedians. Sometimes for people to get the message, they have to use real life experiences. Should it happen, just look straight ahead and no one will know it is us. Don't worry about what he might say though; I will handle him in the gym or the ring another day."

"Thanks. You got me boo?" I asked.

He smiled at her calling him her boo and replied, "Yeah, I got you." Suddenly he remembered part of the reason for his call in the first place. "Oh before I forget, I want to bring up one quick thing before you run off to dance with some buffed up guy." he supposed.

"I don't quite think there will be any buffed guys dancing Salsa tonight. Besides, I have my eye on a heavyweight Deacon at my church."

"Is that right? Better not be any buffed guys. I can fight just a little. Scratch that, I can fight!"

"That's right. This guy I have my eyes on is sort of stalking and threatening me. In the meantime, what is your question?" I asked.

"While Tre and I were out earlier today, I realized I have not treated myself."

"Oh!"

He cut her off. "Listen. I was thinking about a coming out present."

"Well." I replied closing my eyes at the thought.

"I wanted to know what you thought would be a sufficient gift to give myself?" he asked.

"Hmm, a new pair of gloves," I guessed.

"WHAT?" he said sounding surprised and disappointed by the answer?

"You heard me."

He sighed, "Can I send you a picture?" His voiced pleaded.

"Sure, go ahead" I said. My phone chimed as a new message came in. "Hold the line." I opened the attachment. "Oh hell naw!"

Startling Paige with my scream, she shouted, "What's wrong?"

My mouth dropped wide open as a lemon and a lime Lamborghini appeared on my phone.

"Why not?" He begged sounding like a little boy.

"Randall, where is Hunter?" I demanded.

"Tre," he called out as he placed my call on the speaker.

I started in immediately, "My answer is no. The last time you two were together he came back with an Aston. You are sitting over there so worried about what he is doing with me until you are not looking at what you are doing with him. I'm checking you Pastor. My final answer is HELL NO! Did you two hear that loud and clear?"

Looking over at his friend, pitifully, he said, "Will you at least think about it?" he asked forgetting the fact she just said no.

"Boy, don't make me cuss!" I yelled.

"You already did," he said with a little bit of an attitude.

"Do I need to quote scripture?" I asked.

"Go right ahead," Trevor gladly chimed.

"Be a good steward. He who is faithful over a little will be ruler over much." I scripturized without skipping a beat.

"My bible scholar!" Hunter laughed so hard until he was almost out of breath. While it was annoying RW.

I said, "Bye" but before I could hang up Randall took me off of speaker.

"Danielle."

"What now, baby?" I said in my Auntie sarcastic voice.

"Be safe and call if you need me. You know I will not sleep until I know you are home, so please let me know when you make home safely. Kiss the girls for me. I love you."

"Thanks, I will." Right then I planted a kiss on Paige's cheek and she screamed. "I love and need you too." We hung up. "Bye Sade!" I shouted.

Looking as if her feelings were hurt. "Why I got to go away?" she shouted back.

"Because you left Leigh by herself," I reminded her. "Not to mention because I said so."

As soon as she was out of ear range I spoke, "Paige I do not think he has ever been with another woman."

"Serious?"

"Yes, girl. Really."

She nodded her head and raised her eyebrows. "Well that may not be a bad thing," she said.

"No, I do not think it is, but how do I handle it?" I asked.

"The same way you would handle any other guy."

I didn't think that helped so I asked, "And?"

"Act natural."

Shaking my head. "I just don't get it. How is it that a well-acclaimed fighter has been with only one woman, but an a-round-the-way hood goon has been with every trick on the block, her sisters, and her best friends? Got the tats, the babies, the drama, and the stories to tell."

She pointed at me and said firmly, "We don't roll like that. Be happy you have landed a real man. A praying man and an honest man."

"You're right. Four years is a long time. He got me beat. And who would have thought that me with my two boyfriends had somebody else beat? This is a shame?"

"Lame not shame honey," she corrected me.

"Huh?"

"Y'all lame."

"Thanks Sissie. That made me feel better! Let's go."

I texted him.

> I think either lambo is out. Let's strive for that after winning the next fight.

> Can you just look at them?

I was not about to give in.

> Nah that would be a sucker move.

> You run a tight ship Mrs. Washington.

> I do. Always remember that.

We hit all the stops and danced the night away. My feet were swollen, but I kept the heels stacked as we hit one club after another. Finally, we jumped in the car to stop by Mikey's on the way in. I wanted to call Randall so bad while on the road, I really wanted to hear his voice. Instead I gave my full attention to the conversation in the car.

We walked in Mikey's. "Ladies!" Mikey called out, excited to see us.

"Papi!"

"Uncle Mike-Mike."

"Let me get you something. Where y'all been?" he asked observing us closely.

"Salsa dancing," Leigh said exhausted.

"Where is the riff raff?" he joked. We all knew to whom he was referring.

"We left him home," Leigh replied. "Girls night out."

"At whose house? He let you out?" he asked with his back turned to me.

"Let me? Come on Michael." We all laughed. "You know me better than that."

"Okay, okay, what will you have?" he asked us.

He took our orders while we enjoyed the music and each other's company. At two AM sharp, my phone chirped a text. Not only did I look, but everyone stopped what they were doing to view my text.

> Hey babe. I know you are having fun. I am missing you. Are you close to calling it a night? We both have to be up early. Let's try to get a few hours of sleep. Please!

I read it and could not decide if I wanted to respond right away. I looked at Sade and she asked, "Is that our call to go home?"

"Yep. I think it is," I answered honestly.

Rolling her eyes she said, "This dating thing has too many limitations. I can't live like this. We are tracked, followed and stalked all day," she pouted. "It's like I am dating him too."

Leigh got her clutch, "Well I'm leaving," she said. "I'm not getting in any trouble dealing with you three. I am staying on his good side. I will be getting my Vegas fight tickets!"

Sade and I both started counting to one hundred. We had a rule that we were not to respond right back to a text to avoid looking desperate. Unless of course, it was one of us calling or texting. We counted real slowly.

> We are at Mikey's preparing to take it in.

He didn't fight by the same rules. He quickly hit right back. In his profession when you hit, he hit back.

> Great! You know what to do.

We finished our plates, said our goodbyes then went to the car. We laughed all the way home. It was a good night and we all enjoyed ourselves. The moon was bright, the sky was clear and love was in the air for me. As we hit the heart of downtown, I couldn't help myself. I found myself doing something I always ended up doing whenever I entered this part of town at night. I asked Sade to pull over.

I stood in the seat of my car and looked at the skyline. The majority of the buildings that had been constructed within the last ten years had my footprint. If not mine then it was one of my mentors' buildings. Most of the cranes were erected to prepare for a D-RO original footprint. Right at that moment, I felt as if this was my city, my town, my skyline.

"Leigh give me your camera please," I said. She handed it over and I snapped and snapped with the camera. Then I grabbed my iPhone and took more pictures until I could not any longer. All my shots were practically the same.

I looked at my girls and said, "So sad. It's true Sissie. I am such a lame." I gave a weak smile.

"We are proud of you Auntie," Sade said.

"Thanks baby Sissie." Sade always thought that was a compliment, but it wasn't. I wasn't calling her my baby sister, but rather my sister's baby. A replica of my sister. This equated to a baby Sissie.

"I couldn't do any of this without my right hand," and leaned over to Leigh who was snapping too. "It really is a shame. I have the ability to design and build the most amazing buildings any one could imagine, but I could not get a man. Now I have managed to stalk one down, who happens to be designed to my blueprint and specifications but he is married." It was suddenly a depressing moment. My fun escaped quickly.

"Wrong approach," Paige said. "Change your thought pattern."

Yeah I said to myself. "Easier said than done." I felt like a drug abuser although I had no real idea of their world, but right now all I know is I was addicted to someone that may not be good for me. Someone I technically, legally, and morally could not have. His situation was not promising. I rode in the back seat in complete silence on the ride home. I flipped through the camera and attempted to pull my laptop out and download right there in the back seat.

Leigh, however, stopped me. She looked at me and said as politely as she always does, "No ma'am. Not tonight."

At that moment I really wanted to cry, but I held up. I scanned the photos in my phone and picked the one that had the most lighted background and forwarded it to Randall. The caption read: I Built This City!

He hit right back.

> I am proud of you. Even if I have never told you. Your talent is spectacular. I admire your work.

> You haven't really seen my work.

Within minutes he sent a slideshow of my work and posted it as a flipagram. *That's from the thousand-dollar book I sold him* I thought to myself.

> I will autograph that for you one day.

> I would like that. You can do so in the new house you will build for us.

As I was smiling inside and out I remembered something.

> You do know I do not have an autograph from you?

> You will have a million cards and notes. Until then, I will make it my business to provide you with something more personal.

I didn't respond. I just laid my head back on the headrest and closed my eyes. I was not sleepy, but just needed to think in darkness. When we made it home I decided to give him a call while the girls and I were changing out of our clothes in our respective bathrooms.

"Hey," I said when he answered the line.

"Hey babe," he replied.

"Are you asleep?" I asked. I knew he would be wide-awake at least until he had heard from me to let him know we made it in okay.

"No, I'm still up. I was about to blog," he said.

"About what?" I asked curiously.

"That it was three AM and I didn't know where my baby was," he replied.

"You are so full of it!" He laughed. "You sound tired," I noticed the difference in his voice.

"You know Danielle, I am for some reason."

I figured I knew the reason why and simply stated, "Hunter."

"What about him?" he asked.

"Let's just say that he can drain you," I replied honestly.

"How so?" he questioned.

"If he chastised you in the way that he lays it down in the pulpit, then it's draining. It's consuming, but in a good way; if you know what I mean."

"I am not sure about all that, but I will admit I am tired."

"You are not planning on running in an hour are you?"

"No."

"Good," I said. I was glad that he was going to allow himself some rest, but I was a little surprised.

"I don't want to leave RJ alone and I am sure he would not be happy to be awakened at the crack of dawn to lie in the truck or go running with me."

I thought about what he said for just a few seconds then asked, "Is that so?"

"Yeah," he replied.

"Well Randall, if this is the case then he needs to be over every night," I stated.

"You have no idea how much I wish my son could be with me every night, but for now, I will just have to come up with a different plan for when he is here."

"I should have known," I said. Knowing full well there was no way he would not train at the crack of dawn every day.

"What time are you hitting it in the morning?" he asked.

"I am about to break the boot camp news to the girls now," I answered.

"I guess I'll see you in a few weeks after you recover," he teased.

"Big Mama Rose always said if you run the streets all night then you should be able to get up in the morning and handle business. I got this," I shot back.

"Okay then. Text me back and let me know how it goes," he said.

"I will. Good night Sweetheart."

"Good night my love."

We both held the phone like a couple of preteens, no one wanting to say anything more to the other. Although we both wanted to hear it, needed it and felt it. Love was in the air.

Everyone met back up in the living room with our blankets and pillows. The television was turned down low and all phones were on chargers. I flicked the Mac on and immediately got an ugly look from Sissie. I decided to put it down for now but I knew it would only be a matter of minutes before they would be asleep anyways.

"Good night sisters. We are not listening to that damn pecking all night either Danielle," Paige said.

"Good night friends," Leigh replied.

"Sleep tight," I said.

"Don't let the bed bugs bite," Sade chimed.

I waited a few minutes until it was completely quiet in the room and the phones backlights had dimmed. I then said, "I love you all. Boot camp at six AM."

"WTFH?" Sade blurted.

Leigh sat up and asked, "Did she say Boot Camp?" she looked around in the dark for a few seconds then said, "I am not going!" As she laid right back down.

Paige asked, "Why you didn't say this earlier? You just had to go and ruin the night. I don't want to get up in two hours. Is the instructor fine?"

"Love you too."

"Ihateyou.com." Sade growled.

I texted Randall.

> It didn't go over well but not too bad.

"STOP!" Paige screamed. "If y'all do this texting and blogging all night then y'all need to be together. I don't want to hear it."

I closed my eyes. I did not think sleep would find me, however, it did. Obviously, just like Randall, I was exhausted; Salsa did me in. It seemed that no sooner had I closed my eyes, I was awakened by his ringtone ringing in my ear.

Saturday

"Hello," I said groggily.

"Babe."

"Yes?"

"You still asleep?" he asked as if it was unusual.

"I guess so," I replied. I'm sure it sounded as if I was being sarcastic, but I really wasn't. "Wow, I didn't even realize I had fallen asleep."

"I'm sorry sweetie. It's almost six AM," he said.

"Oh crap, we about to miss boot camp!"

"I thought you said six?"

"I did. That is when we needed to be up, but it doesn't actually start until seven. They must have poisoned me for me to sleep late."

"Get ready. Hit me back once you get moving. By the way, Keith is outside waiting to chauffeur your girl's day."

What! I jumped up and went to the glass door and sure enough a Hummer Limo was parked out in front of my door. I could see Keith standing outside the truck.

"Take your time. He will be waiting. He is all yours today."

I was so surprised. I said, "Randall, you did not have to do that."

He smiled. "I know. Enjoy. I wanted too."

"Randall!" I still couldn't believe it.

"I know. I will miss you too," he ignored my last comment.

Full of emotions I replied, "Aww."

"Now that I am being a punk let me get this boy up and wrestle with him before you know who shows up."

Seductively I said, "I will wrestle with you willingly."

"I would love for you too," he replied.

"Have fun and don't tell him you spoke to me this early," I said referring to Pastor Hunter.

"Are you asking me to lie to my Pastor and best friend? I will do no such thing. As soon as he walks in the door I am going to spill the beans."

"Why?" I asked like a little kid.

"He is still my best friend."

"Oh, so are you going to kiss and tell too?" I asked jokingly.

"Probably," he replied honestly without thinking twice about it.

"I am not and I refuse to go back in that office ever again for disciplinary reasons," I growled with all seriousness in my voice.

He laughed a hearty laugh.

"Good bye." I said sarcastically. I hit the iPod and blast Set It Off.

That woke em up! "What is going on?" The three non-morning people asked.

"BOOT CAMP! Let's get it!" I jumped up like I was a drill sergeant ready to get the troops in line.

"NO!" Sade screamed like a two year old having a temper tantrum.

"HELL NO!" Leigh said. "I will never do boot camp again in my life."

Paige said, "Lord why me?"

I said, "Come on the driver is outside."

"Driver?" Sade jumped up and looked out the door. She hit the alarm and opened the door. "Who is that?"

"Keith."

"I know that smarty, but why is he here?" she asked suspiciously.

"To take us to boot camp, come on let's get ready. You can sleep in the car."

"Come on Leigh, this might not be so bad after all," Paige encouraged.

Leigh mumbled, "I will ride but I am not participating in no boot camp."

We all got dressed and threw our bags in the back. You could tell Keith was not use to being with this many women at one time alone. I'm pretty sure it probably sounded like a good idea to begin with, but now if he wasn't already, he would soon hate the idea.

When Leigh approached the Hummer, she mumbled something that he may have taken for a good morning. Paige practically growled at the man. Sade gave him an up and down through her David Yurman shades and said, "Nice Keith. Real nice." I don't think he got it, but it was a compliment.

It was then my turn. "Keith! What do I owe the pleasure?" I said, sounding every bit like a hyper hyena.

"It will be my pleasure," he replied in his monotone voice.

"Are you sure you want to be bothered with four old birds all day?" I asked.

"As sure as I can be."

"Have you gotten enough sleep?"

He looked a little nervous now and replied, "Didn't know it was going to be dangerous."

"Get ready," I said. "I hope you have some form of energy drink, you'll need it. It is going to be a rough ride for you."

"Looks like we will be stopping at the store to fuel up," he was talking my language.

"I will pick these girls up some manners too."

He laughed, "They are cute."

"They bite," I said.

"I bite back," he replied quickly then laughed.

"How did you get stuck with us?" I asked sincerely.

"King and Tony are stuck with Hooks, Tre, and RJ. I got lucky I guess."

"It sounds more like you got punished. You can kick us out anytime you feel like it," I told him.

"My orders are to not let you all out of my sight."

"We may have to blind fold you then," I laughed.

The rude one yelled out, "Are we going to sit here all day while you two talk? We could have stayed asleep!"

"Say something else and sleep may be permanent for you." I leaned in and said. "You got a long day ahead of you Keith. I hope none of this is being taped. Speaking of which," I said pointing to the bags, "Hey, grab those two bags and never let them out of your sight."

"I take it those are your computers?" he asked.

"Yes, and cameras."

"You know I was told to not let you have them," he said.

"I won't tell if you won't tell." I smiled a million dollar smile trying to win him.

"We will see how the day goes. Do you ladies have an agenda?"

"Not really," I answered wondering if he was really expecting an itinerary. That may be the Hooks way of doing things.

"Good, I have your tentative itinerary," he said then pulled out a sheet of paper and closed the door." He entered in the driver's side, rolled the glass down between us, and asked, "What would you all like to listen to this morning."

"Ying Yang Twins," Sade announced dryly.

Keith shook his head, but seconds later it was blasting. It reminded me of back when Sade was in high school, we listened to this type of music traveling to, and from her many activities, band, cheerleading, track, etc. Yes, the Ying Yang Twins definitely worked. By the time we pulled up to the gym we were crunk to def. Leigh was still adamant about not doing boot camp though, so we compromised and opted for yoga. Yes, one may say I settled, but really the truth of the matter is I was out numbered. One thing was for sure, we were not doing Paige's option of hot yoga.

Keith opened the door for us and grabbed the bags. He got his water and what appeared to be several newspapers. He pulled a chair from somewhere and took a seat right there in the room. I didn't think that it truly constituted him actually sitting there watching us the entire time. *Like really? Who wants to do anything to us? Never mind, that's a bad question. There is someone somewhere out there that would love to catch us in a dark alley.* After the class he picked up his chair and once again grabbed the bags. This time; however, I took one from his hand. We did a bag shuffle. "We can carry our own bags," I protested.

He pulled back and waited until we got all our stuff and went directly to the locker rooms with us. He propped the door open and sat inside the door. Not caring that other women would be inside dressing and undressing. It was more than obvious Keith had never been assigned to work for a bunch of girls before. This was going to be a very interesting day for him.

Of course, we did what girls do and took our sweet little time changing and getting dressed. I threw on some shorts and a colored tank. We all came out at the same time. He stood and immediately followed behind us. We got to the truck, the rest of the girls first and just as the last time, I was the last one in.

"Ms. Danielle, what's next on your agenda?" Keith asked.

"Oh," I leaned in the truck. "What's next?"

He said, "Never mind. Hooks has it covered."

From the looks of everything, it appeared as if he did have it covered. I glanced at my watch. It was still early, but that still didn't stop me from wanting to call him. I didn't want to disturb his time with his son and his best friend.

Instead, I did what everyone else would do. I texted him.

> Hey, just checking in. How's your morning going?

> Hey babe. Excellent! Everyone is behaving on my end. How are you?

> We ended up doing yoga instead of boot camp. I am thinking Keith may need a bonus or a Percocet after today. Why is he being punished? LOL.

Randall concerned about Keith's day he thought deeply before he texted.

> He may not show it but I think he is excited. He probably rather be with you all than us. I don't go too far without King. I do not think you have met Tony. Since you've worked with Keith before I felt you would be more comfortable with him. He has been assigned to you until you meet the other guys. Besides I do not think you like King.

I was called out.

> No, I like King a lot. I appreciate the fact that he has your best interest at heart. I'm just hoping he will pipe down a little and realize I am not out to hurt you.

I think she partially told the truth about King.

> I think he knows you are not out to hurt me. He has to get use to this like me. He has never had to share me. This is all different to us. I think Tre is feeling it too. We will talk about it tomorrow. We are still on right?

> Of course.

The girls were busy talking, texting, and emailing; I was the last thing from their mind. When I looked up, I thought *OH CRAP! They are going to lose it.*

Keith stopped the truck in front of our breakfast spot. Leigh and Paige picked up on it immediately.

"He is crazy!" Paige said.

"My kind of guy!" Leigh added with a wink.

"I'm bout sick of him, you, and this healthy life crap!" Sade grumbled. Keith extended his hand to help her out the car, but she wouldn't budge, "I refuse to get out of this vehicle until someone promises to take me to Waffle House!" Paige pushes her out.

As she grabbed Keith's hand he said, "I got you baby girl."

She smiled and said, "It looks like we may be friends after all. Why does Uncle Hooks own a juice bar?" she asked me.

"I don't know," I replied. "I didn't ask him."

"Keith can you answer that question?"

"Yeah, he drinks a lot of fresh squeezed juice," he replied.

"Has he not heard of the bullet? I mean, he had to go and purchase a juice bar. I eat a lot of chicken but I don't own a chicken shack or a chicken coop," Sade said sarcastically.

He smiled. You could tell he wanted to laugh but was trained not to.

We walked in and to my surprise, and the girls, there was actually food available too. We hung out there until it was time for us to go to the Spa. I hoped the employees and patrons did not think we were a rowdy bunch. Although we tried our best to behave, we were still a little rowdy I'm afraid. It wasn't until we pulled up to the spa that I realized no one paid for their breakfast. *I am going to get Randall.*

We all walked in like a posse. We checked the menu and stated our services. I offered Keith a service, but he refused. He said, "Maybe next time. I would love to, but there are too many of you all here for me not to pay attention. I am sure I will regret declining it tomorrow."

"I think you will too," totally understanding his position.

The spa was able to accommodate us and even put everyone in the same room, despite our different services. I just knew this was going to be the perfect opportunity for us have a little girl talk without the extra set of ears, but I was wrong. Keith followed us to the room. Once we were inside and prepared to change, he stepped outside the door. After the room quieted, he knocked and entered. We were all lying on our respective tables. I was laying there preparing for my relaxing body wrap.

"Come in," Paige said.

"Man in the room," he said and sat in his chair.

Where is he finding all these chairs? I almost felt like he was bringing these chairs into the different places with him, although I knew he was not. Moments later there was another tap on the door.

"Yes," Paige said. Four people entered the room.

"Sir, we have room for you too," a voice attempted.

"No thanks. I am on duty," Keith replied in a tone that said there would be no further communication.

All the ladies, myself included, lifted up our bodies when the group entered. There stood three sexy men and one lady. The lady looked at me and immediately walked over.

My eyes got big as I figured out what was going on. "Oh hell naw! No offence Olga but I will take the cutie," I said.

Keith did a poor job hiding his smile as he said, "Sorry, Ms. Rose. Orders from the boss."

"You lying to me?" I asked.

"No ma'am." He never looked up from his paper, but I could see the smile on his face. With an attitude, I lifted my body from that plastic with the sheet, went over to slap the light switch off and grabbed my phone.

The girls laughed. "Sorry Sissie," Paige said through her laughter.

"The down falls of being booed up," Leigh chimed in, cracking herself up even more.

"I'm sorry Auntie D."

I looked at my masseuse and she looked and me. I said, "This is some BS. Straight BS. I guess we are stuck with each other. One thing is for sure, if I am stuck with you then he will surely not be reading the paper today," I said referring to Keith and the reason I cut the light off.

I laid back on the table and immediately texted Randall: INSECURE?

Then I heard a noise, but it did not come from my phone. I lift up and flashed the light from my phone in Keith's direction.

He winked. "What's wrong D?"

"I hope not what I think," I replied. Who gave him permission to call me D?

"Yeah it is," Keith said in almost an insulting tone. I rolled my eyes and said, "Don't get on my bad side Sir."

"What's going on?" Paige asked annoyed as if we were disturbing her deep tissue massage.

"I texted Deac but he texted Keith back instead," I said.

"What does the text say Keith?" Sade chimed in taking my side.

"Shh."

Blank stare. "Did he just shhs us?" Sade asked. "You don't even know; we will jack that phone from you."

"Now text that back," I said and rolled my head in the other direction.

"He wants to know if you are pissed," he said. Right then Keith had a feeling he was going to spend the day relaying all the messages that came from Hooks today.

"And?" I asked.

"And what?" he said dumbfounded.

"What are you responding Keith?" I asked annoyed.

"I said not really," Keith said snidely.

Just then my phone chirped. Randall was finally responding to my text.

> No. I am not insecure. I am simply avoiding having a reason to be.

> If I can't have a guy, then I am not paying for this.

I texted that as if I was hurting his feelings or his pockets.

> Not a problem. The day will come real soon where a somewhat handsome guy will give you as many massages as you want.

> Yeah, yeah, yeah! Let me speak to Pastor.

> Can't do that. I'm just getting him off my back.

He texted proudly. I laughed to myself.

> Not a problem I will see him for myself tomorrow.

> Have fun!

I texted with sincerity.

> Keith may have a black eye the next time you see him.

Not even a second later Keith's phone sounded. "Is that right?" he asked me. "YEP!"

"What now?" Paige asked.

"I am over here getting threats!" he said.

"Oh, from who?" Leigh asked unaware and concerned.

"Your sister over there just told my boss she was going to give me a black eye."

"Only one? A pair would be much nicer," Sade said. "You always do everything in pairs Auntie."

We finished our services in peace and quiet, however, I did manage to sneak and check messages. I think the rest of them were asleep. Keith actually stood and held my phone and then got my laptop for me to work. *I could so get used to this.*

When it was time for me to go shower Keith stood right outside the door. Luckily the shower was in the same room. If it had not been, I am not sure what he would have done. After all, he could not be in two places at one time. Or could he?

Once we were all done we hit the steam room for a few minutes. Low and behold, Keith came in with all his gear on. He removed nothing. Not even his hat.

We finished in the steam room, exited and headed to the locker rooms. He spoke in a tone that I hadn't noticed before. It was his bodyguard voice. He went inside to check the ladies room. He then said to our masseuse, "Stay here. No one is to enter this room."

He went on one side, turned on the shower, and quickly changed his clothes. He was still dressed before any of us. Once he got dressed, he opened the door for the other ladies to enter. You could tell they were a little perturbed they had to wait, but after they saw him it was evident their curiosity was sparked as to why a guy was in the women's locker room. It was then I realized how handsome and fit Keith really was. If you like the muscular type, then he was a hottie. As for myself, I preferred thin guys. Randall was fit and ripped, but appeared thin at a glance.

We dressed and I went to sit on the bench to review my calendar. I checked the time and was trying to see what was next on the agenda.

We were outside when I realize I did not pay again. I quickly turned back to go inside. "I will be right back," I said to the crew.

"The bill has been covered Ms. Rose." Keith said reading my mind.

"He makes me sick!" I growled.

We got in the car and I looked for the button to roll the window down in between us.

"Where are we going?" Keith asked.

"Hair salon. Can you get Randall on the line please?"

The phone rang over speakers in the car. He picked up. "My main man. How is it going?" he asked, assuming it was Keith calling in.

"Hooks!" they all sang.

"Hey ladies! Y'all are like Hooks Angels."

I sat back while they all conversed, loving every minute of it. I liked the way they all took to each other. It is usually hard to get everyone to agree on the same guy. *This was going to be a killer if nothing further happens*, I thought. I didn't know which was worse, my crew, or the fact that he had a crew everywhere he went, or that his best friend was a Pastor. Not only a Pastor but his Pastor and mine too. We had some tough challenges in front of us.

We both had a package deal that came with this relationship, although they varied for very different reasons. Mine was because they were my family and loved me. His was because they had become his family and it was their job to cover and protect him but in the meantime they had grown to love him too. Suddenly, Thanksgiving dinner crossed my mind and I smiled. *How uptight that will be? I better plan a trip.* I always wanted to travel on a holiday, but we never had reason too. Our family was here. *This year we may be travelling*, I thought.

"My love," he said, interrupting me from my thought.

"Yes," I replied.

"Are you okay?" he asked.

"Oh, yes. I'm fine."

"How was your massage?"

"Body wrap," I corrected him. "A little disappointing," I said, thinking back to having the only female masseuse.

He smiled; he knew why she said it as the thought of her having her body wrapped pleased him. "I am sure it was fine."

"She wasn't fine," I replied.

"Good," he said then laughed.

"You are such a smart ass," I threw in.

"Thank you," he replied as if he just received a sincere compliment.

"How are you?" I asked.

"Good."

"What are you and the boys doing?"

"I just got out of the barber chair."

"Are you skinned to the bone?" I smiled at the thought of him with a fresh cut.

"Just like you like it babe."

Immediately I heard Pastor say, "Watch it son in the background."

"Can I speak to him?" I asked.

"NO!" he quickly replied.

"Uncle Hooks Why are you with Pastor? Are you in trouble?" Sade questioned in a kid friendly voice.

"Kind of."

"Are we seeing you today?" she asked.

"I don't think Danielle wants me to intrude on your girls' day. Speaking of which how is Keith working out?"

"He is a little possessive, but I guess he will work; unless we have another choice," Sade said as if Keith could not hear her. They all laughed. Keith looked up in the review mirror and scolded us with his eyes.

"You didn't say if we are seeing you Uncle Hooks," Sade questioned again.

"I wasn't planning on it. I know you all need your "girls" day. Plus, I have my son and I am with Tre all day. He is doing everything in his power to keep Danielle and me from each other."

"Aww. That is Pastor, always doing right. I do not even like kids or Pastor's. They are both scary. What the heck, you can bring them too," she said.

"No, I'll let you ladies have your day. I will see you all tomorrow. If my calculations are correct tomorrow is dinner at D's."

"Yeah baby!" Leigh said.

I had not even thought about that. CRAP! I thought to myself. "You all will be having pizza!" I said quickly.

Looking up from her Kindle, "Pizza on Sunday?" Paige yelled rolling her eyes.

"Why?" Sade simply asked.

"I will not have time to prepare a menu," I replied.

"I got you tomorrow babe, but it will be kind of late. I will take RJ home around four and I will be there about five, but no worries, I have you all covered."

"You do not have to do that," I quickly said. "You have done enough already."

Not in agreement, "Like?" he asked.

"For starters, you are ruining Keith's day." Hearing his name, he looked in the review mirror. "He set breakfast up and I am going to make an assumption you paid for the Spa." I said.

Leigh sang, "Thanks Hooks!"

"Thanks Uncle Hooks!"

"Ditto Randall!" Paige chimed not looking away from what she was reading.

"You're welcome Angels! Don't say another word D. I have dinner tomorrow. It will be from the grill. You do have a grill right?"

"FUNNY!"

"Just asking," he said, not meaning to offend her. He looked up and noticed he was being watched. He said, "Babe, let me run; Pastor is looking right down my throat. I will see you all tomorrow. Yo Keith!" he called out. "Keep up the good work. You *can* handle a bunch of girls." He laughed. "Babe?"

"Yes."

"I will talk to you in a little while."

"K."

"Bye."

"Bye," I replied back. I held the word a long time.

Keith looked back at me through the rear view mirror again. My head rested on the headrest. We held eye contact for a moment. It was as if his eyes had something to say, but I couldn't figure it out. I made a mental note to be sure to ask him later.

The girls ragged me all the way there. "Why didn't one of you say I love you?"

"Because he is married," I said.

"And?" Paige asked.

I couldn't believe she questioned that. "That's a big *and*," I said.

"Why?" She said.

I lifted my head off the headrest and looked at her directly. "It is a no no as far as I'm concerned. We can't just freely sling around the word love and he is still married. That is asking for trouble, legally and emotionally. I don't think I want to put myself in that position."

Leigh looked at me and quietly asked, "Do you love him?"

"I do not think it really matters right now," I replied thinking.

"Yes it does," she said in a tone that demanded an answer.

"Not really, like Tina said, what's love got to do with it? What's love but a second hand emotion? Who needs a heart when a heart can be broken?" I had started something for sure because they all started singing. I reached down in my handbag and pulled out my iPod, attached it to the adapter and turned to Tina as we sang all the way to the salon. Keith made eye contact again and although I still could not read his mind, this time I am sure he read my mind. He read my heart rather. He gave me the hood nods up which was cool.

The girls were so into singing Tina's song that they didn't even get out of the car when we first pulled up to the salon. Once we were all out of the car Keith came inside also. He took numerous calls and he even had the chance to read his newspaper. The afternoon had come really quick and before we realized it, we were just about finished. Suddenly I got a text from a number I didn't recognize.

What's next?

I looked up and around, then at Keith. He gave me the nods up and I knew then it was from him.

Pottery a few blocks down.

POTTERY?

Yeah it is relaxing.

You relax?

I looked directly at him while texting.

YES I DO! Do you ever relax or are you always this uptight?

That is surprising.

I did not respond after I rolled my eyes at him. He did not answer my question about him relaxing or his crew but I didn't pry any further.

When we were done we left and went to do pottery at this quaint little pottery studio just a few blocks away from the salon. We were so excited, you would have thought we were a group of five year olds instead of adults.

"Keith would you like to join us?" I asked.

He smiled although he looked appalled and said, "I think I just may. I have never done this before." I guess the excitement had gotten to him and he had to try it out.

We had a great time, made some really cool and some rather unique pieces. When we finished painting, we decided we needed to eat.

"Where are we going?" Leigh asked always excited about food.

"It's your time to pick Paige," I said.

"I thought you had the day arranged," she replied sharply.

I sighed. "Why do I have to do everything?" I asked. "Fondue."

"Cool!" Sade said. "We will just be hungry when we leave like we always are."

Keith looked in the mirror. "Fondue?" he confirmed.

"Yep." If we were going to make a day of it we might as well do all the things we don't normally do.

As we were riding, my mind wondered as it often does. I then realized I had no clue what I was wearing to church. I leaned up in my seat and asked, "Keith can you stop on exit two fifty two?"

They already knew where I was headed, "Oh no!" They shouted.

"I know, I know!" I said. "Twenty minutes max. I promise." I told them.

"We are timing you."

As we pulled up to Smith's I thought, *I better get something to wear to church tomorrow. Hmm, they have a lot of new stuff today, I might need to stop and get Randall some ties to match.* I picked out orange, purple, light blue, black, and royal blue. All of the suits were nice, but I was really feeling the orange specifically for church tomorrow. I finished talking to Smith, checked out and went to the car.

"Do you all mind if we stop and get him a tie?" I asked.

"No Auntie. Call Saad and let him know we are on the way," she suggested.

We pulled up to the front entrance of the mall and Keith got out and opened the doors for us. I quickly grabbed my suits and exited. *Oh no they didn't.* It looked like I was the only one getting out. I leaned back in the truck. "Oh no you all don't. We are doing this together," I said.

"You don't need us." Paige insisted still engulfed in her novel.

"Y'all come on. Please!" I whined pitifully.

Keith stood there, I knew he wanted to laugh but his face was as stern as any solider outside the Buckingham Palace.

When they finally got out he closed the truck door. He was a bit taller than I thought. I looked him dead in the eyes. "You are coming too. Park the truck," I said.

He looked as if to say, where do you want me to park? "Where?" he asked mildly.

"Valet, I suppose." I opened my wallet and gave him a bill. He shot me a look like I had insulted him. "Fine. Stay right here. I have to do everything!" I snapped. I stepped inside the double doors and found Security on the other side. "Excuse me Sir."

He looked up at me and replied, "Yes ma'am. How can I help you?"

"It appears there is nowhere for the Limo to park and I need the driver to escort us in. We plan to be in no more than twenty minutes. Can we leave the car here on the curb? You can call us in the men's department should an emergency occur. I am leaving you in charge." My statement didn't come across as a question, but rather an assignment. He smiled and I politely smiled back. *Apparently, I've been around Randall too long. I was giving out commands like he does.* I had to laugh at myself a little.

"You have twenty minutes," he said.

"Thank you," I said. "You are the greatest!"

I called out for Keith and told him, "We are good. Lock it up."

The girls were already with Saad the personal shopper for the store. Saad had unfortunately become a person I had to call upon for numerous unexpected events. Mostly work related but he always faithfully came thru for me. There have even been times in which I have dressed, had makeup and hair done right in the mall and managed to make it back to the building to entertain; as if I knew about the soiree months in advance. Keith stepped through the door with a questioning look on his face that asked what did I do to get the security guard to oblige. Hooks wasn't the only one that had the power to make things happen.

I looked at him and answered his nonverbal question, "I handled it," I said. He eyed the security guard like he was giving him a death threat and I peeped it. "Not my type." I said. He was a much older gentleman.

Keith said, "I know and now you will no longer be his type either. I wasn't informed I was going to be breaking necks in the mall. I thought it would be more like at the club."

"The night is still young," I said. I walked fast since this wasn't in our original plans. I certainly didn't want to spend a lot of time taking away from the girls' day."

When I made it over to the ties they had laid out a very nice selection. "I need shirts too," I said.

"You didn't say that!" Leigh said, "But we got you." Saad immediately disappeared to retrieve some shirts.

I examined them closely by putting my suits up against each tie. I looked at Keith and asked, "What do you think?"

The orange tie they selected was nice. That is the one I really needed if nothing else considering I wanted to wear the orange tomorrow. I was thinking the orange and light blue tie. These were certainly two colors I would not have ever put together. It was beginning to be a tad bit of a challenge trying to mentally figure out what he needed to wear as well. Originally, I was thinking chocolate but I came to the conclusion the orange and light blue was not going to work with chocolate. Then I came up with khaki or taupe with an ivory shirt with this tie. Nah, it was still not pulling together for me. Black and blue would be too dark. I wasn't quite sold on it yet, not to mention Deacon Washington and Pastor Hunter were very on point when it came to their wardrobe and accessories. I knew he would wear whatever I gave him, but if I wasn't fond of it in the store I am sure he would not be either.

Saad and the girls busily brought out other options for me to choose from. They placed next to my purple suit a tie with different shades of purple, lilac, and lavender. The royal blue had some funky colors and the black one had tons of nice options.

"Saad, let me get a lavender shirt, a light blue, a black and a dark gray," I said. "I am still uncertain about this orange."

"You better pick something Auntie," Sade said. "You know Deacon Washington is not going to wear it unless you get it right. You know how he and Pastor are very fashion conscious. "

"I know right," I replied. "This may not be a good choice after all. I may have to go with one of these other colors. I can do the purple or royal blue. Umm, let's see, the royal blue would work as well."

"What don't you like?" Saad asked.

"I don't know. It is just not flowing smooth. It is not saying what I want it to say." I looked at all the different combinations spread out before me trying to make a decision.

"Let me look. Danielle, tell me what you think about this?" Saad asked, putting another set of shirts in front of her.

"Oh nice Saad. I think this will work. He brought me a pale orange shirt with white collar and cuffs. This may be what I need to tie all of this together," I said with a smile. "I will take them all. What's the time?" Twenty-seven minutes had passed. "Are we good?" I asked.

"Yeah I think so Sissie. You do not have to rush. Take your time if you are not sure."

"I think I am good."

"Saad, can you press the orange please?" I asked.

"I will take care of it for you," he replied.

He wraps up my purchases, I pay him, and we head back to the limo. We decided to go eat at the Melting Pot, the best fondue restaurant in the ATL. Keith sat at the table with us for the majority of the entire meal. We had real girl talk just as if he wasn't there. Our topics ranged from who would put chocolate on whom, to who would lick, touch and whatever else to whom? It was our typical girl time together, nothing but one hundred percent keeping it real girl talk.

Once our dinner was complete and paid for I could tell Keith didn't want to interrupt, nevertheless he asked, "Are we ready ladies?"

Sade gave him a flirtatious look and said, "Come on Hercules."

I gave her the look of death. "Behave!" I said in a tone only she could hear. Then she mumbled something under her breath that I could not make out.

"I can hear you," Keith said.

We all snickered.

"Where to?" he asked.

"Heavy Weights," Leigh answered.

We all looked. This was different. "Why heavyweights?" Paige asked.

She shrugged her shoulders and said, "It is too early for Mikey so where else do you want to go?"

"The restaurant?" Keith confirmed.

Sarcastically Sade replied, "Yes Hercules."

On the ride to the restaurant, we cut up all the way there. We rolled the limo window between us and Keith up and down, up and down; it is a wonder we did not kill the motor. Our conversations were something that no guy, other than Mikey, had heard. While we were so busy trying to make sure Keith didn't hear us, I would not be surprised if this back seat was being taped anyway.

We pulled up to the restaurant and it was a little more crowded than I expected. Keith escorted us inside and I realized I had never been through the front door. We sat at the same booth Randall and I sat in when he first brought me there. *Where is the music?* I thought. It seemed a little odd that there wasn't any playing.

"Hey," I said to the guy on duty at our table.

"Yes, Ms. Danielle," he answered.

"Please, call me Dani," I said. "I need to get in the truck."

"Hold on let me get someone over here." he spoke into his earpiece and immediately one of the security guys came over.

I nodded hello and he nodded back. I have seen him a few times, but I do not think I have been formally introduced. I followed him out to the truck and retrieved my laptops. On the way in I stopped by the bar and asked what time would the DJ arrive. The chick said, "About another hour." I thought *WHAT?* Suddenly it dawned on me I had not heard from Randall in quite a few hours. I didn't know how I felt about that. I pointed to Keith and then to the DJ booth.

"What?" he mouthed from across the room.

"Let's get this party started," I said as I meet him midstream. I walked inside the DJ's booth. I had been in there once before. I knew how it was set up but I did not know how it all operated. I put my iPod in and found the playlist I wanted with all the new hits. I let it rip through the speakers. I then hooked my laptop up to the ports, went to my iTunes and complied a playlist really quickly. I entitled it Heavyweights.

Keith looked at me and asked, "Do you know what you are doing?"

"You hear music don't you?" I snapped back. "He pays you for security not music or sarcasm." I wasn't being a smart ass. I am after all an engineer. Didn't he know that? If you can't figure it out as an engineer then you redesign it.

He looked like he wanted to shoot back, but decided not to. He wasn't sure how cool we really were yet. I scheduled enough music to last longer than an hour. As we walked back across the floor to the booth, my song came on so I stopped and started dancing. There were a few people already dancing. Keith stood back and just checked the scene. My phone chirped. I had a text but I didn't check. I was doing what girls do; dance alone. Some dude came up and started dancing with me. I threw my hands up to the crew like come rescue me. Keith quickly stepped on the floor in between us.

"My bad," dude said and backed off.

Keith did not say a word. "Nice save," I said. He gave me a face like this is the last time. "If he is cute next time just stay back okay?" My phone chirped a third time.

I still didn't look. I was going to check it when this song went off. Next thing I knew my girls were out on the floor too. Security had heightened in the room and all of a sudden I felt someone's hands on my waist dancing with me. I looked for Keith before I looked back when someone spoke in my ear.

"Why are you not checking your phone?" Instantly, my body temperature rose. I took my time to turn around. When I did our faces were extremely close. I pulled back and took my phone and looked at his messages.

"Don't let it happen again," he said in a tone that I could not understand.

"Jealous and possessive. Where are RJ and Pastor?" I asked.

"Pastor left to go put the finishing touches on his sermon for tomorrow. I think he was tired of me anyways."

"Where is RJ?"

"Playing video games in my office, but I am about to take him home," he replied. He took my hand and pulled me off the dance floor. Keith and King both came tagging along. We stood in the same hallway that we did before. He stood on his side of the wall and I stood on mine. Keith and King stood at the top of the hallway not letting anyone through.

"I didn't know you were coming here tonight," he said.

"It was not in the original plan. Leigh decided to come."

"How was your day?" he asked.

"It was great. I have a bone to pick with you?"

"Now?"

"Yes sir, sure do," I said.

"What am I accused of?"

"Why are you paying for everything?" I asked.

"I want you to have everything."

"Now you sound like TIP." I said smiling from ear to ear.

"So you say. There is a big difference between me and TIP."

"How so?"

"I am here with you and he is not," he winked and smiled back.

"You have a small point. How was your day Sweetie?"

"It is always a great blessing to spend a day with my two favorite guys."

"I'm glad. Oh by the way, I got you something."

He looked surprised. "What and why?" he asked.

"Well, since you asked, I took it upon myself to get you a shirt and tie for tomorrow."

"You didn't have to do that."

"But I wanted to," I said. "Don't get too excited, you paid for your own."

He pulled my hand and drew me closer. "What color are we wearing?" he asked.

"I hope you like orange."

"Are you wearing it?"

"Yes."

"Then I love orange. What else do I need to wear?"

"Nothing will be fine, but if you must beige, khaki or taupe. I laid my head on his chest." I was embarrassed that I actually said what I really felt. *Talk about things you might think, but dare not say; too late now,* I thought. He put his hand on my face just as his phone chirped. He checked his phone.

"What's wrong?"

"Nothing," I replied sadly. There really wasn't anything wrong, as a matter of fact, everything was just right.

"Yeah it is. This is your heart rate." I smirked and dumped my head in his chest again. "Do not be bashful. This is mine." He looked and sure enough, his was just as high as mine. I did not realize that the levels were texted to his phone. *OMG!* I thought. *How clever is technology and how sneaky is he. I can't do anything without him knowing it.*

"You never answered my earlier question."

"Which one babe?" I asked.

"Lemon or lime?"

Seriously, I thought. "What is your accountant's name?" I asked, ignoring his question for now.

"Schlossenbloum," he replied proudly looking at me like he knew what I was up to.

"Get him on the phone," I demanded.

He gave me his phone and I scrolled through the contacts. I found the name and hit send. It rang a few times and then a voice picked up.

"Hello. Gregory Schlossenbloum."

"Hello Mr. Schlossenbloum, this is Danielle Rose. I apologize for calling you so late on a weekend; however, I would like to speak to you about Randall Washington's finances. I am concerned for a few reasons and I will try my best to be brief. Number one, I want his finances to outlast his career. Number two, he is interested in returning to the ring again. Lastly, number three, you are not sure what the financial outcome of the divorce between him, and Mrs. Washington will result in. We need to discuss a few things with him because he has free access to his money, as he should because it is his money. I think we both can agree that he worked for it, but there should be some limitations and budgetary constraints. For example, he just bought a two hundred thousand dollar Aston Martin a few weeks ago and today he is interested in purchasing a Lamborghini. We need to discuss getting him on a budget plan that is within reason if that is possible. I am not trying to overpower him or to tell him what to do with his money, but I would like for him to understand the importance of having these finances throughout his career, retirement and his life span. I want to make sure he has proper allocations for his son, RJ, and that everything has been allocated appropriately."

There was a silence, and then he replied, "Is he available?"

"He is standing here with me. I do not think he believed I would call you for real."

"I am a little shocked to be getting this call Ms. Rose. However, I am pleased; but shocked still the same."

"I suggest we set up a meeting at your earliest convenience. I think this is an appropriate time considering the divorce and his return to the ring."

"How did you know about that?" I asked looking at Randall.

He whispered, "He was here Thursday. The guy wearing the suit."

At the same time Schlossenbloum also said, "I was there on Thursday."

"Oh okay. I am sorry I didn't get to meet you. It make sense now." I looked over at Randall who was no longer looking me in the eyes. "You are the last person he would want me to meet," I said giving Randall attitude.

"I am glad we have met now. I assume you were the beautiful hostess?"

"Beautiful is a matter of opinion and a nice compliment. Hostess yes. No need to compliment me Mr. Schlossenbloum." I said his name real slow to ensure that I did not butcher it up. "We are setting a budget whether you two like it or not."

"Is he there?" he asked again.

"Standing right here looking pitiful. I can tell you now; I am not changing my mind."

"May I speak to him please?"

"Sure."

I handed over the phone and gave him a look as if to say, don't try me!

"Yes Sir," he said very upbeat holding the r on sir.

"Hey Champ!"

"I am not feeling like a Champ right now," Randall acknowledged.

"You are always a Champ."

"Thanks man. I am over here getting beat down by a girl."

"Yes sir, sounds like she is cracking the whip already."

Randall sourly agreed, "Yeah I agree."

"What is that about?" he asked with laughter but sincerity.

He looked at me before he spoke, "I think this may be the future Mrs. Washington."

"If that is the case, then we need to get her in here and set a plan immediately. I agree with her on this one," He declared expecting Hooks to oppose.

"I guess so. Or that is what I am being told."

"Are you comfortable with her knowing your finances?"

"If I wasn't she never would have called you. Much less this late on a Saturday night."

"I'm impressed Randall. This is a first," he reminded his client.

"Me too." he smiled. He was impressed with himself that he not only was interested in Danielle, but she had his best interest at heart. He was willing to listen and take her suggestions.

"I take it you are not getting the Lamborghini?"

He looked at me and said, "I am still working on the car."

I shook my head no. That was still my final answer.

"I will speak back to her please." Randall passed the phone back to me.

"Hello," I said cutting my eyes at Randall.

"Shall I call you Mrs. Washington?"

"Ms. Rose is fine for now."

"What day would you like to meet?"

"I do not have to be present. You two can meet. I trust you two will allocate the budget so that cars are not purchased weekly, monthly or quarterly for that matter," I said firmly.

"He has given permission for you to be in attendance."

I cut my eyes at him. "I do not think it is necessary."

"If you are going this far you may want to have a clue of the numbers you are dealing with. You have no idea. I am impressed you care enough for him to restrict him. A man that fights one night and is looking at getting a record one hundred million probably feels he deserves to by a two hundred thousand dollar vehicle when he wants too. He really does not spend a lot of money on anything other than cars.

He doesn't travel a lot. Not a lot of social functions. He only has one kid. He is really a good guy and not too flashy. He deserves it. But I also respect your point."

"Umm hmm." He was not extremely flashy, but he did however have expensive and flashy taste and tendencies.

"I will get your information and set something up." the attorney said anxiously.

"Thanks for your help in this matter and for receiving my call at such a late hour. I do apologize. But I do want to disagree with you on one thing. He owns a jet. I think that is a tad bit flashy," I added.

He laughed, "Not a problem. Anything for the champ. Have a good night."

"You too."

I handed him back his phone. He looked so disgusted. "Well?" he asked.

"Well what?"

"Lemon or lime?"

I rolled my eyes and neck too this time. "Don't try me man," I said

"Now that I am hurt, I guess I will take the child home."

"Let's walk."

We headed back through the crowd. Once I got seated he said, "Ladies, I will see you all in a few hours. Be safe, have fun, and treat Keith nicely."

He leaned his forehead on mine. "Good night my love. Call me if you need me."

I took the deuces, kissed them, and placed them on his cheek.

As soon as he stepped down I thought to myself, *that is my man*. I looked at the girls. "All I need is a biscuit and a jar of Karo syrup and it is a done deal."

Keith held his head down and covered his mouth while he laughed.

"What?" I said to Keith.

He shook his head, still laughing. "Nothing girl. Handle your business," he said.

I tilted my head to the side and shrugged my shoulders, "I'm just saying."

"You do the doggone thang!" Keith replied through his laughter.

"Just give me some time." They all talked trash. We stayed around until the DJ arrived. I then got my iPod and laptop and we left to head over to Mikey's. When we got in the car Sade asked, "Auntie did you know Hooks was going to be there tonight?"

"I thought he would have been home by now since he has his son. Unless someone told him we were coming." I looked over in Keith's direction, totally insinuating him.

I rolled the window down. "Keith," I called out.

"Yes ma'am," he answered quickly.

"Did you tell Randall we were coming?"

"No, I did not. He said they were leaving there hours before we showed up."

"Either way Auntie I swear he is really feeling you."

"I agree," Leigh chimed.

"I disagree," Paige said calmly.

We all looked at her like she had just spoken some strange unknown foreign language.

She smiled big and said, "He doesn't feel you. He LOVES you baby girl. You can see it in his eyes and the way he gazes at you. I think he LOVES you." she held the word loves.

I said, "I hope he does. But, he got one more time to roll up on me like that and I swear!"

"You swear what Auntie?" Sade said like, yeah right.

"I swear I'm going to lick him ten different ways to Sunday!" I replied. We all laughed.

"WELL DAAAMN!!!" Leigh exclaimed.

I rolled the window up. Immediately Keith rolled it back down. "What? You ain't seen nothing yet."

"What Sissie?" Paige asked.

"Let's just say that eyes have not seen, nor have ear heard, or has it entered the mind of man; what I plan to do to him."

"You may need a refresher course," Paige frowned. "And I do not mean bible course."

"It's like riding a bike baby. Once you get back on it you never forget the motions. You can either ride or be ridden right?" We all squealed and high fived it all around.

Sade said, "That's what I'm talking about Auntie. Put it on him!"

"Make us proud!" Leigh said.

"I am pulling out all the tricks. We both may have to take the week off to recover."

Paige said, "Just kiss and tell. Do tell."

"I may have to keep some of this a secret, but you will know. Once he takes his shirt off it is going to be all over. I'm licking peanut butter and honey off them abs. Sweaty and all! Girls, I can tell you now, I don't know which one will be more worn out; me, my tongue or him. I may have to take this old school and put the bed on cinder blocks for reinforcement."

"Girl, sounds like the neighbors are going to know your name when it is all over."

"Damn right and they are a mile away. Whew! I need a cigarette just thinking about it." I motioned like I was smoking a square. "Whew!"

"Me too! A cigarette and a strong drink right out the bottle," Sade said.

"Shall I pull over ma'am?" Suddenly it got quiet. Real quiet. We were all shocked that Keith had just heard the entire conversation. We forgot he was there. Leigh started taking shots of our faces and Paige quickly dived over to roll the window up. We laughed like thirteen year olds. I hate he heard it, but I surely wasn't taking any of what I said back.

Mikey was at the bar when we walked in, as he always is. "Right on time ladies. I need some help. Who that?" he said speaking of Keith.

"Security, driver, body guard," I snarled.

"Pimp? I am the pimp! He needs to step off."

"Umm no," Mikey was something else.

"Snitch?" Mikey questioned referring to Keith telling our every move to Hooks. "Probably."

"I am sure you all have given him enough to write about. Ask secret service if he needs anything."

I motion for Keith to come over. I made the introductions. "Keith this is Mikey. Mikey this is Keith. They shake hands. "Mikey is my best, best friend. He owns the place. I, or should I say we, spend a lot of time here. If you are going to be assigned to me get used to being here. Let me show you around."

He asked Mikey a couple of questions about his crowd, his exits, and his security. He asked about his occupancy allowance and several other questions that would seem strange to the average person. But to a security person they were very much relevant. I showed him around Mikey's place, the attic, basement, and emergency secret exits. We came back around the bar.

"About time," Mikey rumbled.

"What do you need me to do Mikey?" I yelled.

"Sade is in the booth. Leigh is on the floor with the camera. Paige is at the door. I need you either at the bar or kitchen."

"I did not come to work tonight Mikey!"

"Well what did you come for?"

"Fun!"

"Whatever! Take your pick," he offered. "Kitchen or bar? Fun was not one of the options."

I reached under the counter and pulled out my flats that I kept there. "Give me a shirt honey."

He took his shirt off and gave it to me. He was left wearing his jeans and black wife beater. One thing about Mikey, he stayed fresh and clean. ALWAYS! He was always blinged out too. Tonight he was wearing a huge chain with a blinged out medallion. He would make someone a wonderful husband if he ever felt the need.

"I'll take that too," I said. He leaned his head down and I ripped his neck clean of his chain.

"I'm going in." The orders in the kitchen were out of control. I jumped in and before I knew it an hour had passed. I stepped out the door to see what everyone was doing. I motioned to Mikey for a drink for me and Keith.

Keith got water and I got my De'licious. Grapefruit, pomegranate, and a splash of sprite, virgin of course. I would have taken an alcoholic version if he didn't put me to work, especially since I had a driver. So much for that.

I finally got the kitchen to a good point, so I considered my job done for the evening. When the last call for food was announced I decided I was going on the dance floor. I planned to enjoy some of my night. I passed Keith and pointed to the floor. "Has he called?" I questioned.

"No."

"So I can hang all night then," I said dancing.

"If you choose, but I will be taking you home soon. We have an early morning."

I cut my eyes at him and said, "Party blaster!"

I stopped by the DJ booth and talked to Sade and the DJ and then hit the wood. One of Mike's regulars came and started dancing with me. He was pretty cool, however, I got the feeling he did not truly like girls but had not given up on the notion yet. As we danced he put his arm around my waist. Just like clockwork, I knew it was going to happen; security man came over and slapped his hand down. I saw him coming a mile away.

The patron whispered in my ear a few minutes later, "You got a date tonight?"

"More like a chaperone," I bellowed.

"Let him know I am the least of his concerns. It is the other guys in here that are too shy, too scared of Mikey, or just too dumb to dance with you. Those are the ones he needs to be worried about."

Immediately, Keith came over and did his finger like no whispering. He then stood right there on the dance floor next to us.

I can fix this, I thought. I motioned to the DJ that there was a drink on the floor. The water Keith was holding. He blast me back.

"We see you Ms. D. dancing with one while the other one holds you down. You go girl."

I stomped off the floor while Keith stood there and laughed. It was his intentions to get the guy away from me and I guess his plan worked anyways. I went to the bar and motioned to Mikey. He knew exactly what I wanted. He passed me a wet wipe so I could wipe my face.

"What's wrong?" he teased.

"HIM!" I said, pointing at Keith.

He looked at Keith who held up his empty water bottle. Mikey reached in the cooler and gave him another one. "Three dollars!" I yelled.

He threw a five on the counter. "Keep the change."

"JERK!"

Mikey winked at me. "I love you boo," he tried to console me.

"She is a little irritable. It has been a long day. I think we are calling it a night," Keith decided.

I rolled my eyes.

"Let's go," Keith said and grabbed my arm. I looked down at his hand on my arm and looked up at him. "I am just doing my job. It is getting late, much later than he would have you out." I jerked my arm back. "That's going to bruise," he said to Mikey. "Give her some ice." He pulled out his phone and began strolling.

"Who are you calling?" I demanded.

He looked over his eyelids, "I think you know."

"YOU PUNK!"

I leaned over the counter and kissed Mikey. He passed me my bag and shoes and I handed him my standbys. I leaned my head down and he grabbed the chain off my neck. Then I held my arms up and he got the shirt off then threw it over his shoulder. "What I owe you Dani?" Michael asked very appreciative of his friend's help.

"Love forever."

"You got it babe. Text me when you get home," he said.

"You know it."

Convincing himself, "I'm shutting her down at four fifty nine."

"We will see. Love you." That place will remain open until the last person goes home and Mikey knew it.

I held up my arm, threw the deuces and yelled, "Whoodie Who!" and proceeded to stomp to the door.

"WAIT Danielle!" Keith yelled.

I looked back and threw up my fist to my hand and drew an imaginary line on the floor.

Mikey yelled out, "You got trouble man!"

Keith knew it and replied, "Pray for me," and proceeded to follow me out.

He got next to me and said. "It is one fifty eight. Take your tail home. You know what time we have to get up?" He had no idea Danielle would be such a handful.

"All right, all right, all right! FINE!" It took the crew a few minutes before they got to the door.

"Everyone good?" Keith asked as he got in the driver seat. "Other than D?" He cut his eyes in her direction through the rearview mirror.

"What happened?" Sade asked him.

"She is mad at me," he answered.

Getting a little alarmed, "What did you do?" Paige asked fiercely as she leaned over the entire seat.

"I called it a night."

"Well it is early for us," Leigh replied.

He looked in his mirror, and if looks could kill, somebody would be dead right now.

"Sorry," Leigh muffled.

"Hooks gone kill us all!" he said.

I embarrassed him. "Tell the truth. You had fun with us Keith didn't you?"

He smiled at that. "I did. I would rather be with you all than those boys all day."

"What goes on with us stays between us," I said. He looked like, oh crap! "What did you do?" I asked containing a yell.

"He already asked me and I answered him."

"Stop the truck!" Paige hollered. He pulled over. "Swear right now that what is said and done between us stays between us."

"Sorry, I can't do that Ms. Paige."

"Why not?"

"He will ask me and I have to tell him something."

"Client confidentially," I said through gritted teeth.

"Yeah, that sounds nice and all, but I don't think that will work. I work for Hooks."

"You just let me handle him," I responded.

"If it is not harmful why do you have to tell him anything?" Leigh inquired.

"It's my job."

"No, your job is to protect. It says nothing about snitching," Sade added.

"You all didn't do anything that was bad," he tried to say.

I could not concentrate. "We know, but that was today. There is no telling what we will do and say in the future."

"How about this Keith," Sade said. "If he doesn't ask you don't tell."

"We will roll with that."

"No we will not!" Paige shouted. "What goes on between us stays between us! That is the rule. Otherwise, we can't roll with a driver."

"Girls, you did nothing bad," he insisted.

"Keith," I said. "If I ask you questions about him are you going to answer?"

"It depends," he answered honestly.

Sade started to speak and I threw my hand up to stop her. "Who is he sleeping with?"

"Now?" he asked taken aback by my directness.

"Period!"

"Ms. D," he said intensely.

"Keith." I gave him back his same tone.

"I can't answer that."

"My point exactly. If you can't answer for him then don't answer for me."

"It is different."

"Why?" I demanded.

"I work for him not you."

"Oh, we can solve that then," Leigh interjected.

"Where is my check book little girl?" I asked. She pulled it out. "How much do I owe you?"

Holding his hand up as if to say stop, he said, "I can't take your money Ms. D. He would really have a conniption. Okay, let me just tell you this; I have never been on girl patrol. He has never had the need. Every now and then one of us ends up on kid duty to chaperone RJ at the skating rink, a party, game, or dance. So he may not even ask. Let's just wait and see."

Sade gave a smirk, "You would not tell us the truth anyways," she retorted.

"You make me sick!" I said.

"I know," he replied sarcastically and unmoved by my outburst.

"Relax. He may not even ask. Besides, he knows you all are with me; so you won't be out of control doing too much bad. He must not be concerned because he has not checked in since eleven. It's all good," he reassured.

I could not take it, "All right Keith. We don't want to have to F you up."

"Snitches get stitches!" Leigh added with all of us laughing.

"Let's go. I got to drop y'all off. Go home and get ready for tomorrow too."

"Who is at your house?" Paige asked. We all exploded in laughter once again.

"Keith that was a come on line in case you missed it."

We arrived safely home and Keith instructed, "Text him immediately before I do to let him know that you are home."

I took my phone and sent the text. "Thanks for everything Keith. I am sure it was a sucky day for you."

"I liked it actually. I hope I am assigned to you again," he admitted.

"Good, me too," I said as I reached up and hugged him.

He said, "No one in years."

"Huh?" I said, not having a clue as to what he was talking about. I'm sure I stood there with a crazy look on my face.

"You asked who he has been sleeping with. No one since his wife. I don't think it is a secret." I gave him a pound. "Keep it that way Ms. D," he said very sternly.

I loved the fact that they all had him covered. "I got you," I replied. "I guess Pastor Hunter got to you too?" I assumed.

"Not yet. I am sure I will be questioned tomorrow or as soon as he finds out I escorted you all today. It's cool. He wants Hooks to do the right thing and so does Hooks. We want him to stay focused, and if that means I am on girl duty and sitting outside your bedroom door to make sure he is not sneaking in, then I am on it."

"I am so glad everyone is going above and beyond to make sure my chastity belt remains untouched. Where were you all ten years ago?" I teased.

He laughed, "Good night." He did not leave the door until he made sure I locked the door and set the alarm before walking back to the car.

After I took a shower and started to get my stuff together I realized I still had Randall's shirts.

> I have your shirt.

> I'll pick it up in the morning before six.

Sunday

At five thirty my phone rang his ring tone. "Hello," I answered.

"Good morning. I apologize, I know it is early. Can you unlock the gate please?"

I jumped up and ran to the bedroom. "Sade get the door," I said.

She said sleepily, "Why?"

"Randall is coming to get his shirt," I answered.

"GRR," she growled, but got up to answer the door anyways.

Randall stood there smiling all bright and cheery, "Good morning Sade," he greeted.

"I feel like you may have spent the night and you two are running game. I am not six anymore. I know how this works," She rolled her eyes.

"Here little baby." He hands her a bag of Waffle House. "Where is D?"

Pointing to the back she said, "Bathroom. I wonder why?"

"I'm going back." He walked to the bedroom door. "May I come in?" he asked.

"Sure," I replied. He catches me in my bathroom, sits a smoothie down on the counter, and hugs me.

"I miss you," I confessed.

"I miss you too, but I have to run. We are on for tonight remember? Do not forget I have dinner covered. I am gone. My Father's business calls. I will see you in a few." I gave him a hanger with his shirt and tie.

He left the bedroom and walked through the living room. "Ladies breakfast is in the bags on the table. Get it up! If you all can hang out all night dancing with some unknown guys then get it together for church. We have a date. I will see you in a few hours," he said before heading out of the door.

Again, his ringtone came through my phone. He must have called the second he stepped foot out the door.

"Yes, everything okay?" I answered in a panic.

"Yes, everything is fine. I left the Maybach outside. The keys are in it."

"WHAT?" I asked.

I started walking towards the door immediately as I slapped Sade's foot. "Shh. Get up." I pointed towards the door. I looked out the door and said, "No Sir. Come and get this car." She looked at me like WTH are you saying?

He replied, "You wanted it. There you have it."

"Come get this car Randall. You are still not getting a Lamborghini."

"No, come on to church."

"No I can't. I need a lesson before I drive it." I knew the rule in my house. You break it you buy it and today was not a good day for me to purchase a Maybach. Although financially I could.

"Fine! Turn around!" he instructed to whomever was driving him.

He came back and got the Maybach while I was standing in the door. He walked up the cobblestone and handed me the keys to the Benz. "Happy now?"

Sade's mouth ran a mile a minute while we ate. "You can tell us Auntie. I swear you gave him some last night while we were all asleep, didn't you? You know we have the tapes. All we have to do is run them back."

I was extra careful in his car. When I pulled into the lot the parking lot guy stopped me. "The Deacons will lead you in," he informed me. I followed the directions. Once I arrived to where they were instructing Keith and King were there to open the doors. I looked up just in time to notice Pastor's Bentley pulling up behind me. I was too busy checking emails to pay close attention. I saw him getting out and they took his shirt and hanger out of the back of the car. He was wearing a white tee and his slacks. Randall was wearing the same thing when he arrived at my house. I wondered if they knew how sexy they were. I looked back down and continued composing my email. I had not even noticed that the girls had gotten out of the car.

"Who are you texting, your boyfriend?" Randall leaned in and asked.

"Why? Are you jealous?" I said and looked up. He looked like a totally different person than an hour or so ago. Then he was Randall, my baby. Now he was Deacon Washington. He was wearing the orange shirt, orange and light blue tie, khaki pants, and a vest. He did not have the jacket on. His cufflinks almost put my eyes out when he leaned over in the car.

"That was not the right answer," he said.

"What? Am I not supposed to have a boyfriend?" I asked.

"I don't want you to," he answered honestly.

"You have a wife," I said. He knew it was the truth, but it hit him like a blow below the belt. I felt the air coming from his lungs. I wasn't taking it back nor smoothing it over because it was true.

Once he got his composure back together he said, "If you do, why don't you make arrangements to introduce him to me so I can let him know his time is short?"

I wrinkled my nose, "Doesn't really sound fair. You get a wife, but I can't have a little boyfriend," I repeated.

Frustrated with this conversation he said, "Get out the car please." I took his hand and exited the car. He smiled from ear to ear. "You look beautiful."

I smiled back, "You look sexy and handsome Deacon Washington." Of course, he blushed; just as he does every time I tell him that he's sexy.

He loved how I could switch him to the place he was. "You like this shirt?" he asked seeking confirmation.

"I sure do."

"My baby picked it up for me."

"How do you feel about it?" I asked him.

"I love it and I love her," he shyly replied.

I pointed at him and said, "You better watch what you say on sacred grounds mister. No take backs."

"I don't need to take it back."

I could hear the footsteps behind me. I looked down on the ground and could tell from the quality of the shoes who it was. I spoke first without looking back. "Good morning Pastor."

"Ms. Rose, Deacon Washington, good morning. Nice coordinating attire," he pointed out.

I was looking ahead and rolled my eyes. King was facing me, which meant he was also facing Pastor and knew exactly why I rolled my eyes. He smirked but didn't say anything.

"What's up?" Deacon Washington said.

"It looks like a lot," Pastor said sarcastically.

I rolled my eyes again. I turned around and gave him a look letting him know to cut it out immediately as I walked off. King followed behind Randall and me closely.

Pastor spoke real soft. "I have security too."

I rolled my eyes directly at him this time.

"I will see you before you leave Danielle," he said in that famous Pastor Hunter voice.

I huffed and I pouted. "Why and how do I always end up in his chambers?" I questioned as he walked away.

"Never mind him," the Deacon said.

Paige laughed as we entered the church. This was not the regular door in which Pastor normally came through. I figured it all had to be a set up to talk trash to me. *UGH! Why did Randall have to be best friends with the Pastor? How inconvenient.*

"You all finally ready Uncle Hooks," Sade asked. "I mean, if you two are going to creep all night then get people up at the crack of dawn and make them come to church, the least you two can do is let us get to our seats so we can go back to sleep. And I am not sitting on that front row with Hunter walking and talking in front of me disturbing my sleep either."

"I will make note." He leaned over in my ear. "We are on." We walked in the sanctuary as if we were husband and wife. I can see how people would easily mistake it. Once I got to my seat he said, "I will be back. I am on duty today. Let me know if someone tries to hit on you while I am gone."

"Yeah, and don't let me catch you out there flirting," I replied.

That caught him by surprise and suddenly a rush of thoughts came to mind. *Does she think I am a flirt? I need to be more cognizant of my conversations. That is the last thing I need to be referred to. The Flirting Deacon. Everyone should know I have never had a long or inappropriate conversation here with anyone. Mental note, I need to discuss that with her today too.*

When he arrived back at his seat he was wearing his suit jacket. When I looked over my shoulder he gave me a wink. Pastor Hunter laid it down as he always does. I purposely made eye contact with him thinking I would mentally trip him up, but it was of no use; he was ready. That was part of his job and he was good at it. It would be like him coming into my boardroom trying to stare me down. It would probably annoy me, but ultimately it would only cause me to perform harder. I think that is exactly what my deliberate direct eye contact did to him. Right when he was in the heart of his sermon he came down from the pulpit, as he does regularly, and stood in the isle between Randall and me. He managed to put his hands on both of our shoulders. I wished at that moment that clip on microphones had never been invented. He pressed so hard on my shoulder; if the camera had not been on us I would have been tempted to lay him out. *Now he know he ain't right.*

When he walked back down the aisle Randall stuck his foot out in the aisle. I looked down as I rolled my eyes yet again. He smiled. It was his friend so it didn't bother him. What I really wanted to ask him was why he didn't stick that leg out there two minutes ago? Deacon Washington leaned up on his knees as he often does and kept going like nothing happened. Then it dawned on me what Pastor was trying to do and it worked. He was trying to make me uncomfortable, and I was. He knew that he was not making headway with Randall so he must have figured that he would go after the girl. I just shook my head. I have watched enough television to know how this operates. If you keep pressuring one of them would break and he obviously felt as though I was the weakest link. He knew good and well that his boy was not going to ever be uncomfortable in what he did, but me on the other hand, he knew I would. Why, because he was my Pastor. That reigned supreme over being Randall's best friend. I just could not foresee him ever being Tre to me. That was like calling your mother, doctor, or kindergarten teacher by their first names. It just wasn't cool.

After service I didn't want to hang around. Maybe I was merely trying to rush away to avoid Pastor. Right as my hand touched the vestibule door a gentleman touched my arm. "Pastor asked that you wait in his chambers."

I sighed. "Really?"

"Yes ma'am."

"Seriously?" I asked. I wasn't in the mood to be stuck in his chambers again being reprimanded.

He looked at me as if he wanted to say, like why would I lie to you.

I told the girls, "I will be back. I am being summoned again." I am not sure who had the keys to the car but they would figure it out. I knew the drill. He punched in his code to let me in the office and I sat there waiting. I did not even bother to observe the room.

I heard the doors open. "What are you doing in here?" Randall questioned.

I looked up at him and replied, "Top Flight stopped me and brought me in here."

"Let's go." He laughed and reached out for my hand as I stood up.

"Thank God," I said, thankful for the rescue.

As soon as we got ready to walk through the door, however, Pastor entered. "Where do you two think you are going?" he asked, looking us up and down as if we had been in some devilment.

Before I knew it, I rolled my eyes so hard until I got a quick migraine.

Furious Randall said, "Man go head on."

"I just want to talk to her."

"Tre!"

His eyes got big, "What Son? You got something to hide?"

"Naw." Randall threw a fit.

"Well why can't I talk to her then?" They went on back and forth as if I wasn't even there. I felt like we were a couple of fourteen year olds getting busted by my dad. It was ridiculous feeling this way as an adult.

Putting my hands up in between the two, I said, "Excuse me. I am right here. Now I am a little confused. Is this a Pastoral conversation or a let's embarrass RW and Dani meeting?"

"A little bit of both," Pastor answered annoyed that I had the audacity to ask.

"I am honored." Randall laughed although I did not find any of this humorous.

"Thank you," Pastor said looking at Randall as if he was being dismissed.

Randall huffed, "If she is staying then I am staying."

"Fine, take a seat. However, we do not need you," Pastor reassured.

As expected Randall countered, "Make it quick I have things I need to do."

"I didn't get the memo," Pastor said with his arms folded and a huge smile on his face.

I didn't respond. I knew clearly what he was referring too.

"Which was?" Randall asked.

"The color scheme memo," he said while pointing at our clothing.

"Aww man, are you serious? Man stop," he retorted.

He replied cool and calm, "I just want to let you two know how it looks."

"How does it look Trevor?" Hooks said with a raised voice.

"In-a-ppro-pri-ate," Trevor answered enunciating every syllable.

"So you can enunciate." His face displayed his disgust. "The praise team was dressed alike and no one seemed to care," he slammed back.

I saw this was about to turn into a boy fight so I said nothing.

"I don't like your tone RW."

"Well, I don't like your accusations Tre."

"Look, I am not accusing anyone of anything. You two are dressed alike. If I am not mistaken that was your ride she pulled up in right? It seems cut and dry if you ask me."

"Tre if I wasn't your boy you would never notice any of this. It is not going to go away. I, or should I say we, appreciate and have taken heed to your advisory. We are still in order. Let it ride man. Let it ride," he warned politely.

"Pastor, it looks like you two boy scouts have this under control. Do you need me for anything? Otherwise, I have my crew waiting on me," I finally spoke out. I was ready to go and didn't want any parts of what was going down between the two.

"Make sure I get the memo next week on the color scheme," he shot at me.

"Will do," I said and rolled my eyes as he nodded his head.

Randall laughed again. "Didn't work."

"What?" Pastor asked looking confused.

Randall continued, "You can't force one of us to break. We haven't done anything wrong."

"I'll keep trying. If nothing else I will prevent anything wrong from happening. Every time you two get close to each other you will see my face and not each other's. I am going to stay on you two like white on rice and I mean it."

"Continuously seeing your face will make me vomit," I said gagging.

Randall smiled, looked at me and said, "Nice jab babe," and pounded me.

"Watch it Ms. D," Pastor warned.

"Oh no, you started this war. Don't let me spray paint your wheels. You will know what the color for next week will be. How's that for a memo?" I added.

"You will need me Ms. D. I guarantee you will need me. Tread lightly," he advised snidely.

"Yes, of course I'll need you. To officiate the ceremony and dance at the reception. Which by the way, will be held here at the church. Do you think it's possible for you to be the best man and the Pastor? I think it can be done. Other than that, you need to tread lightly. Currently you are stomping with the big dogs," I replied.

Now he was irritated, "Out! Out!" he ordered.

"I go in peace," I said and winked my eye real hard.

"Hey, I will call you later. Let me handle this issue," Randall said to me.

"Okay."

"Oh, let me walk you to the car. How rude of me?"

It seemed as if tons of people stopped him along the way. There were all sorts of questions referencing lost and found, dead batteries, parking cones, petty cash, and troubled teens. He said very politely, "Can you please give me a minute and I will handle that?" I looked back and I could tell immediately that on the other end of the corridor stood his son. I turned the corner quickly to not be seen by him.

Once he turned the corner, the girls were there. He clapped his hands like he had not seen them all day. That was one of the things I loved about him, he was so animated and caring. "Ladies, any request for dinner?"

"Yes. Solid food!" Sade said.

King laughed.

"Yeah, I agree," Leigh stated.

"I was thinking solids too," Paige chimed in.

"Okay, anything in particular?" he asked getting their point.

"Nope. Just something we can chew will be fine," Paige added.

"Is fish good?"

"That will work. Although it does not require much chewing," Leigh said.

"Any food allergies or anything special I should know?" he asked sincerely.

"No," I said. "You don't have to prepare dinner you know."

"Oh, but I do. And ladies after dinner Danielle and I have a conference."

Did he just say a conference I thought to myself?

"We are not leaving you two alone!" Paige said firmly.

I looked at him and said, "Geesh! Does anyone trust us?"

"NO!" he screamed. "I am just about sick of it."

With raised eyebrows Leigh asked, "Are you putting us out before the event begins?"

"No you don't have to go home, but you got to leave the house. I'll give you until seven."

"Dang, we got a time limit too. Sounds like another booty call if you ask me."

"SADE!" I yelled, "You are at church little girl!"

"AND?"

"Ugh! Ihateu.com!" I mumbled through clenched teeth.

She then gave me the same look I had just given her. "You are at church Auntie!" she mocked.

I didn't even bother to respond. "Let's ride," I said instead.

The parking lot guys carefully guided us out. Before we could leave the premises good, Paige asked, "What do you two have to talk about?"

"I am not sure," I said. "He is the one that wants to talk to me."

Persistently she asked the same question again. "About what?"

"Don't know," I said in a tone that suggested I had just answered that question.

"So, he didn't say?" Leigh leaned up and asked.

"No, not really." I answered.

"Either he did or he didn't Auntie."

"Okay. Well, he didn't." I replied annoyed with their interrogation.

"You sure?" Sade asked.

"What is going on? Why am I being harassed today?"

"Answer the question then," the eldest insisted.

"I don't know for real! I asked him a few questions on Friday about his social life. He kind of chumped me off, or at least that's my take on it, and he just said that he needed to talk to me about it in person. Not really sure of the outcome; whether it'll be a bad talk or good conversation. However, I guess we'll see tonight."

"I think whatever he says is sincere and truthful," Sade said picking sides.

"What makes you say that Sade?" I asked.

"If you just watch him closely you will see how sincere he is."

"He can be that sincere with anyone," I replied.

"With who?"

"Whomever. She doesn't have to go to the same church. She could be anyone. Who knows; she could go to the gym or anywhere."

"Nah Auntie, you can tell just by the way he talks to you. He always seems interested and concerned in what you say or do. Not to mention his proximity. He stands so close to you until it makes me nervous and sweat. When he moves, you move back and then he moves forward; like y'all are in perfect sync with one another. He stands so close until he practically pushes you through the wall! A guy that is not interested would not stand that close. If he had a boo at the church he would definitely would not be standing that close. If he had someone else then why would he walk you in, then go out and come back to you again? I mean, you two even wear the same colors and sit on the same row. All I know is that if there is a she, then she is dumb if she doesn't notice all of this."

"It may not be the fact that she doesn't notice; she may not very well care. She may be out for the loot. You know how some chicks are. If he got bank, he can do whatever as far as she's concerned. Why should she be of concern with another side chick if she is getting her needs met? Let's not forget he is married. That is who she is concerned with; the wife not me."

Shaking her head, "I just don't see it," Paige said.

"You may not get it, but take a moment to look at the big picture. He is a boxer and to say he is banked is an understatement. Why would a chick care about another chick as long as her time, loot and whatever else ain't interrupted?" *This was really not the conversation I anticipated on having and to be honest, I had never really thought about him having someone else until now. Sure, Keith had kind of confirmed that he did not a few hours ago, but right now it was on the top of my thoughts. I couldn't shake it.*

When we arrived at the house I was so distracted I decided I needed to go for a walk. I went to my room, changed my clothes, and hit the track. Initially I was going to take my car, but felt the need to be close to him so I took his instead.

I realized my phones were not charged, but I didn't even worry about it. The way I felt right now, I needed to focus and not bother with texts or emails anyways, so I left them in the car. At least my iPod was fully charged. I pulled up my playlist and strolled around, and around, and around. I wasn't keeping count or anything and had no real idea how long I'd been walking. I had it bad; I could not get him off my mind. My thoughts were running rampant and I found myself wondering if he really was the church flirt. I thought of all the female encounters I had seen. I thought, *maybe he is sincere. Maybe I should pull back. If it is meant to be then wait until his divorce is final. One thing is for certain, Hunter is not going to lie back calmly and watch this unfold.*

■■■■■■■■■■■■■■ ■■

The house phone rings. "Hello."

"Hey it is Randall."

"Hey it is Leigh. What's up?"

"Nothing."

"You re-nigging on us?"

"No. Why would I do that? Is Dani there?" he asked.

"No, she is at the track," Leigh replied.

He felt something wasn't quite right. "I see. Okay. I will call her phone. See you at five."

"Bring food and cupcakes," she called out.

He chuckled. "Man cannot live by bread alone."

"Bye. Don't forget the cupcakes."

A look of worry set upon his face. "Why is she not answering her phones?" he spoke out loud.

"Make a U-turn guys," he ordered.

"Where to." King asked?

"To the track please."

"Is everything okay?"

"I hope so," he replied unsure while tracking her device.

• •

I was rounding another corner when I noticed a car coming into the lot. A nice car, I might add. I continued on my walk and when I looked again I saw a person standing on the track as if he was waiting to fall in line. *It's Randall.* He was still wearing his suit. His vest was unbuttoned, his tie was loosely knotted, and his shirt hung outside his pants. I could tell, even from a distance, that his shoes were top of the line. I walked up on him and said, "Hey." He fell into line and did not say anything. He had his hands in his pockets and his head hanging down. *Goodness gracious, he is such a gorgeous man!* My thoughts were all over the place. *He could be entered into a sexiest man alive contest. Mmm, I really wouldn't mind seeing him without those clothes,* I thought, however, I didn't know if my heart rate would be able to take it.

I didn't know what to say. He had not responded so we walked in silence for a brief moment. We got half way around the track then he said, "Danielle, can I ask you a question?"

"Sure."

"Why aren't you answering your phones?"

I looked at him and said, "You came all the way up here to ask me that?"

"Yes, as a matter of fact I did."

"They are in my car. Sorry your car."

"Why Danielle?"

"They are dead."

"Hmm."

I could tell he wasn't buying that. "What's wrong?" I asked.

"Why are they dead?" he asked suspiciously. He figured it odd that I would not have my devices charged considering how much I utilized them.

"We were out late last night and I didn't charge them and I didn't put a charger in your car."

He then asked, "Why are you walking and not resting?"

I sighed, "I have a lot on my mind."

"Like what?" he asked with concern.

"Life," I said upbeat.

Really? He thought to himself. "And?" he waited for me to elaborate.

"Just in general," I said. I knew I was being vague.

He looked upset. "Don't do this Danielle. What is bothering you?" he asked wondering why she always worried.

I did not hesitate. "Hunter and our conference today."

"Why?"

"I don't know," I replied. It was true; I didn't know why his little meeting with me had me feeling some type of way. I couldn't even articulate how I was feeling about the whole ordeal.

"Yes you do." He still had his hands in his pockets and his head low not looking at me.

"No, I really don't."

"Why do you think?" he continued.

"Because I feel as though I am stuck between a rock and a hard spot," I replied honestly.

"I am sorry. I understand how you feel. I am stuck in the same spot. I have no clue what to do either. I trust Him and hope you trust Him and me."

"Yeah."

"Look at me," he said.

I looked at him. "Yes," I said as I blinked my eyes.

"Do you trust me?" he asked sincerely.

I walked for over a quarter of the lap before I spoke. I know the silence was deafening. I watched his son and King. This was so much for me to take in. "I have no reason not to," I finally said.

He put his hands over his face. As if to say thank God. As we slowly approached his car he said, "Danielle, promise me you will go home and get some rest. I will be over at five. I need to see you, talk to you, and do what I can without stepping outside my boundaries. I am still going to prepare food as I promised, but I need to get RJ back and just clear my head before I get there. We really need to set the record straight. I may even need to talk to Trevor before I come over to make sure my thoughts are in line vertically and horizontally."

"Unfortunately, and as hard as it may seem we can control our feelings. We may have to get them in check for the time being," he told me.

I looked at him real sad, thankful that I was wearing my shades. I am sure my eyes were brick red and seconds away from dropping tears. I tried to speak, "What are you going to do about your car?" I asked.

"You can have it for all I care. Right now I need to worry about you. Me and you. I will worry about that car later. It is just a car," he replied.

I felt like crap. I dropped my head and said, "Okay." I came out here to get my mind right. I had no intentions of him coming out only to clutter it up again. No matter how much I was around him, he still made me extremely nervous and right now was no different.

He grabbed me as sweaty as I was and hugged me. He then kissed my neck and my forehead. "My love," he whispered.

I stood there with my lips poked out as he lifted my shades and saw the redness. "Danielle, don't hurt me like this right now. I can't be weak. I have my child with me.

Give me a few hours and you can cry as much as you want. I will wipe each tear. You can yell as much as you want or curse me as much as you want," he paused. "Please just help me Lord," he said silently to himself but she heard his prayer.

I nodded again. He let me go and sighed so hard until it was as if it was his last breath. I was still standing in the first lane as he stepped through the fence. I fell in the grass feeling as though someone had taken the life out of me. Why was this so hard and getting harder? Whatever Hunter was trying to do was working. It was entirely too much work to be at peace. I was going to set up the next meeting with him myself. I needed to talk to him, although I was not sure if I needed to talk to him as a Pastor or as Randall's friend. This was difficult to say the least.

I lay on my back in the grass with my knees propped up and my hands over my face. I sobbed hard. Maybe that was what I needed. *How did I let this happen?*

Apparently, he looked back. "King, I will catch up with you down the street." I heard him say. I am sure that was to come back, but to not let RJ see what was going on. I could not look up or move my hands.

"Danielle, get up. Let me take you home," he said as he leaned over me.

"No thanks. I'm good," I said, but was I?

"No you are not! I will change the plans and talk to you now. This can't wait until later."

"It can. Just let me get myself together. Go on and do what you have to do and I will be fine when you see me this evening," I said trying my best to reassure him.

He looked at me lovingly and said, "I can't leave you in the grass like this."

"I came out here to be by myself. To think alone. I am okay I promise."

"I am not leaving until you are ready to leave."

I got myself together. He then picked me up and carried me to the car.

"Go home please. I will call you. Lie down until I get there."

"I will see you in a few hours." I felt like someone was taking him away from me and never bringing him back.

I drove home and once I got to the driveway I had somehow managed to get myself together. I wanted to lie in my bed and sulk so bad, but I knew it would be rude. I had not been in my bed in three days almost. Instead I showered and lay across it for an hour and then went to join the others, but it was no use because I was asleep before my head hit the couch.

At four the phone rang. "Got it. Hello," Leigh said in that cheery voice of hers.

"Hey, yeah she has been asleep for a while. I think we all may have dosed in and out, but she is still sleeping. Okay we will see you in an hour."

I did not even hear him come in. I do not know who opened the gate. All I heard was something falling in the kitchen. I needed that sleep. Mentally I needed it. I clearly understood what he meant about not being mentally ready. I opened my eyes and saw all of them in the kitchen and hoped they did not see me because I really wanted to close my eyes again for at least another hour.

I could hear them whispering something. Actually, it was Paige's voice I heard. She was always giving some kind of instruction and over ruling everyone with age, motherhood, or seniority. She was speaking in that stern, I got it, you all do not know what you are doing, motherly tone she often uses.

I let them go on for another minute or two and then mumbled, "What do you all need?"

"We can find it," Paige said with confidence.

"Let me help you," I said. I started to get up when I realized that the boy was sitting on the other end of the couch. He held my feet down as I tried to get up.

"They can figure it out. It will be fine," he whispered trying to soothe her worry.

This was one of the reasons why I loved him. I needed someone to tell me to sit down and be still every now and then. I waved hello and closed my eyes back. Maybe fifteen minutes later I smelled smoke.

"What's on fire?" I asked jumping up from the couch in a panic.

"The grill," he said calmly. "Don't worry, it is under control."

"Who is watching it?"

"Me," he said.

I gave him the side eye. "You are sitting down," I replied.

"I know and you are supposed to be asleep. I will wake you up when your plate is ready."

All I could think was what are they burning? I wasn't too panicked because I know Paige is capable. The other three, however, I wasn't sure they could boil water without instructions.

I did as I was instructed and closed my eyes. Twenty minutes later I decided I should get up. It was six o'clock. No one was in the house. There was one rose lying on the floor at my feet. It made me smile and hurt at the same time. I could so get use to this, which is why it made me smile, but when I asked myself if it was realistic, that brought pain. Not that I didn't think his gestures were sincere. I did. I imagined he would continue the same forever. He didn't seem to be the type of guy that did it to get a girl and then pull back. Was it realistic that he ever could? Would he ever divorce and become available; and if he did would I still be available?

No one was in the house. *Did they leave me?* As I walked through the kitchen there sat the largest colored bouquet of roses and baby's breath. *Now did they get a picture of this?* I got my camera and took a picture then stepped out the door to see them grilling and listening to the iPod. Sade was looking through a magazine, he was on his iPad, and Sissie had a book in her hand. I have no clue what Leigh was taking a picture of, a bug maybe. She had the camera pointed to the ground.

"My people!" I called out.

"Hey there sleepy head," Leigh said.

"Whatever. Hey Y'all. Hey Chef," I said to Randall.

"What's up babe? Dinner is in two minutes. I told Sade to set the table twenty five minutes ago and she hasn't," he added.

"Liar!" she barked.

"Watch it!" Paige snapped. "It was more like eight minutes ago." she snitched.

"Whew. Y'all are body slamming out here," I said laughing but glad they all got along.

He walked up real close to me as he always does and said, "Join me in the kitchen please. Are you rested? Do you feel better?"

"Yeah. Lack of sleep makes you crazy." *And emotional* I thought.

"Or lack of."

I put my finger up to his lips. "My word Mr. Washington. Does your Pastor know you speak to the ladies like this?" I teased.

"Food. I was going to say food. And it is lady. Not ladies."

"Yeah right," I replied.

"Speaking of which, they get one hour and they are out of here," he said.

"Dang! Drill Sergeant!" I said jokingly.

Being transparent, he responded. "I know but this waiting has driven me crazy."

"Do you have that locator on?"

He looked at his wrist. "Yeah why?" He looked at me strangely.

"Hunter may show up," I said frantically. Although, I was hoping Pastor Trevor Hunter never darkened my door unannounced. That would mean nothing but trouble.

"I would have to disregard the cloth today and knock him out for a few hours. At least until this conversation is over."

I laughed, "You are a dirty fighter."

"No, I am real. Remember I started fighting in the hood before I ever hit the ring and organized fighting."

"Keep it real for the conversation later," I told him raising my eyebrows.

"I wish pillow talk," he mumbled. "Hey, speaking of which, I got you a present. Let me go get the stuff off the grill first."

There was a bag on the counter I didn't notice before. I opened the bag and fell to the floor. He saw me from the door and knew exactly what I was laughing about. I pulled it all out and took a picture. *I know damn well we told Keith that what goes on with us stays with us.* I then remembered that I had Keith's number in my phone. I dialed. I don't think he even let it ring.

"Ms. Danielle," he answered.

"Yes!" I snapped.

"I have been waiting on this call all day," he stated humorously.

"Have you now? Why would that be?"

He paused for a second then said, "I am sure I am fired."

"Understatement!" I replied.

"He told me he was going to do that at five AM this morning and I thought he had it when he came by earlier to get his shirt. I take it you just got your package."

"Yes I did."

"What was it?" he asked as if he didn't already know.

"You do know you can't hang with the ladies again right?"

"No, I happened to say that before we had our conversation," he tried to explain.

I cut him off, "Oh really?"

"Yes really."

"You are still fired."

"Mrs. Washington?"

I smiled. I liked the ring to that. "Don't try to butter me up," I said.

"I think syrup was the word you used."

"You know damn well that is the last time you roll with us."

"I know but let me explain," he shouted.

"Go right ahead."

"This was before we had our conversation and after we did, I felt so bad until I answered your question about him. It was fair. Just to let you know, he didn't ask. He called and asked how things were going. That's when I said other than you being sopped up with a biscuit and Karo syrup, nothing."

My eyes bulged, "You said what?" I screamed. *No he didn't.*

"I thought it was cute and complementary to how he feels about you; that is all I am saying."

"Who pays you to think?"

"Watch your mouth young lady. You will ask me a question again and only I will know the answer. What was in the bag?" Keith probed again.

"I will send you a picture," I said. It was five cans of Pillsbury Grand's biscuits and five bottles of Karo Syrup. Karo original, dark, lite, light brown sugar and pancake.

They both were wrong for that. It was so cute though, I had to admit. He was so thoughtful in everything he did. I didn't know how to handle it. That is why we needed to talk. I walked outside with a suspicious look.

"Dinner is on the table," Leigh said.

Paige looked at me and stood up and said, "What's wrong?" I handed her the bag. She looked very intimidated. She opened it and hollered.

I looked at Randall. He raised his eyebrows as if he was innocent.

She passed it to Leigh. Who looked at Randall and said, "Get him on the phone."

"What?" Randall asked like he had done nothing. Which technically, he had not, but Keith sure had. He had committed a cardinal friend sin.

"Please just do what Leigh asked?" Sissie said in that big sister don't F with me tone.

"What did he do?" he asked sincerely.

"He knows," I said with a smirk.

Leigh and Sade rolled laughing.

"Dani already called him."

How did he know that? I wondered.

"I didn't ask you that!" she barked.

He dialed.

"Speaker please," Leigh instructed.

"What's up?" Keith answered after the first ring.

"Not your clown butt. What did you do?"

"We discussed this," He said laughing.

"Who is we?" Paige asked.

"Hooks. Help me," he pleaded.

"Can't do it man. I do not know what you all discussed," Hooks replied innocently.

"What can I do for you girls?" he said all business like.

"Just tell us why you snitched," Leigh yelled at the top of her lungs.

"It wasn't snitching at that time. I know better now."

The conversation went on for a few minutes. We said good-bye and prepared to eat. I sat in my usual seat at the head of one end of the table and Randall automatically took the other end of the table.

"Let's pray," he said. We all bowed our heads and I held Sade and Paige's hand. Sade held Leigh's and Leigh held Randall's who held Paige's other hand. As he prayed he thanked God for this family. I think we all squeezed each other hands at the same time. Family was where my thoughts pondered. The next thing I knew they were saying Amen and dropping my hands.

Dinner was salmon, tuna steak, corn, grilled vegetables and cabbage. I needed this diner. It was healthy and fulfilling. I really wanted comfort food, but for the time being this would have to do. If I must admit, it was rather good.

"Hooks this is decent," Paige said. "Are you sure you cooked it or was it already prepared when you got here?" she asked alluding to the fact that he could not possibly have cooked this meal.

"Not another one?" Sade said rolling her eyes at each of us especially Randall and me.

"Another what?" He defended himself while completely puzzled at their conversation.

"Another Auntie. Always pretending she cooked something. We never see her cook and we never see when or where she buys it from." Sade accused. "The food magically appears."

"Pretending?" Leigh said. "It is make believe food. The Food Network fairy prepares whatever she puts on the menu."

"I do not think she can really cook," Sade said with conviction stuffing her mouth.

I sat there listening as if they were not talking about me. We ate, laughed, joked and fellowshipped. We had good, clean, wholesome fun. I was very tempted to look down at my watch to see what time it was, but I didn't. It seemed like hours passed or maybe I felt that way since I had a lot on my mind.

Then the time finally came. "All right ladies." He made the shots ring by clapping his hands. "You do not have to go home, but you know the rest."

Paige stood up and said, "Let me clean up." That was just a front to buy time.

"No thanks, we will take care of it," he said.

"No we have it," she replied. "I insist."

"We will take care of it!" he said in his Deacon Daddy voice.

"I feel like we are being put out, Leigh said creasing her brows.

"Not quite," he replied. "Remember, the original plans."

"I have been put out of better places," Sade said.

"I am sure you have," he said agreeing with her.

"Oh is it like that Hooks?" Sade gave with much attitude.

Sternly he spoke. "Sade."

"Yeah?" she placed her hand on her hip and rolled her neck.

"You know what time it is," he said.

"You and Auntie doing something you know you don't have no business doing?" she insinuated still in a tone that projected much attitude.

"Not this time. Not this time," he replied once to her and once to himself.

He left himself open and all of them took punches on that statement.

"Okay ladies, let's ride since we are being put out," Sissie said with the pouty mouth.

I decided to interject, "Come on girls. Let's play fair."

Waving her hand, "Yeah, yeah, yeah whatever," Sade dismissed.

They started walking towards the door as I got a plate to put in the sink. He placed his hand on my waist and said, "Leave them there."

We walked them to the door as if it was our door. We stood on the front and watched them pull off like we were a couple. After they were out of sight we both stood there lifeless, as if afraid to move. Truthfully, I was afraid to move. The time had come and now it was the moment of truth.

"Come on let's clean these dishes up," he said as he placed his hand around my waist and led me back to the kitchen. We washed the dishes and put the food away. I sat on the counter and watched him. He was the man of my dreams. Once he finished wiping the last dish he passed it to me and I placed it in the cabinet next to me. He leaned on the counter while I sat there. We both stared at each other. It pained me terribly.

"It's such a nice night would you prefer to go outside?" his voice trembled. I could tell he was nervous.

"That will be fine," I said calmly. However, I was extremely nervous too. I wasn't sure where this conversation was going, how it was going to end, or the method of getting there. We walked out on the balcony; I sat on one chaise while he sat on the other. It was a good arrangement. We were not face-to-face and I didn't have to look at him if I choose not to.

He jumped right in. "Danielle what's bothering you?" he blurted out to start the conversation.

"Nothing," I said. He waited and waited then realized I was not going to speak any time soon.

Speaking sternly, "Don't do this Danielle!" I still said nothing. He sat up but I did not look in his direction. "Talk to me," he said.

I closed my eyes.

He spoke just above a whisper, "Danielle."

"Yes," I replied also in a whisper.

"Please tell me what is bothering you. I can't fix it if I don't know what is broken."

"I really don't know where to start."

"Anywhere," he begged.

"I do not think I can do this," I painfully admitted.

He dropped his head.

"I have worked hard and long to avoid being hurt," I said weakly.

"Danielle, I have no intentions on hurting you. That is not my desire."

"I do not think most people set out to hurt anyone. It just happens."

"I never want to hurt you," he said with sincerity in his voice.

"Doesn't mean it won't ever happen."

In sheer disappointment, "what am I doing to make you think I will hurt you" he asked.

I dropped my head into my hands, "You are not doing anything. The situation is just overwhelming." I explained.

"Overwhelming? I was not expecting that word," he responded sounding hurt and defeated.

"I wasn't expecting for anyone to show up in my life and flip it upside down in an unusual way."

Trying to remain calm, "is that unusually good or unusually bad," he asked.

"Option two."

"Why did you use the term flipped upside down and why is it bad?"

"Come on Randall let's be real," I said almost with laughter in my voice.

"I thought we were."

"When Randall?"

"All the time," he said perplexed.

"That may be where the issue is."

"I do not follow you," he replied.

I took a deep breath, "I said flipped upside down because I care for you a lot. I think, or maybe I hope, you feel the same way. Which makes it bad."

Out of curiosity, he asked, "if I could make this divorce happen today would we be having this conversation?"

"No, we would not, but can you even make it happen period? If it hasn't happened in three years, I have to be honest and say that I do not foresee it happening anytime soon."

"Four years," he corrected feeling exasperated already.

"I stand corrected. The issue still exists. Randall, I like to live a simple life."

His eyebrows rose at the words simple life insinuating I did not live a simple life.

I ignored his accusation and continued on. "I work hard and play hard. Drama has no purpose in my life. I like it like that and I plan to keep it like that. The last thing I need is some BS. I got Pastor riding me like a jockey in the Kentucky Derby. My heart is racing like it is in the Indy 500. To make matters even more difficult, this might be all over a guy that may one day be available or may not."

As confused as he could be, he needed to know, "what is this really about? Me, You, Tameka or Trevor?"

"Actually, all three play a major role."

In his commanding tone he clearly stated, "Disregard Tameka. Ignore Trevor. Now what?"

"You don't understand. It doesn't really work that way. I do not want to get caught up."

Each of her responses led him to another question. Why was she making this so hard? "Caught up in what?"

"Mess, drama, BS or whatever you want to call it."

"I have none that follows me," he said.

"Oh, I beg to differ."

"Name drama that surrounds me."

I said nothing. I saw that we were not going to see eye to eye on this at all.

"I will speak to Trevor and ask him to keep you out of this. If there is anything he wants to say he needs to direct it to me."

"It still does not change the facts Randall."

"I am trying to change that too," he said in desperation. It was painfully obvious he was used to being the one to try and fix it all.

"In the meantime maybe we should pull up," I said regretfully.

He sighed and sat back. "What do you mean by pull up?" He was getting irritated and upset. He covered his mouth when he spoke. If he was trying to muffle the irritation it did not work.

"As little or no contact as possible," I hesitantly told him.

"What is that supposed to do?" He paused quickly, "Regardless, I do not see that happening Dani."

"It will remove our feelings from the equation. It will make sure we stay on the friend level," I said, sounding as if I was simply trying to convince myself.

"I don't see how it will work. All it is going to do is frustrate us even more. It doesn't work like that."

"If I recall correctly you were the one who said we can control our feelings."

He laughed because he knew he said it.

"I need a redo," I said sourly.

Trying and successfully containing his fury he asked. "Exactly what would you like to redo?"

"A lot."

"Starting from where?" I was really irritating him at this point and this comment was not about to make it any better.

"The day I pulled up to the church parking lot is where it all began," I said. "I would not be in this situation if I had stayed home that Sunday morning."

"Do you not like it? I am in the same situation with you," his voice was elevated.

"Like has nothing to do with it. I can't do what I want to do. I can't be who I want to be. I have to continuously look over my shoulder, always making sure I am saying, and doing what is appropriate for two friends. I have to make sure no one is rolling up on me. It's overwhelming," I said.

"I am hurt," he said lowering and shaking his head. He did not see this coming.

"That makes two of us," I responded.

"Please let's stop using the word hurt," he suggested.

"It is what it is."

"Why?" he asked as solemnly as he could.

"Randall!" I said for the first time raising my voice. I caught it, paused, and then took it back down. "Because I can't do any of what I want to do. I am not in control. I can't touch you if and when I want to. I can't show up to your gym with lunch if I want to. I can't show up to your house with dessert when I want to. All I can do is follow your lead. I didn't go this long to turn my life around over something that may or may not happen," I said stressing the words may not happen.

"This is so messed up."

"It is a very bad situation that can change at any given moment in any given direction. I'm not so sure if I want to wait to see what will happen."

"I do not know what to say."

"Just say you understand Randall."

Understand? "I can't because I am not sure I do. I do understand your point. Maybe I do not understand how you got here. Danielle can I tell you something?"

"Sure. Why not?" I replied.

"I love you. I love you right now just as we are. I love you more than I have ever loved anyone in my life. I appreciate your honesty and concern. I respect it. Promise me that you will keep me informed on how you feel. Promise me you will be honest. Promise me if your interest change you will tell me. I promise you that you are the only person I am interested in. I promise to make you happy always. I promise to be faithful, loyal, and honest at all times. I promise to be there for you. I promise to do all I can as expeditiously as possible. I will keep you informed and abreast of whatever is going on in my life. I do not want to hide or keep anything from you unless it is a surprise for you."

"Danielle, I need you. I can't let you go right now. I can't walk away. That would be impossible. It would destroy me, but I have to do what makes you happy first. I will sacrifice my all for you. I do, however, want to address a comment you made."

"Which was?" I asked with raised eyebrows.

"You called me the church flirt."

I looked at him for the first time since we came outside. "Well are you?" I asked expecting an answer.

"Why would you ask me this?"

"Curiosity," I said.

"I have never ever had a conversation other than normal church business with any one there. You are the first and last female at the church that I have called and spoken to outside of those walls. I have never and I still do not have the need or desire to talk to anyone. I will not talk to anyone if it makes you feel better. You just say the word." He threw up his hands.

"If truth be told, you are the youngest and I may be biased, but also the most handsome Deacon in the group. You are also a Champion Boxer in case you are not aware. Why wouldn't a chick try to holler? Regardless of being in church or married for that matter. Chicks will be chicks and groupies will be groupies whether it be in church or not. A come up is just that, a come up."

His frustration level had just hit about an eight point five on the Richter scale. He said, "I am going to say it again; I have never hollered at any of them. Those days are long gone for me. Let me rephrase that; I have never had those days. Flirting is out! If I can't have you then I'm done. I can crawl back to the cave I was in when I met you. I was fine there. I was minding my own business, not thinking about boxing, dating, flirting, or any of that nonsense; and I didn't have to ask anyone if I could buy a car with my own damn money that I fought hard for. Literally!" The conversation shifted gears. He was heated.

"I am not sure how to handle this situation in decency and in order," I said calmly.

"We are friends Danielle. How much order does everyone want from me?" He yelled.

"Yes by virtue we are friends, but if truth be told are we really friends?" I asked. I still remained calm.

"What have I done to make you think I am not your friend?"

"I did not say you were not my friend. Underneath the surface, you and I both know that we are more than friends," I answered.

"What in the hell am I supposed to do Danielle!?" he yelled. You could hear the frustration in his voice.

I looked out of the corner of my eye and folded my arms. I was at the point where I was finished with this conversation. I felt it coming on, the shutdown that is, with one simple word. Fine. Everyone knows when a woman uses the word fine, it ain't ever fine. Ask Paige and Mama Rose. They used it regularly and Sade and I HATED IT!

He covered his face for a second. "I am sorry. Excuse me for yelling. I am very sorry. That was rude and inappropriate," he said a little calmer.

I rubbed my forehead. This was not going anywhere and it was going quickly. Why was he so uptight? What part of this was he not getting? I really wanted to take a time out. No, I needed a time out.

"What do you regret?" I asked looking down.

He threw his hands in the air and stood up. "What kind of question is that?" he asked even more annoyed.

"A sincere one and one I want to know the answer to?" I replied.

"A lot of my earlier years. Well, mostly Tameka in my earlier years. Some of my boxing, I could have done differently. Wait. Is this about me or is this about me and you?"

"The latter."

"If that is the case then I regret nothing."

I raised my eyebrows this time.

"Should I be concerned that you have regrets?" He was looking at me but I refused to look back at him.

In my mind all I could do was wish I was not in love with him. I didn't want him to hurt me. "If only I could rewind and redo," I said shyly.

He reached his arm out and pulled my chair directly next to his. He jerked it rather. I was surprised it didn't collapse. It caught me off guard and if I wasn't sitting down I would have lost my balance.

"I am trying so hard to remain calm, but you are making this extremely hard." You could hear the restraint in his voice.

I spoke not a word.

He spoke slowly, "What exactly do you mean rewind and redo?" he spoke each word clearly as if he was trying not to get angry.

I did not even debate mentally on if I should speak, I just told the truth. "If I could redo it all I would have gone with my first mind and turned around from the parking lot the Sunday I arrived at church."

At that, he pointed his finger at me. I looked at it crossed eyed. He was pissed by now. "That's," he paused looking for the right word, "Jacked up!" he yelled in a tone he had been trying to avoid.

I still avoided eye contact. I wasn't sure what I wanted to say or how I was to say this.

"I wish you would say something to help my confusion," he said passively.

"Confusion?" I said abruptly. "You have no idea what that word means." I was so close to him until I could see the pulse in his neck jumping, his chest rising and I could hear him grinding his teeth and gnashing his jaw. "Deacon Washington."

He snapped abruptly, "RANDALL! Don't ever call me that when we are on a personal level. Especially at a moment like this!" he yelled at me.

Whew! His mood swings were currently giving me whiplash from snapping my neck back and forth. I think my eyebrows were going to officially be stuck like the joker once this conversation was done. "Randall," I said slowly enunciating each syllable. "This is probably one of hardest things I may ever do. You asked me to promise you that you stay behind the friend line. Today I am assisting you in doing so. Yes, our actions say that we are still friends, but our hearts loudly speak something different. To help you conform to the promise I think we should pull up and pull back. You have more to lose here than I do. You are in the process of a divorce that has the potential to get nasty, ugly and flat out obnoxious real quick; and even more so due to our apparent, unapparent or assumed relationship. In other words, this could get real ugly. Not to mention your best friend is a Pastor, my Pastor, and your Pastor. He is not going to let you slip one tenth of a millimeter. Lastly, you are a man of God. You have accepted a position that requires you to remain in line and in order. I do not want to compete or come in between you and the kingdom. Neither do I want to be splattered all over the tabloids as a home wrecker. The last thing I want is some misconstrued picture of us on a front cover. I hate drama and I do not have time for it. I can't afford it in my life."

Challenging her use of words, "compete? Did you use the wrong word?"

I gave him a look like do not interrupt me.

"If you do not mind, let me worry about all of these things. I am fully aware of my divorce. I have offered Tameka absurd amounts of money. I would give it all to her if she would just go away. It is not about the money for her however; she is just being down right mean. I know my kingdom assignment and I am aware of what I need to do and can't do. Trevor, umm, yes my best friend. There is nothing like him. I would not give him up for the world. He is a friend that can pray and expect mountains to be moved on your behalf. And you know what? Whether I believe it or not, once he prays those same mountains are in fact moved. He is truly a man of God and a great friend indeed, my best. No matter what time of day, no matter the issue, he is available. He is a man after God's heart. A man that has the ability to be a mere man and shoot pool on Saturday afternoon and be anointed on Sunday morning in the pulpit. I do not have to sell him to you. You have seen it and know all these things to be true. I just hope and pray that he and I are cut from the same cloth."

"Have you ever seen me or my name in the tabloids? I do not think I have ever. I have no intentions either. Drama, I do not do drama either. I could easily subject myself by entangling myself with Tameka's BS, or any other chicks. I could be a baby daddy to numerous babies. But I won't; therefore, I stay drama free. I cannot tell you of any time in my life that I have had "drama." It's not my character. Let me be the man in this situation and until I am out of line, let me be me. I am the man right?"

He was testing me and before I knew it, I fired back, "I would love to be me too. But right now, I think you (I pointed my finger and emphasized the word you) need to remember what Paul told Timothy in reference to a Deacons position. Deacon Washington," I said with attitude.

"Low f'ing blow! Maybe you missed it the first time so let me reiterate it. You will call me Randall!" His tone was concise. He emphasized the word will. *Did he check me?* Right as I was about to interrupt him he was saved by the bell.

His phone rang, but he hit ignore without looking down. Then he shot a quick text back. "Excuse me please. Let me send Trevor this text before he shows up." He spoke the words into his iPhone instead of typing. I am sure there was a purpose for that.

You have great timing. Why are you my friend? Right now you have made my life miserable. I am with Danielle being quoted scripture."

Pastor typed right away, A girl after my own heart.

"Is it just me or are you upset?" I asked mildly.

"No, it's not you. I am upset. One second from being irate. Truthfully."

"Why?" I asked as if I didn't know.

"I don't know what to say or do," he said. "I do not know if I am being accused or what."

"Do I have a reason to accuse you of anything?"

"No!" he yelled.

"Are you sure?"

"I swear on all things good and true. Where is this coming from Danielle?"

"Where?" I asked.

He looked like duh?

"Randall," and I took his hands and looked him in the eyes and said, "Maybe you have misunderstood what is going on here. I love you. I don't want to get hurt. I don't want to hurt you or your family either. I do not want to disappoint God or man. I want your credibility and name to remain unblemished. I do not want to deal with groupies. If I don't back out now, I don't think I can ever live without you."

He placed his head on my hands. He sighed hard and exhaled. "Oh Danielle, what am I to do?" He put his face in his hands. "F**k!" He said it over and over again.

I couldn't move. I was shocked. I had never heard him say that word or too many other curse words. I sat still.

He bit the bullet and asked her a question he necessarily did not want to know the answer to. "Do you not want to see me anymore?"

"I want to see you every day. From the rising of the sun until the going down of the same. But I can't."

"But you do? That was the question."

"Yes. Do you want to see me? What do you want from me?" I asked.

"I want to see you all day every day. Any and everything else please let me worry about it. Relax."

"I can't. This is too difficult for me."

"Why?"

"Because I want to hug you, kiss you, tell you I love you and I can't."

"How do you think I feel? I want to do the same. I want to make you smile. I want you to be happier than you could ever imagine," he confessed.

"So what do we do in the meantime?"

"Take it day by day," he said.

I think I already knew, but I asked anyways, "So I take it you are not pulling up?"

"Umm, hell no! We have a busy week next week," he replied as if nothing had just transpired.

"What?"

He grabbed me and gave me a nuggie. "Right now would be the point where I would kiss you and take your clothes off. So, let me just do this."

"Get out!" I said, playfully hitting him.

"I think about you so much!" he confessed.

"Ditto."

"I respect what you are saying and how you feel. However, I do not think I will be able to just walk away. I do not think I can tread lightly at this point. I can't adhere to your request. Like I said, I have a lot of things planned for us this week. I was going to tell you about them tonight, but you are such a dream snatcher. I will wait until tomorrow." He waited and asked, "Do you want to spend the rest of your life with me?"

I tried to break the tension and said, "I am not answering that. I plead the fifth amendment."

"Why?"

"Pastor Hunter may be hiding in the bushes, and if I answer that he will be throwing oil and holy water on us. You got me bent." We both laughed.

"Are you sure you and he are not friends? You know him too well."

"He will show up at my door to give me the third degree," I laughed.

"That's your boy." He took a pen and a piece of paper. He wrote do you want to spend your life with me? Check the box.

I drew my own box, wrote maybe, and checked it. I handed it back to him. He looked at it. Smirked and put it in his pocket. We sat there in silence listening to the music for another thirty minutes or so.

He reached out and held my hand. "I better go."

I nodded. We both moved as if leaving each other was the last thing we wanted to do. I walked him to the door and we stood there staring at each other as if meeting for the first time. "Good night Danielle."

"Good night Deacon. Thank you for dinner."

"Thank you for everything," he said. "Oh, by the way, I will have a word with Keith tomorrow."

"Ah, he is sorry. Don't hurt him," I said.

"I will try not to."

"Get some rest," he said gently.

"You know what to do."

He walked slowly to his car. He got in and backed up and began to pull off. "Go inside, lock the door, and set the alarm," he said before he drove off.

"Okay. Hey, what are you going to do about your car?" I called out.

I could tell by the look on his face he hadn't even thought about his car. It must be nice to have so much money until you forget about an entire car. A luxury car no less. I had never thought about his finances other than when we called Schlossenbloum. He was truly paid and his answer proved it.

He looked at it in the driveway. "I will get it later. Keep it here. It looks nicer here with you anyway."

I threw up my hand bye and watched as he pulled off. I took a shower and tried to lie across the bed, however, the thoughts of the conversation were still annoying me. No matter what he said I needed to pull up. More than likely, I was going to be the one hurt in the end. Tameka would get a fat check every month and a hefty settlement with all the perks of still being his wife. He would begin to train and have less time for me and I would be the one crying myself to sleep every night. Weeping may endure for a night but joy cometh in the morning. I did not even want to go that route again. Been there done that.

He texted: I am home. Are you asleep?

No, of course not.

I texted the girls: Goodnight ladies.

I realized his car was still outside so I went to go put it in my garage. I got in, cranked it, and sat there with my head on the headrest thinking about him. He was smart. I know he purposely left his car so he would have a reason to come back. I didn't know from past experiences, but I knew of people that would somehow forget a toothbrush or pair of shoes at your house. It was kind of like marking your territory so to speak. It let others know they had been there and it gave reason for them to come back. I gave him his props on that tactic. "Clever guy," I said out loud. I sat there in his car wanting to be close to him. I wanted to think of him and that is exactly what I did.

Finally, I went in and crashed on the bed. My phone chirped at three nineteen indicating he had just blogged. It read:

> I may look like the life of the party but I am hurting. To tell the truth, I have been hurting for a long time. Tonight was no different. I smiled and hid the pain, but my voice and anger revealed it. I have done all I can do. Now it is time to be true or back away. The second is not an option. I am a winner! There is no way I will be defeated. I know this is not a game, but I must treat it that way until I have won. I have to do what I have to do in order to get ahead. Even if that means devouring the enemy. Everything and everybody that stands in my way will go down. Bro, that means you too. I can't stop won't stop until I have reigned. Mark my words; the battle has just begun. All obstacles will be destroyed. I will not let this moment pass me by. My life of making mistakes and settling for less is over. This is the start of new beginnings, a new dimension, and a new life. Here's to my new vision and my future wife.

Go to bed.

Then I rolled over like a dog being patted and smiled myself back to sleep. He texted back but I was so engulfed in the heat of the moment until I not only missed his text, but Sade's too.

WEEK 16

Monday

He blogged again at four AM.

I am cool by myself but I am much better when were together. Like hot and cold, neither are great by themselves but work well when mixed together. You take me higher. You make me. With you, I bring out the best in me. Give me time. Before long, I will change your life. They will call you the Deacon's wife.

Sometimes those short quick snoozes are all you need. I woke up about forty minutes later feeling well rested and ready to rise. I spent time with the Master and pressed on. I wanted to call him in the car but I choose not to. I really needed to focus on my final touches for this presentation tomorrow. If I landed this it would be the largest project we not only have going on right now, but one of the largest in the history of the firm. I was pumped although I knew I would spend tonight doing last minute cramming, drawing, and redrawing all night.

I pulled up to the office and as I strolled down the hall, my phone rang in my bag. It was his ringtone. "Hello."

"Good morning."

"Good morning. How are you?" I asked.

He hesitated for a brief moment then said, "Danielle, I am a little tired today."

I was shocked to hear that response. I stopped dead in my tracks. "Why?"

He took his time and hesitated before he responded. "I am not sure."

Feeling a little suspicious of his answer, I asked, "Are you sure you are not sure?"

Against his original plan, he confessed. "Well, our conversation troubled me last night and I hope I did not anger you."

"About?" I asked raising my eyebrows.

"Yelling." That was not in his personality and he really was stressed about it.

"Not necessarily," I said.

"I apologize. I am just stressed about this and spoke out of character."

"Is that your true character?" I quickly asked.

"No it's not."

I sighed deeply.

"Well I know you have a busy day. I wanted to talk to you briefly about tomorrows events."

"Umm okay. Go ahead, I have a few moments." Besides, I was curious as to what he wanted to discuss.

"I need for you to be at the gym when you leave work," he instructed sharply.

"Any particular reason?" It caught him off guard. I do not think he had rehearsed an answer to that question.

"I think Keith has some things he needs to go over with you."

"Oh."

"Yeah, and you need to bring the girls," he added.

This was getting more confusing. "Do we need to come in workout clothes?" I gently asked.

"No actually, you need to come in something you want to be photographed in."

What in the world is he talking about? "Oh the paparazzi will be there getting the tabloid pictures," I joked.

He didn't find it funny and ignored me. "Don't stay late tomorrow. You'll need to get out of there so you can be here by six." His tone was back demanding.

"Dang okay. Instructions. Instructions. Do you have a busy day?" I asked trying to change the subject and get the focus off me and the things he was directing me to do.

"Somewhat. I am about to plan the week so I can put it on your calendar."

"Oh really?" I said wondering what all would he be placing on my calendar.

"I may have to get with Leigh and Sade to confirm."

Now I was beyond curious. I asked, "Confirm what?"

"I do not know all the details yet, but you will soon know. Right now, focus on your presentation. I think you are a winner," he encouraged.

"Well Champ, thank you for the encouragement. However, I think you are the winner between the two of us, but to make it simple, just call me the Deacon's wife." I snuck in.

You could hear him blushing through the phone. Although he has already told me more than once men do not blush. I pictured his face, his smile, and those beautiful teeth. I was glad to make him blush. I mean he was the one that wrote that in his blog last night correct?

"You need to not be up on the internet in the middle of the night." He said knowing I had read his early morning blog.

I quickly lied. "I was not. I was asleep."

Knowing I was not telling the truth he asked, "You read it this morning?"

Trying to deflect the conversation from me I asked, "Why were you not asleep is the question?"

Shaking his head he replied, "one day you will learn. But I think I asked you a question first."

"What?" I tried to play it off as if I didn't know his question.

"Did you read it this morning?"

"No actually a few seconds after you posted it. But I rolled over and went back to sleep."

"I see."

"Now what is the motivation behind it?"

"You are the motivation behind it. It expresses how I feel and gives a prophetic declaration."

"Prophetic declaration?" I was surprised he used those words. "Okay Pastor. More like wishful expectations," I said.

"Are you denying prophetic declarations First Lady Washington? I receive it. If I can only get you to receive it also then we will all be on one accord."

"Which part are you asking or insinuating I should receive?"

"Just as I spoke it. In decency and in order. Originally, I said the Deacon's wife but notice you spoke Pastor in my life. I guess you can say that changes your title in due time. The Mrs. Reverend Washington. I like that," he replied.

"I do not think you can properly use both of those titles. You have to pick one or the other."

"I regret to inform you, but I do not think anything we are doing is going as planned by Danielle's Book of Etiquette," he said with a chuckle.

"Neither by Emily Post, but that is neither here nor there. The future is yet to be determined sir. The correct format was the first way you said it, First Lady Washington."

"The future was just stated. I told you what will happen. And for future references, I can call my wife whatever I choose to and whenever I choose to. Do we have an understanding on that?"

I liked his comment a lot, but I still had to stand my ground and remember he was a married man and it wasn't like we could jump the broom tomorrow or next week for that matter. "Let me address something right now Pastor Washington. You seem to show traces of a slight temper."

He laughed. "You are right. I am exemplifying signs of being a little temperish. I need to watch that. I can promise you it is not my normal behavior. I'm really a nice guy."

"Now what I need to know is are these sincere behaviors? If so, then we have an entire new set of issues that need to be addressed."

His tone lowered. "No, we should not have a problem," he answered.

"I am holding you too that."

He thought to himself. *I need to pull up on my behavior. I yelled yesterday and today because I am getting frustrated. It is not my personality. I think this Tameka situation has me so uptight that it is frustrating me and it is surfacing when I discuss things that it hinders. I am calling Tre immediately.* "Well now that I have gotten myself in a little trouble I better go and let you work."

"Okay dear."

"I will talk to you later and do not forget tomorrow and the girls," he reminded.

"Got it covered." *I don't but it should not be a problem*, I thought to myself. I pulled out my phone and started texting immediately.

"Have a good day my love," he said.

"You too Champ!"

"Bye."

I texted the crew.

> Girls, we have been invited to meet Keith at the gym tomorrow, Tuesday after six. No clue about what. Currently it is Monday 6 AM let's get it cracking!

I sat at my drafting table and opened the blinds to wait for the sun to rise. I studied, made changes, and perfected them until I heard a tap at the door.

"Hey friend," a raspy voice said. I looked at my watch it was seven twenty seven and Leigh was there. She said, "Shut up. How can a person sleep when someone is texting them at ungodly hours?" she asked.

"It was business hours," I replied.

"Where, in Europe?" she shot back after rolling her eyes.

"Tst tst. Don't count this as overtime," I teased.

"Not planning on it. I am trying to be an overachiever like you," she said smacking her lips.

I was still looking down at my drawings. "Umm hmm. You would still be about two hours late," I replied.

"Doesn't matter. Once you get married and no longer have the need to show up at the time most strip clubs and bars close, I will be able to work the hours I choose. Preferably, ten to two."

I had to laugh at that one. "In your dreams!" I said through my laughter.

"Dreams do come true. Would you have ever thought you would be marrying a boxer?" she asked startling me.

I turned around on my stool just as she was going out the door. I yelled, "Check on the model for tomorrow!"

"It will be here at ten," she said real sassy insinuating she was not starting work until ten o'clock.

"Are you free?" I started, but before I could finish she jumped in.

"For Keith at six tomorrow? Now that's overtime."

"It was Randall's request. Send him the bill."

"I don't care whose request; it still needs to be noted on my check."

"Get out and good bye Oscar the grouch," I said. She hated when I called her that. She mumbled all the way back to her desk. "Good day to you too!" I shouted looking down at my plans. I was being sarcastic and annoying. I am sure she wanted to slap me by now.

The next interruption from Leigh was at a minute after one. "Sarcastic Sally," she said.

"That is me," I respectfully replied. I was still looking down and threw up the peace sign behind my right ear.

She cleared her throat. I took my time and slowly turned around. There it was a model of the building I had in mind. I loved looking at the Mini Me's. I jumped down from the stool and ran over to the cart. I pulled up the presentation so we could practice on our time. Leigh knew just what I was doing and walked out. I yelled, "You started it sir. Fight fair!" *Why does she never want to go over this with me? She always says it is like rehearsal. It is a presentation not a chorus line she would say. You overachiever.*

She shut the door and continued to mumble, "She makes me sick!" *I do not have time to discuss anything. I need to be studying this plan inside out. I will have the client all day tomorrow trying to sell him on this design.* Right then my phone rang so loud until it scared me. "Yep," I answered.

"Auntie D!"

"What's shaking?" I asked.

"A little of this and a little of that. What happened last night? We did not get any updates, but I do see Hooks blogged in the three o'clock hour, so we assume the rendezvous was over."

"Who is we?" I asked. Just then, I looked back and noticed Leigh at the door. "Y'all make me so sick! Nothing!" I yelled sounding guilty.

Sade sighed, "Come clean."

"I am!"

Leigh said, "Something had to happen in order for him to say you are going to be the Deacon's wife."

"He is going to stop this blogging immediately!" I said. "Sade why are you up before lunch?"

"Low blow. I do not sleep in late every day. Besides, I have a little job I am going to be in charge of today," she said. "And furthermore it is after one."

"What?" She knew I would ask.

"I don't know yet, but I am sure it will be something BORING!"

"Are you getting paid?" I asked.

"Don't know that either."

"What do you know?" Leigh said laughing.

"I know you have been around Auntie too long. Double team!" she replied and clicked the line off.

We both laughed and went back to what we were doing. *I think I will do a quick hour work out on demand and work all night. Besides, that will give me a good reason not to see Randall.*

Leigh grabbed some food, brought it in for lunch, and plopped in my chair. That was the only break I had all day. I heard her saying bye and asking, "What do I need to have for tomorrow night?"

"Good question. Let me find out," I answered. I realized I did not have any information about tomorrow.

"I better not have to prepare a speech or anything," she said seriously. I think that referred to her speaking or me speaking.

"I am sure that truck load of cameras will be all you need."

"See you in the AM. Take it home at a respectable hour," she instructed.

"Will do," I replied.

She looked at me with suspicion and said, "Before the sun goes down D."

She knows me well. "Gotcha," I replied. That would be close to nine so I was cool. I did not want to text him. I had not spoken to him since twoish. I was trying to pull up but I guess she had a good point. We did not have enough information for tomorrow. So I cheated and texted. Texting was the greatest thing since sliced bread for me.

> Hey, do I need to do anything, have anything or wear anything particular for tomorrow?

> Nothing!

My mind went there. I debated on responding or calling. I broke and called.

"Hey babe," he answered.

"Do nothing, bring nothing, and wear nothing. Do I understand you correctly?" I asked.

He laughed that robust laugh. "That is fine with me," he said still laughing.

"Is that not what you said?" I confirmed.

Embarrassed by his comment. "It is."

"I'm simply trying to abide by your instructions," I teased.

"If you do please know that there will be trouble and I can't guarantee I will be able to contain myself."

"Do what you need to do," I said.

He laughed again, "Get behind me Satan."

"Umm okay. It is going to be a little difficult with me behind you unless you know something I do not know. But I will try anything once," I threw in and laughed.

He was stunned and had to walk away from the group. He was blushing from ear to ear now. "WOW! I was not expecting that Ms. Rose. You have completely left me speechless," he said.

"And to think we have not even started yet," I said with confidence.

He exhaled really hard. He laughed gently this time. It was almost a smirk as he ran his hand across his face and head. "Babe, I am in the middle of something. I am not sure I will be able to concentrate now but can I call you when I am done?" He had to end the call; otherwise, he would no longer be able to finish the remainder of his day.

"Yeah sure."

"Are you still at work?" he asked.

"Yes."

"It's after six," he informed me.

"I know."

"You know tomorrow you are to be here at the gym at six," he reminded me again.

"I will."

"What time are you leaving tonight?" he asked.

"Leigh said before nine," I replied exaggerating the truth of what she said.

"Nine?" he said sounding surprised. "That is ridiculous. I am coming to get you and taking you to dinner."

"I have to get this done Randall."

He sighed harder this time. "And you have to eat too."

This time I sighed.

"Well that gives me three more hours to finish what I am doing. I will call you at nine and you had better be in the car. I want to hear the engine and flasher."

I thought to myself, *I will have to get a sound bite of an engine and a flasher.* "I will do my best," I said. I'm not sure if he was convinced.

"Nine Danielle!" he said in that Deacon Daddy tone.

"Nine Danielle," I repeated sarcastically. We hung up.

"What she say Uncle Hooks?" Sade questioned.

"Nothing," he replied.

"I am surprised she hasn't called me. She must be really busy with that project," Sade thought out loud.

"You don't think she is stressed about it do you?" Randall asked with concern in his voice.

"I hope not. I will call her in a little while. I just don't want her to ask where I am and I have to lie. You know she is smart. Knowing her, she will pick up on your background noise being the same as my background noise or something. How lame."

"Then maybe you should text," he suggested.

"We will see. We have one more place to stop. This is going to be so awesome. I hope she wins the project and then the surprise will just be icing on the cake."

"You think so?" he asked.

"Yep. Auntie needs some surprises," she answered knowing full well Danielle hated surprises. It eliminated her ability to be in control.

"Really? Why you say?"

"Because she works all the time. She works entirely too much if you ask me. She needs some fun and for other people to do nice stuff for her. She is always doing stuff for people," she replied.

"I hope to one day surprise her, do nice stuff for her, and make her happy every day."

"You know what?" Sade asked.

"What?"

She smiled and said, "I think she will like that and I will too."

"Oh you think?" he said returning the smile and happy that she agreed.

"Of course Uncle Hooks." She punched his arm laughing.

"Girl we got to toughen you up," he said making comment on her weak punch.

"Shut up!"

"Let's roll," he said. "You are breaking me."

"I'm doing my job and you still ain't getting that Lambo," she confirmed.

"You don't think she will give in?" he asked seriously.

She gave him a, you got that right look then said, "You will learn."

Dropping his head, he said, "I take that as a no."

She laughed and replied, "You are brilliant no matter what they say about jocks."

"What do I have to do to get the Lambo?" he asked. He wasn't about to give this up easily. He was determined to get that car.

"Probably sell five other cars," she replied.

His eyes got big. He said, "Dang all of that? I do not foresee that happening."

"You may be able to ask her tomorrow if she has had a good day and a Delete," she suggested.

"I am going to try it at your suggestion," he said.

"If she says no then it will be no different than the answer you have now."

"You are right," he dreaded.

• •

It was now after eight and I was still reviewing at my drafting table. I had not eaten much or worked out today and figured it was time to start shutting down. I will follow the instructions I was given earlier. I got in the car right at eight fifty two and I debated on calling him. I really needed to pull back; so I texted instead and he hit right back.

I drove home in a daze, not sure if I was feeling lethargic due to work, hunger or from him. I may not want to admit it to myself, but he was the man of my dreams. A dream I hadn't had in years. I cared for him, I loved him, and I needed to get myself together.

Once I got home, I was like a zombie. I did not want to talk. I was starving, but I did not want to eat. I sent one text to all. Home.

I contemplated turning my phone and the locator off. I needed the time to just think and rest. I opted to leave the phones in a separate location from where I was. They were in the kitchen and I was in the shower. Feeling as though I needed to be alone in silence, I laid across the bed thinking. I wanted to make sure I was ready for tomorrow at work and at the gym. I had no clue what was up. I hoped the early part of the day went extremely well. I closed my eyes and prayed. When I opened them again my house phone was ringing off the hook. I had no clue where I was, what time it was and what was going on. "Hello," I said just above a whisper.

"Open the gate please."

"Huh?"

"I am at your gate. Can you please open it?"

I pressed the buttons and ran to the bathroom. Before I could accomplish anything, he was already at my door ringing the bell. I was so groggy when I opened the door. He looked in amazement as if I might have been sleeping for two days in a row. He grabbed me and hugged me.

"I am going to be honest. I am not going be able to pull up like you suggested. It is ten fifty. I went as long as I could. Does that count?"

I smiled. I was so sleepy. I felt the same way, but right now, I did not have the strength to discuss it.

"I will let you go back to sleep," he said. He took my hands and kissed them over and over again.

Why? I thought to myself. *Why Lord? I am half-asleep and the man of my dreams is kissing my hands.*

"Go to bed my love. You have a long day tomorrow. I wanted to come by and say goodnight and good luck tomorrow."

"How can I not love you?" I asked in amazement of this man.

"I hope that you do," he said.

"Good night."

"Good night," he replied then left.

I was back across the bed for the count, or so I thought. My mind raced a mile a minute, all I could do was think of him.

He blogged at five after eleven:

> If I had known this was coming I would have been prepared. My status would have changed long ago. I have been blindsided in the best imaginable way possible.
> BY LOVE!

Tuesday

Before my feet hit the floor, I spent time with Him in prayer. When I finished, I arose feeling refreshed. I looked in the mirror quite a few times confirming the bags under my eyes were gone. This was a big day for me. I was debating on changing the suit that I had previously selected, but decided to go with my first mind. I moved the mouse on my laptop posted in the bathroom and as I stepped in the shower, I realized he had blogged.

Quickly, I jumped out, caring less that I was wet and the shower was running. I ran over to the keyboard barely avoiding a slip and slide incident across the marble. That would have required a lengthy explanation. I raced to read his additional blog at two fifty eight AM.

> If loving you is wrong, I don't want to be right. I have done all I can to avoid it. I have done all I can to show it. Today, I will do all I can from this moment on to prove it. I hope you go to bed tonight as happy as I am now. Today, it has cost me a lot, but it was well worth it. I have done it all for you my love.

What in God's name does that mean? I sat in the middle of my bathroom floor naked and wet. My bare bottom touching the cold floor with a hot laptop on my wet thighs. I am sure this has to be a safety hazard. I sat there confused, happy and in love. I knew I needed to get up, but my heart would not let me at the moment. I had plenty of time, but I wanted to get to the office early to make sure my head was clear. However, I could not move. *Am I the only person that reads this stuff? Other people have to be reading this other than my crew and me. I wonder if Pastor Hunter read this. He had to; he is his best friend after all. How are we pulling up but he writes this.* I just sat there still for a long time. It hit me, *who said he was referring to me?* The thought made me sad. I read it once more. It was six minutes after four. I had no care for etiquette. I hit his speed dial.

"Ms. D!" King said as if it was four in the afternoon.

"Hey, good morning," I replied.

"You good?" he asked abruptly.

"Umm, I am great," I said.

"What can I do for you?" he asked as if to say why are you calling this early.

"You can put him on the line please."

"It's Ms. D." I heard him say to Randall. "He said why you are up and can he call you back in a few minutes?"

"No."

"No, what?" King asked puzzled.

He slowed running so he could hear King.

"No, he can't call me later," I clarified.

"I thought you said you were okay?" King replied confused.

"I am but I need to speak to him now," I said calmly.

He handed the phone over without a word. That was a first.

"What's wrong?" Randall queried immediately after placing the phone up to his ear.

"Good morning," I replied casually.

He stopped running, stood still, and shrugged his shoulders to King. He repeated himself, "What's wrong?" he asked a second time.

"Who said something is wrong?" I told him.

He sat on the curb. King looked over and opened the door to the truck and Randall motioned he was good. "I guess no one," he said cautiously.

"Can't I just call you to say good morning?" I asked.

"Yes, you can," he replied. *But you not only called you also demanded you speak to me. And interrupted my training.* He thought to himself.

"Well then."

He laughed lightly. The call and urgency was still pressing upon him as a potential problem. "Maybe I got the wrong impression. You never tell King you need to speak to me now."

"Well from this point on maybe things will change," I said.

"I hope it is for the good. Good for me at least," he said hopeful.

I replied, "Well you will have to just wait and see."

"How long is the wait?" he asked.

"It is not me you are waiting on." I said matter of factly.

"Who is it then?" he asked unaware.

"I think you know who and why."

He rubbed his head, another one of his nervous habits. "So what's up?" He questioned still not understanding why she called unexpectedly like this. There had to be more to just wanting to call and say good morning.

"Really?" I asked.

"Seriously," he replied.

"I want to know the answer to a question Randall."

"Okay?" he asked raising his eyebrows.

"Okay what?" I felt like we were in high school.

"What is your question?" he asked also feeling like they were teenagers.

"Who are you blogging about?" I asked.

"Oh, that," he said. "My life." He rubbed his head again. He was not prepared for or expecting that question.

I said nothing. I was trying to decipher if he was being sarcastic.

"What?" he asked with a laugh to his tone.

"I think you know what I am referring to," I said getting a little annoyed. "You have not answered the question."

"Yes I did," he replied with another slight laugh to his tone.

"No, my question was who?"

"Danielle, when I write these blogs, it's my way of speaking to you. Things I want you to know. We have had this conversation before, remember, at the Aquarium?"

"Why can't you directly say them to me?" I asked.

He took a few seconds to gather his words. "I am trying to be proper and within the confines of our friendship. I do not think it would be proper to confess my feelings openly, so I write them," he replied.

"How do I know if you are speaking to me or someone else?"

"You trust me."

"Was that a statement or a question?"

"It was a statement. It should not be questionable."

"Humph." I had to think about that one; allow it to sink in.

"Sounds like you are questioning?" He held his head down and rubbed it again.

"If you say so," I said.

"Unacceptable," he replied.

"What?" I asked a little thrown off by his choice of words.

"If I say so; it's unacceptable. Do you feel so? Do you or do you not trust me Dani?" he asked.

"I simply had a thought," I replied.

Truthfully, afraid of her response, "what thought," he asked.

"That you may not be referring to me. That maybe I am being egotistical," I answered honestly.

"Ego-tis-ti-cal?" he sounded each syllable stunned. "Please don't take this as not answering you, ignoring you, or trying to upset you, but can we discuss this after the event? I know you have to get to the office and pound yourself over the head as if this is the first time you have done this."

"Is that an insult or encouragement?"

"It was said with love and encouragement."

"Thanks. Maybe I am nervous and freaking out a little."

His thoughts were *maybe she is nervous because she feels the same way I do*. "Can I help you with that?"

"I beg your pardon."

Suspiciously, he asked, "Is your mind in the gutter?"

"I am naked on the bathroom floor. What do you expect?" I replied.

"Crap, my mind just joined yours let me savor this moment," he paused. "Can I tell you something?" he asked.

"Do you have to ask?"

"You had to ask if I was speaking to you when I blog," he reminded her.

"I needed confirmation," I clarified.

"I love you. Is that confirmation enough?"

I paused.

"D?" he called out.

"Yeah?"

He paused.

"Randall?"

"Yes?"

"I love you too," I confessed.

He lay back on the curb. "Call me when you get in the car. I will be right here sprawled out on the curb thinking of you on the bathroom floor naked."

"Good bye," I said laughing. He was laid out on the curb sweaty and I was laid out on my bathroom floor naked. I finally got up, showered, dressed, and made it to the car. I gave him a call as instructed.

"Hold on," King said as he answered the line.

"Yes ma'am," Randall answered.

"Hey," I said sweetly.

"Hey, I had to go back and reread what I wrote. Why didn't you think I was speaking of you?" he asked curiously.

"You don't specify," I said.

"Okay. We will see what tonight brings," he said with anticipation in his voice. "If specifications are what you want, then specifications are what you get. I forgot I was dealing with an engineer," he laughed. "Specifications are all you know."

"Oh ghee. Don't have me in the Pastor's office," I warned him.

"Don't change your mind now. I like to give the people what they want," he said mocking me.

"Oh boy." My mind went there.

"It's all good," he chuckled.

We talked all the way, until I made it to my job. Just as I was in the elevator, the phone hung up. He called right back. "Yes Babe," I answered.

"Sweetie. Have a great day. Call me if you need me. Good luck and go sell a building or two," he said.

"Randall thanks so much for your support."

"It's nothing."

"I will talk to you later."

"Six D," he reminded in that demanding voice.

"I know." Six was pushing me to the limit.

Leigh arrived at seven forty five as if it killed her. She gave somewhat of a good morning greeting, if that is what you call it. It sounded more like a grumble as she went straight to the conference room to set up. The guest arrived promptly at nine. I escorted them in and we immediately began. I was much calmer than normal. I was positive that was due to my conversation earlier. I was working the slides, the pointer, and remote control. I had a house full consisting of the guest and in house groups too. *If I had known in house would take over the room, I would have rented the Fox Theater* I thought to myself. Leigh took my goblet and held it as if to say take a breather. Today I pulled the Waterford out. Here go these vultures that show up unannounced with plastic bottles and paper cups of water at my table. I had lunch being catered on china and silver serving trays and these idiots are killing me. Anyone that really knows me knows I love china and crystal. I was not trying to impress the client. However, if it were up to me we would drink and serve off fine China and Waterford daily.

I sipped my water. The room passed a few words amongst groups. "Do we want to take a break?" I asked. They said no but I insisted, "Let's take a ten minute break. We still have a lot of ground to cover before lunch." I checked the camcorder to make sure it was recording correctly. The house secondary photographer was photographing since Leigh was assisting me.

We started back on time. Moments after starting back up I realized my remote was moving slowly I held it up to Leigh and shook it a few times. I heard her texting. I am sure she was texting me, or rather she better be confirming that she's getting batteries delivered to the room. As I stood in the back of the room, I am not sure, if I am too far or if the batteries are actually going out. *This cheap mess*, I thought to myself.

"Next slide please," I said with my arms folded and full of confidence. I continued my presentation and by the time I got close enough to Leigh, I dropped the remote on the table.

"They are coming," she whispered.

That is why I loved her and paid her well. It was cool. It gave me time to move my arms around anyway. *I should not have agreed to something at six. I will need to go work this tension out at the track*, I thought. It won't be tension per se, but I did feel the need to get back to me. Right now, I was strictly in selling, work and business mode and I knew that I was going to need to reprieve. I was thinking and hoping Leigh could read my mind and get us out of this. I really needed to take this group to dinner. *Love makes you say anything. I should not have agreed*, I thought again.

I was ready for lunch to come and go. I planned to jet out and get some D time and then come back and eat or pick over my food with the crew. I wanted to go look at the model again. I had it illuminated with lights. I was very excited about it. Leigh then showed me where Randall had texted three times. I nodded my acknowledgment. We had signals for everything. I so wanted to talk to him right now. I loved this man so much. If no one else knew it, I admitted it to myself. I was madly in love with him!

"Next slide please." It was so fascinating until I purposefully stood all the way in the back of the room. I signaled to make sure photos and recording were good. I wanted to capture their impressions. Once she went to the next slide you could hear them and see them sitting on the edge of their seats. I was impressed at the slides myself. It looked totally different on a ninety-six inch screen opposed to the fifteen or so inches I normally looked at on my monitor. I thought about his car still being in my garage. I snickered. I patiently waited and let them all take it in. It was amazing.

I leaned in, "Has Deac, Sade, or Paige called?" I asked.

"No but I think they are aware that you had a big day today. He did text three times. Good luck, a six o'clock reminder, and some other mushy nonsense."

"Send a text back please," I instructed.

She knew where everyone was and what was going on. I was the only one left out of the loop. Which was not unusual. It was getting time for lunch. We were having it served in a different conference room.

I went over a few particulars and then asked, "Are there any questions? Leigh, how are we with lunch?"

"Three minutes," she said.

"Great! I think this is the perfect place to break. Let's reconvene here in forty five minutes." I let someone else escort them. I raced to the ladies room and my office and I dialed Deac.

"Hey," he said rushed.

"Hello," I said in return.

"How is it going?"

"Good, but long and stressful," I answered.

"You can handle it. Don't forget six Danielle! Okay?" As she cut her worry short.

He said Danielle. "All right I will see you then," I paused. "Is there any way we can do it later or another day? I really think I should treat this group to dinner?"

"Meet me here at six and you and I can feed them anything they choose. My treat."

I grumbled, "Okay." I am sure he could tell I was not happy. "Bye," I said quickly.

"It will be fine sweetie. Do your thang," he encouraged me.

Replying hesitantly, "I will. Thanks."

He hung up. "What she say?" Sade asked as soon as he hung up the line.

"Call Leigh now and ask her what is going on," He demanded rubbing and shaking his head. This was not going as planned.

"This is Leigh."

"Can you talk?" Sade asked.

"Yes, for now," she replied.

"Click off if you have to. What is going on? Hooks said she called wanting to cancel for today."

"Everything here is going good. Great actually. You know how she is when she is not in control. There was an issue with the batteries in the remote control. Otherwise nothing. What did she say?" Leigh asked.

"She wants to take them to dinner."

"Well we are still cool. She has no clue. A few more hours and I think she will be fine," Leigh reassured.

"That's it? He told her to meet him and they can take them to dinner anywhere of her choice."

"How are we going to do that?" Leigh asked.

"The plan is that you'll take them to the restaurant supposedly and she will meet you there," Sade explained.

Shaking her head, Leigh said, "Y'all get me in the middle of all kinds of BS. Let me go. I am sure she is calling Paige right now and you know your mama can't hold water."

"She is your friend," Sade said.

"Your mother," Leigh reminded her referring to Paige's inability to keep secrets.

"She is my Auntie's sister," Sade threw in and they hung up the line.

"You think this will work?" Randall asked. "I feel bad lying to her."

"I think it will be fine."

"So what's up with the job baby girl?" he asked.

"I am trying Uncle Hooks," she whined.

"What's the hold up?" he questioned.

"I don't know," she replied wanting the change the subject.

"Well, what are you looking for?"

"Something related to journalism."

"And what is your strategy?"

"I just finished with a special project not too long ago," she said.

"Why didn't they hire you?"

"It was a special assignment. There was not a permanent position and the funds were not in the budget."

He continued to question her on her job search, "So they had no other positions available until the budget changes?"

She replied, "I wished."

"So what else are you looking for and where?" he continued with his questions.

"I do a lot with Leigh and Auntie in hosting the website and the photographs they take and the recordings. Auntie keeps me busy just with that alone. It is good experience and exposure. I also get to edit comments and label the films and photos. I post them and forward or download them where she needs them to be."

Curiously, he asked, "Umm. How do you like that?"

She smiled at the thought and said, "I like the job a lot."

"So why can't you find a real permanent one?"

"It's five jobs for every five thousand applicants in Atlanta and I am not sure I want to move. I am considering it for a few years to get something under my belt. However, can you imagine the three without me?" she laughed.

"No, I actually can't. But more so the other way around. You without them."

"Whatever! Now, that you have fallen from the heavens I am sure she will let me leave," she said.

"Why do you say that?"

"Just look at you two! I think y'all are going to get all booed up," she said sarcastically. "Pretty soon she won't have time to work and will be paying me to help Leigh; and the next thing I know; she will become the Deacon's wife." As she said that last statement, a huge grin came on her face just watching him turn red in the face.

He smirked and blushed in embarrassment.

"Why are you tripping? You did blast it over the internet for everyone in the world to see," she reminded him.

"You are right," he replied. *Even for my current wife to see*, he thought to himself.

"I think you have it bad," Sade said while shaking her head.

He lied, "I do not!"

She replied, "You know you do," and poked him in the side.

Curiosity had gotten the best of him. He could not take it any longer. He had to ask. "Did you have anything to do with the portrait she gave me?"

With disgust at how much they were alike, she lowered her head in disbelief. "UGH! You two belong together. I say picture, but you two say portrait. Who says that? How lame!"

"Tomato tomato!" he said and laughed still requiring an answer to his question.

"Ha!" Sade laughed pointing at him.

"Well did you?" he asked again a little more serious.

"Depends," she said suspiciously. "Did you like it?"

He raised his eyebrows. Now he was the one in disbelief that she even had to ask that question. "I love it!" he exclaimed.

She smiled big and replied, "If that is the case then of course I did. But I can't take all the credit. It was a group effort."

Fighting back the tears in his eyes. "It is awesome."

"Yeah, it turned out great. It was a lot of hours of pulling pictures and cropping them in a short amount of time, but I must say I'm happy with the way it turned out."

Still feeling emotional from the other night. "You all did a great job!" he complimented again.

"I'm glad you like it nerd boy."

Not even knowing it, she took his emotion level back to zero with one sentence. "Let's go child."

As they walked through the mall, he wasn't sure who got the most attention, King and Keith or Sade. He knew it wasn't him and he liked it like that.

"Ay shawty!" Sade turned around and just as quickly as she turned, Hooks pulled her arm back.

Honored and embarrassed all at the same time. "Aww, man. Hooks, my bad," the young fellow said.

"This is my daughter son. Do we have an issue?" Hooks said sternly making direct eye contact with the hooligan.

"No sir. I apologize," he said immediately with just as much fear in his eyes as was in his voice. But he was going to be sure to tell his crew he had a run-in with Hooks Washington at the mall over his daughter. No one was going to ever believe this. Especially, when he brags about standing his ground.

"I am sure you do," Hooks replied all the while mean mugging the guy. Sade stood there for a moment as if she wanted to holler at the dude. "Let's go," he told Sade as he walked off. Keith and King stood right there and waited for her to drop her gaze and take movement.

Once she caught up to Hooks she said, "Hater!"

"Call it what you want!" he barked totally unapologetically.

"How you gone be all booed up with Auntie D and I can't even holler in the mall?" She was seconds away from throwing a temper tantrum.

He looked at her as if she had just lost her mind. "Not the right one," he said in that don't try me tone.

Insinuating the small amount of relationships Hooks had been in she asked, "How do you know?"

"Shawty, first off. Secondly, he is in the mall in the middle of the day. What does that tell you?

"He may be at lunch. Besides, we in the mall also," she said. "Duh!"

He stopped walking and leaned in close to be face to face with her. "Little girl, think for a moment! He is not at lunch from a job. Neither are you and I at lunch from a job. Either way it goes, he is not dating you if he is referring to you as shawty. Case closed!" he said sternly in his Deacon Daddy voice with his eyes radiating fire as he gazed in hers.

She pouted and stomped away. Leaving him standing there. He shook his head and ran his hand over and down his face. "Lord help me," he mumbled wondering how he got himself in this. Life was so much easier with boys. You either break up the fight or let them fight until one gets hurt or they wore themselves out. Now he had to deal with attitudes, personalities, shopping events, temper tantrums, and everyone wanting to do what they wanted when they wanted. There was no discipline.

King looked at Keith and said, "Man how are we going to deal with girls?"

Keith laughed. "They are all good. You have to learn how to deal with them. Especially these four."

"Punk!" King yelled in the middle of the mall.

Hooks tried to be the peacemaker knowing full well he did not have a mean bone in his body and yelled out to Sade, "I love you too baby girl!"

Keith caught up to her and continued as if nothing happened.

● ●

Lunch was just about over. "Leigh don't look at me in that tone. Randall is insisting I am at the gym by six. I have no clue what's going on. Can you take them for a drink and meet you all around sevenish?"

Leigh sighed and said, "You are killing me. Just kidding. My pleasure," she smiled at her boss and friend. She didn't mind at all. Little did Danielle know but things were going as planned. Just not according to her plan.

"Thank you so much," she said gratefully. "Heaven knows I do not need to be stressed on this last leg. Three more hours and we can call it quits. We will let them check in at the hotel and then head to dinner. Speaking of which, he wants to go too. Should I take him?" I asked.

"It may be a good move to close the deal," Leigh said. "Who knows, they may think you have done work for him and be impressed."

"Or think I am his mistress," I said.

"Well you are aren't you?" Leigh said. "Let's go crazy."

I did not like her response. The truth really does hurt. Since it made me a little more nervous I made the decision that I would not allow him to come. I gave small talk and an icebreaker once we all returned. I had some of the City's most famous decadent desserts arrive to include a chocolate fountain with fondue and a cappuccino machine in the conference room. "Let's indulge," I said already regretting the calories.

Leigh was in heaven. I thought I was going to have to stop her, but I was too busy having a tasting contest with myself. Just when everyone was getting good and full, as the old southern folks would say, I told Leigh to bring it in.

One of the guys rolled in a cart with a cover draped over it. My signature item, a variety of roses, lay beautifully all over the cover. To date I have no idea as to how many roses I have received or given away in my life thus far. Of course, they are my favorite flower.

"Lights please," I instructed. No one had seen this replication except Leigh and me. It was awesome! I do not know if the building was that great or if the replica made it that great. Either way it went, this one was going home with me. Never mind I had not considered where I would even put it, but it was surely mine. I would have no choice but to have something else made for their souvenir.

"I present to you your future project by Danielle Rose of Sanders, Carmichael, Morrison and Shwatz." I removed the fabric allowing the roses and petals to fall where they may and exposed the illuminated building. It was the best reaction I had ever received from any of my work. I swear it was the model that did it! It looked like something from Universal Studios. I motioned and signed to Leigh to send the guy over who had done the amazing job making the model something special. To think he was a recent graduate. He was my new vendor for sure. Matter of fact, I am going to request that we hire him. I was concerned he would not be able to get this to me in a timely manner and was prepared to present without. This boy sold the job. I felt like I needed to buy him a BMW or something based on the reactions. Cameras were snapping all over the place and even Leigh started taking pictures. She acted as if she had never seen it before either. That decided it. It was going in my bedroom so I could look at it all night. Maybe I would finally get some sleep. This would be like a night light until I had a real reason to sleep, Randall in bed with me.

The showing of this cancelled the presentation although I was nowhere near finished. They ate, drank, and observed. Leigh gave a thumb up and Sanders motioned as if he hit the jackpot. I was for certain his net worth just doubled if not tripled.

"Can you design a theater?" the client asked. Obviously beyond impressed by what he had just witnessed.

Without hesitation, "Tell me what you want, and I can do it," I responded confidently.

"We are also interested in a district with brownstones to shop and work," he thought aloud.

"Easy. That is not a problem. Do you have the land or am I winging it?" I responded.

"You draw it up, tell us what we need and we will worry about the land," he replied.

I motioned for Leigh to take notes. She placed the tape recorder on the table and continued to take pictures in between scribbling. If you have ever seen Leigh's hand writing you would know why I use the word scribbling.

I looked and she gave the sign that she was ready. I went to the back of the room, allowing them to have the light and glory. I didn't mind staying in the shadow. I heard my phone chirp from receiving a text.

"Respond back please." Leigh knew I was speaking to her. I didn't know who it was but I assumed it was one of the crew.

Leigh texted, Another winner.

Once I had gotten their attention, I said, "So guys, tell me about this theater. What are we looking at?" I sat in front of my dessert while they threw out ideas. Leigh wrote while I chilled. Her laptop was there but I'm not sure why she was writing. I was cool though and besides this was over. From the looks of it, a job was won and two more forecasted. Today was a good day!

I may be on schedule after all. It was four before I knew it. "I hate to cut this short guys but I think I have tons to work with. I am going to let you go check into the hotel. Leigh will meet you at the restaurant at six and I will join you around seven. Some of us have to continue working," I said with a wink.

As we dismissed Sanders followed me. My head was really too high in the sky to talk to the boss right now. At this moment, I was the boss. As usual, he didn't state it in the conversation, but he was pleased. I went back to my office, checked messages, and loaded the camera to my desktop. Leigh would do her thing with the photos but I had to have a copy too. I called Paige.

"Hey girly," she said as she answered her phone.

With sheer excitement I replied, "Hey Sissie!"

"What's up? How was work?" she asked as if she didn't already know.

"I think today was the best day ever!" I said with excitement.

"Dang girl. You do what you do! Danielle the builder. I knew those Lego's meant something to you!" she replied matching my excitement.

I laughed aloud. She always said that and it always made me laugh. I still had those Legos and I frequently bought new ones. "Don't you ever forget those Legos," I told her.

Excitedly Paige spoke, "I know gym at six. Is he proposing?"

"He better not!" I said.

"He may be divorced and you don't know it."

"Yeah right! I maybe Mother Theresa too," I replied doubtful looking out of my office window. "I am not sure he could keep it a secret that long anyways."

"Mother Theresa. Well that wouldn't be far from the truth since you have become so lame now," she laughed. "Wouldn't that be the icing on the cake?" she continued to think to herself what if Randall did propose to her baby sister.

"Umm no," I said in return.

I could picture Paige waving her hand at me as she said, "Whatever!" she then asked, "All jokes aside, would you say yes?"

"Heck no!"

She laughed then said, "Liar! Are you leaving now?" she asked knowing I was lying.

"Not yet."

"Just be later than me no matter what you do."

"This is impossible." Paige was always late. Even when she was early, she was still late.

"See you soon girly," she said as we disconnected the call.

I dialed Randall from my desk phone. He answered after the first ring. "D. You should be gone," he said condescendingly convinced she would be late.

I looked at my watch and replied, "I still have time."

"Do you?" He checked his watch.

"Over an hour," I answered nonchalantly.

"D!" he said rather fiercely.

"I got you. RELAX! Ask me how my day was? Do something boy. I have been busting my tail." I told him.

"You see a boy kiss a boy," he said smartly. Then he asked me, "Danielle, how was your day sweetheart?"

"It has been an absolute EXCELLENT day!" I said excitedly. Then commenting on his see a boy kiss a boy statement she became serious again. "You did not specify where, how, when and how long. I have free reign."

"Great news! Congratulations! We will have to celebrate! Good, now get your you know what over here! NOW! You owe me a long, intense, passionate kiss. French kiss that is. Anywhere I choose," he smirked mischievously.

Instantly, my body tingled. The muscles in my private area flexed at his words and the thought. Once I closed my eyes, my body shivered. "DANG!" I was really thinking dang to myself but it came out. "You are rude and demanding."

Sade sent me a text.

Breaker, breaker one nine. What is your location?

My office. Ten four.

> You have two minutes and you need to
> be headed out the door sweet pea.

Ugh. I was tired of people checking me. *What is going on with everyone today?* I found myself getting worried as if something was about to pop off. I didn't want to leave. I only wanted to sit back and process it all, but I had no choice so I left.

Wouldn't you know it, of course only because I needed to be somewhere, traffic was a mess? *Did I just hear they landed an aircraft on highway eighty-five? What in the whole wide world? Someone was bound to call before I pulled up to the gym.* These last eight minutes to get there would seem like eternity. Since traffic was at a standstill and it was safe to do so, I sent a quick text before they sent out a search party.

> Exiting the highway.

It was three minutes after six when I hit the pavement of the lot. JJ damn near bomb rushed me out of my car. He was standing outside when I pulled up. *This is too much excitement for one day.* I walked in still kind of hyped and discombobulated. I spoke and JJ kept pulling my arms. I didn't really pay a lot of attention, but I did notice that there was something different in the atmosphere. *It is usually nosier or something*, I thought. I was still too hyped to focus in, however. Suddenly we appeared to be going into an elevator, which was odd because I didn't remember an elevator being there before. I was an engineer; I would have noticed that. It was strange.

JJ hadn't said a word now that I think about it and just when I got ready to speak the doors opened to our destination. I glanced and saw the people. Leigh first, but it did not sink in until after they said, "Surprise!" I jumped.

Now they all knew I had an exciting day. What were they trying to do to me, kill me? "What the hell?" I said, truly surprised, as I held my chest. It felt as though my heart was about to beat out of the cavity that housed it. It wasn't my birthday. The elevator doors closed and then I held the closed-door button.

"What is going on?" I asked JJ while we remained in the elevator. I did not see Randall in the mix.

"It's a surprise. You will have to see," he said calmly.

"Is this what you rushed me for? I am not getting off this elevator until someone tells me what is going on," I demanded folding my arms and moving far in the corner.

He smiled instead of giving into my demands and said, "Why don't you go see?"

The doors opened again and Randall stepped inside. It was like they were trying to get the cat out of the tree. The elevator door closed once again.

I was so confused. "Is this in honor of celebrating my work today?" I asked dumbfounded looking from one to the other. The door opened and JJ stepped off.

"No. You'll have to go see. It just coincidentally fell on this day."

"You do not play fair," I said reluctantly.

"Let me change your thoughts," he said. "I don't want to be categorized like King. I think you will love it and I hope you will utilize it forever. I hope we can together. You inspired me to do this for you. I hope you like it and I am glad it falls on such a great day."

"So you didn't plan this?" I asked.

"Yes, but not to happen on today," he patiently replied.

I held out my arms and we embraced. You could hear Sade talking on the other side of the door loud as ever. My twin was about to freak out if I didn't come out of that elevator. I knew once the door of that elevator opened snapshots were going to be taken. *Am I really ready?* The doors opened, and yes, we were hugging as the cameras fired. *What am I walking into?*

I dunked my head in his chest. He pulled my arm to pull me out. I quickly identified the many different faces. A lot from my office, the people I presented to today and Hunter. I think I saw Mikey too.

"What is going on?" I said sternly and slowly.

He whispered in my ear while they snapped shots. "It is the grand opening of the Rose Hall Track."

"Excuse me?" I said. I was unsure if I had just heard him correctly or clearly. *Did he just say Rose Hall Track?*

"Check it out!" he said, proudly smiling from ear to ear.

There was a track in the roof of the room. I had drawn something like this a few times. A few larger gyms and recreation centers had done it to save space. Actually, it was something I originally wanted in my house, but the county denied it.

I looked around slowly observing every detail. I walked up to the wall and reviewed the murals. The room was extremely quiet; you could hear a pin drop. Everyone seemed to follow me with their eyes, except for the few that followed me taking pictures, Leigh, Sade, and the videographer. Randall was directly behind me. Every step I took he was right there on my heels. I looked back at him and kept walking around the room. I noticed there was a loft space and I really wanted to get over there, but these walls had me mystified. *Who did this? Who knew all of these things?* I could not remember where I had written this, drew this or to whom I told; but someone had recreated my thoughts perfectly. It would literally take me hours to learn everything on these walls. I think I was more impressed with the walls than anything else. I looked over at the clients from earlier and shook my finger at them. I pointed at Hunter.

He leaned in my ear. "It took your painter almost two weeks working every day and numerous hours to finish this. That was the hold up."

I looked through the crowd, found her, and blew her a kiss. I was still trying to get over there to the loft area. It looked interesting to me. I glared at Paige.

He was directly behind me, the same way he always held me down. I leaned back into him and said, "You are in big huge trouble Mister. BIG TROUBLE!"

"Punish me!" he said very seductively. "I pray that I am not led into temptation." He smirked.

He always looked the same. I stared at him intently. I cared less who looked at this point and you had better believe all eyes were on us. I wanted him and everyone in the room to feel the way I felt; and that was to know I loved him. He was thirty years old, but right now, he looked like an eight-year-old kid. He was clueless. He had no clue how my heart was melting.

"I hope you like it," he said like the child who drew their mommy a mother's day card.

"I love it," I said as I dunked my head into his chest again.

Grabbing my hand, he said, "Walk the track with me."

As we walked, he explained all the details. There were four corners of the track like the ceiling of the room. Each corner had a street sign; a real sign in which all of them contained a rose. Danielle Lane, Rose Avenue, Angels Way, and Loves Court.

From the way he explained the details, I think he was more excited than I was.

Each lane had roses painted on the floor. It was marked like a real track, but all the markings were hooks and roses. There was also a mural on the wall that read "Hooks N Roses," with hooks and roses painted and intertwined.

"Four laps equals one mile. I know you count laps; therefore, I made sure it was four lanes. It was difficult to make four lanes. I also did it so you can have your girls walk too if they choose." He pointed to the ceiling at all the speakers and the monitors. He pointed out the ventilation system. "I wanted to give you a way to walk the track safely. I don't have to worry about you anymore," he said.

"So can I give you back the 007 locator?" I asked.

"No ma'am," he replied as he bumped my shoulder. "You can show up at four AM or ten PM if you choose, and when you do, I have a locker room for you also."

"Are you aware that I created this?"

"Umm yes. I have paid for the design. I think Leigh may get fired and Sanders and Carmichael will probably blackmail me forever for authorizing the release of your plans without your approval. I hope you are not upset, and if so, hopefully only with me."

"So is that why they are all here?" I asked still in shock and not really knowing how to respond just yet.

"Yep. This way you don't have to kill them tomorrow," he said.

My eyes had been focused between the murals and an area I could not see well. "What's that area over there?" I pointed with excitement.

"You don't even want to know," he said with just as much excitement.

"You follow instructions well huh?" I teased.

"Call it what you want. I call it being a sucker. You are making me weak and turning me into a punk," he sighed. "If truth be told. I love it."

I looked over the railing to the gym below and walked faster in my five inches to get over to the loft. Once we got there, I was like a three year old on Christmas morning. I had to keep myself calm and not be rude by speaking to my guest, but I had no interest in anything they were saying. I was trying to see all the goodies.

Knowing me as well as she does, Paige immediately handed me a water; I was sweating and not from the lap. I stood there and looked at the television, sofa and oversized chairs. There was even an awesome office area with a beautiful drafting table and bookshelves galore. *Who would really work in that space?*

"Come on Auntie," Sade said while grabbing my hand. There was a small nook with a bed and a luxurious bathroom, that if I recall correctly, he referred to as a locker room. I can see why he called it a locker room since it had four showers, but it was nowhere near a locker room. I then looked at the custom-made closet and it was even nicer than my closet at home. I glanced around for a while and then went back out. I grabbed him and Hunter and fingered for Mikey to come along.

As Hunter came in he said, "This is the first time I have been allowed this far."

"And the last time!" Hooks snapped back. "It is too girly."

"Boys play good in the penthouse or else you both will get sent back to the dungeon!" I warned.

"Oh my area is the dungeon now?" He asked laughing that laugh I so loved.

I bucked my eyes. We walked in the closet. I was surprised to find it full of clothes of all sorts of tennis shoes, dress shoes, workout clothes, and formals. "What is up with this?" I asked.

Coyly and blushing he replied, "What" as if he had no idea what I was talking about.

"You know what!" I said with sheer laughter in my voice. I could not contain it any longer.

Trying to play like he was disgusted. "Talk to Sade. She swindled me into all of this nonsense fru-fru stuff. That girl needs to be stopped. You are aware that she is on our hands forever right? There is no way anyone is going to ever marry her. You all have spoiled her! Her taste is too expensive, she is too demanding and turns me into a push over like her Aunt does me." He bumped my shoulder again while Hunter gave us a look.

"We taught her well," Mikey said.

"Take it all back!" I said with laugher again.

"My pleasure!" he said quickly. "But you have to pick out one of those things over there," as he pointed at the dresses. "For Friday," he said.

"Why?" I asked.

"If you would do me the honor, I would like for you to accompany me to The Fight for the Cure benefit," he said.

"Such a worthy cause, I definitely could not say no." The pun was wonderful. I loved it. A fight for the fighter. I looked over at Hunter as if I had to get his permission.

"This is nice," he said in his Trevor tone. "If there is anything you do not want just put it in my car and I will present these as gifts to First Lady."

I smiled a mischievous smile. "I'm picking one dress and the rest is going back."

Shaking his head amazed that he and his team had pulled this off without her knowing and surprised she had not snapped yet. "There has got to be a million pairs of shoes over there! I guess you can call them shoes. More like straps with stones and nails for heels."

I smacked his arm. "You want me to look nice right?" Knowing he loved her heels.

"Just explain all of this to Schlossenbloum please. He is going to lose it once he sees the bank statement."

"Oh no," I said. "I had nothing to do with this."

"Yeah right. You like it? We can change anything you want if you do not like it." He said not imagining what she could possibly want changed. But then again he was not a girl.

I looked at Hunter, "Don't look at me in that tone." I am sure my look was serious. Neither of them could read what I was thinking or about to say. Unexpectedly, I jumped up on Randall and wrapped my legs around him; catching him totally off guard. I was over taken by his surprise, his generosity, and his love for me. At this moment, he was physically overtaken by my response and his male parts indicated it.

"Damn! Keep it all!" he yelled. "Sade, we have another shopping spree tomorrow if this is the thanks I get." I kissed his neck and face over and over again. The next thing you know, Sade came running with that camera in tow; snapping away.

Hunter cleared his throat, I guess as a reminder that he was in the room.

I jumped down, straighten my clothes, rolled my eyes, and said, "Let's eat. GHEE! Why is he always around?"

"I heard that," Pastor Hunter said as if it was my goal for him not to hear me.

Mikey yelled, "Dinner is served!" When I looked down the gym had miraculously turned into a dining area with chiavari chairs and linen. Paige had done it again. Who would have ever thought Hooks Gym would contain fine china, table linen, crystal drink ware, and chiavari chairs. I could only imagine the guys were having a hard time stomaching this. They were about to be bulls in a china cabinet.

We all gathered downstairs and Pastor Hunter being as shocked as I was finally regained himself. "Let us bless this addition and the meal."

He grabbed both my hand and Randall's. The three of us held hands and everyone else held each other's. Leigh and Sade continued taking pictures and you could hear the steady snapping of the cameras. We had a blast all night. I glanced over at Randall, taking in his handsome face and told him, "you are in big trouble."

He rubbed his head and face then replied, "I know." He was not agreeing to the same reason she was. This time he was not even concerned with living this down with his boys. He was more concerned with how he was going to live with Danielle. Every time she was in close proximity of him, she did something to his body that his mind was not always able to control. It was a feeling he liked. It was something he looked forward to enjoying. This was a feeling he lacked for a long time. It was a feeling he did not know how he was going to contain. He confessed to himself that it was desire he craved and needed and he was well aware it was going to be his biggest challenge to refuse and not make known.

Pointing at him and then over to Sade. "You and Sade are never allowed to be alone again," I ordered.

"Help me!" he said out loud. Again referring to his male physical state and not what she was referring to.

"Oh, you better believe I will."

That was not the comment he neither needed nor expected. He quickly changed his thoughts. "Don't forget Leigh and Paige helped with the furniture," he threw in trying to preoccupy his mind elsewhere.

"Oh! So they all were in on this too? Huh?"

He frowned out of strain. "Of course. Mikey, Hunter, First Lady, JJ, King, and Keith. I am not going down by myself. I refuse!" He looked like DUH as he ratted out everyone involved wishing his man parts would go down.

"No worries, I got all of you," I said.

"I know. We will pay for it." As he sat there being tortured by her presence as she was clueless.

"Now what else is up for the remainder of the week?" I asked.

He laughed out loud at her statements, which seemed to be in sync with his mind. "Well one of the other blackmail events from your office is that I am to run in some race you are walking in on Saturday," he replied.

The surprises just kept coming. "You are?" I said with probably too much excitement. I tried to tone it down a bit and calm myself.

"Yes."

"GREAT!" It did not work and just like a little kid finding out they were going to Disney World. I reached over and kissed all over his face again. I was so excited!

"Hey, hey, hey. We have guests," he said blushing.

"Forget them," I said sitting back in my chair as he stood to escort me back upstairs to be alone.

"I am a little disappointed that you didn't invite me yourself," he said.

"Sorry, I didn't even think about it."

"I hear you put this walk on every year."

"Yes," I replied. "I have done so for years."

"Well Hooks Gym will be there every year from now on."

"Really?"

"Yeah."

"Wow!" My excitement level was way over the Richter scale and it was noticeable. "Everyone?" I asked.

"I think the entire gym. Vickie has the details. Some shirts are being made and some more crap I don't even want to be involved in. You need to quit that job," he said.

"Why?" I asked.

"Everyone there will take advantage of you. They will blackmail you and make you go broke."

I laughed, "I think it is only you. Don't let them do that to you."

"I have had to donate a flight also," he told me.

"Oh God! You do not have to do that."

"To make you happy. I have no problem doing that and more. Let me figure out the next tactic to see you smile and on top of me again," he said with a smile plastered all over his face.

"No tactic needed," I winked as my body agreed. He laughed that robust laugh that I love. I was flicking my new remote not looking in his direction. "Randall."

"Yeah babe," he said distracted admiring the drafting table.

"I love you!"

It caught him off guard. "I love you too," he said as he ran his hand across the handcrafted wood that cost him a fortune.

■ ■

When I got home later that evening and began to reflect, I wished everyday could be like this. This was a happy day. I couldn't help to wonder why life hadn't been this grand and great before. *It doesn't matter. I am grateful for it now. Don't know what I did to deserve it, but I loved it.* I was appreciative, happy, and blessed. All I wanted to do was just enjoy the moment and hope it could last forever.

It was a little after midnight when I decided I was going to do something I hadn't done in a long time, sleep in, and arrive after noon. I opened my garage and looked at his car. I wished it could stay in my driveway forever. Not that I wanted his car, but rather, I wanted him with me forever.

I showered and got my clothes together for the next day. I was going in with jeans on then realized it was going to be Wednesday and if I was going to work late then I may not have time to come home and change for church, so I change my wardrobe.

I sent out a group text.

> Thanks everyone for everything. You all are the greatest. You have gone above and beyond to make me happy. I was surprised and overwhelmed. Today was the greatest! Good job, great friends and a loving family. I send my love to all of you. Good night.

I then sat back and actually watched television! I did not work; check emails, draw, or surf the net. It was one thirty seven AM when I heard the familiar chirp on my phone.

He blogged. Everything feels right. I forget about what makes this wrong.

I publically responded to his blog and posted. I love you.

He responded to the post. I love you too.

Then there was a post from Hunter. Enough Beloved, go to bed.

He texted me this time. DAMN!

I texted back quickly. WE ARE IN BIG TROUBLE!

I do believe so.

Why is he up?

I have no clue.

Good night.

Sweet Dreams.

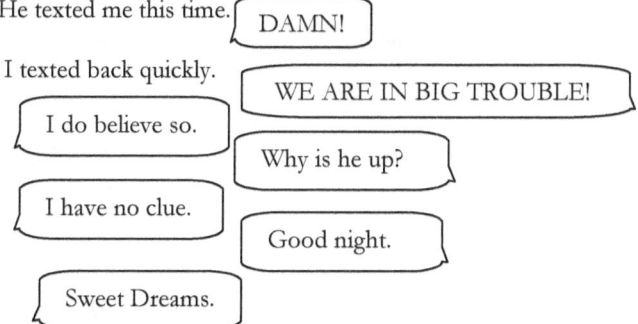

Wednesday

I woke up and I felt different; almost like a new person. It was similar to the way one feels when they first give their lives over to Christ. That's how I felt, although I couldn't understand why. *Surely, there is no way this could be from Hooks. Or is it?* Now I was playing word games with myself. Referring to him as Hooks gave the impression he was just Hooks, the boxer. Referring to him as Deacon Washington kept him in the confines of the church and the title he held. However, when I referred to him as Randall, he was mine. From now on, he was going to be DW or Hooks, nothing more or nothing less. *A man builds me an indoor track and I cannot morally tell him how I really feel without feeling guilty,* I thought.

I was not allowed to put my arms around him, look him in the eyes and tell him my true feelings or plant a huge kiss on him. *This really sucked!* Who followed biblical principles anymore and why were we insistent on doing so? Maybe it had something to do with our upright relationships. Truthfully, that was the case; however, a huge part of it was his best friend. It seemed the more Trevor did the worse I felt. Not that

I didn't appreciate it, I did, but I was still not in control. *Lean not unto your own understanding.* All I could think about was *I am being set up and punked.*

Maybe the presentation had me zoned. I have yet had the opportunity to enjoy it. Since the television was still on from last night, I found something to watch and chilled for a while. I was determined to take it light today. Who knows, maybe I would not even move from this spot, go to church or brush my teeth. *Hmmm, I might even dip Doritos in the ice cream straight from the carton. Yeah baby!* Today would be a good day. *Let me shoot a blast text.*

> I'm vegging out. Call only in emergencies.

It was four in the morning so if I decided to go in I still had time to chill. Around eight AM I had had enough. The party was over. Leigh and Paige had texted and DW had already called twice. I let him know I was still in bed. He asked if I felt okay. "I feel great! I'll call you later," I told him.

Oh well, let me jump up and get to it. It was a nice thought and maybe one day I will follow through. I was in a good mood but extremely mellow. I called everyone responsible for last night and personally thanked him or her. I called DW and thanked him as well. You could tell he was thrown off by me calling him DW, but he didn't respond. I do not think he even has a clue where it came from. Deacon Washington. DUH!

I went to work; however, I sure didn't accomplish much. *I should have stayed home.* I was technically a day behind from presenting, but it was all good. I debated around five if I should go to church. That would be the right thing to do. Besides, how would I justify not going? The truth? I am trying to pull back from DW. Not acceptable, so I mentally prepared myself to go.

I arrived in the vestibule, snuck in and went straight to my seat. Why did I think I could pull that off? Who was I fooling? Of course, he was somewhere monitoring or had someone watching for him. My rump had not hit the seat well before he tapped my shoulder.

"Slide over," he said. Praise and worship had not begun yet. I slid over and he sat down. "How was your day?" he asked.

"Great," I replied.

"Good." He responded sitting up on his knees looking directly at me and me trying to focus elsewhere.

I nodded.

"Everything good?" he asked.

"Yep."

"You sure?" he asked.

"Yep." I was still thinking to myself. *This is crazy. Dani just give in. Who cares? It is the twenty first century. People do not do stuff the way they use to. Confess your sins later. You are making matters worse. What are you proving?* Then just as quickly as the thought came, reality set back in. *No can do. Besides, I do not think he would go for it either. This was a good thing. If he was this strict and by the book with me, hopefully, he has been this strict with all women. This is pretty much what he has proclaimed.*

"Okay. I will be back," he said reluctantly to my curt responses.

"Okay," I said, still not looking in his direction.

He sat there a little longer and then said again, "I will be back. Let me go. I'm on." You could tell he was nervous. He did not know how to respond.

"Okay," I replied again.

"I'll be back," he said for a third time trying to get my attention.

"Great." I said with excitement. I could see his expression from the side of my eye; it was like WTH? As soon as he walked away, I realized I had not spoken more than one word for each response to him all day. When he came back, Hunter was already in the pulpit. He was coming in later than normal. I didn't pay much attention. He grabbed my hand in the middle of a clap, but I didn't acknowledge.

Praise and worship was going on. He participated and was completely engulfed. I could see him from the corner of my eye; however, I was not making much contact like I normally would. His arms were raised and his head was bowed for an unusually long time. He had my attention. He did not move. He was motionless for minutes. I looked back and I didn't see anyone. Anyone like the crew that is.

Then I felt like crap. I hope this feeling was not Danielle initiated. I searched the entire room and could not find one person that could help me. Hunter seemed emotional also. Then I wondered, hoped, and prayed that it had nothing to do with me. Immediately, I snapped my neck. He had fallen to his knees.

My eyes grew large and I looked up at Hunter with bulging eyes. He was calm and cool. He glanced at him and kept it moving. I searched the room again. No one from his crew was around either. The more they sang the worse it got for him. He was on his knees. The only indication of life was the tears streaming down his face.

Hunter begins to pray, but I didn't close my eyes. He didn't either and I hoped he understood that I was not being rude. I needed to support Randall and I needed to have my eyes open to do so. Hunter stood over him, speaking softly and slowly. Pastor Hunter and I made eye contact as he placed his hands on his head. I looked around again and noticed that King, Keith and the others, whose names I did not know, had finally arrived. That made me feel a little better, not good but better. I hope I had nothing to do with this. I hoped it was all in the spirit.

Hunter then placed his microphone in the chair and began to speak over him. Randall didn't move much and the way his boys were standing; you had to be really looking hard to find him or Hunter. They had the pulpit covered and on total lock down. I was not sure if this was to protect them both while they were down or to hide him at a weak moment. Either way it went nothing was about to pop off. You had to be a fool to even try it.

I stepped out from in front of my seat just a tad to see what was happening. It didn't appear at first glance that he was that close, however, he was now leaned over at the altar. All he had to do was bend his torso and he would actually be laying on the altar. I began to panic. Not out of fear, but for helplessness. I could help but was this the right place and would this be a good decision?

Hunter prayed and Randall received. Keith, King, and the others were so close until I could not see him and I was just less than two steps away. What was troubling him or what was pleasing him? I wanted to know. I needed to know.

I stretched my hands towards him and started to pray. King didn't leave his side. He sat in the chair with me. He knew him much better than I did and he knew something was wrong. Whatever it was, it had a hold of him. Be it good or bad, either way it goes; this was a stronghold. He was being obedient by being in the house of the Lord and following the spirit.

The guys were posted around the room at every door. I glanced around and for the first time, I realized just how many of them there actually were. I didn't like to refer to them as bodyguards or security so I thought of what he refers to them as, the guys. They were there and had his back. He began to move as if he was about to get up and just like that; JJ snatched him up like a rag doll and placed him in his seat. I could have sworn someone else was seated in the seat next to him, but now I realized it was JJ. Keith was not very far away at the closest exit. You could see Jon Jon standing in front of him but was blocked by a column and David and Lefty were on that same side. The pity of it all was that none of us could really get to him like we wanted. However, he was getting to whom he needed to at the moment. All we could do was stand on guard. Not guarding because he was in danger, but rather, guarding his post.

This was my first time seeing him so full and emotional in the house. I had seen him emotional at the gym when he wanted the opportunity to fight again. At that time we all knew why he was so emotional, but right now, I don't think anyone knew why. Others may have known but I didn't. I don't think he held his head up but once through the first thirty minutes of the sermon. I made sure my face was the first face he saw. I was not trying to compete with others, including Hunter, but their faces would be stern. It was their jobs. He barely looked up, but I still gave him the largest smile I could offer and winked. He looked like he lost his best friend and it hurt him just too even keep his eyes open. His eyes were completely blood shot. Before he could lower his head, the tears fell like crocodile tears. King was now standing behind him and Keith sat in the seat next to me.

Moments after he dropped his head my tears began to fall too. Keith handed me his handkerchief. I think the sniffling is what gave me away or Keith was really good. It could have been a combination of both. He never lifted his head again and for the remaining of the service, I just observed the view. I listened but I thought about him.

There were a lot of people here with him. I had to question whether they were here because they were working, being supportive or here to worship with the rest of us. Although I understood, they could not show visible signs of worship; I couldn't help but to wonder. I thought again about how much it takes to make what he does seem simple and easy. I looked at each guy until they gave me eye contact including Hunter and Keith. I thought of all the work, time, and money he has invested. Everyone else in the room got to go home to their kids, family, pets and spouse at the end of the day. Yet he on the other hand, practically lives at the gym and spends his waking hours running, punching, jumping, or beating a bag, eating the bare minimum and rarely sleeping.

He paid a very high cost to be the boss. Fame, fortune, money, power, and strength still didn't buy happiness and love. Even building indoor tracks, spontaneous flights across the country and landing on the roof of churches did not pay the price for love. I realized at that moment all he needed was the same thing we all need, what I needed. Love! I was so glad, oh so glad, that he knew the God I knew. He knew how to find Him and meet Him in the place He always showed His presence. I was happy to know that he was a man not ashamed or afraid to praise God. He was not going to let Him go until He blessed him and answered his needs. I naturally assumed something troubled him. If he knew what I knew, and I believe he did, he was well aware that weeping may endure for a night but JOY cometh in the morning light. He was at his set time and his set place and God had already worked it out. This may be all a surprise to some, but God had this planned on the calendar some years ago.

I sat right there in my chair and continued to pray for him. I prayed fervently. He was my friend so when he hurt, I hurt with him. Keith could hear me. The tears were rolling down my face as if I was attending a funereal. Deacon Washington's posture was fuel for Pastor Hunter's sermon. It seemed the more he wept, the more I prayed and the harder he preached. If his message did not reach anyone tonight, it reached his friend.

When asked to stand for altar call, he didn't stand nor did he move for the rest of the service. The guys covered him. You had to be paying close attention to notice he was still seated; head bowed and was still as hardening cement. Pastor gave the benediction and the crowd poured out, yet he sat there motionless. I didn't move either; and neither was I until I knew he was fine or someone asked me to move.

I turned back to reach for a Kleenex. Keith was next to me and as I reached, I could feel and see the motion from the corner of my eye. They all moved suddenly. Randall had fallen out right there on the altar. I think they were concerned that he was hurt. He was alert however. JJ got down with him to see if he was okay and he moved his head up and down as JJ spoke. Hunter was in the middle of greeting members of the congregation when he looked over and noticed him. I could tell by the look on his face that he could not take it any longer and had to check on his friend.

He could no longer be Pastor right now, not when his friend needed him. He called Elder over as if it was a tagged effort and he moved. It was Wednesday and although he was not suited, he did have on a blazer. He threw it across the pulpit and motioned to make way. He then kneeled down next to his friend. You could see the concern on his face, although he remained calm and collected. His tone was so low until I could barely hear him. He motioned for the intercessor and the prayer warriors to move quickly. When they prayed; baby, the earth shook and trembled; the foundations of heaven moved and crumbled! He had the right people on his team for a set time as this.

He lifted his body up and grabbed Hunters neck then proceeded to sob like a sick toddler. Hunter looked me dead in the eyes just as Deacon Washington turned his head and responded back. My eyes were so red and teary until I could barely see. Hunter looked back; he looked so sad. I gasped for air and I didn't know what was going on. His shoulders dropped. This was extremely overwhelming. Deacon Washington lay out on the floor limp. He had been incoherent the last two hours and now here was Pastor stepping outside of his pastoral duties and being a good friend, but at the same time giving me the look of death. He motioned for Keith to come over.

"Don't move." Keith commanded me in that tone they all knew how to use.

I stood still. My feet were so numb until I thought they were bleeding. I think it was more fear than pain or hurt at this point. *What am I afraid of?* I didn't know and that was the fear. I was afraid that whatever it was I couldn't fix it.

Keith turned around and suddenly all eyes were on me. I could not see my eyes of course, but I felt them rolling around from side to side looking at everyone as best as I could. The warriors were praying and JJ was still trying to get him to lift up off the stairs from the way he had fallen. I've been in church all my life and I've seen a lot of stuff, but I've never seen anyone hurt themselves while they were praising God. Sure, I've seen a lot hit the deck but nothing was ever missing, broken or lacking when they rose again. As a matter of fact, most of the time they rose and recovered the spoils.

"Sit down," Keith instructed. Someone brought over bottles of water which he unscrewed the top to one and tossed another to one of the guys standing at Randall's side. He then gave me another Kleenex. He looked at me as if he knew what he was going to say was going to cause me pain.

Instantly my breathing sped up. I looked at my watch and it was doing something I had never noticed before. I think I was hyperventilating. *Of all the days for the girls to miss church.* As Pastor always says, "You never want to miss church because you never know what might happen." A few of the ladies I was friends with and a prayer warrior were on guard. I still had no clue what was happening. I almost felt like I was having an out of body experience. I was hoping this was only just a dream.

Keith paced the floor. I didn't get what was so mystifying. Why was he nervous? He waited until I got my composure. I looked at all the guys specifically. They all looked like something was truly wrong.

"Are you okay?" he asked.

I nodded yes and then no and then yes again. But the true answer was no. I think I understood why Keith was pacing; however, he wasn't used to dealing with girls on this level. This was either too much, too emotional or just not what he bargained for when he signed on. "Danielle!" he said harshly.

I slowly answered, "Yes."

He asked again, "Are you okay?"

I just answered this same exact question. "Yes," I answered again.

"Are you sure?" He looked like Lord help me. I was too afraid to tell him the truth that I wasn't okay. I was panicking. I am glad they were all right here and no one was watching the watch. I was so afraid they were about to tell me he was reconciling with his wife. I felt like I was going to faint. This was not going to be good. Neither option was good; that he went back, she came back or that I fainted. My breath was shorter and shorter and I was visibly shaking. Hunter was staring me down and it was not from animosity. Not that I think he could ever exemplify any but more for concern. He couldn't be in both places at one time. Right now, he needed to be with Deacon. Someone had brought Pastor Hunter's wife back to the sanctuary but I don't even remember seeing her come in. She was seated in a chair next to him praying. Strangely, I wished someone was taking a picture. I know it was inappropriate but I wanted Randall to see the support he had. He probably could not feel it right now, but the glory of the Lord was in this temple. He filled the room like a cloud. I realized they had secured the doors so no one could come in.

Keith was still pacing. He then came up to me and said, "Danielle, he wants me to take you home."

I was shocked and hurt. "NO!" I said very sternly.

He paced away as if he expected that reaction. He remained calm as ever then came back. "It was not an option," he said.

I was determined however to not leave him. "I am not leaving. I refuse to," I said defiantly.

"He is going to be here all night," he tried to reassure me.

I wasn't about to budge. "Then we will do what we got to do."

"He is not moving until you leave Danielle."

"Well, I am not moving until he tells me to do so himself!" I said in an extremely defensive voice for someone crying her heart out.

"He can't right now," he said as he resumed pacing the floor profusely. He looked like he really wanted to make me go, but he could not because he was in the sanctuary. I was a girl and he was trying to be patient with me. He pointed for me to look at Pastor Hunter.

I sat down so I could be eye level with him. He shook his head confirming what Keith said to be true. I shook my head no. His shoulders dropped again; he knew this was not going to be an easy task.

He held Deacon's head in his lap as he knelt, JJ was speaking to him, and the warriors were crying out. JJ and Pastor both motioned for me to come over. I was trying to be strong but by the time I was just three short steps away I almost collapsed. Deacon grabbed my hand. His hand was limp, not a fighter's grip.

I leaned my face into his head. My face was in Pastors lap also. Under any other conditions, I would have said, "UGH!" My lips touched his ear and I told him, "I am not leaving you." My tears ran all across his ear and head.

"I'm fine," he said in a much stronger tone than I assumed his voice would have projected at this particular time.

"No you are not!" I sobbed.

"Go home Danielle!"

"Not until you look me in the eyes and tell me you are fine," I replied.

"I can't right now." He squeezed my hand. I was lying on the floor like I was the referee and Pastor had him in a headlock.

"Oh God!" he called out. "Have mercy upon me!" he wailed. "O LORD; for I am weak: I am troubled, O LORD, heal me. Help me!" he cried out to God.

I held his face over Hunter's grip. Someone finally thought along the same lines as I did initially and began snapping pictures. I could feel their feet standing over me as they snapped again.

Hunter spoke ever so softly, "Danielle he will be fine. Go get some rest. We will be here until he is fine. I will call you myself. I think someone is going to take you home and make sure you eat." There was not a sign of worry in his voice. It would be difficult to not trust him. If God had an earthly voice, I imagined it to sound like Hunter's. Just then, I shivered as I listened to God speaking directly to me. They had better be glad He did; otherwise, there is no way I would be leaving on my own.

God confirmed, *"Yes, you heard correctly Danielle that was my voice speaking through him. He is fine my child."*

I whispered in his ear, "I love you and I need you." I didn't care if Hunter heard or not. My hot tears ran down his ear. A piece of me touched a piece of him.

Keith gently pulled me up and someone had already moved my stuff. As we walked out, he held me up. He realized that I was reaching for my handbag and gave it to me. I put it down on the floor, squatted over it, and dumped everything out. I scrambled through the contents and found both cameras. I pulled them out and waited until they turned on. I then motioned to Keith to wait one minute. I walked up and started shooting. I was on my knees using both cameras.

After about fifty shots, I realized I needed to go to the car and get my good Cannon. I quickly changed my mind; however, as that might appear to be very rude. I decided to go home instead. As I got closer to my bag I saw that Keith placed everything back inside and zipped it, just as he once told me to always do. I unzipped it and dropped the cameras in, but this time I zipped it back. I looked up at him and he gave approval. I reached in both pockets for my keys just as he held them up. He was going to be good at this even if he himself doubted it.

Once in the car and off the lot I said, "Pull over please." We turned into the Chick Fil A. Not only did I plan to eat, but I ordered a milkshake too.

"What?" he said surprised.

I replied, "I know right. Are you eating?"

"I think I will," he said second-guessing his decision. We ordered, paid, and pulled off.

He broke the silence. "Can I ask you a question?"

In the middle of my waffle fry, I responded. "Yep."

Appalled, he asked, "What's up with the cameras and gadgets?"

"Gadgets, you never know when you need to send an email, check an email, log on to something or research something. Sorry I am sort of a nerd like that," I answered honestly.

"The camera?" he said not wanting to comment that she carried two.

"Pictures are worth a thousand words. Sometimes there is no way you can ever recreate a moment. A snapshot captures it and even if you hold the moment in your heart forever, the picture shows all the details. It never forgets."

"I agree but."

"But why did I take pictures tonight?" I finished the sentence for him. "How rude was that right? He needs to know and see the support he has. The only way for it to be known is to visibly see it. We would tell him and try to recreate the moment, but the photos will show the proof."

"I guess you are right," he said. "It looks like the video ministry started a recorder back up also."

"Good." We rode the remaining way in silence. When we pulled up to the house I said, "His car is still here."

"Good. I will take it back."

I gave him the keys and opened the garage.

"Ms. D."

"Yes," I answered.

"He is fine." he said it like it was nothing. He too had no concern in his voice.

"I hope so. Do you know what is wrong with him?" I asked.

"It could be a lot of things or it could be nothing."

"I'm trusting you," I told him.

He nodded. "Get some rest."

"I will," I said as I went inside.

It was almost eleven o'clock. I had not responded to a text or answered a call in hours. I ate, showered, and began to work. It was hard.

At three AM, my phone rang, startling me a little. "Hello," I quickly answered.

"Sorry to call you so late this is Trevor," he said.

"It's not a problem," I said. I had been waiting for his call. "How is he?" I asked.

"He is fine. I am just leaving the church. I am sure he will give you details, but he has something weighing heavy on his heart. He is aware that God is in control however."

"Thank you for being a great an awesome man of God and a wonderful friend," I said meaning every word.

"It's nothing. I am sure he appreciates you being there too."

"Thanks."

"Good night."

"Good night and drive safely." I tried to close my eyes. I knew Randall as a mere man; however, others saw him differently. He may even see himself differently. After today, the clichés and proverbs were all true. Money didn't buy happiness or love. He was the strongest in that sanctuary tonight but he laid face down reaching for the help he needed. He knew King, JJ, and even Trevor couldn't provide it. We all panged as he wallowed and bellowed knowing there was nothing we could do. Like a child having a seizure, all you can do is wait it out and hope they don't harm themselves. I only hoped that he left revived and in receipt of what he needed. He was a true mighty man of valor. I do not think I was asked to leave because he didn't want me to see him in this state. I think I was asked to not subject myself to undue turmoil and agony.

He didn't want to hurt me. Tonight I received a revelation. I have prayed and asked God to tell me why did we meet? Why was he in my life? What was it for? The answer was revealed that it was to strengthen my brother. I was here for this season in his life. I was just the stair step to help him over this hurdle. I may be wrong, but I felt like tonight may be the last time I see him other than for two hours of service on Sunday and Wednesday. Just as I promised, I would not let his presence interfere with my worship. I was making the same promise again today. I was going to continue to worship there. Maybe not sit in the same spot. Possibly run in and run out until the pain subsided. As of tonight, I accepted the fact that we may never be nothing more than friends. It hurt but I felt good about it. I saw the change in his life. If I gained nothing, who cared? I gave all I had and he gained it all. His growth and happiness was much more important than mine was right now.

He needed it more and it was more valuable to who he was. I could build buildings sad, miserable, and sorrowful. I know because I have done so for four years. He; however, could not fight in that state. The fight was back in him. His warfare was not carnal and I do believe he showed that tonight. I prayed the strong hold had been pulled down and removed. I hoped he was at peace and he had everlasting joy.

I felt as though our season had ended. We have known each other right at sixteen weeks. Our time together was just that, a season. I enjoyed every moment of it and I must say I was blessed by it. I had nothing else in me, so I buried my head in my pillow and sobbed.

I tried to nap but I was too wired. I tried to work but decided to work out instead. I did have fries and a shake to work off. I popped a tape in. I wanted to go to my track but right now may not be the best time. I am sure he was there. I was doing my tape when my house phone rang. It was ten before four. What does Sade want and where is she coming from or going to? "What do you want child?"

"Hey," he managed to mutter.

I was surprised to hear his voice. "Oh! Hey! I thought you were Sade calling."

"Why are your lights on?" he asked.

"Because I am working out?" I replied.

"Now?"

I knew the answer before I even asked him. "Are you stalking me?"

He didn't answer. Instead, he said, "Come to the door. Please."

I powered down the alarm and opened the door. I was glad I was a stickler and followed Mama Rose's rules. Always have clean underwear on and always look like you are expecting company. Otherwise, at three fifty ain't no telling what I could have looked like.

I opened the door. I stood there for a moment with the doorknob still in my hand. He would not look up at me. His clothes were very wrinkled from lying on the floor. You could see the visible movement from his chest rising up and down. Just then, I realized he wasn't going to move. I stepped outside to close the door so that I would not let the air out. You know Mama Rose would pitch a fit with that door being open that long letting all the good air or heat out. Once I stepped outside, I was so close at this point until I could feel his breath on my face. He still did not move.

I wanted to blatantly ask what was troubling him but I didn't think this was the way to handle this. He leaned his forehead on mine. I leaned on the door. I hoped and prayed this glass could hold the both of us. *Who cares? It's just a piece of glass.* I hoped we didn't go through it, but right now, my friend needed me. I had to call the man I loved friend.

After an extended silence he said, "I am sorry."

Rubbing his face, I asked, "For what?"

"For everything," he said.

"Why are you sorry?" I asked paranoid. My chest was heaving as it did in church earlier.

"To put you in the middle of my catastrophic life. For you seeing me like I am today. For shipping you home last night. For doing things that have caused me to step over the boundaries. Things that I wanted to do. Things that have made me attached to you. For wanting and for loving you when God knows I can't," he said with so much pain in his voice.

I sighed heavily.

"I am sorry to stalk you. I had nowhere else to go. I had no intentions on being here when you left. But you turned the lights on. I am sorry I came through your gate without calling. Your remote was in my car." He grabbed my hands. He squeezed them until they hurt. It wasn't malicious. He didn't know his own strength.

He then fell down to his knees and I went with him automatically. Technically, I had no choice; he was still squeezing my hands. We stayed there for what seemed like hours. All you could hear was him sobbing and breathing. I still had no clue as to what troubled him.

"Come in let me get you a bottle of water," I said.

He said, "Okay," but he never moved and neither did I. Then movement in the neighborhood begins. It had to be after five or closer to six.

He too realized morning was near and I did have somewhere to be. "Get up so you can get ready for work," he said softly.

"I am not leaving you here," I said without a second thought.

"This is amazing. You are so good to me," he spoke barely above a whisper.

"Why do you say?" I asked.

"You have said that twice in eight hours without having any knowledge of anything," he humbly answered.

"I trust you. I am not leaving you Randall."

"Thank you for being here for me. Thank you for your love and support. Thank you for understanding."

"You do not have to thank me or apologize to me. No matter what happens, I will always be your friend. I will be here for you," I said.

He was slightly concerned with her statement. "What do you mean no matter what happens?" Avoiding any concern in his tone.

"Just that."

"Let me do what I am doing. Allow me this time to weep. You do just what you are doing; be my support until this is over. I am not going anywhere and neither are you. The timing is beating us up, that's all. Let me worry about all the particulars."

My look was of panic.

"Go get dressed. I am going to be right here when you are done," he said.

I did what he asked me to do. Told me rather. My eyes were bloodshot. When I returned he was laid out on his back on the porch. He could hear my feet. He moved his arms and I reached down and handed him my hand to pull up on.

He looked me in the eyes. "I am fine," he reassured. "This will all make sense soon. I promise I am not holding anything from you. As soon as I am mentally ready I will speak to you about it."

"You need some food and rest," I told him.

He rubbed his head and face then replied, "I am sure I look like hell."

"When was the last time you slept?" I then asked.

"I don't know."

"Please go home and go to bed. Get in the bed and do not run this morning." Not sounding too convincing, "I will try."

With sincerity in my voice, "Promise me you will Randall!"

"I will try."

"If you love me you will," I pleaded with him. "This is a two way street. The same way you ask me to do things is the same way I am going to ask you."

He said, "Don't," but I immediately cut him off.

"Shh. You asked me to go home last night so I did. You asked me to go get dressed, I did that too. You asked me to be patient; and with everything in me, I have. You just asked me to let you do what you need to do and I am. Now I am telling you to go home. Not to the gym. Eat. Do not drink a shake or juice. Lastly, get in the bed and not in the chair or the sofa. I mean this Randall."

He touched my nose. "You got all of your stuff?" he said as sarcastically as he could right then.

"No."

"Let's get it." He laughed shaking his head. He knew I was right in my request. I drove to work as he drove home. I wasn't sure what would happen from this day on.

Thursday

I was exhausted mentally.

Leigh came in. "Hey," she greeted warmly.

When I looked up her entire demeanor changed.

"Oh crap!" In addition, she slammed my office door. "What happened?" she asked alarmed.

Rather calmly, I replied, "I am not sure I can talk yet."

"Nothing bad is it? Everyone is alive and okay?" she asked while going to get that damn camera.

"Yeah, yeah."

"Don't scare me!" she yelled back.

"I will tell you all at one time," I told her.

"What can I do?" she asked full of concern.

"I do not know yet." We both sat there in silence. This is what friends did. Her silence and presence right now was golden.

After a long time of silence. Leigh said, "Do you think you need to go home?"

"I want to but I am the same useless there as I am here right now."

Around eleven he texted me.

> I am just waking up. I think I am going to shower and lay around. I plan to chill here. Other than going to get my tux, I will be here all day today. Call me if you need me. Thanks again.

> You are welcome.

> I am sure Tre will pop over once he finds out I am not at the gym.

> Call me if you need me also.

At noon, I called Leigh back into my office and got the other two on the phone. I explained the entire night, no one interrupted, and no one spoke a word.

"What are you going to do Sissie?" Paige asked in that motherly tone.

"This is so difficult. I can do nothing. Let me rephrase that," I said, knowing I needed to correct myself. "I can do all things through Christ who gives me strength, but in this situation, nothing."

"I am speechless," Leigh said. "Did he say what is troubling him?"

Shaking my head, "No."

"All we can do right now is pray for him and sometimes prayer is all that's needed." I lowered my head.

Leigh shook her head in agreement and Paige chimed, "I think you are right."

Leave it up to the child. Sade broke the ice and made me spit my water all over the desk when she opened her mouth. "Auntie D let the man get the Lambo! I would lay over the altar too if I had deal with Auntie about buying a car, with my own money, that she had nothing to do with. I know how he feels. Shoot, I have to ask if I can have my weekly fix from H & M. I would buy both colors and show her tail. Now what? Where they do that? Go Hooks Go!"

She then started mumbling as she always did, "How you gone tell that grown A' man what to do with his money? Like you the wife, you ain't the wife yet. That is probably some mess the wife would say anyways. Then here comes your hot tail thinking you running something. That man ain't studding you. He was probably praying to figure out how to get rid of your controlling tail. He was wishing you would go away. You stalker! He probably hoped you would see this side of him and back off. Now, here you go trying to have a prayer vigil for him. She didn't get it Hooks. She is very smart but she can't read in between the lines. She only reads blue prints, black, or white, not gray. I swear, common sense ain't common. Now those are the words from Mama Rose."

She paused. We all waited to see if she was finished with her soliloquy. She took a breather, but low and behold, she picked up where her mumbling left off. "Humph. He trying to have fun and live life and you asking him to be responsible and think about the future; like he bout to marry you. He doesn't want to do that. He is trying to get away from marriage. Besides, you come with too much baggage Auntie. You got all of us. What man wants to marry all of us? Not even a champion fighter. That's a damn shame. Humph. What is we gone do? Gheez Louise! We can't even get a lame Deacon from church! If I were allowed to curse, I would right about now. How sad!"

There was silence. Then we all fell out laughing. "If he wants his bread to ever be buttered he knows what to do?" I said laughing.

Leigh yelled, "Bread?"

"Hooks ain't ever eaten bread! Does he even know what it is?" Paige added to the laughter.

Sade screams in the midst of the laughter. "Shut up! He does eat bread."

"Have you seen him eat bread before?" Sissie asked both concerned and sincere.

"Party is over," I said. "Triple team. Out Leigh. Bye girls."

"Wait!" Sade yelled. "Where is he now?"

"Home," I replied.

"Okay. I have to do everything. I'll take care of this. I let you all go to church one night by yourselves and you two come back looking like you been in a fight. Does he still have teeth?" she asked being funny yet concerned.

"Umm yeah. JJ was concerned about that too. I am sure he will have his mouth piece in on Sunday's from now on." We all laughed. I guess it's true; a merry heart doeth good like medicine. I really needed the laughter. I felt better even if I didn't know what troubled him. "We are sick. Bye." Here we were on speaker, Skype, and trying to Tango. To make matters worse, we were only five to ten miles away from each other. Technology made us have it bad.

It was five. Leigh asked, "What's up for the night?"

"I better work out," I hesitated.

"And then?" she waited for a response.

"Don't know."

"Are you leaving soon?"

"Maybe in an hour. I think I am going to go try my new track out. Come by if you can." I said.

"I better if we are walking a race on Saturday."

"Yep. I will be there a few hours today and tomorrow."

"No ma'am," she said quickly.

"No ma'am what?" I asked looking up from my computer.

"You have a benefit tomorrow so you will be out of here at three for hair and nails," she reminded me.

"DAMN! DAMN! DAMN! DEACON! This dating stuff may not be for me after all. It interferes with me working." I nearly forgot about the event.

"What did you say the wife's name was?" she asked.

I thought it odd she would ask that right now. "Why?" I asked.

"Let me pay her to sign. Sister needs to get a life. We are not going to spend our lives working all day and all night," Leigh said.

"Who? Me or you?"

"Both of us!"

"I hinder you from having a life?" I asked. I hadn't really thought about it like that.

"Umm yeah!" Leigh replied as if I asked a stupid question.

"You love having that camera in your hand?" I asked.

"I do not think I will ever be Leigh Cannon Nikon."

Leigh was hitting home hard. "For the second time today get out of my office!"

"I'm gone! I'll be by the gym. I guess I am going to have to get me a boo there," she said while heading out the door.

I did what I said and at three minutes after six, I was shutting down. I hit the ladies room, observed the bags under my eyes, and headed to the parking deck. It was six seventeen when I got to the car. I didn't mind traffic this evening. Actually, I didn't notice it. I popped in the CD from last night. I realized I had two. I do not remember how I got them. Deacon Washington surely didn't give them to me and when Keith and I left, the video ministry was long gone. I am glad they have a backup plan because Deac normally shuts the bookstore down.

I listened closely, carefully and loud. I wanted to make sure nothing happened that I missed. I knew that was not the case because no one else got what Deacon Washington got last night either.

I pulled up to my spot and rested my head on the headrest. He said he was staying home today. From where I am parked, I can't tell if he is here or not, considering he parks under the building.

"Jerk face!" I spoke out loud and jumped out the car. I hit the trunk and then realized I had an entire wardrobe of new clothes inside in my loft. I got my handbag and went inside.

"Good evening Ms. D," I was greeted by Mimi.

"Hi. How are you?" I made it a point to stop and hold a conversation with her today. I didn't want to seem like all I did was brush by her. Actually this is what I did, but not by choice. She was very nice. I enjoyed our conversation.

"Enjoy your track."

"Hey thanks. I will let you know how it walks. What time are you out of here?" I asked.

"Eleven," she said counting down.

I looked at my watch and said, "Girl, you are pushing me to stop early tonight." We both laughed.

"Shall I request your dinner?" she asked.

"No thanks. I can do it. I have a bottle of water here with me which will probably be dinner."

She laughed. "Well let me know if you need me to show you how to operate the phones up there. I think you have a dedicated line and a central line."

"I'll have to check out the amenities. As long as I have enough receptacles and data ports, I should be fine. I am sure you all have me well taken care of."

"Have a good work out," she called out.

I smiled and said, "Thanks," in return.

I spoke as I entered the main gym area. I peeped at the guys then headed up the stairs. I went first to my office area, plugged in, and logged on. *He and I will need to talk about a little more technology I need.* When I walked into my closet it occurred to me that I had not decided on what to wear tomorrow or if I could wear any of it. I sent him a text.

Can you take the dresses back I don't wear?

No.

Oh wow!

He thought about it for a minute then replied.

I can but I am not. Eventually you will need them all at some point.

Oh. How are you?

Good. You?

Good.

Sorry to scare you last night.

No, you didn't.

He really did but I wasn't going to tell him that.

Liar

Huh?

I will send you your levels.

Ugh! Figures! YOU MAKE ME SICK!

I LOVE YOU TOO!

I melted on the floor. I text the girls.

EMERGENCY! HELP! What am I wearing tomorrow night?

Leigh called. "I will be by there in a little while. I think Paige is still at work. Sade is at the salon. We will be by there. Hold on sunshine. Help is on the way," she said in her reassuring tone. I had the best girls ever.

"Thank God!" I said. "See you soon!"

I put my iPod on and begin to walk. I emailed Leigh at the office to talk to her about the stuff I needed there like iPod, voice activated computer, televisions needed to be data linked as monitors and they also all needed to be linked to a disc player with all my software downloaded to the desktop. Leigh was going to hate me after she and I spend a week getting this all together and synced up to my home and work stuff. This was a great idea he had. It made me want to call him.

"Hey Babe!" he answered.

"Hey Sweetie."

"How is the track?"

"These are some snitches around here." I leaned over the banister and shouted. "Snitches get stitches where I am from!" A few of the guys looked up. I bucked.

"I leave you alone one night and you are trying to start a fight."

"Who called you?" I asked in a demanding tone.

He laughed, "I'm not snitching."

"How are you doing?" I asked still looking trying to figure out who was the snitch since I already knew who the stalker was.

"I'm good babe. Thanks for asking."

"Are you sure?"

"Yeah."

"You sure you sure?" I asked.

He laughed. It was a church statement he knew all too well. He had been friends with Trevor long enough for me to guess this was not a new statement for Trevor. He always said people would say they are fine when they are not. Make sure they are fine. Ask them are they sure when they say fine. Help your brother or sister in need.

"Remember you promised," I said.

Huh? "Promised what?" he asked not recalling his promise.

"That if something was wrong you would tell me."

"D, you are right. I did and I will. Just not today," he said dryly. This confirmed something was truly wrong.

"Well, tell me the truth," I said.

"About what?"

"Are you all right Randall?"

"I'm good."

"You are lying," I told him.

He was quiet for a second then said, "Okay. I am not good but I am not bad. I am sure that does not make sense."

"Yeah it does. Well kind of. Actually, no it does not. Now I probably make as much sense as you do," I said shaking my head.

He laughed.

"Why are you laughing?" I asked. I thought we were having a serious moment.

"You make me laugh," he perked back up.

I raised my eyebrows. "Oh really?"

"Actually no," he said seriously then he laughed again.

"There you go again." He laughed a lot. Not to annoy you nor was it a nervous reaction either. It was silent. I wondered did anyone else make him laugh this much. "Hello."

"You," he said.

"Huh?" I asked; I hadn't a clue what he was talking about.

"You make me happy," he said.

"Wow!" Wow to his response and wow to the fact that he made me wonder if he could read my mind.

"What?" he said.

"You kind of caught me off guard."

"I like to do that and I hope I can do it often and always. Why are you caught off guard?"

"Well you just said you are not good or bad but I make you happy."

"I'm not. You are the reason for these emotions," he said, not realizing he had just answered the question I had in my head.

He slammed me with that. Somehow, his statement had a sting to it; not so sure that's good or bad, could go either way. In other words, I could be good for him or bad. This was getting more confusing.

"It is a good thing," he said. I guess it was my hesitation that led him to confirm that; or either he truly was a mind reader.

"You almost made me forget why I was calling. You probably already know," I said jokingly.

"What? To tell me how much you miss me, need me, and want to see me?" he stated.

"Umm no," I said sternly.

"Kick a man when he is down why don't you," he joked.

"I called to say thank you for the track. I love it."

"Are you sure?" he asked.

"Umm, yes. Absolutely sure!" I reaffirmed.

"Positive? Everything is fine? You are sure?"

"Well there are a few things I need to do," I said, thinking of some of the technology things I needed to add.

"Like what?" he asked sounding a little disappointed.

"I need to have these televisions in sync. I need an iPod adapter to the Bose system. I need to add some data ports to the television and load some software and."

"Stop it right there!" he said in that Deacon Daddy voice.

"Huh?"

Firmly, he stated, "you are not adding any work related stuff! Clear?"

"I need it." I said softly.

"Oh hell naw! You bout to make me cuss!" he replied.

"I think you just did," I acknowledged.

"Yeah, I heard it," he replied disgusted.

"To answer you, yes it is work related stuff I need in order to successfully work," I said as if this would make a difference to him.

"No ma'am. You are supposed to be relaxing there."

"There is an office in here right?" I asked to justify my need to the technology upgrade.

"No!" he yelled.

Looking at the office I replied, "I beg to differ."

"There is a desk. It is for decoration and not for working," he barked.

"Okay, now that we have that resolved, can you explain the drafting table please?" I waited for his response because this time I knew I made a valid point.

"Bye Danielle. Have a great next forty minutes. Enjoy the desk and table. It will be removed tomorrow," he said rather nonchalantly.

"Wait!" *Did he say he was removing my desk? The devil is a lie.* "Which one of these dresses do you prefer I wear?" I asked.

"Do you have to wear any?" he asked.

I laughed so loud. "Oops."

"Surprise me," he said.

"Are you taking the others back?" I asked again.

"No!"

443

"The benefit is for Breast Cancer correct?"

"You are correct."

"What are you wearing?" I figured I could match him.

"At this point all black unless you prefer for me to wear something different. I think Vickie ordered me a pink flower and you one too. Unless you prefer to wear a pink ribbon instead?" he teased.

"Let me decide what I am wearing and I will let you know. I think I would prefer the pink ribbon," I said just to mess with him since he did not specify it was a pink rose.

"Either one is fine with me, just let me know."

"Good bye meanie!" I told him.

"No working in the gym," he reminded me again.

I mumbled. "You work in the gym."

"And Danielle," he called out.

"Yes?" I answered.

"I will let you know when it is resolved. You will be the first to know. By the way, the gym is my job." He tried to check me and then hung up.

"You okay up there Ms. D?"

"Other than the snitches, yeah, I'm good," I said.

"Is it too hot?" she asked.

"No. Thank you for asking."

"You have a Bose system up there if you want to turn it on."

"I have my iPod."

"Let me know if you need anything Ms. W."

"Sure will." I walked for another thirty minutes before the girls showed up. You would have thought I had never been to an event before. I jumped in the shower so I could try on dresses. I tried on several dresses, but hands down we agreed on the Marchesa tiered pink silk gown and Manolo Blahnik rhinestone buckle sandals. I was pleased with all the options he and Sade had picked out and purchased. I asked Sade, "How much was actually spent?"

"Auntie that is such a rude and inappropriate question," she replied in disgust.

"You make me so sick!" I told her. She was right, but I still wanted to know.

"I hate you too twin," she smarted off.

They left around ten and I changed and started right back at it. Around eleven, the girl from the front came half way up the stairs and spoke. "Ms. D," she called out.

"Yes."

"Good night," she said.

"Good night. Drive safe."

"Mr. Hooks called and said that he wants you to go home," she relayed the message.

"I know." That was not a surprise.

"Good night." She disappeared as if she wanted no further participation in this conversation.

Maybe twenty minutes later and I'll be dammed if he didn't show up! I heard the commotion, looked over the banister, and saw him coming. I walked right to the dressing room and started gathering my things. I knew what was about to happen. "I'm ready!" I shouted before he could make it up the steps.

"Why did I have to drive up here for you to leave hardheaded?"

"You didn't," I said giving him a smile.

"It's midnight," he said while looking at this watch.

"The gym is open twenty four hours right?" However, it was not quite midnight.

He bit his lip before he spoke. "For you, no."

"It is my track?" I asked condescendingly.

"Let's go," he demanded.

"My place or yours?"

He laughed. "Why we gotta leave?" he flirted back.

"Boy stop," I said seductively.

"You see a boy slap a boy," he said mocking me.

"Don't tempt me." I held up my index finger. "Don't do it to yourself."

"Call me now," he said as I got in the car and called him. "I was at home chilling all day until I had to come make your butt go home," he chastened.

"Yeah, yeah, yeah." We talked all the way to our respective homes.

Friday

I made it an extra early morning at work. I knew I had to leave early in order to do all of my girly things before the event this evening. I was somewhat glad that I did not go with a form fitting dress considering I didn't work out much this week. My phone rang. "Yes Randall."

"Good morning to you too."

"Morning."

"What is up with this? I detect a little attitude." I'm glad he noticed.

"I already know what you want."

"What do you think I want?" he stressed the word think.

"You are calling to give me an absurd list of instructions for tonight." I smiled because I knew I was right.

"Do you really think you know me that well?" he asked me knowing full well I did.

"Am I right?" I asked instead of answering his questions.

"Slightly." he said shyly. Although there is nothing shy about him at all.

"Slightly my foot!" I said pumped up while he laughed.

"I wanted to say hello and give you some instructions." He stressed hello this time.

"Instructions? No, I am not wearing a bulletproof vest under or on top of the dress. That is absolutely out!"

"Girl!"

I cut him off. "I got your damn girl."

"Watch your mouth! Listen," he said holding in his laughter.

"I am listening."

"I have to be there at five."

Really now? "Five PM?!" I basically yelled.

"Yes," he replied as if this did not affect my plans.

"Whew. You are trying me." *Why in the heck didn't he tell me this a week ago? How in the world am I gonna manage this,* I thought. Now I had the attitude he mistakenly detected.

"You do not have to if you don't want to. It will make for a long night. I am sure you will still be at work anyway," he assumed accusingly.

"Excuse you. I will not. I have a hair appointment at three. Thank you."

"Like I said, you will not be ready at five. I can leave after the photos and come pick you up or send someone to pick you up," he suggested.

"I can drive. Tell me where I need to be."

"I am going to ignore that statement. Remember this is a public function. There will be a lot of people. People with cameras. All kinds of people," he stated. "Just to ensure we cover everything, I have to let you know a couple things. My guys will all be dressed in tuxedos. You will know them by the pink rose on the lapel and the pink ribbon attached. You will probably be the one person who can identify them. They will be securing the room, outside and in front of the venue. It will be different from what you have seen before. Your monitor will still need to be on. If you tell me what time you will be ready, I will send someone for you."

"What is the actual time of the event?" I asked. This whole change of plans made me nervous. *Was he avoiding arriving together? Was he avoiding being photographed?* Right at that very moment, I felt like what I was; the chick on the side, I confessed to myself.

"Seven until midnight," he answered.

"This is not going to present a problem for you is it?" My curiosity got the best of me so I had to ask.

"I'm not trying to be a jerk, but if it was a problem for me, I would not have invited you."

"Thanks. Can I give you a time later?" I asked.

"Yes. I will have Keith pick you up when you're ready," he said.

"Please don't wear Keith down messing with me," I said.

"I think he will be fine. Actually, I think he likes being assigned to you."

"You are not going to be angry if I am not there at?"

That question startled him and he didn't let me finish. "Why would you not be there?" he asked.

"I was going to say at five before you cut me off. Five is early," I said.

"Get there when you can. Are you trying to back out?" His voice showed anxiety.

"Of course not. I just don't want you to be pissed if I am later than I originally say."

"Take your time. I am blessed you agreed to go."

"Thanks for asking me to go. I am flattered." However, I was still the other chick on the side and that fact weighed in my mind.

"Wait until the event is over. You may change your mind. Remember, this is work for me. However, I do it because I want to. It is a charitable event that I am not paid for, but I am still on the clock. There will be a lot of cameras, recorders, and questions. I have not been to an event in years. This will be a shock to most. I am prepared for thousands of questions. Daniel Khrittyleberrg, my spokesperson and my staff will be present. My staff will be sure to help instruct me when to speak and when not to. It will be a different event than what you may expect. I normally would not ask all of them to join me, but since this is my first time back in the lime light I want them there. The number one question will be when I will fight. Of course, I can't and won't answer that yet. There may be a question of who you are as well? I will purposefully try to avoid that. Not for shame, but to keep you and your name out of this."

"Then again, no one may notice that I am with you. You will have an entourage yourself. I am sure you will hate that. Keith, Nate, BJ, and Lefty have been assigned to you. They will escort you everywhere. Even into the ladies room. Be prepared."

My eyes widened, "I think I can use it by myself," I stated.

"You think?" he laughed. "Yeah, I know. They will all be together when Keith picks you up. I am going to do all that I can to make sure I spend as much time, if not the entire time with you. That is one of the reasons I am going at five. So that I can get the majority of the questions, the press and photographs out of the way. I don't want to bore you with that. Besides, I knew you would not leave work to be there that early. You and I will definitely eat together. I have requested no cameras or media while I eat. I also requested that I eat in a secluded area and not the public ballroom. Of course, the food will be scanned, double scanned and triple scanned. I was going to request Mikey come and prepare our food, but I waited too late to get hotel clearance and approval and I didn't want to rush him to get the appropriate paperwork returned to them. You can advise him that I am working on that for future purposes however. If Vicky has everything she needs on file it won't be a problem other than scheduling his time. I am sure Vickie has made arrangement for something to be brought in for us."

"Are you going to eat?" I asked.

"With you, yes. I requested a vegetarian plate without oils, fat, butter etc. A large fruit ensemble and a chicken and fish plate for you and the guys."

"Will I be on a date with the guys?"

"No ma'am! You are on a date with me. The guys are working and are getting paid for tonight's events," he said although he was not being paid.

"You do not have to pay anyone on my behalf. I can drive my own car and entertain myself. Remember I have had to do so for a long time. I have been dateless at numerous events on many nights."

"We will talk about that one day soon, but note this; you will never be dateless again," he said.

"Is that because of you or The Crew?" I asked.

"Again, let me express this. I pay the crew for every action, event, and detail they perform. When we are out, no matter how many are around, you are with me. They are working and getting paid. Quite nicely, I must add. Now I am a little concerned that you may not feel the same."

"Well, I do want to specify whether we are on a date or not," I said.

He laughed a small version of that robust laugh. I was learning him well. When he chopped it off, I knew it was either because of sarcasm or because of nervousness. This time nervousness.

"Minor technicality at this time."

I gave a laugh back and he caught my sarcasm. It was not minor to me by any means and neither was my sarcasm. "I will take that as I am working also."

He frowned.

I shrugged my shoulders as I said, "I mean you did provide the attire."

He laughed again. You could tell I was hammering him. "Are you on my payroll?" he issued with the little temper I detected he had.

He obviously didn't know me as well as he thought he did. Since he gave it to me, I was definitely the one to give it back. Do unto others, as you would have them do unto you. "I do not think you can pay me my worth, but it is evident that others will lower themselves for your gratification and accept payment. My firm that sold you my plans without my knowledge or permission for example." I dished it out; however, my intent was for that to sound softer than it came out.

He paused for a long moment. I'm sure he was wrapping his mind around what I just spilled out. I spoke first. I probably should have remained silent but I knew I had to smooth my last statement over. "It was a good payment acceptance; I am glad they did so. Neither do I think it was malicious on anyone's part."

He proudly announced. "A day will come, but somehow; I feel it has already arrived. I am sure it will greatly gratify you to boldly and proudly accept my payment offer or offers." He knew right then and admitted to himself that Dani was different. Maybe a little more than he bargained for, but he was not turning back now. He couldn't. He was in too deep.

No he didn't strike back!

"Now, as I was saying before Danielle so rudely misspoke," he continued.

Why did he speak of me in the third person? I missed the next part of his sentence. I was thinking about the fighter. Today was his day to shine. There was silence. If I was supposed to answer back, I missed the question. Instead, I asked a question. "So what's up with Keith?"

"He is stuck, tied, and permanently assigned to you. If you don't like him I can get you someone you like worse."

I frowned my face, "And why do I need someone?" I asked sharply.

"Safety. Like I said for public purposes, we are two friends attending an event. That's how I feel and I am sticking to it." However, he thought to himself, *she is more than my friend. She is my love interest. If I can only break these shackles off my feet.*

"Humph." That statement was a harsh and hurtful reality. It cut deeply and yet, I couldn't dispute it. I knew it, but to hear it from him was painful. I knew the arrangement and I agreed to it.

"You disagree?" he asked.

"I just want to make sure I have the facts right." I said sourly trying to contain my hurt.

"The facts are that I love you and I hope to God that one day you can and will love me in the same manner." He said this out loud before he knew it and wished he could retract it.

"Bye Deacon."

"Have a great day sweetheart." *Why did she have to do that? It was snide, cheap and unfortunately, it was right. It confirmed her current attitude.*

She had just put him back in place with the Deacon reference. Why did they meet at church? Why was he so attached to Trevor? Furthermore, why was he still married?

• •

It was weird how I thought about him all day, even after he blatantly said we were not going to be on a date. I almost didn't want to go. In my mind, I thought of this like we were going to the prom. He should be very glad he was married.

Otherwise, this would have been a lucky night for him. No matter how much Pastor Hunter would have taken over my mind.

I didn't eat lunch; I couldn't. I was nervous even if I didn't admit it. I lied and told Leigh I wanted to finish what I was working on. Which was nothing, as it had been all day. *This is preposterous. Why am I acting like this? It is a Breast Cancer Benefit. I have been to numerous benefits.* Then I caught myself. *But you have not with a champion boxer and the man of my dreams I corrected myself.*

I packed up and left at one o'clock. "I'm gone!" I called out to Leigh.

Jumping from her chair shocked. "What the?" Leigh stammered.

"I am going to try to get to the salon a little earlier so I can get in and get out. Plus I have to get my nails and feet done too," I said rushing out the door.

"Okay. See you around five. You need to eat," Leigh said.

"I have a bar." I held it up. "I will stop and get a salad from Chick Fil A."

"Promise?"

Why did she always do that? Make me promise? Now I had to stop and get a salad. Once I got to the car, I was still nervous. I decided to call him.

"Ms. D," JJ answered his phone.

"Yes."

"He is in the barber chair," he informed me.

Hesitantly, I responded, "Umm okay."

"You want me to relay a message?" he asked letting me know he was not giving him the phone.

I was a little disappointed. "I guess not."

He noticed the pause and said, "You hesitated. Are you sure?"

I hesitated again. *Were they all this observant? I guess so it was their job.* "Yeah."

"Nope, hold one. You don't sound sure." He handed the phone to Randall.

"Excuse me," I could hear Randall saying getting up from the chair and walking away. "Hey babe what's wrong?"

"Nothing," I replied.

"You good?"

"Yeah. I just wanted to call you and say hello. You didn't have to stop getting a haircut," I said sadly.

"Danielle, I look forward to the day that every time you call I stop and desist everything I am doing to give you my undivided attention."

"You are killing me."

"Why?" he asked speaking from his heart.

"Just cause," I said.

"I know. It's because I am telling you the truth and not holding back any punches. No pun intended."

"None taken, and yes." He hit the nail right on the head; that was exactly why.

"You will learn that I am very honest, open, and straight forward. I rarely hold back."

"I like it," I said.

"I hope you like all of me," he replied.

OMG! My mind went there, yep right there! "Well I won't hold you. Continue on."

"Where are you?" he asked.

"I am on my way to the hair salon."

He was impressed. There were some things that moved her to leave work early. "I can't wait to see you tonight. I am almost a little nervous," he admitted.

Did he say nervous? "Why?" I asked.

"I don't know. Seeing you in that beautiful dress and, and, and I don't know," he stammered.

"Umm is Hunter with you?" I asked.

"Yep."

Quickly I said, "Bye."

"I'll call you once I am done here."

He walked back in and snarled at Trevor.

"What? I am sitting in the chair getting a cut and this is what I get?" Trevor asked playing innocent.

"Stop praying so much bruh?" Randall said.

"Why? Is it working?" Trevor said through a laugh.

"On your behalf, yes. For me, no."

"Yeah it is," Tre happily said.

"I will let you know when I need prayer," Randall said acting angry.

"You did already."

"Not what you were just praying about."

"It's my job," Tre replied.

"Be a failure sometimes. Over achiever." Randall said.

"Can't do it."

"I wish you would."

"Will not."

"Can you pray for someone else then?"

"I was." Tre told him.

"Other than her and me."

"I do."

He looked at his friend and asked, "When?"

Tre laughed a little. "All day every day. I am praying right now."

"What? To ruin my life?" Randall asked.

"No. I was praying that this conversation will end soon," he said.

"DONE!" Randall shouted.

Trevor continued to antagonize his best friend. "You will thank me for this one day."

"Don't foresee it. I don't foresee it," Randall said shaking his head in thought.

"Sooner than you think bruh."

"I'm giving away a friend. Any takers? He is a prayer warrior. He will be a blessing to you. Please somebody take him," Randall joked.

"Looks like you are stuck with me dawg," Trevor said laughing and taunting Hooks.

• •

I called the makeup counter and changed my appointment from five to six forty five. There was no need to back track. The event was right down the street from the mall. *I might as well go there dressed.* I thought. It was a good thing Sade had taken my dress down there, so they had the colors already picked out. All I needed to do was show up. I settled for an up do at the hair salon. I left there, swung by Chick-Fil-A as promised, and got a salad; never mind I only ate one piece of chicken out of it as I drove to the nail salon. I knew I needed to eat, but my nerves would not allow me do so. Once this first event was over, I should never be nervous again. I got a soft nude pink polish on my nails and toes. It was similar to cotton candy. Then proceeded to the house in good time.

My phone rang. It was the ringtone from my house. "Hey."

"Where are you?" Sade asked.

"Minding my business staying out of yours." Click. "No that! UGH! I am going to kill her! Rude, disrespectful heathen. I hate kids!" I dialed it back.

"Hello." She boldly answered as if the deed to the house was in her name.

"Let me tell you one thing." My other line rang. "Let me call you back heffa."

"What?"

I clicked her off. "Hello."

"Hey babe."

"Hey. I will be ready when Keith arrives." I cut him short so I could get back to Sade before I blew a blood vessel.

"I know. I just wanted to say I can't wait to see you." He was nervous. He was always so confident and on point; therefore, this nervous energy was odd to see coming from him. However, it was natural to be nervous; I was nervous too. We were probably nervous for different reasons. Him because it was his first time in the spotlight in years and me because I did not want to be looked at or referred to as a home wrecker. No matter what you say, people will not understand our relationship. I did not understand our relationship.

"Thanks. Same here."

"I will let you get dressed. Behave with the guys."

"Will do." He could hear the tone of my voice that was more Sade's doing than anything.

"Let me rephrase that. I want them to come to work tomorrow and the next day. I really do not want to have to punch either of them if I don't have to."

"Got it," I replied trying not to misplace my anger in his direction.

I walked in my house. Everyone was there ready for the transformation. As I came in the door, I yelled, "Sade!"

"Yes ma'am."

"Get out of my house!"

"When pigs fly."

I put all the stuff on the counter and before I knew it, Leigh went straight for the bag of food.

"No ma'am. Sit your tail down and eat before you do anything," she ordered.

"Why do I have friends?" I huffed like a two year old. I was blessed to have friends and family that loved you enough to chasten you and tell you the truth. Even when you didn't want to hear it.

I spread the salad around the plate several times before I bit the bullet and chomped down. "Satisfied!?" I yelled. This was already starting wrong and to think I had a group of boys to deal with next.

"UGH!" They all rolled their eyes at me. "I hope they get stuck." I headed for the shower. This was always the tricky part. Making sure a strand was not out of place. Luckily, I had a pin up. It's a good thing I didn't have makeup already. I sat with my undergarments on, the monitoring device mounted around my waist waiting for Keith to get to the gate, and then I would step into the dress. I had my shoes on trying to break them in. *Why in God's name didn't I do this last night?* I could hear his ringtone as I was stepping into the dress.

Leigh started taking pictures while Paige zipped me and Sade went to the door. I stared in the mirror to make sure you could not see the imprint of the device around my waist. Once I came around the column, Keith did a double take. It made me self-conscious. "Do I need to change?" I immediately asked as if something was wrong.

"You are fine," he said. You really didn't know what that meant coming from him. Keith never showed any expression. Which made him good at what he did but it sucked if you were trying to read him.

"Are you sure?" I was in a panic.

"I am sure." He looked me over. I knew immediately he was looking for the device.

"It is on my waist."

"Is it secure and monitoring?"

"I think so." I said as he checked his phone and felt my waist to confirm it was secure. Once he gave me the nod that it was okay, I spoke. "I have one problem."

He looked like ah hell. "That would be?" He asked in his same tone.

"I need to stop at the mall for makeup," I said.

He raised an eyebrow. He had no clue what that meant or what he had gotten himself into. "I don't see that being a problem."

"It wasn't an option," Sade said.

"Okay. Have fun," Leigh said diffusing the potential battle be it verbal or nonverbal.

Paige leaned in and gave me my handbag, sorry Judith Leiber, which was no ordinary handbag. She looked at Keith but spoke to me, "I have you some pay phone money in there just in case they try to get brand new and you need us to come get you." The line her and Mama Rose always said when I went on a date when payphones were still in existence and on every corner.

My girls always have my back! I laughed at the thought of them coming to get me and turning up.

Keith didn't find it amusing. He had his game face on. "Is Mother Hen coming too?" he asked looking at me but side eyeing her back.

We all laughed because Paige was Mother Hen. I got to the door and stood there. So did Keith. I could tell that he didn't know what I was expecting so I held my elbow out for him to grab it. He did.

"I'm not holding that," he said pointing to my handbag.

"Maybe not, but you will escort me since we are stuck together. If you are following me to the ladies room tonight, then let me warn you now so you're prepared, yes you will hold it."

"I'm glad to see it is snapped up," he noticed.

"Your number one job is to never let me slip, fall or be left alone. My hair should not be out of whack; there shall be nothing in my teeth or nose. Are we on the same page?" I asked.

The look on his face said, "Why did I get picked for this?"

I replied, "Why don't you ask him?"

"Ask who what?" He snapped back.

"Hooks. Why did he choose you?"

"Hell if we know," Paige said. "Kevin Costner was much better at it."

He smirked. "If I recall correctly he got some too." Keith said in Paige's direction.

"Well that ain't happening!" I interrupted. "UGH! And he got shot!" I interjected.

"I'm glad it ain't." He responded to me but was still looking at Paige.

Paige smarted off, "It is happening. Just not you with her."

That had to be her best come on line for the year. We all looked at her but he didn't get it.

"Good night ladies," he said breaking the sudden awkward silence.

As we walked down the steps, he looked down and blushed.

"She is single you know. I'm just saying," I smiled.

"No, I didn't know," he said with a trace of a smile.

His phone rang and he clicked his ear. "Cinderella is entering the pumpkin," he announced annoyed.

I frowned at him. "The Princess is entering her Chariot!" The Maybach was a long way from a pumpkin.

"Let me get her in the car and she can call you back Hooks."

Did he just tell my Boo I had to call him back? Well damn! When I got into the car, it was just like he said earlier; two of the other guys were in the car. Keith put me in, went around the front, and said, "Stop at the mall please." He got in the back next to me. I laid my head on the headrest and closed my eyes all the way to the mall. Ignoring my phone.

Once we got to the mall I saw that it was my house number calling. I called the makeup counter and said, "I am getting out of the car." Lefty stayed at the valet with the car while BJ and Keith escorted me inside the mall. Keith in front and BJ in the back of me. It took all of twenty minutes to put a face on my face. I liked it. It was soft and natural. I almost didn't know makeup was there.

"I need to purchase this gloss when I pay," I said to the artist.

"Your services were paid for by the guys," she nodded over in the guys' direction.

I looked at Keith. Of course, he would not make eye contact so I grabbed his arm.

"I am just security." He handed her a card for the gloss.

"You look beautiful Ms. D. Have a wonderful time," the makeup artist said.

Keith and BJ were acting like they never wanted anyone to see them at the makeup counter at the mall. I kind of stomped ahead of them breaking my shoes in and then turned back and said, "You two may get some boo's if you stop worrying about who sees you."

"Why me?" Keith said frustrated referencing why he had to be placed with the girl.

"To whom much is given much is required," I quoted.

"Amen," he agreed.

We got back in the car and drove in silence. As we began to pull up to the venue, he chimed through his wrist, "Cinderella." I snapped my neck and he whispered, "The Chariot with the Princess has arrived." he said it like the words hurt.

Something was said in his ear and he barked back. "Those were her words," he literally barked it back.

We pulled up extremely slow, but as we got closer to the entrance, I could see why. They were waiting on all the other cars to move. Once they did, I was able to see other well-known Atlantans. But more so, I could see King, JJ, Black, Sammie, Nate, and Randall on the steps. He was in the middle. They were all on a step to his left and right. All of them dressed in their tuxedos and wearing the pink rose just as he stated. The rose was the best pink rose I had seen in years. It reminded me of the roses in my Dad's Rose Garden as a child. I took a second and allowed my mind to flashback. As I was deep in thought, I realized I was strategically placed so I would be at his side when we arrived. Keith walked around and opened the door. Nothing moved, not a soul stirred, and not a camera flashed. They were doing exactly as he instructed. I just hoped that no one tried it. I didn't want a camera to get smashed on my behalf.

Keith handed me his hand. By the time I stood fully out of the car and Keith moved from in front of me Randall was right there at my side. He said nothing. Keith handed him my hands and he gently took both of them and said, "Hello."

"Hello."

Keith reached across, handed me my handbag, and closed the door. King and JJ turned and walked up the steps in military formation. No one and nothing, other than us, moved. Keith walked directly behind me, his steps in my footsteps. Closely, the others followed suit and by the time we reached the top step he leaned in and said, "You smell great and look amazingly beautiful."

"Thank you. You look handsome as well," I acknowledged.

He smiled then said, "We are on." He nodded to King to open the door.

It started out a little uncomfortable. He didn't know how to walk in with me. Next to me, holding hands, arms locked, in front of or behind me. As we started walking in, he and I were in the middle of the group. King on his left and Keith on my right. He finally decided to take my arm. As soon as he did, a camera flashed. I swear Keith broke it. He pushed it back so far until by the time the flash sparked I am sure it got the ceiling.

"The Champ only! You should have been here at five for the photo shoot. If you missed it then you will have to wait until he is ready again." Then he got all up in the guy's face and said, "Are we clear?"

The guy nodded but actually, he was busy trying to get his camera back together. For his sake, I hope he was listening. I locked arms with Keith too. Technically, they were all my dates since I could not claim one particular person as a date.

I had not been nervous up until this point. I realized there was a strong possibility that this could be a public spectacle. Photos could be presented and slanderous things could be said. I leaned into Keith and asked, "May I have my phone please?"

"It is not ringing," he said.

"I know. I need to send a text." Randall pulled my other arm like he was a little jealous. I looked at him and said, "Give me your phone." He reached in his pocket and gave it to me. In turn, I gave Keith the NOW WHAT look. I found a column to lean behind and I texted superfast. They all stood on the other side of the column. It came right on time. He was allowing photographs while I texted the girls for direction.

> Hey it's me. What am I supposed to do for the photographers? We didn't think this out! We didn't plan well. This can get disastrous. HELP! Hit back both phones.

Paige texted right away.

> No worries. Be camera shy and if they happen to catch you, just smile.

Sade typed a bunch of acronyms.

> IDK, ICD, OS

Leigh translated Sade's response.

> Sade said, I don't know. I can't deal. Oh s**t! Let Randall and Keith know you prefer not to be photographed and they'll handle it.

This was the same type of event I have attended on behalf of the firm; however, tonight I was there in a different capacity. I could not really talk to anyone and the queen's guards would not allow anything more than a simple hello. They would intervene anytime the conversation got far enough that someone may ask who I was or to whom I was there with. The four of them did not move from my side. King and JJ were with him at all times. The other six were scattered throughout the room.

He was very charismatic by nature. He was the same person no matter where he was. The gym, church, or here in a ballroom. An overall great guy. He managed to mingle, converse, pose, and accommodate my needs. At one point, I was speaking with one of the local politicians I knew from the community and work related projects. I saw Keith's movement, which let me know he was speaking into his ear.

As soon as he was able to break free, he came over. "I didn't know you were interested in the political type," he said quietly.

"I didn't know you were such a jealous stalker," I said with a smile on my face.

"Don't make me not vote for the man."

"So are you admitting to being jealous?"

"I am admitting that while I am working and you are being flirted with. I am out here doing all of this for you."

"I beg to differ. Dr. Jekyll and Mr. Hyde here along with his compadres will never allow anyone to think they are flirting with me."

"What did you just call my guy?" He knew I was referring to Keith.

"You heard me."

He pulled me away from the guy's ear range. "You are crazy."

"Well he is. One minute he is cool holding my handbag and the next, he is about to rip someone's throat out. I think you need to let them out more often. Keith has a lot of pinned up frustration."

"He is doing his job girl. You ain't seen nothing yet. Wait until they are all off and can really cut up or something really pops off."

I cut my eyes and said, "I don't want any part of that."

Another local Pastor stood to pray over the food. Immediately after the prayer, a staff of the venue came over. "Mr. Hooks we would like to escort you to your private dining area."

Sol, Vic, BJ, and Jon Jon went in first and examined the room. Once they deemed it was safe we were allowed to enter. Then they began to scan the food, which took some time, much longer than I ever remembered. Finally, we got the okay to eat.

I noticed that he, nor his crew, was eating so I opted to pick over my food. For the first time banquet food was actually delicious and I opted to not eat too. I did get a few bites of the halibut and the asparagus before I realized they were not eating. Then I convinced myself I did not want to drop anything on my dress so I didn't eat either.

In all reality, I was not eating because he was not eating. I was starving though! My salad had worn off. The question was why was he not eating? He did not appear to be as small as most fighters, but then again he was not a light or middleweight either. He was a small guy; however, I think the height and muscle had something to do with his weight class. Regardless, he was as fine as the day is long. Yep, he is fine. He is sexy. I like to refer to it as being super sexy. That is just beyond fine. You know like LL Cool J, President Obama, Paul Walker, and Nelly to name a few. DAMN is all you can say. After thinking about this, I lost my train of thought. *Dang! What was I thinking? Oh, he really should be eating.*

"Hey, why aren't you eating?" I asked.

"Huh?"

"Why are you not eating?" I said slower. Why did people do that? He heard me the first time and I knew he did. He asked huh like I was going to change the question and I spoke slower as if he was going to tell the truth. The truth was he doesn't eat.

"I'm not that hungry," he answered.

There were no way liquids kept him full three hundred and sixty five days a year. "You do not want anything?"

"Naw, I'll pass," he said.

"You know we have a walk tomorrow. You may want some nourishment," I said as mildly as I could. What I really wanted to say was, "Eat the damn food Randall! I am hungry and I want to eat. I will look like a pig if I am the only one eating and why did you have them prepare a room and something different if you knew all along no one was going to eat it?" *I should have brought a Little Debbie in my bag. Next time I will know.*

He smiled first. Then he showed his teeth. Then he laughed that robust laugh. I knew where his mind went. But I asked any way. "What's so funny?"

He laughed and raised his eyebrows. "You don't want to know."

"Yeah I do."

He looked at me like you asked for it. "The nourishment I need is at the table, not on the table," he replied and in sheer embarrassment as he stood up. "For your information I will not be walking in a walk tomorrow."

I thought to myself, *WTH? Yes he is.* "Excuse me?" I said sternly and with much attitude. We had a deal or he made a deal with my firm.

"What?" He tried to act as if he didn't know what I was saying to him.

"What do you mean?" I asked firmly.

"I'm not walking," he said flatly.

"You said you were," I said in a tone only Danielle could make.

"No I did not."

"Yes. You did." *And don't dispute me!* I thought to myself. *I know what you said.*
"I never did Danielle. Sorry."

"That's jacked up." I guess he could see my disappointment.

"I am running. You and your crew can walk," he said with a smile.

My face relaxed. I was relieved, but he was playing with my emotions.

He moved across the room and King leaned in and said, "You may want to eat."

"I'm good," I lied.

"Remember you will be walking in a few hours. He is use to it, but you may not be."

I looked at him and asked, "Why are you not eating?"

"After ten years of this you learn to follow his lead. When he moves you move. If he ain't eating, you ain't eating. No matter what. No matter how hungry you are. The slightest thing can transpire while I am lifting a fork to my mouth. When he sits still, I sit still. When he pees, I pee. When he prays, I stand guard. When he sleeps, I sleep with my eyes open." King explained things in a way I hadn't considered.

"That's interesting. I didn't realize he has been doing this for ten years," I said.

"Longer than ten years. I am sure there are a lot of things you didn't realize about the Champ."

"I take it you like your job," I insinuated.

"Not really," he surprisingly answered.

My eyebrows rose.

"I love the job. I love the sport, I believe in him and he believes in me. I trust him and he places all his trust in, on, and with me." Then King leaned in real close, almost intimidating. "I won't and will not let him down. He has placed a lot of trust in you and I don't expect you to let him down either. Are we understood?"

I could tell all eyes were on us. They left the poodle with the Rottweiler; or so they thought. I didn't think King was being rude. He was being protective. I respected it and it was complimentary that he cared so much for Randall. But being Danielle; and as it is customary in my house, he bit so I bit back.

I smiled politely and leaned in even closer. I looked him directly in the eyes and said, "I'm glad we have that established. Once the new sheriff is given her badge, the new laws will be established. Hopefully, you won't have a problem with them. Deputy Barney Fife, thanks for letting me know your expectations. I trust that you will honor and accept mine. The first one starts now. At all times and by all means necessary Danielle and Randall will shine. Notice I said Danielle first. Furthermore, when I call, you get him. When I speak, you listen. When I need, it is provided. Hopefully, the same respect and protectiveness you have for him, you will exuberantly display for me. Exuberant, in case you don't know what that word means; it means cheerfully, happily and over joyed! I think we are going to get along just fine Mr. King now that we have a clear understanding of our expectations of one another."

He was not expecting my bite, but I wasn't expecting his either. We were face to face like two pit bulls.

Out of nowhere, someone clapped. "Down King!" Keith said.

"Wait a minute. You may want to talk to the lady first." he snickered as if I was supposed to be intimidated.

I snapped, "He started it. I think we have it under control." Our eyes and positions still locked as if we were about to go to war with one another.

Keith mildly barked at King. "Any problems come through me or the Champ."

Randall shouted from across the room as he stood watching us intently holding a bottle of water. "No they don't."

Keith said, "You gave me a job. Let me do it. If I have to be in charge of a girl then I have to be defensive just like King. The same way he got you, I have to have her covered."

"It will not be necessary because I hope they both said all the words they need to say. I think they have been waiting to chump at each other for a minute now. The tension should be released. Where is JJ?"

"Outside the door," Keith replied to answer Hooks' question.

"Call him in and let him know I think he is next on the chopping board. You good D?"

"I was testing her and she snapped. My bad," King said with laughter in his voice.

"This ain't what you want King," I said. "And yep I'm good, I can hold my own. I am not new to punks like this."

"I see. She is all good," and King hugged me.

Then I realized he was really pulling my chain. I think he meant it but he was jerking it a little. I didn't blame him. He had a six million dollar man on his hands. He had to make sure he protected him by all means. I also have to keep in mind that the guys haven't had to deal with a female around them like this; so having me around was new to everyone. I just hoped he checked any and every one that was around him the same way he checked me.

"King!"

"Ms. Rose."

"Can you get with Pastor Hunter the same way you just got with me?" I asked.

"Do I need to?"

"Yes."

"The reason why?" he asked.

"To keep him off my behind," I said honestly and without any remorse.

They all laughed.

"Ms. Rose," Lefty said. "I think staying on your behind ensures the Champ will stay in line. We do not trust the Champ right now. At least not alone with you."

"ENOUGH!" Hooks said. He came over and grabbed me and we walked over to the couch in the room we were in. We sat down. He slouched and told the guys, "Y'all better watch it. She got a girl crew backing her up." He held up his phone. You have some interesting texts coming in."

Oh shoot, I forgot to delete the ones I read and to tell them to send to my phone only. Sugar smacks! There is no telling what they were responding. I hope I will not be embarrassed.

"Are you okay?" I said.

"Yeah."

"Are you tired?"

"Not really."

"What's wrong?" I asked.

"I do not understand why wasn't King getting with Tameka like that? If he had, I would not be in this dilemma," he said shaking his head.

"Maybe he likes her."

That was far from the truth. "Maybe I should have a talk with him about his behavior."

"It's cool," I said.

"It's unacceptable is what it is."

"We got it under control. He is looking out for you," I said totally convinced.

"Now is neither the time nor the place," he replied.

I rubbed his hand, "I do not think he was being malicious."

Taking his other hand and rubbing his head. "You know what D?"

"What?"

"This is why I care so much about you?"

"Why?" I asked.

"Why?" he said puzzled.

"I mean I am glad you do, but why?"

"You can handle anything. You make it seem trivial and easy. Like that was nothing."

"It was nothing. I can handle King. I can run with the best of them," I admitted.

"It didn't look like you were intimidated."

I shook my head, "I wasn't."

"It is just too much at one time. We have Trevor riding us and now King is riding you. They all need to pipe down."

"Relax. It's all good. They all love you."

He reached over with his other hand and placed it on top of mine. "I hope you do too."

I made a noise with my mouth like a sigh. Really, I opened it to responded and decided not to.

"Come on let's go socialize. I am still at work you know. Are you okay?" he asked.

"Yep."

"No, are you really okay?"

"I am fine. Really," I answered sincerely.

"Are you fine that I am working?"

"It is your job. One day you may have to accompany me to a work social event," I raised my eyebrows curious as to how he would answer.

"I do not mind. Just let me know when. We can leave anytime you want to."

"I will let you know."

"Great. I am glad you accompanied me. You look beautiful. Thank you."

"Thanks. I am glad you invited me." *I wanted to say I look hungry.*

We stepped back into the ballroom with the others. We walked in as if we were together. There were many well-known faces there, some of the city's big names. There was also some other a-listers in attendance that did not live in the city. King was on his left and Keith was on my right. The others behind and one in front of us. Someone stopped him. He stopped to talk, but I kept moving; or rather Keith and I. We mixed in and out of the crowd.

Somehow, Keith and I ended up standing on the dance floor. I tapped his shoulder.

"No," he said without looking at me.

"No?"

"I'm on duty?"

"I didn't offer you a drink. I asked you to dance," I said pouting.

"No ma'am." Therefore, I danced by myself, as he stood there clearly evident that he was paid to watch me. I could see Randall trying to move across the room. The more he moved the more the cameras moved and the more people stopped him. He kept looking over at me until finally he made it over. The cameras were still on his heels. King shook his head no to each camera. Keith stood side by side with King for reinforcement.

"Excuse me. May I have this dance?" he asked.

I swear I felt just like I was at the sock hop and my crush asked me to dance. After we danced, we strolled the room. He went to another area of the ballroom and took more photographs. I watched. They had all sorts of props and make up there. It became more apparent that he wasn't just a regular guy. He was a Champ. A well-known Champ that just so happens to be a genuinely nice guy that a lot of people loved.

He took pictures for almost an hour. His personal photographer was there and he was the only one allowed to snap me. He snapped the entire crew. I was hoping I would be able to get copies of these. Leigh would greatly appreciate it.

His smile was so radiant. I was mesmerized. I don't know if he could tell I was mesmerized or not. Unexpectedly he looked over at me and said, "That's it for the night guys. Thanks. I want to enjoy my beautiful date." My heart melted!

He said it. Date! I smiled from ear to ear. As soon as we entered the ballroom, again they announced the Champ was back and the cake could be cut. The cake was in layers that went from the floor to maybe six feet tall. It was made of shades of pink trimmed in pink icing ribbons.

I looked back at the photographer and said, "Make sure you get plenty of pictures before he cuts this cake." He did as I requested.

Randall took the knife and sliced a nice piece and to my surprised, he handed the cake to Keith who in turn passed it to me.

I looked up and he nodded. I was not sure if I was supposed to eat it or not. He cut the next slice. It was a nice size also. He took a chunk of it and ate it slowly while the camera snapped. "You all should be able to handle the rest," he said. "I am going to indulge."

He had such charisma. He knew damn well he didn't want the cake. Nor did he probably eat it. As he walked around the side of the table, King handed him a napkin and he handed King the plate. That is where it happened. He spit the cake in the napkin and handed it to Jon Jon who was standing by. He grabbed my arm.

"Has that cake been checked," I asked.

He smiled, "You learn quickly grasshopper."

It was checked before it ever came out. The piece I just gave Jon Jon and King will be checked right now.

"I saw that move," I said.

He was surprised that I paid attention. "Did you?"

"Yeah I did. I must say it was pretty smooth."

"I have to do it regularly."

"Don't eat it," I said.

"I can't all the time. I try not to. We have an early morning. Let's get out of here."

We walked back through the ballroom hand in hand. I asked, "What time is it?"

"Ten fifty eight," he said.

"Is that cool?" I asked.

"If you are ready," he replied.

"Yeah. It's been a long evening." I was not exhausted but I knew what I had to do in just a few short hours.

"I want to enjoy you alone," he said while looking directly in my eyes. He said good night to the people as we passed back through the crowd. When we got in front of the hotel, the Maybach was already out front. Keith opened the door to let me in the back. "I'm driving," he said. "I will see you all in the morning. Four AM."

"Four?" I quickly repeated.

"Not you," he said to me. "You all can follow behind until you feel it is safe to fall off," he told the guys.

"Are you sure?" King asked with hesitation and concern.

"Yeah."

King was not happy with this decision considering they were coming from such a function on a Friday night in such a high traffic area. "Let me drive you Champ." King pleaded without making eye contact.

"I want to be with my date alone," he said for the second time tonight.

They all looked at each other not knowing how to respond or either they were too scared to. He closed my door, got in on his side and we pulled off. We chatted all the way to the house. He really had a set of lungs on him. He could use them and they worked. He helped me out of the car. I walked in and cut the alarm. He came in behind me.

"I am not going to stay long. We have to be up early," he said sadly.

If I thought it was safe and appropriate I would have offered him to stay and chat. I wasn't worried about tomorrow. Neither of us slept anyway. "Yeah I know. Another good cause. When you do things for good reasons you don't grow weary."

"You are right. Preach on it," he encouraged me.

"No need, I would be preaching to the choir."

He changed the tone of the conversation. "I am very happy you agreed to go tonight."

"I am happy you invited me. I had a great time."

"No you didn't," he scolded.

"Yes I did."

"If I choose to go to another event or function would you do me the honor of accompanying me?" he asked hesitating.

I really wished he asked would I go on a date with him but he did everything in decency and in order. "Of course I will," I smiled.

"Are you sure?" he asked.

"Yes," I answered.

"Thank you so much," he said as he laid his head on my shoulder. This time something was different though. I couldn't tell if he was less stressed or more stressed. His body language was telling a story I didn't quite grasp.

"I will see you in the morning," I said while hugging him. I laid my cheek against his and had both of my arms around him. He had one hand in his pocket fidgeting. The other arm was around my waist. We stood like this until he left.

"Let me get your devices out of the car." He ran to the car and returned with my phones.

I was so in awe until I did not even remember that the girls were at my house. After he left I stood at the front door until I heard Paige's voice. "Did you have a nice time?" she asked.

I turned around facing her and said, "Wonderful!"

"You hungry?" she asked.

"Starved! What's on the menu? I didn't eat. He doesn't eat, so they don't eat, therefore I didn't eat either."

Paige said, "That is crazy. Pizza, wings, ice cream and chips. Want some?"

"Run it." I went to disrobe. "Where are the girls?" I called out.

"Clubbing."

I had flashbacks of club life. "Remember those days?" I asked.

"YEAH! I do. It is still early we can hit the town."

"Let's do it," I said when we both knew, good and well, that we were just playing.

Before Randall could text me to let me know he made it home, I was half-asleep with a plate in my hand. I heard it. I saw it. I read it. But I was too sleepy to respond. I didn't even hear the dynamic duo arrive. However, at seven minutes after three, I heard my phone chirp, letting me know that he was blogging.

> Everyday gets better and better. She makes me better. The man I am today I have never been. This life I know now I never knew before. It is like a baby eating table food. They never want a bottle again. Now that I have come from the dark side, I will never leave the light. I thank you for coming into my life. I am grateful for you. You are a blessing to me.

> Go to SLEEP! I will see you at seven. Don't show up a minute

> King and I are working out at four.

> Tell that Bully to go to sleep too.

> You should be asleep.

> I WAS!

> Sweet dreams my love.

Now how in the hell am I supposed to sleep after that? I cheated and got in my bed and left Paige and the girls on the sofa.

Saturday

At five fifty, my eyes popped open. This was considered late for me. I laid there thinking, *I have to go deal with three of the most non-morning people in the world. How am I always stuck with them and morning events?* I laid there and meditated. At five fifty nine, my phone rang his ringtone.

"Good morning," I said as if I had been up for hours.

He replied, "It's time."

"Thanks Sweetie. If you are tired you don't have to participate," I said.

"Good try. That will never happen."

"I'll see you soon." The thought alone made me excited.

"By the way your ride will be there in forty minutes," he said before I could hang up.

"I can drive myself," I told him.

"Not today." He hung up and I did not even get the chance to really protest.

"CRAP!" I jumped up. Hit the lights and walked in the living room.

"Ay! Get up. We have thirty minutes to get ready. We are rushing. AGAIN!" I turned to walk back to my bathroom to get ready. Not a creature stirred. I turned back around. "Ay. We got to get dressed." I heard a mumble. I would bet it was Paige but no one moved. I set the alarm off and walked away.

Paige yelled, "Sade make that noise stop!"

She got up with an attitude, stomping and hitting the alarm all crazy. Leigh sat straight up with an attitude of her own. "All right toddlers now that I have your attention, let's get moving. The driver will be here in ten minutes." They all took their time getting dressed. At six thirty five, my phone was ringing to open the gate. "Let's go kids," I said sounding more like a drill sergeant than the caretaker of toddlers.

"Kool Kids!" Sade mumbled.

When I opened the door, Keith was getting out of the car. He looked like he had a full night's sleep when I knew there was no way he could have possibly gotten more than six hours. "My favorite protector!" I said.

He smiled, "Ms. D. You doing well this morning after last night?"

"Like a million bucks," I said.

"That's what I am talking about." Then we pounded.

The girls looked at eat other. Sade was her typical self. "What the hell ever?" she mumbled.

Paige leaned in and asked, "What's up with you and Keith?"

I looked in the review mirror and saw him looking. "Nothing," I replied.

"Liar!" Sade blurted. That child knows she didn't know how to hold her tongue.

I rolled my eyes, "Keith please tell them."

"Tell them what?" he asked.

"I guess what they want to know," I replied.

He wasn't sure what they wanted to know. "Ladies?" he asked.

"What happened last night?"

"Nothing."

"Come clean Keith," Leigh said.

"Nothing particular. Normal stuff." Now he figured out what they were talking about.

"Normal?" Leigh said in disbelief. "We can see right through that. Now y'all best friends. Besties and stuff. Come on man."

"I will let D tell you."

They all said, "D," at one time.

"Damn Keith!" I shouted.

"Oh my word!" Leigh said as she rolled her eyes.

Sade nudged me hard in the arm and asked, "Auntie what happened?"

"Keith what are you referring to?" I asked innocently. I knew exactly what he was speaking of.

"You and the argument," he said.

"It was not an argument!" I corrected. "It was an established understanding."

Leigh said, "Tell the truth Keith. Shame the devil."

"D," he said.

I looked at Keith in the rear view mirror. "My friends call me D." Then I looked at the girls. "Y'all make me sick! We had dinner separate from the others. While we were in the room and supposed to be eating, I noticed no one was but me. King sat next to me and I asked him a question. He answered, but then he got real fly at the mouth." I then paused and looked at my girls like, "now y'all know me right. So, anyways, I was not going to take that like a punk so I got back with him. Nothing major."

"That's not how I would tell the story Ms. D," Keith said.

"That's why you are not telling it," I said with an attitude rolling my chap stick across my lips.

"Tell your side of the story Keith," Paige said and hushed me before I had a chance to rebuttal.

"It was more like she got all up in his face? Hooks had to break them up from across the room."

"Gosh! Keith you know it wasn't that serious." I laughed it off. "You are blowing this out of proportion. Dude come on?"

"Yeah it was," he said adamant about what he witnessed.

"Tell on Keith," Leigh said giving me a look I didn't understand.

"What?" I said still holding my stance that it was nothing.

"So Hooks calms it down. Then I said if you have anything to say to her you need to go thru me to King. Hooks said that won't be necessary. So I said if I am in charge of the girls then it is my job to cover them the same way he covers you."

"Y'all don't know how to act anywhere." Leigh laughed.

Sade excited about the drama, asked, "What else did Uncle Hooks say?"

"Ms. D told King he was Barney Fife." You could tell he was holding in his laugh. "He is pissed about that statement," he let his laugh out.

"Keith you talk too much!" I yelled.

He rolled the window up between us and locked it.

Paige tapped in the window, "Keith let this window down immediately!"

"What else happened D?" Leigh asked.

"OMG!" I slid down in the seat. "OMG!" is all I can say.

"What? What!" Sade slammed back to back.

"That man! That man! Oh gee. Lord that man!" I yelled.

"What? Tell us!" Sissie asked in such suspense.

"I do not know what to say. He has so much charisma and he is so sexy! I almost feel like I can't breathe with or without him. I can't sleep without him, eat without him; I can't live without him! I know it sounds so silly and lame but that's how I feel. I got it bad! How am I going to shake this? I know I have to, IMMEDIATELY! This is so not good. Damn! I love that man. I wish you all could have seen the photo shoot. Leigh you would have been in heaven. I'm pretty sure I'll get to see them first and then the two of us will decide which ones should be used. I know I'm all over the place, but y'all what am I gone do?"

The car was silent. Real silent. Keith rolled down the window. "Am I interrupting?" he asked.

"No, what's up?" Paige said in her solemn tone from reflecting on what I just confessed.

He handed her the Saturday's paper sports section. It read, Randall "Hooks" Washington appeared last night at a local breast cancer event to fight for the cure. He was the guest of honor and keynote speaker. He opened the floor to photographs and questions. However, there were two questions he refused to answer. When are you fighting again? His response was, "I am fighting now to help find a cure," and he elaborated on his volunteer activities that encompassed this research.

The second question was are you being escorted tonight by the lady in pink. "His response was escort? I choose not to answer that question in the regards that I may incriminate myself because of the negative meaning of escort. Besides, there many ladies here tonight in pink. I would hate for the next word you use to be gigolo."

My apologies for the wrong choice of words. "Are you on a date?"

"Actually, I am on duty." The Champ responded eluding the question at hand.

He never really addressed the question. Either question to be exact. So, we still want to know. When will you fight again and who was the lady in pink? From what we could tell, a female wearing pink accompanied him. She could not be photographed. They did not arrive together, but were seen leaving in his million dollar Maybach together after the event. They were unaccompanied by his staff when they left. His bodyguards followed closely as they pulled off in separate cars. His security staff heavily surrounded the mysterious woman in pink the entire night. She appeared to be comfortable and familiar with them all and was not shy to the crowd or the camera. When one photographer made an unwise attempt to take her photograph, his bodyguard tried to break his camera.

We have spoken to the cameraman and confirmed that no charges will be filed. We have not been able to get a statement from the Champs spokesperson; however, he was present at last night gala as well.

"I will give them a statement," Keith said. "I did not try to break his damn camera. I could have easily done so if I wanted to. The next time I will break his damn neck. Let's see who writes that."

We all looked at each other and laughed.

"Sounds like there was some highlights to last night's event!" Paige said with excitement. "We need all the details."

"Other than him looking scrumptious, there are no more details." I slid down in the seat and they all laughed. "You all are laughing but I am so serious. That man, that man, that man! He gone make me lose my mind up in here up in here!"

We talked and laughed during the remainder of the ride. When we pulled up Keith opened the door and Randall was standing there waiting. Someone else took the car and Keith walked with us. I knew from that moment on that Keith and I had connected.

"Did they eat?" he asked Keith. *Why couldn't he ask us?*

"No."

He handed us all a bar, a banana and a bottle of water. They were all groggy. I was discombobulated and in love.

"Hey babe," he said. "Why not?" he said looking at Keith as if it was his responsibility to make sure we ate. Maybe it was.

"Hi."

"Are you ready?" he asked me.

It was just like another switch kicked in. I got crunk up. "YEP!"

Paige looked up from her bar like she really didn't want to eat it. She then asked, "Hooks what happened last night between King and D?"

He looked at me and I pointed to Keith. Something happened? Keith was now my BFF. I hoped that was a good thing and long term.

We hung out until it was time to go to the line up to begin the walk. He gave his rendition of last night's events, avoiding as much of me and King's squabble as possible. It was nice; my crew and his crew, just chilled while the sun came up. I got my bag and passed out shirts. I gave my crew their shirts and Randall passed out shirts to his crew. The girls and I wore tanks with my firms name and Hooks gym imprinted on the front. The hook on my tank; however, was blinged out with rhinestones and a blinged out rose hung from the hook. I did tell King my number one rule right? Danielle will shine. Cameras flashed and Leigh was pissed. She began snapping pictures too. Both of our crews were on the front row. He said he was running and that meant his crew ran too; based on the information provided by King. I think Paige and Leigh were running, but Sade and I were definitely walking. Walking, talking, people watching and eating cupcakes if we could.

The shot fired, he looked at me, but no one moved. "Be safe. I love you," he said. "I will be back to walk with you across."

This time he nibbled my neck. King yelled, "Delete it," when the camera snapped. He let Leigh keep her photo.

He let my neck go, threw up the deuces and the crew followed behind him. King was less than a step behind him. All others that were running began. I stood there stunned.

Move Danielle. One foot in front of the other. You can do it. I said to myself. The next thing I heard was my hateful niece in my ear.

"There is a puddle underneath your feet. You leaking. You soaking wet." Then she walked off briskly.

I stood there for a minute. "Ugh!" I groaned and begin to run to catch up. I did check the ground first though. The walk was nice. They all ran and Sade and I listened to our iPods and talked. She gave me all the details of her night and I gave her all the details of mine. Next thing I knew a handsome, sweaty man smiling from ear to ear was on my side.

"Hey you!" he yelled out.

"Hey!"

I looked at Keith and he nodded like he knew exactly what I was thinking about. I wanted to make sure they had not overhead my conversation with Sade. I was beginning to like Keith after all.

"Are you done?" I asked.

"Yeah. I told you I would be back to walk with you," he answered.

"Good job. What was your time?"

"It is no big deal. I let King keep up with that kind of stuff," he said unaware.

I looked at Keith, but he didn't speak. I looked at King and his lips were closed too. "I hate you!" I yelled and ran off. I didn't run far. I realized years ago I was not a marathon runner.

Once the walk was complete, we did the photo thing again. Someone came from a local television station and wanted to interview Hooks, but he refused to do so. All he said was he was doing this for a worthy cause and on behalf of my firm. Then he said, "Let's go," and everyone followed his lead.

We ended up at Mikey's. This time everyone ate something. He, of course, had a huge plate of fruit. Once we were all ready to leave, he placed his forehead on my head. He left it there until King said, "Let's roll."

Randall told me, "Thanks for invite."

If I recalled correctly I did not invite him. He was blackmailed. "No. Thank you for joining me," I replied. It was not like I invited him to something fun. Well, then again, to him this was probably a highlight for the day.

"Go home," he instructed like he usually did.

"I will. You make sure you do too." I said in return.

●●

Once we got to my house, everyone went their own separate ways. They all needed to go to the salon; I did too, although I had just gone yesterday. I was not in the mood of sitting there again. I showered and tried to relax. I turned all the phones off, but it was useless.

I decided to do one of my favorite past times. I dropped the top and hit two-eighty-five. I rode and stopped where I saw my buildings and snapped shots. I loved this city. These were my buildings. I brought my dreams to life. My dreams and my buildings both stood life size over the city.

If JD was the Mayor and TIP was the King, what did that make me? TIP said he laid the foundation. If that is the case, then I designed, engineered, orchestrated, and built this city. Call me the Queen. I had forgotten my status.

This city belonged to me. My name was plastered to almost every building in some form or fashion. You know what I loved the most? Each time I saw these buildings it was like seeing them for first time. Now that I thought about it, he was like my buildings. All I could do was stand back in the shadow and admire him.

After rounds and rounds of pictures, I moved on. I drove the scenic route where I had a lot more things to see. I took a break and pulled up at the car wash. As they were washing my car, I started working and responding to emails. A builder's work was never done. There was always something to do, questions to answer, an addition to design, a deadline to meet or an inspector to argue with.

I heard a roaring engine. I squinted my eyes. I was trying to concentrate. *Who on earth is roaring that engine that loud? Don't they see I am working? How freaking rude! Some people should not be given a license to drive.* This person was annoying me with this noise. I finally looked up, and low and behold, it was him in the Ferrari! I shook my head. I think he could see me from the distance. He parked, or rather he stopped, but he surely he did not park the car.

I knew right then that the GPS attached to my wrist did much more than what he told me. This was either interesting or a mind game. The man I was thinking about and running from was tracking me and showed up to where I was.

WTH? He came and sat next to me. Neither of us spoke to the other.

"Ms. D!" One of the guys yelled.

"Yes? Can I ask your friend a question?"

I laughed. *Did he just really ask me is he could ask Randall a question?* "I don't see why not," I said shrugging my shoulders.

"Mr. Hooks, how can I earn your business and clean your car?" he politely asked him.

I looked over at him waiting for his response.

"It is clean, but since I am here," he handed over the keys. "Why aren't you answering your phone Danielle?" he asked in a humorous tone, covering his real emotions. He had no problems talking or asking questions, or giving orders.

"I turned them off. I just want to chill." I said mildly as if I hadn't committed an offense.

Sensing my tone and body language, he had no other choice but to ask, "Am I disturbing you?"

"No. Actually, this is a pleasant surprise." I said because it was.

Not totally convinced, he countered with a second question. "Are you sure?"

I smiled looking in his eyes, "Of course I am."

"You can tell me. It will hurt my feelings, but I will survive," he said.

"I am not that shy," I said laughing.

"I don't think you are shy at all," he said back jokingly.

There we sat in silence on a beautiful Saturday afternoon; it was golden. A few minutes later, the same guy came back over. He handed me a bottle of water and tried to pass one to Randall, but he shook his hand no politely. "Can I get you two anything while you wait?" he asked. The Champ was there and the red carpet was being rolled out. When I am there alone I get thrown a juice, a crumpled up newspaper and a side table with an extension cord for my laptop.

"We're cool," Randall replied.

"Your usual Ms. D?" he asked.

I nodded and he brought back a newspaper, a television table, and a grapefruit juice.

"A regular I see," Randall replied, noting they were contributing to her lack of ability to ever relax. *Is there ever a time or place where she does not work?* He thought.

"Sort of." *Who else is going to wash my cars?* I thought to myself.

"We will have to change that," he said.

Neither of us looking away from our iPads. *Was he reading my mind?* "So what else can you tell?" I asked.

"Tell about what?" he looked at me but I didn't give eye contact in return.

"Anything," I replied.

"I'm not following you," he said with unwanted confusion.

"What else does this gadget reveal?" I held up my wrist like it weighed a ton.

He thought cautiously before answering. *This would not be the time to lie or give up too much information.* "This gadget serves for thousands of purposes that I have yet to figure out," he said avoiding the real question.

"Oh, so I take it I am the guinea pig?"

"I do not think I would refer to it as that. Are you upset that I have showed up unannounced?" he asked sensing this from her question.

"No, I have nothing to hide. If I wanted to hide something I would have turned it off too," I said.

"I have left you several messages and texts. I even left you a message stating I would be arriving here in a few minutes and to remain here. I take it you have not checked any of them."

"Nope, not a one," I admitted. *The one time I cut the phone off and he rings it off the hook.* No pun intended. *Then they don't understand why I never turn them off.*

"You don't have an app that sends your voice messages electronically from your phones to your email accounts?"

I looked up at him. *Was he serious? Was there such a thing and I didn't know about it. I was going to have a word with Sade and Leigh. Why didn't I know?* "Is there an app?"

"I figure you would know or invent it."

Don't try me. "Maybe I will."

Trying to carrying on conversation without appearing flustered, he then asked, "So what have you been doing?"

"Enjoying the day. What about you?"

"Honestly, looking for you. Worried about you. It is unusual for you to do that," he continued.

Don't get too excited Danielle. Stay calm. Look casual. Act normal. He is stalking you girl in a good way. "Sorry you worried. Where is protector man?" I asked, speaking of Keith.

"He should be pulling up momentarily. He was concerned too," he said.

"Hit back and tell him I'm good," I instructed.

Just as I said it, Keith was already pulling up. "He is going to get the car washed while he is here too."

"Oh cool."

"You didn't go to the hair salon?" He made note of my same ponytail from the race earlier.

I looked at him not knowing if that was an instruction or an insult. "Naw, I sat there yesterday. I don't think I can handle two days back to back. Don't fret. I won't embarrass you tomorrow at church."

"I could care less about that. You won't embarrass me. This is by choice. I know you will have it neat and in order tomorrow. I just wanted to make sure you were fine. Once I could not reach you and noticed your location was continuously over two eighty five for the past two hours and then you stopped; it really concerned me."

"Thanks for your concern. You are really a stalker," I said and laughed.

Keith got out of the car. "Ma'am," he said as if I had some explaining to do.

"I am sorry," I said to him and then I looked at Randall. "I am sorry if I worried you too." I made a face like a kid caught with her hand in the cookie jar.

"We will have a discussion later," Keith stated furiously.

"Oh boy! I am so looking forward to that," I replied with my eyebrows touching but never looking up to give him eye contact. I wasn't that brave today.

"Or you can be given an additional phone. Have it your way. This will not be hard for me." He emphasized the words will not.

Keith was starting to work my nerves, although he was good at what he did. He was genuinely concerned. "Understood!" I said.

"Now that we have that covered let me see if I can get the pumpkin cleaned for Cinderella," he said joking.

"CHARIOT FOR THE PRINCESS! Does anyone ever listen to me around here?"

Randall sat straight up and raised his eyebrows. He pulled my chair next to him in one swoop. He was a little guy but very strong. He looked me in the eyes with his eyes as wide as they could go and ask, "Do you want to talk about it?"

I looked at him stunned. I wanted to laugh, but considering he was actually serious, I held it in.

"Maybe." I spoke too strongly, but I immediately tried to soften it. "I'm good," I said. Both of them at once was a little intimidating. I was just glad the terminator was nowhere to be found.

"Remember our promise to each other." With that, Keith got up and walked away not wanting to intrude.

"There you go running my help away," I said to Randall.

"Your help?" he said loudly.

"Yes."

"Not long ago you cringed at him. Now he is your help?" I snickered. "That's an improvement."

"You stuck us with each other we might as well be cordial," I replied.

"That's all it better be is cordial. As a matter of fact. It needs to just be business," he said sternly.

"Jealousy."

He replied, "Call it what you want, but know I am serious."

"Really?" I asked.

"Really," he repeated.

"Seriously?" I asked.

He looked at me and replied, "Definitely seriously."

"Okay. What are we really serious about?"

"Don't play with me Danielle!" He yelled gaining more attention from others in close proximity.

"Umm, I have a slight feeling that you may be insinuating something between Keith and me?" I said in a joking tone.

"I am not insinuating. I am stating that he is your security! I hope we are clear on that."

"So is he not allowed to be my BFF?" I could see him glaring at me out the corner of his eye. "I mean King is your BFF?" I got in.

"NO! Trevor is. King is my trainer!" He forcefully spoke through clenched teeth.

"Well who is your security?" I asked.

"I don't need security," he stated furiously.

"Humph, well I do not recall asking for security either," I said.

"You didn't. I pay Keith to do a job that I expect to be done in decency and in order."

"I did not know King was a volunteer?"

"You are killing me Danielle!"

There we went with Danielle again. I noticed when he got upset with me I was always Danielle. "Let's be fair Randall," I said.

He kicked the table like a little spoiled brat. I knew where we were going and I also knew where his mind went. I stood up; he jumped, but didn't stand. *That was unusual.* I went inside the door, "Keith," I called out to him.

"What do you need?" Keith asked.

"Watch my stuff," I said as he followed me outside. I quaffed my juice. "Let's go," I said to Randall as if I was speaking to a defiant child about to get a spanking in the restroom.

At my command Randall looked up from the ground as if he had a crystal ball there giving him his next intrusive instruction. "Where are we going?" He asked timidly as if he was suddenly afraid to go with me.

"Get up!" I now demanded. My tone was beyond harsh. *Now I know good and well that I said I wanted to chill. Ain't nobody got time for this!* He looked like damn! But he stood his narrow tail up. "Keith, if I yell whoodie who find me please," I instructed.

"Gotcha Ms. D."

"We will be back," I told him.

"Not! Hooks is not leaving and neither are you without me," Keith said.

"We both arrived here without you," I informed him. I grabbed Randall's hand and we began walking down the street. We walked down the driveway and turned right.

He looked at me and turned his head really quick. "Am I in trouble?"

"YES!" If only he knew how much trouble he was in.

"I'm sorry!"

"What in the hell was that statement supposed to mean?" I asked.

"I'm sorry," he said hesitantly.

I cut my eyes and shook my head. "No, the f'ed up statement before that."

Hesitantly, he asked. "Which was?"

"It better be all business," I repeated. "That was the statement you made correct?" I questioned.

"I didn't intend to offend you," he back peddled.

"I do not intend to offend you either, but let the record show you stuck Keith with me. I do not think I need Keith. I can handle my own. Now, that I have been "assigned" to him you give me grief. I almost resent your remark, but I forgive you." I stretched my hands towards him. "Forgive him Father, for he knows not what he says. Just to clarify, I can holler at whom I choose to holler and when I choose to. Unfortunately, for me I am not interested. For you, on the other hand, that may be a good advantage." I mushed him in the face. "But don't push me son because I'm too close to the edge. Don't ever try me again boy! I'll jack you up! Remember you are the one with the stipulations." I walked off a little faster than him. "Oh how soon we forget," I mumbled as I stomped off.

Did I really just mush a champion boxer in the face on a busy public street? Yeah I did. I was just a few steps ahead of him as I continued to rant, "Men kill me! They think they run this world. Ha!" I laughed so loud. "They don't know squat, nothing, nada! They're the ones with the biggest baggage and then want to throw it off on you. The devil is a liar! I don't have to hide or lie about anyone I choose to be in a relationship with. I'm bold enough, honest enough and woman enough to tell you, or any other jerk face for that matter, what I want them to know. Moreover, if I should choose to date Keith, a balling baby daddy, a rich old man, or any other dude, it is no one's business but mine. I hope that is crystal clear!"

He jumped at my words. I could see him out the corner of my eyes. I turned my neck slightly and bucked my eyes. When we made it back to the car wash, I asked cheerfully, "Am I ready?" As if I didn't just finish showing out a few seconds ago.

"Yes Ms. D."

"What's my tab? I got the little red, whatever that is, and that monstrosity over there," I said.

He stepped up and practically pushed me out of the way. "You have already ripped my butt from California to New York and now you insult me and my whip? Get back and give me a break," he said now annoyed with me.

I walked over to my car. I checked it slightly. Sat down and let my top back. As soon as he walked over, I threw up the deuces and said, "Thanks and I'm gone." I pulled off. I didn't give him time to speak. I got him pegged.

I was PO'ed. *Here it is I am riding around town because I am head over heels with a married man and he practically accuses me and his hired hit man of improper relations! Did he really have the nerves to say that I must remain on a business level? Aww hell naw!* I needed to simmer down a little because it was obvious my blood was still boiling. *What kind of mess was that to say? Men are so freaking clueless!*

I rode a little longer and as the sun began to set; I took it on to the house and chilled. It was around ten. I was good and Lifetime bound when my house phone rang. Just then, I remembered I had not cut my phones back on yet. It had been a nice quiet evening. "Yes," I answered.

"I am sorry to bother you but your phone is still off," he informed me as if I didn't know.

"Yes," I said sternly. I was well aware.

"We did not coordinate for tomorrow," he informed me.

"Oh," I replied. We discussed colors and I told him thanks and good night. I didn't give him time to respond before I clicked off. I wasn't really that angry, and in actuality, I wasn't pissed off any longer, but he had to feel the pain. I could not let him know he had me eating out the palm of his hand. *Yeah, he might have to sweat this one out this time*, I thought.

He, on the other hand, felt it. He ran for the next three hours. I watched television and chilled. I finally fell asleep. At his house, he could not sleep. It troubled him that his bad choice of words had him walking on eggshells.

Sunday

When I arrived at church, he was at the door. "Good morning," he greeted.

"Good morning Deacon."

He leaned in and said, "You can call me Randall here."

"I wouldn't dare in the confines of these walls. How disrespectful that would be?" *Didn't we just have a fight last night? You are back to Deacon.*

He laughed. "I hope you will accept my apology," he said.

"For?" I said with raised eyebrows.

"I think I spoke out of context yesterday."

"Apology accepted." *What a cheap shot. Like I could really stand in the vestibule of the church and say, no I do not accept your apology.*

"I want to clear up that I do not think that way. My thoughts came across differently verbally than they were mentally," he tried to explain.

"No hard feelings. My thoughts came out just the way I intended." I was not wavering.

He smiled that beautiful smile and extended his arm. He walked me to my seat. This time I was in the chair next to the chair that I normally sit in. "Keith will be here today and maybe from now on. I am under praise surveillance," he whispered.

I laughed. I couldn't be mad at him. I was a sucker for a man in a suit.

"You say the word and I will kick him off this row immediately."

Prayer went on. Praise and worship started as normal and the next time I looked Keith was next to me. A few minutes later Deacon Washington was on his post and King and JJ were next to him. I checked the spots and the remainder of the crew were on point.

The first song went on and I barely glanced in his direction, and when I did, he winked. I smiled. Keith cleared his throat and I looked at him oddly. The next song started. Praise was going on in full effect. I looked over at him and held my wink. He gave it back. I was engulfed over the next few minutes. When I glanced over the next time, he was on his knees. His arms stretched out and his palms up. He was crying out to the Lord. *How and when did this happen?*

I looked at Keith but he never moved, nor did his expression change. He gave one quick nod as if to say, we got this." Praise went on, we were rocking the house, and it was all good. The next time I saw movement out of the corner of my eye, he was prostrate.

I push the buttons on my watch and immediately Keith touched his ear. "She is fine, Hooks is down." I nodded to the guys at the door to come over. They must have spoken in Keith's ear because he pushed his hand toward me like we got this.

I looked at the intercessors next to my row and nodded letting them know I needed help. I dropped to my knees, stretched my hands toward him, and began to pray. I dropped so quickly and suddenly until Keith bent forward.

I prayed fervently. At some point, I moved my body back and Keith caught me. It shook me from my concentration. I realized that the crew had made it and the intercessors were covering him. Keith handed me a bottle of water. When I cleared my eyes enough to look up, Pastor Hunter was coming out of the door. It caught him off guard that his best friend was laid out in his pathway to the pulpit. He stopped and did a double, triple, and a fourth take. He got down on his knees then gave instructions to the intercessors. He laid his hands on Deacon Washington and prayed. Keith raised me to my knees and pointed to my chair.

Hunter instructed the Elder to take the microphone. He did so and the praise team continued after his prayer. Once their song was over Hunter took the microphone.

"Beloved, if I were you I would not miss this moment. I think the praise team and Deacon Washington have set the atmosphere. They have ushered in The Spirit of the Lord. Position yourselves. Deacon has positioned himself." The praise team was on their knees also. "They have positioned to receive the blessing. Deacon has assumed the position to get the answer to his questions."

"Some of you have been waiting on an answer from God. Some of you need an answer from God. Those of you that I am speaking to; you need to get to the altar right now to bask in His glory and posture yourselves. You do not want to miss this opportunity. Weeping may endure for a night but if I were you, I would not miss the joy that is at this altar this morning. Don't worry about Deacon Washington. Step over him. Lean down behind him or next to him. You just get to this altar. There is room at the altar."

The next thing I knew the altar was full. The entire area except where Randall was. They did not let anyone too close to him. I could not breathe. I drank the rest of the water. As soon as Pastor finished I was going to get water and to the ladies room to wash my face. I think I was hyperventilating again. *I am going to mess around and have a female securing me when this is all said and done. Keith is not going to be able to handle me emotionally. Right now, I cannot handle me.*

I was so limp and full until I really could have laid across the seats since there was nowhere at the altar to lay. I am sure I was not sitting in the chair lady like by any means. One thing was for sure, when you are in The Spirit, you could care less of how you look. Just like a woman in labor. She could care less who sees her and how she looks throughout her travail.

Hunter gave a prophetic blessing upon those at the altar. He prayed for them and sent them back to their seats. Deacon Washington was still lying prostrate and motionless. No one from the crew moved. Not even as Pastor began to preach.

"Well Beloved, I came prepared with ten plus pages of notes, but The Spirit has led me to change my sermon. My message was tight! I labored before the Lord for this message as I always do. As you know in this house, we follow The Spirit of the Lord. When He moves," he pointed to the crowd to complete the sentence. He did his famous clap and finished the sentence. "We move. At this time, I would ask if you are able to please stand for the reading of the Word as is customary in this house."

"Praise team I like that. Continue to sing that softly. If you will, turn in your bible with me to the book of Psalm chapter thirty and I will read verse five in your hearing. Video ministry I know this is not the scriptures I provided, but we will give you a minute to change directions."

He flipped his bible. "If you have found your place let me know by saying Amen."

The congregation responded, "Amen."

"Video ministry you all are good. You are right where we need to be. Thank you for your obedience."

"Scripture reads. For His anger endureth but a moment; in His favor is life: weeping may endure for a night. Y'all missed the place to shout right there. I will say it again. I do not know about you all, but that right there blesses me. Maybe I just came to bless Deacon Washington. I think I will." He went and leaned over the deacon, his best friend. "Weeping may endure for a night, (he claps) but joy cometh in the morning."

It touched me so. *If God is angered only for a moment so should I be.* I wasn't and I couldn't be mad at Deacon.

"For the sake of a subject this morning The Spirit has led me to speak to you about Weeping May Endure for A Night. You may take your seats."

He began to preach. I could hear myself gasping for air and hyperventilating. I really needed to walk out but I could not leave him there. He was in good hands and in the right place, but I needed to be there when he stood and regained himself.

Hunter carried on. I was listening, although I didn't take notes and seemed to be panicked. It was amazing that he shifted gears and changed sermons at the drop of a dime. That is why I loved him. That is why he had the followers he had. This was an important trait for a pastor to have. Yes, all Pastors could and should be able to do it. However, could they and keep the attention of the congregation, make sense and get the point across to a seven year old child and a seventy year old adult? That was a different story. I was glad I was a member and looked forward to greater things with Pastor Hunter. He had only just begun to see the fruits of his labor.

"I hate to be the one to tell you beloved but sometimes you gone go through. This is not a message we can shout on. I got to tell you. I love you too much to lie to you. Sometimes you gone go through doing exactly what it is you are supposed to be doing. Darkness will fall over your life at any given moment without rhyme, reason, or notice. In the midnight hour some nights, many nights and every night you may find yourself troubled, dismayed and confused. But whatever it is that you do, know this; weeping may endure for a night."

He paused and changed the octave of his voice. "I just stopped by today with the help of the good Lord and my friend (he pointed down at Deacon Washington as he stood over him) to tell you and encourage you that surely I say to you weeping has an expiration and that joy will come in the morning light. I don't think you heard me; joy will come in the morning. I didn't say it might, or possibly, one day or maybe. What I did say was it WILL come. Look, it's in your bible. The bible in your lap! It has been there all this time. Please know during the midnight hour that you have a weapon in your tool belt. You have several. You are equipped! You have faith and prayer just to name a few. During the midnight hour if you position yourself accordingly. If you get down low. Get down on your knees. Bow down to the Lord and bellow in His presence. Drop yourself as low as you can go and call on Him until you can't call Him anymore!" Hunter was down too giving an example and eventually ended up lying next to Deacon Washington.

Right then Randall quivered. He had movement so I nudged Keith. He did a hands down motion to me again like I got this. He moved again; this time like a newborn baby trying to wake up. If you stay still maybe they will go back to sleep, but if you move they will wake up wailing. He tried to move again. Keith stood and helped Pastor Hunter up. King and JJ bent over and snatched Randall up. Each one held him under his shoulder. They did not pick him up. They snatched him up so quickly until I sighed loudly. He backed up to his seat and sat down.

He had travailed. I did not move my eyes and I waited and waited for his eye contact. When he looked up, it destroyed him. I wasn't sure if his devastation was because he had to face me or if it was because at that moment I looked just as bad as he did. He dropped his head low again. He could have easily tipped out of the chair. I sat for a moment trying to catch up to Hunter and gave in. I could not take any more. I needed to get myself together so I could help him.

I didn't know if I was going to be able to do it but I stood up. Keith looked. I took my time to get myself together. I held on to the back of Keith's chair as I passed it and made my way down the aisle. It was a long aisle, but right now, it appeared to be ten times longer than what it truly was. My eyes were blurry and I could not focus clearly. There had to have been a few thousand people in here. Once I got on the other side of the door, I leaned on the wall for a minute. Then I proceeded to the restroom, holding the wall for a far as I could. Once I got there, I leaned over the water fountain and sucked up as much H2O as I could. I lay on the wall until I slowly slid down to the floor. I covered my eyes. Left hand over left eye and right hand over right eye and sobbed. *What was happening and why?* I needed some help. All I could do was remember Mama Rose.

Psalm 121 - A Song of Ascents.

I WILL lift up my eyes to the hills -From whence shall my help come?

My help comes from the Lord, Who made heaven and earth.

He will not allow your foot to slip or to be moved; He who keeps you will not slumber.

Behold, He who keeps Israel will neither slumber nor sleep.

The Lord is your keeper; the Lord is your shade on your right.

The sun shall not smite you by day, nor the moon by night.

The Lord will keep you from all evil; He will keep your life.

The Lord will keep your going out and your coming in from this time forth and forevermore.

A Mother's love was powerful. There was one thing more powerful, and that was the love from God, Agape love. When you put those two together with faith, you could truly move mountains. I focused hard on clearing my mind. I had pulled up one of the scriptures Mama always recited. At the same time, I had called on my help. I knew my help came from the Lord.

Immediately, at the same moment I felt a body sit very, very close to me. Our shoulders touched. God was good. He sent help for that set moment. Although, I had not looked up and didn't hear him coming; I knew it was Randall. I could smell him. I could tell from his breathing. He sat next to me as still as I sat next to him. He had one knee bent and one leg stretched out. His head was resting on the wall. His eyes closed.

I have no clue how many minutes had passed. I just knew that I was calmer because I could now hear Hunter over the speaker in the hall. When I first sat there, I could hear nothing.

Randall said, "Danielle, I am fine."

"You are not okay. It troubles me that you are troubled and don't trust me enough to tell me what's wrong," I shared my true feelings with him.

"I don't know right now. Let me get through this; when I know, I will tell you everything. What you said is not true. I trust you with everything I have. I trust you with my life. I'm wrestling with flesh and I'm waiting on God to speak to me. I need you. I trust you, but I need Him more now than I ever have. I'm asking for direction and I'm not going to stop. I am not going to let Him go until I hear from Him. Until then this is who I am. A weak, humble, yet bold man searching for wisdom and knowledge. I'm useless to you until I get the answers I need. I am going to wait on the Lord and be of good courage, and He shall strengthen my heart. I'm not letting Him go until then. I am fine. Don't worry about me, please. I'm dealing with this the best way I know how. I am relying on God. He is my source, my help and my provider. I'm working this out. It is between God and Randall. It has nothing to do with anyone or anything else. Don't hold this against me. It's nothing bad. I just want to move on with my life. It's time. I need to and I have reason to."

"Danielle, He promised me life more abundantly and I want it. I desire it and I long for it. What you see today is the half of it. You see the guys aren't touched at all. They have seen this behavior for the last few weeks. I am pressing and pressing. I haven't told you, but I have spent much more time on this altar than you have seen. I have been here late nights, early morning and some nights, all night. I am going to keep lying here until my blessings come. I know this display of praise may seem frightening. It may seem like it is in response to a bad situation, but in the big scheme of things, it is in response to a good thing. A very good thing indeed. God is so good. I have a lot of strange things going on in my life but I surely have a lot of good things to be thankful for. I have to give Him the praise due His name. If only you knew how you have saved my life. I have so many confessions I want to share with you. I am sorry to frighten you. I am fine. I am better than I have ever been in my entire life. I want to stay this happy forever."

He held my hand. I tried to get it together. He was right. I was seeing his praise as a moment of trouble or weakness. He was seeing his praise as giving glory to God. He admitted that he was waiting on an answer or answers, but in his heart and in his mind everything was going to be all right.

I felt a ray of hope and relief come over me. Was I completely satisfied with his soliloquy? No! Was it a start to an explanation? Yes. I continued to hold his hand.

"You know what?" he asked.

"What?"

"You surely have my back," he realized.

I tried to laugh.

"I understand last week you got a little ticked off that no one ran to my rescue. I also saw your hesitation and frustration when I asked you to leave."

"Yeah and so what of it?" I smarted off.

"You are a mess. You know that?" he said.

"Well your little crew ain't the only ones that have your back," I told him.

"Little crew? I see. I think you feel as though you can take them out," he said with a smirk on his face as if I was entertaining.

I look at him and raise my eyebrows. "I can!"

"Oh Lord. Let's go," he said laughing.

As he began to stand, I heard Keith running down the corridor and once he got to us, he helped him up and snatched me up.

"Can I wash my face?" I asked knowing I looked horrible.

"You can do anything you like," he replied.

He came in the ladies room with me. I washed my face and then he looked at his and decided to wash his too. It was a good idea after all. We walked back in the sanctuary. It looked totally different. I had been up and down that aisle hundreds of times. It never changed, but it surely looked different than it did twenty minutes ago. This time I sat in the same seat I was seated in as he pointed to Keith to take his seat and Randall sat next to me.

He was back to Deacon Washington. He looked directly at me, winked his eye, and then leaned up on his elbows like he always did.

"Deacon Washington you are back right on time as I come to a close. Twenty minutes ago, you were prostrate waiting on the Lord. I do not know if He answered you yet. You were weeping, but now you are smiling. The point taken. Joy will come in the morning light." He jumped and stomped his feet on the pulpit. His voice changed. He was excited. "If you just keep the position. Keep your eye and ear gates free, clear, open, and wait on the Lord. He will not only speak to you, but to your heart. He will remove the mountains in your life. He will make the rough smooth. The crooked straight. He will bless you."

He calmed down. He stood directly in front of Deacon Washington. "Keep your position. Stay in the word. Stay connected. Keep the faith."

Deacon had his hands held up and once Pastor finished talking to him he said, "I receive it in the name of Jesus."

"Stand to your feet."

The praise team began to sing a song that reminded you that trouble was not permanent. The benediction was given and then Randall did something he had never done; he walked me out of the sanctuary. Normally, he is busy with his other duties.

Today it was me, him and the good Lord. We walked out together and solemnly. We got close to the door and he said, "I will get you a CD."

"Thanks," I told him.

"What are you about to do?" he asked smiling.

I smiled then said, "Walk my track."

He loved the way I referred to it as my track. "Why don't you go home and get some rest. It has been a long week," he said.

"I may do that later," admitting to myself he was correct.

He sighed unhappy with my response, "I would feel better if you did it now."

"Yeah, but I want to walk for a little while."

He hesitated before asking, "Are you going to work too?"

"Nah. Probably not." I answered honestly.

"What?" he was shocked at my response.

I laughed out loud, "I know right!"

"All right but you will leave the gym when I leave here?"

It wasn't a question. With Randall, it never is although I answered it as if it was. "I will try. What are you going to do?"

"Go home," he replied.

"Home where?" I asked.

"To the house I pay for," he said hesitantly as if unsure.

"Which one would that be?" I asked.

He looked confused. *Is she implying I pay for other houses?*

I spoke to clear the confusion. "Are you going to the gym or the physical house with a bed?" The look on his face told me that cleared it up for him.

"The place where there is a bed." He laughed.

"You are going home?" I asked shocked.

"I am going to the place I own, pay the bills and where there is a bed," he reassured.

"Really?" I asked. I saw clearly that we were playing word games. All of that house and it still didn't feel like home. They said money can't buy happiness. It was true.

"Yes."

"Seriously?"

"Yes!" he said for the second time.

"Why?" I asked.

He gave up that robust laugh for me. "If I can be transparent with you for a moment," he paused. "I have sweated my suit out. I want to take a shower, lie down, and just go to sleep. I am exhausted. Service has taken a lot out of me today. I need some rest."

"Yes you do," I agreed. "I am glad you realize it." When we reached my car, he stood over the door on one side and I stood over it from the inside of the car. Our arms touched. He exhaled and then he reached for my hand. I could tell that what he was about to say was difficult for him.

"Thank you Danielle," he said.

"You are more than welcome. Thank you for all that you do. Be blessed. God has worked it out," I encouraged.

"You too," he said.

I looked him in the eyes without a blink and said, "You know God loves you, and so do I."

He was still full and I wasn't helping the matter any. He just nodded. His eyes immediately turned red. I didn't want to embarrass him or push him any further than he wanted to go. Whatever this was, it was difficult for him. I sat down in my car. He held my door obviously deep in thought and I held my thought.

Dang, he is one sexy man, I found myself thinking. The weaker he was. The more he prayed. The harder he pushed. The more tears his eyes made. The sexier he became and the more I desired him. *I probably could really take advantage of him at this moment.* That is what I wanted to do but I couldn't. *Danielle clear your mind* I said to myself. Actually, what I thought was, *Danielle Jade Rose you might want to get your mind right. Here the man is in tears and you have mentally stripped him down and seduced him.*

"Are you going to be okay?" I asked.

"Sure," he said in a forced voice.

"Call me later," I told him.

"I will," he promised.

He closed the door, but just stood right there in the same spot. He stayed there until I could not see him any longer in my rearview mirror. I did go to my track but I didn't stay too long. I am sure they called him and told him I was there. The last thing I wanted was for him to show up after he said he was exhausted. I wanted to go lay down myself. My thoughts were out of control. I was no more good for the day.

It was afternoon when I returned home. I was too lazy and my mind was too boggled to even eat. I started out on the deck, then the chaise, the couch, the bed and finally the floor. I still couldn't sleep. I was extremely restless. Restless in a strange way.

I didn't want to watch television and believe it or not, I didn't want to work. I just wanted chill. I realized I couldn't and apparently, I wasn't going to. I was stuck between a rock and a hard place. I had never really dated anyone other than my two college and high school boyfriends. Now, here I was madly and deeply in love with a married man who just so happens to be a Championship boxer; and most of all, a man of God.

How did this happen? I thought to myself. My mind raced in a hundred directions. These were not my intentions. When I was instructed to park in the field early that Sunday morning, exactly fifteen weeks ago to the day, I had no idea my life would change. I hoped and I prayed I would be a bigger and better person, but never did I imagine my heart would get involved. I came here to find a church home. I went to learn, to grow, and to share the gospel with my fellow man. Along with that, I have stumbled up on more than I bargained for. I found the man of my dreams. I found the love I have been waiting for. My heart was located. It had been shredded to pieces. I did not know if it would ever mend. The jacked up part of it all was it mended too quickly. Just as a wound heals. It scabs on the outside but it is still infected on the inside. It causes more trouble and pain. That is what has happened to my heart. It mended, but it causes what will possibly be more trouble and pain.

We were two broken vessels super gluing each other back together. *I have got to walk away. I have got to remove myself. I must govern myself accordingly.* I just couldn't wrap my mind around being able to continue to worship there and nothing happening between us. Or worse, something does happen. Something inappropriate happens. Something bad. Something that my mind is stayed upon. *I can't let it happen. I can't face Pastor*

Hunter. I can't face the congregation. I would no longer be able to walk down that aisle and sit in the same seat as if nothing occurred. Truthfully, I knew I would feel like death if I placed that upon him. If I had to allow him to walk in that sanctuary to face his best friend the people he loved. Standing in front of his God as an adulterer. He took that position seriously. He took that title seriously. I could not interfere. My heart would not allow me to do so. I could not destroy his character. He had years of opportunity to do it himself and he didn't. There was no way I was going to change that.

He had a wife and a son. As a woman, I felt as though I could not interfere. I had to back up. I promised to be his friend. I promised to let him know what bothered me. I wasn't sure how I would tell him this, but I knew in my heart I had too. I had to let him know what bothered me and why. I didn't know how I was going to say it. I hoped it didn't come off as rude. I hoped I wasn't misleading. I had not done the right thing. I prayed God forgave me. I wept. I felt what he felt this week and clearly understood why. It suddenly made sense why he was unable to talk and why he laid himself on the altar. Regardless, of our feelings being the same, were they appropriate? Were they in line with God? Were they in decency and in order? Were they selfish? Were they of the world and of the flesh? Was I content and happy because I now had someone to love me? I had someone interested in me. I was no longer alone, but I was also no longer at peace. I was concerned about him. I was concerned about encountering a situation with his wife. I was concerned about us eventually no longer being in control of ourselves.

I liked him. I liked him a lot. He made me happy and he made me smile. He was the first man that had done so in four years. I needed him and wanted him to need me too. I wanted, desired, and loved him. I loved him. I loved him with every inch of my heart and every movement of my body. With all the depths of my soul. I loved him from the crown of his head to the soles of his feet and every inch in between. I would have loved him if he wasn't a fighter. I would have loved him if he wasn't a Deacon. Something about him drew me near immediately. *Why was he chosen to address me that Sunday morning? How did we get stuck together? Why have we or did we attach from the very first moment?* I wished I could go back to the night before we meet. I wish I could redo. Even with all the wishes, I still didn't wish I didn't love him.

I didn't know what to do. So I did all I knew how to do. I prayed, "Forgive me Father, for I have sinned. I have lusted. I have committed adultery with my eye. My flesh is weak"

I lay prostrate on my floor and I cried out to the Lord. "Father, please have mercy upon me. Forgive me Lord, for I am weak, but in You, I will claim that I am strong. I know You will increase my strength and make me strong where I am mentally and physically weak. Make me whole. Help me Father!" I wailed.

After all my wailing, nothing changed. I still loved him and I couldn't turn it off that quick. One thing was for sure; I was going to speak to him as soon as my courage increased. As soon as I could, I was going to shut him out of my life. It would hurt me. It would certainly devastate me, but I could not see him anymore and I could not be a member of Hunter's church. It was going to pain me but I had to do it. I had to save him and me. I did not want to. But I could not go on like this. Pastor was a blessing in my life. Even if he chasten and disciplined me. I needed it and I respected it. In order to save face I knew I had to walk away. He would not understand and it would hurt us both. I hated to know that he would be hurt. We both have waited so long. Four years for both of us, and it still wasn't right.

Hunter quoted the Word of God, that weeping endured for a night but joy comes in the morning. I prayed for joy. It was hard not to grow weary in well doing. Earlier Hunter spoke this to his friend. Little did I know that hours later I would replay the sermon in my head; that I would be the one weeping?

I didn't know how much time had lapsed. It was now dark outside. I rolled over on my back and laid there looking at the ceiling. I could hear my phones ringing. I could not move and so I didn't. These were my Confessions!

WEEK 17

Monday

You would have thought I had been out drinking all night, as I have no clue of last night. It is all a blur. *What did I do?* Not only last night, but yesterday all together. From the way my stomach was rumbling, I do not think I ate at all.

My feelings had not changed though, that I was sure of. No matter how much it hurt me and bothered him, I had no choice; I was going to have to pull up. Two things made this difficult. One, I was not going to be able to worship where I was being fed and two; I was surely not going to be able to utilize the beautiful track he built me. I was going to have to figure a way to get through this. *This too shall pass.*

I refrained from calling him. Lord knows, it took everything in me not to call, but I needed to place as much space as I possibly could between us. If I did my part, that was a start. Once I got in the car, I felt empty. I could only think of him. I checked all the voice messages. I did everything to occupy my mind. I could not give in. So far it worked. I put the radio on blast.

The office was quiet, but of course, it was five AM. This was going to be a long day if it was only five and I was already having withdrawals. I tried to make a deal with myself.

Then I just said *stop it Danielle, you are going to have to take this hour by hour if you insist on going cold turkey.* This is what I planned on doing until I was able to get the right words to speak to him.

Dani girl, you can find some messes to get yourself in. How do you do it? I laughed out loud at myself. It made me smile although I still felt like crap on the inside. I started to work, knowing from that moment on, work was about to be my life again. I was back on the grind. Hustling every day. I was not going to force Leigh with me this time. She had a life. I was the destitute one and none of this was her fault. Then I thought, *maybe this will work out after all. If I am grinding like I am known to do, I can pop in church, pop out, and hit the track he built me after ten PM every night. He would surely be gone.*

I felt like I had a plan. I looked at the stuff on my desk and I could see how I could make this work. *Mind over matter. Out of sight out of mind. If I can successfully stick to the plan, I could do it. If I sit in an inconspicuous place in the church, he would not see me.* I was hyped about this plan until my phone ran his ring tone. My heart raced.

He could see I was at work so it would be cool if I did not answer. I quickly turned my desk phone off so that it would go directly to voice mail if he called it. He called the next cell. It seemed like it rang ten times. I picked it up to answer and just as I did, he hung up. I was spared.

I scrolled to missed calls. I contemplated and contemplated on calling back. *D, don't be checked by a married man.* Then it sounded. The tone to alert a voice message. I clicked it and then hung it up. *It is too early to punk out on the plan.* I didn't check it right then.

I waited an hour and texted. It was a cheap shot but that was the entire reason it was invented. To have a conversation without saying a word. Texting and the internet were the greatest inventions for me.

> Hey. I see you called.
> Is everything all right?

> Good morning Danielle

He was not responding. Instead, he was forcing conversation. *I guess I did come across rudely, but I was trying to push back right?*

> Good morning Randall.

> How are you my love?

> Fine. Thanks and you?

> Blessed. Blessed to be a blessing and blessed to have you as a blessing.

Why is he doing this to me? He is making this extremely difficult.

> Thanks.

> Are you okay?

> Yeah. I am slammed. Just trying to catch up.

> Have a wonderful day and call me when you can talk. I miss you my love.

There he goes again. Love is like being on a diet. The more you try to avoid it the more you are tempted with your favorite fattening foods.

> Will do.

I really felt like crap for blowing him off like that. *What's a girl to do?* How long would he allow it before he questioned it, showed up or worse? I had to take my chances.

• •

I hope I did not upset her. She has been distant all weekend, he reflected back on Friday night and Saturday morning. It seemed like ever since then she was not the same. *Was something said or done inappropriately? Yeah, I did make a stupid remark but I thought we had that cleared up.* He thought about church. *What could I have done that would upset her? Maybe I was wrong for not confiding in her.* I really didn't know what to confide. That I was confused. That I wanted, begged and prayed that God would make Tameka sign so that I could spend my life with her. That it troubled me the choices I made early in life were effecting me now. That I wanted an undo button. I wanted to erase most of the last fifteen years. Truthfully, I would give up all the boxing if I could erase Tameka. How I prayed God changed my heart. How I needed Him to strengthen me so that if I ever had the opportunity, I wanted to be the best man I could be for her. How if I had the power, the money, and the chance, I would buy the world and place it in her hand. I could not tell her that. I could not tell her how bad, how much and how I longed for her. I just couldn't. I called Keith instead.

"What's up?" Keith picked up.

"Get in my office now!" Hooks yelled loudly.

Keith scowled at the demand. He immediately thought, *what did I do? This assignment may not be for me.* As he entered the office, he felt as though he needed to be cautious. He said, "Yes sir," and looked around as if someone else or something else was in the room, although he knew Hooks was alone.

Keith could see his temples moving. "Sit down," he demanded in a stern angry voice.

Keith sat down reluctantly.

He leaned on his desk. He waited a very long time before he spoke. He was trying to figure out if he missed anything. "Replay the weekend's events," he said looking down.

"Starting from where?" Keith asked.

"Where the weekend began," Hooks said obviously frustrated already.

"Why?" Keith asked. Now he was a little nervous.

He stood up. "Because I asked you too!" he yelled.

"What are you looking for?" Keith asked suspiciously, but calmly trying to figure out what was going on.

"Don't dispute me right now. Just do what I asked you to do. What happened out of the ordinary this weekend?" he asked.

Keith looked at him as if he must be crazy. "The entire weekend was out of the ordinary."

"Meaning?"

He looked insulted that he was asked this question. "Meaning you went to a benefit. You haven't done that in years. You shut the gym down and we walked a charity walk. You haven't done that ever. You laid on the altar two services in a row. You haven't done that publicly. Not sure which part seems out of the ordinary to you, but it all seems strange to me." Keith answered him truthfully and he hoped it was what his boss was looking for.

He thought about it. "I was speaking of unusual with Danielle," he said lowering his tone.

Now he really looked at him as if he was crazy. "Everything with Danielle is unusual." He said like *DUH!*

"For example?" he persisted.

"She is an unusual character if I must say." Now he was annoyed. "Everything about her and every aspect of her," he declared.

"Is that good or bad?"

"It depends," Keith answered honestly.

Hooks was annoyed at Keith's responses. "Depends on what?" He barked.

Trying to be respectful Keith replied, "Your position."

He motioned with his hand for Keith to elaborate.

"Meaning for you good. For me bad."

He looked as if he was trying to understand what that meant. "Why?" Hooks continued to probe.

"Because she has no interest in me protecting her; just like I have no interest in spending time at the makeup counter and following after her temper tantrums," Keith said.

Hooks raised his eyebrows and babbled, "Tantrums?"

Keith shrugged his shoulders, "Well, that's what I call them. I need her to do what I say and when I say it with no questions. No talk back and no hesitations. She is just a girl doing what girls do though."

"What do you need her to do?" he frowned.

"Listen, pay attention, leave the gadgets alone, stop working, concentrate, slow down, focus, and follow my instructions," Keith rattled off the list.

Hooks understood but he also knew Danielle enough to know getting her to comply would be a challenge, "That ain't happening. But I will talk to her," he added knowing his talk was not going to change behavior.

"Just put someone else with her," Keith demanded.

"I can't do that."

"Why?" Keith asked him squarely.

Hooks was asking the questions today. "What else was strange?" He avoided Keith's question.

"These last few months have been strange. We have been with you for years and we have never had an experience with females. Now her." He stressed the word her.

"Because I am deciding to finally get a life you all consider it strange?"

"Yeah and you do too, hence the questions."

"No the questions stimulate from Danielle's behavior," he said as if trying to convince himself.

"Her behavior doesn't shock me at all," Keith said.

"You don't know her like I do," Hooks replied.

Raising his eyebrows, Keith quickly commented. "Oh I am sure you do."

He rose up. "What the F is that supposed to mean?" he asked.

Keith looked like he wanted to bark back. "What is up with that?"

"What?" Hooks ask clueless.

"Why are we dropping the F bomb?" Keith could not recall a time he had ever heard Hooks use the F word.

"All you are to do is protect her," he said.

"I don't want to do that! All I do is get attitude from her! Welcome to my world. By the way, what did I do to get crappy estrogen detail anyway? Bob the builder never had an attitude," he compared.

"She doesn't want you around either. It is a job none of you probably want. Nevertheless, one of you has to do it. Before it is all over all of you will do it and love it. I think with your attitude and her attitude, it may actually work. The way you snapped at King is the way you are to snap at the enemy. Once she sees you in action and can trust you, then it will be easy to add others to her protection. Right now, I think you are the only one that can handle her. You see how she and King barked. I think it will be like that for all the other guys."

"Whatever," he replied. Obviously, what Hooks was saying didn't make him change his mind about this assignment.

"Again. I ask what happened strange."

"Why are you asking this question?" Keith asked Hooks.

"Danielle has been distant since Friday night. Her phones were off Saturday. I heard nothing else from her after church yesterday. Today she clearly does not want to be bothered."

"Well, what did you do?" Keith asked.

He looked at Keith. Went to the other side of this office and began to pack up his stuff. Keith sat still and thought. *This is the number one reason why I did not want to be bothered with this girl. Now he is all out of whack because a chick is not speaking to him. We cannot let this happen when it is fight time.* "Hooks get it together!"

"I'm going home. Call me only in an emergency on the house phone," he said.

Keith looked stunned. Then looked around as if there were hidden cameras and he was part of some kind of prank.

This was serious. He needed to be at home. He got in his car and did what she did. He cut his phones off and drove home. He got home and lay down until he fell asleep.

I gave in. Around four thirty, I checked his message. It was tender. I could not have a heart if I didn't respond. When I called him back, his phone went directly to voice mail. I thought nothing of it. I left a message and shot a text. *This may not be as hard as I imagined it would be.*

I finished my day. Went to my old track and headed home. Around eleven forty five I realized I had not heard from him. I called again and got the same outcome as earlier. It was all good. Maybe he felt the same way and was shutting me down too. I was cool with this. I waited all night for my phone to chirp once he blogged, but it never did.

Tuesday

I immediately checked every site and every phone to see if he had called, texted, blogged or emailed. "Wow," was all I could say. *Did we have the same change of heart?* I felt like crap. I do not know why but I did. I headed to work. I gave in and I sent a text first.

> I'm worried about you. Call me please.

He wasn't the type of person that played get back. At least I didn't think he was. This was strange. If I didn't hear from him by noon, I was calling the gym. I got a lot of work accomplished considering the circumstances. At noon, I debated and debated then called. Again, his phone went directly to voice mail. *WTH?* I did what I said I was going to do and called the gym.

"Hooks Gym."

"Good afternoon. May I have Randall please?"

"Who's calling?"

I pulled the phone away from my face and looked at the screen display as if I had the wrong number. *What kind of question is that? Who calls him there other than me?* "Danielle," I answered.

"Ms. Rose he is out of the office right now."

They all were playing games with me. *You knew it was me when you answered the phone. You knew he was not there when you asked who is calling.* "When do you expect him to return?" I asked.

There was some hesitation, "I am not quite sure," Mimi replied.

That was complete BS. "Has he been there today?" I asked in a tone that denoted I knew she was lying.

"Yes ma'am he has," the receptionist answered.

She was very smart and well trained to answer only what she was asked. "Do you know who he is with?" I asked.

"I was not here when he left Ms. Rose."

What a crock of s**t! She may very well have not been there, but there were only a few choices. I was getting a little perturbed with the word game. "So you don't know who he is with?" I asked again hoping she got my tone that I knew she was lying.

"I surely do not. I can have him call you once he returns," she added.

"And you don't know when he will return?" I was heated now.

"No ma'am, but I will request he return your call promptly."

I suggest you do! "Please do." *Smarty pants.*

"Thank you."

"Good day." *What the hell is going on,* I thought. Then I slammed my desk phone down. I waited another hour or so before I remembered I can check his watch too. I went on line to check it and I'll be darned if it was off. *What is going on?*

I thought, *what can I do?* I made a promise that I was not doing this again. It could drive a person crazy worrying about someone. What they were doing? Where they were? Who they were with? I wasn't doing it!

At three, I called King. I didn't want to have to do it. He did pop up on me at the car wash. It was only fair. I just hoped I did not hear something I didn't want to hear. I wasn't concerned that he was hurt. At this moment I was more concerned he may have had a change of heart and no longer wanted to talk to me. "Yeah," he answered.

He was so rude. "Hi King," I said.

"Ms. D." he said void of emotions.

"I have been trying to track down Randall for the last twenty four hours with no luck." He said nothing. I guess I didn't ask a question so he had no reason to respond. "I did not know he was allowed to turn his watch off?" I asked.

"Yes, he can turn his off," he confirmed.

Really? "Well, is he all right?" I asked.

"He is fine. Excellent as a matter of fact. He is in the other room," he informed me.

Now, this seems odd. "Can I speak with him?" I asked.

Void of emotion King responded, "He is in a meeting."

"What?" I said out loud before I knew it.

"In a meeting," he repeated as if I didn't hear him the first time.

I changed my tone. "Is everything okay?" I asked again. I didn't believe him. Something definitely was going on.

"Yes," he replied rather curt.

"Why is he not answering my calls or responding to my texts?" I asked with the same tone.

"An emergency came up," King answered boldly.

"Is he in town?"

"Yes, we are in the city."

"Do you know how much longer he will be?" I asked.

"No."

King offered no more than what I asked and that was like pulling teeth with a pair of plastic tweezers. *Where did he get this crew from?* "Can you have him call me please?"

"I am sure he will," he said.

"Thanks King." I responded although I was not convinced.

"No worries. Have a good day Dani."

Was that a consolation prize? No worries. Was he serious? I hung up totally confused and perplexed. I didn't know what else to do. I did all I was going to be able to do. Now all I could do was wait. I decided I was going to the gym. I packed up and got in my car. It was after four. I would at least be there if he showed up. I felt like a true stalker. A bona fide groupie. At four forty seven PM, my phone chirped indicating I had a text. It was him! My heart was racing.

It's final! She signed.

I pulled over on the highway. A lump rose in my throat. I quickly sent an email to Paige. She signed the divorce papers. How do I respond? She is always so eloquent in these matters. I changed directions and stopped by the house to change. I did not change, but instead, I grabbed a red dress and shoes. *We are celebrating!* I picked up a bottle of low calorie nonalcoholic champagne. *I didn't know they made such a thing.* And I headed over to Randall's.

I was shaking the whole way there. I had no idea what to say. I didn't know how to feel. *Was this really happening?* Paige had to be in a meeting. She did not respond right back. I am sure as soon as she reads this it will be an all call text or conference call. I was so nervous. It was like he was immediately a different person to me.

I dialed his phone. I was shocked he answered. "Hello."

"Can you open the gate?" I asked.

"Are you at my gate?" He ran to the monitor to check. I could hear the buzzer opening the gate.

Before I could pass the gate and drive the distance to the house, he was already standing outside. I got out and walked up to him. He did not say a word. He looked different; relieved is the word. He looked revived. He had bags underneath his eyes but he seemed like a weight had been lifted off him. "CONGRATULATIONS!!!" I screamed.

"Hey, I am so shocked to see you here. What are you doing here?" he asked.

"Am I not invited?" I asked.

"You do not need an invitation," he said.

"I came to celebrate if that is okay?" I told him.

"It's great," he said excited.

I pulled out the champagne. He hugs me. "Nonalcoholic and low calorie. Whatever!" I said with excitement.

"You are so thoughtful. Today I would drink alcohol. It has been a long time coming and a long two days."

He escorts me in the house and to the kitchen. He places the bottle on the counter. It looked like he was sitting outside from the way the door is open. I walk over to the door and glance at the pool. I have my bag still on my arm.

"Let's celebrate!" I said.

"I'll get dressed," he replied.

I pulled my bikini out of my bag and held it up.

He was shocked. "What in the hell is that?" he questioned.

"Swim suit!"

"Says who?"

"Shut up! Says Victoria Secret. We are going swimming. Change your clothes!" I told him.

He said, "Why," and walked through the kitchen to the pool and jumped in with all his clothes on.

I followed suit and did not even give it one thought. When I rose from under the water, we were face to face. He leaned his forehead on mine. Our lips gently touched.

"Can I kiss you?" he barely whispered.

"Do you have to ask?" I said as we kissed for the first time.

THE END!

EPILOGUE

You have read your first book in The Confession Series®. It laid the foundation for the remaining books. In order to build anything, you must start with the foundation. The foundation is the most important part of a structure, as it must be strong enough to hold everything above it. Most foundations are seen on the surface; however, they go deeper in the ground than we could ever see with the human eye. So as in our lives. We do not see our foundations, but they are like roots. They are deep in the ground and growing daily, although we never see them. Our foundation is our vertical relationship. If you keep that in order and abide in Him, everything else in your life will fall into its proper place.

As you read, Randall and Danielle haphazardly crossed paths. In an instant, they were drawn to each other. Circumstances prevented them from forming an intimate relationship. These issues have now been removed and they get to formally date and proceed with their lives. It will not be easy. The struggle will surely begin. The key to it all is to maintain their individual and collective vertical relationship. With this, along with prayer and confessions, all things are possible.

BENEDICTION

We all have been given gifts and talents. The source and resources needed are in place to successfully accomplish them. Reach deep inside yourself and discover your talents and abilities. Once you put them to work for the kingdom, your life will forever change. Be blessed and be a blessing to others in the process.

> I pray.......
> Your life has been touched.
> Your heart is new.
> Your body is whole.
> Your walk is Godly.
> Your witness is genuine.
> And your faith is unshakable!

PREAMBLE TO RINGSIDE CONFESSIONS©

We kissed so passionately! It was long overdue. I could not believe it was happening; it was like a dream! I almost wanted more information or details. I knew he was not lying. I just could not believe it was true. Tears ran down his face. It was finally over! I kissed each one of them as they fell.

"This is why I care so much about you Danielle," he said while looking me in the eyes.

I asked, "Why?"

"I can be myself. I can laugh. I can cry. I can pray. I can be weak. I can be strong. I can be transparent."

The more his tears fell, the more I kissed them away. Then mine began to fall.

"Why are you crying?" he asked while gently wiping my tears away.

"I don't know." I spoke barely above a whisper.

"Tell me please." His voice and his eyes pleaded with me for an answer.

"I am happy. I am very happy for you."

He placed his lips on mine gently. We were breathing each other's breath. They touched. They separated. They touched and separated again. Finally, he kissed me beyond passion. It was a forceful kiss. A kiss that said I want you desperately. A long over-due kiss indeed!

Before I knew it, my back was up against the wall of the pool. We were engulfed in each other. Our bodies were not only wet from the water. I had not been kissed in years. It was just like riding a bike though, and let me tell you, I had not forgotten. Our breathing was extremely hard. My heart was beating so fast, hard, and loud until I swear I could audibly hear it. His was too, as I felt it beating on my very own chest.

No matter how hard I tried not to moan, I did; it could not be contained. It was a soft, gentle, erotic moan. He groaned an exasperated and long awaited moan. I never wanted this moment to end.

He kissed my lips, neck, ears, and my chest. My body fell limp. I leaned my head back while he kissed my chest. The back of my head was in the water. Pool and shower romance was the best. It was indescribable, sexy, provocative, and irresistible. In order for him to keep my balance, I wrapped my legs around him. He pulled back instantly. I thrust my pelvic into his pelvis area. He groaned. He immediately let go of my waist. Thankfully, I had my legs around his waist and my arms around his neck. He put his hands in between us and readjusted himself. The back of his hand slid down my pants before he was able to gather himself. I inhaled and held my breath.

He was fighting me. He was fighting his body and mine. I kissed his neck and forcefully grabbed the back of his head. He gave into me; his body parts touched my body again. This time more powerful than the last time. He grabbed my buttocks and pulled me in closer to him. The only thing separating us was cotton. Wet soaked cotton. I was overwhelmed. Overwhelmed with his statue and the situation at hand. This morning I never suspected my day would end like this. Air was the only thing that separated us. He thrust himself back into me again. I made a loud moan and gyrated at the same time. At that point, we were still fully clothed, but no doubt about it, we had just made love. Mentally, emotionally and practically physically. I think we both climaxed.

Ringside Confessions© Coming Soon!

www.ingramcontent.com/pod-product-compliance
Lightning Source LLC
Chambersburg PA
CBHW020627020726
47494CB00001B/81